KIRSTEN KRUEGER

Kirsten Krueger

NERVE

✦ AN AFFINITIES NOVEL ✦

NERVE: An Affinities Novel

ISBN: 978-1-7329014-2-1 paperback
ISBN: 978-1-7329014-3-8 ebook

Editing by: Mikaela Pederson, A Step Up Editing
Cover by: Damonza.com
Formatting by: Damonza.com
Interior Art by: Ilona Parttimaa

To my sister Heidi, because she was mad that I dedicated Blood to our other sister instead of her

AFFINITIES NOVELS

AFFINITIES NOVELLAS

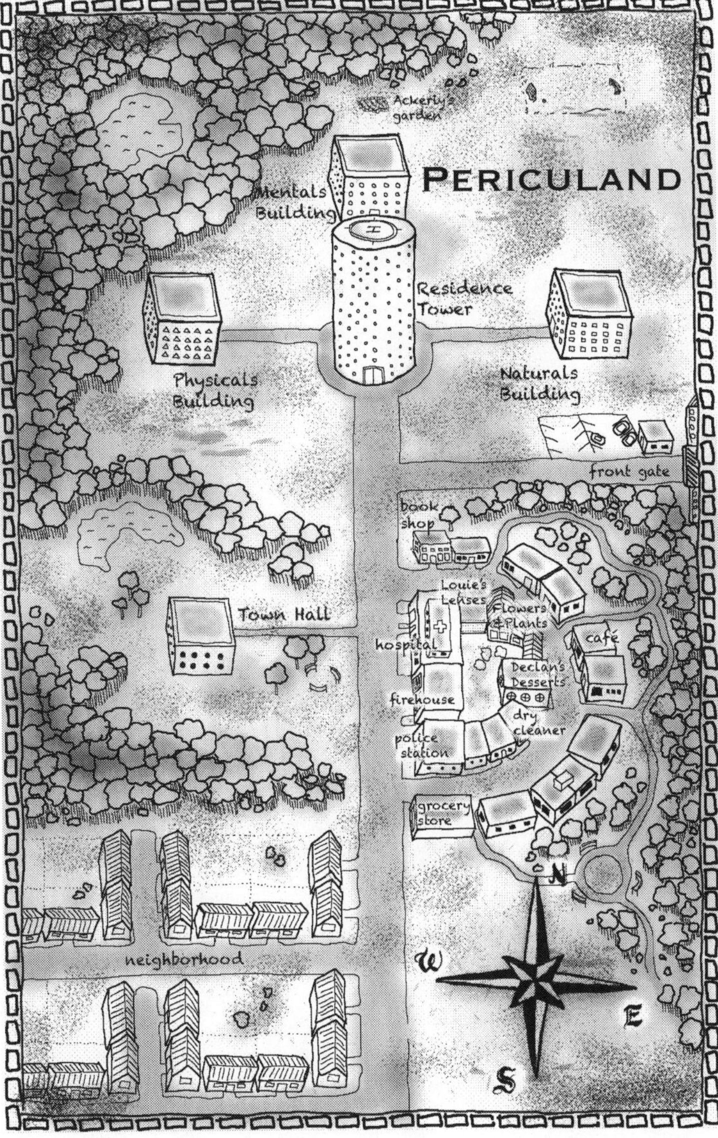

Ackerly's garden
PERICULAND
Mentals Building
Residence Tower
Physicals Building
Naturals Building
front gate
book shop
Louie's Lenses
Flowers & Plants
hospital
Town Hall
café
Declan's Desserts
firehouse
dry cleaner
police station
grocery store
neighborhood
N
W
E
S

1
The Fire Internal

A grunt reverberated through the dank little chamber as Madella Martinez yanked at the manacles encasing her wrists. Her concept of time had deteriorated, but she must have spent weeks in the Wackos' captivity—or months.

Knocked unconscious the moment she'd been teleported into the van, she'd awoken some time later in this windowless room, the metal door her sole hope of escape. She lay on a slanted slab of cool steel that made her normally pliable limbs immalleable, rendering her Affinity useless. After such a prolonged period of this mind-numbing torture, would her power ever work properly again?

At first, she'd been certain Jamad, Zeela, and Avner would rescue her. She had cried, screamed, and fought for hours to wrench herself from the restraints until her voice disappeared and her strength diminished, leaving her hollow and defeated.

Someone came in each day to feed and clean her. The tall silhouette blocked out most light from the external hallway, and once the door was closed, the darkness made him indistinguishable. Whenever his hands brushed her sullied flannel pants or grimy skin, he grunted in disgust, though she'd never heard him speak. Why would he talk to someone so subhuman and soiled?

Today, though she wasn't sure which day *today* was, a tinier silhouette appeared when the door swung open. Maddy stopped thrashing and cleared her throat, but the visitor had no conversational intentions. With the flick of their hand, the cuffs snapped, dropping Maddy to the ground.

Pain sparked through her joints as she collided with the stone, and her atrophying muscles strained to function as she rose to her hands and knees. Wisps of burnt-orange hair fell over her face, and she pushed aside the greasy strands with her trembling hand. Her fingers tingled with the sensation of touching something other than the frigid metal.

The stranger had disappeared, giving way to a long, empty hallway. Glass panes lined either side, divided by pale walls too bright for her eyes to handle. Failing to stifle her groans, Maddy pushed off the ground and used her slanted metal bed to stand. Her arms sagged too long and her legs wobbled in unstable strides. The tile in the hallway warmed her bare feet as she stumbled through the doorway, and the balmier air rejuvenated her taut skin.

Beyond the glass panes lay small, vacant cells, all clean and well lit, unlike hers. In the last cell on the left, a prisoner slept against the wall, thin arms hugging his legs. His mohawk, which faded from black to blue, wilted over his forehead, as unkempt as the dark makeup smeared on his cheeks. It took a moment for Maddy to recognize him in his withered state, but this was the Wacko who had broken into Periculand—the one with an Affinity for putting people to sleep.

"Do you have somewhere to be, Madella?" a voice asked, jolting her. The volume hadn't been loud, but any sound was jarring to her underused ears. Ahead, in the open doorway, stood the speaker: a young man, arms crossed to display his tattooed arms.

Ink covered the entirety of his skin, black patterns with random splotches of reds, oranges, and yellows, in small explosions bursting from his flesh. Dark spirals and flames crept from beneath the neckline of his t-shirt, snaking up to his prominent jawline. Though he seemed at ease leaning casually against the doorframe, what terrified her was the hue of his eyes: radiant orange, streaked with lines of white and yellow.

A silver hoop glinted when he raised his eyebrows. "You wouldn't have a few moments to chat, would you?" Maddy's wide eyes flew toward the cell the other Wacko slept in, and the man before her flashed a crooked smile. "Worried about Josh, are you? He's suffering only a mild punishment compared to what he did." When she blinked at him, his smile became patronizingly sympathetic. "Of course, you have no clue. Come, I've made you coffee. We'll talk."

Without another word, he retreated through the doorway, which led to a grand office. An elevator was positioned in the closest corner, and though Maddy wanted to dart for it, she knew that, in her current state, she was no match for this healthy man. Instead, she followed him toward his wooden desk, the gaudiest object in a mostly barren space. Two bookshelves towered against one wall and a massive flatscreen television hung on the other, the only adornments in sight.

He motioned for her to sit on the leather chaise before his desk while he sat in the chair beyond. As she stumbled onto the chaise, she was startled to see a tinted window at his back. Thick vines covered the glass, mostly blocking her view of the endless body of murky gray water in the distance.

"Lake Erie," he said when he saw her staring. His words were polite, spoken almost kindly, despite his obscene tattoos and punkish fashion. As he pushed a black mug of equally black coffee across the desk, he added, "If you look through the window at the right angle, you can see Cleveland. Have you ever seen Cleveland before?"

Nodding, Maddy grabbed the coffee mug. The liquid splashed against the ceramic walls as her hand quivered.

"It's nothing spectacular," he drawled, leaning back and raising his own mug to his lips. "I'll level it if I get the chance—perhaps rebuild something that's even better than Periculand." He paused as she forced the scalding liquid down her throat. "Aren't you going to say, 'There's nothing better than Periculand?'" When she didn't, he sighed. "You aren't much company, are you? I see why your friends allowed you to be taken so willingly." Her jaw clenched as weeks of building frustration surfaced. He grinned. "Ah, there we are. Seems I've hit a nerve. You'll be pleased to know your friends *did* chase after you, but our van left far before they could catch up.

"I tried bargaining with Angor Periculy to exchange you for the woman he's captured, Naretha. He didn't take to the offer. The reason for Josh's punishment, in fact, is because he did nothing to bring Naretha back to us. He simply left her there. He left my girlfriend there." His fingers whitened around the handle of the mug, and he hastily placed it on his desk before assuming a more lax posture.

Maddy was too focused on her memories to ponder the waver of his composure. She recalled the last JAMZ session she'd been to, when the two Wackos had barged into the basement. One, apparently named Josh, had knocked out students with his sleep Affinity while the other monstrous Wacko charged at the rest of them. With the help of Avner and Jamad, Maddy had subdued and contained the monster on the mat, but then the teleporter arrived. Tangled with the monster, Maddy had been swept away to the Wackos' van and transported here. She had no idea a third Wacko had been left in Periculand.

"I would punish the teleporter, as well," the man across from her continued now, "since she did nothing to retrieve Naretha either. But, alas, she's my grandmother, and she has memory issues. I couldn't punish my dear grandmother for forgetting about Naretha, nor could I punish her for forgetting what Periculand even looks like.

"If you were curious, that's why we have not reentered to save Naretha. My grandmother can only teleport to a location she can picture in her mind, and since she has forgotten what Periculand looks like, she can't go there again. Josh and Boyd were both stupid enough to delete the picture from their phones—that was how she got into the town. Josh took a picture once he was inside; it was a fine plan, until he left Naretha behind."

Maddy bit the inside of her lip, tempted to ask more but knowing it wasn't her place; she was a prisoner here, not a guest. She wanted to know who Boyd was, or more important, why the Wackos had been so eager to kidnap the young primary Hastings Lanio—or even why she had been freed from confinement.

As if reading her mind, the Wacko smiled slyly and said, "We infiltrated your town to acquire Hastings. You know his Affinity, I'm sure." Her brow furrowed and he cocked his head with intrigue. "You *don't* know? That's surprising. I assumed he would have told you, considering he's your cousin." Maddy's body went stiffer than it had since before she'd acquired her Affinity. "You didn't know *that*, either? Well, this is a day of discovery for you, Madella. Your mother never mentioned her dear sister, Jocosa,

Hastings's mother? You didn't attend your aunt's funeral when your young cousin murdered her? Ah—excuse me. *Murder* does imply willingness. Hastings didn't *mean* to kill his mother. It was a fault of his uncontrolled Aff—"

"H-he *killed* his mother?" she blurted out, her voice scratching her throat. Speaking felt unnatural after such a lengthy silence, but she couldn't help her incredulity.

"Didn't you ever wonder why Hastings was in prison for ten years? I guess you didn't, since you didn't seem to care much about him at all."

The Wacko basked in his superior knowledge, but this information was too profound for Maddy to be piqued. She had a cousin she'd never spoken to, even though she'd had plenty of opportunities. Did he know? Did he hate her for never reaching out?

"We wanted Hastings because he has the rare ability to burst blood vessels," the Wacko informed her, stroking a silver ring on his finger. His tattoos became a distorted blur in Maddy's vision as she inhaled this startling fact. "We always love to recruit those with…useful Affinities. His first task would have been to tear out the blood of that petty cop, Mitt Telum.

"Since you're so oblivious to everything, I assume you're also unaware that Telum *murdered* my father in September." Maddy gaped but was unable to produce a sound. "Yes, I do hate Telum." His fiery eyes glared beyond her as his hand formed a fist. "I suppose I'll have the pleasure of eradicating him myself. The only good that came from my father's death was my own ascension." He gestured around his office, though there wasn't much admiration in his sour expression. "My older brother tried to claim the position as leader of the Wackos, of course, but he's not cut out for leadership."

"*L-leader*? You're—you're—"

"The leader of the Wackos, yes," he droned, apparently bored of his own title. "My father, Ephraim Mayer, founded our organization—named it Affinities for Freedom. I prefer *Wackos*. It suits our unique tastes better.

"In September, my father was raiding an Affinity research facility to free captured Affinities but found it abandoned. He discovered some information on one of the lead researchers, Linda Stark." Maddy's shock must have shown, because the Wacko's grin broadened. "You know the Starks? Young Tray and Seth—my father and his team read all about them in Linda's files. They decided to pay a visit to her home, perhaps to torture some information out of the rotten Regg. Again, they found it deserted, but Mitt Telum caught them breaking in. My father shot him, but Telum absorbed the bullet and then shot it back out. Punctured my father's heart—killed him. And, now, here we are; I'm leader of an entire organization of Affinity 'terrorists' at the age of twenty-two."

Swallowing, Maddy clutched the coffee mug against her chest, letting the warmth comfort her as she prepared her next question. "Where…exactly…*are* we?"

"Underground." He stretched his arms and laced his fingers above his hair, crushing the wave of dazzling flames. Even the undersides of his upper arms were completely inked with tattoos; Maddy quickly deflected her vision when she noticed a pile of skulls within the fire and explosions. "This is the official Wacko Headquarters, set in one of the little cliffs on Lake Erie's coastline. It's a miracle no one's ever noticed it before. My father was a fool for installing this window." He nodded back toward the glass. "It's a nice touch aesthetically, though. This office is so plain and unappealing. I think I might hang Telum's skull right over…there."

Maddy's eyes bulged as he pointed toward an empty spot on the wall beside the bookshelves, and the Wacko chuckled. "There are plenty of other Wacko hideouts throughout the country, if you're wondering," he said as he swiveled his chair back and forth. "We've infected all of the big cities, though our largest concentrated population dwells here, in this underground lair. Once all the Reggs are dead, I think I'll relocate to somewhere less dreary, like Washington DC or New York City. Naretha would enjoy living closer to the ocean, with her salt Affinity. Although, judging by her current situation, who knows if she'll ever make it back here alive? Or if I'll have the patience to wait that long… Perhaps it's time to find someone new."

It was nearly impossible for Maddy to suppress a shudder as he wiggled his eyebrows at her. She hid her discomfort by downing the rest of her coffee. The caffeine had sparked her awareness, but hunger hollowed her stomach. Part of her wished she were still strapped to the metal slab, eating the tasteless food spoon-fed to her by the mysterious silhouette.

"Is…that why you brought me here?" she asked. "What are you going to do with me?"

"Oh, we're going to torture you, obviously."

She dropped the mug, and it shattered into thick ceramic shards at her bare feet. One thinner piece stabbed her big toe, but she hardly felt it. "I-I don't have any information. I don't know any—"

"Only joking, Madella." He sighed, leaning over his desk to see the mess. "You *have* destroyed one of my favorite mugs, though, so maybe I *should* torture you… Still joking," he added when he noticed the tears welling in her eyes. "We wouldn't torture *you*. No, no. You're an Affinity—you're one of us." She wanted to point out that he already *had* tortured her, but her heart beat too fast for her brain to focus. "Besides, I don't think my brother would let me, since he's become quite fond of you."

Blinking back the wetness, she fought to comprehend his words. "B-brother?"

"The scrawny thing that's been feeding you? That's my brother, Zach," he clarified, eyes glowing mischievously. "As I've said before, he's not the leader type—too soft, too sentimental. He's got a freaking *cleaning Affinity*, as if that should exist…"

A faint smile surfaced as she recalled the way her feeder, Zach, had made disgusted noises when touching her dirty skin. Of course someone with an Affinity for cleanliness would find her state of hygiene fouler than anyone else. "What's…your name?"

"Danny," he responded, kicking his feet onto his desk. His shoes were much too formal for his otherwise casual attire. "Danny Mayer, the Wackiest Wacko, I've been told—though I'm certain there are plenty of freaks here who could claim that title."

Maddy had barely heard a word he'd said after his name because the sound of padding feet caught her ear. When she glanced down at the source, she saw a tiny white-furred dog scampering over the shards from her coffee cup. It growled up at her in a way that was oddly cute.

"Come here, you little bastard," Danny groaned. The dog scurried around the desk and sprung into his lap with an impressive amount of agility for its small stature. Even though it had walked over the sharp ceramic fragments, it didn't have any injuries.

"He—he walked over the splinters…"

"He's not the most cautious." Danny stroked the little dog's silky hair. "That's probably how he gained his Affinity."

"Affinity?"

Haughtiness entered the man's vibrant eyes as he lifted his chin. "They never told you animals could gain Affinities in *Pericu-*

land? What a shame dear old Angor has sheltered you so. But yes, little Shards has an Affinity for sharp objects. We've even stabbed him and he's been okay. He just absorbs whatever punctures his skin—like *Mitt Telum* does, probably."

Maddy eyed the dog warily, wondering if Danny spoke the truth or if this, along with everything he'd said to her, was a story he'd fabricated.

"I assume you're wondering why we held you in that horrible chamber for so long," Danny said, his vision focused on Shards. "Naturally, Zach wanted to let you go, or at least place you in a more humane condition, but I'm not so naïve. With an Affinity like yours, you would have found a way to squeeze out of our normal cells… Now, though, everything is different. Hastings is, unfortunately, dead, and Naretha—"

"Hastings is *dead*? How? When—"

"Don't interrupt me." Danny's face was eerily rigid when he glared up at her. Blinking once, she pressed her lips together and restrained the numerous questions on her tongue. "Hastings's death was, frankly, very political and far too complicated for you to understand. It shouldn't matter to you, anyway; you didn't care about him until I told you he was your cousin five minutes ago."

Though Maddy's lips parted, she couldn't think of an adequate response.

"As I was saying, Naretha is no longer in Angor's captivity—one, because Angor is no longer in charge of Periculand; and two, because a few of your little friends broke her out of prison and, I assume, are bringing her here to exchange for you. So, at this point, I don't really care if you escape. You're no longer a bargaining chip."

"But…won't you need me to get, um, your girlfriend back from my friends?"

Danny waved his tattooed hand dismissively. "You should know I don't play *fair*. A trade sounds too boring. Besides, what reason would you have to go back to Periculand now? Your friends will be here, and if you go back there, the Reggs will suspect you conspired with us 'terrorists' and throw you into *another* prison. No, Madella, your future is here. Call it fate, destiny, chance—*something* brought you here, and now you have two choices. Either join us in our quest to eradicate the Reggs and gain our deserved freedom, or...go sit in that cell, manacled to that uncomfortable table."

"For...forever?"

"Until your friends arrive. The least we can do for a fellow Affinity is give you the opportunity to die amongst friends." His eyes blazed brighter than before—not like a fire necessarily, but like a cataclysmic explosion pouring from his irises. He seemed to know the answer, but still he asked, "Which will you choose?"

"I'm pretty sure this is illegal," Adara Stromer said as her vision flew from her cellmate to her friends on the other side of the electric bars.

Tray Stark seemed unperturbed by her statement, his brown eyes narrowed without sympathy. She wasn't sure where he'd acquired his suit, but its fanciness didn't hide any of his nerdiness. Lined up beside him, Lavisa Dispus picked at a scab on her hand, Ackerly Terrier's earthy green eyes winced behind his glasses, Hartman Corvis bounced with jittery nerves that made his freckles vibrate, and Eliana Mensen glared at Adara's cellmate with the same enmity she felt.

Upon awakening a few minutes ago covered in a thick layer of soot, Adara had found the primaries standing outside her cell in

Periculand's police station. All five wore black mourning clothes for the upcoming funeral—Hastings Lanio's funeral.

"Mitt," Adara prompted now, her focus shifting to the police officer leaning in the entrance of the corridor. His arms were crossed and his silver irises glimmered as he watched her. "This is illegal, isn't it?"

Sighing, Mitt stood straight and took a few steps closer to the cell's bars. "Probably," he admitted, "but I was instructed to place both of you in this cell by the Rosses."

"Freakin' Reggs," Adara muttered, bitterly recalling the two Regular ambassadors who had apparently taken over Periculand after the former principal attempted to assassinate them. Angor Periculy's mind control hadn't worked on Hastings, though, and now the young boy was dead while his murderer sat ten feet away from her. "They can't place an innocent underage girl in a holding cell with a murdering psychopath."

"I have murdered no one," Angor insisted, thin hands folded peacefully in his lap. He lounged in the other corner on a metal table identical to hers, wearing the same parchment-colored outfit. The rings of exhaustion under his eyes were darker than his pink hair, giving him a gaunt, powerless appearance.

Adara felt no pity for him—not when he had caused the death of poor Hastings. Her insides blazed with rage at the thought. She wanted to erupt in flames again—to finish what she'd started when she'd tried to climb over Angor's desk and set his flesh on fire—but the idea of that fire froze her to the core.

"You murdered *Hastings*!" Eliana exclaimed when Adara said nothing. The mind reader's voice reached an unexpected volume, and her bright blue eyes were full of zeal as she took a step toward the bars. "You wanted him to kill the Reggs and he wouldn't, so he had to kill himself. He became a martyr because of you, you sick, deranged *monster*."

Mitt cleared his throat, and Tray gingerly placed his hand on Eliana's shoulder in an attempt to calm her. She shoved him off and hugged herself, blinking back the wetness in her eyes as she stared at the floor.

"I'm sorry," she whispered. "I just… This is just…*wrong.*"

"You're correct, Miss Mensen," Angor spoke up, swinging his long legs over the side of the metal bed as he stood. "This is all very wrong. Hastings was a pure soul—one who wanted to do good but was plagued with an Affinity for evil…"

"He wasn't," Eliana snarled, her venomous eyes darting to meet his. "He didn't only know how to burst blood vessels; he knew how to heal them as well. He could have *helped* people, but now he never will because he's *dead.* He shouldn't have had to die."

"I agree," Angor said, his voice emotionless even as tears spilled down the girl's cheeks. "Hastings never wanted to harm anyone, and that was what killed him in the end."

"*You*—"

"*I* had nothing to do with it," Angor interjected, causing an immediate uproar from all the students. Until now, they'd been quiet, but Adara recognized the hatred they radiated, akin to her own. He shook his head as they refuted his claim and hastily amended, "I do blame myself for putting Hastings in that situation. Had I not asked him to attend that meeting, he may still be alive."

"If you hadn't asked him to murder the Reggs, he would still be alive," Lavisa corrected, picking her scabs with more vigor.

"I never asked him to kill—"

"You forced him to," Tray spat. "You forced him with your Affinity."

"I forced Hastings to do nothing," Angor stressed with a hint of agitation. "I only asked him to save this town. I asked him to become our weapon against the Wackos if the time came. He was reluctant, but he agreed that, if the Reggs insisted every Affinity in this town go to war, he would kill the Wackos single-handedly to save Periculand. But then *someone*—I'm still not sure who—used their mind controlling ability to manipulate him into becoming a murderer."

"Don't say *someone* as if it wasn't you," Adara snapped.

"It *wasn't* me. I don't have a mind controlling Affinity," the man persisted. "If I did, do you think I would be trapped in this cell right now? Of course not. I would have convinced everyone in my office yesterday that I wasn't the one to murder Hastings."

"Isn't that what you're trying to do now?" Hartman asked, orange eyebrows furrowed in confusion.

"Am I succeeding?" Angor countered. "If I had a mind controlling Affinity, you would believe me—I could easily make you believe me—but you don't, and that in itself should be enough to prove I am not what you think I am."

"Let's say you don't have a mind controlling Affinity," Tray suggested diplomatically. "Let's pretend you didn't try to convince Hastings to kill the Reggs. Who *did* try to make him kill them? And what *is* your Affinity?"

Angor exhaled a dramatic sigh, bringing his fingers to his chin as he began to pace the cell bare-footed. When he approached Adara's bed, she emitted a growl that he ignored as he spun to walk the other way. "I don't…*know*. Olalla wouldn't and *couldn't* have, for that matter. Her Affinity is for peace; if anything, her presence probably made the entire situation better than it should have been. The Rosses were the targets, and…and I was the only other person there, so it does make sense that you blame me… I suppose it could have been one of *you*, but none of you have a mind controlling Affinity, nor would you, at such a young age, have the ability to compel someone as mentally skilled as Hastings. It must have been someone who wasn't there."

"This is ridiculous," Tray fumed, motioning exasperatedly toward Angor. "Is he seriously trying to convince us he *isn't* guilty?"

"You were the one who proposed the idea," Lavisa reminded him dryly.

"Is…is there anyone in this town who *does* have a mind controlling Affinity?" Ackerly asked. "Hastings *was* acting a little weird even before he went to your office. We—we were out in the gardens and he suddenly stood like he was in a trance."

"I'm sure *he* could have possessed Hastings from that distance." Eliana jabbed her finger in Angor's direction. "He has a strong mind; I can feel it."

The principal paused his strides, pivoting his calculating gaze toward the blue-haired girl on the other side of the bars. "Ah, yes, mind reader. You should be able to read the truth in my brain, should you not?"

"I'm…not that strong," she admitted feebly, shuffling where she stood. "There's…a wall around your mind, and I can't penetrate it."

"Hm, I do feel that, as well." His eyes squinted as he rubbed his temples. "But it's not a wall I forged… Strange. I've always been skilled at combatting mind readers, but I *want* you to read my thoughts and still you can't. Mind readers… Aethelred! Yes, yes." He halted and looked up at the five primaries with feverish eyes. "Aethelred is one of the few in this town who know my Affinity, and he knows it's not mind controlling. Speak with him—he will get to the truth of this. Bring him here, if you must. Let him delve into my past, and then, Miss Mensen, you can look into his brain—"

"If your Affinity isn't mind controlling, what *is* it?" Tray repeated.

"I have no idea," Angor said, his brow creased worriedly. "It's as if a hand has reached into my mind and stolen all evidence of it. There is a blank spot—a black hole..."

The primaries stared at him, uncertain and skeptical, but then Mitt cleared his throat, cutting through the tension.

"You should get going," he advised. "The funeral will start any minute."

"Oh, yes," Angor said, breaking out of his reverie. "I would like to pay my respects—"

"Not you," Mitt warned as the principal took a step closer to the humming bars. "Or you," he added to Adara when she shifted. "You're confined to this cell until further notice. The Rosses will come soon to determine what to do with you—both of you."

Adara huffed a caustic laugh but produced no snide comment as he opened the door to the main office. With an almost apologetic glance in her direction, he led the other five primaries out of the jail.

All of her friends avoided her eyes, except Ackerly, who grimaced as if it physically pained him to leave her. "We'll be back to visit," he assured her before disappearing through the threshold.

Her hands clenched into fists when the door closed, but other than that she didn't move. Of course he would abandon her—of course they all would. Everyone always found a way to leave.

Sighing, Angor resumed his lounging position on the other side of the cell. "This is quite the predicament for both of us. I do believe I would care more about our current situation if Hastings were alive, though. The fact that he is dead...has hollowed me."

"Shut up," she said with an eye roll. "You may have come close to convincing them, but I'm not so easily fooled. You put on a good act, but you're the king here. Why would you care about one measly peasant who failed to do your dirty work?"

"I thought it was obvious. Did my son not resemble me?"

Adara blinked slowly as her head rotated to face him. The gleam in his pink eyes was eerily curious—and honest. "Did *what*?"

"Did Hastings not resemble me? Our skin tones were different, yes, but he inherited the darker hues from his mother. I liked to believe we had a similar jaw shape, at least—"

"*What* are you talking about?"

"I'm talking about Hastings," Angor said. "I'm talking about my son."

2

The Future and The Past

November weather didn't normally inspire much creativity in Eliana, but the pale gray clouds casting gloomy light over the field fit her mood perfectly. She wished she could be at her desk, painting this sullen scene rather than standing amidst it. Hastings would have mentally mocked her if he'd discovered her creating something so dismal, but now he wasn't here to share his cynical thoughts—to grumble about the frivolity of Periculand's citizens as they gathered in this park to mourn a boy they'd never known.

The town's park, situated across the street from the hospital, was a vast plot of land outlined with barren trees and scattered with picnic tables. A small playground was stationed at the center, but no one played today; any children present huddled by their parents, sniffling over the fresh mound of dirt that was Hastings's grave.

Their grief was shallow. It infuriated Eliana that they could all look so solemn over the death of Periculand's "martyr" when, on the inside, they were only concerned about themselves.

Who will protect Periculand now?

Who will take charge of this town? Will it affect us?

When will all this fuss be over so I can go back to the lounge and play video games?

That last thought belonged to Dave Byle, the acid-spitter, and Eliana almost marched over to him and drove her pointed heel into his groin as soon as the thought hit her consciousness. She'd never been inherently aggressive, but part of her wanted to attack all of these people, if only so she could have a few moments to respect Hastings without their incessant internal ramblings.

Instead, she stood at a distance, staring at the white marble headstone through bleary eyes. She and the other primaries had stopped by on their way to the police station to look at it this morning, and the image of his epitaph was so ingrained in her brain that she didn't have to see the words to know what it said.

Hastings Salvator Lanio
March 14, 2001 – November 9, 2016
BELOVED FRIEND, HEROIC MARTYR

He hadn't had any friends—*she* had been his only friend. The other sobbing students were just trying to get attention. All the people speaking over his grave thought more about the consequences of his death than the fact that he was gone—that he had been *murdered*, forced to become a martyr.

She hated that word, *martyr.* It immortalized him as this deity—turned him into a hero they could all pretend they had always been fond of. His sacrifice should not have been forgotten, but neither should his life, his kind soul, his desire to be good. All of that was irrelevant to these people, though; the only part of his existence that mattered to them was the moment he ceased to exist. She really, really hated that.

There was one other headstone beside his, dedicated to an Affinity named Bertha Hopkins who had died of old age only a year ago. Her mound was already flattened and overgrown with brittle grass. Eliana wondered how long it would take for nature to erase Hastings's mound—how long it would take for the memory of him to fade from this town.

As if the ground had read her thoughts, a few small flowers began to bud out of the earth at her feet, sprouting from green stems into orange and yellow petals.

"Asclepias curassavica," Ackerly's nasally voice said as he appeared beside her. She should have mentally felt his consciousness nearing, but she was too distracted and numb to concentrate on anything specific. "They're sometimes called bloodflower. Thought it would be fitting, considering..." He glanced at her through the lenses of his glasses and grimaced. "They'll die in a few minutes, I think. They're native to the tropics..."

"They're beautiful," she said, meaning to sound grateful but mostly sounding empty. "It makes sense that they'll die soon. Hastings...died before he should have. Angor shriveled the life from him like the cold will shrivel the life from this bloodflower. They would have lived long, beautiful lives if they hadn't been planted in a cruel, selfish place—"

"I...didn't really mean for it to be so metaphorical." The way she scowled at the flowers must have unsettled him, because Ackerly cautiously added, "I'm really sorry about Hastings. None of us knew him as well as you, but...we liked him, and it's not fair—what Angor did to him, I mean."

"It just...disgusts me that he *denies* it. What could his Affinity be if it's not mind control? And who else would want to kill those

Reggs as much as he does?" Eliana's vision slid across the crowd of gathered mourners to where the Rosses stood, shaking hands and bowing their heads somberly, as though they'd known the deceased personally. Her jaw tightened.

"*You* look like you want to kill them," Ackerly noted awkwardly.

"They should be the dead ones, not Hastings. *They* should be..." She shook her head, clearing her racing thoughts. "This is the way he would have wanted it. He...he would have rather died than have killed someone else."

"Like he killed his mom..."

She nodded once, reading his mind and seeing how he'd discovered that specific fact in Fraco's files. "This is the way he would have wanted to go—saving people. But...it still aches to know he's gone...that he'll never get to heal people like he wanted."

"Whoever did this will pay. Tray will make sure of it."

Following the boy's green gaze, Eliana found the Stark twins conversing with Aethelred near one of the picnic tables. Abandoning the dying bloodflower, she slunk closer to them, hearing their conversation not audibly but through their thoughts.

"*Were you very close with Hastings?*" Aethelred asked Seth. Today, like everyone else, he wore a dark suit that brought out the true redness of his hair and eyes, giving him a menacing appearance despite his inherent placidity. Though the Stark twins were fairly tall for sixteen-year-olds, the chief of Mentals towered a head over them, dwarfing even the muscular twin.

"*Not really,*" Seth said, his verbal statement as transparent as his thoughts. "*I always talked to him, but he never answered. I did like him, though. Right* now, *I don't like him so much, because his death is forcing me to wear this uncomfortable suit.*"

Eliana was relieved to see Tray roll his eyes as his brother squirmed. "*You're so inconsiderate.*"

"*I'm just* joking, *bro. Trying to lighten the mood...*"

"*There's nothing light about this*," Tray grumbled. For the first time, his moodiness was actually appropriate for the situation.

"What are they saying?" Ackerly whispered to Eliana, who jumped at the realization that he'd followed her to this shady cluster of trees. All three of their faces were visible from here, but the sound of their voices was still faint.

"Just bickering. C'mon." She motioned for him to follow her through the trees until they were at a better vantage point, hidden by the brush but close enough to hear the conversation with their ears.

"What did the Reggs ask you in their interrogation?" Tray asked his brother, who had finally stopped his obnoxious fidgeting.

"Lots of pointless stuff." Seth shrugged and then scrunched his nose at the constricting fabric of his suit. "About Hastings's routine, his meetings with Angor—why would I even know about that? They also wanted to know if Adara was somehow in on the whole thing, as if her becoming a fire monster to kill Angor wasn't proof enough that she was pissed. They're just looking for an excuse to keep her in that jail. How's she doing, anyway?"

"When she woke up, she was just as pleasant as usual—spewing profanities, mocking everyone who breathes..."

"She's awake? Damn, I need to go see her." Seth stroked his chin as he glanced up at the teacher standing between them. "Am I allowed to go see her?"

"Normally, yes, with an adult escort, but now that Mr. Periculy is also in jail, I am unsure as to how the rules will change," Aethelred explained, studying the Rosses where they stood across the field. His mental wall was fortified enough that Eliana couldn't glean specific thoughts, but the aura of distrust was evident.

"Angor's in *jail*?" Seth blurted incredulously.

"What else would you expect them to do with a murderer?" his twin questioned. "They even put him in the same *cell* as Adara, so that shows you how dangerous they think *she* is."

"Adara's in a cell with him—*alone*? We gotta go bust her out!"

"I don't believe Mr. Periculy to be as much of a threat as everyone thinks," Aethelred cut in pensively. "He was never fond of the Reggs' rules, but he never expressed any desire for violence. I've known him for many years, and he has made mistakes but none this grave. He will not injure Miss Stromer. I find it hard to believe he would have even put Mr. Lanio in such a dangerous position…"

Eliana didn't find it hard to believe, and Tray was just as skeptical. "The important question now is *could* he have put Hastings in that position?" he asked. "Does Angor have the ability to control minds?"

Aethelred's red eyebrows creased in contemplation. Even from this distance and even with the wall, she could detect a different sort of block around his thoughts—one similar to the shield and void in Angor's brain. "I…am not entirely sure," he finally admitted. "He is a Mental, and I know his Affinity…or I should…but it's as if someone has removed the knowledge from my mind."

Tray exchanged a look with his brother but then remembered Seth hadn't been present when Angor had said almost the same thing about his memory. "So…" Tray started slowly, "you don't know what Angor's Affinity is? But you did…and you think someone erased your memory?"

"It seems that way. I don't doubt there are those with an Affinity for erasing memories. I believe the same thing happened to Miss Stromer, actually. When I saw her past a few days ago, portions of it had been tampered with—blocked from view almost. This feels the same."

"So, you think someone has the ability to block memories, but you *don't* think it's Angor?"

Aethelred opened his mouth to reply, but Eliana already knew his answer: No, he did not believe Angor could block memories. He didn't even believe Angor could control minds. But…*how*? And *why*?

"Mr. Certior!" Fraco Leve hissed loudly, his frantic thoughts breaking Eliana from hers. The greasy man scampered over to where the Starks and Aethelred stood, and the crowd parted for him, none wanting his oily suit to brush against them.

"*I'll mull it over*," Aethelred muttered to Tray, the volume too low for Eliana to hear outside her mind. Though she sensed his thoughts had drooped into consternation, he met Fraco with a cordial smile. "Mr. Leve. Is there a problem?"

"Is there a problem?" the vice principal mimicked boorishly. "There are several problems, Mr. Certior. Our leader has been hauled off to the very prison he built, and now the people of this town are worshiping the Regg ambassadors as if they are gods! You know as well as I that there is no possibility Mr. Periculy is guilty."

"What makes you say that?" Tray asked, eyes narrowing.

"Because, for one, Mr. Periculy is an upstanding citizen and valiant leader. Two, Mr. Periculy is a man of strategy, not violence. Three, Mr. Periculy did not care for many people in this world, but he did care rather ardently about Mr. Lanio. And four, Mr. Periculy does not have a mind controlling Affinity. That should be enough proof to sway you, Mr.—"

"What is his Affinity, then?" Tray interrupted.

"It's…" Fraco's confidence wavered immediately as his dark eyebrows wrinkled. That strange wall settled over his mind, foreign and formidable. "It's…it's not mind controlling, and that's all you need to know."

"You can't remember, can you?"

"I—remember perfectly..."

Tray wasn't listening anymore, though; he and his twin actually exchanged looks now, and they aimed one at Aethelred as well.

"Mr. Leve," the chief of Mentals interrupted over Fraco's stammers. "Is there something you wish for me to do?"

"I—I *wish* for our leader to be freed from jail. Stromer can rot in there for all I care, but Mr. Periculy must be released. Certainly, we are the two most powerful people in this town now. Can we not do it?"

"In Mr. Periculy's absence, it would appear *you* are the principal. Why are you asking me what you can and cannot do?"

"Because...because..."

"Because everyone likes Aethelred and no one likes you?" Seth offered, making Fraco seethe.

"Shoo now, both of you!" he fumed at the twins, waving them away with his oily hands and spraying droplets on their faces in the process. The Starks complied, wiping their skin as they departed from the authority figures.

Eliana tapped Ackerly's arm and prompted him to trail her through the trees until they were only paces away from the twins, who were still removing Fraco's grease from their eyes. They were so blinded by it that neither noticed their friends about to emerge from the woods, nor the person who had sauntered up to join them, halting Eliana before she could reveal herself.

"Wait," she whispered, grabbing Ackerly's arm and nearly throwing him into a tree. His grunt was drowned out by Calder Mardurus's wry greeting.

"Starks. I would offer to clean your faces, but water and oil don't mix."

Tray blinked his eyes open and frowned at the sight of the

smirking secondary. "I don't want any of your water near my face ever again. What is it that *you* want, exactly?"

Calder cocked his head to the side, shifting a few wisps of his deep blue hair. "Rumor has it you two were there to witness..." He paused, all humor dying from his expression. His mental shield was thick, but Eliana still anticipated his next words. "You were there to witness Hastings's death. I want information."

"Is Nero asking?"

"I'm not Nero's secretary."

"Kinda seems like you are," Seth noted.

"I'm not—" Calder cut himself short and ran his hand over his hair, stopping when he hit his bun. "Where is Stromer?"

Tray raised an eyebrow. "You haven't heard Avner broke the Wacko free and fled town to save Maddy?"

Calder shook his head dismissively. "I don't care about him—I'm talking about his sister. One of you must know where she is, considering you're both dating her."

"Whoa, whoa, whoa," Seth said, appalled.

"Please," Tray groaned, massaging his temples. "Don't ever even *think* there's a possibility I could be romantically involved with Adara Stromer."

"Yeah, she's like a sister to us," Seth insisted. Eliana almost felt sorry to know it was true, given the way Adara thought about *him*.

"Like the kind of sister you got stuck with and could never get rid of, even though you hate her," Tray added. Eliana almost sensed that *wasn't* true, but his sentiments toward Adara were too convoluted to decipher.

"I like my sister, so I can't really relate," Calder mused with a shrug, though the nonchalance seemed forced. "And I always know where she is, so you two must know what happened to Stromer."

Having simmered down from their minor outburst, the Stark

twins glanced at each other knowingly. "Who's asking?" Seth finally said, crossing his arms.

"Me?"

"Why do you want to know?" Tray pried, adopting his brother's stance.

Calder rolled his oceanic eyes. "Because everyone's saying she's in jail, and if she is, then I have some payback to dish out."

Seth's head thrust backward in confusion. "Payback?"

"You two were there when I got locked up and she came to mock me." Calder averted his gaze momentarily and then added, "I just want to return the favor."

"Oh, well in that case, she's in jail, first cell on the right—same one you were in," Tray said without hesitation. "Give her hell for me, will you? And let us know if Angor's killed her yet."

"Angor? She's…in jail with Angor?" The intensity of the boy's dread seeped through the bricks of his mental wall. "She was in on it then, the attempted murder?"

"She was not in on it," Seth scoffed. "Where the hell are people coming up with this crap? Adara tried to murder *Angor* after what happened with Hastings. She became a raging fire demon."

Calder's wall began to crumble with his nausea. "She did? Like when Aethelred touched her the other day? And when…" He glanced down at his suit, unable to verbalize the way Adara had burned a hole in his shirt during their skirmish in the library.

"Worse," Tray clarified grimly. "Her skin became…dark, like hardened lava, and the blaze was so strong we could barely see her through it."

"So, she's in jail because she's dangerous?"

Seth laughed. "She's probably the most dangerous person in Periculand, since Hastings is dead. At least *he* knew how to control his emotions; Adara doesn't even know what the word *control* means."

Calder actually winced at that. "Hopefully Periculy will be able to contain her with his mind controlling Affinity."

"*If* he has a mind controlling Affinity…" Tray said, but his words were unheard by the others when Kiki Belven scurried up to them and yanked on Seth's arm.

"I need to talk to you," she demanded, digging her black-painted nails into his bicep. She'd clearly done them to match her dress, but the dark hues didn't compliment her pale skin and hair well. Even so, she wore no makeup over her mildly freckled cheeks or around her vibrant blue eyes, and there was something appealing to Eliana about her natural beauty.

Seth wasn't fazed by her looks or her clutch on his arm. "About what?"

"Everything!" she exclaimed, but her frantic energy subsided when she noticed the third boy among them. "Ooh, and you, Nero's cute friend—I'll need to talk to *you* later."

Calder's expression remained indifferent with her request. "Okay."

Kiki shot him a flirty wink before issuing one final tug on Seth's arm that forced him to comply. They weaved through the crowd until they were on the outskirts of the park, sheltered beneath a large, dormant tree. Eliana could have revealed herself to Tray now, considering Calder had also strolled away, but something drew her deeper through the trees, like a magnetic force attracting her mind.

"So, you're into Calder now, huh?" was the first thing Eliana heard Seth say once she was within earshot. Ackerly hadn't joined her this time, and it left an uneasy feeling in her gut. Listening to the twins discuss relevant topics like Hastings and Angor was justifiable, but eavesdropping on Seth and Kiki's personal conversation? They had *dated*, and, though Eliana had overheard plenty of their thoughts about each other, this was intentional and immoral—but she didn't even start to walk away.

"I have no interest in him," Kiki insisted, rolling her eyes.

Seth squinted in what Eliana realized was an attempt to study her irises, because he was convinced there was something different about them. Intrigued, she positioned herself behind a tree where she could better see Kiki's features. Still, the only change she could deduce was in the girl's demeanor. Around the others, she'd been superficial, but now her panic was evident, her capacity for substantial emotion revealed.

"Then why did you say you'd have to *talk* to him later?"

"Because I have to make myself seem normal, Seth, so people don't get suspicious. If everyone realizes I'm not interested in boys anymore, they're going to know something is wrong."

Seth blinked, baffled. "You're not into boys anymore? That's... unexpected—but hey, there's nothing wrong with being a lesbian. I'd prefer it, I think, because then I'll stop taking our break up as a personal slight—"

"That is not what I am talking about!" she hissed. "I just don't...I don't care about having a boyfriend or hooking up with anyone or any of that, really, and you know that's always been my top priority. There is something wrong with my brain, Seth, and it's distracting me from my top priority."

"Kiks, you know you can be honest with me. If you're attracted to girls, I'll support you all the way—"

A loud, shrieking groan escaped her lips, drawing a few confused glances. "I am not talking about my sexual orientation," she whispered irritably, almost too low for Eliana to hear. "I am talking about...well, I don't really *know*. All I do know is...is that I knew this was going to happen, Seth—all of this." She motioned toward the funeral and the crowd, stopping at last on Hastings's grave.

"I saw this in a dream. I knew Hastings was going to die. I don't know how I knew, but I didn't tell anyone and I feel awful. I'm such a bitch."

Eliana had been still before, but now it was more paralysis than an attempt for stealth. Kiki had *known* Hastings would die? Eliana had always gotten a weird vibe from her brain, but she'd never gathered any information regarding Hastings's death. Was that why Kiki had been straying away from their group?

Tentatively, Seth met his ex-girlfriend's desperate gaze. "Well…I've never wanted to say you were a bitch before, but if *you're* saying it…"

"This is no time for jokes! Hastings is *dead.* Maybe he was a quiet loser, but…he thought I was funny, I think. He would always snort at me in our Mental Class, and…and I'm going to miss being laughed at by him. How pathetic am I? I actually liked that freak! I sat in our classroom and cried all last night—so much that my eyes were too swollen to put on makeup this morning!"

"I…I'm upset too," Seth managed, speaking honestly. "We didn't talk much, but he was my roommate, and he wasn't a dick like everyone at our old school."

Kiki bit her lip, eyes darting for any sign of eavesdroppers. Luckily, Eliana was still too frozen to be detectable. "I…agree," she admitted, causing Seth's eyebrows to perk. "Everyone here feels *real.* Hastings didn't care what people thought of him. He was always truthful, when he actually talked, and he *died* to save two strangers. I would never do that, Seth. Hastings was so much better than me—better than all of us—and he's gone."

Eliana could feel the ache in Seth's chest. Everyone thought he was as shallow as Kiki, and they *were* equally shallow—but also equally not shallow. Beneath their good looks and cool-kid facades dwelled two fragile souls, surviving this world in the only way they knew how.

"You said…you knew he would die?"

Kiki's blonde curls bounced as she nodded. "I saw it in a dream a few nights ago. I've been…seeing a lot of things recently. That's what's wrong with me."

"All of these things you see…*happen*?"

"Yes. The first thing I saw that happened was those Wackos breaking in last month. Since then, I've seen small things, like predicting what you'll wear the next day or a lesson we'll learn in class. I saw…Adara exploding in flames. I thought it was a nightmare."

"They're not dreams," Seth said warily, voicing exactly what Eliana had concluded, "and it's not what's *wrong* with you, Kiki. It's…your Affinity."

She blinked her wide blue eyes, and through Seth's thoughts, Eliana registered what had altered in them: They were streaked with pink, like two rings of cotton candy.

"You can predict the future."

"You didn't know," Angor concluded as he swung his legs over the side of the metal table to face Adara. She had already jumped off her own table and couldn't decide if she wanted to punch him or puke.

"Of course I didn't know! Hastings barely ever *spoke*—and you two weren't exactly the perfect father-son duo. Did *he* even know?"

"He was a smart boy; I assume he suspected, at least. I never forthrightly said so—"

"You never even *told* him you were his father? Well, this is further proof you're a jackass. You were going to throw your own son into the Wackos' nest without even batting an eye."

The man wiped a hand across his brow, as if the heat of her words had induced perspiration. "I never *wanted* Hastings to have to kill the Wackos, but I believed it was what he was designed for."

"Ah, so you believe in fate, do you? Where the hell is Nerdworm when we need a logical mind?"

Angor stood now, towering over Adara with his lankiness. Though he was far less intimidating in his prison garb than in his usual purple suit, there was still something menacing in his unnaturally pink eyes. "Hastings was the most skilled student in Periculand. He could have annihilated the Wackos and walked out unscathed. It would have been immoral, perhaps, and I would have loathed to see so many Affinities perish, but it would have saved millions of lives. I'm unsure of what you know about the new leader of the Wackos, but he has killing capabilities you couldn't even begin to fathom. We're talking about the extinction of this entire—"

"The Wacko leader is *more* deadly than Hastings?" she interjected doubtfully.

"Far more deadly and far more temperamental. Without Hastings, I fear we don't stand a chance. That was why I was so adamant about sending him in, rather than risking our entire population in a futile fight. If we stormed the Wackos' headquarters, their leader would know in an instant and we would be dead. If Hastings had slipped in unnoticed, however, the leader would have died without warning."

"And you would have had him murder hundreds—maybe thousands—of Affinities. How *righteous*."

"They are terrorists and many are fanatics," Angor sighed in exasperation. He ran a hand through his hair, which looked nearly as greasy as Fraco's, and began to pace the cell. "If Hastings only took out the leader, any of the others would have risen in his place—they would have wanted to avenge him. The current leader *is* actually seeking vengeance for the death of his father, Ephraim Mayer. That officer who was just in here, Officer Telum—he was the one to kill the last Wacko leader."

"Mitt killed the Wackos' *leader*? Damn, I underestimated him. So, he's like, an American hero then, isn't he? Why hasn't the government set up a shrine in his honor for us to worship?"

"Because he is an Affinity. He's lucky he wasn't sent to a lab for testing. I would have been interested to see how his ability does work, though…"

"You condone torture—excuse me, *experimentation*—on Affinities? Well, that just earned you a point in the guilty category. And now I'm back to believing you're full of shit and Hastings was *not* your son."

"I was thirty-five when I met Jocosa," Angor began dramatically, and Adara emitted a groan.

"I don't want to hear your whole life story, Your Highness. I just want some form of proof that Hastings was your son."

"She was a waitress at one of my favorite dives," he continued, ignoring her interruption. "She had no clue I was a successful millionaire; I kept my wealth a secret, though I always did tip her well. I was always revered and feared in my work life, and I enjoyed going to a place where I could relax, be casual. The fact I'm an Affinity is obvious"—he motioned to his pink hair—"but at the time, the public hadn't really made the connection between the hair and eyes and powers. Jocosa was always fascinated by me, but she never pried or intruded. At first, she thought me a friend, but I fell quickly in love with her."

"So…then you screwed her and out popped Hastings?" Adara guessed, causing Angor to purse his lips and halt his pacing.

"To put it bluntly, yes. I became obsessed with her when

I realized she had my child inside of her. I started spilling my secrets—my dark secrets—and she slowly distanced herself from me, quitting her job at the restaurant and moving out of town. I lost track of her—not before I told her that I hoped we could name our son Hastings, though. It was the name of the street I had lived on with some of my close friends in my youth, a wonderful place. Even if she wanted me to have nothing to do with him, I was content when I discovered she'd at least given him that name.

"When he was sent to the detention center, I made an effort to visit him, but it was right around the time Affinities became the government's enemy—because of the Wackos, of course. Ephraim always had a desire for chaos… It reverted my attention from Hastings to my dream of Periculand. I spent much of my time fighting for Affinity freedom while also trying to track down Wackos. I regret that time I could have spent with my son, and above all, I wish I had told him the truth. He would have scorned me, most likely, for abandoning him, but…"

With a raspy breath, Angor plopped down onto his metal slab and rubbed his temples. "You can confirm this story with Aethelred, if you please. He knows. Fraco knows. Hell, the *Wackos* know. Why do you think they wanted to capture Hastings in October? Yes, he was powerful, but they wanted him specifically as leverage against me. They thought that, if they could kidnap and corrupt him, I would be swayed to their side. Now they have Madella, which I am aggrieved about. If I had married Jocosa, she would have been my niece."

Adara was so dumbfounded by this tale that she almost didn't catch the implication. "The stretchy girl…is Hastings's cousin?"

"*Was*, more accurately… It's a surprise they haven't tried to use her capture against me. I have no doubt they will, but I suppose I'm no longer a threat to them. If they want Periculand, they'll have to woo whoever takes charge next."

With slivered eyes, Adara surveyed this broken man, wondering how someone with so much power could lose it over what he claimed was a lie. "Even if Hastings was your son, I still wouldn't put it past you to sacrifice him to kill those Reggs. You wouldn't have expected him to use his power against himself, anyway—you sure as hell looked shocked when he did."

"I've never been on fine terms with Artemis and William," he agreed, nodding as he stared at the ground. "And I wouldn't put it past me, either. I've done worse."

"So, you're admitting to it then?"

"Do you think I'm so reckless? I knew you and all your friends were listening out in the hall. I sensed you mentally as soon as you arrived—"

"With your mind controlling Affinity," Adara finished, raising an eyebrow.

"With…my Affinity," he said, nearly choking on the words as his face contorted. "The Affinity I still cannot recall. Regardless, would I have attempted to murder two people in front of your eyes? I only asked Hastings to pop my blood vessels as a display of his power, not to harm the Rosses. Young people should not have to endure such trauma—hurting others and witnessing death. I did, and you see how I turned out."

"Yes, you're a murderer. Good thing we only saw our friend die, rather than two snooty strangers."

Angor loosed a breath and met her dark eyes with his light ones. "What can I say that will sway your mind? I have admitted I am a bad person, but do you believe I'm evil?"

Adara chewed on her lip, tasting the remnants of ash that had seeped into her flesh. "I believe that I need to have a word with Devil-Red. Oh, Weaponizer!" she sang, directing her call toward the closed door Mitt had disappeared through not too long ago.

"I have a few requests to make! They include donuts, a shower, our favorite red-eyed person—"

"You have red eyes now, if you were unaware," Mitt pointed out as he poked his head through the doorway, his silver eyes studying her with a mixture of agitation and amusement.

She had *not* been aware, but…it wasn't completely surprising. "Well, then our favorite red-eyed person who isn't me. Can you summon him?"

3

Another Thieving Stromer

Avner Stromer was really starting to develop a detestation for the countryside. For the past day, his surroundings had been characterized by nothing but fields, farms, and tiny towns. He, Jamad, Zeela, and their prisoner Wacko had spent the first night of their voyage hidden in an abandoned barn, the teens forced to take turns on guard, in case Naretha attempted to flee. During the day, the Wacko insisted on staying away from main roads to remain *untraceable*, but Avner was convinced this was a tactic to tire them so she could escape.

"You know, I'll move a lot faster if you take off these handcuffs," she said, not for the first time, as the four walked along a dirt road. She lifted her hands, cuffed by silver metal that barely glimmered in the overcast gloom.

Judging by the faint glow of the descending sun, evening approached, bringing with it the pang of hunger. Avner hadn't thought to bring food—or money. It hadn't taken long for him and his friends to realize they were ill prepared for this expedition, and Naretha knew it.

"*You know*, you're a Wacko, so no," Jamad countered with an icy smile. Overnight, his facial hair had grown into a thin layer of blue over his chin, pale in contrast to his brown skin. Like his friends, he wore lightweight black clothes unsuitable for the chilly November air. The cold didn't have an effect on him, but Avner and Zeela shivered continuously, as did Naretha in her flimsy prison garb.

"There's a town ahead," the Wacko said, narrowing her salt-pink eyes at the landscape before them. The farms were mostly barren this time of year, and beyond this field lay a village that appeared to be just one street of buildings.

Jamad scoffed. "You can barely consider that a town."

"There will still be people," Naretha snapped as she tried to yank her hands from the cuffs. The red marks on her wrists proved this wasn't her first attempt. "Any Reggs who see us will report us."

"So, we go around." Avner nodded toward the path they walked on.

"Can't," was all Naretha said before she bent down, scooped a handful of dirt, and flung it at Jamad's head.

Dust smothered his face and hair, forcing him to spit before he rounded on her, seething. "Give me one reason I shouldn't freeze your—"

"You need me," she said. "And we *all* need to cover our hair in dirt. If we don't, the Reggs will definitely call the cops. Trust me, this isn't the first time I've been in public the past three years."

Jamad glowered through his dirty eyelashes, but he wasn't the one to speak.

"We're *so* impressed that you're *so* skilled at being wanted by the government," Zeela drawled, though she had already sprinkled dirt over her white hair. She rubbed it in, transforming her into a light brunette. "Why is entering this town necessary?"

"Wacko Headquarters is almost two hundred miles from here," Naretha said as they began trekking across the desolate field. "Do you *want* to walk for days, or do you want to rescue your friend tonight?"

"Are you suggesting we hail a cab?" Jamad questioned condescendingly.

"I hope you're not that dumb," the Wacko snorted while awkwardly smacking dirt onto her pink head with cuffed hands.

Avner studied the buildings materializing before them. Most appeared to be residential, but between two houses stood a lone gas station plucked straight from the 1970s. Angor had really done a spectacular job of locating Periculand far away from civilization, considering this was the most they'd seen since their departure. "Do you know someone who lives here?"

"Hopefully not," Naretha said. "The last thing we need is to be recognized."

"Do you think Angor sent out messages telling people to watch for us?" Jamad asked, looking to Avner.

"I'm…not sure." He crumbled dirt in his hair, hoping it would be enough to conceal the electric yellow. "I think if he wanted to find us, he would have by now. Maybe he *wants* us to save Maddy."

"He could have easily conducted the exchange himself," Zeela pointed out.

"Yeah, but…I feel like Angor's always got some hidden motives, you know? It seems like him to pretend he didn't want this, even if he did. Maybe it's some kinda power move against the Wackos."

"Let's not talk about it *in front of* a Wacko," Jamad suggested with a wary glance at Naretha, who was more interested in the town ahead. They'd nearly reached the road, and other than the few cars parked at the gas station, there weren't many others in sight.

"How skilled are you with your Affinity?" she inquired, glancing sideways at Avner.

"He's the *best* at wielding electricity," Jamad stated proudly. "Never met anyone better."

"I don't think you've ever met anyone else who can control electricity *period*," Zeela said, but the argument ended when they stepped onto the pavement and she took in the village through her sunglasses. "This looks like Watertown."

"It is," Jamad confirmed. "We're close to Beverly."

Naretha's head perked up in alarm. "Who's Beverly?"

"It's the town we grew up in," Zeela said. "If we're going north, we'll probably pass it."

"We should see if my 'rents will let us borrow their car!"

Naretha tore through Jamad's enthusiasm instantly. "We'll avoid *Beverly* at all costs, and we will not ask your *'rents* for anything. We can't give anyone the means to track us. We're gonna steal that car." She motioned toward an old station wagon with a broken taillight and sagging front bumper parked at the gas station across the street.

If anyone were outside, they would have heard her plan to thieve, but there wasn't a living being in sight—in a normal human's sight, anyway. Avner could tell by the crease of her eyebrows that Zeela saw something they couldn't.

"There's a man inside the gas station store. He'll see us if we steal it."

Avner crossed his arms over his chest. "Even if he *doesn't* see us, it's still wrong to steal."

"You broke a 'terrorist' out of jail," Naretha reminded him dryly. "I think you're past the point of fretting over the law, little one. Have you ever used your Affinity to start a car?"

"We're *not* stealing the—"

"I'll take that as a no. It shouldn't be too difficult, if you're careful. You'll need to use the right voltage or you might fry the battery."

"I'm not stealing a car."

"All right, I'd like to make it known that I'm not really *against* stealing this piece of junk," Jamad interjected, hands held before him in innocence. "I mean…I don't think anyone's gonna miss it much. But Av is never gonna go along with this—it's futile to even try. Let's just walk to Beverly."

"Do you *want* to involve your family in this?" Naretha demanded, her impatience opening the door for ruthlessness. "Do you want them to be questioned and imprisoned when the government finds out they were accomplices in this? I might not believe my cause is one of terror, but everyone else does."

"We can plead with my parents for help," Zeela offered with a shrug. "They probably won't, but I wouldn't be too concerned if they went to prison—they always looked down on me for being blind, and they thought Eliana was clinically insane."

Naretha's tone was breezy as she said, "You might say that, but you don't mean it. If you won't start the car," she added to Avner, "I'll break into that store, kill the man, and steal the keys and the car—and you'll be forced to watch."

"How are you gonna kill him in handcuffs?" Avner asked skeptically.

"You think these handcuffs disable me from using my Affinity? Children, I could kill each one of you if I really wanted to, but I *don't*. These are Regg cuffs—they aren't doing much, other than bruising my wrists. Don't test me. Will you start the car, or are we gonna keep standing here like a bunch of suspicious creeps?"

"He hasn't seen us yet," Zeela noted, peeking between the man in the store and her boyfriend. "He might not notice if we're quick."

"I've never started a car *with* keys before. Why are you so convinced I'll be able to magically start one with electricity?" he asked Naretha.

"Because it's not *magic*; it's science. You'll need to send a current to the battery, which is essentially what the key does. That'll start the engine, theoretically."

"That sounds oversimplified," Jamad said, stroking his dirt-covered stubble.

"Would you like me to get technical, or would you like to go save your friend?"

"Stop pretending to care about Maddy," Avner said, more as a command than a statement of annoyance. "We know all you wanna do is get back to your Wacko boyfriend. *I* want to save Maddy, though, so...we'll steal the car."

"I was really hoping you'd say that." Jamad clapped his hands together in excitement. "I've always wanted to steal a car."

"Really?" Zeela mused, raising her white eyebrows behind her sunglasses. "I've known you for fourteen years and I've never heard you once express an interest in becoming a car robber."

"I meant it more as I've always wanted to steal a car since the Wacko suggested it a few minutes ago," he amended, unfazed. "Seems pretty badass—especially if Av's gonna use his Affinity to do it."

"We'll see," Avner grumbled, not bothering to look before crossing the street. There had been no passing cars so far and, for their sake, he hoped none would drive by to witness this experiment.

The station wagon had probably been white at some point but was now a dull yellow with enough nicks and scratches that it almost looked like an intended design. Avner shot an instinctive glance over his shoulder before approaching the driver's side, but as before, there weren't any spectators to be concerned about.

"The guy still hasn't seen us," Zeela assured him, her white eyes fixed on the store.

With a deep breath, at which Naretha rolled her eyes, Avner grasped the handle and yanked open the door. It squeaked loud enough that Jamad cringed beside him, and he had to be delicate with it as not to tear it from its rusting hinges.

As he slipped into the driver's seat, Avner noticed the interior was as unappealing as the exterior; holes, stains, and claw marks riddled the seats. Grease smeared the rearview mirror, filling the car with its stench, and the steering wheel was sticky when he placed his hands on it.

"Stop looking so disgusted and start the damn thing," Naretha griped, hovering beside the car. "Be gentle but not too gentle—"

"You're not helping," Avner sighed as he brought his finger to the metal keyhole. He could feel the battery buried within the same way he sensed electrical sockets and anything that held a charge. Screwing his eyes closed, he tried to gauge how strong the voltage was—how many amps of power he would need to exert to trigger the battery. Naretha released an agitated breath at his side just as the current shot from his fingertips, snaking through to the battery in the briefest instant.

As the engine spurred to life in a fit of coughs and wheezes, Avner scrambled from the car, certain it would explode. Jamad's hands sprang up, prepared to freeze any unwanted combustion, but then the noise lulled to a purr, like an angry cat awoken from a deep slumber.

"Huh." Naretha eyed the car rumbling before them, impressed. "I didn't even think this old thing would work—nor did I think your electricity would start it."

Avner's eyes widened. "Were you hoping it would explode and kill me?"

"*Hoping* isn't really the right word..."

"He heard it," Zeela said, staring intently at the store and the man within. "He's coming."

"Get in the car now!" the Wacko ordered, sliding over the hood to the passenger's side.

Avner glided back into the driver's seat as Zeela and Jamad squeezed into the rear. There weren't any seats in the back, leaving a muddy floor for the two to plop onto as the car's doors slammed closed and the store's door flew open. The man ran at the car as fast as he could with his oversized gut, yelling, cursing, and waving his cell phone, as if any of these actions might purge them from the vehicle.

Naretha grabbed the gear stick and shifted the car into reverse. "Drive!"

"I don't know how!" Avner admitted, eyes darting between the steering wheel and the rapidly-approaching man. "I never even got my learner's permit!"

"Hit the gas and turn the wheel!" she shouted, leaning toward the driver's side as she attempted to aid him while still cuffed. She managed to spin the wheel to the left so, when he finally pressed his foot to the gas pedal, the car swerved in a backward arc, nearly colliding with the screaming employee.

After slamming the brakes, Avner pivoted to see the man raise his fist to punch the back window. Jamad yelped, but before the man could swing, Naretha clumsily shifted the car into drive and cut the wheel to the right. Without hesitation, Avner hit the gas, thrusting them forward.

"Why don't you know how to drive?" the woman demanded, flopping back in her seat as she glared at him. The old car jolted in confusion when he tried using both feet to operate the pedals, and even with both hands on the wheel, he veered in unpredictable directions on the linear road.

"I was too young to get my permit when they took me to Periculand!" Avner exclaimed, inelegantly twisting the steering wheel. Though the vehicle threatened to deviate from the road and into the grass, the Wacko only rolled her eyes, void of concern and full of annoyance.

"Do *any* of you know how to drive?"

"I'm blind, so no," Zeela answered flatly.

"I, um, failed the written test…four times," Jamad confessed. "I drove a tractor once, though."

"My God—you country kids," Naretha groaned, closing her eyes, likely to combat nausea. "Uncuff me, someone."

"We're not uncuffing you," Avner said, his voice rising to a higher pitch at the end when he nearly drove them into a ditch. Luckily, her eyes were still shut, so she didn't see. "We don't trust you."

"What do you expect me to do?" Her eyes flew open, too harsh for such a pale pink. "Take you to the Wackos' evil lair? Oh, that's right—we're already *going there*. We all have the same objective right now, and I'm the only one who can get us there, considering none of you little twits are competent enough to *drive a motor vehicle.*"

"I drove a tractor," Jamad repeated.

The sudden flare of sirens drowned out Naretha's ensuing grumble. Her head whipped back while Avner peered through the mirror, which reflected an approaching police car. Panicked thoughts flashed through his mind—of them being linked with the Wackos and going to *jail*—but Naretha's aggressive punches tore him from his hysteria.

"Drive faster!"

Zeela and Jamad toppled over in the back when he slammed his foot on the gas.

"We're not going to be able to outrun the cops! I don't even know how to drive!"

"*Uncuff me*!"

"*No*!" Avner barked, but Jamad had already pulled the key from his pocket and shimmied through the gap between the front seats to grab Naretha's wrists. "J, *no*—"

"She's right, Av," he said apologetically. "She knows how to drive, *and* she knows how to get to—"

"Two more cop cars coming," Zeela announced, her sunglasses now abandoned as she focused the full force of her powers on the road behind them.

"Shit, I didn't even think that little town would have a police force," the Wacko muttered.

"It doesn't. Those are state troopers. That guy must have called and reported us," Zeela assumed grudgingly.

"We'll lose too much time if we switch spots," Naretha said to Avner, who barely managed to keep the car on the road as they zoomed at its maximum speed. "Keep driving as fast as you can and follow the road."

"What do you think I've been trying to do?" he complained, but Naretha ignored him as she unbuckled and climbed into the back. "Where are you going?"

Again, she disregarded him, instead directing her attention to his friends. "Hold on to the seat belts—*now*."

Though attempting to keep his eyes on the road ahead, Avner did see Zeela and Jamad exchange wary looks as the Wacko crawled toward the rear of the car. Neither hesitated to grab a seat belt, though, when she kicked the trunk door open.

At the speed they cruised, the rusty old door flew off the hinges completely, slamming into the road and partially obstructing the police cars' path. Avner watched in near paralysis as the cars swerved behind them to avoid the heavy, metal door. They would *definitely* go to prison now—if not for that stunt then for the fact that Naretha now had one hand secured around an overhanging handle and the other aimed out the gaping hole, as if she intended to *assault* the officers.

"What the hell are you doing back there?" Avner shouted, glancing anxiously over his shoulder. Wind whipped through the opening, muffling his voice and blowing the dirt from his hair.

"Destroying our enemy!"

He fought to keep the vehicle driving smoothly, despite her jarring words. Two of the three cars had made it past the wreckage and were catching up fast. "You can't kill cops!"

"I'll tell them you advised against it if we find ourselves in prison," she assured him before conjuring a stream of thick salt crystals that spurted from her free hand and blasted the closest police car. Naretha wasn't near enough to inflict any damage beyond scratching the glass and denting the metal, but a few of the crystals popped holes in the tires, and they gradually deflated, rolling the vehicle to a bumpy stop.

"Are they dead?" Avner blurted out in dismay.

"Yeah, that slow deceleration *killed them.*" Naretha let out a sarcastic laugh and tightened her grip on the overhead handle. "If *you* slow down, I'll kill the ones in the next car."

He clenched his jaw and kept his foot steady on the gas.

"Beverly's up ahead," Zeela said as she peered out the front windshield over Avner's shoulder.

"Dammit, I wanted to avoid Beverly." The Wacko squinted at the houses and buildings on either side of the road ahead. At that moment, the first car they'd seen thus far whizzed by in the opposite direction, and Avner swore as he turned the wheel too hard, almost spinning them off the road. As he resumed a straighter path, he distinctly heard Jamad retching from behind.

Zeela was unperturbed by the movement, her gaze steady on her hometown. "The only way to avoid Beverly is to go into a small development, where we'll get caught by the cops, or to run ourselves into the Muskingum River and hope this thing floats. Neither seems promising."

"We can't ride this piece of junk all the way to Cleveland," Naretha said, as if thinking aloud. "The cops have probably seen the license plate by now. We'll be lucky if we make it past Beverly before we're caught by another police force…"

Jamad's head rose high enough that Avner could see him through the mirror, his dark skin abnormally pale and features screwed in nausea. "We're going to Cleveland?"

Naretha groaned as she ran her free hand through her short, greasy hair. "We need to ditch this car and find a new one."

"How do you propose we do that when we've got cops chasing us?" Avner questioned, referring to the one persistent police car still on their tail.

The woman looked to Jamad, whose brow furrowed at her smirk. "You might be better with long range than me."

Avner watched his friend swallow and consider; he then watched him sit up with a new wave of confidence and aim his arctic blue eyes at the approaching vehicle. Just as Naretha had done with her salt crystals, Jamad produced a gust of frozen mist, which shot from his fingertips and solidified as it struck metal.

The wheels stopped turning and the police vehicle came to a sudden halt as it consolidated into a block of ice.

"*J*!" Avner scolded in astonishment as the frozen car faded into the distance.

"That'll buy us some time," Naretha reckoned, seemingly unimpressed by the teenager's display of power. "Now to get rid of this car and any evidence that *we* were in it."

"I have an ice Affinity, not a fire Affinity," Jamad stated blandly, though his eyes were still bright and sparkling like fresh snow.

"Maybe we should have brought *your* sister along, Av," Zeela joked, but he was past the point of humor—and past the point of caring to rebuke her assumptions that Adara had a fire Affinity. His mind ran frantically around the direness of their situation—the possibility that his girlfriend might be injured or imprisoned or *killed*.

"You want to burn this car and then what? *Run* to Cleveland?" he demanded, glaring at Naretha through the mirror. Her focus was trained on the river ahead, popping into view beyond the buildings and trees.

"No, we drown this car, run into town, and hide," she answered simply. "They don't know what we look like, and they'll be too preoccupied with recovering this car as evidence to search for us right away."

"Run this car into the river?" The rate of Avner's already racing heart escalated. He'd never properly learned how to swim; the few pool parties he'd attended had abruptly ended after he dipped his feet in the water and his friends complained of a mysterious shocking sensation. Submerging in a river didn't appeal to him, especially not while they were trapped inside a car. "*How*?"

"Unbuckle," Naretha ordered. "Kick off your door—"

"I'm *driving*!"

The Wacko's patience hit its peak, and instead of arguing, she pushed Jamad aside and slipped her arm through the space between Avner's seat and the door. Before he could comprehend what was happening, she yanked on the old door handle, but the pressure from the rushing air was too strong to allow the door to open.

"Shit, we're going too fast," she muttered so quietly that Avner could barely hear. "You're gonna have to jump out the back, like the rest of us."

"I can't keep my foot on the gas pedal if I'm climbing into the back!"

"I know, I know. I'm thinking we'll probably leave you to drown."

"You're kidding," Zeela snarled, her white eyes like slivered almonds.

"Someone has to be the sacrifice."

"Then it'll be *you*."

"*I* am the only one who knows how to get to Headquarters—"

"Screw this," Jamad interrupted as he shoved Naretha in the same way she'd shoved him. Without explanation, he leaned over Avner's shoulder and projected a spurt of frozen mist from his hand, encasing his friend's foot and freezing it to the pedal as a chunk of ice.

"Dude!" Avner exclaimed, accidentally jerking the wheel. "What the—"

"I only froze your shoe, man," Jamad assured him with a clap on the shoulder. "Take your foot out; the ice should be heavy enough to hold down the pedal."

"You can't seriously agree with the Wacko. We can't drive this thing into the river!"

"It's the only option," Zeela admitted remorsefully, gazing

ahead at the bridge looming above the river. Civilization congested the landscape now with residential and commercial buildings crowding either side of the road. Cars slowed as they neared the bridge, but since Avner's shoe was iced to the pedal, there was no stopping the station wagon as it zoomed at an unsafe speed down the street.

"Once we cross these train tracks, you'll need to veer off to the left through that parking lot," Naretha said, pointing toward the upcoming auto parts store. "Then drive through that other parking lot across the street, and from there it'll be a straight shot to the river, as long as we don't hit any trees…"

"This plan is becoming progressively more horrible," Avner said as he pulled his foot free from his shoe. As Jamad promised, the pedal remained flat to the floor, keeping the car moving at its full potential. "And I liked these shoes, J. You owe me."

"If we make it out of here alive, I'll buy you a new—"

"*Now*!" Naretha exclaimed as the car practically jumped over the train tracks. Ramming Avner's arm, she swerved their vehicle into the parking lot across the street, nearly taking out another car driving in the opposite direction. Zeela clung to the passenger's seat while Jamad gagged again, but the Wacko was unaffected by the recklessness.

As they plowed through this parking lot and the next across the street, fumbling over curbs and dodging parked cars, Naretha finally aimed the vehicle at a wide gap in the line of trees that separated the second parking lot from the river.

"Move to the back!"

Avner started to scramble from his seat, but the car struck a slight bump in the terrain that acted like a ramp, propelling the station wagon into the air and slamming all four passengers into the ceiling.

Screams, grunts, thuds, and moans filled the air as the car plunged on, ignorant to the people struggling to right themselves within. The earth was rougher than the pavement, jerking them around as Avner, dazed and bleeding, crawled toward the back to join the others. A screech surprised him as the left side of the car grazed the trunk of a tree, the metal tearing across the bark, and he found himself wedged between the two front seats when the station wagon descended into the water.

The actions that ensued were too rapid for Avner to process. Naretha was already rolling out the back as the car slammed into the water while Zeela and Jamad yanked frantically on Avner's arms. At the abrupt deceleration of the vehicle, his girlfriend's head banged against the ceiling, and her eyes rolled back, either in severe disorientation or complete unconsciousness. As her body slumped against the door, Jamad finally hauled Avner into the back, but it was too late; the car had fully submerged beneath the surface, and water surged in through the massive gap, drenching the three of them as the dying vehicle sunk deep into the murky gray river.

Avner scrambled to grab any part of his girlfriend, but the violent influx thwarted him. Within seconds, she became lost in the flood, and as everything blurred beneath the dark veil of water, he did, too. All he knew was that even if he possessed the ability to swim to the surface, he wouldn't let himself without Zeela.

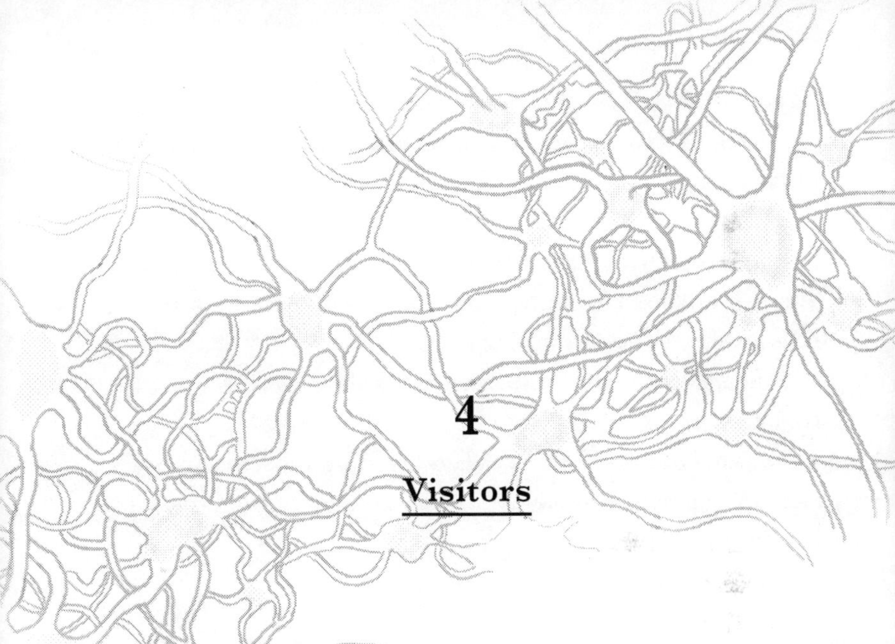

4

Visitors

"I never thought I'd say this, guys, but…I'm not hungry." Seth sighed, dejectedly staring at his full plate of food. The entire school was packed in the cafeteria, which, despite its colorful tables and chairs, embodied gloom. Typically, the noise and chatter of students was overwhelming; tonight, however, tones remained hushed.

Thoughts still assaulted Eliana, though. Hastings wove through everyone's minds, and the constant reminder of his absence provoked queasiness rather than hunger. Like Seth, she'd barely touched the meatloaf on her plate, and even Kiki on her left had eaten more.

"Try to look at the bright side," Tray advised as he shoveled meat into his mouth. "Everything might be awful, but at least Adara isn't here."

"Adara not being here is the reason I'm not hungry. She should be right *here*." Seth motioned to the seat between him and Eliana, in which Kiki currently sat. After a blink of her multi-colored eyes, she shot him an affronted glare that didn't penetrate his awareness.

"If she were here, she'd probably be sitting next to Ackerly," Lavisa commented as she nodded to the empty chair on his left. The green-haired boy munched on broccoli like a rabbit, but he paused when she spoke his name.

"Adara's probably…fine," he said weakly. "We'll go visit her after dinner."

"I wouldn't worry about Adara," Kiki drawled, leaning back and twirling her curly blonde hair around her finger. "I *saw* her future; she won't be in prison forever."

"What did you see?" Seth questioned.

Kiki's gaze dodged his as she uncomfortably said, "I…saw her surrounded by fire. Maybe she'll burn her way out of jail."

"I have no doubt about that," Tray grumbled through aggressive bites. "She'll definitely make a dramatic exit."

"Can we talk about the fact that Kiki can *see the future*, or are we gonna avoid the subject forever?" Hartman prompted, orange eyes darting around the table. Everyone waited awkwardly for Kiki to respond, and Eliana could feel irritation building defensive walls around the blonde girl's mind.

"No, we're not going to talk about it," she finally snapped, standing to tower over the table in her black heels. "I'm beginning to remember why I stopped hanging out with you losers."

"Kiks," Seth pleaded, but she shunned him and strutted off. She had nearly reached the cafeteria's exit when the glass doors swung open, admitting the chilly November air, as well as two cold-aired humans: the Regular ambassadors.

The Rosses' emotionless gazes swept the room, and Kiki's strides halted at the sight of them, her fear strong enough to reach Eliana even with the many minds between them. Artemis

Ross stood six inches shorter than Kiki, but the woman's authoritative aura shrunk the teenager to the size of a worm. As the two Regg ambassadors glared at her with dark eyes, she slowly slunk back toward the table until her bottom was planted in the seat between Seth and Eliana. None of the primaries asked her why she'd rejoined them; the imposing presence of the Rosses alerted everyone that whatever they were about to declare must be heard by all.

"Ah, Mr. and Mrs. Ross," Fraco greeted as he scampered to them. "I was under the impression that you'd already left, otherwise I would have prepared dinner accommodations."

"We have no intention of leaving," Artemis replied stonily. A knot at the base of her skull contained her slick, dark hair, pulling the wrinkles of her round face back and giving her a younger appearance than her taller, leaner, and grayer husband.

The vice principal hesitated to answer Artemis's bold claim, giving William the opportunity to say, "You may resume your seat, Fraco."

At the faculty table across the room, Aethelred was the only teacher to maintain poise; the rest defaulted to suspicion while Fraco descended into dismay.

"I-I am the acting principal—"

"You've been relieved of your duties," Artemis assured him without any friendliness. He staggered back, as if stabbed, but he didn't retreat to the teachers' table before someone else beckoned for his attention.

"Hey, Fraco!" Nero Corvis called from the far corner. Surrounded by his gang of smirking comrades, the bulky bully held no respect for the arrogant adults. The only one of his group that appeared less than amused was Calder, whose eyes aimed enmity at his leader as he bellowed, "What's with these plastic utensils?"

Fraco squinted, as if trying to physically see the question. "The…utensils…"

"Are we trying to kill the environment now, or can we not wash the metal utensils because of a water shortage?" Nero jeered as he snapped every plastic fork and spoon in reach.

"A water shortage seems impossible to me," Nixie Mardurus said, flicking the broken pieces of plastic her boyfriend dropped on the table. Like everyone, she wore black, but her lacy, gothic dress was adorned with dark blue accents that matched her spunky hair and sly eyes.

Artemis frowned at Nero's careless wreckage. "You can thank Adara Stromer for the new plastic utensils. We were informed she stabbed another student with a metal fork; therefore, they have been deemed dangerous."

"Dangerous," Calder repeated with a condescending laugh. "She barely broke my skin. And I healed, for the record. I'm not a pu—"

"A wuss," Fraco interjected, predicting what the boy had intended to say. "You're not a wuss, Mr. Mardurus—we're all aware. Thank you, Mr. and Mrs. Ross," he added to the Reggs, now recovering from the bewilderment that had petrified him, "for your consideration of our students' safety."

"Where are those lousy Stromers anyway?" Nero asked loudly to no one in particular. Attention flew from the empty table that Avner, Zeela, and Jamad had always occupied to where Eliana and her friends sat near the buffet. She hated the shallow pity her peers vaguely felt when their gazes paused on her.

"The Stromers are no longer students here," William announced, causing a murmur to wave around the crowd. Eliana knew Avner had gone and Adara was in jail, but for these Reggs to declare they weren't students, as if they'd been permanently expelled...

Even Nero's thick eyebrows creased at this news. "What is that supposed to mean?"

"It means both siblings are criminals," Artemis informed him. "Avner Stromer has aided in the escape of the captured Wacko, Naretha Salone. If he is found, he will be imprisoned. If he returns here, he will also be imprisoned. Adara Stromer, on the other hand, is a suspected accomplice in Angor Periculy's recent assassination attempt against my husband and myself. She has been placed in jail, along with Angor, until we can determine her—"

"Adara didn't try to murder you!" Seth exclaimed, jumping from his seat. "She tried to murder Angor after he tried to murder—"

"Regardless," William cut in sternly, "she is a danger to this town."

"Adara Stromer might be a...a witch," Tray stammered, "but she's all talk."

"No, no, Stromer is dangerous," Nero piped up, nodding with eyes widened in fake fear. Though Eliana wasn't a fan of his morals, she did have to admire the way he could spin any situation to his advantage. "She should stay in that jail forever, I think."

"You're just scared, 'cause now she might actually beat you in a fight!" Hartman called over to his stepbrother, who abandoned his act of apprehension and aimed his slivered gray eyes at the younger Corvis.

"I could still beat her, but she could hurt other people, and I care a lot about other people."

Tray snorted audibly, but Artemis spoke before he could jump back into the argument.

"You are all aware by now that Angor Periculy's assassination attempt resulted in the death of Hastings Lanio."

"His death was tragic," William said, dipping his head solemnly. Eliana's body involuntarily stiffened at his manipulative sympathy. "Mrs. Ross and I have been instructed to ensure nothing of the sort ever befalls Periculand again."

"How do you plan to do that? Do you have an Affinity for preventing death?" Tray challenged, but Eliana shook her head at him. Even through her anger, she'd been able to read William's thoughts, and she knew exactly what their plans were.

"No, we are fully Regular," Artemis replied, "but we have been appointed as the new overseers of this town."

Fraco had to clasp a chair with his slippery hand to prevent himself from falling. "O-overseers?"

"Technically, we are the new principals," William explained with little care for the oily man's mental health. "You will remain vice principal, Fraco—*our* vice principal. You answer to us now."

Fraco's entire face twitched as his hand slid over the chair, but instead of stumbling, he straightened his posture and gave the two Reggs a smarmy bow. "Of course."

"*Of course*?" Seth hissed, spinning to face his twin. "He's just gonna let Adara sit in jail!"

"The next few days will be a time of mourning and adjustment," Artemis declared, vanquishing the whispers throughout the room. "Mr. Ross and I will assess the situation here in Periculand and determine our next course of action. We ask for your full cooperation through this process. We are here for your safety and security."

"So, what are the *rules* now?" Nero asked as he stabbed broken pieces of the plastic utensils into his uneaten meatloaf.

"For now, the rules will remain the same," William said, "but we believe this school has been run poorly under Angor's authority, and we plan to make changes."

"Well," Lavisa droned, her boots up on the table as she picked at a scab on her calf, "if the rules are the same, that means Corvis will break them just as he always has."

Nero snarled from across the room, but Seth was the next to speak.

"If the rules haven't changed, does that mean we can still visit Adara in jail?"

"That is the one rule that has changed," Artemis countered without remorse. "The prisoners of Periculand's jail will receive no visitors until we can determine the danger they pose—and ensure there is no one here who would dare to help them escape."

"Was there ever a point when you hated Hastings for what he did to your lover?" Adara asked, genuinely curious, as she stared up at the plain white ceiling. Again, she lay on her "bed," the metal slab cold beneath the warmth of her ash-covered skin. Angor sat in the other corner of the room, looking like a little boy with his knees hugged against his chest.

"No," he sighed, ignoring the pinkish hair that fell in strands over his face. "I blame myself for Jocosa's death. If I had not impregnated her, our son never would have killed her. If *I* had not impregnated her, perhaps her son would not have had an Affinity. If I had been there, at least, I could have trained him, worked with him…" Shaking his head, he stretched out his long legs and pivoted his head toward Adara. "That's why I was so adamant about training him when he arrived here—why we had so many meetings. I didn't want him to do what he did to Jocosa to…anyone else."

Adara's eyebrows shot up as she glanced at him from the corner of her eye. "Is there someone specific you're referring to?"

Though Angor pursed his lips, he was unable to voice a response before the door beyond their prison cell opened and Mitt peeked through.

Adara inclined her head slightly to look at him. "Is Devil-Red here?"

"No, I've received word from the Rosses—"

"Of course they remain," Angor said with a dramatic breath. "Have they claimed themselves the rulers of this town yet?"

Mitt shifted uneasily. "Yes, actually. And they've decreed that none of Periculand's prisoners are allowed to have visitors."

"Of course they have," Adara grumbled as she banged her head back on the metal. "Did you come to bring me donuts then?"

"Well...no. I came because you have a visitor."

Springing upright, Adara locked her gaze on where Mitt was positioned in the threshold, shielding the visitor from sight. "Seth?"

"Um—"

"No, it's Prince Charming," a slippery voice said as he pushed past Mitt and waltzed into the hall. Still in his suit from the funeral, Calder Mardurus stepped up to the humming metal bars and flashed a cocky grin that gave light to his deep blue eyes. With him, he brought the scent of outside's downpour—the fresh, damp fragrance Adara had come to recognize—and though the rain should have soaked him, every inch of the boy was perfectly dry. "Cue the clapping and whistling."

All elation extinguished as Adara rolled her eyes and flopped back against the wall to stare at the ceiling. "God, I've had this coming for me, haven't I?"

A sassy retort from Calder was expected, but his haughtiness had withered and a hint of trepidation now characterized his features. "Your—eyes," he choked, struggling to regain coolness.

"Oh, yes, I've heard they're a hellish red. I'm pretty *hot* now, I guess."

"Aethelred can pull off the red eyes," Calder began, appraising her carefully, "but you look like a full-fledged demon."

"Demon*ess*. Yes, I've been informed," she assured him with a dismissive wave. "Have you come here only to say things I've already heard, Pixie Prince?"

"Mostly," he said, shrugging in a way that restored some of his confidence. "I had plans to come here and mock you with the same words you used to mock me when I was on the other side of these bars." He reached out, as if to touch the electric metal, but then he withdrew with a lofty smirk. "What do you think of these duck slippers, Stromer?" Involuntarily, Adara's jaw dropped at the sight of the yellow slippers she had once stolen from Kiki to taunt Calder with now on his own feet. "Jealous?"

"Where did you get those?" she demanded, hopping off the table to approach him.

"You were supposed to say, 'Should I be?'"

"Should I *show you what my Affinity can do*?" Her jaw clenched at the instinctive burning of her skin. It wasn't a painful sensation, but flames itched to burst from her flesh, and that sickening thought alone chilled her.

The building fire must have been apparent to Calder, because he licked the derision off his lips. "I raided your dorm before coming here. For all the Reggs' talk about not being able to visit prisoners, I had no problem sneaking over here. Maybe I'm just naturally stealthy, though."

"They actually took over? They run this town now? What are they saying about *him*?" When she threw her thumb over her shoulder in Angor's direction, Calder noticed him for the first time, and the Pixie Prince's humorous expression morphed into a scowl.

"They're saying what I assume is the truth—that the mysterious Angor Periculy attempted to murder the Regg ambassadors with his mind controlling Affinity but killed Hastings instead. And then *you* erupted like a volcano of flames," he added, almost delightedly. "Let's see it, Stromer. Don't worry about setting the jail ablaze—I happen to be an expert firefighter. We wouldn't want to let you burn down the prison, would we?"

"I don't—I can't—" She cut off her stammers and tightened her hands into fists at her sides. "I don't have a fire Affinity."

"No? Well, did you jump into a chimney then? You *are* covered in soot, if you were unaware."

Adara snarled through bared teeth, but before she could voice a retort, Calder lifted his finger and sent an invisibly thin jet of water at her face. The liquid streamed across her forehead in an intricate design that she assumed were obscenities carved from the ashes.

"What the hell?"

"Don't touch it," Calder reprimanded, swatting her reaching hand with another spout of water. "You'll ruin the masterpiece. It says 'LIAR,' if you're curious. I was going to write, 'I'm a foolish, reckless, fire-breathing liar,' but your forehead's not *that* big. What do you think, Telum?"

Mitt scratched his chin as he surveyed her. "The simplicity of it works. Stromer always *has* been a liar. I'm sure you've heard her deny that she set Kiki Belven's house on fire a few months back, but given her Affinity, we all know that was a lie."

"If I'd wanted to set Kiki's house on fire, it would be a pile of ash," Adara scoffed, blinking furiously as a droplet from Calder's water-writing slipped onto her eyelashes; the rest had dried instantly upon meeting the unnatural heat of her skin. "And I'm not the liar here; the King is the one who's spitting lies. Says he's innocent—didn't try to kill those Reggs. Claims he doesn't have a mind controlling Affinity, and that Hastings was his son."

Mitt blinked his bulging silver eyes while Calder scrunched his blue ones in skepticism.

"I appreciate that you have no qualms with spewing my secrets to whomever enters this room," Angor intoned. "Considerate, Stromer, very considerate."

"My brother's the nice one, Your Highness."

"How can Periculy be the king if I'm a prince?" Calder asked.

"*That's* what you're wondering?" Mitt blurted out as he paced toward the cell. "I wanna know how Hastings could have been his son."

"That's actually the only part of this asshole's story that I find somewhat believable," Adara said with a distasteful glance back at her cellmate. "If it is true, though, then the rest…starts to make sense. I need to talk to Aethelred—confirm the facts. I need you to bring him to me." Her harsh glare was trained on Calder now, and she fidgeted when his lips curled back over his teeth.

"Desperate, are you, Stromer? You must be if you think I'll meet your demands."

Adara strolled back to her metal slab in lazy, calculated steps. "I'm not demanding anything, Pixie Prince. I'm perfectly content with allowing this creep to rot in his cell, even if he's innocent. You should know by now that I have no care for justice."

"You don't care about other people receiving justice…but what about for yourself? You know they're saying you were his accomplice, don't you? If Periculy burns, so do you."

Feigning indifference, Adara plopped onto her bed and

stretched her arms behind her head. "I hope that pun wasn't intended, because it was lame. I have no problem with lounging in this cell for the rest of my days—no school, no Tray, no Kiki, and until now, no *you*."

Calder studied the bare walls, unconvinced. "You bore easily. You won't do well in here."

"What makes you say that? All I've ever wanted was to do nothing. This is my dream come true. Could use some donuts, though," she added with a pointed look at Mitt. "Or a freakin' shower."

Friskiness readjusted Calder's features. "I can arrange that, if you get undressed—"

"All right, time for Mardurus to leave," Mitt announced as he grabbed the boy's elbow and hauled him toward the exit.

"It was a *joke*. There's no attraction between us—we're opposites."

"Opposites attract," Angor put in thoughtfully, and Adara rolled her eyes. "Your water Affinity is impressive, Calder, as is Adara's fire Affinity, but there is always room for improvement. If you agree to fetch Aethelred—if you help us escape from this jail—I will agree to train both of you, together."

Calder released a tactless laugh. "I'd rather dance with the devil than train with the Fire Demoness." Adara's gaze rose at that, and she fought not to display any hint of emotion. "Besides, based on her words, she enjoys being cooped up in this little hellhole. Then again, who believes the words of a fire-breathing liar?"

5

Velkommen and Un-*Velkommen*

A cocoon of comforting coldness enveloped Avner, but it ruptured when his body met frigid air. Teeth chattering, he flopped onto the muddy earth and hacked up river water for a few agonizing minutes. When his lungs were finally clear and his eyes focused on his surroundings, he found his companion looked equally unwell.

Faint beams of moving headlights lit Jamad's blue hair as he shook water from it. To their left loomed the bridge they'd skirted, busy with passing cars, but Avner knew no one would spot them by the river's edge. The darkness of evening concealed them from view of spectators or searchers.

"Cops," Jamad coughed with disdain as sirens blared in the distance. "This could have been avoided if they hadn't chased us."

"This could have been avoided if we hadn't *stolen a car*." Avner pushed to his knees, joints creaking and head throbbing. Slowly, he pivoted into a seated position and stared at the deep gray water. They'd washed up on the opposite side of the river, and there was no trace of the vehicle beneath the surface. With sudden alarm, Avner realized there was also no trace of the girls. "Where is Zeela?"

"Uh..." Jamad scratched his head and winced as Avner jumped to his feet, one shoe still missing. "Let me get that ice off you—"

"Where is Zeela?" Avner repeated, ignoring the frost numbing his body.

Jamad scrambled to his feet. "She...passed out in the car—hit her head, I think. I pulled you both out, but Z got caught in the current."

"Why would *she* not be your priority over me? J—"

"I saved your life, man," he said softly, his brow wrinkled with hurt. "And of course I care about Z, but...I saw the Wacko grab her."

"*What*?"

"Naretha—she...she got out of the car before it crashed, but then she jumped into the water to save Zeela. They were behind me for a while, but..." Jamad's hopeless gaze raked over the water. "We've been here for over five minutes and I haven't seen them."

"God," Avner moaned, gripping his icy hair and pulling at the frozen strands. "This is all my fault. We never should have done this. I'm going back in."

"Av," Jamad pleaded, placing a hand on his friend's arm. As he did, he absorbed some of the ice, slowly thawing Avner's frozen form. "You...can't. When you were in the water—when *we* were in the water—you kept...electrocuting me. Pretty badly, too. I don't think I would have made it if I wasn't used to your voltage, or whatever. You know this dirty water's a conductor, and...I don't know how far it extended—if it affected the girls..."

Avner's ears deafened to outside noise as his heartbeat escalated to a roar. He scanned the river, the shoreline, the bridge, but his sight was clouded with panic. Zeela could be dead and it would be his fault. He shouldn't have sanctioned this mission, he shouldn't have allowed them to steal the car, he should have been more careful—

"Avner, look!" Jamad gripped his elbow and hauled him along the bank, closer to the bridge. So dazed by worry, Avner almost didn't notice the two figures approaching as Naretha dragged Zeela by her forearms. His girlfriend's face had paled to the hue of her hair, and she didn't even flinch as the Wacko heaved her over roots and rocks.

"What happened?" Jamad demanded once the Wacko stood before them. Her dirt-drenched hair lay unflatteringly flat against her head, and her thin prison garb would have been nearly transparent in daylight. When her pink eyes slid up to the two boys, they did not harbor nearly as much anxiety.

"I hate water," was Naretha's acidic response. An involuntary shiver overcame her, forcing her to drop Zeela's arms. Avner fell to his knees as his girlfriend hit the ground and then brushed frozen hair from her face.

"Is she…alive?" he asked, fingers trembling as he attempted to find her pulse.

"She better be, considering I risked my life to save her," Naretha grumbled, ruffling her hair. Jamad had removed the frost, drying her, but goosebumps still covered her skin.

"Can't you revive her, Av? Restart her heart?"

"Her…heart is still beating."

"Then give her a little jolt to wake her up?" Jamad suggested, earning a brief scowl before Avner brought his attention back to Zeela's face. Her sunglasses had disappeared in the crash, unveiling her delicately closed eyes, and she looked as peaceful as always, almost as if she *were* dead.

"Did I… Did you feel any electricity in the water?" Avner asked the Wacko.

"No, it was just *cold*." As a bitter afterthought, she added to Jamad, "Of course *you're* fine."

He shrugged, but his grin didn't remain when his eyes found Zeela again. "Do you want me to carry her?"

"No, I—" Avner began, but his voice died when Zeela sprang upward, instantly regurgitating river water. Hastily, he rolled her onto her side, and Jamad set his hand on her forehead to thaw her flesh. After a few moments, her breathing resumed its normal rhythm as her eyeballs slid around within their sockets.

"I…I'm blind," she croaked, and the boys exchanged a smirk.

"We know, Z—"

"*No*, I'm *blind*! Everything—it's all mixed up—I can't see anything clearly," she stammered, squinting and shaking her head. All smiles faded, and when the boys looked at each other this time, their eyes were full of unease.

"Well, help her up," Naretha said impatiently. "We need to get moving before we're spotted. I'm not sure if you've heard, but sirens have been blasting since I surfaced. I'm sure the cops are searching this town for us."

"Beverly," Jamad sighed wistfully, peeking through the trees that lined the river to the residential area beyond. "Never thought I'd see it again."

"I guess I *won't* see it again," Zeela muttered, rubbing her forehead as she leaned on Avner for support.

"This is just temporary," he assured her, but it felt more like reassurance for himself. "You're just dazed. Your sight will come back."

Zeela grunted but made no reply as they climbed up the slight incline and through the trees. They soon found themselves at the end of a cul-de-sac lined with old houses that fit the country landscape. Avner recognized none of it, but Jamad's scanning eyes stopped on the remodeled colonial with white siding and burgundy shutters to their right.

"Z, I see your parents' house."

She scrunched her face, straining to see, but her head wasn't even aimed toward her former home. "Do you see *them*?"

Jamad shook his head but then, upon realizing her vision was useless, added, "No. They're not home."

"Good. They'd report us if they saw us out here."

"We need to keep moving," Naretha said with a wary glance at the Mensens' house. "Even if they're not home now, they could come—"

"Where are we planning on going?" Avner interrupted. "We don't have a car, and if the Wacko hideout is in Cleveland, that's at least a two-hour *drive* from here. We can't walk. Zeela can't see."

"And Avner's bleeding," Jamad put in, deepening the Wacko's frown. "We need to stop somewhere—and we need to eat. You've never been a teenage boy, so you don't understand, but the hunger is real."

Naretha hummed as she surveyed the Mensens' house. "Does she know how to break in?"

Zeela expelled a humorless laugh. "We are not breaking into my parents' house. They would never stop until they found us. And it doesn't look like much, but they've got it secured like it's holding treasure—alarms, cameras... How close are we to it? Last time I was here, they had outdoor cameras."

"Shit, I forgot about that," Jamad muttered as he retreated a few steps. "And I forgot your parents are psychos. If we're not gonna raid a store, *my* parents' house would be ideal. If they're home, they'll be happy to see me, and if they're not home, I'll leave them a note and they'll understand."

Naretha's jaw shifted in skepticism, but after another shiver, she crossed her arms and nodded. "Lead the way."

Flashing his teeth, Jamad motioned past the Mensens' house to a dark, grassy field. The distant lights of the town weren't very bright, allowing visibility of the stars shining around the crescent moon as they trekked through the empty meadow.

"Do you remember walking this way when you used to sneak over to my house?" Jamad asked Zeela, who used her boyfriend's arm as a guide.

"Yeah, I remember," she said, her eyes shut. "Your street is straight ahead."

"She's lying about being blind," Jamad whispered loudly. "Doubt she's ever *really* been blind enough to know what it's like."

Her lips slid upward. "I just remember the feel of Beverly, J. How could I forget our hometown?"

"Yeah, how could you forget such a God-awful place like this?" Naretha chimed in.

"All right, so Beverly's *small*," Jamad agreed, "but it's got character. It's a quaint, stress-free place—the kind of place you probably want to blow up with your terrorist buddies."

"I don't hate it because I want to kill people; I hate it because we got stranded here and it happens to be a town in which you two know people. That makes us easily recognizable, easily traceable. This is an undesirable location for us."

"It's a great town—"

"If I ever have an unwanted child, I'm naming it Beverly."

"An unwanted child with the Wacko leader?" Jamad suggested with a wiggle of his eyebrows.

"Let's hope not," she mumbled as she squinted up at the stars. She hugged her torso with her thin arms, attempting to ward off the cold, but Jamad didn't offer her warmth as Avner did with Zeela. Instead, he badgered her with more questions.

"How did you end up with the Wacko leader, anyway? What's he like, huh? Is he old enough to be your dad?"

Naretha snorted. "Danny is younger than me, actually."

One of Jamad's light blue eyebrows shot up. "How much younger?"

"Not as young as you, little one."

"How does a guy younger than twenty-five find himself in charge of an entire terrorist organization?" Avner asked, peeking over Zeela's head at the Wacko.

She ran a hand through her lusterless hair. "It's a long story."

"Classic excuse. We have approximately two minutes until we arrive at my house," Jamad said, consulting his invisible watch. "Tell away."

"It's too complicated for you little teenagers to understand."

"Fine, then explain why you saved me," Zeela demanded. "We all saw you escape the car before it went under. Why come back in to save me, rather than cross the bridge and return to your Wacko hideout alone?"

With a lick of her lips, Naretha rather gruffly repeated, "It's complicated."

Zeela emitted another spiteful laugh, but she didn't pry any further, since they'd reached what Avner assumed to be Jamad's street. Based on the way he gawked at the small, red-bricked ranch across the pavement, this was his childhood home.

"It's… It looks the same, Z—just like when we left it three years ago. Dad got a new car, though, which is surprising."

"Mm, he did love that old Volvo."

"Lights are on, unfortunately," Naretha observed. "How long

do you think it'll take them to notice if Sparky starts the car and leaves with it?"

"Probably less than a second, considering this town is so quiet—and considering they're looking at us right now." Avner tilted his head toward the house, where two silhouettes watched from the front window. Jamad balked at the sight of his parents, so Naretha shoved him forward.

"Fine, let's go meet our doom," she grumbled and stalked across the street.

"Jamad's parents are nice," Zeela defended, since he was too overwhelmed to speak. "Although I wouldn't blame anyone for being mean to you, since you're a mass-murdering terrorist."

"Don't get testy with me, Blindie. I saved your—"

"Just be quiet," Avner hissed as the four stepped up to the front porch. The white railing was old but sturdy enough for Zeela to use as a crutch, allowing Avner to release her. "And whatever you do, Wacko, they can't know who you are."

"I'm not an *idiot*—"

The wood door beyond the screen flew open before the bickering could intensify. On the other side stood a Caucasian couple wearing pajamas and baffled expressions. Avner and Naretha blinked in mutual surprise.

After a long minute of silence, the Wacko finally said, "I think your parents moved, Snowman."

"*Snowman*?" Jamad repeated from behind her. "That makes me sound rotund. What about *Ice Beast*?"

"Jamad," the woman in the doorway breathed, her accent distinctly French. With golden eyes that rivaled Orla Belven's, she peered over their heads at Jamad, who pushed through Avner and Naretha to face the adults beyond the screen. The man's lips cracked into a grin, and he flung the door open before throwing his arms around him.

"*Gutten min*!" he cried, squeezing Jamad like a child, even though the teen was a few inches taller. He pulled away to reveal a curly blond ponytail and eyes nearly as blue as Jamad's, though it was the only trait they shared. From their pale skin to their calm vibe to their Regularness, these adults didn't resemble Avner's best friend at all.

"Are these…" the man began again in a Norwegian accent, gesturing to the other three.

Jamad glanced back, pausing for a second on Naretha. "My friends? Yeah, Dad. You guys remember Zeela, right?"

The woman gasped even before Jamad shifted to reveal her. Zeela's eyes were still sealed, but she stood straight and took a step toward the sound of their voices.

"Hi." She stumbled into Jamad. "Um, I'm blind."

"As if that's a surprise to anyone," he joked, but neither of his parents laughed. They were still shocked by the sight of the girl they had known for so many years, standing on their porch so altered.

"Your hair," the woman whispered, reaching for Zeela's white locks. "And *your* hair." With a step closer to Jamad, she stroked her thin fingers along his fuzzy blue hair and smiled sadly. "You grow so tall. I remember when you were here." She motioned to below her chin, and Jamad let out an emotion-filled laugh before he wrapped his arms around her. The embrace lasted for a few tear-filled moments before the woman pulled away and took his hand, leading him into their home.

"*Velkommen*, friends of my son. Come in, come in," the man beckoned, stepping out of the way so they could enter.

Avner aided Zeela over the shallow step but didn't bother holding the door open for Naretha. Likely wary of accepting the hospitality of Reggs, she remained on the porch for a few extra moments while the rest submerged into the warmth. Though Avner didn't particularly care for her, if she escaped them now, they'd have no bargaining chip with which to retrieve Maddy—or any means of finding the Wackos' hideout. That was why, when Naretha prowled in, scrutinizing the house with distaste, Avner was mildly relieved.

"This is my dad, Elias, and my mom, Colette. And this is Avner, my best bro," Jamad introduced, prompting him to shake hands with both Solberg parents. "And that's Naretha."

The Wacko didn't smile when everyone glanced in her direction. She did frown, though, when Colette whispered, "Girlfriend?"

Jamad laughed heartily. "No, no, Mom, but she would be if I wanted her to be." The wink he shot Naretha elicited a growl, but he ignored her as he bragged to his mother, "I get *all* the girls in Periculand. Well, except for Z. She's strictly Avner's."

"Are you all hungry?" Elias asked, provoking the immediate response of "*Starving*!" from Zeela. As he retreated from the room for the kitchen and Jamad exchanged a few words in French with his mother, Avner watched Naretha stalk the perimeter of the living room. An ancient television sat in the front corner, surrounded by plaid couches and a tacky rug. Paintings of mountains adorned the wood paneled walls, and from afar, he spotted a photograph of Elias and Colette's wedding. Jamad stood between them, so young and different with his dark hair and eyes.

Ten minutes after entering the house, the four Affinities were seated at the old wooden dining table, and Zeela had somehow acquired two eye patches to help with the headache that seeing induced. One had the Superman logo while the other was simply SpongeBob's face.

"You look like a prophetic pirate," Jamad observed.

"I can still kick you, even though I'm actually blind now." Her pursed lips indicated that her eyes were narrowed, even if the childish fabric obscured them. Avner couldn't stop snickering about it.

"I had glasses as a kid," Jamad explained to Naretha, who surveyed the eye patches with disgust. "Had to wear those patches sometimes. It should have been embarrassing, but I thought it was pretty dope."

"Clearly," the Wacko droned, arms crossed over her filthy prison shirt. Neither of the Solberg parents had mentioned it, so Avner assumed Jamad had told them it was a strange clothing trend. "Explain to me how you have a Norwegian dad and a French mom but your lineage is clearly African."

Jamad leaned back in his chair with a skeptically furrowed brow. "We don't *know* that my lineage is African. I could be… Jamaican, or—"

"You know what I mean," she interrupted through gritted teeth.

"Well, they didn't birth me, if that's what you somehow assumed." He stretched his arms behind his head tauntingly. "I was abandoned by my biological parents. Apparently, I was an *unwanted child*." His eyebrows perked at that, and she stiffened. "Elias found me alone in an alley in Chicago when I was about a year old. He was only twenty-six and a recent immigrant from Norway, and he tried to find my real parents, but when no one claimed me, he kept me as his own. He got a job near Beverly not long after that and bought this house when I was about five, which was also when he adopted me formally. He was always Dad to me, though."

"Since I don't see skin colors—or any colors—the way you guys do, I thought J was Norwegian when I first met him," Zeela said with a reminiscent smile. "It was our first day of kindergarten, and he started talking to me in Norwegian and I had no idea what the hell he was saying."

"Yeah, so she started speaking to me in *Japanese*," Jamad added, as if it were ridiculous. "That was when we realized our only common language was English."

"Mm, what a strange concept in *America*."

"We always spoke Norwegian at home—"

"*Anyway*," Zeela cut in dramatically, "I didn't put it together that Elias wasn't Jamad's father for a few years. My Affinity didn't kick in too much until I was about eight, and then I started to recognize that their facial features were different. I had no idea about their skin, though, until Jamad told me. I still don't really know the difference."

"Dang, I had no idea you were even adopted. Never thought to ask," Avner mused as he drummed his fingers on the scratched wood. "Guess I shouldn't be surprised by the interracial family, though. My foster family was black."

"*Really*?" Jamad sat forward in his chair. "Why didn't you ever tell me?"

"Why didn't *you* ever tell *me*?" Avner challenged with a knowing smirk.

Resuming his slouch, Jamad waved in surrender. "Touché, my friend. I guess it never mattered to me what color skin they had or where they were from. Elias took me in when no one else wanted me, and when Colette showed up, she immediately treated me like her own. They love me, so they're my parents."

"Same. I've missed my foster family these past few years... Adara always hated them, but I think that was only because they made her eat healthy and do her homework. Plus, she hates everyone."

"Your sister's the little brat with the red hair, right?" Naretha clarified.

Avner shrugged one shoulder and winced. "One could describe her as such."

"How else would you describe her?" Zeela questioned, cocking her head to the side.

"I mean...her hair's not really *red*," Avner said uncomfortably, earning a chuckle from Jamad, "although it probably will be once she harnesses her Affinity."

"Her fire Affinity," Zeela coughed, and Avner shot her a playful glare. He still wasn't convinced his sister's Affinity was fire, but if it was, it would certainly be more intense and deadly in her hands than anyone else's.

"If we ever make it back to Periculand, I'll train with her," Jamad assured him. "I have a feeling I could quench a fire pretty easily."

"You cocky teenagers will be the death of us all," Naretha sighed as she picked dirt from her fingernails. "You still have a long way to go with your Affinities."

"And *you're* an expert?" Jamad countered sassily.

"*No*, but... All I'm saying is each of you could improve if you chose to work with us."

Even with her eye patches, Zeela's disgust was evident in the dropping of her jaw. "Are you suggesting we *join* a terrorist group?"

"It's not—" Naretha began but stopped when the Solbergs emerged from the kitchen with plates of steaming pasta in their hands. After placing one in front of each Affinity, they assumed their respective seats with beaming smiles.

"Eat, eat, please!" Elias insisted, but not before Jamad shoved his first forkful into his mouth.

"Still the only dish you can make right, huh, Dad?"

"His cooking is improving." Colette gave her husband an encouraging pat on the shoulder. "But not much."

Elias's laugh came straight from his belly. "It's not so bad," he said, mostly to Naretha, as she was the only one who hadn't picked up her fork. After the scrutiny from the man, she reluctantly took a bite.

"We did not think we would see you again, Jamad," Colette said as she fiddled with the hem of her sleeves. "Why did they allow you to leave?"

The blue-haired boy choked on his pasta, but Avner quickly flashed a charming smile. "Can you tell us the story of how you two met? I'm intrigued—was it in Europe?"

Colette's mouth drooped, taken aback, but Elias eagerly clapped his hands before diving into the tale. "You must know that Jamad and I enjoy mountain climbing, correct?"

Zeela nodded while Avner gaped. "I, um—no, I didn't know," he admitted with a confused look in his friend's direction. Jamad refused to tear his focus away from the pasta.

"I have always loved adventure," Elias explained with a genuine smile at his son. "Jamad and I traveled the world when he was young. We were visiting the Great Wall in China, and she was visiting the Great Wall in China…" He gestured animatedly toward his wife. "Jamad and I ventured off the Wall and climbed one side of Mount Tai, and when we looked across the mountain range to the other side of the Great Wall, we saw her standing at the peak, so beautiful…"

"Oh, that's a bunch of bull, Dad." Jamad laughed before swallowing his food. "We *were* at the Great Wall, but we first saw Mom when Dad was trying to get a picture of the mountain and then backed into her and nearly broke her foot."

"Romantic," Naretha commented as she munched loudly on her pasta. Avner couldn't decide if her tone was sarcastic.

Elias smirked, his blue eyes sliding to his wife. "She was very gracious—did not yell at me."

"I wanted to," Colette teased, lightly punching his arm. "He was very kind, though. He gave me his phone number, and we planned to meet again. After the accident, I rushed to see them—"

"What accident?" Avner inquired as Zeela's fork scraped the bottom of her plate. Even blind, she'd eaten all of her pasta, and now, without anything to do, her demeanor shifted into intense awkwardness.

"She means incident, I think," Elias said, brushing a blond curl from his forehead. "It was not an accident, but it was unfortunate—"

"What was?"

"Gunnbjørn Fjeld. Jamad has surely told you the story of our time there." As he inclined his head toward his son, the boy sunk low in his seat and trained his vision on the food before him. "Have not you told Avner of the day you saved us from the ice?"

Avner's eyebrows creased as he pivoted toward his guilty friend. "I thought Jamad acquired his Affinity when he slipped on ice?"

"You told him *that*?" Zeela blurted out. "That's an awful lie. I'm surprised he bought it."

"*You* know about this…this *field*—"

"It's a mountain." Jamad released a breath and dropped his fork carelessly onto the table. "Greenland's highest mountain. Very remote, very hard to climb, very *cold*. Dad and I were traveling the world the summer before fifth grade. We'd climbed plenty of mountains—plenty of icy mountains, too—but a storm hit when we were on Gunnbjørn. We would have died if my body hadn't adapted—if my Affinity hadn't given me the ability to fend off the ice and snow."

"Well, that's one of the more intense Affinity stories I've heard," Naretha put in as she twirled her fork in the spaghetti. "And I've heard quite a few intense stories. What made you think slipping on ice would sound cooler than that?"

"It's not really a day I like to recall," Jamad snapped, his usual coolness cracking. "And…I don't like when people look at me with pity. I'd rather have them laugh about how I'm an idiot than act like I have some tortured past."

"Most Affinities do," Naretha reminded him before slurping the noodles. Avner continued studying his friend with a sense of distance he'd never experienced between them.

"You all have powers, yes?" Colette prompted, quenching his dismal thoughts. "We know Zeela is not really blind."

"I am now"—she tapped her eye patches—"but usually I'm not. I've been told my hair is a different color than it was when I left Beverly."

"Yes, it is white now. It was gray when you left, and Jamad's hair was much darker blue. How strange…" Colette's words trailed off as she looked from Jamad to Zeela to Avner. "And you? What is your superpower?"

"Electricity," Avner replied absently. "Not sure how I got it. Probably stuck my finger in an outlet when I was young or something."

"And you?" Colette asked Naretha.

The Wacko flicked a finger over her plate and watched as tiny salt crystals showered over the pasta. "Salt."

Elias's head bobbed back. "Salt? I did not know that was a superpower."

"It is, and I could probably kill you with—"

"Sorry," Jamad apologized before the woman could finish her threat. "She's a little, well… Uh, thanks for dinner. Real good, Dad—"

"Will you sleep here?" Colette interrupted anxiously. "We were not expecting you. I am scared we are not prepared."

"Don't fuss, Mom. We can all sleep in my room for the night. We don't plan to stay long."

"I wasn't under the impression that we were staying at all..."

Jamad either didn't hear Naretha or ignored her, too intent on observing the silent conversation between his parents.

"You will not be able to sleep in your old room, Jamad," Elias admitted, "but we can arrange something in the living room."

"I...won't be upset if you got rid of all my stuff," Jamad said, but Avner detected the lie. "I expected you to, honestly. You had no idea when I'd come back—or *if* I'd come back."

"We kept your stuff." Colette tucked an already-tucked lock of brown hair behind her ear. "It's in the garage, in boxes. You cannot sleep in your room because...it is not your room any longer."

"Did you turn it into an office, or..."

With a deep breath, his mother stood and motioned toward the door to her right. "You will have to see it to believe it."

Tense and confused, Jamad rose from his seat and walked around the table. Naretha was intrigued enough to follow, so Avner stood as well, trailing her until Colette opened the door to the dark room.

When his eyes adjusted to the lack of light, he saw the walls were the same shade of pastel pink as Naretha's hair, adorned with flower designs and cheesy quotes about *babies*. The reason for all this lay sleeping in a small bed across the room: a toddler with dirty blonde hair and a face that resembled both of Jamad's parents but nothing of Jamad. It was the Solbergs' baby—their biological baby.

"She is your sister, J," Colette cooed, stroking a hand along her adoptive son's arm. "She is named Jade, to remind us of you. She's almost three years old now, born not long after you left."

"Didn't wait long to replace me, huh." His hollow words were not a question, but they baffled Colette like a complex algorithm.

"R-replace?"

"I was kidnapped by the government, so you had to have another kid to replace me—I get it. You thought that, if you gave her a similar name and put her in the same room, she could replace me. Well, you were wrong, because she's *better* than I ever was. She's really yours. She's not some baby you found in an alley or were forced to adopt because you were in love with his father."

"*Jamad*!" Colette gasped in outrage, but he shook his head, backing out of his old bedroom as if it harbored a disease.

Avner and Naretha parted for him, eyeing each other with the same uncertainty. Jamad didn't seem to notice them, though; he met no one's eyes as he stalked through the dining room and said, "I need some cold air," before exiting the house entirely.

Frantically, Colette grabbed a coat before following him into the night, leaving the three Affinities alone with the Regg man at the table. Avner's plate was still half full, but when he and Naretha sat back down, he had no motivation to finish.

"Should we…"

"*Nei, nei*," Elias dismissed as he eyed the front door with disinterest. "This is common. Jamad is the queen of drama."

"King, you mean," Naretha corrected, but the man shook his head.

"No, I mean *queen*. I know English well. I often exaggerate my accent, so Colette doesn't feel as insecure about hers. Jamad is a drama *queen*."

"I've never considered Jamad *dramatic*," Avner said. "He's always been very…collected at school."

"J's been trying to impress you since we met you in Fraco's

van three years ago," Zeela droned. "*I* didn't tell you that, though. He's sensitive about his sensitive side, ironically."

"You didn't…really have another kid to replace Jamad, did you?" Avner asked Elias warily.

"No. Colette was pregnant with Jade two months before Jamad was taken. We planned to tell him, but then he left… We had been trying for years. We always thought Jamad would enjoy a sibling." With a shake of his head, his longing expression faded into one of seriousness. "Now, you all didn't really come here for a social visit, did you?"

Zeela pressed her lips together as Avner scratched his greasy head, leaving Naretha to answer with a rather blunt, "How do you say, 'I'm a Wacko and these three broke me out of prison, so we could travel to Wacko Headquarters together,' in Norwegian?"

Elias blinked, and then he blinked again. When he sat up in his chair, his back straight and blue eyes wide, he stuttered, "Th-the terrorists? You are part of the terrorists?"

Zeela kicked Naretha under the table. "What happened to *stealth*?"

"After assessing this situation, I've decided a scare tactic will work better."

"She's…well, she's telling the truth," Avner admitted, at which Zeela dropped her jaw. "She is a Wacko—a terrorist—but we aren't with her. Well, technically, we are…"

"Children," Naretha groaned, throwing her head back before turning to a gaping Elias. "I'm a 'terrorist,' but they're not. The only reason I'm with them is because they need me in order to save their friend, who was captured by the other Wackos. They're all noble and good or whatever. Your son is a perfect angel."

"I-I don't know what to think," Elias stammered as he staggered out of his seat. "This is a lot…"

"You'd better not go shout this information to the world," Naretha warned. "My threat to kill you with my pathetic salt superpower still stands."

"I have no plans to tell anyone of this. It would only be detrimental to my son. I don't approve of his choice to work with a terrorist, but...you say this is to help his friend?"

"She's practically his girlfriend," Zeela affirmed, causing Naretha's smug expression to fade. "She's been our best friend since our first year at Periculand, and the leader of our town refused to save her from the Wackos, so we decided we would. You can see how that's something Jamad would want to do."

"Yes," his father agreed, stroking his chin. "I imagine he would do the same for you, me, or anyone he cared for. He has always been reckless."

"And dramatic, apparently," Avner muttered.

"We need a way to get to the Wackos' hideout, so we can save our friend," Zeela told Elias. "I know it sounds insane, but...will you help us?"

6

Alien

"Okay, so, zombies, aliens, or Wackos?" Seth asked without preamble as he led his friends up the Residence Tower's spiral staircase. From the end of the line a whole floor beneath, Eliana could barely see him climbing the steps backward, and the clamor from below overpowered his question.

As usual, enthusiastic chatter filled the lounge, but instead of discussing the recent presidential election, the Regg ambassadors were the topic of interest. Most thoughts about the shift in power leaned toward apprehension, but some students, like Nero, anticipated that this new dynamic might benefit them. Right now, Nero's ascension seemed the only way Eliana's life could worsen.

"Aliens!" Hartman's voice startled her back to the primaries' conversation. One second, he bounced on the stair before her, and the next, he'd teleported to the step below Seth, bringing the other Stark twin to a stop. "Aliens are *awesome*."

Tray's scowl was as black as his funeral attire—and his mood.

"Aliens aren't *real.* Even if they were, they hold no relevance at a time like this."

As the line started moving again, Ackerly said, "Are you, um, asking which group we would want to invade Periculand?"

"No, of course not," Seth scoffed. "We're playing Kiss, Marry, or Kill."

"Right, because that's the most important matter in our lives," Tray grumbled as he passed the second floor.

Hartman scratched his chin in contemplation. "You have to admit it's a hard decision. Aliens are obviously top of the list, but zombies and Wackos are equally as bad."

Ahead of Eliana, Lavisa snorted. "If zombies existed, they would clearly be worse than a group of terrorists."

"A group of terrorists with superpowers, though? They're just as deadly as zombies."

"You're telling me you'd want to kiss a dead and decaying human that wants to eat your brain?"

Ackerly's green eyebrows furrowed as he attempted to work out the logic of this conversation. "Wait…how can you kill zombies if they're already dead?"

"This is all just theoretical—"

"How can one kiss or marry a collective group of beings at once?" Tray demanded over his brother's explanation.

Seth sighed as they reached the third floor. "Fine, there's only one zombie, one alien, and one Wacko."

"Male or female?" Hartman questioned. "And what do they *look* like? The alien's hot, right? She's not a *creature* alien, is she? She's, like, a humanoid being with blue hair and a nice bod, right?"

"You mean, like her?" Lavisa inclined her head toward Eliana as she joined the rest of the group on the third floor.

"Maybe she *is* an alien," Hartman suggested, wiggling his eyebrows at her. Eliana couldn't manage a reaction to his joke. How could they all remain so blithe when Hastings was *dead*? It had only been a day and they were already acting like he'd never existed. Perhaps to them, he hadn't, but for her, he had been a part of her life every day over the past two months. What was Periculand without him?

"My door is back," she observed absently, surprising the others with her random comment. She avoided their concerned gazes by focusing on that new metal door with the number 305 printed in black.

"Great, just as soon as Stromer isn't here to annoy us all." Though Eliana had concluded that Tray was nearly heartless, she was grateful he didn't pity her like everyone else.

"I'm gonna miss having conversations with Adara from across the hall." Seth glanced between his door and the one that was now only Eliana's. After a moment of recollection, he shrugged off the memories and asked, "Is anyone gonna answer my Kiss, Marry, or Kill question?"

"It's not relevant," Tray snapped before Hartman could open his mouth. "What we should discuss is the fact that two of the government's pawns have overthrown our town and aren't going to let us see Adara."

A crafty grin spread across Lavisa's lips. "Do you *want* to see Adara?"

"N-no." The faintest bit of color surfaced in his cheeks, but Eliana's brain was too muddled for her to discern or even care if Tray was lying. "I just—There might come a time when we *need* to visit her. And if the Reggs are so quick to take away one privilege, who's to say they won't make other, more impactful changes?"

"The Rosses are all about intimidation, from what I saw."

Strolling away from the group, Lavisa opened her door. "All they'll do is sit up in Angor's old office and avoid social interaction, just like the last principal. Everything will be the same as it has been."

"Yeah, except that Adara's in jail and Hastings is *dead*. Sorry," Seth added, but Eliana was actually relieved someone had finally mentioned it. "I just don't see how anything will ever be the same."

Tray cleared his throat and nodded toward the door to room 305. "Will you…be okay alone?"

Knowing how hard it was for him to contrive a sympathetic question, Eliana forced the briefest smile. "I was alone last night. I do best alone."

"I've already disproved my previous statement that everything will be the same," Lavisa announced from her dormitory's doorway. "Kiki ditched Periculand."

"What?" Seth hurried over to Lavisa and peered into her room. Through his mind, Eliana vaguely saw the empty side that Kiki had previously occupied, and her stomach dropped. Of this entire group, Kiki was the only one Eliana felt a connection with. Could she really be gone?

As if hearing her mental question, Seth shook his head. "She…she was with us twenty minutes a—"

"She's not gone." That familiar consciousness hit Eliana with a wave of relief, radiating like a beacon—from *her* dormitory. With mechanical movements, she turned the knob of her new door and revealed Kiki within, redecorating Adara's side with her own belongings. A single, carelessly packed box contained Adara's possessions, leaving ample space for Kiki's posters, magazines, and makeup.

As Eliana had sensed, Hartman's roommate was present, servilely aiding Kiki. What she had not expected was that the Belven girl wore only a t-shirt and purple underwear, exposing a generous portion of her legs and…bottom.

When Hartman stepped up beside Eliana, his eyes nearly popped from their sockets. "*Carrick*? What are you—and whoa, Seth, will you punch me if I say your ex-girlfriend is sexy?"

Seth jogged over. "Is she clothed?"

His brother grimaced at the sight of her. "Barely."

"Oh, hello," Kiki greeted, briefly glancing at the visitors. Carrick handed her a skimpy blue dress, which she carefully hung in her new closet.

"Why aren't you wearing pants?" Ackerly asked, eyes darting around uncomfortably. "Are you…trying to become Adara?"

"No." Kiki snatched another dress from Carrick. "It's just overly warm in here. And this is my sleep attire—my non-sexy sleep attire."

"Can we see your *sexy* sleep attire?"

Seth elbowed Hartman in the gut. "She's my ex, man."

"Hold on," Tray said with growing uncertainty. "Did…Adara walk around in just her underwear in front of you, Ackerly?"

"Well, no, but she didn't care when we all saw her naked after her clothes burned off."

"Stop talking about Adara," Kiki snapped. "She isn't here anymore."

Biting her lip, Eliana eyed the posters of pop bands and magazines full of celebrity gossip. "Is that why you're taking over her spot?"

"You can read minds; you should know I hate Lavisa." This was said while Lavisa stood in the doorway, within Kiki's line of sight, but both girls seemed unruffled. "I could move into Seth's room, since Hastings is…" Her words came to a halt, along with her movements. Instead of finishing her thought, she simply continued with, "But he's my ex, so…eh."

"This has ended well for me, but it's unfortunate for you," Lavisa said to Eliana. Though her tone was emotionless, Eliana heard a sincere apology from her mind before she disappeared.

"I wouldn't want to move into my room either," Seth agreed as he leaned on the doorframe. "Was gettin' some weird vibes in there last night. Do you think it was Hastings's ghost? Can you sense that kinda thing, Ellie?"

"You're being insensitive, Seth," his twin groaned with an apologetic look in Eliana's direction.

"It was an honest question. Would you rather me ask her personal details about her relationship with Hastings? Don't you think it'd be *more* insensitive if I asked her if she banged the guy before he died?"

Tray choked out a cough, Ackerly fidgeted with his glasses, and Hartman vanished from the room entirely. Eliana wished she had an Affinity for melting into the wall.

"I don't know why you're all being so uncomfortable about this," Kiki said. "We all want to know; Seth's just the only one indecent enough to ask." With a conniving smirk, she pivoted toward Eliana. "If you didn't at least get a little sexy with Hastings, you were really wasting his talents. I mean, he could have given you a hickey and then erased it with his Affinity! If I'd known what he could do, I would have probably hooked up with him myself. Or, um, you know—gotten him to heal my hickeys."

Evading Seth's gaze, Kiki turned back to the closet and resumed organization. After working through the logic, he finally asked, "Since when have you gotten a hickey? I haven't given you one since before we came here."

"I was talking about the future, Seth. Like...when I date someone new," she replied, her voice muffled beyond the closet walls within which she intentionally remained.

"Date someone new? I thought you were done with boys? Have you *seen* yourself with a new boyfriend? Or a new *girlfriend*?"

"Shut up, primies!" a voice called from beyond the wall, accompanied by a bang.

Kiki jumped, but Eliana was accustomed to Calder shouting at Adara through the wall. "That's Adara's Pixie Prince."

"That guy still scares me," Ackerly whispered, wincing at the wall as if he could see him through it.

"I can hear you!" Calder yelled with another bang. "You primies are more annoying than Stromer's sleep-complaining!"

"We should probably go before he comes in here and tries to drown us," Tray muttered. Less grudgingly, he met Eliana's eyes. "Are you sure you're all right?"

The boys' concerned thoughts flowed freely from their minds; even Seth seemed worried for her, but whether because Hastings was dead or because Kiki was her new roommate, she couldn't exactly be sure. Either way, her situation seemed grim, but she broadened her shoulders and nodded at Tray.

"You should leave, too," he advised Carrick before departing with his roommate and brother. "You don't need to be Belven's slave anymore."

"Slave!" Kiki's outrage was the final push Carrick needed to scamper from the room. "I was going to pay you!"

"I'll help you," Eliana offered as she closed their new door, sealing her dormitory for the first time in over a month. "Did you, um, ask someone to fix this?"

"Obviously. Do you think I want to be *watched*?"

Gingerly, Eliana picked up a shirt and brought it to the closet. "Well...you seem like the kind of person who wouldn't mind."

When she presented the shirt, Kiki snatched it without any

gratitude. "You don't help me, okay? You're my friend, and I don't force my friends to help me."

"Um—"

"Stop acting confused. You can read my mind. What am I thinking?"

Eliana's eyebrows screwed together as she stared into Kiki's eyes. The cool blue was streaked with highlights of pink now, and she could mentally detect the shift in the girl's mind, a result of her Affinity's discovery.

"You, uh...*saw* us as friends?"

"Can't you see it, too?"

"Not exactly... I can tell you're thinking about it, though."

With a dramatic sigh, Kiki plopped onto the bed that had previously belonged to her childhood enemy. "I've never had real friends, but when I *saw* this—this blurry vision of you and me together—I knew that was what it was like to have a friend. So... you might think I'm a rude, selfish bitch now, but one day you won't. I just have to impatiently wait for that day, because...that's all I've ever wanted. I don't want everyone watching me all the time. I want one person who knows me and...cares about me. I thought being popular would win me at least one true friend, but—"

"What about Seth?" Eliana knew the answer to this question, but she also knew Kiki's expression of emotion was wildly different than Hastings's. Where he had chosen to convey his most intimate sentiments mentally, Kiki's thoughts were far less organized, making verbal communication the best means through which to articulate her deepest concerns.

Even so, she struggled to produce a coherent sentence, and after crossing and uncrossing her legs five times, she finally groaned.

"Seth didn't care about me—not *really*. He was the closest thing I had to a friend, I guess, but...he always liked Adara more."

"Which was the real reason you always picked on Adara," Eliana said as Kiki's memories flooded her awareness. "You always had a crush on Seth, so you always despised Adara."

Kiki hugged herself defensively. "Don't act like I'm a criminal. You know Adara's more of a bitch than I am."

"Well, her thoughts are often far less...tender than yours are. Her mind is guarded almost always. Yours is raw...and broken."

Puffing out a breath, Kiki jumped off her new bed and threw a pair of purple cargo pants at Eliana in the process. "Stop reading my mind and start helping me. We aren't friends yet. As the gracious prophetess I am, though, I should probably let you know that I *saw* your sister—"

"Zeela? You saw a vision of her?"

Kiki padded over to the closet again, careless and elusive. "A vague one. It was...blurry, like most of them are, but in it she was with that pink-haired Wacko, or she *will* be, I guess."

With Hastings's death, Eliana had forgotten about her sister's request for her to join them in breaking the Wacko out of jail. In hindsight, it was for the best that Eliana hadn't helped, otherwise she'd be in a cell with Adara, but she still felt guilty for failing to aid her sister. "Is she okay? Did they make it to the Wacko hideout?"

"I...don't know," Kiki admitted with a hint of remorse. "But in the vision they were both smiling, so...probably."

Though finding Maddy and the Wackos would bring happiness to both Zeela and Naretha, Eliana couldn't imagine either of them succumbing to their emotions in such a tense situation. She couldn't predict the future, though—only Kiki could—and so she hoped that, wherever her sister was, she was safe.

The nighttime air felt colder now than it had when Avner had emerged from the river a few hours ago. Perhaps it was Jamad's presence chilling the atmosphere; his mother had been unable to thaw his strong frigidity.

Colette had returned inside after half an hour of arguing with Jamad, tears frozen on her cheeks as she retreated to her bedroom without a word. Elias had put an end to their discussion to console his wife, leaving Naretha to make a few rude remarks while Zeela implored Avner to confront their friend.

On the front porch, Jamad leaned over the white railing, gazing out into the grassy field they'd trekked through. In that moment, Avner realized the boy he'd known for the past three years was only a fragment of Jamad Solberg. There were layers beneath the frivolousness of his friend—layers he had buried with no intention of unearthing.

Avner stepped next to him and placed his elbows on the icy railing. "Naretha's probably gonna kill Zeela in there."

"Then why did you leave them alone?" He recited the words as if they were part of a script he had no interest in.

"Z told me to," Avner admitted reluctantly. "She thinks I'm angry with you."

"Are you?"

Sighing, Avner fixed his vision on a light in the distance—one of the houses beyond the field, maybe the Mensens'. From here, Beverly felt like an endless chasm they were trapped in, sirens still echoing through the quietness. The police would probably find them soon and they would probably go to jail, but this...tension between him and Jamad seemed like the most pressing issue.

"I should be mad, I guess, but I'm mostly just...confused.

You were adopted, you were stuck in a snowstorm, you're a drama queen—"

"My dad said that?"

"Yeah."

Rolling his shoulders, Jamad stood straight and stretched his arms behind his head. "He always says that, and maybe it's true. I dunno… Would you be upset if you found out your parents replaced you?"

Avner raised his eyebrows. "You're really asking *me* that?"

"Right, no parents." Jamad released a breath and dropped his arms, staring out at a barren tree. "I am a shitty friend, aren't I?"

"I never told you much about my foster family." Avner spun around to sit on the railing. "We both suck at communicating. And, for the record, I probably wouldn't have cared if my foster parents replaced me. They probably have by now. They always had other foster kids—always tried to help everyone. It was nice, but it didn't make me feel…special or loved. *You* are loved—your parents love you, man. Don't you see that? They didn't want another kid to replace you; they wanted her *for* you. Honestly, though, little sisters are a pain."

Humor didn't meet Jamad's eyes when he snorted. "Nothing feels the same as it used to. Everything looks the same, but it's all different."

"Maybe you're just different," Avner offered, studying his friend's light blue features. "When I met you, your hair and eyes were darker. You weren't as good at your Affinity, and you definitely weren't as cocky."

"It's not cockiness if I'm as awesome as I think I am," Jamad said, drawing a grin from his friend. "It just sucks being here. I've wanted to see them for years, but now…they barely feel like my parents anymore, and that baby…she doesn't feel like my sister.

She's almost *three* and I didn't even know she exists. I'll never watch her grow up. If I ever see her again, she'll probably be a grown stranger. It just feels...wrong."

"If it makes you feel better, I'll probably never see Adara again."

"Oh, bull. You'll see her when we get back to Periculand. Not sure if that's a good or bad thing for you, though, brother."

Avner licked his lips and peeked past Jamad through the window, where Naretha listlessly sprinkled salt onto her plate. "We can't go back to Periculand, J. We broke a Wacko out of jail. Even if it was something Angor wanted to do himself, he'll have to punish us. We're fugitives now."

Crossing his arms, Jamad leaned back against the brick wall. "So, what? We join the Wackos?"

"No, we'll...figure something out. For now, we need to focus on getting to the Wackos and saving Maddy. We talked with your dad a bit; he said he has a few connections in town who might be able to get us to the hideout without raising suspicion. Naretha said, 'The shadier the better.'"

"Of course she did." Jamad turned his head toward the window to observe as the Wacko flicked crystals of salt across her plate. "Why'd she save Z earlier? Why didn't she ditch us?"

"Figured she wouldn't make it to Cleveland alone? Has a crush on you?"

"You're probably right. Who *doesn't* have a crush on me?"

"Well, I'm hoping Zeela doesn't." At Jamad's cheeky grin, Avner kicked him in the shin. "Thanks for the reassurance, J."

His friend's laugh softened any remaining coldness between them. "In all seriousness, though...do you think Naretha's got some hidden motive? What if she doesn't bring us where she says? What if Maddy's not even where she assumes she is?"

Avner drummed his fingers on the railing as the same worries wove through his mind. “I don’t think we have any option but to trust Naretha at this point. Our main focus should be leaving Beverly. Your dad said we could stay for the weekend, just so we have everything prepared.”

“That’s…nice,” Jamad said, but he squirmed against the wall. “I’d like to leave as soon as possible, though. There aren’t a lot of crimes around here—I bet the cops will be coming door to door soon, trying to find us.”

“I don’t like the idea of sitting around, either, but it’ll be better if we’re thoroughly prepared before departing. That way, maybe we can avoid a repeat of today. We weren’t ready for this mission.”

Longing was etched into Jamad’s face as he gazed into his childhood home, likely remembering better times. “No, we weren’t.”

7

Usurpers' Dominion

Eliana's bare feet mounted each step of the spiral staircase with gradual precision. Not one thought penetrated her awareness, and the absence of minds resulted in a startling quiet. The incandescence of the white stairs was stark in comparison to her wispy dress, strewn from the same fabric as her darkest thoughts.

Strange.

These little details, coupled with her inability to slow her ascent, alerted her that something was fundamentally wrong, even before she reached the third floor of the tower and discovered a ghost.

Facing her new door was Hastings Lanio, his posture as guarded as always with his hands in the pockets of his purple cargo pants. His pants, however, weren't fully purple. They kept oscillating between purple and another color—one that made Eliana's head ache.

Trying to read his mind was like trying to claw through a cement wall, so she gingerly approached, waiting for him to hear her delicate footsteps. When he didn't turn, she reached out, but her hand flowed freely through him, confirming the truth that he was not present. He continued to stare at her door without any inkling that she loomed behind him. Her voice was inaudible when she tried to speak, but his voice echoed through the corridor, its origin everywhere but nowhere all at once.

"Did you really think that was me?" he asked, clear and blunt. "Did you really think I would want to return to this life, even if I could? I murdered my own mother. Did you think *you* could change that? Did you really think you could ever make me happy?"

Frustration bled into his words, but the shell of Hastings standing at her door was cool, steady, and emotionless. Eliana wanted to study him—wanted to draw the angles and lines of his body, to sculpt him back to life—but her eyes darted frantically instead, searching for the voice's source, the true Hastings.

"Where were you when I almost murdered again? Why didn't you help me when she took over my mind? You were the only weed that could kill the root of my anger, a beautiful weed—"

"What are you talking about?" Eliana cried as her voice broke free from her throat. "Weed? Are you...talking about Ackerly? The flowers he grew at your grave..."

"You're missing the point, Eliana."

"Are you *blaming* me? I never wanted you to die. And I'm not—I'm not replacing you with Ackerly now that you're gone!"

"The point is you don't know why I'm gone. You don't know the reason behind my death."

"Angor! Angor is the reason behind your death!"

A laugh echoed through the room, more prominent that Hastings's typical snorts. "You were always so jealous of him—of the time I spent with him. It's only logical you assume he's evil."

"He is! He was the one controlling your mind and—"

"He?" the voice repeated, now much too sinister to belong to Hastings. "But didn't you hear me? Didn't you hear me say *she*?"

Eliana scrambled to decipher his thoughts and find an explanation for this, but the walls closed in around her mind and body. Before she could think to scream, her awareness was sucked from the dream and inserted back to her rightful body, where it lay in bed.

"I'll get it, since you're so *lazy*." That voice belonged to Kiki, who'd rolled out of bed to stomp toward the door. Apparently, someone had knocked.

It took a moment for Eliana to reorient herself in this reality—the one in which Hastings was dead and not a talking phantom. A full day had passed since the funeral, two full days since his death, and classes had been canceled, leaving the students to roam aimlessly around town. Kiki had spent the majority of the day organizing her excess belongings while Eliana reluctantly accompanied Seth, Tray, and Ackerly in their attempt to visit Adara. It wasn't that Eliana missed her old roommate; she didn't, really, especially not since Adara had been so insensitive about Hastings's death. Then again, she *had* tried to avenge him by attacking Angor as a ball of fire.

The former principal was who Eliana had hoped to see—to pry into his mind and gauge the truth of his guiltlessness. Aethelred had admitted to the Stark twins that he didn't believe Angor's ability was mind controlling; now, after this dream, her need to invade his mind was more vital than ever. It had been a dream, yes, but if, in that dream, Hastings confessed he had been possessed by a *she*, and if, in real life, Angor denied the ability to possess minds at all…

"What do you want?" Kiki snapped when she opened the

door. Her annoyance immediately dwindled into disbelief, and she gawked through the crack at their visitor.

"Who is it?" Eliana asked, sitting up.

With a wide-eyed glance over her shoulder, Kiki hastily said, "No one," before disappearing into the hall.

Her unguarded thoughts made her hysteria evident to Eliana, even with the door closed between them. Upon approaching it, she heard panicked panting on the other side. When she finally dug into the visual cortex of Kiki's mind and saw through her, Eliana's own alarm spiked to the point of paralysis; Kiki, somehow, stared into familiar *living* blood red eyes.

It was thoroughly impossible, but every inch of him was distinctly Hastings, from the messy hair and bronze skin to the nubby fingernails and expressionless face. He was more vivid now than in the dream, but she was still certain he couldn't be real. She must have read Kiki's vision incorrectly—something must have been amiss in the connection between their brains.

"What is *happening*?" the blonde exploded in a whisper, confirming that she indeed saw Hastings as well. "Explain to me exactly how you are here while I focus on not thinking about the fact that you're here so Eliana doesn't find out." Moaning, she rubbed her fingers over her forehead and strained to think other thoughts. Eliana wasn't sure whether to be grateful for her new roommate's atrocious control. "God, this is awful. I thought my Affinity was predicting the future, but now I'm seeing *dead people* again. Tell me this is a dream."

When he didn't answer, she touched his hard jawbone and soft cheeks. Eliana closed her burning eyes as she felt the warmth of his flesh beneath Kiki's fingertips, real and tangible and alive. The way his lips curled in response, though, forming a smirk too sly for Hastings, provoked Eliana's eyes to spring open with newfound caution.

"I didn't know you could predict the future," Hastings mused in a voice unlike his own. It was less raspy but still familiar. "That makes you a *prophetess*, doesn't it?"

Kiki's small nostrils flared as she crossed her arms. "Only *I* can call myself *prophetess*, creep. How aren't you dead? Everyone saw it, and I *saw* it."

Hastings's eyes raked over her half-exposed body, and Eliana almost blushed—until she remembered she was seeing through Kiki's vision. Then she couldn't decide what disturbed her more: that Hastings was looking at *Kiki* like that, or that *anyone* was looking at Kiki like that. "Did you, now? Tell me more, Prophetess."

Perhaps it was Kiki's irritation or perhaps it was her own, but either way, Eliana had had enough of idly watching this scene unfold. With a burst of indignation, she yanked the door open, clearing the threshold to witness Hastings with her own eyes. As soon as she did, she recognized it was not him—not *her* Hastings. The dramatic shock on his face never would have been displayed by the real Hastings, nor would his thoughts have been so exposed and vulnerable.

"I just dreamt that Hastings came to our door," Eliana said slowly, absorbing every detail of his appearance to find some flaw. In the dream, his pants had been purple, but they were now orange—the burnt orange of the Physicals. "And now he's here."

Kiki tightened her folded arms. "What does that *mean*?"

"I don't know," she admitted, "but I do know this isn't Hastings."

"I'm…sorry," said the boy before them as his deep red eyes flickered into a stormy gray. "I…didn't think you would come out here. I was just—"

"Trying to frazzle Kiki," Eliana finished for him, her voice soft but her smile wry. "You succeeded."

"What is *happening*?" the blonde girl repeated as the boy's physical features morphed.

His skin darkened to the hue of midnight, his lengthy limbs condensed into toned muscle, and his hair shortened to black stubble. It was the boy who was Lavisa's brother but who didn't look like he should have been.

"*You*!" Kiki gasped, as if he had committed the most heinous crime. "You're that bitch's brother!"

"Well, no, I'm not Avner, but I could look like him, if you wanted me—"

"I'm talking about Lavisa! Adara is old news, and she's in prison, so she's basically dead!"

"While on the subject of dead people, I'm sorry again," Ruse said to Eliana, his composure restored. Even if his tone had not been sincere, she would have believed him simply because the thoughts in his mind confirmed the truth of his statement. "About pretending to be Hastings and about the fact that Hastings is dead… I have news that'll cheer you both up, though."

Kiki smiled, sarcastically sweet. "You're leaving now?"

"Yeah, actually. I'm heading down to JAMZ," Ruse explained, glancing at his little sister's door beside theirs. "Since the founders left, Nero decided to run it tonight. I heard him talking about it up on our floor, and he said he doesn't want any primies showing up, so I figured I'd ruin his night by specifically ensuring all the primies come."

Eliana gnawed on her lip. "I'm…not sure I want to see what JAMZ looks like with Nero in charge."

With a nod of understanding, Ruse turned back to Kiki, an invitation in his cool gray eyes. She examined him with distaste.

"What happened to the blue eyes?"

He shrugged. "You didn't like the blue eyes; figured I'd try something a little different. Lavisa still seems to dislike me, no matter what form I take, of course, but—"

"Hm, my enemy and I have something in common," was Kiki's only comment before she spun on her heel and vanished into room 305.

Eliana eyed the new door, now closed, for a moment before looking at Ruse. "I'll come."

"Really? You're not too depressed?"

Flattening some of the creases in her purple flannel pants, Eliana inhaled and said, "I'm not going to let…what happened affect me."

"Right…" Ruse eyed her, unconvinced. "Well, it affected me. Not Hastings's death, but…other deaths…of people important to me. So, it's okay to mourn."

Eliana knew exactly what this referred to, based on his unhindered thoughts, but she didn't acknowledge it, knowing he would have specified if he'd wanted to. It wasn't her place to leech off the emotions of strangers, but it calmed her—this reassurance that someone else understood the war of denial, anger, and sorrow raging in her mind.

"Let's go wake my sister, shall we?" Ruse prompted, slicing through what he perceived to be an awkward silence.

Eliana gave him a polite smirk before following him to room 304, Lavisa's dorm. "Why did you choose this as your default form?" she asked before he could rap his knuckles on the door. "It's clearly not what you actually look like, unless Lavisa's not your biological sister."

"She is. If you want the truth—which you could definitely discover by reading my mind, so I'll just tell you—I was in Kiki's dorm once, when she shared it with my sister, and saw some posters of a famous guy who looks just like this." He motioned to the defined muscles and richly-colored skin. "Figured she thought he was hot, so here we are."

Eliana masked her budding protectiveness and quietly asked, "Why the interest in Kiki?"

His expression darkened as his thoughts descended to the past. "I see the way she ogles Nero during training. Not many girls do, once they realize he's with Nixie—or once they realize he's a barbarian. I figured, if I distracted her enough, she'd be less preoccupied with him—wouldn't wanna get involved. I've seen primies get ensnared in Nero's posse, and it's never a good position to get stuck in."

"You don't have…a crush on her?"

"She's *physically attractive*, obviously, but…is it even possible to have a crush on someone with such an attitude?"

Eliana recalled Seth's infatuated thoughts of Kiki when they'd been dating; even then, the sentiments had been shallow because Kiki's outward demeanor was shallow. The only reason Eliana hadn't begged someone else to become her new roommate was because she could see past the surface, and the depths implied a potential no one else could comprehend.

By the time Lavisa answered the door wearing tight, black clothes that looked more like fighting gear than pajamas, Ruse had morphed his appearance once more. Blinking, Eliana found one of the Stark twins at her side. With his styled hair and aura of agitation, he resembled Tray perfectly.

Lowering the knife she'd pointed at them, Lavisa glanced between the pair. "If you're going to ask me if I can leave my room so you can use it for sex, the answer is no."

Eliana gaped while Ruse tried his hardest not to giggle, as it would have been very un-Tray-like. Lavisa noticed the unnatural response from the boy who should have been appalled and, with the sniff of her nose, narrowed her eyes. "Brother. Have you finally decided to stop evading me?"

The resulting transformation of Ruse's physical attributes—the darkening of his skin to the shade of Lavisa's, the brightening of his hair to a warmer brown, and the shift of his eyes to a shimmering bronze—didn't alter his sister's dry look.

"I don't remember you being this handsome." His sister's jab didn't dent his cocky grin. "You're being a bit generous, don't you think?"

"Is this…what you really look like?" Eliana asked.

Lavisa rolled her eyes. "We had much darker hair as kids—and darker eyes. The rest is…close enough." With a pause, she glanced between them again. "You two aren't…"

Eliana shook her head violently. Unfazed, Ruse drawled, "We're going to JAMZ, sister. If Nero decides to continue with the team idea Avner started, you and I could partner up."

"What use would you be in combat? Can you shift into anything deadly?" Her brother opened his mouth, but she continued before he could speak. "Are the others coming?" Eliana nodded. "And Nero's in charge?" Another nod. "And does he want us to be there?" She shook her head this time, and Lavisa's dull eyes flashed at the implication. "Then let's go."

The chilly basement of the Physicals Building had warmed substantially since all of Periculand's students trickled in—all except the primaries.

Nero's other followers had been ecstatic to hear his plans to revamp JAMZ with his own violent edge. Nixie had even convinced the core group to wear dark gray bands of cloth around their foreheads, a tribute to the might of their leader. Calder found the hype a bit ridiculous. He did wear the gray cloth and he did stand on Nero's right, like the intimidating groupie he was supposed to be, but his mind had been elsewhere the entire day.

Even Nero announcing the JAMZ session this morning at breakfast hadn't been able to regenerate a sense of normalcy in Calder's gut. He could personally attest to the fact that students had been placed in Periculand's jail before, but never had they *kept* students there for more than a few hours of punishment. Adara had been there two days now, and the *principal* was there with her. Never had anyone challenged Angor's authority—and if he truly had a mind controlling Affinity, no one should have been able to.

But the Reggs had.

Calder had heard what Tray Stark mumbled at the funeral yesterday—his doubts that Periculy had a mind controlling Affinity at all. The principal had claimed his innocence as well, and the strangest part was that Adara Stromer *believed* him. Though he sincerely hoped the Fire Demoness never escaped that prison cell, part of him wished she were here, so he could at least hear *why* she believed Angor's story—so he could determine how much of a threat these Regg ambassadors were.

The two Reggs had no clue that most of the school was huddled in this basement, but the primaries did. As Nero quieted the crowd, his least favorites stalked into the room, invoking absolute silence.

"Tray Stark," he greeted, cordial but aggressive, as the twins and their group of primies marched up to the opposite side of the orange mats. An extra boy was among them, but even with his unfamiliar features, Calder recognized him as the shapeshifting prick, Ruse. Judging by the self-satisfied smirk on his lips, he'd informed the primies of this event; even without looking at his leader, Calder felt the agitation seeping from his pores.

"Nero," was Tray's curt response. Wearing his school uniform, he was the only one of the group other than Lavisa not clothed in pajamas. As his brown eyes surveyed the crowd of upperclassmen, any who were loyal to Nero, including Calder, bared their teeth in feral grins. Those who had been Avner's friends shifted with discomfort. "No invite for us tonight? Were you too scared to fight Lavisa again?"

Nero snarled as his granite eyes settled on the yellow-haired girl. "I'll gladly pummel her again, right after I explain tonight's rules."

"Rules?" his stepbrother questioned with the raise of his orange eyebrows. "Didn't realize you were so civilized now, big bro."

"Tough words for such a small boy." Nixie swirled water through her ringed fingers in a threat. "Why don't you teleport over here and say that to his face?"

It was impossible to tell if Hartman's answering vibration was a result of his Affinity or his fear.

"We won't mind destroying you all, so please, stay." With a gesture too gentle to suit him, Nero motioned for them to join the crowd. Obediently, the primaries and Ruse blended into the throng, where all oddly-colored eyes watched Nero step onto the mats. "It's no secret that douchebag Stromer and his little friends ditched town to join the Wackos, so this isn't *JAMZ* anymore; it's Nero's Dominion now.

"The rules are simple—much simpler than the long list of don'ts Stromer always had us conform to. There will be no intentional murder. Accidental killing…" His lips slid into a devilish grin. "Well, there's nothing we can do about that. As for maiming, no one's allowed to hurt anyone beyond the point of Jason

Pane's repair. Since Dr. Pain can cure practically anything besides death… Who wants to fight first?"

Calder almost wished the rest of the students would walk out in fear, but then Seth Stark strode onto the mats, and Calder decided he was the stupidest primie of them all.

"I do." His proclamation quenched the murmurs of trepidation. Based on his brown hair and blue eyes, this Stark twin hadn't learned his Affinity, but his muscles filled out his t-shirt enough to indicate that his strength might last a few seconds longer against Nero than Lavisa's Affinity had. "I challenge you, and I want to raise the stakes. If I win the fight, you have to break Adara out of prison—by punching the walls down with your fists."

Out of Nero's minions, Nixie's cackles rang the loudest. The only silent two were Nero, stone-faced and contemplative, and Calder, attempting to conceal his dread.

"No!" Seth's brother hissed, stomping onto the mats. "Adara needs to stay in prison!"

Lavisa joined the twins with far less dramatics. "*That's* what you're worried about? Not that your brother's about to be pulverized? How about"—she paused, twirling on her heel to face Nero—"we do teams? Primaries vs. Nero's friends."

"Allies," Nero corrected tightly, "but an interesting proposition, Dispus… If we're making bets, what do *we* receive when you children lose?"

"I'll owe you a debt," Seth offered, surprising Calder with his boldness. Did he really think they could win?

"You're practically a normie," Nero scoffed. "I want a debt from someone of actual use. I have super strength, a mind reader, and fighters; I don't want my pathetic brother, and no one needs plants, but…I don't have anyone who could utterly incinerate my enemies. If we win this brawl, Adara Stromer owes us a debt when she's released from prison."

There was no way the Stark kid would approve of this. Adara would burn down Periculand before she would agree to heed any of Nero's commands, and Calder wouldn't be able to douse a fire that size. Since the primies were guaranteed to lose, they had to say no.

But then Seth *nodded.*

"Deal."

Tray complained, obviously, but Seth didn't really care. His brother's freak-outs were common and typically an overreaction. This was their one shot to free Adara from jail; he hadn't questioned his choice for a second.

"You can't make decisions on Stromer's behalf," his brother said immediately after Seth agreed. His objection wasn't loud, but Nero and his posse still waited on the edge of the mats, as if to see what Tray might declare—as if Seth's word had no authority.

"*Relax.*" He ushered Ackerly, Eliana, and Hartman onto the mats with a wave. "We aren't gonna lose. And if we do, you know Adara'll burn Nero to ash before paying some meaningless debt."

"We accept," Lavisa called to Nero as she tightened her hand wraps. "We have six on our team, so you can only have six on yours."

"No problem there." The brute cracked each of his knuckles and joined the primaries on the mats, five of his group following without instruction.

The Pixie Twins flanked him while the acid-spitter, Dave, prowled beside Calder and the boulder-boy stomped on Nixie's other side. Seth remembered boulder-boy's ability to conjure massive rocks and had to swallow his apprehension, reminding himself that he had super strength—*probably*.

Behind them strolled a girl Seth had often seen with Nero's group but who he had yet to personally encounter. Turquoise freckles speckled her dark skin, matching the bright hue of her hair and eyes, and a thick chain of metal links hung around her neck like a dog collar. She whispered something to Nixie as their group halted before the primaries, and when her malicious gaze fixed on Ackerly, he recoiled.

"We aren't gonna play with a *ball*, as if this is some sport," Nero announced, voice booming through the hollow basement. "You're eliminated when you step off the mats—or when you're too weak to get up. The last group standing wins. You have one minute to prepare before Watkins starts the match." He nodded toward a boy standing on the edge of the mats, pink eyes dull and mouth slightly ajar to reveal large teeth.

"Nero's mind reader," Eliana mumbled, her eyes on the apparent referee as Seth pulled them all into a huddle. "Keep your minds guarded."

"We shouldn't have to worry about that, or any of this. You're dumber than Adara," Tray sneered at Seth. "We're about to *battle* with Nero—possibly to the death, since he doesn't care if he 'accidentally' kills us…"

"We've got a mind reader"—Seth nodded to Eliana, who looked paler than usual—"the best fighter in Periculand"—Lavisa's lips pressed into a tight line—"a teleporter"—Hartman's freckles quivered in response—"a kid who could probably strangle someone with his plants—"

"Well, I don't know about that," Ackerly piped up uneasily.

"And two people with super strength," Seth concluded, ignoring everyone's distress. There was no reason for them to be afraid;

they all knew their Affinities. Though it should have been discouraging to know even *Kiki* had discovered her power by now and he still hadn't, Seth believed his super strength was buried somewhere inside, waiting for the perfect moment to emerge. "We might be younger," he went on, "but we're tough, and we all love Adara."

"*You* love Adara," Tray corrected. "*I* certainly don't, and I can't imagine any of these other level-headed individuals do, either."

Seth challenged each of them with arched eyebrows.

"She's, um…" was all Eliana came up with.

Ackerly's face scrunched in a half-smile, half-grimace.

"She's dangerous," Lavisa put in, tightening her hand wraps again, "and she needs to be contained, but I admit your ploy was a clever one. If Nero breaks her out, they'll probably throw her right back in and lock *him* up, as well."

Tray's eyes protruded as her words sunk in. "I…hadn't really considered that…"

"Neither did I," Seth admitted with a shrug. "But once Adara's out, I'm gonna make sure she stays out. We can free her."

Ackerly adjusted his glasses and winced. "I just…don't want to see how many buildings she burns down when she finds out she owes Nero a debt."

"Agreed," Hartman said with a vigorous nod. "Let's try to win."

"There's no 'try' in winning," Seth began, but he didn't get to continue his inspirational speech before Watkins called for the match to start. Then Nero's force was upon them.

Dave hurled an attack first, aiming a wad of acid-spit at Hartman, who teleported just in time to miss the blow. Relief washed over his face as he popped up beside Lavisa, but his optimism died when boulder-boy launched a rock the size of a fist at them. Though Lavisa was swift enough to dodge it, Hartman's teleportation had disoriented him, and the stone slammed his forehead, sinking him to his knees. Nero's chuckles overpowered the thud of his stepbrother's body hitting the mats—and fueled his minions to strengthen their assault.

Boulder-boy pummeled Lavisa with a rapid slew of rocks, rendering a counterattack impossible. With Hartman groaning on the ground, Dave's new target became Tray, who hopped around like a bunny to escape globs of acid. Nixie swirled water around Eliana's head, threatening to drown her and killing any hope Seth had that their mind reader would warn them of oncoming attacks. Ackerly attempted to hold his ground as the turquoise-haired girl advanced, a malicious grin splattered on her lips. She uncoiled her metal chain from around her neck and whipped it at him, wielding the weapon with supernatural grace.

On the opposite side of the mats, riding the edge, Calder stood motionless, watching Seth as he crouched in an offensive position, prepared to win this fight for Adara. Seth knew he could sack him with ease; this water-boy was smaller than most of the football players he'd gone up against in the past. So inexperienced with combat, Calder didn't even flinch in defense when Seth plowed forward to tackle him. At the last second, the younger boy realized why he'd been so slow to react. With the flick of his hand, water slipped into Seth's nose and mouth, obstructing his airways.

Coughing and spitting, he halted and strained to remove the water. Calder closed the gap between them to grab his chin, forming an orb around his face. Seth had never been one to panic, but maybe he'd never had much to panic about. Super strength couldn't rip the water from his lungs. He kept his lips sealed until the need for oxygen overrode his will. Water didn't flood his throat when his mouth opened, though; it was air.

None of the spectators, some standing only feet away, noticed what Calder had done, nor did they hear him when he quietly growled, "Pretend you're scared."

"I-I think I am scared." Seth's words warbled beneath the orb, sending ripples through the water.

"You need to pretend to struggle, and then you need to kick me off the mats." Seth's eyebrows shot up, but Calder continued his instructions, quick but clear. "Dave doesn't secrete acid on his legs, so grab him there. Haldor"—he motioned toward boulder-boy, who still flung rocks at Lavisa—"is ticklish behind his kneecaps. Don't ask me how I know. Demira"—he nodded toward the girl chasing Ackerly with the chain—"can control metal. She'll be tricky to beat, but if the plant kid can keep her distracted long enough, you can shove her out. Don't be afraid to hurt her. But Nixie—if you hurt Nixie, I'll slaughter you. She'll fight you, but she's enough of a twig that you can just pick her up and place her outside the perimeter. Do all of that, and the six of you might stand a chance against Nero. Five, I guess, since Little Corvis is pathetic."

As if hearing him, Hartman groaned on the mats, repeatedly struggling to sit up and then flailing back to the ground every time.

"Why are you helping us?"

"Because"—Calder clenched his hand into a fist at his side, discreetly thwarting Nixie's efforts to taunt Eliana—"you might be as dumb as a pile of bricks, but your brother's a genius, and if anyone's gonna figure out what's going on in this goddamn town, it's him. And I want to know when he does."

Swallowing, Seth gave his best attempt to look like he was drowning—which probably wasn't a very good attempt at all, but Calder went along with it. The secondary's face twisted in concentration, and he feigned fury when Seth finally kicked him into the crowd.

It was Nixie whose reaction mattered, though; at the sight of her brother being assaulted, all of her vicious attention honed on Seth. Before he could lunge toward Dave to grab his legs as Calder had instructed, Nixie rushed toward him, a torrent of waves swarming around her.

Seth opened his mouth to swear, which was probably the most idiotic thing he could have done, considering it made Nixie's job of snaking water into his lungs laughably simple. The panic this time was as real as the last, only there was no hope for mercy from this Mardurus twin. He stepped toward her, prepared to lob a punch, but she pushed him back with a strong burst of water. Every attack she would deflect, especially since he couldn't *breathe*. He was certain he was going to die here without ever even unleashing his super strength—until Eliana picked up one of boulder-boy's rocks and chucked it at Nixie's back.

Her scream had Calder shouting from the sidelines, but Seth ignored it as he hacked up water. Once air flowed freely into his body, he plunged through the melee and scooped Nixie into his arms. Though she punched and kicked and squirmed, Seth swiftly jogged toward the mat's edge and deposited her beside her fuming brother.

With only four opponents left, Seth whirled around and soaked in the details of the brawl. Eliana heaved Haldor's rocks at Dave to stop him from attacking Tray, who caught on and joined her. The two drove the acid-spitter off the mats and then turned their attention to Demira, still hunting Ackerly with her chain.

She took the stoning better than Dave. Abandoning her chase, she released her chain from her hand and guided it toward her two assailants. Neither Tray nor Eliana knew how to react when that metal, floating through the air as if by magic, wrapped around their wrists and forcefully jerked them toward the edge. Seth didn't have the chance to attack the turquoise-haired girl before his two teammates were disqualified from the match—not that he would have been able to anyway, since Nero had finished cracking all of his joints and was ready to avenge his girlfriend.

Seth had faced enormous opponents before, but none the size of Nero. Now that his only equal in strength, Tray, was out, and it was three against three, Seth had no choice but to fight the beast.

He would do it—for Adara. She was his best friend, and she didn't deserve to be in jail. Well, maybe she did deserve to be in jail, but not for what they'd placed her there for. If his super strength wasn't developed enough to free her, he'd have to ensure Nero did.

Although a face-off with only the brute had seemed daunting, the task became borderline impossible when Seth realized he'd also have to fight boulder-boy. While he'd assessed the best method, or if there even *was* a method, to defeat Nero, Haldor finally managed to pelt Lavisa with a rock weighty enough to knock her off the mats.

Leaving Seth and Ackerly alone to fight off three aggressive Affinities—or die.

Terror radiated from the two primaries stranded on the mats, and guilt radiated from Eliana and Tray for allowing the turquoise-haired girl to catch them off guard. Her wrist throbbed from the metal chain, but she knew the pain was trivial compared to what Seth and Ackerly were about to undergo.

"The pathetic plant kid and the normie," Nero mused, shaking out his meaty arms. His muscles undulated with the movement, and Ackerly slowly backed toward Seth at the sight. Eliana heard them both swallow as the three upperclassmen closed in. "This should be enjoyable."

Ackerly eyed Haldor's endless rocks, Nero's ruthless fist, and Demira's deadly chain. Eliana knew there were a few seeds tucked in his pockets, but she also knew the frantic thoughts flowing through his head: That he'd never practiced growing a plant without dirt or water or sunlight, that he had no chance of protecting himself in this fight, and that he didn't *want* to fight.

"I surrender," he said, holding up his hands. None of his friends reprimanded him when Nero nodded in acknowledgement and allowed him to scamper off the mats. Eliana would have done the same in his predicament, even if it meant abandoning Seth.

"Say goodbye to your twin, Stark," Nero sneered at Tray, who was nearly pulling out his hair at Eliana's side.

"Seth—"

"I've got this," the foolishly cocky Stark insisted, resuming his crouch.

"Stand down," Lavisa commanded as Haldor summoned a boulder bigger than his head. "It's not worth it."

To Seth, however, it was—to unlock his Affinity, to become his brother's equal, to become *useful* in this place where his existence didn't seem to matter. Eliana read all of these thoughts seeping from his brain, but that wasn't the reason she decided not to interfere on his behalf. She sensed another consciousness stirring and scheming, and she knew even before it happened that Hartman, still lying on the mats, would grasp Seth's ankle and teleport them both into the safety of the crowd.

She didn't anticipate how much this would infuriate Nero—or Seth.

"What the hell, dude?" he barked down at Hartman, who

now lay on the concrete floor among the students. "I was gonna beat them all and save Adara!"

"I'll save her," Hartman croaked, his mind hazy from the hit to the head. "Just be…patient…"

Lavisa wove through the crowd to confront them. "We need to take him to the nurse. Tray, carry him."

"No, just leave him!" Seth snapped at his brother. "He ruined *everything*!"

"Seth," Tray started, the pity clear in his inflection. His twin didn't hear his consolation, though; in a fit of despair, Seth shoved through the throng and stalked out of the basement.

"Poor cry-baby Stark," Nero cooed as the Mardurus twins and Dave rejoined him on the mats. "Which team wants to challenge us next?"

None spoke up, nor did anyone dare to look directly at the primaries as Tray hauled Hartman into his arms and the five trekked toward the exit. Eliana looked back before they reached the doors and her eyes locked with Calder's. Though his posture was lax, she saw the rage festering deep within him—the need for revenge.

With a voice clear and practiced from his interactions with Nero's mind reader, Calder sent his thoughts to her without any room for interpretation.

Tell Tray Stark we need to talk—in private. And ask yourself, Mensen, the next time you attack my sister, if you'd enjoy death by drowning.

8

Information Breaker

Since his near-death experience with Calder a few months ago, Tray had been careful to avoid him. This had proven difficult, considering their separate dorm rooms shared a bathroom, but he'd managed it—until the morning after the disastrous session of Nero's Dominion.

When Calder picked the lock to the bathroom and barged in, Tray almost tripped over the toilet in terror. To his fortune, he hadn't been *using* the toilet, though he was wearing only his boxers. With barely enough space for a shower, sink, and toilet, the bathroom was tiny for one person's use; for two boys, it was near claustrophobic. In this close proximity, the way Calder appraised his body with mild disgust made him squirm where he stood.

"I thought you'd be more muscular. You aren't the dumb twin, are you?"

"No." The word was muffled as Tray covered his mouth and nose with a hand, as if that could prevent Calder's water invasion. "What do you want?"

He leaned casually in the open doorway, his black hoodie and jeans giving him a much darker vibe than his school uniform. "The mind reader didn't tell you I want to have a chat?"

"She did," Tray replied, gradually lowering his hand. During a brief, whispered conversation the previous night, Eliana had told him what Calder had thought to her—and what he'd unintentionally let her glimpse when he'd been too busy during the brawl to shield his mind. "I didn't think this was the place you had in mind when you said *private*."

"Well, we can't be seen conversing in *public*. I want to know what you know about Periculy, the Reggs, this town—all of it."

Crossing his arms over his bare chest, which, until Calder's rude comment, he did think had gained a considerable amount of muscle, Tray nodded. "All right. And I want to know why you visited Adara in jail two days ago—and how."

At first, Calder cocked his head in confusion, but then his expression soured. "Mind readers. God, they're a pain in my ass." He rubbed his forehead and exhaled. "I can't break Stromer out of jail for you, nor do I want to. Your brother was idiotic enough to strike a bargain with Nero, and if the debt he wants Adara to pay… She's better off where she is."

Tray's eyes narrowed as he contemplated the secondary's words. "What is he gonna make her do?"

"Her fire Affinity mixed with Nero's bloodlust… Maybe we'll get lucky and she'll kill him instead of complying."

"You…don't like Nero? Aren't you his closest friend—or ally, or whatever he likes to call it?"

Calder's nose twitched, but he didn't answer that inquiry. "I walked right off campus to the police station. No one stopped me. The Reggs can't be everywhere at once. And, for the record, Stark, I went to *mock* her, not *visit* her."

Tray was unconvinced, but he didn't bother to question it. "The Regg government plans to train us to fight the Wackos. Angor wanted Hastings to kill all the Wackos on his own, so none of us would have to fight. The meeting he had with the Reggs to propose the idea was when someone took over Hastings's mind. I was certain it was Angor, but now... Someone erased his memory—"

"And you think it could be the same person who controlled Hastings," Calder concluded, scratching his chin. "Who else was at the meeting?"

"The Reggs, Olalla Cosmos..."

"She *is* a Mental, but her Affinity is peace. Think it's possible she can cause peace *and* discord?"

"Based on what I've researched, no. Mind Affinities are usually too specific to have multiple facets. And, though she *did* seem to have some negative history with the Reggs, she was more opposed to Angor during the meeting and his plan to use Hastings."

Calder's deep blue eyes bored into him, saying what neither wanted to voice aloud.

"No," Tray shook his head. "The Rosses are *Reggs*. It's a fact. Neither have weird hair—"

"Artemis's hair matches her eyes perfectly. Your color is brown—plain. Hers could be, too."

Tray gnawed on the inside of his cheek, calculating the probability. "But Artemis seemed like the victim. Hastings was demonstrating on Angor, and then her blood vessels began bursting as well."

Calder's eyebrows perked up. "But Angor's ceased popping?"

"Well, no. His kept popping, too..."

"What if," Calder said, standing straight, "Artemis forced Hastings to pop her own blood vessels to deflect attention away from the fact that she was the one doing it?"

Tray scowled, peeved not because of the notion but because he hadn't thought of it first. "What reason would the Rosses have to kill Angor?"

A spiteful laugh erupted from Calder's lips. "Isn't it obvious, primie? They wanted to take over the town, and that's what they did. This way probably worked better for them, honestly. If Hastings had lived, he would have had the opportunity to tell everyone the truth. With him dead and Periculy in jail—and without any memory of his Affinity—no one can prove he didn't do it and Artemis did. I don't particularly care what happens to you, but if I were you, I'd start learning how to combat Mental Affinities. If this 'Regg' can control minds and she's ruthless enough to use an innocent boy and let him die for her cause, we're all screwed."

Strangely, Tray agreed, but he felt uncomfortable saying so, especially to the boy who hadn't had any qualms with nearly killing *him*. Instead, he asked, "Should I expect you to tell Nero what I told you?"

Calder flashed a complacent grin. "I don't answer to him."

A knock sounded behind Tray, not on the door to the bathroom but on the door to the corridor. Ackerly would deal with it; Tray's focus remained pinned to his strange, new ally. "I know Seth couldn't have beaten you last night. He...doesn't know his Affinity, and you're powerful..."

"I appreciate the compliments, Stark, but—"

"You let him beat you. You wanted us to win."

Calder's lips pursed with the implication, but an alarmed voice beyond the door thwarted his response.

"Um...Tray?"

The two boys exchanged a wary glance before Tray hurried out of the bathroom, expecting the worst. When he entered his dorm, still in his boxers, Ackerly stood unharmed near the open doorway in which the Regg ambassadors waited.

The look Tray shot Ackerly surpassed scathing, but the Reggs seemed unperturbed by his lack of clothing; they merely stared at him with those blank, unfeeling eyes. The only solace Tray could find was that, from their vantage point, the Rosses couldn't see Calder lurking in the bathroom, listening.

"Tray Stark?" Artemis's eyebrows perked slightly, as if the tightness of her bun pulled them. When Tray gave her a slow, perplexed nod, she continued. "We require your assistance, Mr. Stark. How well do you know computer systems?"

"Would you be able to decode a password?" William asked, his tone as severe as the streaks of gray in his dark hair. "Have you ever tampered with security systems?"

Tray really wished he were wearing clothes for this conversation. "I... Are you...blaming me for something? If anyone's done something illegal, it was probably Adara Stromer."

After a shared side-glance, the Rosses attempted the most pleasant smiles their taut lips could manage. "We are having trouble with some of the school's security systems," Artemis explained. "Mr. Periculy did not give Fraco Leve the knowledge to fix this problem, and we were informed by Mr. Leve that you are one of the smartest students at this school."

"Well"—Tray's chest puffed up—"he isn't wrong about that."

In his periphery, he noticed Calder roll his eyes, likely fighting off a snide comment.

"So, you will help us?" William clarified, struggling to hide the hopefulness in his voice.

Tray's haughtiness deflated as he recalled the conversation he'd just had—the one in which they'd determined these Reggs could very well be more dangerous than they seemed. "Oh, well... How would it benefit me?"

Artemis inhaled sharply, warding off impatience. "If you know how to fix our problem and refuse, you will not be fond of the consequences."

"In that case, I've never touched a computer in my life. Can I get dressed now?"

Though the Rosses saw through his lie, they surrendered with a nod. "We'll go speak with Angor then," William said to his wife just loud enough that Tray caught his words.

"What's going on?"

The Reggs nearly jumped at Hartman's voice. Behind them, he lingered in the hall with Lavisa, who appeared far less sociable than her companion. After the initial surprise waned, Artemis narrowed her eyes at the gigantic welt on the boy's forehead. Although Tray had carried Hartman to the nurse's office the previous night, Jason Pane had been out working at Periculand's hospital, which meant he'd been unable to heal the swelling mound.

"Where did you get that?" William asked, studying the injury critically.

Hartman's carefree demeanor plummeted, and he gaped. "I... teleported into a wall."

Lavisa's eyebrows jumped dully. "Does sound like something you'd do."

The Reggs weren't convinced, but they simply eyed the students with warning before stalking toward the spiral staircase. It wasn't until the sound of their footsteps became inaudible that Calder slunk out of the bathroom to confront the primaries. Hartman yelped at the sight of him, and Lavisa, though not wearing her hand wraps, immediately lifted her fists in defense.

"Relax, Dispus," Calder droned as he strolled toward

them. "I'm not here to fight you. Stark and I are working together—temporarily."

Lavisa's eyes widened at Tray, but she averted her gaze upon realizing he was barely clothed. "Working on what?"

Ignoring her, Calder said, "If the Reggs are going off campus to speak with Periculy, this would be a good time to snoop. Corvis, go fetch the mind reader."

"E-Eliana?"

"What do you need her for?" Lavisa demanded. "Are you planning to kill her for hurting your sister last night?"

Calder's jaw shifted in irritation. "No, I need her to alert us if anyone's coming. And I'll need you two to hang out in the library and be on guard."

Lavisa matched his agitation by placing her hands on her hips. "What makes you think you can tell us what to do?"

Again, her inquiries were ignored as Calder met Hartman's orange eyes. "You can teleport, can't you?"

"A whole *twenty-five feet.*"

Calder's expression remained bland. "I don't know why you find that impressive."

"I've gained an entire *five feet* in the past three days!"

"Then you'll have to teleport in twenty-five-foot increments to reach us—and alert us if you see anyone who might interrupt us," Calder concluded, massaging his forehead in exasperation.

Lavisa's defiance still radiated. "Where will you be?"

Cutting his eyes to the right, Calder surveyed Tray and Ackerly. The former's mouth went dry when he realized he would actually have to work with the boy who had nearly drowned him—the untrustworthy secondary who seemed interested in someone as deviant as *Adara*. His unease heightened at the formation of Calder's grin and subsequent utterance of the words, "In Fraco's office."

Three days had passed since Adara was thrown in jail. Three days since she'd woken up to find her friends on the other side of those bars, all dressed in black. Three days since the Pixie Prince had visited, taunting her with those duck slippers in a way that, though she would never admit it, had been highly entertaining. Three days of no responsibility, no school, no Tray, no Kiki—

And Adara Stromer was bored.

She'd always thought her life goal was to do absolutely nothing, but being cooped up in this cell without anyone to start fights with had her beyond restless. Yesterday, Friday, she'd tried grabbing the bars to pry them open—as if she had the strength to bend metal—and had been severely electrocuted. At least her involuntary nap had killed a few minutes of her miserable existence.

Now it was Saturday, and she should have been out in Periculand, roaming the streets with Greenie and causing some mayhem that would give Nerdworm a heart attack. Instead, she lay on her back, soaking in the cold of the metal slab and staring blankly at the white ceiling.

Angor sat on the opposite side of the cell, probably probing his mind for knowledge of his Affinity to no avail. As he'd repeated to Adara numerous times, all of his memories that involved the use or mention of his Affinity had been skewed and distorted, leaving a hole that tore through the majority of his mind. Every time he grew closer to distinguishing it, that void would consume him; still he persisted, though, inducing agitated insults from Adara at his strange meditation techniques.

Other than the times she contrived one of those sarcastic quips or an inappropriate question that the principal refused to answer, the two prisoners didn't converse much. That was why, when the Regg ambassadors unexpectedly arrived that morning, Adara was actually ecstatic to see them.

"Ah, the Reggs," Adara greeted as soon as Mitt guided them into the hall outside her cell. His expression was far less bright than his ugly orange uniform, and he remained in the doorway, observing them with wary vigilance. "How convenient that you've come at this exact moment. I was about to ask Mitt to unlock the bathroom door for me." She motioned with her foot to the plain, white door beside her metal slab, which led to the tiny toilet she and Angor were only permitted to use when Mitt electronically opened the door with a button outside the cell. "But, now that you two are here, I think I'll enjoy pissing on you much more," she finished with a wicked grin.

Mitt scrunched his nose, but the Reggs were unfazed.

"I would advise stepping back," Angor warned the Rosses when Adara swung her legs over the side of her bed and stretched into a sitting position. "She isn't bluffing."

"You two deserve it for locking me in a cell with a *murderer*." Her red eyes must have appeared particularly demonic with that comment, because it provoked the Reggs to take a wise step away from the bars, which she approached on bare feet. "When are you pricks gonna let me out of this hellhole? Mitt won't give me donuts."

William's chin remained high as he looked down on her. "Your confinement here is based on the possibility that you may have conspired with Angor in his attempted mur—"

"Bullshit—you're just afraid of me. But I have news for you: *I don't have a fire Affinity*. Whatever you think happened in that office—it didn't."

"When you erupted in flames before our very eyes, you mean? That didn't happen?" Artemis challenged, raising an eyebrow.

"You'll remain here until we've had enough time to organize the mess Angor's left in his wake—and until we can determine whether you will be a liability to the rest of the people in this town."

"*Of course*. You couldn't have me incinerating your army of teenagers that *you* intend to kill by throwing them to the Wackos for slaughter."

The Rosses bristled at that lick of knowledge—the truth she shouldn't have known.

Intrigued, Angor stood and paced toward her, stopping a healthy distance away. Meeting her gaze, he implored her not to divulge what else she might know, but she ignored him and rolled her eyes back to the Reggs.

"And now I'll be here forever, won't I, because you don't want everyone else knowing your dirty little secret?" Her gaze darted between them, but neither showed any hint of emotion.

"We repaired the damage your fire Affinity inflicted on the principal's office," Artemis informed her before redirecting her vision to Angor. "But upon sealing the hole, we found we were unable to reenter through the doors. They've been locked, and we don't have the code."

"Oh, I never created a *code*." Angor simpered, even though he smelled of body odor and had been degraded to the garb of a prisoner. Somehow, despite this setting, when he stood with his hands folded behind his back, he still exuded authority. "The only way to open the doors is through the computer within, or by voice recognition."

Clearly the Reggs had not anticipated this, for both of their expressions turned acidic. "So, only your voice can open the doors?" William clarified.

Now it was Angor who frowned, and Artemis caught onto that brief displeasure. "Is there someone else who can open it?"

All he gave them was an ambiguous, "Perhaps."

"Fraco told us he was not informed of any code," Artemis said flatly.

"No, he never was, nor does he have the ability to enter the office without me. His voice cannot open those doors."

"But he is your vice principal. Is he not meant to fill in for you in your absence?"

Angor resumed that presumptuous smirk. "I never had any plans of being absent. Now that I am, it appears Fraco didn't rise to my position regardless."

Artemis looked poised to lunge at the bars and grab Angor by the throat—and, judging by Mitt's guarded posture, he likely wouldn't have warned her of the electrical consequences. Before she could, Angor asked, "What reason would I have to inform you of how you can infiltrate my office and overthrow my town? The logic isn't there, Artemis."

"If you bring me donuts, I'll torture it out of him," Adara offered with a wiggle of her eyebrows.

Both Rosses pointedly disregarded her as William said to Angor, "It would make you seem less suspicious. If you oppose us, it only adds to the argument that you attempted to murder my wife. If you cooperate with us, perhaps we will consider your plea."

"I don't believe you'll free me from this cell, no matter what I do. How would you ever rule Periculand when its founder is an innocent, free man? No, you will keep me here whether I'm proven guilty or innocent." Artemis's lips pursed, as if to refute, but Angor continued. "I will tell you who can open my office if you agree to free Adara from this jail."

The girl slowly pivoted her head toward the principal and cocked it to the side. "Did you not hear me when I offered to torture you for donuts?"

"Maybe that's *why* he wants you out of this jail." Mitt's suggestion earned a middle finger from her.

Artemis eyed her husband, brooding. "We could always cut another hole in the ceiling of Fraco's office to get into Angor's."

"You'd rather destroy the damage you just fixed than let me out of this place?" Adara questioned in dry disbelief. "The only person I would burn *if* I had a fire Affinity would be Nero Corvis. And probably Kiki Belven. And *maybe* the Pixie Prince, if he's being particularly an—"

"We will free her if you tell us," William conceded with a sigh. Adara blinked at the same instant Artemis did, both in shock.

"Good," Angor said, though he hardly masked his astonishment. "If you must utilize my office, you may speak to…Jeannette Alberts. Her voice can open the doors. She will know I have approved it simply by the fact that you have this knowledge."

Adara's mouth fell open. "The *librarian* is the only person in this freaking town who can get into your office, other than you? What, are you *banging* her? The *librarian*? Isn't she a bit young for you? I pegged her at thirty-five, *maybe* thirty-fo—"

"Thank you for the information, Angor," William interrupted with a curt nod. "We will return in a few weeks to discuss your trial."

"Have fun in solitude, Your Highness. I'll tell the *librarian* you miss her," Adara crooned, stepping up to the bars. "All right, Weaponizer, open it up."

"That won't be necessary," William assured the officer before he could reach for the electronic keypad on the wall.

Artemis's countenance shifted to relief just as Adara's shifted to dismay. Clenching her fists on the hem of her flimsy shirt, she growled, "What do you mean it won't be necessary?"

"We *will* free you, eventually," William informed her with a pitying glance. "Just not now."

A torrent of fury swelled in Adara's chest. Her freedom—her chance of escaping this pit of boredom—had been dangled in front of her nose, only to be cruelly snatched away by these freaking *Reggs*. It wasn't her animalistic snarl that made the Rosses pause in the doorway; it was the crackle and glow of flames.

From her fists budded two separate fires; with cores of whitish-yellow that cascaded into orangey-red, they heated the chilly jail while scorching the edges of her shirt. If she reached forward, she probably could have melted and bent those bars as she'd wanted to earlier, but the sight of that *fire*, morphing her hands into flesh like hardened lava, searing through her clothes, threatening to consume her…

She staggered back, and the flames extinguished with her anger, subsiding into nothing and leaving her hands soft but covered in a fresh layer of soot. The loss of warmth hollowed her soul, and that lingering panic numbed her senses—to the point that she didn't even notice as the Reggs scurried from the room and prompted Mitt to close the door behind them.

Alone with only Angor, who studied her with an experimenter's eyes, Adara shook off her anxiety and padded back to her metal slab. The coolness lessened her fiery rage, but she still had enough left to glare at the principal. "Even though you tried to save my ass, I still don't like you."

With an exhale born of numerous disappointments, Angor retreated to his own bed of metal and said, "I didn't expect you would."

9

Shifting Allegiances

"What the hell happened there?" Calder asked as he peered up at the massive patch of spackled drywall on the ceiling.

"Adara happened there," Tray grumbled, shoving past him to enter Fraco Leve's office. Upon arriving a few minutes ago, the door had been locked, prompting Calder to utilize his mysterious lock-picking skills. None of the primaries asked him where he'd learned the trick, and with the venom that flared in his eyes every time they fell on Eliana, she was too afraid to pry into his brain and figure it out.

After discussing the plan for far too long, Lavisa had finally acquiesced to help by sitting with Hartman at one of the tables near the front door of the library, monitoring for any signs of Fraco. It hadn't taken much to convince Eliana to join them—not with the threat of drowning, of which Calder had politely reminded her.

"Fraco got a new desk," Ackerly remarked as he and Eliana

trickled into the office behind Tray. The Stark twin had already stalked to the right side of the room, where the wall was shielded by endless filing cabinets.

Tray yanked open one of the black drawers and said, "Also because of Adara." After ruffling through the files and then pulling open another drawer, he slammed them both shut. "Fraco didn't label these *or* put them in alphabetical order. The lack of organization…"

"Damaging Fraco's property won't keep us inconspicuous, Stark." Calder raised his eyebrows at the dents Tray had put in both drawers.

Alarmed, Ackerly's eyes protruded behind his green glasses. "Oh, weeds! He's gonna know we were here!"

"He's gonna know *someone* was here," Calder corrected, "but if we're lucky, he'll be too frazzled by the Reggs' hostile takeover to notice. Maybe you should take a seat, Stark, unless you think your super strength will break Fraco's chair."

"Do you know where we can find Angor's file?" Eliana asked Ackerly in an attempt to assuage the tension.

"We'll…probably have to check them all for *P*, unless teachers and administrators have an entirely different section…"

Ackerly winced at the drawers, which Tray had resumed jerking open, purposely oblivious to Calder's admonishing glares. His expression mollified when the Stark twin pulled out a green folder and waved it at him. "Found your file."

"Put it away," was all Calder said before searching other drawers.

"Adara almost destroyed your file last time we snuck in here," Ackerly recalled with a nervous smile as he opened what appeared to be the *A* files.

The secondary's reaction was far more severe than Eliana had anticipated as his head whipped toward the green-haired boy with barely restrained ire. “You snuck in here before and *didn’t* find out what Periculy’s Affinity is?”

Tray snorted. “Adara was in charge of that excursion. You can imagine there was no logic behind it.”

“It was before…the incident,” Ackerly explained. “We were just trying to discover…Hastings’s Affinity.”

He peeked fretfully in Eliana’s direction, expecting a negative reaction. The other boys waited for it, too—the moment Hastings’s name would provoke a violent outburst from her. Due to years of emotional suppression, she maintained neutrality and continued flipping through files. It wasn’t until she noticed something unusual that she turned to the boys with a frown.

“I just looked through the *S* files… Adara’s isn’t here.”

Instead of looking to Eliana, Calder and Tray both glanced at Ackerly in inquiry.

He swallowed. “She…didn’t take it when we came. She didn’t even want to look at it.”

Unconvinced, Tray mumbled, “Wouldn’t put it past her to return here and steal it on her own.”

“The last time we were here, it looked like someone had tampered with some of the files,” Ackerly remembered with growing dread. “Do you think they stole hers?”

“With what purpose? She didn’t know her Affinity at the time, so it wouldn’t have been in the—”

“I found *P*,” Calder announced, jaw tight with displeasure. “Periculy’s isn’t here.”

“Maybe someone stole both?” Ackerly offered weakly.

After moving to the next drawer, Eliana tugged on it and found it wouldn’t budge. “This one’s locked.”

“Let me open it,” Tray said, but Calder intercepted him.

"Remember what I said about not leaving traces of damage, primie? I'll do it."

Grumbling, Tray allowed the blue-haired boy to pick at the lock until the drawer swung open, revealing files of all three symbolizing colors, as well as names that began with all twenty-six letters of the alphabet. Most of the teachers' files lay within, but there were also a few student names scattered throughout, like Nero Corvis, Madella Martinez, and both Stromers.

Without searching for Angor's file, Calder extricated Adara's. Though muffled by his mental block, there was a hint of excited interest in him as he sifted through the pages.

"Wow, her birthday really is on August fifteenth," Ackerly noted, standing on his toes to scan the first page over Calder's shoulder. "You'd think that would be something she wouldn't have remembered correctly, being so young when her parents left her…"

"Adara Stromer is too much of a narcissist to forget her own birthday," Tray said. "And Avner was old enough to have told her. Does it…*say* anything about her parents?"

Calder flipped to the next page, which gave information on Adara and Avner's father. "Casimir Stromer," he read with a furrowed brow. "That's an odd name."

"Says the guy named *Calder*." Tray's retort lost its edge when he spotted the page on the man. Most of it was blank, some spaces appearing to have been purposely whited out.

"My parents were high when they named me," Calder stated without emotion.

Eliana tore her focus away from the file. "They were high when you were *born*?"

"You can read minds; figure it out on your own," he countered, blue eyes still roving the page before him. "Look—the section about an Affinity. It's marked 'Yes.'"

With the questions tumbling through his mind, Tray's voice came out absently. "Adara's father has an Affinity—or *had*, if he's dead—but it doesn't say his ability."

"Check Avner's," Eliana suggested, prompting Ackerly to withdraw the other Stromer's file. When he filtered through it, she saw the page on Casimir Stromer was exactly the same.

Ackerly shuffled through a few pages that detailed his electricity Affinity. "Th-the information on his mother is missing."

"So is Adara's," Tray noted when Calder flipped through her file and found only a few blank pages that had yet to be filled with information on her fire Affinity.

"In the other files, there are always pages about the mother, even if they're blank," Calder said. "Whoever tampered with the files must have taken the pages on the Stromers' mother."

"Why?" Eliana asked quietly.

After a moment of deep thought, Calder shook his head and returned Adara's file to its drawer. "I don't know. But we need to find Periculy's—"

"Whoa!" Eliana spun around to find Hartman standing on Fraco's new desk, feet slipping as he fought to steady himself. "This desk is slick with oil. But, hey—guess what? I think I got *twenty-seven* feet just then! It's hard to tell—"

"The Reggs are back," Eliana said, reading Hartman's frenzied thoughts before he could voice them. "They're…dragging the librarian up the stairs—"

"And Fraco's with them," the teleporter finished as he hopped down from the desk, wobbling.

After grabbing Avner's file from Ackerly's hands, Calder hastily shoved it back into the drawer and then sifted through the remaining folders. "If Fraco comes in here, can you teleport us all out at once?"

"Me?" Hartman spluttered, but he composed himself after the secondary aimed a vicious scowl over his shoulder. "Uh…no? I've only ever teleported one person at a time."

Calder jerked his head toward Ackerly. "Then get started."

Teleporting a few feet toward them, Hartman grasped Ackerly's arm before the green-haired boy could protest, and the two of them disappeared, as if they'd never been there at all.

"I see why Nero constantly has the urge to beat that kid senseless," Calder commented, still focused on his task.

"Not everyone's attention span is as refined as yours."

Eliana muttered the words so softly she believed he hadn't heard, until he said, "You're riding a thin line, Mensen. Just because your boyfriend died doesn't mean you can say whatever the hell you want and get away with it. Periculy's file isn't here."

Infuriated, her jaw had dropped, but then she caught his last sentence and stifled her irritation. "I just sensed the Reggs and Fraco—and the librarian. They're on the floor above us, in Angor's office."

Tray ran a hand through his hair. "Angor actually told them how to surpass the security system. Why would he hand Periculand over to them so easily? Especially if he has a mind controlling Affinity…"

"Check if any of the other drawers are locked," Calder ordered as he closed the one with Adara's file and worked to relock it.

"I think the librarian knew the code," Eliana said in answer to Tray's question, squeezing her eyes shut to focus on the minds above. "We're too far for me to get anything clear, and—and they all just…disappeared." Movement halted, and when Eliana pried her eyes open, both boys stared at her.

Tray was the one to blurt a baffled, "What?"

"All of their minds are gone. I—I can't sense any of them."

"Maybe they're coming back down."

"They're not anywhere in this building." Shaking her head, Eliana strained to search for the four minds. "It feels like...I've been blocked, somehow..."

The boys shared a knowing look as their minds converged to the same assumption: If Artemis had a mind controlling Affinity—one that could even erase memories—then it was quite possible she could block mind readers.

"I sense them again," Eliana said, interrupting the boys' ruminations. "The Reggs are still in the office with the librarian, but Fraco—he's coming back down the stairs."

"Where the *hell* is Corvis?" Calder asked, just as the orange-haired boy materialized on Fraco's desk again. Before he could brag about his teleportation or spew nonsense, the secondary snapped, "Take Stark. Now."

Tray backed away from Hartman when he teleported to him. "Me? Why?"

"Because you're nothing more than a sack of muscle. Mensen can alert us if Fraco's coming back."

"He's not." After opening another drawer, Calder paused at Eliana's statement. "He's...looking for Nero. The Reggs...want him, for some reason."

"Corvis, take Stark."

"*No—*" But Hartman, perhaps in fear that Calder would provoke his stepbrother to pummel him later, hooked his arm through Tray's and vanished from the room before the stubborn Stark twin could object.

"When Little Corvis comes back, he'll teleport me to intercept Fraco and Nero on their way back up to Angor's office,"

Calder explained, kicking one of the drawers closed and abandoning their fruitless mission. "*You* will trail us and listen in on whatever meeting happens up there. I want you to figure out what's going through the Reggs' minds while I focus on the verbal conversation. We'll confer after."

"And I assume you'll drown me if I refuse?" Eliana asked with all the boldness she could muster.

Calder just rubbed his temples. "You spent too much time with your old roommate."

The primaries were harder to work with than Calder would have liked, but after hashing out his plan with both Eliana and Hartman, he convinced the teleporter to jump him down the hall. From there, he intentionally bumped into Fraco and Nero in the stairwell on their ascent to the fourth floor. Knowing the smaller Corvis had teleported back to the library and his involvement would remain unknown, Calder met his ally and the vice principal with calm indifference.

"Mardurus," Nero greeted when their paths intersected on the second-floor landing. "I've been looking for you all morning."

"Floretta summoned me to her office for a scolding," he lied smoothly. "Apparently, I'm not allowed to drench primies that irk me."

Nero chuckled, but Fraco vibrated with annoyance.

"Out of the way, Mr. Mardurus!" In attempted intimidation, the man swatted Calder with his greasy clipboard. "We have business with the principals!"

"They've adopted that title, have they? How quick you are to change allegiance, Fraco. What will Master Angor say when he discovers you've abandoned him?"

The conflict was clear on Fraco's face, but he didn't have the opportunity to defend himself before Nero said, "Mardurus comes with us. I want to have back-up, in case things go south."

The man huffed a sigh and plowed past Calder. "I have no idea what you assume is going to happen up here. The Rosses are respectable, professional—"

"They're the *government*." Nero began climbing the stairs; he didn't have to beckon for Calder to follow. "I'm not going back to prison."

"They have no intention of imprisoning you, Mr. Corvis," Fraco assured him, likely to alleviate the hint of aggression.

Though not the brightest, Nero had enough brains to be wary, and he nodded to Calder before they entered the office—a silent command to drown everyone in sight if these Reggs tried to restrain him.

Calder had never stepped inside Angor Periculy's quarters before, and the sheer size impressed him upon first glance. A wall of books comprised the right side, while framed degrees and awards littered the left. The posterior wall, like that of Fraco's office and the library, was composed entirely of glass, encompassing a view of the barren forest at Periculand's northern border.

At the center of the office dwelled a lavish, wooden desk behind which the two Reggs stiffly stood. It wasn't the sight of them that caught Calder's attention, nor was it the librarian who stood by the wall of books, purposely removed; instead, it was the patch of wood before Angor's desk that didn't match the reddish hue of the rest.

"Stromer really ruined this place, didn't she?" he mused with a pointed glance. The Rosses did not look nearly as entertained, but neither voiced a word before Fraco scurried into the room.

"I apologize. Mr. Corvis insisted on bringing Mr. Mardur—"

"They both may stay," William said, nodding to the two empty chairs on either side of Adara's circle. Nero stomped to the vacant seats, threatening to crack the new wood with his heavy footsteps. His massive form barely fit between the arms of his chair, while Calder's lithe body slipped into the other with ease.

"Close the doors, Fraco," Artemis commanded, and the vice principal—*their* vice principal—obeyed without question.

Nero fidgeted in his tiny seat. "There's a button for that, you know." When the Reggs stared at him, bemused, he nodded to the computer monitor on Angor's desk. "There's a button on the computer that'll electronically close the doors."

Suspicion swam in William's dark eyes. "How do you know?"

"I served my share of punishments in this office," the boy replied, flashing a brutish grin. Neither of the Reggs seemed to want to know more.

"Upon entering this office a few moments ago, we were met with surveillance footage of an…event that occurred in the Physicals Building last night." Artemis twisted the computer screen so both boys could witness the video of the brawl. Although the volume was muted, it was clear from the visible recording that Nero was in charge of the gathering—and that he commanded a horde of formidable teenagers. "What is the purpose of this?"

"An underground fight club." Nero shrugged one of his meaty shoulders. "We get more intense in there than we do in training, since Fraco won't allow violence."

William looked to the oily man positioned behind the boys. "You won't allow violence?"

"I—well, Mr. Corvis has a tendency to severely injure other students!" Even Calder had to admit that this accusation, albeit true, was petty. "Training is a place for students to practice their Affinities in a safe—"

"Not anymore," Artemis cut in. "The conduct of this school will change come Monday. Angor has kept the purpose of Periculand a secret, but the government allowed him to build it on the premise that the young Affinities would be trained to combat the rising Wackos." Nero's eyebrows perked at this new knowledge, and Calder feigned surprise by parting his lips. "The current president is lenient, but the president-elect will not be. Upon Angor's imprisonment, Emmett Ventura instructed my husband and I to seize power over this town and conform it to the standards on which it was built."

"You two work for Ventura?" Calder blurted out, unable to contain his revulsion.

"Yes, they do," confirmed a voice that boiled his blood. When the face of Emmett Ventura appeared on Angor's computer monitor, canceling out the view of Nero's Dominion, Calder didn't even try to hide his antagonism.

"Damn, I hate this guy. He's such a p—a wussy, as Fraco would say."

"I-I never—no—never—" the vice principal stammered, but the president-elect had no care for him.

Ventura's lips curled with equal distaste as he realized the boy who'd squirted water at him sat on the other side of the screen. Calder could at least find satisfaction in that he'd managed to make this asshole feel so much chagrin.

"This—this boy cannot be the leader I prompted you to find," the man insisted, struggling to maintain poise. His office gave him the illusion of professionalism with awards covering most of the wall behind him. Sun shone through a window to his right, lighting his brown eyes to gold while his hair remained purely black. To Calder, it was not the Regg features that signified his cowardliness but the recollection of the man's terrified face when he'd been *splashed* two months ago.

"No," William replied from behind the monitor as he tilted it to face Nero, "this is the leader we found."

When Ventura appraised him, Nero's eyebrows inched even higher. "Leader?"

"This is Nero Corvis," Artemis informed the president-elect. "He is a well-respected student here at Periculand Training Sch—"

"Because other students fear him too much to oppose him!" Fraco scampered to get in the camera's view but halted when Nero eyed him with the promise of violence. "I-I… What I mean to say is that Mr. Corvis has many enemies here."

"As far as I know, all my enemies have either fled this town or are rotting away in prison," the brute countered coolly.

Artemis continued as though the outburst hadn't happened. "Nero is practiced in leading students. He has formed his own version of training for students that allows them to express their Affinities in a more impressive way than Angor ever consented to."

"Nero's Dominion, I call it," he added. Calder was tempted to make a comment about JAMZ, but it didn't seem in his best interest.

Fraco, apparently, had forgotten himself entirely. "Mr. Corvis will not be a positively influential leader! He spent many years in a juvenile detention facility and has been deemed—"

"Juvie?" Ventura repeated, not appalled but intrigued. "For what?"

Nero straightened, unashamed. "Domestic violence. *Severe* domestic violence."

The Rosses both remained silent, harrowed by this awkward information, of which they'd clearly had no prior knowledge.

Instead of dismissing him immediately, though, Ventura asked, "What is your Affinity?"

"Strength."

Dipping his chin, the man contemplated a moment. "No other student would challenge your authority?"

"Not unless they want to be pulverized," the boy said with a menacing jump of his eyebrows.

Though it was true that his main opposition, the Stromers, were out of the picture, Tray Stark still existed, and it took all of Calder's self-control not to remind his leader of this fact.

Folding his hands atop his desk, Ventura met Nero's eyes through the camera. "I will become president in two months. My predecessor has done a lousy job of containing the Wackos, and I want my legacy to be one of eradication—of the Wackos, I mean. I want you, Nero, to be the fist that squashes them. With your history, I believe you would be an excellent commander in my army of Affinities. You will lead ruthlessly, and you will destroy the Wackos without remorse. Does this appeal to you?"

"Nero," Calder hissed, watching in horror as a grin spread across his ally's face. "You can't work for this douchebag—"

William cleared his throat, interrupting Calder and prompting the gray-eyed boy, who stroked his wide chin, reveling in the suspense.

"I think, Mr. President, that there isn't anyone else fit for the job."

Ventura slapped his hand on his desk in enthusiasm. "Excellent! Mr. and Mrs. Ross, you will instruct Nero on his task, yes? And Fraco, as you are frequently involved in student affairs, you will ensure that all heed Nero's commands. And you"—his gaze settled on Calder again with growing hostility—"what is your purpose here?"

"Mardurus is my strongest ally," Nero answered before Calder could contrive a snarky remark. "He could drown fifty Wackos in a matter of minutes."

Ventura hummed in skepticism. "He is obedient to you?"

"Mardurus is like a dog. I keep him on a tight leash," Nero assured, triggering a deluge of rage that Calder had to hinder by forcing a smirk.

"Make it tighter," was the president-elect's last comment before dismissing the boys and Fraco from the office. Eliana wasn't in the hallway, but Calder didn't need her mind reading to hear Ventura say, "Tell me what you've learned from Angor Periculy's file," before the doors slammed behind them.

10

Parental Love

After numerous arguments, Zeela, Avner, Jamad, and Naretha finally came to the conclusion that they would have to spend the weekend with the Solbergs. It was less than a three-hour drive to Wacko Headquarters, Naretha claimed, so if they left with Elias's car early in the morning, they would be able to return that same evening. Unfortunately, Jamad's father worked on weekends, which meant they would be unable to borrow the car until Monday morning. Zeela just hoped that, when the time came for them to drive again, Avner wouldn't be the one behind the wheel.

Surprisingly, Jamad seemed the most chagrinned by the delay. Avner was too worried about Zeela's temporary blindness to rush the departure, and Zeela was too enthralled by Jade to care about leaving. She spent the majority of the three days playing with the toddler, while Jamad spent it avoiding all interaction with her. Naretha, who had been initially opposed to the postponement, had become so engrossed in watching the Solbergs' ancient television that she might not have been bothered if they waited an extra week to leave. In the end, Jamad's restlessness, along with his friends' desire to retrieve Maddy, propelled them to set Monday morning as their departure.

Late Sunday night, after the Solbergs had gone to bed, Zeela lay in a sleeping bag on the living room floor among the other Affinities, unable to sleep. Her jumbled brain still pounded, but she had to feign painlessness to stop Avner from fretting. He'd taken an injury to the head as well, and though it had ceased bleeding, she knew he would neglect his own wounds to tend to hers. So, in everyone else's minds, her eyes were improving; in her mind, however, she'd begun to worry her Affinity was broken.

Between Avner's deep breathing on her left and Jamad's ridiculous snores beyond him, Zeela knew they'd fallen asleep. With Naretha's silence, she'd assumed the Wacko had, too, until a quiet voice filled her ear, soothing her jarred senses.

"I haven't watched TV since I was eight. Ephraim never allowed them at Headquarters. I should tell you he hated them because he didn't want to promote Regg actors or something, but…he just hated technology—never even had a cell phone. He was livid when one girl with a tech Affinity revamped the entire compound to include electronically-coded doors and computer systems. Everyone else was pleased, at least."

This was the most the Wacko had said to any of them. Carefully, Zeela asked, "Who's Ephraim?"

"The leader of the Wackos—or former leader, I should say. He was murdered in September by a cop. That's why his son took over, Danny."

"Your boyfriend."

"Yes," she ground out. Zeela could tell the agitation wasn't aimed at her.

"What kind of Affinity did Ephraim have?"

"That's a secret." Naretha sighed, shifting in her sleeping bag. "But now that he's dead, I guess it doesn't matter. He had…a *fruit* Affinity."

"A-a what?"

"He could grow fruit—and vegetables, when he really concentrated. And that was it; there was nothing deadly about it. He didn't even start the Wackos, which used to be called Affinities for Freedom, with any intention of violence. But he *was* skilled with guns; I'll give him that."

Zeela's head spun with even more intensity than before. "Affinities for Freedom? That's what…you call it?"

"Not anymore." Bitterness laced through Naretha's inflection. "Danny officially declared that we're the *Wackos* when he took charge. It's…fine. Our goal is still the same: to be recognized as *people* by the government. If we have to be aggressive to get to that point, we will."

Though Zeela didn't agree with the ethics, she didn't bother to argue. "How long have you been with the Wackos?"

"My parents handed me over to Ephraim when I was eight. They were Reggs."

"They didn't like that you had an Affinity?"

"No, they didn't like what the government would do with me if they found out I had an Affinity. They knew I'd be safer with Ephraim. They gave me up because they loved me." Naretha's voice broke slightly at the end, and she cleared her throat, playing it off as nothing more than a voice crack.

"But you didn't love them?" Even without the ability to see auras—or anything, for that matter—Zeela could feel the resentment in the air…and the sorrow. "Is that why you stayed with the

Wackos? Is that why you want to fight against the Reggs? Because your parents—"

"I loved my parents," she growled. "When the Regg government found out they were helping Ephraim, they kidnapped, tortured, and killed them."

Zeela's eyes flew open in shock. "Wh-when?"

"Shortly after the Wackos became public, ten years ago. I'd already been living at Headquarters for seven years, but I was… close with my family still. My older brother was the one who gave me my Affinity. We were toddlers and he poured salt in my eyes, that little bastard… We were always friends, though, and when they took my parents, they took him, too. When I found the names of those involved… They didn't enjoy their deaths."

This outright admission to murder took Zeela a moment to process. An adequate response didn't enter her mind before Naretha asked, "Were you born blind?"

"I…was. My Affinity developed so young, though—I don't know exactly what it's like. If this is anything like blindness, what's happening to me now—it's not pleasant."

"I can't even fathom an Affinity like yours." Zeela assumed the ensuing rustling was Naretha shaking her head against her pillow. "What's most impressive is that I couldn't even tell you saw differently, before now."

"My Affinity compensates well enough that I can piece together the shapes of the world. Heat, X-rays, auras…and I can focus my eyes on distant objects, like those cop cars a few days ago."

A snort escaped the Wacko, and Zeela heard her head turn again, likely in her direction. Was Naretha looking into her eyes, the pure whiteness that so many found disturbing? She tried to discern just one shape, but everything was a pulsing array of blinding colors and grotesque figures.

"I see color, but it's not like yours. When I first began seeing auras, I didn't know what they meant or how to label them. I began experimenting, deciding which auras correlated with which moods, and I labeled them according to which colors seeing people associate with each. Jamad always said red meant angry, so now the color I see when people are angry is red, to me."

"Trippy." There was a bit of wonder to that comment.

"Getting a feel for how people's faces are structured was tricky. I know what Avner and Jamad look like—and Maddy, too—maybe almost to the same degree an average person would. I didn't have enough time to study your face before my mind blew up." Rubbing her temples, Zeela closed her eyes again and sighed. "You have short hair, don't you? And a thin, long nose?"

"I don't think I wanna know how I look in your mind, Blindie."

Whether it had been a joke, Zeela smirked anyway. "Your hair is pinkish, I know, and Avner always says pink is a sweet color, but to me—well, maybe it is best I don't tell you how you look in my mind. What does Avner look like to you? Is he aesthetically pleasing?"

Naretha's normal sarcastic voice resurfaced. "You're asking me if a tan kid with neon-yellow hair and eyes is aesthetically pleasing?"

"Um, yeah? I don't really know if those traits clash in everyone else's eyes or not."

"They do clash. His hair should definitely not be neon-yellow, nor should his eyes…but it's that way with most Affinities. I've never seen someone with pure white hair who isn't elderly."

Zeela's eyebrows shot up, even though her eyes remained sealed. "I look elderly?"

"You have white hair and you're blind—of course you look elderly."

Rolling her eyes behind their lids, Zeela asked, "Well, what does your boyfriend look like, the Wacko leader? Is *he* aesthetically pleasing?"

"Danny is the most attractive person I've ever met, physically and personally," Naretha stated, her inflection dry and unfeeling. "He's also the most dangerous person I've ever met. Maybe that's what *makes* him attractive. He's ruthless, but he's not. He's passionate, but he's not. He just…doesn't make sense."

"Well, I don't think *you* make sense," Zeela countered, voicing her next words tentatively. "I still can't decide why you saved me in the river instead of running back to the hideout on your own."

Tension wafted off the Wacko, and she was immediately guarded. They hadn't spoken this much or revealed details so intimate, and if Naretha planned to spill the truth, it would be now—

A sudden bang jolted the small house, interrupting Jamad's snores and intensifying Zeela's headache.

"What was that?" she asked, but her question wasn't answered verbally. The only sounds that responded were that of bodies scrambling from sleeping bags, Naretha's bare feet padding across the wood floor by Zeela's head, and then a second bang, originating from where she assumed the front door to be.

With no context as to what caused the banging or if it had inflicted damage to the house, Zeela was subjected to lying there motionlessly, listening as Naretha and one of the boys tiptoed across the room. When someone placed a gentle hand on her arm, she burst upright.

"Hey, it's okay," came Avner's voice, confirming it was Jamad who had joined Naretha. "I think someone's at the door. You… Can you see at all?"

"A little," she lied, straining to piece together the images before her. Directing her eyes toward where she hoped the front door resided, she added, "I think someone is at the door…"

"Z…you're looking at the dining room table."

Whipping her head in the opposite direction, where she now knew the door must be, she found that everything still looked as incoherent and sighed. "Am I looking at the door now?"

"That you have to ask makes me think you're not." His wry smile was clear in his tone.

"Av, throw me my sweatshirt," Jamad called from a few paces ahead. Avner shifted away from Zeela, and a moment later she heard the whoosh of the sweatshirt flying across the room, followed by Jamad's grunts as he shrugged it over his head. "Whoa, Wacko," he said, as if seeing Naretha for the first time. "You look like a boy in my old pajamas."

Zeela touched the soft flannel pants Jamad had given her for sleeping. "Do I look like a boy, J?"

"Nah, you're actually pretty." He paused and then added, "Oh, right, you can't see. I'm winking at you and Av. And now I'm giving the Wacko a shit-eating grin."

Another violent knock split the air before Naretha could retort.

Jamad spoke quieter than before. "I see…a vehicle outside, and there's—there are a few people on the porch. At least three."

"Wackos?" Avner's dread was palpable.

Naretha's gruff response overpowered her light footsteps. "We'll be lucky if they are."

"Did you *tell* the Wackos to come to my house?" Jamad hissed in outrage. "You have no right to put my family in—"

"Open the door!" a voice shouted, accompanied by another obnoxious bang.

"What will you do if we don't, asshole?" Naretha yelled.

"Mom, Dad, get back in your room!" Jamad whispered frantically. Apparently, the Solbergs had heard the commotion and slipped out to investigate. "Wacko, got your salt crystals ready?"

"Yes—" The word had barely left her mouth before a cataclysmic explosion boomed through the air.

Zeela knew it must have been the old wooden front door flying off its hinges and erupting, because a few stray splinters managed to graze her skin before Avner jumped over her in a human shield. Colette's screams were muffled from afar, and Zeela imagined her burying her head in Elias's chest. Grunts emitted from Jamad and Naretha, both likely pelted by the door's shards.

"Are you okay?" Zeela breathed to Avner as he uncurled from the shell he'd formed around her.

"Yeah, fine," he panted, still gripping her hand. "J threw up a wall of ice to protect us."

"Is he okay?"

The stomp of heavy boots drowned out her inquiry. "I was almost done breaking the lock," an unfamiliar feminine voice griped. It sounded like she spoke though some kind of device.

"I was provoked," a man replied—probably the one who'd destroyed the door.

Hastily, Avner whispered, "There are three of them. They're wearing these black suits with helmets—I can't see their faces at all. They—they have weapons, Z. You need to stay back—"

"Avner!" Jamad called in panic. "They've got electric guns over here!"

"Don't move." He squeezed Zeela's hand before scrambling up and disappearing from her awareness. Without his body beside hers, she felt stranded and disconnected from the chaos unfolding just a few feet away.

Crawling forward, she quickly found the wall of ice Jamad had constructed. It must have been inches thick and feet tall—a solid defense for defenseless Zeela. Pressing her back against the cool, melting surface, she closed her eyes to block out the jumble of nonsense and pictured what was happening based on sound.

Crystals clicked against each other in endless waves, likely Naretha's salt and Jamad's ice. The mumbled curses that flowed from the Wacko's mouth indicated the two Affinities were unintentionally counteracting each other, the salt melting the ice and resulting in useless pools of sludge. Their lack of success clearly delighted the intruders, because three ominous cackles wove through the air, along with the crackling of electricity.

"Blast 'em, Av!" Jamad yelled, followed by an increase in the sparking noises. When he and Naretha both cried out in pain a moment later, though, Zeela knew Avner had been unsuccessful in his attempt to attack the intruders.

"J! Dammit! Z, they're immune to my Affinity! Jamad and Naretha are down!"

"I...am not...down," Jamad grunted, his words strained from the effects of the stun-gun. He was accustomed to Avner's Affinity but not enough to be completely resistant.

"No, get back in your room!" Avner demanded, probably to the Solbergs. Colette's muffled sobs were still audible, but Zeela assumed Elias would at least attempt to help—not that he could if even Avner's powers were ineffective. "J, can you st—"

A new weapon fired, one that Zeela guessed was some type of dart-gun. As soon as she heard the dart penetrate flesh, she scrambled along the ice wall to find the end, desperately trying to view what was happening on the other side. When Jamad shouted Avner's name, she stilled, paralyzed by the insinuation. Had Avner been shot? Was he...dead?

"Please!" Colette wailed as a body wilted to the floor with a thud—*Avner*. "Please, do not take him! Only them!"

There was a pregnant pause in which Zeela couldn't even breathe. Jamad's disbelief mirrored hers. "*Take us*?"

"We received a call earlier, notifying us that three fugitive Wackos were here," a masculine voice droned, likely originating from the intruder who had demolished the door.

"I'm not—we're not—none of us are Wackos!" Jamad stammered. His incredulity lingered, but Zeela had pieced together the harrowing truth: Colette had called the government to apprehend her, Avner, and Naretha. Colette, who had been like a second mother when her own had been so unloving, had turned them in to become prisoners.

"They must go, Jamad!" she cried, remorse and fear evident through the thickness of her accent. "They have ruined you. You are not the same boy!"

"No, I'm *not* the same boy!" he barked, the room chilling a few degrees with the coldness of his words. "Did you expect me to come back here after three years as the same kid I was before? *I* definitely didn't expect to return to find I have a *sister*!"

"Jamad," Elias pleaded. "I did not want this, but…let them take the three Wackos. Stay here, with us."

"No, *no—*"

"Glad to hear you don't want to stay," the female intruder interrupted. "We wouldn't have let you, anyway."

Zeela squeezed her eyes shut at the sound of the dart whizzing through the air. Jamad grunted as it perforated his skin, but she knew he must have passed out, because after his body thumped to the floor, he was silent.

"Please, please!" Colette begged, her words nearly inaudible between her sobs and her accent.

The intruders ignored her, and Zeela had to swallow her hopelessness as she heard them dragging the three immobilized bodies out the front door. Were the intruders even aware that she was curled up here, behind this wall of ice? Was it opaque enough to hide her? All she knew for certain was that they planned to kidnap Avner and Jamad, and based on the fact that she still sat here, unharmed, they had no intention of hauling her along with them.

If they took her two best friends—after the Wackos had already taken Maddy—and Zeela was stuck here, completely *blind*...the guilt and helplessness would consume her.

So, when the female intruder commented on how the boy with the blue hair wasn't the third Wacko Colette had called about, meaning there must be another, Zeela crawled over soggy splinters toward that voice. When they spotted and electrocuted her, she didn't fight back.

"Can you see?"

The whispered words hit Zeela's ears when her senses finally rejuvenated. The world was hazy for a few moments, but then shapes and colors began to materialize before her—not in the same fashion that normal eyes perceived but in *her* normal vision of heat and X-rays and auras. Naretha lounged on the floor beside her, oddly calm considering their predicament.

"Yes," Zeela confirmed quietly, absorbing the details of the van they sat in. Unlike the ones Periculand used to transport students, there were no seats for them, no view of their captors, and no windows. With her reacquired vision, she saw three bodies seated in the front, all swaying, as if... "Are they *dancing* up there?"

"And singing." A second later, Zeela indeed heard some

cacophonous vocals. "They're so obnoxious. At least they couldn't hear me rummaging around back here."

Following Naretha's nod, Zeela twisted to find cabinets bolted into the walls behind them. She couldn't open any, however, because her hands were tied with rope behind her back.

"Took me forever to even open one." The Wacko wiggled her bound arms, proving she was just as incapacitated. "Once I did, though, I found a bunch of medicine—weird shit I've never come across. I injected you with the one labeled 'Concussion Cure,' and—"

"You injected me with a foreign drug?" Zeela repeated, eyebrows arched.

"It *worked,*" Naretha mumbled as her gaze drifted to the unconscious boys slumped on the opposite side of the van. "I don't want to try anything on those two. They were tranquilized, judging by the darts hanging from their chests. Normal tranqs don't work that fast, though."

"If they have drugs that can cure a concussion, I'm not surprised they have rapid-acting sedatives. Do you think the boys will be all right?"

Naretha shrugged. "They're both breathing. The real issue now is how we're gonna get the hell out of here. I don't know what this rope is made of, but I found a knife in one of the cabinets and it won't cut through."

Zeela peered behind her back, where she fruitlessly rubbed a knife against the bindings. In her vision, there was something unnatural about it—something she couldn't quite pinpoint.

"I can't focus on anything outside the van long enough to figure out where we are," Zeela said, "but I know we're going fast. If we tried to jump out now, we'd die."

"God, I hope we haven't left the state," Naretha groaned,

banging her head back against one of the cabinet's metal doors. "We shouldn't have bothered leaving Periculand. Danny would have razed that place to save me, and we wouldn't be stuck in this van, headed to some research facility."

"Is that where we're going?" Terror gripped Zeela at the thought of scientists prodding at her eyes. She didn't want to think of what they might do to Avner and Jamad.

"Most likely. Why imprison us when they can experiment on us? It's sick, but…I see why they do it. They need to learn as much about us as they can in order to build weapons to use against us. I've heard horror stories about these places from Affinities who escaped and came to the Wackos for refuge. None of them are right in the head."

"Are any Wackos right in the head?"

"Remind me not to save your ass ever again—and remind me never to listen to Snowman ever again," Naretha added, jabbing her chin toward sleeping Jamad. "His parents shouldn't have been trusted; we should have left that night. It was one of them that sold us out, wasn't it?"

"His mom." Zeela let out a weary sigh. "She was always so *kind*. I…can't believe she betrayed us like that. Don't be a bitch to J about it, though. He's gonna be…unwell for a while."

The Wacko snorted, shaking her head. "I don't care how unwell he is. All I care about is escaping before they cut me open to find out where my salt crystals come from."

"Is there a specific place they form?"

"No, but that's the point. The Reggs think they can do some experiments and then know all there is to know about Affinities, but our powers are complex—they defy the rules of science…or rewrite the rules, at least. Every human has sodium chloride in them, and somehow I can make it grow and flow out of me. If they can figure out how to hinder my ability or replicate it… They're gonna *love* you, if you hold the cure to blindness."

Zeela's jaw clenched at the prospect. "When I was young, doctors did love me. They didn't suspect I had an Affinity; they just thought my blindness had worn off, somehow. They always did tests on me—nothing intrusive, but…I always knew they wished they weren't confined by ethics. When my sister started hearing voices, we hid it from my parents as long as possible."

"Just as a reminder, the *Wackos* don't experiment on people."

She rolled her eyes. "They do kill people, though."

"Semantics."

Although Zeela knew she was kidding, Naretha really did believe the Wackos were justified in their terrorism. She opened her mouth to question it, but then a hole slid open at the anterior of the van.

"They're awake," the woman said, peering through. She wore a helmet, but beyond it Zeela detected an unflatteringly flattened nose to compliment her sneer.

"Gas them," one man said while the other continued to sing.

"Like hell!" Naretha staggered to her feet and lunged toward the opening. The woman slammed it shut, and before the Wacko could move her bound hands into a position to reopen it, clear gas seeped from the vents. "Chloroform," she choked, eyes fluttering closed as she dropped to her knees.

A moment later, the sweet-smelling chemical hit Zeela's nostrils, slowly lulling her senses. As she collapsed onto her side, she could only allow the cool metal of the floor and the discordant warbling of their captors to soothe her into the realm of unawareness.

11

The Enslaved and The Escaped

Calder avoided the primaries for the rest of the weekend, despite their efforts to communicate with him. Apparently he'd gathered enough information from his meeting with Nero and the Reggs that he didn't need Eliana's input on the situation.

In truth, she hadn't grazed even one thought during that meeting. As soon as the doors to Angor's office had shut, her powers had been rendered useless, as if a shield blocked her Affinity—or, perhaps, all Mental Affinities. Tray agreed that, if Affinities existed, scientific ways to combat them must have also existed.

"That's probably why you suddenly couldn't sense any brain activity when we were in Fraco's office," he contemplated at breakfast on Monday morning. "They must have closed the doors to Angor's office."

"Do you think they know the office can do that?" Eliana asked, peering around Lavisa to look at Tray. His cereal was soggy and untouched before him, his brain too involved in rumination to crave sustenance.

When he considered her question, the answer ran through his mind with as much logic and rationality as all his thoughts. *If Artemis has a Mental Affinity, she knows what the room can do; if she's truly a Regg, then she doesn't.*

The confirmation of either of those facts grew increasingly vital, yet Tray didn't mention it to the others. Eliana had gleaned a general sense of his suspicions, since he wasn't skilled enough to form a complete mental block on his mind, but he avoided thinking about it around her in the hopes that she would remain oblivious, which she was also aware of. Instilling panic in their friends wouldn't help this already-negative situation, so Eliana maintained the façade of naivety.

"Let's hope not," was Tray's vague response as he leaned back in his seat and avoided the others' gazes.

The six primaries sat at their usual blue table in the cafeteria, a somber ambience hanging around them. Everyone anxiously awaited the Regg ambassadors' arrival and the announcement of how Periculand would change under their rule. Even Kiki was unsettled enough to have claimed the seat on Eliana's right rather than sit alone. Seth, however, was nowhere to be seen.

After the events of Nero's Dominion, the dejected Stark twin had holed himself up in his lonely dormitory, ignoring his brother's periodic knocks. Lavisa had suggested Hartman teleport in there to ensure he was alive, but the orange-eyed boy was convinced Seth's grudge against him for teleporting them off the mats would prompt a physical fight. Eliana, who could read every thought that went through Seth's unguarded brain, didn't disagree. That was why, when the glass doors of the cafeteria burst open, the six of them were almost disappointed it wasn't the Reggs.

"Seth!" Kiki called as he stalked toward the buffet. Unkempt hair hung in his eyes, stains riddled his white t-shirt, and he still wore orange pajamas rather than cargo pants. When his blue eyes locked onto his friends, void of his usual enthusiasm, Hartman began to tremble.

"Don't call him over here," the teleporter hissed at her from the opposite side of the table, but it was too late; Seth had altered his trajectory and approached his ex-girlfriend, who plastered a sweet smile on her glossy lips.

"Seth." She gestured to the empty chair beside hers. "Why don't you sit? I got you some bacon."

Blinking, Seth glanced down at the plate full of bacon before her, none of which she'd eaten. When Eliana read the thoughts flowing freely from her mind, she shot Tray a look that nonverbally confirmed the truth: Kiki had, somehow, bribed Seth into coming to breakfast this morning, his first meal in days. The glare Eliana threw at Hartman quelled his quivering, and he tried to act as normal as he possibly could.

"Thanks," Seth said absently as he plopped down in the vacant seat. His eyes evaded all others as he munched on the bacon strips.

"Seth," Kiki prompted again, folding her hands on the table, "why don't you tell the orange-haired loser what I told you this morning?"

His gaze darted briefly up at Hartman, now wide-eyed in his seat beside Ackerly. "Kiki saw a vision of the future…where I apologized to you for being an asshole."

"'*Stupid* asshole,' were the exact words," Kiki corrected.

Sighing, Seth bit into another piece of bacon. "I'm sorry for being a stupid asshole."

"*And*?"

"And thank you for saving someone as pathetic as me."

Kiki beamed smugly as she patted Seth on the back. "Exactly how I saw it. I'm a genius."

When her eyes locked onto the other Stark twin across the table, Tray, for the first time, actually believed she was. He knew as well as Eliana, who simultaneously read both of their minds, that Kiki hadn't *seen* a vision of this precise moment. That she'd convinced Seth of it so easily and contrived the plan so flawlessly defied all of Tray's knowledge of her character. A satisfying flutter of emotion built in Eliana's gut at the prospect that Kiki had finally embraced the deeper, brighter side of her personality.

"I, um—yeah," was all Hartman could say, his freckles stagnant for once. "I'm...glad you're alive."

"I'm not." Seth slumped back, nibbling his bacon with less fervor. "Adara's still in *jail.* I failed her. I'm the worst best friend in the world."

Lavisa raised her eyebrows knowingly. "She would've been more pissed to hear you'd let Nero murder you. At least you still have the opportunity to break her out."

"Don't encourage him," Tray snapped, receiving an eye roll in response. "Adara's imprisonment is the least of our worries right now. We need to figure out what went down in that meeting between Nero and the Reggs."

"I think we'll find out soon," Ackerly mumbled as the glass doors opened once more, this time admitting Artemis and William Ross—with Nero and the Pixie Twins at their backs.

Nero's expression was far more smug than Kiki's had been moments earlier, and with every student who withered under his gaze, the arrogance magnified. Nixie reveled in the apprehension as well, tauntingly erupting cups of water at every table they passed.

"I don't think I've ever been afraid of a girl in pigtails before,"

Hartman whispered as the five intimidating figures neared the center of the cafeteria. Unlike his sister, Calder's method of instilling fear was in the form of apathetically surveying the crowd, so contrary to the inspired, almost righteous way he'd looked at the primaries in Fraco's office.

"Nixie's not what scares me about this," Tray muttered, watching closely as Nero took a spot beside the Reggs, as if he were their equal. The Pixie Twins stood at a distance, like bodyguards, scanning the quickly quieting scene.

"Attention!" Artemis droned, although they clearly already had it. "We have a few announcements to make."

At the answering silence, students glanced around in concern. Typically, Nero would defy the authority in some crude fashion, but now he was *with* the authority. And without the Stromers to oppose him…

"As you all know," William began, rotating as he spoke in order to view the entire cafeteria, "my wife and I have generously agreed to run Periculand with the unexpected villainy of its former leader. After reviewing Mr. Periculy's files and performing a thorough evaluation, we have come to the conclusion that the conduct of this town has not been to the government's standards."

"The United States government sanctioned the development of this town under the condition that its students be trained as weapons to combat the terrorist Wackos." Artemis's addition provoked whispers of alarm.

Tray clenched his jaw and muttered, "At least they're finally being honest about it."

William called for order and waited until the chatter subsided. "Mr. Periculy obviously did not follow this guideline. None of you are even close to ready for confrontation with the Wackos, which was demonstrated when they invaded this town last month.

The only ones capable of capturing a Wacko were the few who stand around us—Nero and his friends."

Nero held up his hands, as if to settle a crowd, even though acid-spitter Dave was the only one to applaud.

"Adara was there, too!" Seth defended, waving a piece of bacon in the air to draw attention to himself. The Rosses ignored him, but Nero scowled.

"Stromer didn't do shit to thwart the Wackos." His friends, seated at their usual table, snickered in support. "*I* took down that Wacko, and then the other Stromer helped her *escape*. Anyone who associates with that family should be locked—"

"Nero, unlike others, has made the safety of this town and its inhabitants his utmost priority," Artemis cut in, barely hiding the strain in her tone. "This is why we have agreed that he will be this school's student leader—a commander, per se, in the war against the Wackos. He has mastered his Affinity well, and you will all learn from him. His authority is to be treated as equal to that of a teacher—"

Tray spluttered, springing upright in his seat. "Excuse me?"

"You're excused, Stark," Nero sneered, nodding toward the doors. "Maybe you should leave before I give you detention."

"Are you blind?" Tray demanded, his attention on the stone-faced Reggs. "You want to give *him* power?"

William's composure didn't waver. "Nero is exactly the kind of leader this school needs. He understands that weakness cannot be tolerated if we are to win this war."

"It doesn't sound like *you* intend to do any fighting." Lavisa narrowed her yellow eyes in a challenge.

"Our job is to organize and instruct," Artemis said, "which is what we will do, starting today. We're aware that this school has put an emphasis on classroom education while lacking in the area of improving your Affinities physically. That is why, from now on, all classes have been canceled. Instead, students will spend eight hours a day in the training gymnasium."

"That's ridiculous!" Tray exploded, his chair flying back as he stood from it. "Our mental education is far more important than our physical education! Most of us aren't even old enough to join the army!"

William licked his lips, the first sign of agitation. "You have been gifted with an ability that can save this country from ruin. Your knowledge of science, mathematics, and history is irrelevant, as is your age. All students in Periculand, as well as all citizens, will be expected to march against the Wackos once the president-elect is inaugurated in January, and any who resist will be treated as terrorists themselves."

"And what do you plan to do with the terrorists you apprehend?" Tray questioned through his teeth.

"Confinement with the possibility of execution." Artemis stated this without shame or remorse, her dark eyes boring into him. To Eliana, it didn't seem like mind control necessarily, but Tray felt no inclination to argue. "In preparation for this conflict, Periculand has been placed under the protection of armed guards, who will monitor the perimeter of the town, as well as scout the campus for any signs of intrusion. These guards have been outfitted with gear designed to withstand all types of Affinities, so although they are Reggs, they will stand a chance against the Wackos in the event of an attack."

"If you can make Reggs equal to Affinities with these suits, why do you need a bunch of dumbass teenagers to fight your war?" The familiar voice diverted all attention to the girl seated alone at a red table in the corner. When the Rosses registered the cherry-tinted hair and eyes of Adara Stromer, clean of soot and no longer sporting her prisoner garb, they didn't take a moment to observe that her cargo pants were orange instead of green.

"Apprehend the criminal!" None of the seated students moved at William's command, but Nero rapidly prowled across the room, Nixie at his heels and Calder following hesitantly.

"Shit." Adara fumbled out of her chair and darted toward the kitchen door. Before disappearing, her eyes flitted back to the primaries, but she didn't wink at Seth or Tray or Ackerly—she winked at *Lavisa.*

Her mustard-colored eyes were still wide with realization when Nero and Nixie flew by their table and followed Adara into the kitchen. As soon as they did, the panicked screams of the cooks wafted out along with the smell of freshly cooked food.

Calder paused in the open doorway, his eyes on the scene within but his thoughts carefully aimed at Eliana. *It's not her, is it?*

In the instant he opened that question to her, Eliana also collected the speculations that had led to the recognition. He'd noticed the orange cargo pants, the too-dark hue of her eyes, and the fact that she hadn't even looked in his direction—as if looking at Calder was the first thing Adara Stromer would have done upon escaping from jail. Eliana smirked at that notion, and Calder seemed to understand what she'd glimpsed, because he swiftly shut off his mind as a frown formed on his face.

Though he'd concluded, along with many others, that Adara would have been idiotic enough to publicly announce her breakout, he hadn't needed Eliana to shake her head in affirmation to know the person fleeing from Nero was Ruse Dispus. He also didn't seem particularly disappointed when, a few moments later, the brute pushed through him to reenter the cafeteria with murder written on his face.

"She got away."

"Search the town for her." At Artemis's command, the gray-eyed boy dipped his chin and beckoned the Pixie Twins to follow him. "Everyone else, search the campus. Fraco, alert the guards of the prisoner's escape."

Nodding servilely, Fraco scurried from the cafeteria after Nero and the twins, the rest of the school trailing fervently behind. Eliana knew no one really planned to apprehend "Adara" if they found her, but they were all excited to watch this event unfold.

"My brother loves to cause a scene," Lavisa mused as the seven primaries rose from their table and trickled out of the cafeteria last. To combat the cold weather, students had been granted white sweatshirts with the Periculand Training School logo, but the November chill still bit at Eliana when they passed through the double doors of the Naturals Building.

As they paused on the path, Lavisa watched the Reggs and Fraco scamper around campus in search of the escaped prisoner. The other students stood by the Residence Tower, observing with their own silent amusement. "He's probably pissing his pants with hilarity right now."

Kiki flipped her hair in admonishment. "Your brother is an idiot. *He's* gonna get arrested for pissing them off."

"No, he'll shift into some other form and they'll never find 'Adara,'" Hartman said, bouncing on his toes. "Well, they *will* find Adara—in jail, where she's been this entire time."

"Won't they know it was Ruse, though, when they realize Adara never broke out?" Ackerly's question was directed at the culprit's sister, who just shrugged.

"Probably. I won't break him out of jail if he finds himself there."

"Hopefully he *does* get thrown in jail," Seth said before

receiving an incredulous look from Lavisa. "Then Adara will have company. She must be lonely."

Eliana's focus trained on the police station, barely within sight at this distance. "Don't forget Angor's there."

"Yeah, but that guy's a murderer."

"Seems like the type of company Adara would enjoy," Ackerly piped up timidly.

Before Seth could retort, his twin shook his head vigorously and snapped, "Stop talking about Adara. As I've been saying for days, we have more important issues, like the fact that *Nero* has been given authority! But not only that—he's *answering* to the Reggs! Nero's never bowed down to anyone before."

"It's hard to say never when we've only known him for three months," Lavisa countered. "What do you think, Hartman?"

The teleporter licked his lips, orange eyes darting toward where Nero and the Mardurus Twins had disappeared into town. "Tray's right. Nero's never accepted authority; he's always wanted to be in charge. He didn't even listen to his own mother when we were young, and I think he might have actually cared for her, so…"

"He survived juvie," Seth reminded them, waving that flimsy piece of bacon around as he spoke. "Maybe this is how—by getting in with the right people, even if it meant groveling."

Tray blinked in bemusement. "I didn't know you knew the word 'groveling.'"

"My life's gotten so boring without Adara that I've resorted to reading dictionaries for fun."

"I always knew her absence would be intellectually beneficial for you."

"Nero survived juvie with his strength, not through groveling. Hastings…" Eliana started, but she was unable to finish her sentence—unable to dredge up those memories of Hastings telling her things, of Hastings talking and being alive.

"Well..." Ackerly awkwardly cleared his throat. "If Nero's never bowed down before, why bow down to Reggs? Doesn't he... hate them?"

Tray scratched his chin, brooding. "They must have given him a good offer. Eliana, were you able to read his mind?"

"He knows how to block me...because of his mind reader friend." She nodded toward the crowd of students at the center of campus, where Nero's pink-haired mind reader stood tall and expressionless. "And, er—Calder has been avoiding me, I think. He won't tell me what happened during the meeting. William's mind was fairly open, but he wasn't thinking about it at all...and Artemis's mind is...strange, like Angor's."

"Her...mind is like Angor's?" Ackerly's green eyes brightened with the realization. Tray tried not to cringe as his roommate discerned what he and Calder had suspected. "What if Artemis... has an Affinity? A Mental Affinity? A...mind controlling Affinity? What if they're *forcing* Nero to work with them?"

Hartman shook his head. "Nero would crush their skulls."

"He wouldn't be able to if they had control over him," Lavisa reminded him. "If she's a skilled mind controller, he wouldn't even know he was being controlled."

A memory struck Eliana suddenly, and the implications of it were harrowing. "I-I had a dream...of Hastings...the other night. He said *she* when referring to the person who controlled his mind. What if Artemis is not only controlling Nero now but was also controlling Hastings then? What if she wasn't the target, but she was trying to murder *Angor*?"

Groaning, Tray massaged his temples. "I miss having only Seth and Adara as company. You people are too intelligent." They all looked to him in bafflement, so he sighed. "You all know I suspect that Angor doesn't have a mind controlling Affinity, but on Saturday, Calder and I came to the conclusion that it could be Artemis. Seth and Adara never would have had the brains to figure—"

"Why isn't this information you would pass onto us immediately?" Lavisa demanded.

"Because it's just a theory, and I didn't think they would use it to get *Nero* on their side. Now…it seems like the only viable option."

"Hastings's murderer…is walking around *free*?" Eliana's voice remained deadly calm, even as rage swelled within.

"*And* running this town, instead of the man she accused as his murderer," Hartman added. "Should we start a protest? Expose her? Boycott training? March around with posters?"

"No, we should do something that will actually lead to progress—something that won't waste our time," Tray dismissed as he monitored the new security guards who now stomped around campus in search of "Adara." Their suits were solid gray, exposing not even an inch of their skin. They wore tinted helmets atop their heads and had *guns* slung over their shoulders as casually as backpacks. "I wish I could get a good look at that gear—the anti-Affinity material. I want to see what it's composed of."

"Okay," Lavisa said, startling Tray out of his pensive trance. When he saw the impassive expression on her face, he glared.

"Don't get Adara-sassy with me and just say 'okay' to every word I say to piss me off."

"No, I meant I'll get it for you."

Tray's lips parted. "You'll get…"

"I'll get the gear for you," she repeated slowly, as if speaking to a toddler. "Just give me some time to assess the situation and find the perfect timing. Hartman, I'll probably need you."

"Oh, yes!" He teleported around them in excitement. "Is this plan progressive enough?"

"It's...a start," Tray replied, eyes drifting toward the Naturals Building. "I'll need to steal some equipment from the science labs."

"Stealing, Stark?" A smirk spread across Lavisa's face as she backed toward the town's entrance, where there would surely be a concentration of guards. Hartman teleported after her in three-foot spurts.

"I... You're stealing, too," was Tray's lame response, eliciting only an impish eyebrow jump from Lavisa before she spun on her heel and stalked toward her mission.

His twin clapped him on the shoulder. "I'll come with you, bro. I'm probably the only one who'll be able to keep you on this path of immorality."

"It's just borrowing," Tray insisted with a cough. "Ackerly, I'm assuming you'll be more useful in collecting the right equipment than my brother?" After fidgeting with his glasses, Ackerly acquiesced. "And you two will deflect attention from the fact that we're not present?" Eliana gave him a nod while Kiki rolled her eyes.

When the boys departed, leaving the girls on the outskirts of the crowd, Eliana wasn't quite sure what to do with this vague task. More than anything, she wanted to get in a room alone with Artemis and delve into the woman's mind, thoroughly exploring every crevice until the truth was unveiled.

Kiki had other plans of interrogation. Grabbing Eliana's arm and demanding she meet her eyes, the girl hissed, "What's going on with us?"

Eliana's mouth opened in surprise. "With...us?"

"You have a dream about Hastings, and then he shows up at our door—"

"That was Ruse," she said evenly, banishing any hope that Hastings could ever come back. "It was probably just a coincidence."

"Just like it's a coincidence that, in your dream, Hastings said *she* and now everyone's suspecting Artemis killed him?" Her eyebrows perked, daring Eliana to refute the logic. Within a few days, Kiki's hair and eyes had changed colors rapidly, the blue and blonde now nearly a dusty rose-gold, and if that meant her Affinity was accelerating as well…

"You think…I'm subconsciously interpreting your subconscious visions of the future…and they come to me in the form of dreams?"

"I was *going* to say you're *stealing* my dreams, but if you want to put it that way, sure. Our minds are…connected, or something."

Eliana bit her lip as she surveyed the girl before her. A few months ago, she never would have thought a person like Kiki Belven would give her a second glance—but Kiki had *wanted* to be her roommate, and she'd expressed a desire to be her friend. She had psychologically tortured Adara, Eliana knew, and she still wasn't a kind person, but if the two of them could find a way to work together, perhaps to prevent calamities like Hastings's death…

"We should…explore this connection more," Eliana finally conceded. "And I should teach you how to block mind readers. I…almost always know what you're thinking."

Color crept onto her pale cheeks, but Kiki kept her posture dignified. "You can't blame me for admiring your hair color, okay? I would choose blue over pink any day."

Eliana smiled coyly, knowing the other girl's opinions of her appearance were rooted deeper than shallow envy. "Thanks, I think…"

It hadn't been difficult for Calder to convince Nero to let him stop by the police station and ask Officer Telum about Adara's location; so hell-bent on finding her, the brute only grunted before continuing his prowl through town. Adara would hear about this shenanigan, even if Calder wasn't the one to tell her, but he *wanted* to be the one to tell her. Though Ruse had done it merely for fun, this felt like an unexpected gift to counteract the otherwise dreadful direction of Calder's life.

"Telum," he greeted the moment he barged through the front door. The officer lounged with his feet propped up on his desk and a small device in his hands, but he swiftly scrambled to a more proper sitting position. "Are you...playing handheld Yahtzee right now?"

Awkwardly, Mitt glanced down at the red piece of plastic. "It was the only electronic device they'd let me bring into town."

"This is what they're paying you to do? Play electronic board games?"

Silver eyes slivered, Mitt stood and chucked his little game onto the desk. "I *would* be patrolling the town for danger, but I'm required to be here at all times now that we have prisoners. They won't even let me leave for ten minutes to go find a book in the library. They bring me my food and the prisoners' food, and I sleep on the floor." He motioned toward a pile of blankets and pillows in the corner. "Don't tell Adara; she'll make fun of me."

"Because *you're* as much of a prisoner as she is? *I* might make fun of you for that—and for the fact that, while you were playing Yahtzee, Stromer managed to escape."

Mitt blinked once, processing Calder's words and complacent expression, and then he whirled around and darted into the back corridor where the jail cells resided. Calder followed at a leisurely pace, pausing to lean on the doorway and watch in cruel amusement as Mitt realized Adara was still locked behind bars, lying on that metal slab and staring up at the blank ceiling.

"Something wrong, Mitt?" she droned without bothering to glance in his direction. Her eyes *were* strikingly red in comparison to the shade Ruse had given them. Calder wondered, if it weren't coated in soot and grease, what color her hair would be now.

"You—you—" The officer spun toward him, simmering. "Get out."

"I wish I could, Mitt, but only you have the power to free me," Adara sighed dramatically.

"*Get out.*"

Before she could give another sassy retort, Calder finally replied, "It was an honest mistake, Officer. You see, Adara Stromer really *has* been running around Periculand, causing mayhem—"

"Pixie Prince," she breathed, springing up to meet his gaze. There was undiluted enthusiasm in those red eyes—an expression he'd never quite seen on her—and it made him pause a moment before dipping his chin.

"Fire Demoness."

Composing herself into a state of antagonism, Adara swung her legs over the side of the slab and padded on bare feet toward the bars, halting a safe distance from the electrically-charged metal. She surveyed his white sweatshirt, green cargo pants, and plain black shoes with displeasure. "Where are your duck slippers?"

"I was in too much of a rush to retrieve them. Shapeshifter Dispus disguised himself as you, leading the entire school to chase 'you' around town. I'm intelligent enough to know the difference, so when they told me to check the jail for you, I figured I'd stop by to inform you of the chaos unfolding in your name."

"I'm gonna get so much shit for this..." the cop muttered, rubbing his forehead.

Adara's lips flared into a grin. "Did you get it on video?" she asked Calder. "Are the Reggs pissing themselves? I bet Tray is *fuming...*"

"Stark knew it wasn't you." He sniffed, inhaling the prisoners' grungy odor. "Nero's gone on a rampage, though, ransacking the town to find you. Even when he knows it wasn't you, he'll probably *still* come in here and try to destroy you."

"I hope he does," she said with an appreciative glance at the electric bars. "Well, Pixie Prince, aren't you gonna go make it happen? Aren't you gonna go report to your master and tell him I'm here? You are *Nero's Minion*, aren't you?"

Calder's lips curled downward with that. His vision flickered in Angor's direction, where the ex-principal relaxed on his slab, listening with intrigue. "Nero's the Reggs' minion now. He's agreed to be the commander in their army—Emmett Ventura's army—against the Wackos. Once this issue of finding you is resolved, Nero'll be in charge of training the other students for the remainder of today...and every day."

Angor sat upright, running a hand through his dirty pink hair in dismay. "This is precisely what I aimed to avoid... Do they not see the students are children—that they are sending untrained children to war with psychotic terrorists?"

Calder shrugged. "I don't think they give a shit about who dies, as long as none of them are Reggs. They don't see us as people; they see us as a means to their desired end. And Nero sees allying with them as power."

"What do *you* see it as?" When he refused to meet her eyes or answer her question, Adara added, "Sounds to me like you and Big Boy are on the verge of a break-up. How heartbreaking."

"I don't have to blindly agree with him to be on his side." The defensive response was instinctive, but after a pause, he rethought his predicament. "The Reggs aren't the issue, it's *Ventura.* I can't stomach working for that guy. I told him next time he comes back here, I'd have a host of enemies awaiting him, and now they're all his freaking *allies*."

Adara snorted. "You've screwed yourself, Pixie Prince. Now you won't look nearly as tough as you think you are. *Although*... if you want to defy Nero *and* the Reggs, I think *I* would make a wonderful ally. All you have to do is subdue Mitt with your water magic and press some of those buttons on the wall over there, and then we take this town as our own."

He masked his intrigue with skepticism. "Take it how? By burning it to the ground?"

"I don't have a fire Affinity," she snarled as her hands curled into fists. The movement drew attention to her flimsy prison garb, the sides of which were singed.

"You might hate fire, Stromer, but feelings aren't facts. Your proposition is tempting, by the way, but I don't think I'm ready for this town to be utterly incinerated quite yet. I'll come back when things get dire." He turned to leave but then saw Angor massaging his temples. "I tried to figure out what your Affinity is by sneaking into Fraco's office to retrieve your file. The Reggs got to it first; they have it now."

The ex-principal looked up, weary and distraught. "They are the only ones who know the truth then, and still they have no intention of freeing me. I will order my own death sentence if it is discovered that I do have a mind controlling Affinity—that I did kill Hastings—but as far as my brain can remember, neither is the truth. If it's possible to expose the truth to everyone—to declare me as innocent and the Reggs as liars—will you do it?"

Calder's lips twisted in contemplation. The answer was clear to him, but publicly announcing his allegiance didn't seem like the wisest move, even in front of a crowd with as little influence as this one. "I'll see what I can do."

"Your power is extraordinary," Angor insisted, rising from his perch. "Surely you can use force to bring justice to this—"

"God, Angor. Just when I want believe you, you start saying shit that makes you sound like a murderer," Adara groaned as she paced away from the bars. "The Pixie Prince only resorts to violence for the sake of his precious master." Spinning back toward him, she tilted her head and asked, "Isn't that right?"

"I'm not incriminating myself on the *chance* that he could be innocent." Calder's harsh gaze cut from Adara to her cellmate. "I'll see what evidence I can gather *inconspicuously.*"

"Thank you," Angor said, nodding. "I always did admire your ability. The sheer control you have over water, even from the very beginning—magnificent. If I had been trying to murder the Reggs, I would have used you instead of Hastings."

Upon sprawling on her bed, Adara hit her head against the metal and grunted, "Ow—please don't admit you've considered how you would murder the Reggs if you're ever granted the chance to defend yourself."

"Why?" Calder asked Angor, ignoring her comment.

"Well, Hastings's death by severed blood vessels was nearly instantaneous. He could have drawn it out for torture purposes, of course, but he wasn't yet *that* skilled. *You*...you could drown someone to death over a matter of hours if you wished, inflicting greater suffering and making a grander statement."

After considering his words for a moment, Calder shook his head. "It never would have worked if you'd tried to use me. No one can control my mind."

Adara rolled her eyes. "Nero does a fine job of it, and it's not even his Affinity."

"Nero does not control my mind."

"Then what's stopping you from breaking me out of this prison, hm?"

Calder opened his mouth, but it was another voice that spoke.

"I'd say his penis, mostly. He knows he won't be able to control his attraction to you if you're free, and considering the obvious, none of us really want that," his sister crooned as she appeared in the doorway. Calder had a difficult time suppressing surprise and maintaining nonchalance, especially when Nixie shot him a grin that said Nero wouldn't be happy about this.

Nonplussed by her presence and the words she'd uttered, it took Adara a moment to sit up and meet Nixie's eyes through the bars. "The obvious?"

"You're a lame little primie Nero wants to murder, and if my brother follows through with his attractions, he'll be murdered as well," Nixie droned, as if it really were obvious. "Thanks for telling us about Dispus, by the way." This snide remark was aimed at Calder. "You'd better convince Nero you had no idea—and that you didn't use this opportunity just to flirt with Stromer."

He refrained from scowling at his sister by directing his animosity toward Adara. "Don't tell Dispus to run around in your body again, got it?"

Adara, luckily, had enough brains not to claim she had nothing to do with Ruse's charade, which would have exposed Calder's bluff. Instead, lips curling as her red eyes studied him through her lashes, she mused, "Maybe next time it'll be *you* inside my body, Pixie Prince."

Cackling at the lewd joke, Nixie retreated from the room, beckoning her brother to follow. Calder lingered for a moment, giving Adara a look that was meant to quell what his twin had insinuated. But with the way she appraised him, those eyes sparkling like rubies amid a pit of ash, he almost wished the Fire Demoness's words would come true.

As he departed with a wink, he sincerely hoped Stromer was left with as much confusion about his sentiments as he felt.

12

Another Imprisoned Stromer

Jamad's head ached, but it was nothing compared to the pain festering in his gut, the rage of betrayal ripping through him.

What bothered him most was that he should have seen it coming. Colette had acted strange during their entire visit. Even though Jamad had shown no interest in interacting with Jade, Colette likely wouldn't have warranted it anyway; she was protective of the child, like most mothers were, but that fear had driven her to betray him and his friends.

There would be no forgiveness for this—that decision became finite when he finally opened his bleary eyes and beheld their new location.

Moisture dripped from the stone ceiling, dampening his pale blue hair with water that would have been cold to anyone else. His wrists hung level with his head, manacled to the stone wall behind him by impenetrable chains, and his fingers tingled from the poor blood circulation. Strong rope bound his ankles, restraining him in the same fashion as the other forty people in the room.

It didn't surprise him that the limp hair and droopy eyes of each of them were oddly-colored. It did make him swear, though.

"Glad to hear the drugs didn't kill your pleasant attitude, Snowman," Naretha's ragged voice droned from farther down the wall. Avner sat directly beside Jamad, his yellow head tilted forward in unconsciousness; Zeela was positioned on her boyfriend's other side, blinking; and Naretha lounged beyond her, glaring up at the ceiling as it deposited drops of water onto the bridge of her nose.

Jamad yanked at the chains and shifted on the dirty straw beneath him. "Where are we?"

This had to have been an underground chamber; there were no windows, and the only door was wooden and moldy with decay. Even if the room hadn't been small, the rancid stench of feces would have been enough to induce a sense of claustrophobia. Rat droppings littered the ground, but the people scattered around the walls were arguably more disgusting, each coated in grime with withered scraps of clothes hanging from their thin bodies. None of them were dead, but...a few were certainly close.

"Hell," one man grunted from the other side of the dungeon, his gray eyes more lucid than those of most of his prison-mates. The t-shirt he wore was torn and crusted with blood. Scars lined his square face and once-athletic arms, and his hair, too gray for his wrinkle-free complexion, was a few months overgrown. "We're in hell, depending on your definition of the word."

Jamad should have asked more about their location, but his focus was now aimed at this man's familiar features. "Are you... related to Nero?"

Groaning, as if in response to the sound of his enemy's name, Avner shook his head and squinted. "Nero?"

"You know Nero?" the man questioned with a spiteful snort.

When Jamad just glared at him, he sighed. "No, I'm not related to Nero Corvis. I worked at the juvie he was sent to, though—almost lost my job when he showed up because *they* thought we were related. I feel pity for whoever shares blood with a menace like him."

Naretha studied the matching shade of his hair and eyes. "You have an Affinity?"

Nodding, the man said, "I...used to be able to attract metal, like a magnet. This place has weakened my Affinity, though. I can barely even sense the metal around my wrists anymore."

"How long have you been here?"

"Who knows?" He leaned his head back against the stones. "Is it still 2016?"

"Yes—November, unless we've been here for more than a few weeks," Naretha said.

"If my perception of time is right, it's only been a day since they threw you four in here. I've been here since August. There was a...fight in the juvie. It was my fault—I let some Affinities in to retrieve this kid, Hastings, and there was a brawl between the Affinities and Regg prisoners. My superiors didn't care much about my Affinity before the incident, but after... Well, I don't have *proof* they turned me over to experimenters, but I was kidnapped a day later and woke up here."

A grimace had progressed on Avner's face throughout the tale. "Was one of the Affinities you let in a girl with reddish hair and endless sarcasm?"

After a moment of recollection, the man sat straighter. "Yes, actually."

"My sister," Avner sighed. "I apologize."

Naretha spat and, for a moment, Jamad thought it was because of Avner's politeness, but then he realized water had dripped into her mouth. After spitting twice more, she asked, "Have you just been sitting here for months, or do they experiment on you?"

"You'll find out soon enough," the man said with an exhale of defeat. "They'll likely take you today. They enjoy new subjects."

Jamad shuddered for the first time since acquiring his Affinity. "This is messed up. We need to get out of here."

"There's no way—"

"We'll fight our way out," Naretha growled, cutting off the man. "We aren't just gonna give up."

"They pump gas into the air to suppress our Affinities," he explained, unwavering in his dejection. "You might be the strongest of us now, but not for long."

"He's right," Zeela admitted, still blinking. "I can see everything in here—vaguely—but my X-ray vision won't penetrate the walls."

Jamad leaned forward as far as he could to shoot her a questioning look. "I thought your Affinity wasn't working anyway?"

"Naretha cured me in the van."

"I don't remember a *van*. Damn, that tranq really got me." Jamad rubbed the sore spot beneath his clavicle with his chin. "Anything else I missed?"

"Your mom's a bitch, if you weren't aware," Naretha replied, earning a scowl from Zeela.

"I am aware." The thought made him want to release his icy anger, but like Zeela, his Affinity was dwindling. "I'm…sorry I brought us there. It was a stupid move."

"Mm."

"My parents wouldn't have been any better," Zeela said, clearly resisting the urge to kick the Wacko beside her. "They would have called the cops the moment they spotted us."

"In the end, it made no difference," Jamad said, his scathing tone directed at his mother—and his father, for that matter. "Reggs will be Reggs."

"J—"

"It's true, Av. I never wanted the Reggs to be our enemies, but...they are. They hate us, all of them—even the ones who used to love us."

Avner pressed his lips together, silencing his tongue. In his eyes, Jamad was probably some criminal now for thinking lowly of Reggs, but amidst this dire situation, there was no use in arguing about their differing ethics.

"I always thought that, out of us Stromer kids, Adara would be the one to end up in confinement," Avner mused, shaking his head. "If we ever make it out of here, she'll never stop mocking me for it... How many researchers are there in this building?"

The man closed his eyes at the memories. "Whenever they bring me to the lab, I'm too drugged up to count."

"There are two," a weak, hoarse voice piped up. Upon pivoting to the right, Jamad found a girl about his age with pale skin and striking magenta eyes that matched her dirty hair. All she wore were bedraggled undergarments, the bra and panties both too small for her form. Judging by the way her skin clung to her jutting bones, she had lost weight but had grown in stature, as if she'd been captured before puberty truly hit.

"Only two?" Jamad repeated, unsure if he was more bewildered by the state of her appearance or the words she'd uttered.

"Two who conduct the research," she repeated, clearing her throat. "Four guards. One overseer."

Naretha sprung forward until the chains prohibited further movement. "That's it? That's pathetic. Even if we don't have our Affinities, we can easily take them. You two have gotten into fist fights before, haven't you?"

"If fist versus ice counts," Jamad answered with a wince. "And the fist was Nero. He destroyed me, for the record."

"Nero's the buffoon who looks like him?" Naretha asked, jerking her chin toward the man across the room. "I wasn't even impressed when we fought him, and if you can't beat him… God, you are screwed. I'm gonna bust out of here, though, with or without the rest of you."

The girl beside Jamad shook her head incessantly, pink eyes bulging in terror. "You can't defeat them. They are indestructible."

The Wacko rolled her eyes. "They're Reggs. I'll demolish them."

"You'll be optimistic today, but tomorrow…" The man stared at the wall, ghosts swimming in his eyes. "The hope doesn't last long."

"How long have you been here?" Jamad asked the girl. Her body was so marred with bruises and scars that it was difficult to determine how pale she really was. Currently, there was a vicious gash in her abdomen still oozing blood, even though most of it had clogged. "Shit, what happened?"

"Don't get near it," she warned when he shuffled closer. "They will *know*." Brow furrowed, Jamad scooted away again, eyeing her warily. "I have been here as long as I can remember. There is no way to escape."

"I'll make sure you escape," he insisted, glowering at her wound. That this deep slice was so *common* to this girl… He would slaughter these researchers for the way they'd tortured all of these Affinities. "I'll make sure we all escape. Z, you have no idea what's on the other side of these walls?"

"Dirt, mostly—but there's a hall beyond the door and some other rooms, I think. I can't get a clear image of anything."

"Do either of you have an idea of the layout?" Jamad asked, glancing between the man and the girl.

"Meredith does." The man nodded toward her. "She's been here the longest—or has survived the longest…"

"I'll tell you anything you want to know," Meredith confirmed, meeting Jamad's eyes earnestly. "But *they* can't know."

"When they know, it'll be because we want them to. How can we get out of these chains?"

"More important, if they take us from this room, how can we turn the Affinity-suppressing gas off?" Avner asked. "And do you know where the exits are?"

Jamad tapped his fingers on the metal chains, letting it cool his agitation. "We can't wait for them to haul us out of here. We need to free ourselves and surprise them."

"There's no way we're getting out of these manacles, J. Even someone with a magnetic Affinity hasn't been able to break loose. Our best bet is to go along with this until we can form a tactical—"

"So, we're just gonna let them cut us up?"

"*No*—"

"Better think of a plan fast then," Zeela said, fidgeting to sit in a more defensive position. "Someone's outside the door."

Indeed, a moment later, a key clicked in the door before it flew open. Cold fury spiked in Jamad's chest as two men in tinted helmets entered, invoking memories of their kidnapping. They wore the same dark, impenetrable suits, though now, with all the Affinities stripped of their abilities, the suits probably served as more of a barrier against the toxins in the air than as a means of defense. Beyond the men, the corridor was too dimly lit for Jamad to make out the details, and he doubted Zeela could glean much, either.

"Samiya will enjoy her," one guard said, his voice distinguishing him as the one who had wrecked the Solbergs' front door. If his parents hadn't been the reason they were in this situation, Jamad might have craved vengeance for how these men had charged into their home; now, however, he focused on the guards' future offenses as they stepped toward Zeela.

Avner tugged on his chains in an attempt to shield her body with his. "Don't you dare touch her!"

"That's not a very malevolent threat," Naretha said, her words pausing the men. "How about I'll shove salt down your esophagi and he'll electrocute you both to death afterward if you touch her?"

The door-destroyer chuckled and the other shook his head. "Our suits are designed to resist all Affinities. Besides, the air has rendered you harmless. You're no match against us."

Naretha and Avner kicked their bound feet at the men and Jamad willed his body to produce some type of ice, but all efforts were futile. His body felt unusually hot—perhaps with nervousness or anger or despair—as his childhood friend struggled against the Reggs. One of the men used a syringe to subdue her while the other unlocked her fetters and hauled her over his shoulder.

Even as Avner grunted and shouted and wrenched and writhed, the guards didn't hesitate to depart the room with Zeela, carrying her to some torture chamber. Jamad was thankful when the pipes began to pump out gaseous sedatives to quiet Avner, because the stone walls weren't as thick as they'd originally thought, and Zeela's screams snaked through every crack.

Zeela was blind—again.

It was as if a vacuum had sucked the universe out of existence, leaving only this hollow void, or as if her eyes had been carved from her skull. With the pain radiating from them, weaving through every fissure of her brain, she wouldn't have been surprised if they had.

The two guards had hauled her down the hall ruthlessly, even as she'd thrashed and clawed. Perhaps she could have willed herself into a calm state if she'd been more aware of her surroundings, but one of the men had thumped her on the head two steps into that dirt corridor, disorienting her to the point that what little eyesight she'd regained was again lost.

Zeela had never been one to scream, but when they'd shoved her into a frigid room and strapped her to what she assumed was a metal table, she'd let her voice reach a volume she'd never thought imaginable.

"Shh, shh," a feminine voice had cooed in her ear. Heat signatures flashed around her, but nothing had been coherent. "You don't want to worry your friends."

Zeela's mouth had clamped shut at that. It was a tactic to get her to shut up, she knew, but it had worked. There was nothing Avner and the others could do to save her, so she took the pain in silence, only crying out when the agony became particularly unbearable. Whatever the researchers did to her wasn't pleasant.

The woman and what sounded like a man prodded at her eyes, injected needles in her skin, and scanned her with foreign machines. There was no way to free herself from this table; her wrists ached from trying. Wetness seeped down her cheeks—blood or tears, she couldn't tell. And her scalp felt unusually cold, as if they'd shaved off her hair at some point and she hadn't quite noticed.

If she survived this, she would not be the same. Maybe she should have been thankful to have lost her sight after all.

13

The Science of Defense

"You're thinking…that you hope Nixie never comes back, so you can have Nero all to yourself," Eliana concluded, proceeding to gnaw on her lip as she side-glanced at Kiki.

The blonde girl threw her head back with a groan, curls spilling behind her shoulders. "Why do you have to be so talented?"

Eliana fought to subdue her rising blush. For the past thirty minutes, she and Kiki had sat on the orange bleachers, waiting for the first day of all-day training to begin. The Rosses and Fraco still hadn't returned from their hunt for "Adara," but Nero had, and he and his entourage stood at the center of the mats, Dave groveling at his side while the pink-haired mind reader surveyed the room with boredom. Evidently, the Mardurus twins were absent, which had prompted Kiki's most prevalent thoughts.

"I'm not *that* good… I can barely read the Rosses' minds," Eliana added, hushing her tone so none of the other students would hear. Of their primary friends, they were the only two attending training, but a group of tertiary boys sat within hearing distance, and she didn't want them to guess what they suspected of the Rosses. In some selfish, twisted way, she didn't want *anyone* to know what they assumed about Artemis because, if it were true, Eliana wanted to be the one to exact justice. Her demeanor might have been as docile as her Affinity, but she would make an exception for this.

"I don't care about that," Kiki dismissed, craning her neck to scowl at Eliana. "I care about *me*. How can I block you?"

"I…I'm not really sure." Eliana combed some of her blue hair behind her ear. It was such a vibrant shade now, so different from the black color she'd been born with, that she was often shocked when the brightness fell before her eyes. "I know you need to build a wall around your mind, but…it just comes to me naturally now. Hastings was the most skilled with it. He would have been able to explain it better, but…"

Kiki's pout morphed with a tinge of sympathy. "You really miss him, huh?"

Fiddling with one of the pockets of her purple cargo pants, Eliana said, "He wasn't part of my life that long, but…yeah. It still feels surreal—like he'll walk in here any minute and sit down without saying hello, biting his nails and silently judging everyone…"

"Do I even wanna know what he thought of me?"

"Probably not." She smiled softly when Kiki scoffed. "We were similar in a lot of ways, except…in that he never really liked you. Hastings never wanted to be close with anyone. It was a struggle for him to open up to even me… I'm selective, too, I guess, but I like to have people I'm close to, even if it's just one person. I read enough minds to know people are inherently evil, but…"

"Am I evil?" It sounded more like a challenge than a question.

Eliana barely suppressed a wince. "You did bully Adara for most of your life…"

Straightening with dignity, Kiki huffed, "I'm not bullying her *now*."

"She's not here."

"Don't get so technical. I wouldn't bother with Adara even if she were here. She can have Seth—she can have this whole damn town! I just want one person."

Hesitating, Eliana studied the way the other girl glared out at the gymnasium, pointedly avoiding her eyes. When she followed Kiki's gaze and found who it was trained on, she exhaled with dejection. "Nero?"

Kiki's glossed lips parted, but before she could confirm or deny Eliana's assumption, the gymnasium's double doors burst open for the Pixie Twins. They stalked in with a dramatic gait, Nixie's short pigtails bobbing as she smirked at everyone and Calder's dark eyes narrowing as he glowered at everything.

"Stromer's still in jail," Calder announced, quieting all conversation and drawing all attention. "The girl running around town was...Ruse Dispus."

Eliana sensed his reluctance in divulging that fact, but she couldn't decipher his thoughts well enough to know why he wouldn't want to incriminate Ruse. Perhaps it was the glimmer of giddy sadism in Nero's eyes at the sound of the shapeshifter's name that provoked Calder's desire to protect the other boy. Anyone who received such malicious attention from Nero earned Eliana's pity.

"Dispus," Nero growled, cracking his knuckles. "If I find that kid, I'll pummel him." After scanning the bleachers, he must have decided that, even if Ruse were here, he would be too well hidden amongst the other students, because instead of weeding through the crowd to find him, Nero clapped his hands and said, "Let's begin *training* then, shall we?"

"I believe we should wait for the Rosses to arrive," the history teacher, Than, piped up from the edge of the mats, where all the teachers stood. None looked particularly thrilled at the prospect of Nero leading training—nor the fact that their classes had been indefinitely canceled, making them irrelevant.

"And I believe that I was given authority here," Nero snapped, causing Than to wither slightly. At his side, Aethelred sighed, but he seemed to think this was inevitable, so he kept his mouth shut as Nero addressed the students. "Most of you have pathetic, incompetent Affinities, like doing *math* problems and growing *plants* and 'seeing the future.'" Kiki expelled an affronted hiccup that Nero didn't acknowledge. "Since most of your Affinities will be useless in battle with the Wackos, we're gonna work on a little hand-to-hand combat. That way, when the terrorists outmatch you, at least you're not crying your way to the grave." Murmurs of trepidation danced through the audience, at which Nero's lips spread with wicked glee. "We'll start with a simple punch." He jabbed the air with such force that Eliana swore she felt a breeze. "Who wants to help me demonstrate?"

Unsurprisingly, no one volunteered. Calder looked ready to sacrifice himself just so Nero wouldn't pick some unfortunate kid out of the crowd when the doors were again thrust open, this time granting access to the new principals and their vice.

"Well?" William prompted without greeting, his expectant attention fixed on Nero and his posse. The Rosses both appeared calm and composed, but Fraco panted profusely, doubling over to prop his hands on his knees. Based on the state of his brain, some severe nausea was building within him.

"Stromer's still in jail," Nixie droned, picking at her dark painted nails. "Ruse Dispus was the culprit, impersonating her to irk you. Don't fret; we'll discipline him later today."

The Reggs exchanged a mutually pacifying look before pacing across the mats to join the other faculty. Fraco staggered behind them, woozy and disoriented from sprinting around the campus in search of "Adara." This whole ordeal would have been hilarious to her, and Eliana wasn't surprised that, even in jail, Adara Stromer had played some part in wreaking havoc throughout Periculand.

"I was just calling for volunteers," Nero informed his masters. "Anyone you wanna see me punch?"

Artemis's soulless eyes raked the crowd—probably in search of Tray, Eliana realized with alarm. Who else had been so defiant toward them? Since Eliana had been tasked with keeping the others' absence unknown, there wasn't a lot of contemplation before she lifted her hand in the air.

Calder's eyes immediately protruded, and even Nero looked nonplussed by this turn of events. Her instinct told her to lower her hand—to retract her hasty sacrifice—but as she stood from her seat, the logic of her decision solidified with even more clarity. This would distract the Reggs, and it would also help her determine if their suspicions were valid. If Artemis had allowed Hastings to die for her cause, wouldn't it be equally as easy for her to let Nero beat Eliana?

A petty little part of her was also curious as to how Kiki would react to this: Nero, her obsession, versus Eliana, her roommate and future friend. Eliana didn't want to have to put her in that situation, but she just had to know if Kiki's "one person" was Nero or…someone else.

"Each of you will have to face foes like Nero—perhaps even worse," Artemis said, her deadpan voice echoing through the gymnasium. "The Wackos won't show you sympathy because you're small. I have no qualms with this."

Because you're probably a murderer, Eliana thought as rage coursed through her veins.

For the first time, Artemis met her eyes, and she had to hide the chill that ran down her spine. "You may join Nero on the mats."

Throwing up the toughest mental shield she could conjure, Eliana nodded and then began her descent from the bleachers—just as Kiki snagged the hem of her sweatshirt.

"What are you doing?" she hissed. "You're gonna get killed!"

"At least Nero will still be standing," Eliana said with much more coldness than she'd intended. Kiki's face contorted in outrage, but Eliana slipped out of her grasp and jogged down to the floor. It wasn't until she stood on the mats, only feet from the aggressive brute, that she noticed her roommate had followed.

"Don't punch Eliana—punch me," she demanded, pausing her strides once she was positioned between Nero and Eliana, the latter now too paralyzed with disbelief to interfere. "I want to be punched."

Nixie's eye roll was arguably more intimidating than Nero's monstrous muscles. "He's planning to punch you with his fist, not his penis, Belven. You know that, right?"

"*Obviously—*"

"Hey, Kiki!" a smug voice called from behind. Eliana barely had to rotate her head to know it belonged to Kiki's older sister. Lounging at the top of the bleachers, Orla was impossible to miss with hair that shimmered like polished gold and stunning looks that very few were immune to; even Eliana had a hard time concentrating when Orla was in her line of sight. The condescending manner in which she gazed down at her sister was enough to snap her out of the daze. "Stop making yourself look so pathetic by trying to get with my ex and give up already!"

"Never thought I'd agree with a Belven, but I think I do," Nixie said, cocking her head to the side.

"The only thing I want from your boyfriend is for his fist to collide with my face instead of Eliana's." Kiki crossed her arms, holding her ground. "Aethelred! Tell Nero he has to punch me!"

Across the gymnasium, Aethelred squinted at her. "I'm not typically one to condone violence, Miss Belven. If anything, I think the three Affinity classes should be given different drills to perform. For instance, those with a Mental Affinity should congeal in one corner and practice mentally, rather than physically. Don't you think this would be more beneficial, Mr. and Mrs. Ross?"

"Not to offend, Mr. Certior," William said in a tone Eliana found offensive, "but what use would an Affinity like yours be to a soldier? Would knowing the past of a vicious assailant help you in battle? I'm afraid not. Many of the Mentals are at a severe disadvantage, we're aware, which is why we think physical combat training is vital."

"To put it simply for all you bozos," Nixie drawled, "you're gonna have to learn to take a punch. So, let's begin with these two."

Eliana and Kiki both tensed, preparing for a blow from Nero, but then Nixie formed a fist of water. As the liquid coalesced in the air with supernatural beauty, Eliana's jaw dropped in awe. Her lungs were not equipped for the deluge of water that collided with her body and flooded her open mouth, seeping down her throat.

The force of the torrent launched her back onto the mat, but she was too focused on drowning to feel the pain. Hacking up liquid, she flopped onto her side, the beating of her heart so loud that she nearly didn't hear Nixie say, "That was payback for when you pelted me with rocks on Friday night, Mensen—and for the fact that your little girlfriend is a pain in my ass."

Bleary-eyed and dazed, it took Eliana a moment to realize

Kiki was "her little girlfriend." When she sat upright, Nixie's eyes were alight with the use of her Affinity—and perhaps the violence. The annoyance didn't settle in Eliana's core until she noticed *both* Marduruses were smirking at her.

You had that coming, Mensen, Calder thought without remorse. *Never make yourself vulnerable to my sister or Nero. Now you know you're in for a shit-ton of hurt if you do.*

Eliana's lips shifted with animosity, but unfortunately Calder was unable to comprehend any of her hateful nonverbal responses.

"Get off the mats, Belven"—Nixie nodded toward the bleachers—"before I drench you as well."

As if the thought of water ruining her hair and makeup was more terrifying than a punch from Nero, Kiki swiftly scurried to her roommate and hauled her to her feet. Though the gesture was kinder than Eliana would have expected, she did note Kiki was careful not to get *too* close. She wasn't sure if it was because she didn't want to get sopping wet or because the "girlfriend" comment had flustered her.

"Why would you do that?" Kiki breathed once the two were safely seated on the bleachers again. The Rosses beckoned for other students to file onto the mats, forming a line of quivering kids who would be forced to fight Nero. None of it seemed instructive—or ethical—but as was just proven, there was nothing Eliana could do to stop it.

"I just…wanted to see how far the Rosses would let it go," she said, wringing out her hair.

"They would have let Nero murder you if I hadn't stepped in!"

"Which means they would have let Hastings die, too."

Kiki blinked, processing the insinuation. "You… You're sneaky," she finally said. Even if her inflection hadn't indicated it, her baffled mind was thoroughly impressed. "But next time you do something like that, you need to ask me first."

"Ask you…for permission?"

"No, ask me if I'll do it with you," she clarified, shifting with…*awkwardness*. Eliana hadn't been aware Kiki Belven was capable of feeling self-conscious. "If you're going to die, so am I."

"That's…a little extreme." Eliana cringed as she awaited an infuriated reply.

Remarkably, Kiki remained calm and diplomatic. "I hope it's a good enough reason for you not to commit suicide."

"I-I'm not suicidal—"

"Your boyfriend *died*!"

"He wasn't the only person I live for." Her heart pounded now with even more intensity than after Nixie's attack. "I-I'm going to be okay. Thank you, though…for worrying about me."

"I didn't *say* I was worried," Kiki began, but then she saw the smirk budding on Eliana's lips and groaned again. "Stop reading my mind." She swatted Eliana's forearm. Through the fabric of her sweatshirt, she barely felt it, but it was still nice to have some physical contact with another human again. "Ugh, you're soggy…"

"Because of *you*."

At the sassiness of Kiki's eye roll, Eliana actually had to suppress her smile. "Wouldn't you rather be soaked than toothless? I *saved* you, and since I saved you, can you *please* teach me how to stop you from invading my mind?"

Though she nodded in agreement, and though she was capable, Eliana wasn't quite ready to slice the tether that linked her mind to Kiki's. So, as she'd done before, she spent the remainder of training purposely failing to teach Kiki to block her.

"Water resistant: unsurprising, unimpressive. If it's fire resistant, though..." Biting his lip, Tray adjusted his goggles and readied the blowtorch, which he'd "borrowed" from the science labs, along with the goggles. He was the only one in his dorm room wearing them, since the others observed from a distance; only Ackerly dared to stand near Tray's desk as he worked on the Affinity-proof suit Lavisa had stolen from one of the town's newly implanted guards.

How Lavisa had managed to retrieve this suit was a mystery to Tray, but apparently Hartman had actually been helpful. Now the teleporter couldn't stop giggling about how the naked guard would have to report to the Rosses that he'd *lost* his suit. Lucky for that man—and for the primaries—the Regg ambassadors were probably too busy seeking out Ruse to care about the missing suit.

"Do you think the smoke detectors will go off?" Ackerly asked. No one else was in the Residence Tower now, but if they set off the alarms, it would throw the school into another frenzy.

"If Adara was here, we wouldn't have to worry about that," Seth sighed, flipping absently through a dictionary he'd found in his brother's endless pile of books. The only reason Tray paused to look at his twin was because he couldn't get over the fact that Seth actually held a *book* in his hands.

"If Adara were here, we would have to worry about that *more*. She would've burned this whole building down by now."

"No, Adara would be able to quench the fire with her Affinity."

"*Quench*," Hartman repeated with an appreciative nod. "Your vocab is really expanding, dude."

"Maybe it's my Affinity," Seth grumbled.

"Why don't we test the suit with something that won't get us caught if it goes terribly wrong?" Lavisa suggested before Tray could ignite the blowtorch. Leaning on the door to the bathroom, she scratched at a scab on her arm, barely prying her attention from it long enough to raise her eyebrows. "Try ripping it with your super strength."

His eyes narrowed behind his goggles. "Will you mock me if I can't?"

"No. But we'll be able to conclude that it's resistant to super strength if you can't. This is an experiment, not a competition. Just because there's a reason to mock you doesn't mean I will. I'm not Adara."

Pursing his lips, Tray placed the blowtorch on the ground. He was about to tear at the fabric when a figure appeared in the open doorway, stunning him with her violet presence.

"Holy hot," Hartman blurted out upon seeing the former vice-presidential candidate, Olalla Cosmos, enter the room. Her hair cascaded on one side of her head like a cluster of orchids, and though her irises were as piercing and bright, dolefulness characterized those eyes, reflected in her black attire. When her focus fell on Hartman, his orange freckles disappeared in a surge of scarlet. "I mean—hi. We're not—we're just—"

"Studying the Reggs' new suits?" Her lips inched upward as she eyed the clothing on Tray's desk. He hadn't even tried to hide it; this woman was too intelligent to be fooled.

"We're trying to figure out what, exactly, they're resistant to," Tray explained, removing his goggles as he stood from his chair.

"Are you planning a revolt?" she questioned with a hint of humorous castigation.

Warily, Tray set his goggles on the suit. "No, just studying it for the love of knowledge."

Olalla smiled tightly as she folded her hands. "The Reggs have various types of technology to combat Affinities—science they've been working on for years. The government certainly *could* fight the Wackos—"

"Then why don't they?" Lavisa asked flatly. "Why force kids to fight their war?"

"They wish to keep the war contained amongst the Affinities. Harold and I would have prevented that—and this, all of this..." She eyed the suit and then shook her head. "We had no hope, I will admit. I was foolish to think we could have won. Third-party candidates never win, even if they are the most rational option. We would not have had war, but now we will. The Wackos would have reasoned with me. They would have known that I understand their struggle and want to help all Affinities. But Ventura...he hates Affinities. The Wackos will rebel with greater violence than before—especially now that Daniel is in charge."

After readjusting his glasses twice, Ackerly asked, "Who's... Daniel?"

Olalla pressed her lips together and sighed through her nose. "Someone you should hope not to meet. I have not yet apologized to you all. I know you were Hastings's friends. His death pains me, and I imagine it must pain you more. That Angor could do such a thing...it seems unlike him. But people will commit heinous acts for power. He always was mysterious about the nature of his Affinity..." Shaking her head again, she met each of their eyes, not with pity but with empathy. "I wish I could bring peace to you in your grief—I wish I could bring peace to this town, but...my mind feels weary. I can barely find serenity for myself."

Tray exchanged a brief look with Ackerly before asking, "Do you feel like someone is suppressing your Affinity?"

"No, no," she dismissed. "My emotions sometimes inhibit my Affinity..."

Though she was convinced this was the truth, Tray was not.

If Olalla's peace Affinity was weakened, someone with a mind controlling Affinity had to be suppressing it. "Why are you still in Periculand?" he asked instead of delving further into the matter of her mind. "Are you working with the Regg ambassadors?"

"Are you here to drag us back to training?" Lavisa added bluntly.

"I've been at odds with the Rosses for years, you can imagine. We have our separate priorities. My opinions on the matters of Periculand are irrelevant to them now, and yet…they force me to stay. After Hastings's death and my loss in the election, they claim I might be a target—a target for whom, they haven't said. I'm under the impression they don't want me to leave their dominion simply because they fear I will join the Wackos. A ridiculous concept, but…it's for the best that I'm here now, regardless. Angor may have inadvertently led to Hastings's death, but he is not wholly bad. He fought for years to keep the students of this school from war. Without him…well, someone needs to be here to oppose the Reggs, to strive for peace."

"So…you *don't* want us to go to training?" Hartman clarified, still quivering with excitement in the woman's presence.

"I'd like to hear what you learn about those suits," she said, nodding toward Tray's desk. "I've been studying Regg technology myself with the intent of, perhaps, creating fabric that can enhance an Affinity, rather than subdue it."

"Adara could use some fireproof clothes," Seth said, slapping the dictionary shut. "Not that she cares if she burns her clothes off, but I think Tray was disturbed."

"Afraid of a girl's body?" Lavisa challenged, jumping her eyebrows at Tray as he grumbled his dissent.

"I—was—more annoyed that she didn't care," he stammered, crossing his arms defensively. "It's unnatural. And crude. And contemptible."

"Ooh, contemptible—just read that in the dictionary," Seth enthused. A moment of silence ensued in which they all stared at him, waiting for him to recite the definition. "Oh, I don't remember what it means. I just remember reading the word. Spent most of the time trying to sound it out in my head."

"I'm impressed you did that much," his twin mumbled, relieved that the subject had deterred from talk of Adara's nudeness.

"Speaking of Adara, we should go visit her." Seth wiggled his eyebrows at his friends.

"The Reggs outlawed it," Tray reminded him, "and now they have guards everywhere. We're not even supposed to be *here*. There's no way we can get off campus without being spotted."

"It won't matter if we're spotted if we have the Affinity ambassador with us. She has to have the clearance to get past those guys."

"And if not," Hartman chimed in before Olalla could object, "I can teleport us all one by one to the police station."

"Twenty feet at a time," Tray snorted.

"Twenty-*five*—"

"I've been meaning to pay Angor a visit," Olalla interjected, ignoring their banter. "I want to hear from his own mouth how he could have been so foolish as to try to murder Artemis. The guards won't grant me special privileges, so teleportation might be the best—"

"Yes!" Hartman exclaimed before extending his hand toward her. "May I have your hand, m'lady?"

"I think we're all capable of walking down the stairs before we start the teleportation," Lavisa droned, pushing through Hartman's outstretched arm and squeezing past Olalla in the doorway. "Are you gonna join us, Stark?"

Seth discarded the dictionary by throwing it on his brother's bed and then plowed through the room. "Of course! I could never pass up an opportunity to see Adara."

"I was talking to your twin, actually." Lavisa, now in the corridor, peered around Olalla to meet Tray's testy gaze.

"I—no—fine." Sighing, he cast a forlorn glance at the blowtorch he'd been unable to use. Instead, he was being forced to visit a *thing* far more dangerous and far less beneficial to his quest for knowledge. "Let's go visit the demoness…"

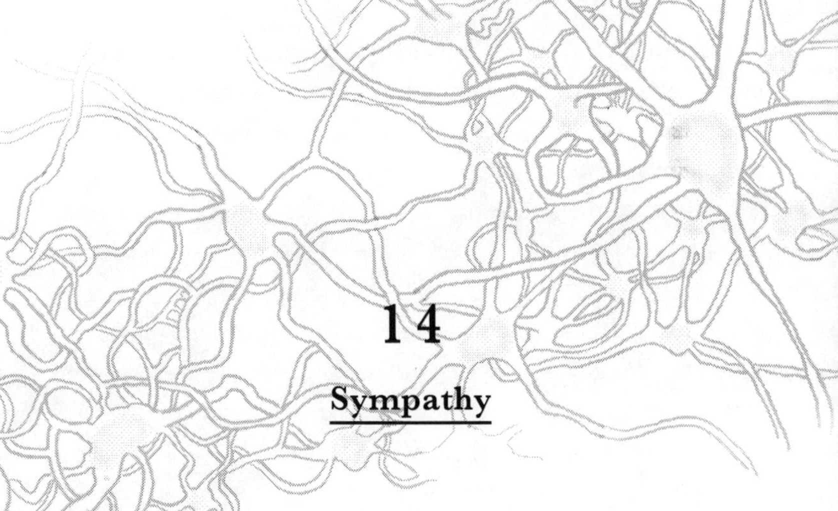

14

Sympathy

"No," Mitt barked before the Starks and their three friends even finished passing through the police station's doorway. He'd been at his desk again, playing handheld Yahtzee since Calder Mardurus's departure a few hours ago, but now he sprung to his feet and planted himself before the back door as they approached. "You can't visit her. Shouldn't you all be in class?"

"We should," Tray affirmed grumpily. Behind him, the teleporter wobbled around dizzily, the intimidating yellow-eyed girl glared with crossed arms, and the plant-kid awkwardly readjusted his glasses. "The Rosses canceled classes indefinitely. Now it's only training."

"Training to be in the government's army against the Wackos," Lavisa added. As an employee of the Rosses, Mitt thought he would have been made aware of this information, but he'd never heard anything of the sort.

"Yeah, those Reggs are corrupt," Seth said. Though the boy

was only sixteen, he was as tall and muscular as a fully-grown man, making Mitt feel far less authoritative as they stood face to face. "They want to use children as weapons—which is why you should defy them and let us see Adara."

Mitt eyed the five teenagers ruefully. "If the Rosses are ruthless enough to train children for war, I'm not sure I *want* to defy them."

With a dramatic groan, Seth rolled his eyes back to his brother. "This guy is an asshole. I take back everything I ever said about cops being the good guys. They are out to get us."

Tray was the one to roll his eyes now. "He's just doing his job. Obviously he'll get in trouble with the Reggs if he lets us see her."

"You just don't want to see Adara."

"True," Tray said, but his focus had shifted to Mitt. "What if we told you we're here on official government business?"

Lavisa pursed her lips. "Are we?"

The Stark twin's nose twitched, but he remained silent as the officer considered his words. After a minute of scratching his chin, Mitt asked, "How official is this government business?"

"Hartman," Tray prompted, glancing back at the panting, swaying boy.

"I can't teleport anymore, man. My *head*—"

"Am I allowed to come in now?" a voice sang as a purple head of hair slipped in through the front door. Mitt blanched at the sight of her.

"Ms.—Cosmos," he choked as the former vice-presidential candidate entered. "I-I voted for you."

"I think everyone in this town did," Tray said flatly. "She wants to see the prisoners."

"Uh—of course." Mitt fumbled for the door handle. "But"—he paused to glower at the primaries—"the rest of you can't come."

Seth's whines of "c'mon" and "please" were instantaneous, but Lavisa was far more collected as she strolled to Tray and said, "Can I execute plan B now?"

"I thought you were morally against hurting innocent people?"

"If he's aligning himself with the Rosses, I think *his* morals are already—"

"Fine, fine," Mitt huffed, clenching his fist around the door handle. "You have fifteen minutes. If the Rosses find out about this, though, I wasn't involved."

Stepping in line with the students, Olalla smiled. "I will gladly take the blame."

Mitt shook his head in awe. "Damn, you are perfect."

"I *know*," Hartman enthused as he bumbled over to the rest of his friends, colliding shoulders with Lavisa.

The teenager's voice snapped Mitt out of his trance, and he embarrassedly opened the door. When he poked his face in, Adara stopped pacing her cell to assess his demeanor. Judging by the excitement that sparked in her eyes, she probably assumed he'd brought Mardurus in for another visit. He didn't miss the dullness that consumed her face upon Lavisa's entrance.

"*More* visitors?" Adara droned as jittery Hartman staggered in next. "For a cop, Mitt, you really like to break the law."

Ackerly winced at her in greeting. "He wasn't really happy to oblige."

"Greenie." All disappointment abated at the sight of his grass-colored hair and matching glasses. "I thought you forgot about me."

"It's hard to forget about you when you're the constant talk of the town," Tray sneered as he marched before her cell's bars.

Adara's lips broadened at his grouchiness. "I'm glad to hear I haven't become irrelevant. Have you missed me?"

"Yes," Seth answered before his brother could open his mouth. Though he wore dirty pajamas, he still had the audacity to sniff at her. "You look as gross as Fraco. Haven't you showered?"

"I'm not *allowed* to shower." She gave a scathing glance in Mitt's direction. "Apparently, I'm too *dangerous* for such luxury."

"The Reggs just don't want you leaving your cell. The showers are down the hall."

"It's not like I'll try to break—" Adara cut herself short when Olalla entered the hallway, peering into the various cells with curiosity. "Damn, I've gone from *no visitors* to *celebrity visitors*. I must be the most sought-after prisoner in the history of the world."

Olalla's eyes trailed her voice to the only occupied cell, and when they landed on the former principal sleeping soundly on his metal slab, they protruded in alarm. "You've put her in the same cell as Angor? This is dangerous, Officer Telum. If Angor has a mind controlling Affinity, there's no telling what he could do to this—"

"If?" Tray repeated. "*You* don't know for certain that Angor's Affinity is mind control?"

"Angor was always very secretive about his abilities," Olalla said, eyeing the man as his chest rose and fell. "But the recent events have confirmed it, I suppose…"

"Why don't we all just admit that no one knows what the hell Angor's Affinity is?" Adara crossed her arms over her chest, exposing the burnt sides of her shirt.

"Did you burn yourself?" Ackerly blurted out, prompting her to lower her arms again.

"We aren't talking about that, Greenie. We're talking about Angor's Affinity."

Hartman steadied himself by holding onto Lavisa's shoulder. "If it's not mind control, it must be something pretty freakin' bad. Nero's scared of it, so it's gotta be as deadly as Hastings's Affinity was."

"Nero's scared of it?" Tray asked, brow furrowing in Hartman's direction. "How do you know?"

The teleporter tried to shrug and nearly lost his balance. "The only way Fraco was ever able to subdue Nero was when he threatened him with Angor. He must have been punished with Angor's Affinity before."

"He must know then," Tray pondered, stroking his finger along his chin. "He won't tell us now that he's working with the Reggs, though. If he had evidence that supported Angor's innocence, he wouldn't want anyone to know, because then Angor would be freed and the Reggs wouldn't be in charge anymore, thus ending his newfound authority."

"Big Boy would never divulge information to you anyway," Adara said. "He hates you. But…if he's prompted to *think* about it, we all know a certain mind reader who can pry the truth from him—unless my ex-roomie has joined the Reggs, as well? I'm surprised she's not here to see me."

"Don't delude yourself into thinking Eliana actually likes you." Pausing, Tray eyed her warily. "But…that isn't…a *terrible* idea. We'll talk to Eliana about it."

"Of course you will," Adara drawled, inhaling as her self-importance swelled. "It's okay to admit that you need me—that you wish I was out of this cell."

"Yes, it would be okay, if it were true," Tray countered pitilessly. "You've already caused enough trouble today, running around town and—"

"I was running around town today?" she gasped in mock astonishment. "*Really*? Tell me *more*."

"She already knows," Mitt cut in as the boy opened his mouth to explain. "Mardurus came here to make sure she was still locked away, and he told her."

Tray's already-disgruntled attitude amplified. "I see."

"Is that a problem, Nerdworm?"

"He didn't…tell me he was stopping by," the Stark twin answered, avoiding her radiant red eyes. "He could have relayed some information. It doesn't matter now, since we're—"

"Hold on," Adara interrupted, taking a slow step toward the bars. "Are you…*working* with the Pixie Prince? Are you two *friends* now? You *are*." She laughed before he could even grunt a reply. "He said he snuck into Fraco's office to look for information. You guys went with him, didn't you?"

"Only for the sake of finding the truth," Ackerly responded hastily. "We aren't…friends with him, though. He did try to drown us that one time…"

"I had nothing to do with him," Seth said, holding up his hands in innocence. "I'd never betray you like that, Dar."

"Thank you, Jockface." The condemning look she shot Ackerly made him cringe. "I'm unsurprised Nerdworm would ally with one of my sworn enemies, but you, Greenie? I'm disappointed."

"If you're allowed to receive visits from Mardurus, then we can work with him during this investigation, okay?" Tray snapped as he scrubbed his forehead. "Is there anything else we need to discuss with Stromer, or can we leave now? This was a severe waste of time."

"Mm, I agree, Nerdworm—talking to you is always a waste of time. Why don't you just leave then, so I can talk to my real friends?"

"Yeah, you can go, Tray," Seth agreed. "I want to stay and tell Adara about how I almost broke her out of prison."

"Did you?" she questioned, raising an eyebrow. "Somehow I don't recall that."

"Well, it happened during Nero's Dominion—"

"Nero's Dominion?"

"Yeah, it's this whole thing—but the important part of it was that I almost struck a deal with Nero that could have freed you from this place. I lost the bet, obviously—mostly because of Hartman—but it's fine, because Hartman teleported us here to see you, so now I forgive him and we're bros again."

Adara pressed her lips together and glanced around at the others, who all sighed—except Hartman, who looked thoroughly befuddled. "I'm not really comprehending the story," she said. "Can you start over?"

"Sounds like a story of forgiveness to me," Angor yawned, stretching as he sat up on his metal slab. "I didn't hear the beginning, though, so I can't quite be sure." Blinking his coral-colored eyes, he roved the group of people before him, unperturbed until his vision locked onto his former associate. "Well, this is an unexpected surprise. To what do I owe the pleasure, Olalla?"

Her expression was tight as she watched him stand on bare feet. "I was curious as to whether the consequences of your actions were adequate punishment. Considering you've been grouped in a cell with this innocent girl, justice has not been served for the death of that poor boy."

"*Innocent* girl? That's a new one," Adara remarked. "Makes me sound kinda pathetic."

Angor's brow scrunched. "If I recall, you called yourself innocent not too long ago."

"She's only innocent when it suits her argument," Tray explained.

"Adara cannot be held accountable for the unleashing of her Affinity," Olalla insisted, her hostility still aimed at Angor. "This school should have prepared her better. Regardless, the event that triggered it warranted such a response. We have disagreed in the past, Angor, but never have I been so appalled by your methods. To try to *murder* the Reggs…and to use *Hastings*—disgusting."

"I agree," Angor said as he attempted to flatten the wrinkles in his prison garb. "I never had any intention of harming the Reggs. The only way in which I desired to use Hastings was to subdue the terrorists—which is why you must believe me when I say I played no part in Hastings's death. I don't have a mind controlling Affinity."

"He's so freaking bad at trying to prove his innocence," Adara sighed before any of her friends could speak. "He always leaves out the vital pieces of evidence—like the fact that Hastings was his *son*. Yeah, I've been dying to tell you all about that one, but you never deign to—"

"What?" Tray breathed as all five of them blinked.

"Oh, did I reveal something important, Stark? I think you'll have to bust me out of here with your super strength if you want me to repeat—"

"You're Hastings's father?" Tray demanded, his rapt attention trained on the former principal.

"Was, but yes. Hastings was my son. I was thirty-five when I met Jocosa—"

"They don't need to hear your sappy love story, Your Highness," Adara intoned. "All they need to know is that I believe you, and I'm too cynical to believe anyone."

"I do see it." Seth squinted through the bars to study the man. "You're, like, an identical version of Hastings—just, you know, old and with lighter hair…and skin."

"Did you know?" Adara asked Olalla, who scrutinized Angor with uncertainty.

"No, I didn't, but…it seems…possible."

"Hastings didn't know who his dad was," Seth recalled, gazing into the distance reminiscently. "I always used to talk to him about my dad, and he once told me he didn't know his. Pretty much the only thing I ever got him to say, but—"

"I didn't know you actually talked to Hastings," Adara mused. "I thought he was too emo for you."

"He was," Seth conceded, "but I used to talk to him before going to sleep, and it made me feel less alone. He never answered, but I still felt like I had a friend. Now I just talk to myself before I fall asleep."

"That's sad—in a pathetic way. Bet you miss chatting with me from across the hall. Did they ever fix my door?"

"Yeah…" Seth answered slowly, "but now it's Kiki's door. She took over your dorm."

"Ah, so I'll be rooming with Mustard when I break out of this pit." Adara smirked at Lavisa, whose expression remained impassive.

"I thought you'd prefer to be Seth's roommate."

"An interesting concept. But, if the Wackos don't know Hastings is dead and they decide to come back here for him, I don't really want to be sleeping in his bed. They could mistake me for him—the reddish hair, you know."

"I could never mistake you for Hastings," Hartman said, still leaning on Lavisa. "He was so bony and you're…well…you eat a lot of donuts."

"You're telling me I don't remind you of Hastings, not because I'm a girl but because I'm *fat*?"

"There's a difference between not bony and overweight…"

"How would the Wackos even know Hastings was in room 302?" Tray cut in, his tone far too severe for the lighthearted banter. "Periculand's location is a secret; I doubt you can look up our room numbers on the web."

"Don't ask me, Nerdworm, but they know. When they broke in last month, they went straight to Hastings's room...like someone told them before they came." Adara's eyes bulged in the same instant Tray's did. "There's a Wacko sympathizer in the school."

"If Hastings was your son, I assume it wasn't you." Lavisa nodded toward Angor, who shook his head.

"I've corresponded with the Wackos on a civil basis, but I have never divulged any information about Periculand. Its location, obviously, is known to them, but I have made it very clear that they are unwelcome."

Tray seemed like he might rub his forehead raw. "The sympathizer could be anyone in this town—any citizen, any student, any teacher..."

"None of my employees have any affiliation with the Wackos," Angor said. "I did thorough background checks before hiring."

"Oh, you did background checks, how cautious of you," Adara derided with a sarcastic smile at her prison-mate. "It's not like people are smart enough not to add 'Wacko' to their resume."

"Don't you think...if the Wackos planted a spy in Periculand...that they would have executed a mass invasion already?" Ackerly inquired. "Why bother sending one of their own here if they only ever relay small information?"

"Valid questions, Greenie," Adara agreed, tapping a finger at him. "We'll need to investigate. Mitt, set me free."

"I'm not going to set you free, Adara."

"There is a Wacko in this town and you're still worried about an *innocent* girl like me? So what if those Reggs fire you? If they're working with Nero, I say we overthrow them and elect the Purple VP as our principal. Then I can call her the Purple Principal."

Olalla smiled fondly at the nickname, but her tone was stern. "We should respect the Rosses' wishes for now. We don't have enough evidence on any front to start a conflict, and though I don't agree with them, we don't want all Affinities to look like terrorists by forming a mutiny against the Reggs."

Groaning, Adara flopped back onto her slab and stared dejectedly at the ceiling. "Fine. Have fun figuring it out on your own, then."

"I doubt you'd help us, even if we did free you," Tray scoffed. "All you want is to get out of this cell. You've never cared about the greater good."

"I just *need* donuts. I'm being deprived of basic human rights in here!"

"We should get moving," Tray said to the other primaries, ignoring Adara's bemoaning. "If we need to search the entire town for a possible Wacko—"

"You don't need to search the entire town." Swinging upright, Adara met Tray's hostile gaze and said, "You just need to suspect the unexpected. So, you know, the nice people—like Aethelred or Floretta or Medea or maybe even my freaking brother. It's always the nice people."

"Your cynicism is showing, Stromer," Tray retorted. "If anything, it's probably someone shady. We'll figure it out."

"You might need me," she sang, but Tray didn't show even an ounce of sympathy at her hopefulness. Mitt only cared because he knew this exchange would worsen her attitude toward him for the rest of the day.

"No."

"Fine, do my dirty work for me. Go, my servants, while I stay here and relax in the company of our enemy." With a dramatic gesture at Angor, she lounged back on her slab and eyed Tray drolly.

He was, obviously, not impressed. "Who are you impersonating?"

"Myself as empress, of course."

"Empress of prison? Not surprised that your aspirations are still exceedingly low." Her following frown inflated his chest a bit. "We'll report back if we find any information on this Wacko sympathizer—or on Angor."

The former principal bowed his head in gratitude. "Thank you."

"Oh, shit, do I have to teleport again?" Hartman moaned as he wobbled away from Lavisa.

"No, I want you to save your strength," Tray ordered as that classic brooding look overcame his features. "There's something we need you to do tonight."

"How was training with Nero?" Hartman asked as he twirled a pencil through his fingers.

"Awful," Eliana muttered, eyes fixed on the piece of paper before her. Over the past few hours, she'd sketched a drawing of Periculand's northern forest, constantly displeased with the state of the depiction. Night had fallen by now, and even though the woods rested directly behind the library, the bare trees were invisible beyond the dark glass.

"Nero gave almost everyone bruises while *demonstrating*," she continued, her gaze flicking up to meet Hartman's. He'd arrived about an hour ago to inform her that Tray had tasked them with prying some information from Nero. Verbally, he had been respectful and quiet, but his mind was as sporadic and unremitting as his physical movements, and his random thoughts distracted her.

"Did he notice we weren't there?"

"No, he was too busy reveling in his power." She paused, assessing him as he flipped the pencil in the air. "Your step-brother…he'll have to be caught very off guard for me to glean any knowledge from him—and he'll need to be actively thinking about it."

"If you're nervous about talking to him…I can try to do it on my own. You can read his thoughts from a distance—"

"No, no…I can do it," she assured him, gently placing her pencil on the table. "We'll have to act now, though. I just sensed him leaving the Reggs' office upstairs."

Hartman inhaled deeply as he rose from his chair. "Here we go then… Get into position. And I know you aren't very loud, but do try to yell for me if you need help."

Her returning smile was soft, but he didn't see it before teleporting twenty-five feet across the library, scaring a group of students in the process. Once he'd disappeared to intersect Nero in the stairwell, Eliana crumpled her hideous drawing and slunk into the nearest aisle of bookshelves, collecting volumes as she walked.

Barely two minutes passed before Hartman's fearful yelps and Nero's rancorous growls penetrated the library's silence. Mentally, Eliana felt the panic surging through the room, and the alarm rooted itself in her brain to the extent that she almost did scream when Hartman and Nero rounded the corner, both Corvises barreling down the aisle toward her. Hartman's expression was apologetic when, only two paces from her, he abruptly teleported, allowing Nero to plow into Eliana at full force. This had been the plan, but as she plummeted to the ground, an avalanche of books raining around her, she realized she really hated Tray Stark's plans.

As expected, Nero didn't profess his sincerest apologies at the sight of Eliana struggling to sit up. She was relieved that he even had the decency to stick around for a moment to see who he'd unintentionally assaulted. Whatever Hartman had said in the stairwell to provoke him hadn't been enraging enough to dispel all of his conscience.

"Little Mensen," he huffed, his bulky body eclipsing the ceiling lights. "Second time you've crossed my path today."

"S-sorry," she stuttered, so focused on gathering the books that she nearly forgot to try to read his mind. The wall he'd built around his thoughts was as formidable as his physical appearance—and as thick. Though a brute, he was not senseless, and his mind reader had probably instructed him to be cautious in Eliana's presence.

His eyes darted around warily, but it wasn't her that he feared; it was the possibility of witnesses. For, when he realized no students were peeking down the aisle, his meaty hands hastily reached down and yanked Eliana upright, standing her on her feet like a doll. She was too stunned by his rough kindness to even thank him. Nero never helped *anyone*. The way he winced down at her now indicated he regretted the decision, but that he hadn't left yet implied this plan might go smoother than she'd anticipated.

"What, um...did Hartman do?" She hugged a book to her chest, awaiting an aggressive reply.

Nero's tone was subdued when he grumbled, "Breathe. That little shit doesn't have to do anything to piss me off."

"He is...a bit...annoying," Eliana admitted. The words weren't entirely false—Hartman *was* a little agitating—but her sentiments toward the younger Corvis boy weren't negative, and she would certainly choose his company over his stepbrother's. For the purpose of this plan, though, Nero had to believe otherwise.

His eyebrows formed a unibrow of skepticism. "I thought you were friends with the runt?"

"I don't...think I have any friends here," she replied quietly. "Hastings was the only person I trusted."

Nero's eye twitched at that, opening the smallest crack in his mental wall. Out of it seeped...sympathy—not enough for him to console her, but enough that a burst of confidence took hold of her tongue.

"I know you were afraid of him..."

"I wasn't *afraid* of him," Nero sneered, crossing his arms defensively.

"I can read minds," she reminded him, lips twisting knowingly.

Refusing to meet her gaze, he snorted, "I'm good at guarding my mind."

"I know...but Hastings also told me you were afraid of him. And...that you're afraid of Angor."

"I have no reason to be afraid of those freaks—*Mentals*." As if realizing who he was talking to, his eyes locked onto her purple cargo pants, but he didn't add, "No offense."

"Well...I'm afraid of Angor," she told him, not giving herself enough time to consider if it was a lie. "Who knows if he'll decide to use his mind controlling Affinity to take back the town? With an Affinity like that, he could easily complete his mission to murder the Reggs."

The notion that Angor could return to his position of power did strike enough fear in Nero to knock holes in his mental block, but his thoughts of Angor were...*muddled.* He did fear the man, but he didn't know *why*. It was as if someone had put a shield around those memories—one that not even Nero could tear down.

"I'm not worried about Periculy," he said breezily, even though confusion still riddled his brain. "He can rot in jail. The Reggs'll restore order to this town, and once I have enough leverage..."

"You...want to take over Periculand?"

Nero smirked devilishly. "You'll be lucky if I do, Little Mensen."

Even as a mind reader, Eliana had no idea what that could mean, but she did comprehend that the wink he gave her before stomping off was a threat. A threat that didn't concern her—not now, when Nero's lack of knowledge gave her all the information she needed.

Because, if Nero had suddenly forgotten Angor's Affinity... and if he was in frequent contact with the two people who wanted to keep Angor in jail...and if Angor wasn't using his Affinity, which should have been able to easily free him from his predicament, then perhaps Angor truly wasn't the one with the mind controlling Affinity.

Perhaps Artemis truly was.

15

Another Fiery Stromer

Avner had never experimented with drugs, and now he knew why it had been a smart choice: whatever chemicals the Reggs pumped through the air vents *hurt*. Invisible hands squeezed his brain, draining his energy, and with the periodic experimentations on his body, he'd fallen into a state of decay.

Days had passed—or maybe weeks or months. His Affinity had curled into a distant corner of his mind, unwilling to emerge even when he begged it to. Never had he felt so disconnected to the charge of energy. Based on what he'd gathered from the researchers' conversations, his ability, at an atomic level, allowed him to separate negative and positive ions in the air and spark electricity between them. He hadn't thought his Affinity was so technically rooted in science, nor did he think he would have the opportunity to use this knowledge to improve. It seemed unlikely he would ever be able to summon electricity again.

As the man with the magnetic Affinity, Charlie, had said on their first day, the researchers always drugged their subjects beyond the point of comprehension; the experimentation room was a cold, metallic blur to Avner. He vaguely remembered them shaving his head, but he might have thought it a dream if his other three companions weren't bald, as well.

There were two scientists, as the magenta-eyed girl, Meredith, had claimed, and they spent the most time on Jamad, trying to discern how he caused water to freeze. Naretha had an untreated incision in her arm, through which they attempted to determine if there was an abnormal amount of salt in her blood, muscles, and bones. The cut looked as infected as the one on Meredith's stomach, which had yet to heal. Sloppy and merciless, the experimenters seemed not to think other humans could feel pain.

This fact had been solidified on the first day, when Zeela returned from her first bout of experimentation, head haphazardly shaven and white eyes oozing blood. Avner had wept at the sight of her, and though she'd been dazed and mostly unconscious, he'd attempted to comfort her despite the restraints. He'd been unable to cry or even produce a sound when she returned from her second experimentation with one of her eyes carved clean out of its socket. Naretha and Jamad had both screamed in rage. Avner had simply crumbled into a pile of sorrow.

None of the other prisoners had been touched since their arrival. Currently, Jamad was absent, likely being cut up in the research room. The emotional numbness prevented Avner from caring. Charlie had been right: This was hell. Was this punishment for breaking Naretha out of jail—for breaking the law? Avner had convinced himself that it was—that he deserved this for being so undeniably stupid. His friends, though…they didn't deserve this. He wasn't even sure Naretha deserved this.

She seemed to have accepted her fate; gone were her snarky remarks and dry humor. Her dull, pink eyes stared lifelessly at the stone walls, as if the researchers had extracted her brain. The only time she showed a hint of emotion was when Zeela returned from experimentation, her appearance even more grotesque than before; then there was fury in the Wacko's eyes.

Now, when the moldy wooden door flew open, none of the prisoners moved. They had probably forgotten about life outside this pit—Avner nearly had. When Jamad made a lame attempt to wrench out of the guard's grasp, however, anyone conscious snapped up in attention, only to be disappointed when the guard tightened his hold on the boy's arms and launched him across the room.

Meredith shrieked when he slammed into the wall beside her, crumbling into the spot soiled by his own excrement. There was a pause during which only his muffled groans were audible, but the guard grunted and retreated from the room without further incident.

Leaving Jamad unshackled.

"Are you okay?" Meredith asked as he unfurled and stared up at the ceiling.

"I'm lying in my own piss and shit—of course I'm not okay." When he noticed her still staring at him with concerned eyes, he added, "Sorry. I'll live. No open wounds—"

"J," Avner interrupted, "do you not know what just happened?"

"Of course I know what just happened." He sat upright and spat into the dirt. A large bruise bulged on his forehead just beneath the light blue hair beginning to regrow. "I just got thrown against a freakin' wall, and I think Meredith's the only one who cares!"

"No, *look*." Avner nodded to his friend's untethered wrists while yanking on his own chains. "They didn't lock you up, man. You're free."

Naretha banged her head back against the wall. "Dammit! Why did you have to be the first one free? You're gonna leave me here."

"If you stop being such a pessimist, maybe we'll consider bringing your Wacko-ass along." With a taunting smirk, Jamad jumped to his feet—and then wobbled. They hadn't been fed much, and after whatever experimentation he'd just endured, the adrenaline pumping through his veins was probably all that kept him upright. "How do I get everyone out of these restraints? Anyone know?"

"You'll need the key," Charlie groaned as he shifted forward. "Which none of us have."

"We won't be able to break out without our Affinities," Avner said, struggling to kick his feet out of the ropes. "Can you cover the vent?"

Jamad's gaze flew to the vent high in the corner. "Yeah…I've got an idea. Sorry," he added again to Meredith.

She winced at the address. "What…are you doing?"

"Taking off my clothes," he said as he began to do just that. "My abs are so hot, they're probably gonna debilitate you."

"Not the time for cocky jokes, Snowman," Naretha droned, her sardonic demeanor more indicative of enthusiasm than displeasure.

"Sue me, Salty. I'm amped," he countered while shimmying out of his sweatpants. Once he wore only snowflake boxer shorts, Meredith did blush, but he didn't make another quip before hurrying to the vent. The duct jutted out enough that, when he stood on his toes, he was able to drape the sweatshirt over the air holes and seal it by wrapping the legs of his sweatpants around the metal.

Without a direct source for the noxious gas to escape through, it lingered in the air, gradually seeping through the cracks in the stone walls. Half-naked but giddy, Jamad used this time to crouch beside Avner and fiddle with the knot binding his legs.

"You smell like sewer, dude."

"I think we all do," Avner muttered, liberating his legs from the rope when Jamad finished untying it. His muscles were sore and stiff from disuse, but as static began to crackle around him, he felt ready to run miles. Jamad shivered in delight, and Naretha grinned like a fiend when she snorted salt from her nose.

Many of the other Affinities stirred throughout the room, awoken by the rebirth of their powers, but Zeela remained motionless, her one eye closed as if she were asleep. Avner knew she wasn't—her breathing was too quick. Given that she'd barely spoken since their arrival, it seemed unlikely she would speak now, even though their freedom inched closer by the second.

"I can probably pull the chains out of the wall," Charlie said as Jamad untied his legs.

"Me first," an old lady croaked. Positioned in the corner, her pale face was inlaid with wrinkles and scars, and her baby yellow hair was a wisp atop her head. When the others glanced her way, she wiggled her frail fingers, which morphed shape as they moved. "I'm excellent at picking locks."

"You can…morph your fingers into keys?" Avner asked.

"I was a bit of a thief in my youth," she admitted, though there was no remorse in her manic grin.

"Free her then," Jamad commanded Charlie once his legs were untied. Grimacing, the man scrunched his face and clenched his fists, bowing the lady's metallic chains toward him. After another grunt of exertion, the shackles ruptured from the wall, showering debris on the woman before her entire body lurched toward

Charlie. She landed face-first on his legs, her arms awkwardly suspended above her as the metal connected with his fists.

"Agh, I think I'm broken," she griped. Charlie released his hands and she flopped fully on the ground. When Jamad gingerly began to turn her over, she swatted him away with the chains. "Give me a minute, will ya?"

"Hurry it up, canker sore, we need to get out of here," Naretha barked as the woman lay limply on her belly.

"That sounds like a point for the 'let's not bring the Wacko' category," Jamad crooned, receiving a snarl from Naretha in response. Her mood mollified substantially when, a few minutes later, the old lady finally mustered the strength to trudge around the room and unlock each pair of shackles with a key-shaped finger.

It seemed a miracle that she could walk at all. Many of the others, even those significantly younger than her, struggled to stand upright on shaky limbs. Meredith was so weak that she could barely roll onto her knees. Jamad stooped down to help her, but she recoiled.

"I can try to carry you, if you want," he offered as she curled into the wall.

"I…can't leave," she whispered, eyes darting around frantically as the other Affinities rose. "They will know."

He studied her stomach wound and her undergarments, too tight for her body. "Did they…put some kind of tracking device in you?" She shook her head, but he continued eyeing her with suspicion. "Well, I'm not leaving you here. We're all escaping and so are you. I don't know how long you've been here, but life above this place is good—you'll see."

Her head continued to shake in earnest, but he ignored her and spun toward Avner. "Can Z walk?"

Biting his lip, he tenderly nudged his girlfriend's shoulder. She still wore Jamad's old t-shirt and flannel pants, but the deadness in her expression when her one white eye flew open was far from cozy. "Z…are you okay to move?"

With an absent nod, Zeela pushed to her feet and Avner followed, watching her warily. She touched her head, coated with barely a centimeter of white stubble, and her lips twisted. "How do I look?"

A smile cracked across Avner's face as he brought his fingers to her jaw, stroking dirt- and blood-crusted skin. "Beautiful. How do I look?"

Her one eye roved in its socket, but she didn't return his affable attitude. "Different," was all she said. Avner wasn't sure he wanted to know what that meant.

As the Affinities congealed near the entrance, Naretha positioned herself at the head of the crowd to survey the moldy wooden door with distaste. "Should I ram my shoulder into this piece of junk, or…"

"I thought we were going for stealth," Jamad grunted as he hoisted Meredith into his arms. Panic characterized her demeanor, but she seemed too paralyzed to fight him.

"You think they aren't gonna notice all of their prisoners leave?" Naretha raised an eyebrow. "I say we bust out of here full force—kill 'em all."

"Great idea, except we don't know if our Affinities will work outside this room," Avner said, weaving through the group to confront the Wacko. "They could be pumping the gas into the halls."

"Not the halls," Meredith said, trembling in Jamad's grasp. "Just the rooms."

Naretha's saccharine smirk radiated. "Good. I have some threats to uphold. The real issue will be removing the guards' masks into order to shove salt down their throats… You up for a little death by electrocution, kiddo?"

Avner inhaled through his nose. "We're not killing anyone."

"Oh? We should let them live so they can find more Affinities to torture? That's noble."

"We only resort to violence if it becomes necessary. If we can sneak out of here unnoticed, that's our best shot of ensuring there aren't any casualties on our—"

"Get ready to resort," Zeela interjected, her eye focused beyond the door. "They're coming."

Jamad swore so profoundly that Meredith hiccupped. "Do you think the guard remembered he didn't shackle me?"

"Doesn't matter," Naretha droned as she cracked her knuckles. "Drop the dead weight and get ready to fight."

"I'm not leaving her—"

"I can walk," Meredith assured him, though her voice quavered. He looked like he was ready to protest, but then the door's lock clicked, signaling that the guards had indeed returned.

Hastily, Avner planted himself between Zeela and the door while Jamad placed Meredith on her feet. Hands rubbed together to spark lightning, and icicles formed in the air, glittering with the promise of carnage. Meredith gawked in awe at the suspended shards of ice, but the others were too busy readying their own defenses to be impressed. Naretha's skin budded with salt crystals while Charlie summoned all of the shackles to his body, morphing him into a metallic monster. Even the old lady prepared to fight, converting her fingers into mini drills.

The problem was that, when the two guards did burst through the door, they wore their typical Affinity-proof suits—and wielded dart guns with tranquilizers. Two prisoners fell before any of them could attempt to employ their powers.

Screams filled the dungeon as more darts zipped through the air, but no one else was shot before Avner's blinding bolt of electricity tore across the room, colliding with the masked men. Though he was skilled enough not to electrocute anyone else in the process, the other Affinities still shrieked with as much fear as they had for the dart guns.

Naretha, obviously unfazed by the deadly lightning, bombarded the guards with thick salt crystals. Jamad mimicked her actions by hurling icicles at the men, attempting to find a weak spot. As they pushed on through salt, ice, and electricity, it became clear there were no vulnerabilities in their suits—until Charlie swung the shackles over his head like a lasso and thwacked one of the guards in the face, shattering the black glass of his helmet.

"Fry him!" Naretha shouted to Avner, who immediately shook his head.

"I'll stun him, but I won't kill him!"

With a loud groan, the Wacko whipped a torrent of crystals at the guard, slamming into every pore and breaching every airway. Even as the man fell to his knees and choked violently on salt, though, his partner did not relent. He continued dispelling tranquilizers from his gun, most missing but a few hitting their mark—like the one that embedded in Naretha's arm.

Her resounding swear was drowned out by the bang of Charlie's metal slamming the back of that man's head. Swaying, the guard wilted forward and landed on his face, glass helmet shattering from the blow. The clamor fizzled, leaving only Naretha's plentiful profanities to fill the void.

"Dammit. Can someone cut off my arm?" she moaned, staring down at the dart jammed in her limp limb.

Zeela yanked out the dart. "We don't need to cut off your

arm. The sedatives in these are weak. They'll drain your strength, but you won't pass out like last time."

"How do you know?" Naretha's tone was skeptical, even as the other fallen Affinities slowly wobbled to their feet.

"I can see it flowing through your veins," Zeela replied, her one white eye roving over the Wacko's body. Avner had never cared much about his girlfriend's appearance, but looking into her empty, blood-encased eye socket was…difficult.

"Right," Naretha mumbled. "Well, let's get moving then."

"Is he dead?" Jamad nodded toward the second guard.

"No," Meredith said, knees quaking as she stared down at the man. "Please kill him."

Initially, Jamad's eyebrows shot up, but then his lips slid into a feral grin as he extended his hands. "With pleasure."

Before Avner could object, ice seeped from his friend's fingers, slithering through the crevices in the man's helmet to consume every inch of his flesh, freezing the life out of him. There wasn't a hint of remorse on Jamad's face when the deed was complete; he simply wiped his hands and then extended his arm to Meredith. Though uncomfortable about his half-naked body, she looped her frail arm through his and allowed him to escort her toward the doorway.

"Don't tell me—" Avner shook his head, running a hand over his nearly bald scalp. Jamad paused and glanced over his shoulder expectantly. "J…that was *murder*."

"Not murder, Av. Justice. For all of us."

"No," Avner insisted, taking an aggressive step over the dead guards, "this is *wrong*!"

"*This* is wrong," Naretha retorted, motioning around the dungeon they'd been holed up in for an immeasurable amount of time. “Let’s get the hell out of here. If you want to stick around and revive the demons, Sparky, that’s your choice.”

Though Avner’s jaw was clenched, he let the group of prisoners trickle out of the room without a fight. He was clearly outnumbered in this argument; none of the other Affinities seemed remotely miffed by the unnecessary murder. Even Zeela, though she did grant him a glance, was unsympathetic to his opinion. Her only response was a blank, unreadable stare before she headed to the narrow hallway.

Without the effects of the toxic gas, Avner now saw the dirt corridor with clear eyes. The door to their dungeon was the only wooden one; all the others were shiny silver metal with electronic locks.

“That’s the experimentation room,” Meredith whispered, motioning toward the next door down. “Samiya and Paul are probably in there.”

“The experimenters,” Jamad commented, and Avner remembered hazily hearing those two names while they prodded at him. Luckily, neither of them emerged before the group reached the end of the corridor, where a switchback staircase resided.

Zeela and Naretha led the pack upward, the former scanning for signs of life and the latter readying her left hand with salt to demolish that life. The stairwell only ascended one flight, and when they arrived at another metal door with a keypad lock, Naretha prepared to punch it.

“The alarms will sound if you try to break through,” Meredith advised, halting the salt-encased fist in midair. “The code is 0121.”

“Well, aren’t you a helpful little thing?” the Wacko muttered as she jabbed her elbow into the numbers on the keypad.

When the door yawned open, Jamad drawled, “And you wanted to leave her behind.”

Naretha rolled her eyes but didn't comment before prowling through the portal. Beyond, the metallic corridor was so dimly lit that Avner barely distinguished the doors lining either side.

"This door's slightly ajar," Zeela breathed to Avner, her lone eye unhindered by the lack of light. Avner stared at the door intently, waiting for someone to emerge, but then Zeela grabbed his forearm, halting him before he could conjure a spark. "There are two people inside—sitting."

Though the two people had yet to detect their footsteps, Avner knew Naretha had no intentions of leaving this place without inflicting more damage. As she stalked across the hall and kicked open the door, he followed swiftly at her heels, hoping this time he could prevent needless death.

Unexpectedly, the room beyond the door was not a laboratory, and the two humans curled up within were not guards or experimenters but prisoners chained to separate beds and gagged with cloth. Even in the darkness, the man's hazel eyes, the woman's blue eyes, and their ordinary brown hair were visible.

"Reggs," Naretha whispered in confusion, eyeing the two with unease. For a moment, Avner was equally as baffled, but then, through their bedraggled appearances and pleading expressions, he recognized them.

"S-Stark," he stuttered, gawking. Linda Stark, Seth and Tray's mother, tried to cry out his name through her gag, but Avner couldn't manage a reply. They were in better conditions than the Affinities had been, but it made no sense that an Affinity research facility would harbor two Reggs.

"Ch-Charlie—Charlie," Avner called, drawing the gray-haired man into the small room. "Can you free them—or get that lady, maybe—"

A deafening blast of gunfire reverberated through the underground complex. Shrieking ensued as the Affinities in the hall stampeded forward, surging the crowd to the opposite end of the corridor through which they'd come.

"Let's go," Naretha barked, hastily departing the room without dragging Avner along. He continued staring at the Starks in paralysis.

Jamad, with Meredith still on his arm, peeked in to usher Charlie out but then noticed Avner was there as well, gaping. "Av, let's *move*."

"We—can't leave them—"

"They're *Reggs*!"

"They're *people*!" Avner shouted, but Jamad didn't stick around to argue. With Meredith, he fled, leaving his friend alone with two helpless prisoners.

The sound of gunshots grew closer by the second, emanating from the stairwell. Cries ripped through the air and then evanesced when bullets ripped through flesh—not tranquilizer darts but *real bullets*. Avner knew he had no chance of freeing the Stark parents without Charlie or the key lady, and if Affinities were dying out there, his duty was to ensure Zeela's safety above all else. Still, tearing out of that room and into the bedlam of the corridor also tore an irreparable gash through his conscience—through his heart.

At least ten Affinities lay dead on the unforgiving floor when Avner emerged. Was that his fault for stalling them earlier by questioning Jamad—for stalling them now by demanding help for the Starks? He didn't want to think about it, and frankly, he didn't have time. On the far end of the hall, the escaping Affinities ascended a second staircase. Now it was just him, ten dead people, and two guards with guns.

The man and woman wore suits like the other guards had;

his electricity wouldn't be able to penetrate them, and with the gunpowder in those metal rifles, any attempts to use his Affinity could explode the building.

He was ready to accept death—to surrender and beg them to kill him, rather than imprison him again—but then the guns suddenly flew from the guards' hands, swooping to the ceiling and sticking there, as if by magnetic force.

Time stopped in the corridor, the living as petrified as the dead as all three stared up at those rifles. Avner understood why it was happening, and with a burst of newfound hope, he spun and darted toward the stairwell, zooming up the steps without glancing back at his pursuers.

When he reached the open doorway at the top, he found himself amidst endless mounds of hay encased within the worn wooden walls of a massive barn. Most escapees had darted for the exit, but Jamad, Meredith, and Naretha remained not far from the stairwell, the three huddled over Charlie and Zeela, who both crouched in the hay. As Avner had suspected, his girlfriend had witnessed the scene below and told the man to use his magnetic Affinity, which glued the guns to the ceiling, saving Avner's life.

Upon his emergence from the stairwell, Naretha shouted, "Run!" but seemed unable to heed her own command; the sedatives hadn't taken her consciousness, but they had slowed her muscles substantially. While Jamad, Meredith, and Charlie dashed toward the exit, she staggered in an awkward jog.

Zeela noticed her lagging and scooped her arm under the older girl's armpits, hauling her along. Avner followed directly behind, shielding them from the oncoming guards. Though they no longer wielded guns, they certainly had speed. With Zeela's lack of fighting experience and Naretha's current state of lethargy, when the guards did catch up, Avner was forced to fend them off alone.

He would not let Zeela die—especially not after she'd wasted precious seconds saving *him.*

Whirling around, he projected two congruous bolts of lightning at the guards, desperately hoping the electricity would find some fissure in their armor. When they plowed on, he knew he would have to fight them fist to fist, a feat he'd never been particularly skilled at.

Aware that his hand would shatter in a collision with their helmets, Avner pretended to ready his fists for a punch, but when the male guard was upon him, he kicked him in the gut, sending the man stumbling backward. Within seconds, he regained composure and latched onto Avner's leg, jerking it upward and flipping him onto his back.

The hay muted the impact of the landing, but his body still ached as he stared up at the two guards, the man restraining him while the woman prepared to pummel his face. In one last feeble attempt to save himself, Avner shot electricity toward the woman, but it missed the target—and hit a pile of hay instead.

Swearing frantically, both guards staggered way from the blazing mound. Avner didn't waste the distraction; scrambling through the hay, he stumbled to his feet and broke into a sprint, distancing himself from the increasing inferno.

Heat permeated the barn, signaling him to flee as fast as possible, but once he reached the rest of the group, he realized they hadn't yet escaped. The Affinities clogged the exit, their path thwarted by three figures in white.

"The experimenters," Meredith whispered to Jamad as Avner joined them, panting. "And the manager, Fryda."

Hearing this, Naretha groaned and mustered all of her

strength to shrug off Zeela. When she reached the front of the crowd, where the three simpering Reggs stood, she spat on the hay at their feet. "This is becoming tedious."

The eldest lady opened her mouth to speak, but Naretha didn't let her utter a word; from her hand, a stream of sharp salt crystals effused and rushed up the woman's nose, shredding through her brain. Before the two researchers could voice their outrage, they met the same fate. The prisoners didn't wait for the corpses' collapse to stampede out of the barn.

"Wish your parents could've seen that," Naretha grunted to Jamad, grinning despite her depleted energy. "I told them I was deadly."

"You've definitely proven yourself an experienced terrorist," he muttered as they finally passed through the barn's threshold. Though the wintery sun wasn't strong, their eyes had become intolerable to the rays, forcing the Affinities to squint as they trudged through the grassy field. Zeela was the only one unperturbed, her wide eye absorbing the scenery.

Through his eyelashes, Avner discerned that the brown barn was positioned at the center of a vast, seemingly deserted farmland, the structure sticking out like a lone ship in an open sea—only now that ship was ablaze, the fire licking out of every window and threatening to consume the wood completely.

"Well, Sparky, looks like you became a murderer today after all," Naretha mused, lifting her hand for a high-five. "Welcome to the club."

Ignoring her crudeness, Avner turned to the group of weary Affinities, many collapsing with exhaustion, immune to the blazing barn only a few paces away. "Does anyone have a fire Affinity?"

"Your sister does," Naretha said when no one responded.

"Adara does not have a fire Affinity," Avner snapped, his anxiety swelling as he watched the roof of the barn cave in. "She hates fire."

"All the more reason for her to have a fire Affinity. I saw it in her eyes—they blazed as bright as this when she tried to attack me in Periculand."

Again Avner disregarded her, his focus entwined with the lethal conflagration. "J, can you put this out? The Starks are still—"

"*Ice* isn't gonna end this, Av. I feel like a melting cone of ice cream right now."

"We can't just let them *die*! They're Tray and Seth's parents—they're innocent people!"

"Did you say Stark?" Naretha perked up from where she leaned on Zeela. "Those Reggs were the Starks?"

"Yes." Avner watched her cautiously. "Do you…know them?"

"This complicates things," she murmured, her nose twitching toward the barn. "I'm not sure if Danny will be thrilled by their deaths or enraged that he wasn't the one to end them…"

"Your boyfriend knows the Starks—and he wants to *kill* them?"

The Wacko opened her mouth, but then Meredith yelped, rousing those who'd decided to rest. "They're coming!"

"Who's coming?" Avner demanded, his heart pounding with the possibility that the Starks had somehow found a way free. Meredith didn't have to answer, however, for him to know how futilely optimistic that thought had been. The two figures materializing from the flames like charred demons were the answer.

"*Run*!" Jamad bellowed, setting the Affinities into a frenzy.

"How are they alive?" Naretha complained as she attempted to keep pace with the group. A few other dart-inflicted individuals straggled as well. It took all of Avner's self-preserving will not to turn when the guards attacked one man at the rear of the pack, his screams echoing through the meadow with infinite anguish.

"They have Affinity-proof suits," Zeela said, her voice strangely level given the circumstance. "Fire is an Affinity, therefore the suits are resistant."

"Well, nothing's resistant to this." Throwing his hand back, Jamad cast a sheet of ice atop the grass. As expected, the two guards slipped on the suddenly slick surface, giving the Affinities enough time to gain more of a lead. Jamad's triumphant laugh resounded through the meadow, as gleeful as Avner's heart was mournful.

He wanted to mention the Starks again—wanted to sprint back there and fight his way through the flames to save them—but even though he'd caused that fire, it wasn't his Affinity. He would have to sacrifice his own life if he tried to spare theirs. Perhaps a sacrifice was in order, though. The Starks shouldn't have perished for his foolish mistake. But how could he abandon Zeela now, after all she'd suffered? How could he sacrifice himself for his own pride and self-righteousness before she found comfort and safety?

He couldn't and he wouldn't. Still, fleeing from that burning barn solidified the permanence of that gash in his conscience, altering the shape of his perfect morality. Zeela had said he looked different, and as his morals morphed, he wondered if she would ever look at him the same—or if he would ever want her to.

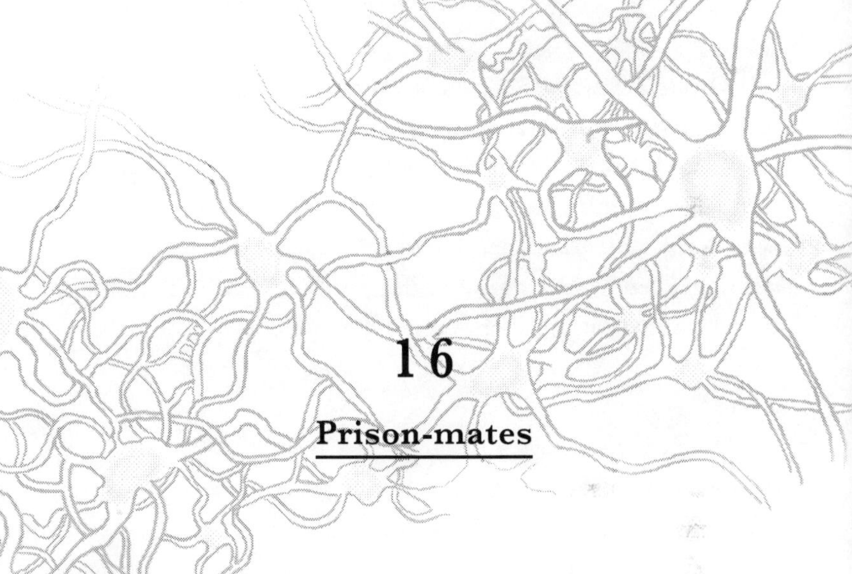

16

Prison-mates

Two grueling weeks of torpidity had passed for Adara Stromer. Other than Mitt, not one person had entered the police station, leaving her with little knowledge as to what was happening in Periculand. From what the officer had told her, none of the students had openly defied the Rosses yet, which was likely a result of their alliance with Nero—or the fact that eight hours of training was far less tedious than eight hours in a classroom. Adara definitely would have appreciated the Reggs' takeover for that.

She knew Nerdworm would be restless without a constant inflow of knowledge, which was why she was surprised he hadn't used his newly acquired free time to visit her and complain about his discontent. None of her friends had visited since the day they'd brought Olalla, and for that reason she'd been forced to seek a tentative companionship with Angor. Though she wasn't sure she believed the King's claims of innocence, she'd realized in her boredom that she didn't care if he was lying. She would have befriended Nero or even *Kiki* just to feel less lonesome.

That was why, when Angor started an exercise regimen a few days after their incarceration, Adara had reluctantly agreed to join him. The routine consisted of movements like push-ups, sit-ups, squats—and then faithfully, at the end of each workout, Adara's last exercise was her plea to Mitt for a box of donuts. One evening, the prisoners were finishing their push-ups when Weaponizer entered the corridor without a summons.

"You need to tighten your core, Stromer. You're flopping around like a fish."

Still in a droopy plank, she readied a sardonic retort, but when her head rose to confront him, she found him smirking along with the three teenage boys at his back.

"Oh, thank God," she blurted out, jumping to her feet and leaving Angor to complete his push-ups alone. "I've been so freaking lonely here."

"You don't...look lonely." Ackerly eyed Angor curiously as the man continued to exercise. As usual, Greenie looked like a humanoid plant, his white Periculand Training School sweatshirt stained with pollen and his green cargo pants coated with dirt.

"Of course she's not lonely," Tray scoffed, arms crossed, as he stomped into the hall. "Look at her—she's *thriving* in prison. I'm not sure why I expected anything different."

Adara met his antipathy with an air of frivolity. "I would probably thrive in a *real* prison. The problem with this prison is there aren't any people in here for me to make fun of. I've already used all the insults I can come up with for the King—honestly, he's too hip for me to come up with much. I need someone like *you*, Nerdworm, for whom there are endless mocking possibilities."

Tray's growl was interrupted by the arrival of his twin, who strolled in with a wooden basket in his hands and an exuberant smile on his face. "Happy Thanksgiving, Dar. We brought you a feast."

"A feast?" Her chest swelled with glee as he set the basket full of food on the floor outside her cell. "It's Thanksgiving?"

"It was on Thursday," Seth said. "We haven't been able to visit, though, because Hartman's been holed up in the nurse's office almost every day. Nero."

Adara's mood darkened at the mention of his name. "That dickwad. If only I could be freed from this prison…then I could beat up that bully and save his victims from peril."

Mitt rolled his eyes when she looked to him dramatically. "I still haven't gotten the okay from the Rosses. For my sake, though, I hope they release you soon."

"You couldn't beat up Nero even if you tried," Tray said. "You'd probably incinerate him instead, and then burn down the whole—"

"I *don't have a fire Affinity*!" she snarled, nearly grabbing the electric bars in rage. Composing herself, she added, "If I'm so evil and you're so noble, Nerdworm, why haven't *you* opposed Nero yet?"

"Because I don't want to end up in a cell with *you*," he snorted, but his eyes were on her prison-mate. Angor had finally stood, brow drenched in sweat. "What are you two training for, anyway—to break out?"

Massaging his biceps, the ex-principal said, "I don't wish to atrophy. I'm no longer as spry as I was in my youth, and given that I can't remember my Affinity, this passes the time."

"And you, Stromer?" Tray prompted with arched eyebrows. "Why aren't you improving your Affinity?"

"Because I don't *know* my Affinity. Besides, I need the physical conditioning; I am getting *fat* in here. Outside of prison, I burned so many calories—"

"Shut up. You never played any sports."

"My sport was taunting people, and it required a lot of exert—"

"*All right.*" Seth waved his hands to interrupt their endless banter. "I think a little booze will lighten the mood."

When he reached into the basket and pulled out a handful of beer bottles, Adara's shock was enough to actually quench her argument with Tray. "Where the hell did you get that?"

"Convinced some guy in town to sell it to me. He was so pissed off about the Reggs' takeover that he didn't mind breaking the law."

"Mm, and you're divulging this information *in front of a cop*." With her pointed look in Mitt's direction, Seth's cheeks paled.

"Uh..."

"Do you have more?" the officer asked as he peered into the basket.

"Yes...?"

After rummaging through the basket, Mitt pulled out a bottle, tipped it toward Seth in acknowledgement, and then retreated to his post by the door. "Thanks. I won't say anything."

"You're allowing minors to drink alcohol, and you're partaking in the event, but you *won't* break me out of jail? Where are your priorities, Weaponizer?" Adara demanded, sarcastically aghast.

"How is it that you have more beer in here than food?" Tray questioned, digging through the basket with a frown.

"I'm not *rich*, bro," Seth said before chugging a bit of his drink. "My boss barely pays me minimum wage."

"Your boss?" Adara repeated flatly. "Are you in a Periculand gang now?"

"No, no—my boss at the cleaner's. I, um...took over Hastings's job there."

Though Angor's expression turned solemn, Adara managed not to flinch. "The Reggs are letting you work in town? I thought you weren't allowed to leave campus?"

"We're permitted to leave with a Regg escort...one of the guards they installed in town," Ackerly explained. "Most students got jobs since they started making us pay for our own food... I work at the flower shop, and it's—"

"Hold up," Adara interjected with such force that Seth stopped drinking mid-gulp. "The Reggs are making students *pay* for meals?"

"And they're rationing the food," Seth added, finishing off his first bottle. "Took away the buffet and everything."

"Damn." Adara shook her head. "That's about the worst thing they could do. I'm glad *I* don't have to work. I just sit here and they feed me for free. How are there even enough jobs in this small town for all the students?"

"There aren't," Tray said. "A lot have resorted to begging their rich parents for more money, like Kiki."

"And like you two? Haven't your parents been sending you money?"

"They were...before the election."

"I've sent them some letters about it, but they haven't gotten back to me." Seth shrugged as he grabbed another bottle.

Though he seemed unconcerned, his twin's brow wrinkled, probably contriving some conspiracy theory or assuming his parents dead. Instead of voicing his rash conclusions, he rested his vision on Angor and asked, "Why didn't we have to pay when you were in charge?"

"Because I paid for the entirety of this town with my personal funds." The man plopped down on his metal slab and wiped perspiration from his forehead. "I instilled mild taxes, of course, but…now I imagine the United States government is stuck paying for the town. I suppose that's only justice for unrightfully placing me in this cell."

Tray cocked his head, skeptical. "One man could pay for all of us but the government can't?"

"The government's a bunch of greedy assholes," Adara reminded him. "Murderers, on the other hand—super generous." Before Angor could defend his virtue, she added, "Joking, Your Majesty. You aren't a murderer…maybe. Still haven't decided if you're a lying scumbag or not. Hey, Nerdworm, if everyone's got jobs, what's yours? Bookstore attendant?"

"Yes…" Tray confirmed uncomfortably, eliciting cackles from Adara.

"You're too predictable, Stark."

"He's been working on the suits, too—the Affinity-proof ones the Regg guards wear," Seth chimed in, now nearly done with his second beer. "He created this device that temporarily disables them—the guards go ape, naturally—but yeah, that's how we snuck out to come visit you."

"*Nerdworm's* been working on a device that helped you come visit *me*?" Adara clarified, her smirk stretching.

"It's also to help us in case the Reggs ever become hostile," Tray huffed. "You aren't as important as you think you are."

"Oh, on the contrary, I'm *more* important than I thought. I've never been under the impression that you cared about me at all, but to go out of your way to bring me company… You are a softy after all."

"I—no—not—not one part of that is true—"

"Did you bring donuts, Jockface?" Adara prompted, ignoring Tray's stammering.

"Could only smuggle one. They don't have them on campus anymore, and the grocery store had limited stock…" Though it was less than she'd begged for, her face still split with undiluted fervor at the sight of that single donut. Seth attempted to hand it to her through the bars but then recoiled when the sensation of static reminded him of the metal's electrical properties. "Mitt, dude, tone it down with the electricity for a minute?"

"So you can break Adara free? No thanks."

"I'm the only one who has the ability to bend the bars, and clearly I have no desire." Rubbing his face, Tray sighed. "Just let her have the stupid donut. Her grin is demonic."

Prying the bottle from his lips, Mitt turned to the console on the wall, where he pressed a few buttons, silencing the electrical buzz that had previously filled the air. Greedily, Adara reached both hands through the bars and snatched the donut from Seth, cherishing it with more care than she would an ancient relic.

"Mm, cinnamon," she hummed before sinking her teeth into its sweetness.

"This is how you get Adara to shut up," Seth informed Mitt as he opened his third bottle of beer. "Your life'll be a lot easier if you feed her donuts."

"Slow down with the booze, Jockface," she said through a mouthful of donut. "Save some for Greenie."

Ackerly's face flushed. "I, um…don't drink."

"Stromer knows—she just likes to make people feel uncomfortable," Tray grumbled as he reached into the basket and grabbed two apples. Ackerly fumbled to catch the one he tossed over his shoulder at him.

Teeth full of donut crumbs, Adara grinned. "You know I love you, Greenie. Hey, speaking of love, did Eliana figure out Angor's Affinity from Nero?"

"Why would love remind you of that?" Tray questioned between bites of his apple.

"Well, I would *love* it if we get all of this mystery shit over with, so I can bust outta here. So, what's the verdict?"

"Ooh, I know that word," Seth enthused after finishing his third bottle. "*Jussst* read it in the dictionary the other day. It means 'green with vegetation,' like my man Ack over here."

"That's the definition of *verdant*, not *verdict*, Seth," his brother corrected with exasperation. "Stromer wants to know if we've found Angor innocent or guilty. The answer is we're still unsure. Eliana said Nero's memories of Angor's Affinity are warped and concealed even from him, which leads us to believe Artemis blocked his memories so he wouldn't realize Angor's innocent."

"Well, Artemis certainly thinks highly of Big Boy," Adara concluded. "I bet he wouldn't have put it together, even if he knew the truth."

"Nor would he want to…with the way the Reggs treat him," Ackerly said before gnawing on his apple like a chipmunk. "Nero would probably support them, even if he knew they were liars."

"Any leads on who the Wacko sympathizer is?" Adara asked, looking between Tray and Ackerly as Seth downed a fourth bottle.

"We've been checking files for shady backgrounds and monitoring the post office for any suspicious mail…" Tray's jaw shifted in frustration as he stared at his apple core. "Nothing yet."

"Maybe I should just start beating people up for information," Seth offered as he tossed an empty beer bottle into the basket. "With my *sssuper* strength."

His twin rolled his eyes. "You're drunk, Seth."

"N-O. That spells no. Because I'm N-O-T. Not." Tray opened his mouth, likely for a condescending retort, but then Seth began again. "I think I'm gonna chug the next one. Yeah? Yeah? Anyone wanna compete?"

"Seth," Tray chided, but his twin ignored him as he retrieved another bottle and began guzzling it. Adara wasn't surprised when, moments later, Seth choked and then upchucked, spewing liquid vomit all over the tiled floor.

"Oh, weeds," Ackerly swore, dancing away from the puke.

"Oh weeds?" Adara repeated while Tray continued to scoff at his brother's immaturity. "Damn, Greenie, you've got a dirty mouth. What should we call it…a garden mouth?"

"I—need a bathroom," Seth choked as he wobbled away from the expanding puddle.

"End of the hall," Mitt said, still casually sipping from his first bottle.

When Seth disappeared, Ackerly awkwardly eyed the floor. "I, uh, have some herbs that'll help with his nausea…"

"And yours?" Adara challenged, seeing the paleness of his face. Nodding, he hurried down the hall after Seth, and she chuckled. "This has been the best Thanksgiving ever, rivaled only by the year I got your Uncle Robert to drink his own piss."

Tray snorted at the memory while Mitt cringed.

"Not sure I wanna hear that story." The officer set his empty bottle gently into the basket. "I'm gonna go get a mop. Punch her with your super strength if she tries to escape, Stark."

"Gladly…" Tray mumbled as Mitt sauntered into the front room. Alone with only Angor, Adara and Tray studied each other with equal suspicion.

"Nice vest, Stark," she said, referring to the ugly puffy vest he wore over his sweatshirt. "It's definitely lame enough to suit you."

Tray narrowed his eyes but maintained his dignity. "I assume you have no concept of the weather anymore, but I'll have you know it's cold outside."

"You must be the Stark Adara often refers to as 'the wussy one,'" Angor commented, inciting a rancorous glare but no verbal response.

"Where's your smart retort, Nerdworm?" Adara stepped closer to the bars. "Aren't you gonna scold me about how juvenile the term 'wussy' is?"

"I have no interest in provoking an enraged response from you," Tray answered carefully, examining her as if she were some foreign, unstable substance he couldn't quite understand or control.

"Afraid I'll shove you into a wall like I did when you sparked an Avner worship-fest during our history class earlier this year? Or has my absence weakened your verbal parrying skills?"

"Your absence…hasn't benefited my life in the way I thought it would," he admitted, nose twitching with the discomfort of his own words.

"Oh? Are you saying you've *missed* me? Are you as drunk as your brother?"

"*No.*" Without much grace, he crossed his arms over his vest. "You're just…the easiest to convince to do reckless things; everyone else is too afraid to snoop around for information. And, with Avner gone, there's no one to oppose Nero."

"I thought *you* were his arch nemesis now? Super strength versus super strength. I'm just a normie to him."

"No one thinks you're a normie," Tray said darkly. "Everyone knows what happened in Angor's office, Adara. You can't deny it forever."

She opened her mouth to do just that, but before she could refute, Mitt waltzed back into the hall with a mop and bucket in his hands.

"This is why teenagers aren't allowed to drink," he muttered, glowering at the puddle of puke. "I assume if you ever become principal again, you'll fire me," he added to Angor as he cleaned the mess.

"Actually, I quite like you, Officer Telum. A man of duty with an honest, human heart. I hold no grudge against you for keeping me here, or for…this." Angor gestured toward the beer with amusement.

"Thanks," Mitt murmured, but his voice was drowned out by the static of the radio at his hip.

"Mitt—Mitt!" a frantic female voice sounded. "There's a car headed toward town! Shit—shit—what if it's more Wackos? They're gonna take over my mind again! Fu—"

"Officer Wright," he interrupted after hastily grabbing the radio. "I'm…with students…and Mr. Periculy."

"Oh…" the voice mumbled. Adara snickered, knowing it must be Dr. Wright's daughter, Ira, who guarded the front gate of Periculand. Clearing her throat, the woman said in a much more formal tone, "Officer Telum, there are intruders. Code gray."

"On my way." As he propped the mop against the wall, Mitt surveyed the others with unease.

"Ooh, Mitt's sleeping with the school security," Adara taunted, wiggling her eyebrows.

"That's all you gathered from that conversation?" Tray spat. "There are Wackos breaking into our—"

"I'm not sleeping with her," Mitt retorted, metallic eyes fixed on Adara. "We're *friendly*. And that's not relevant now. I need to provide Officer Wright with backup—and you need to clean this up, in case I have to bring in prisoners."

"Me?" Tray blurted out, but Mitt had already jogged out of the room. Gagging, the Stark twin retrieved the mop and wiped up the remainder of his brother's vomit without looking at it.

"This is what you get for being the responsible one," Adara sang, reveling in his disgust. "One of the many reasons I enjoy my life as a deviant."

"Why are you so giddy?" he demanded. "We're being invaded."

"True. But if Mitt and Ira are successful, I'll get some new prison-mates. And if they lose, the Wackos will probably demolish this town and the Rosses will crumble. Either way, I'll be pleased."

"What if the intruders aren't Wackos? What if they aren't intruders at all? What if...Avner's back?" Adara's bemused blink roused a triumphant smirk from Tray. "It *has* been over two weeks since they left. If your brother has any intention of returning, now's about time. Given he broke a Wacko out of jail, *he* could be your new prison-mate."

"Come a little closer, Stark," she snarled, clutching the bars. In his haste, Mitt had neglected to turn the electricity back on, allowing her to grip them with relentless ferocity.

"So you can burn me?" He placed the mop in the corner. "I'll pass."

As soon as the words spewed from his mouth, a furious, defensive chasm unfurled in Adara's chest, warming her flesh with what she assumed to be rage. "*Burn you*?"

Tray paused, warily watching her fists tighten on the bars. They were meant to be an anchor for her indignation, but then that anchor began to soften—and *melt*. "Adara..."

Stumbling back, she gaped at the damage she'd inflicted: the metal, now warped and thinned, was like an abstract icicle. She'd *melted* the bars. Her hands were still abnormally dark and blistered, but the volcano of anger within her had cooled and sealed, leaving only a numb sense of fear.

"Impressive," Angor marveled from behind, straightening to observe the bars. "If only you would allow me to train—"

"Shut *up*," Adara growled, but her fury extinguished when the front door of the police station flew open, permitting cold air, uneven footsteps, and whiny voices.

"We *aren't* Wackos! How many times do I have to *tell* you, you unfairly attractive human being? Did you see his silver eyes, Ash? Holy balls, they are gorgeous..."

It wasn't hard for Adara to determine which of the three girls Mitt lugged into the back corridor was the one admiring his features; even as he hauled them by joint chains through the open doorway, she continued ogling him with rose gold eyes. Though a teenager, she stood nearly as tall as the officer. Long, messy locks of peachy-pink hair covered her weathered sweatshirt, the word "Volleyball" barely distinguishable in peeling letters.

"Oh—oh, you're putting us in jail?" she asked when she spotted the cells lining the walls.

Tray, still in the middle of the hall, shifted into a slightly defensive stance, while Adara's face alit with a grin. "Well, well, well. I've always been a pessimist, but dreams do come true," she mused, appraising her three new companions like prey.

Mitt's admirer seemed nonplussed but indifferent about the presence of other humans. The smaller and substantially younger girl in the middle staggered along like a lost kitten, the pom-pom on her knit hat solidifying her youthfulness. She bumped into the first girl when Mitt stopped to open the cell across the hall, and the girl at the rear threatened to flatten them all with her elephant size.

"The monster," Adara said slowly, recognizing the unmistakable mass.

As if it was her given name, the girl blinked her murky green eyes and locked gazes with Adara, brow creased beneath her short, swampy hair. Through her thick lips, her words were surprisingly articulate as she said, "The angry sweatshirt girl."

"Angry sweatshirt girl?"

"You were angry when the water boy ripped your sweatshirt," the monster clarified, her steps reverberating through the floor as Mitt ushered the three into the cell.

"Ah, yes, I remember now. I haven't yet forgiven Water Boy for that offense. Thank you for reminding me. *Almost* makes up for the fact that you destroyed my door. This was one of the Wackos that broke in, Mitt, if you were wondering."

"We *aren't* Wackos," the peachy-haired girl groaned as the officer locked their cell and gave her an unconvinced look.

"You arrived in one of the Wackos' vans, Stromer claims you're Wackos—"

"She's in jail!" the girl exclaimed, throwing up her hands in exasperation. "Why believe her over us?"

"You also admitted that you traveled here from one of the Wackos' hideouts—"

"Where we were *prisoners*."

"Why would the Wackos imprison Affinities?" Tray inquired, scrutinizing her matching hair and eyes.

"Why would Periculand imprison Affinities?" The girl nodded toward Adara and Angor.

"Because they're dangerous law-breakers."

"Oh, well…that's not what we are. We just didn't agree with the Wacko leader, and he's not so fond of disagreers," she explained, glancing at Mitt for some sign that he believed her tale.

His face remained stony, pensive. "We'll see what the Rosses conclude when they arrive."

"*Dog*," Adara coughed loudly. "What? Oh, I was just saying that you're like a loyal little puppy, Mitt—nothing too obscene. Can the truth even be considered obscene?"

"The Rosses are coming here?" Angor asked, hopping off his

slab and padding over to stand by Adara. "Do any of you girls possess a mind reading Affinity, by chance?"

"We already had our mind reader try," Tray reminded him flatly. "Artemis's mind is too clouded—"

"I was hoping they might read *my* mind, actually, in front of the Rosses, in order to prove I am as innocent as I profess to be."

"All I can do is control gases," the talkative girl said with a shrug. "And Cath's Affinity is just being the toughest bitch in the universe." She gestured appreciatively toward the monster. "And then Ashna—"

The front door banged open again, halting the girl mid-sentence. Although they'd expected the Reggs, Mitt's eyes widened at the sight, probably remembering that Tray was here when he shouldn't have been—and that there was a basket of booze in the middle of the corridor. Suppressing a chuckle was nearly impossible for Adara.

"Stark, take the basket to the bathro—"

Mitt's attempts at concealment were futile, though, for the Reggs had already stomped into the hall—with Big Boy and the Pixie Prince at their backs.

"Oh no," Tray moaned as soon as Nero's burly body filled the doorway.

A reptilian grin cracked over the brute's face at the sight of his small rival. "Tray Stark. Breaking school rules? Should I punish him?"

"Not now," Artemis snapped, her focus trained on the three apprehended girls.

Her husband scanned the entire hall until he noticed the incriminating basket. "Has Mr. Stark been drinking *alcohol* in here?" Sniffing the air around Mitt, his ire increased. "Have *you* been drinking alcohol in here?"

"I—well, that's…irrelevant…"

"Enough, William," Artemis warned. "We need to determine the purpose of these Wackos."

Throwing her head back, the tall girl groaned. "We aren't *Wackos*; we were prisoners of the Wackos. We managed to escape and come here, seeking refuge. Isn't this the Affinity town?"

"It is," Adara confirmed, finally drawing the new arrivals' attention toward her, "but now these Reggs are in charge, so you can imagine that isn't going well for us. Nice leash, by the way, Pixie Prince. Servitude really suits you."

Calder's eyes flashed with the most intense spurt of rage she'd ever seen from him; the expression was so venomous that her lips actually drooped. But, as quickly as it had come, the anger subsided, replaced by a look that could only mean, "Keep your mouth shut." Naturally, she didn't heed his silent command.

"I'm caught in a dilemma here, Artie, Willy." Adara folded her hands in a diplomatic manner. "I have information that could incriminate these three, but I'm not sure I like you enough to share it. Maybe if you did something nice for me, like…oh, I dunno, bring me donuts, set me free—then we can chat."

The Reggs' lips curled, but Mitt spoke before either of them had to bargain. "That one is a Wacko." He pointed to the monster, apparently named Cath, and her mouth gaped at the accusation. "Broke into town last month to try to kidnap Hastings."

"*Mitt*." Adara smacked her forehead and dragged her nails down her face. "I thought you *wanted* me to leave, you absolute asshole!"

"Absolutely *attractive* asshole," Mitt's fan-girl corrected as she batted her eyelashes at him.

"Don't look at me like that," he grumbled, fidgeting. "You're, like, fifteen."

"*Sixteen*, actually."

"Wait." Nero stepped forward, his bushy eyebrows furrowed. "*You're* the one who threw me into that door?" When Cath nodded, his face contorted in revulsion. "You're a *girl*? I was—*No*..."

"Yes, yes, Big Boy, you were beaten by a girl," Adara droned. "There's a mop over there for your tears."

"Why is there a mop?" William asked, blinking between the cleaning instrument and the unusually pale officer.

"I—well..."

"Whoa!" a slurred voice exclaimed as Seth came tumbling out of the bathroom. Ackerly was right behind him, his face as green as his hair. "There is a *lot* of puke in there, my friends. Where is that mop... Oh—hey! More people! Holy balls, this is a certified party up in here, ha, ha—"

"Holy balls? You say holy balls, too?"

Adara watched Seth's disoriented vision focus on the girl in the cell, her rose gold eyes protruding with glee. "Well, yeah, whenever I'm really excited...or drunk. Heh."

"Seems we suspected the wrong Mr. Stark," William noted dryly.

"Can I beat this one up instead?" Nero cracked his knuckles, his violent instincts nullifying his previous despair.

"Not now," Artemis repeated, agitated. "We still don't have the information we—"

"Yo, why is your face bleeding?" Seth shouted as he staggered to the girls' cell and examined the slice on the peachy-haired girl's cheek.

"Got attacked by Danny's dog while escaping. I survived, obviously, but that thing is a little devil, let me tell you."

"Who's Danny?" Seth questioned between prolonged blinks.

"Daniel Mayer has a dog?" Angor asked, approaching the bars. He was near enough to Adara that she smelled his stale odor, but her disgust didn't faze him in his state of curiosity. "I wasn't aware that he had the capacity to care for animals."

"Damn, Majesty, your ability to candidly insult is really improving," Adara remarked with a nod of approval. "We all knew your time with me would be beneficial."

"Who is Danny?" Seth demanded with a bit more lucidity.

"We are wasting time," Artemis said, still probing the trio of girls with her eyes. "Tell us your mission and we will discuss the possibility of releasing you in exchange for—"

"Negotiating with terrorists?" Tray questioned. "Why would we return these girls to the Wackos if they're skilled enough to be sent here? We need to deplete the Wackos' num—"

"This is not a decision that involves you," William interrupted coldly. "You boys have no business here. Nero, Calder, escort them back to campus."

"I thought you needed me here for torture purposes?" Nero griped as Tray helped his brother hobble through the corridor.

Ackerly followed, but dazed by nausea, he didn't realize the floor was wet from the mop; with a little yelp, he slipped and plummeted forward, his left wrist colliding with the tiled floor. The crack of his bones invoked a dramatic gag from weak-stomached Tray.

"Sweet sunflowers!" Ackerly cursed as he cradled his arm.

"There you go again with that garden mouth, Greenie," Adara sighed, shaking her head. "This broken wrist is karma for your vulgarity."

"I'll take him to the nurse," Calder assured the Rosses as he roughly hoisted Ackerly to his feet. Adara almost snarled at the

Pixie Prince to be gentle. Her poor Greenie's eyebrows weren't wrinkled with pain, though, but with puzzlement.

"It...doesn't hurt, actually." Ackerly tested his swelling wrist, but even as he stretched and flicked it, he didn't wince. "The pain...disappeared somehow..." Glancing around frantically for an explanation, his eyes landed on the girl in the cell—the smallest one with the hat.

Adara hadn't given her a thought before, but now that Ackerly examined her with such intent, she noticed her eyes, bulging and petrified, were shimmering rainbows. The pastel colors might have been remarkable if her chained hands weren't open and aimed in Ackerly's direction, as if she'd magically removed his pain. The realization dawned in his eyes the moment it solidified in Adara's mind, but the girl's head twitched in response, signaling him not to mention it.

His staring had piqued William's interest, though. "You—what is your Affinity?"

"I...um...can reduce pain," she admitted, eyes sheepishly sweeping the room.

"Through inhibiting nociceptors?" Angor tapped a finger to his lower lip.

The girl froze under his inspection, so Adara asked, "What the *hell* is a nociceptor?"

"A sensory receptor that detects painful stimuli and relays the information to the brain," Tray explained, as if it were common knowledge. Adara was still perplexed.

"She can control pain nerves," Ackerly supplied. "So, even though my wrist is broken and should hurt, the signal's blocked and I don't feel it."

"Thank you, Greenie," Adara said, even though her smile was directed at Tray.

"Can you provoke pain, as well?" Angor asked with an experimenter's inquisitiveness.

Though she seemed fearful of him, the girl, who Adara remembered being referred to as Ashna, stammered, "I—don't know. I've never tried…"

"Like hell you've never tried!" Nero barked, causing the small girl to jump in surprise. "You're a freaking *Wacko*."

"We aren't Wackos!" the peachy-haired girl shouted as she banged the side of her head against the wall. "How can we make you believe us?"

"Would your mind reader be interested in paying them a visit?" William asked Nero.

"He's a fickle bastard, but I'll convince him."

"Ira—er, Officer Wright said that she didn't sense any danger from these girls," Mitt informed the Reggs quietly. "She claimed they don't seem as hostile as last time."

"And why isn't Ira here now?" Angor questioned. "We trust her judgment; she has always been useful in interrogations. Do you fear she will detect that I'm not a threat and expose my incarceration as a sham?"

The Reggs both frowned at his accusation, but neither voiced their dissent before another spoke.

"We aren't with the Wackos," Ashna said, her small voice permeating the room. "They used us and abused us and tortured us." Lifting her chin, she exposed the bruised, raw ring that encircled her throat, as if a collar had resided there. "They forced Cath to accompany them in September because they needed her strength. Her own life would have been forfeit if she refused."

"If you're not willing to die before aiding the Wackos, you're void of nobility," Artemis said without remorse. "By complying with them, you are essentially part of their group."

"That's easy to say before you've been placed in such a situation," Ashna retorted with calm vehemence. "You've never met the Wacko leader. He blew up a building when Naira refused to kill a—"

"Naira," Calder interrupted, his quizzical gaze settling on the peachy-haired girl. "Naira Steele? I didn't recognize you with the light hair... We stopped at your townhouse to pick you up when they brought me here, but you weren't home."

"Calder...Mardurus?" Her face brightened with recognition. Adara told herself it was the girl's disgusting amount of enthusiasm that made her gut twist. "I went to middle school with this kid!"

Coldness enveloped Calder's face. "Fraco said you weren't at your house that day because you'd gone to join the Wackos."

"I *did* join the Wackos," Naira confirmed, shuffling uneasily. "Someone told me about them—told me they were called Affinities for Freedom, and I thought they were just a bunch of activists. When I joined them, though...I realized how bad they were—how corrupt. When I tried to leave, they locked me in a cell."

Adara rolled her eyes. "Likely story. Let's just accept they're Wackos and agree to leave them here. They *must* have Wacko secrets, and I'm sure I can make them talk."

"With your annoyingness?" Tray scoffed.

Calder's lips quirked to one side. "Or your fire Affinity?"

Adara wasn't sure which boy's response irked her more, but no outburst ensued before Ashna said, "We do have some information about the Wackos that we're willing to divulge. If I can see a map, I'll show you the hideout where we were imprisoned. And...I think I know where Wacko Headquarters is."

Artemis's dark eyes illuminated with the prospect. "This could be what the president has been hoping for... Officer Telum, release these girls. Fraco should be here momentarily, and he'll escort them to the Residence Tower. Tomorrow morning, the three of you will come to our office to discuss what you know. Nero, Calder, bring these primaries back to the tower. Punishments will be distributed in the morning. Bring that basket, as well…"

With that, the Rosses shot Angor matching scowls and then stalked out of the police station. Adara was almost offended that she hadn't received a glare of contempt from the two pricks.

"Er—I should go to the nurse," Ackerly reminded Calder when the Pixie Prince aggressively gripped his arm again. "My wrist doesn't hurt, but…"

"I can take him," Ashna piped up as Mitt guided the girls out of their cell. "I…don't know where to go, but I can ward off the pain until we get there."

"Y-yeah." Ackerly cleared his throat. "Uh—that'd be great."

"I should be the one bringing Greenie to the nurse!" Adara fumed as Mitt uncuffed them, the clang of their unclasped chains nearly drowning out her complaints. "I can't believe you're releasing three *Wackos*, but I'm still stuck in here!"

"I thought you were enjoying your time in prison, Stromer?" Calder crooned, jumping his eyebrows.

"How would you know if she was?" Nero growled, draining the color from the Pixie Prince's face.

"Let's go," he prompted instead of answering. Scrunching his nose, he grabbed Seth's arm and dragged the inebriated teen, who still looked like he was waiting for the answer to his question about Danny.

Suspicious, Nero stalked to the bars of Adara's cell and met her fiery eyes with his stony ones. "If I find out you're wooing my best ally with your fire magic, we're gonna have a problem, Little Stromer."

"I don't have any fire magic, so I don't think we will," she responded complacently.

"Let's hope not." His eyes darted cagily in Angor's direction before he clenched Tray's arm and hauled him from the hall.

"Mitt," Adara beseeched once only the three girls and Ackerly remained. "You have to let me out, man. You know this is screwed up."

"Innocent until proven guilty, Stromer. That's the law," Mitt said, but his grimace was apologetic as he guided the others through the doorway.

"Greenie, wait," Adara hissed before he and Ashna could pass through the threshold. "Secret meeting, *now*."

Exhaling, he trudged back to her cell, his wrist still supported by his other arm. "What's wrong?"

"I don't trust these girls," she said through her teeth. "They must be Wackos."

"I dunno, Adara... Their stories are convincing. What if they are telling the truth? We need to give them a chance."

Her lips curled as she glanced knowingly at the girl with the knit hat, who waited in the doorway. "Pretty girls can tell lies. I know from personal experience."

Heat rose to Ackerly's cheeks as he checked to see if Ashna had heard. "Who—um, do you know that's pretty and lies?"

"I was referring to myself, Greenie," she said flatly, but her moodiness mollified when Ashna removed her hat to shake out her long, iridescent locks of rainbow hair. "What the... What *are* you? A magical unicorn fairy?"

Ashna blinked, shocked at being addressed.

"She means that in the nicest way possible," Ackerly said hastily.

"No, that was one hundred percent insult. Unicorns are so happy and optimistic—it's revolting."

Ackerly actually had the nerve to give her a reprimanding glare. "We'll try to find a way to come visit you again," was his unsympathetic reply. He then joined Ashna in the doorway, leaving Adara alone with Angor once more.

She hadn't realized how full she felt in the presence of those people—even her enemies—until the emptiness of the corridor left a void in her core.

"This is why I'm a cynic, Periculy," she sighed, her voice more aloof than her heart felt. "People always find a way to let you down."

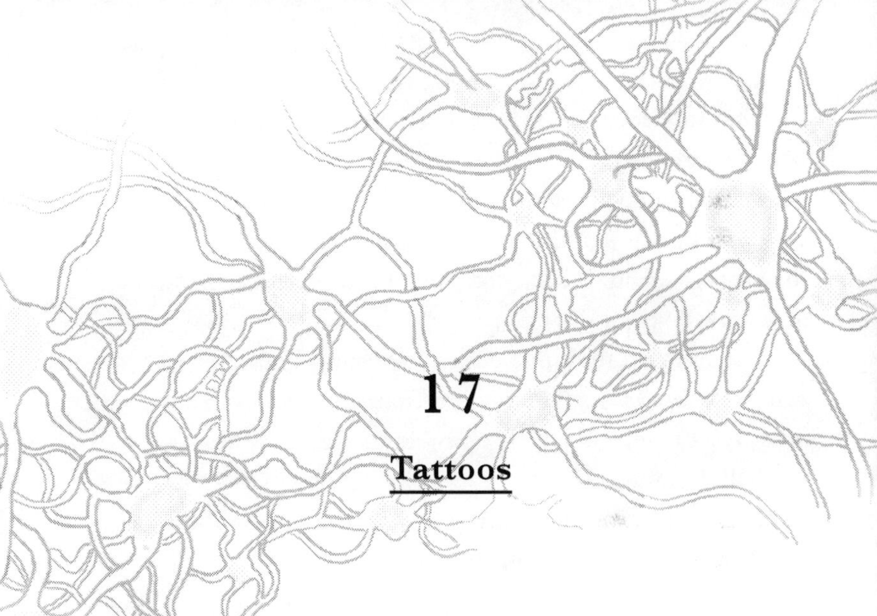

17

Tattoos

It had to have been weeks since the Wacko leader, Danny, removed Maddy from her cell and placed her in one of Wacko Headquarters' dorm rooms—which had become a prison itself. Less torturous, yes, but a guard stood outside the door at all times, and like before, she was brought food rather than permitted access to the cafeteria. Unlike before, it wasn't the mysterious silhouette, carving time out of his day to feed her, but one of the apathetic guards, shoving food into her room without a word of acknowledgement.

Though many would have gone mad, it wasn't the *worst* possible scenario for Maddy. Compared to Zeela, Avner, and Jamad, she'd always been somewhat of a loner, content to dwell in solitude. Someone had deposited books in the room for her, which she quite enjoyed, and now that those nasty manacles didn't confine her, she was free to stretch and practice her Affinity. That was why, when a raucous commotion sparked in the hallway outside her room, she was mildly annoyed.

She was rereading a fiction novel when voices sounded beyond her door, too muffled by the thick metal for her to distinguish. A body then thudded against that metal and shouts filled the corridor, seeping through the plain gray walls. After placing her book on the nightstand, she padded barefoot from her bed to the door and peeked into the hall.

The girl with the bumblebee-yellow hair who had stood watch now lay limp on the floor, her nose oozing blood. Her assailants had fled, likely through the open elevator shaft at the far end of the hall, from which banging reverberated.

It couldn't have been Zeela and the guys, could it? Surely they wouldn't have knocked out this Wacko and then fled without checking the room for her…unless they thought she was down in the cells.

There was no time to ponder these concerns before the second elevator on the opposite end of the corridor slid open, revealing a man in a dark, preppy sweater. She'd never seen his austere facial structure or ash-colored eyes, but his lengthy stature and familiar gait marked him as the mysterious silhouette who had fed her in the dark for a month: Zach, Danny's brother.

Realizing how incriminating this scene looked, Maddy rapidly opened her mouth to defend her innocence, but he spoke first.

"Come, now."

"I—I didn't do it, I swear!"

"Come *now*," he repeated, those light gray eyes glancing back toward the open elevator with apprehension.

"But…I—"

"Have you showered today?" he asked, taking a careful step closer.

"I—what? Yes?"

With a wrinkle of his nose, Zach grabbed her arm and pulled

her toward the elevator he'd come from, his grip so loose that he probably wanted her to wiggle free. She let him guide her along, almost disappointed when the elevator doors sealed them in and he hastily dropped her.

"I didn't see anything!" she blurted out as the elevator jolted upward. "I don't know what happened."

"I do." His eyes remained fixed on the silver doors, as lusterless and pale as his hair—a color too withered for his age. Though his face betrayed no signs of degeneration and she was certain he could be no older than twenty-five, he exuded an aura of sophistication and sagacity that made her feel like a child.

The elevator halted one floor up, but instead of exiting through the doors they'd entered, Zach rotated and punched a few numbers into the keypad, opening a hidden door on the opposite side. Maddy had seen Danny do this a few weeks ago when he'd brought her from her dorm to his office for the *initiation ceremony*, but she was baffled to know it worked in the upper levels as well.

"Am I in trouble?" she asked before he could step through the secret threshold.

Glancing at her from the corner of his eye, he ominously said, "You will be if you don't follow me."

Fearing the door would close behind him, she scurried after him into a room as grand as Danny's, though with far more objects filling the space. The left side was the definition of pristine: sheets immaculately white, dressers dustless and shiny, and every personal accent organized and positioned at the perfect angle. The right side was exactly the opposite: black bedding unmade, dressers open with clothes flowing over the brim, and every item strewn in a disorderly fashion. Zach's face morphed with disgust at the sight.

"Messy roommate?" Maddy guessed, earning a snort from him.

"That's an understatement."

When he didn't elaborate, she gingerly strolled to the uncleanly side, studying the sparkly ebony hairbrush, harsh eyeliner, fishnet tights, and leather skirt in a heap on the floor. "Female roommate?" she asked without thinking, blushing at her own nosiness.

Zach, thankfully, was far less perturbed, his lips twitching slightly as he said, "Not like that."

Nodding to hide her shame, Maddy hugged her torso and avoided his eyes. "So…um…are we waiting for Danny?"

"We came up here to hide from Danny." Zach shifted in place but refused to leave the clean side of the room. "There were some…escapees a few minutes ago. My brother will be angry with Alyssa for letting them get by her."

"Alyssa…the guard outside my room?"

He nodded grimly. "I didn't want you to have to listen."

Although she'd only interacted with the Wacko leader twice, she knew him well enough to understand the implication of that statement. "Will he be…angry with you for removing me from my room?"

"Danny's focus is acute. He'll be too busy worrying about this issue to care. It seems likely that, given the escapees know our location, we'll have to relocate by tomorrow. The government could come for us."

"Do you think they would risk it…with Danny's Affinity? They must know his capabilities…"

"Perhaps."

"You don't seem nervous about it," she stated, studying his pensive expression. "Do you have faith that Danny will save the Wackos, or…or do you not care if we're discovered?"

"We," Zach repeated, closing his eyes to absorb the weight of that word. "My father never would have forced an Affinity to join us. Danny…is a different breed. Can I see it?"

"See what?"

"The tattoo. I know Josh gave one to you. There's no other reason Danny would have released him from his cell after…what he did."

"Oh. Oh, yes, he did." Uncurling her arms, she pulled up the sleeves of her sweater, exposing an intricate design of thick, woven lines. They spiraled and intertwined in a hue of orange much paler than her tan skin, extending farther than she could lift her sleeves. "They cut off at my shoulders, but Danny said one day…he wants them to cover my entire body. For now, he said this is fine."

Zach's rage was well contained but undeniably present. "Have they healed?" She nodded. "Do they bother you when you use your Affinity?"

"No, they just look…strange when my skin stretches. Do you…do you have tattoos to symbolize that you're a Wacko?"

"You don't want to see them."

"I do," she insisted much too quickly. "I mean…I won't judge or scorn you. It seems like you had as little choice in this fate as I did."

"You don't want to see them." That she didn't flinch or apologize made him exhale a bit of his frustration. "It'll be late before my brother is through with his rampage. If you have no aversion for filthiness, you're welcome to sleep in my…roommate's bed."

Maddy smiled softly, knowing the offer was reluctant but appreciating it anyway. "Thanks."

"Just…don't come on this side of the room," he warned, eyeing the empty middle part as if there were a literal line drawn there.

She hadn't encountered a boy afraid of cooties since kindergarten, but she was keenly aware that wasn't Zach's predicament; it had been impossible to forget about his cleaning Affinity—and that he'd defied it by willingly feeding her all those weeks when she was too disgusting to tolerate even her own grime.

"I won't," she assured him. The physical distance was well worth the emotional intimacy his faint smirk established.

Despite his previous sentiments, Avner had not been ready to run miles. None of the former prisoners, with their atrophied muscles and encumbering wounds, had been.

The two Regg guards trailing them hadn't stood after slipping on Jamad's ice. When Naretha lifted their limps heads, she found their eyes impaled by broken glass. Still, she and Jamad ensured they were dead in other ways. Avner hadn't had the breath to scold them—or the will.

Their jogging pace soon lulled into a trudge as they traveled across the open fields, passing through farms and avoiding major roads. Even if the researchers at the compound had died, it wouldn't be long before the government discovered what happened and started a search for the escaped Affinities.

At dusk, the group collectively decided to rest in a wooded area, where the sporadic whoosh of a passing car could be heard from the nearby roads. Many people collapsed against trees, panting heavily, but Naretha, who had used Avner and Zeela as crutches throughout the journey, flopped directly onto the leaf-ridden ground, staring up at the barren trees and darkening sky as if dead.

"We can't stay here long," she moaned as others skirted around her, seeking spots for themselves. "Judging by the highways we've passed, we must be only a two-hour drive from Cleveland."

"Cool," Jamad said as he gently placed Meredith against a tree, "but we don't have a car."

Naretha inclined her head to shoot him a withering look as he plopped onto the ground beside the girl. She had been too weak to walk for the last hour, and Avner had admired his friend's strength and selflessness when he'd scooped her into his arms. He'd then siphoned the coldness from her body, thwarting the chilly air from depleting the last of her energy, and Avner knew he would have offered the girl his clothes, too, if he had any. While none of them had been adequately prepared for this journey, most wearing t-shirts and rubbing their arms, Jamad and Meredith were certainly the most scantily dressed, both in only their undergarments.

"We all have superpowers, Snowman," the Wacko droned. "I'm sure one of us can steal a car."

"We aren't stealing any more cars." Avner crossed his arms and glowered down at her. "And we aren't going to the Wacko hideout. We can't bring a group this size there—it'll draw attention."

"Danny would be more than pleased to have some new recruits."

Irritated and pointedly ignoring her, Avner continued, "We need to get the rest of these people to safety."

"And where is safety?"

"Periculand."

Naretha barked out a laugh as she strained to sit upright and look him in the eye. Even though they'd been in her company for weeks now, Avner still shied away from those pale pink eyes, knowing the violence her scowl promised.

"We are *not* going back to Periculand. You're a fugitive, I'm a terrorist, and Angor practically works for the government. When they hear that we've gone there seeking refuge, we'll end up in another cell, not to mention that, if Angor *does* help us, the government might be pissed enough to shut down the whole town and take all of *them* as test subjects, too. Do you really want to damn them all? Do you really want to damn your sister?"

The possible validity of her words gnawed at him, but he kept his expression rigid and his doubt concealed. "Angor wouldn't let that happen. He's not a saint, but his life goal has always been to protect Affinities—"

"As has Danny's. None of these people will be harmed if we go to Wacko Headquarters. That's where I'm going, whether you're coming or not. At this point, we're about halfway between both locations, so it's your choice, Sparky. It's everyone's choice," she said, her elevated voice quieting the murmurs and the shuffling. "You can go to Wacko Headquarters, where you'll fight for our freedom—fight against the people who did this to us—or you can go hide in Periculand, secured behind those walls, waiting for the day the government invades."

"That's a little biased," Avner retorted, hating the way her speech riveted the rest of the group. "Periculand is a safe place. Not everyone wants violence."

"It doesn't matter what we want, Av," Jamad interjected, idly forming icicles on his fingertips. "The government's gonna give us violence either way. Periculand won't keep us safe after what we did. We made our choice the day we broke Naretha out. We're Wackos now."

The Wacko's lips spread with manic delight, but Avner shook his head in revulsion.

"How can you *say* that, J? Do you—do you *want* to be a terrorist? Do you *want* to kill people?"

"Already have, Av." Jamad's shrug was light, but the iciness in those blue eyes was severe. "And so have you."

Schooling his features into neutrality was a feat for Avner.

That jab cut deep, digging up the guilt he'd spent the last few hours burying. The Starks were dead because of him. Whether they were consumed by the flames, the smoke, or even starvation, they would perish, and one day Avner would have to look Seth and Tray in the eye, knowing what he'd stolen from them. Jamad hadn't known the Starks, and he had the right to be bitter against Reggs, but his total apathy toward their deaths… Avner couldn't be swayed into his friend's line of thinking—and he couldn't stand to join a group of terrorists who aimed to tear more families apart.

"I started this quest to save Maddy," Avner began, his glare unflinching, "and I *will* save her—but first I owe safety to these people. I owe them a chance at a better life—one unmarred by violence. So, whoever wants to go to Periculand, I will take them."

A few appeared relieved, but others, like Charlie, still glanced toward Naretha expectantly. Avner didn't care about that; if Charlie wanted to join the Wackos, fine. What mattered was the decision of the person standing beside him, hugging her arms and staring into the trees with that ominous white eye. When he gradually shifted his gaze to her, she refused to look in his direction.

"Give me an hour," Naretha said to the people looking to her for guidance. "Once my energy's replenished, we'll steal some cars."

"I can lay some ice on the pavement—get the cars to slip enough that they have to stop. Then we ambush them, and *you*," Jamad said, pointing to the lady with the morphing fingers, who was propped against a tree, still out of breath. "You can unlock the car doors."

The old lady nodded, completely unopposed to joining the Wackos. Avner's jaw clenched as he watched his friend take charge of this group with such ease.

"Hey, what's your name, by the way?" Jamad asked the woman as her powder-yellow eyes peered at him through the dark.

"You can call me *Key Fingers*," she replied with a mischievous little grin.

Jamad scrunched his nose. "I'm not calling you that—that's weird. What's your real name?"

"Bethel."

"Oh… Maybe I should call you Key Fingers."

"I've heard of Key Fingers, the jewel thief," Naretha mused with an appreciative glance at the woman. "Nice work. Stealing from rich Reggs has always been a hobby of mine."

"That's how I got caught by those experimenters," the woman admitted bitterly, shaking her head at the memory. "They stole all my stolen jewels, those bastards."

"All the more reason to join our cause," Naretha sang with a spiteful smirk in Avner's direction. "Can you see the nearest road?" she asked Zeela.

"Yes. I can lead you to—"

"Z," Avner interrupted, his voice cautious despite his astonishment. This was what he'd dreaded, but he hadn't seriously thought… "You…*want* to help them?"

She bit her lip but wouldn't fully look at him. "Av…"

"You can't seriously—" The awkwardness of her expression stopped him. She would go with them whether he approved or not; it wasn't his decision to make. He didn't want to control her—to dictate her decisions—but they had always looked to each other for reassurance, and now…

"We still have to save Maddy," she said quietly, decidedly, "and you know we can't go back."

He knew, but he couldn't say he knew. Periculand would be the only safe place for these people—these innocent Affinities who didn't want to get involved in a terrorist group. He had to believe Angor would accept *them*, even if the principal didn't accept *him*.

"I'm sorry," was all Avner could think to say, but he wasn't quite sure what he was sorry for. The list was endless, and that he chose to walk away in that moment rather than persuade her to his cause was only an added offense.

He couldn't just stand there and listen to them plan their villainous journey to Wacko Headquarters, though. Not when it had been so clear that Jamad's intentions were no longer to save Maddy. Not when Zeela would accompany them and, perhaps, join them. Without Avner around, what would stop her? She had never been immoral, but the Reggs had tortured them—they'd carved out her *eye*. Of course she would want revenge—hell, *Avner* wanted revenge, too.

The Wackos promised vengeance, just as they promised destruction. Would Zeela know where to draw the line between justice and cruelty? He didn't seem to; he always stopped too soon, always let the bad guys get away. If those experimenters hadn't died—if they stood before him right now—would he punish them for what they'd done to Zeela, or would he shy away from that responsibility to preserve his conscience?

It wasn't until someone grabbed his arm that he realized how far from the group he'd trekked. When he spun around to face Zeela, he could barely see the pack of resting Affinities beyond her.

"Avner," she said, tentatively lowering her hand, "I know you think Periculand is the right option, but what if we go there and put our sisters in danger? I don't want Eliana to get hurt. I *want* to find Maddy. And now that we've seen what the Reggs are capable of…the Wackos might be good allies."

"Z," he blurted out, bemusedly appalled.

"Naretha's given me more information that leads me to believe they're not wholly evil—the root of their cause isn't, anyway. If we…joined them, we could help their morality… But I'm just speculating," she added, brows creased in a manner of disorientation that was uncommon for her. "Are you really so angry at me?"

"No, I'm not." He swallowed, knowing his demeanor should have been tranquil enough for her to distinguish. "Can you…not tell how I'm feeling?"

Closing her eye, face contorting with pain, Zeela said, "I can't see auras anymore, Avner. When they removed my left eye, that ability went with it. And your features… You're just a blob of heat and bones now."

"You can't tell me apart from…anyone else?"

"Barely," she admitted guiltily. "Your voice, obviously, but… all of the unique and creative aspects of you that my eyesight formed before are gone. I'm sorry."

"No, Zeela"—he squeezed her shoulders—"*I'm* sorry. I shouldn't have let them do this to you. I should have found a way… You said before that you could see the sedatives in Naretha's blood. How?"

"I don't know. I can see…strange things now—biological and chemical things. When the scientists…removed my eye, they said something about how the right hemisphere of the brain was connected to my left eye. Since the right hemisphere is the creative side, it must have been what allowed me to see more definitive shapes and emotions. Now all I have is the left hemisphere controlling my right eye, the logical side that allows me to view what is concrete and objective."

He stroked his hand along her cheek, savoring the feel of her skin. "This doesn't change you, Z—this doesn't change who you are. You're still powerful and you're still valuable. If I need to express my emotions in more obvious ways, I will. You know I'll do anything for you."

"Will you travel to the Wackos with me?" she asked, encasing his hand in hers.

"I can't join a group that seeks to demolish all Reggs," he said softly. "There are good Reggs, even if many of the ones we've encountered were bad. The Starks…"

"That wasn't your fault. You didn't put them down there, and you couldn't have broken them free without risking yourself. The fire…I saw it—it was an accident. If you want to return to Periculand just to apologize to the Stark twins…save it, Avner. Save it for when we can be guaranteed safety. I don't want you to become a prisoner again—ever again."

"It just doesn't make sense," he sighed, finally pulling away to rub his hand over his stubbly head. "I know Tray's gotten letters from his mom. How would that be possible if she's been locked up?"

"Maybe they were captured recently. We don't know how long we were stuck down there. It could have been a while."

"Well, then the other issue is *why* would the Starks be captives of Regg researchers? They were Reggs themselves. Richard was a journalist, and Linda…I can't remember what she did… Regardless, they were a nice couple. Unless the government captured them because of their sons, I don't see their purpose there."

"Naretha said the Wacko leader wanted them dead," Zeela reminded him. "If they were targets of the Wackos, they must have been more than just ordinary Reggs."

"Maybe…it *would* be a good idea to go to Wacko Headquarters then—figure out why the leader wanted the Starks."

Zeela's eye brightened as her lips quirked upward. "So, you'll come?"

His cheek twitched, but he knew she couldn't see his uncertainty. "We'll go back to the group and see what they want. If there are people who want to go to Periculand..."

"You don't even know how to get there from here. The Wackos will know how to get there. They broke in, remember?"

"Considering that incident is the reason we're here, I can't really forget. C'mon." He wrapped his arm around her to guide her back toward the others. Resting her head on his shoulder, she nestled into him, and he realized how utterly exhausted he was.

"I want a bed."

"For?" she mused, tilting her head up to him.

"For sleeping...and possibly other activities..."

She opened her mouth, likely to make a frisky quip, but then dread washed over her face as her eye caught something in the distance. "There's a group of people...coming for our group!"

Avner halted immediately, disentangling himself from her. Though the sound of the forest hadn't altered, he believed in Zeela's vision enough not to question her before breaking into a sprint.

Naretha wasn't really surprised when Avner marched away in a temper tantrum. After only a few weeks of being acquainted with the kid, she was well aware of how self-righteously pissy he could get. He'd broken her out of jail with the intent of bringing her to Wacko Headquarters; at what point had he realized that plan didn't align with his morals?

Danny would be pleased if she brought back a horde of new Affinities, but she doubted, despite the power of Avner's Affinity, that her leader would want such an annoying little wimp associated with the rise of his empire. If Avner convinced Zeela to accompany him on his suicide mission to Periculand, though...

"Zeela's not the type to blindly follow her boyfriend," Jamad assured Naretha, as if reading her thoughts. She *had* watched Zeela trek after Avner through the woods with a bit too much concern, but it still irked her that Jamad read her so well.

Grunting, she flopped onto her back again. "No pun intended?"

"Well, no, that was a bit of a pun. I don't think Z would have followed Avner if she was still completely blind—but I don't think she'll go with him back to Periculand anyway. She'll come with us. Z and I have done everything together since we were kids."

"Since you *were* kids? What do you consider yourself now?"

"Har, har, you're *hilarious*." Jamad's sarcastic attitude fizzled when Avner and Zeela abruptly returned, the couple skidding to a stop before they would have stampeded over Naretha's face.

"People are coming," Avner panted, and she might have thought this was some ruse if Zeela's lone eye weren't staring into the distance with the same level of panic. With curses rolling off her tongue, Naretha sprung to her feet. "There's only four of them, but if they're Reggs…we need to run."

"If they're Reggs, we need to fight and kill them," Jamad said as he stood.

"None of us are strong right now, J, and those suits—"

"Let's *move*," Zeela prompted, her eye still trained on their invisible opposition. "I'll guide the group away from them, in case they're coming from multiple angles."

"I'll stick behind to distract them," Avner volunteered. None of the hastily scrambling Affinities seemed to value his bravery, but Naretha did groan.

"Dammit. That means I have to, or I'm gonna look like a weak pansy." Shaking her right arm, which was partially numb and struggling to regain its functionality after that tranquilizer dart, she glanced toward Jamad. "Snowman?"

"Obviously I'm staying for the action."

"All right, then. Everyone else, come *now*," Zeela demanded as she motioned for the others to hurry ahead.

The elderly Affinities were so freaking *slow*, most bumbling past Naretha like a slushy river of uselessness. Why she would sacrifice herself for these blobs was beyond her. She considered using one as a human shield—especially when gunfire cracked through the air.

Bodies dropped, just like they had in that underground compound, and those fleeing screamed and cried as they stumbled through the trees. Naretha spared only a glance back to make sure Zeela hadn't been shot before blasting salt crystals toward the attackers. Jamad and Avner joined with their Affinities, but the gunshots had been too jarring for any of them to hit a proper target. Salt collided with bark, ice froze a tree trunk, and lightning struck wood, sparking another fire.

The blaze illuminated the four figures darting toward them, none wearing Affinity-proof suits. That fact was seemingly all Jamad needed to know before he launched a stream of icicles at them. Though all four gunmen were stabbed, the brunt of the ice collided with the closest man, and he moaned with rage before collapsing into a pile of leaves.

There was no time for Naretha or Avner to build on that attack; gunfire had resumed, and it ripped through trees, forcing her to fall to her belly in an attempt to remain unscathed. Jamad had found a tree to hide behind, while incompetent Meredith, who hadn't managed to run away, huddled behind a bush, sobbing into her knees. Naretha was about to signal a plan to Avner, lying on the ground only a few paces away, but his attention was focused beyond them—on Zeela, whose right arm had been grazed by a bullet.

"Zeela!" Hastily, he crawled through the leaves toward her. Wobbling, she wilted against the nearest tree, probably too dazed and shocked to hear his voice.

Knowing he would go to Zeela's aid, Naretha prepared to defend them—but then a pair of stubby hands grabbed Avner and threw him against a tree, hindering his crawl.

Swearing under her breath, Naretha clambered across the ground until she reached Zeela. The girl's eye rolled within its socket and blood oozed from her arm like a waterfall.

"You need to run *now*." Naretha yanked her up. "They're dragging the boys away. I'm gonna try to save them, but you need to—"

"No," Zeela croaked, trembling. "I'm not leaving them."

Naretha grabbed her jaw, silencing her. "The day we crashed the car into the river, I could have fled—I could have left you to drown and gone to Cleveland on my own. But I decided that day that I was going to protect you, and if you don't run now, that decision will have been pointless. *Go*."

Her words seemed to awaken her sense of rationality. The last time they'd been in this situation, Zeela hadn't fought or fled when the Reggs imprisoned them, but this time, Naretha needed her to evade capture. This time, Naretha needed her to save them.

As Zeela disappeared into the darkness, Naretha allowed herself a moment to stand straight and exhale in relief. Her arm was still wonky, but she was determined to use all her might to destroy these assholes. Before she could spin and shower them with barrage of salt, though, one of the assailants was upon her, his empty hand at her throat and his gun at her forehead.

When her vision finally focused beyond the gun, she saw it was the same guy Jamad had knocked down with ice shards. His coat was thick enough that the sharp ice hadn't punctured any organs, but blood seeped through the fabric and cuts littered the dark skin of his face. The only features Naretha really took note of were his mauve eyes and matching hair.

"Affinity," she breathed, but he'd pivoted his head toward where his three companions had her three companions locked in similar positions. None of the attackers were particularly old, all likely in their twenties or thirties, but they were clearly skilled in combat. Naretha knew that, with how untrained Avner and Jamad were, and with how utterly useless Meredith was, they would stand no chance against the guns.

"This one's female," the man holding Naretha announced.

"One female over here, too," the woman atop Meredith replied.

"Should we kill the males?" the man restraining Avner asked. He was shorter and pudgier than the others, and his gun trembled slightly against Avner's forehead. He was the weak link, Naretha decided, and possibly their ticket out of this situation.

"No, you idiot, they're Affinities," Naretha's captor snapped. "We take them all."

"Neither of these girls are the one he's looking for," the woman said with a knowing look.

"No one's gonna catch her—you've heard the stories. We take these four back to the house. They must be worth something."

"I've been told I have a personality worth a million bucks," Jamad bragged, provoking his captor to tighten his grip.

"Who on this Earth could ever think such a thing?" Naretha droned, rolling her eyes when the man dug his gun into her forehead.

"Okay, so it was my dad, and given what he did, I don't give a shit about his opinion anymore, but—"

"Enough," the woman snarled as she hoisted Meredith

upright. Tears smeared the girl's face, and her hair was embedded with twigs, but luckily her sobbing had ceased. "Let's get back to the road."

Avner was the only captive who remained silent throughout the trek up to the highway. Meredith hiccupped every time she tripped over a root, Jamad yapped nervously about his hobbies and life goals, and Naretha grumbled at him to shut up. She was so annoyed by these teenagers that she was almost relieved when they reached the shoulder of the highway, where the kidnappers' van resided.

Her satisfaction abated when she recognized the model of this black van—the model Ephraim Mayer had always preferred his subordinates to use.

"You're Wackos," Naretha said as Avner was thrown into the back of the van.

"That does seem to be our official name now," the woman mumbled as she rounded the vehicle to take the driver's seat.

A laugh escaped Naretha's lips as vindictive glee settled. "I was wondering how long it would take for Danny to send out a search party to find me."

The man with the pale purple hair whipped her around and threw her against the van's side. "So, you are one of the females who recently escaped?"

"Escaped?" Naretha repeated, unfazed by the aggression. "Escaped Periculand, you mean?"

"No…escaped Headquarters."

"Someone escaped Headquarters? A prisoner?"

"Three girls," the woman affirmed from her seat in the van. "Broke out earlier this evening. That's who we've been looking for."

"But you escaped from Periculand," the man pinning her down stated, his gaze suspicious. "Who are you?"

"You don't recognize me?" she drawled with a pompous air. "My hair wasn't *that* long before. If you truly are Wackos, you're gonna eat nuclear waste when Danny finds out how poorly you've treated me."

The man pointed his gun at her again as she reached for her shirt, but when she pulled it up to reveal the trail of pink salt crystals tattooed on the skin beneath her breasts, he staggered back in disbelief.

"Does she have a bomb?" the woman asked in alarm as the other men gathered around Naretha, guns raised.

"No." The purple-eyed man swallowed as his companions lowered their weapons with the same amount of reverence. "Devika… she's Naretha Salone. She's Danny's girlfriend."

18

Investigation and Infatuation

Tray thought super strength would have made him immune to pain, but Nero's unrelenting grip still sent pangs up his arm. Their pace back to the school's campus was rushed, and though the older boy had said nothing, Tray noted the way his dark eyes peeked at the basket of booze with delight. Why the Reggs had allowed this underage brute to carry it was beyond him.

At this point, Tray didn't really care about Nero's intentions with the beer; his brain was working through the ways in which he could inconspicuously talk to Calder. With eight hours of training and four hours of work almost every day, Tray hadn't had an opportunity to trade new information with his secret ally—especially since the Reggs now treated him and Nero like their personal guard dogs. Adara hadn't been wrong about that.

Planning to "help" Calder deposit Seth in his room once they arrived at the Residence Tower, Tray let his mind and posture relax—until Nero unexpectedly jerked him along. Instead of stumbling and plummeting to the pavement, Tray took this opportunity to execute a more immediate plan by yanking back. The ease with which the weight succumbed to his will surprised him—and it surprised Nero as well, because he did nothing to stop the basket from flying out of his hands, bottles spilling onto the sidewalk.

"What the hell, Stark!" He shoved Tray violently before rushing to retrieve the rolling bottles. Seth was equally as panicked, his languid state converting into one of despair as he flopped to the ground to rescue the beer.

"What was that about, primie?" Calder demanded, stepping toward Tray with the aggression of a challenge. The water he summoned formed so quickly that Tray barely had time to feel a hint of fear.

"Don't!" he blurted out, gawking at the orb suspended before his face.

Calder's lips curled with malice, but the way he side-glanced at his master was enough to assure Tray that this was an act. "I'll take care of him," Calder told Nero. Even though his Affinity made him physically superior, Tray felt frail and powerless when the blue-haired boy snatched his arm and hauled him toward the Residence Tower.

"You'd better," Nero grumbled from where he crawled around, gathering the beer bottles. Tray hoped the bully and his brother would bond enough over their love for booze that Seth wouldn't receive a beating for his twin's recklessness.

"Way to be subtle," Calder muttered, his gaze fixed on the campus ahead. The three surrounding buildings appeared completely dormant, but a few windows were lit throughout the tower, indicating students were still awake. What could they possibly be doing at this late hour without being required to obtain knowledge? Normal teenagers weren't intellectually advanced enough to study unprompted.

Calder pinched Tray's arm then, dragging him out of his self-aggrandizing thoughts. "Focus, Stark."

"I—am focused," he stammered, shaking his arm lightly. "You can let go now."

"No, I can't. It won't take long for Nero to follow us. He can't think I'm showing you mercy. You're lucky he's not bright enough to realize what your little stunt was about."

"He's definitely catching on to the fact that you've been visiting Adara," Tray retorted, remembering the warning Nero had given Adara upon their departure from the police station.

"I haven't been visiting her." Calder must have known how lame his voice sounded, because he quickly diverted the subject. "What have you discovered?"

"Not enough," Tray admitted with a frustrated exhale. "Eliana hasn't been able to gather anything from anyone's mind. But... Nero *should* know Angor's Affinity."

Nearly halting in his tracks, Calder's grip tightened on Tray's arm. "Of course he should." He rubbed his forehead in self-reprimand. "How the hell did I forget about that? Nero always used to get punished by Angor. He would never say what Periculy did to him, though..."

"Yeah, well, now he doesn't remember. Either Angor blocked it with his mind controlling Affinity...or Artemis did. Even though Eliana's fairly certain it's the latter, I still can't decide. Now that I'm thinking about it, though...it would be hard to torture someone with just a mind controlling Affinity."

"Not too hard," Calder said darkly, his face set in rumination. "I haven't felt Artemis trying to control my mind, but I'm not sure it's the type of thing one *would* notice..."

"We also think there's a Wacko in town."

"Well yeah, genius, there are three, if you didn't just notice—"

"No, someone who's been here, feeding them information. Someone who gave them Hastings's room number."

Calder's strides did falter this time, and his following swears rivaled Adara's in vulgarity. "We're *screwed.* Any leads?"

"No. If anything…I would think it was one of your groupies."

He licked his lips, but the lack of a refute indicated he knew Tray was right. "I'll consult my roommate tomorrow. If anyone here is a Wacko, he'll know." Tray wasn't really sure what that meant, but he nodded regardless. "Any other cheery news, primie?" Calder asked, tugging him toward the tower's glass doors with the newfound irritation their predicament had spurred.

"No, nothing—except I don't think I missed us being allies these past two weeks," Tray grunted, prying Calder's fingers from his aching arm.

"We still are allies." His tone was strong and firm, but his fingers were no match for super strength; by the time they reached the base of the tower, Tray had completely removed them. "Until this is over, we have to be."

"Until what is over?" he questioned, but the way Calder violently shoved him into the lounge—a show for any late-night spectators—was answer enough.

Until the conflicts in this town were solved. Until the conflicts in this world were solved. Until Calder Mardurus could stop pretending to be a bad guy.

"This place is like a futuristic *heaven*," the girl named Naira gushed as her eyes, like medium-hued pink carnations, roved Periculand's buildings. Since Ackerly saw the campus every day, he spent most of their walk focused on the girl named Ashna. She'd covered her hair with her knit hat again, but he couldn't pry the image of that mesmerizing rainbow from his mind. There was no flower he could compare it to—none that grew naturally, at least. He knew enough about girls to acknowledge that staring was creepy, but…it was so hard not to.

Thankfully, Ashna seemed too preoccupied with observing the town to notice. Still, her attention remained partially on him, one hand splayed and slightly inclined in his direction to keep his wrist from aching. Part of him wanted to reach out and hold that hand…but that was silly—stupid. He'd just met this girl, and though he'd been piqued with Adara upon their parting, she'd been right: They had to be cautious of these three.

"Don't get too comfortable here," Fraco snipped at Naira, his suspicion unrestrained. "The Rosses have not yet decided if they wish for you to stay."

The girl ignored him as she ogled the hospital, heightening Fraco's displeasure. At the Reggs' command, the vice principal had retrieved the girls from the police station, but he obviously was not pleased to have been woken up at this hour of night. Ackerly wasn't even sure what time it was; all perception had escaped him in that bathroom. He shuddered at the thought of the vomit.

"Are you in pain?" Ashna whispered, noticing his tremble. "Should we stop here, at the hospital?"

"Uh—no, no…I'm fine." Lamely, he displayed his limp wrist, which didn't help his claim of being fine. "The nurse's office is on campus. He can heal anything quick… You're—um, doing a good job of reducing the pain… Thanks."

She smiled faintly, drawing his gaze to her face, which was marred with a few scrapes he hadn't noticed before. Now that they walked beside each other, he realized she wasn't as young as he'd first perceived. Between Cath and Naira, she'd appeared childishly small, but she was only a few inches shorter than Ackerly, certainly at least in her teens. He wanted to ask her about her age, but Fraco spoke before he could open his mouth.

"There is one vacant room on the first floor of the tower," he announced, referencing his clipboard. "There are only two beds, but…you may break one, anyway." His shiny eyes slivered at Cath, who appeared undisturbed by his comment.

"I don't like beds," she said with a shrug. "Too small."

"What floor are you on?" Ashna asked Ackerly.

With her inquisitive eyes trained on him, he could barely manage to say, "Three."

"I want to be on his floor," she told Fraco, who bristled at the demand in her tone. "We don't know anyone else here. We don't want to sleep among strangers."

"I realize you must be accustomed to hostility amongst Affinities, but here in Periculand, everyone is perfectly—"

"I want to be near…" She paused, looking to Ackerly. His jaw dropped in momentary bafflement, but then he understood she wanted his name.

"A-A-Ackerly."

"Ackerly," she repeated, nodding at him before turning her requesting eyes to Fraco. "Are there any vacant rooms on the third floor?"

"Well," the man began in defeat, "with Miss Stromer's absence and Miss Belven's relocation, there is a vacant spot in Lavisa Dispus's room… And with…the recent loss, there is a vacant spot in Seth Stark's room—but we do not permit co-ed rooming!"

"Who's Seth Stark?" Naira asked, still glancing back at the hospital.

"The—uh…drunk one," Ackerly informed her awkwardly.

This knowledge amplified Fraco's alarm, but he barely spluttered a sound before Naira said, "Ooh, I'll take that room! He seems entertaining."

"We do not permit co-ed rooming—"

"Do you have a roommate?" Ashna asked Ackerly, pointedly disregarding the greasy man.

"I, er—yeah. Tray…Seth's twin—the…temperamental twin."

Ashna's lips quirked in understanding. "Ah… Well, if he doesn't care, I wouldn't mind joining the two of you…until we trust more people here, at least. I can take the mattress from the room Cath's in, since she won't need it."

"If you didn't hear me, girl, I *said* no co-ed rooming—"

"I don't think Tray will mind," Ackerly assured Ashna, whose shy smile brought heat to his cheeks. Though his words were true, what he neglected to say was that Tray would probably approve of this arrangement solely because he would want to keep an eye on these new arrivals.

"Yes, well, *I* mind, and *I* am vice principal—"

"How far are we from the nurse's office?" Ashna questioned, squinting at the campus buildings. Regg guards were positioned around the perimeter, all wearing those Affinity-proof suits. Ackerly was disheartened to see Tray's device had worn off and left the guards acting as if nothing had transpired.

"It's right over here." He pointed to the Physicals Building with his uninjured hand.

Fraco continued spluttering about the impropriety of co-ed rooming, but Ashna gave him an airy wave before cutting away from the group with a vague, "See you later." Ackerly had to skip to catch up with her, carefully avoiding a glance back in the direction of the fuming vice principal. "That man is obnoxious," she muttered as they followed the path toward the Physicals Building. "Is he always like that, or only because he thinks we're Wackos?"

"Always," Ackerly confirmed, peeking over his shoulder to see Fraco ranting to Naira and Cath, all bound for the Residence Tower.

"Hm. So…" Licking her lips, she stared up at the cloudy night. "Why's your girlfriend in jail?"

"G-girlfriend? Adara? No—no, she's not…we're not—"

Ashna's eyebrows perked. "Why else would she be so defensive at the thought of us walking to the nurse's office together? If you're not dating, she must have a crush on you."

"Adara? No—she…" Ackerly paused. Adara's crush on Seth was blaringly obvious, but he still felt it wasn't his secret to tell. "She thinks of me as a brother, I think…a little brother, probably. Or a pet."

"A pet?" Ashna repeated with a laugh. "That's quite a romance you have going on."

"Adara's not the romantic type—especially not toward me. It's more like…she feels the need to protect me."

"Do you need protecting?"

Ackerly winced, his lips shifting as he contemplated. "Probably, yeah."

Instead of pitying him like he'd expected, her lips broke into an exuberant grin. "You acknowledge your weaknesses—I like that. Most people don't. The first step to improvement is acknowledging the problem."

Ackerly tried to smile, but he didn't feel quite as optimistic. "I don't really think it's a problem I can fix. Most people here have…combative Affinities—Affinities they can use to defend themselves. I'm just good with plants."

"Don't say it like it's a bad thing. I—" She halted her words, and while it might have been a sign of awkwardness for Ackerly, he'd picked up on her speech patterns enough to know this was a unintentional pause, as if she had to rework the sentence she'd hastily started. "I like plants. If you're willing to practice, they can be used as a defense."

"I…well…it probably sounds lame, but…I don't know if I'd want to use my plants as a defense. I'd feel guilty if…if a plant died to protect me."

They slowed as they approached the double doors of the Physicals Building, and when they did reach it, Ashna placed her hand on one of the handles, blocking Ackerly from immediately entering. He nearly bumped into her, but she met his eyes, unflinching, despite their proximity.

"I don't think it's lame. I think it's humane—compassionate—and I haven't seen much of that in a long time."

Ackerly swallowed, eyeing the bruise that ringed her throat. It wasn't the type of wound that could have been inflicted on their journey here to verify their claims of imprisonment; it was damage that had been forged over time—weeks, months, or possibly years. A scar that might never heal. Ackerly had never been tortured; the worst he had suffered was the near drowning experience Calder had inflicted. For him, it was impossible to fathom such prolonged pain. Did she even feel it anymore? Had her Affinity formed because of her time with the Wackos? He wasn't sure he wanted to know. Luckily, the opportunity to inquire fled as she opened the door, gesturing for him to enter.

"Thanks," he mumbled as he scurried in. The white-walled corridor was dimly lit at night, but he could see the door to the nurse's office to the right, light streaming through the cracks. "This is…um—where we do our training—in this building, I mean." He nodded jerkily toward the left hall, where the gymnasium loomed. "Hopefully they'll let you stick around long enough to join."

"The two people who run this school..." Ashna started as she followed Ackerly. "They're not Affinities?"

"No...uh, Angor, the guy with the pink hair in jail—he used to run this school, and he built this town, but he was involved with a...scandal a few weeks ago."

"A murder?" Ashna clarified with a knowing twitch of her lips. "I heard things at the Wacko hideout about Hastings's death... But it was Angor?"

"So everyone thinks... We're investigating."

"You are?"

Ackerly blushed faintly as they reached the nurse's door. "Yeah... Me and Tray and a few others... We're not totally convinced it was Angor."

"Who do you think it was?"

He bit his lip, recognizing the extent of her curiosity. This girl wasn't dumb and certainly knew more than she let on. But how much did she know about Periculand—about Angor and the Reggs and everything that went on here? How much *should* she know? Tray would definitely not be pleased with Ackerly if he filled her in on the entirety of their investigation.

Lying did not come easily to him, but he played off his nervousness as innocent awkwardness and shrugged. "We're...not sure yet."

There was skepticism in her eyes—enough that he knew she didn't believe him—but she didn't press the issue before they entered the nurse's office.

No injured students occupied the two beds tonight, but the nurse, Jason Pane, was awake, seated at his desk and rubbing his wrinkly forehead as he studied some files. Upon their arrival, the man's head popped up and he forced a smile, his purple eyes weary. Although Ackerly had always linked the color of the nurse's hair to that of clematis, now he could only think of the bruise on Ashna's neck when he looked at it.

"Good evening, Ackerly," the nurse exhaled, but as soon as his gaze locked onto Ashna, he stiffened. "I've certainly never seen you before… A new civilian?"

"Something like that," she answered with a sheepish shrug. "Ackerly hurt his wrist—fractured it, I think. I've been blocking the pain, but that can only help for so long."

"Blocking the pain?" Jason stood from his chair. "How?"

"It's my Affinity," she said, sounding almost reluctant.

"You can inhibit nociceptors?" the nurse clarified, but he seemed far too puzzled by his own words.

Ackerly couldn't pinpoint why this ability baffled the man so greatly. "Um…yeah…we think so, anyway. It would make sense, wouldn't it?"

Jason's brow remained creased. "Yes, yes, it does… Shall I heal your wrist, Ackerly?"

"Oh, um…yes, please."

Adara had cried out in pain when the nurse healed her nose a few months ago, but as he encased Ackerly's hand in his now, the boy didn't even feel the bones fuse back into their proper state. It wasn't until Jason gently dropped his hand that any sensation returned, and even then it was an ache so dull it could have been general soreness.

"Thanks," Ackerly said, eyes darting between both Jason and Ashna.

"Do you want me to heal your…injuries?" the nurse asked, carefully studying the cuts and bruises that stained the girl's skin.

Her eyes bulged at the request, her demeanor shifting into

that innocent terror that had characterized her in the jail cell. "No—no, thank you. I…can ward off the pain. I don't mind; it's good practice."

The nurse seemed to accept her reason for trepidation as genuine, but Ackerly couldn't. The way she'd said it was too inarticulate—too hasty and choppy—to be the truth.

"Thanks," he repeated to the nurse, waving his newly mended hand before stumbling to the exit. Ashna followed, scratching at her knit hat with clear discomfort, though Ackerly doubted it was physical discomfort. Something about Jason's request had unsettled her; once they departed the office, however, she dispelled the unease with a sigh.

"Sorry, I just…" She trailed off, wringing her hands before stealing a glance at him. "I don't like to be touched. I haven't retained many positive outcomes from physical contact in…a while."

"Oh." Having assumed more nefarious explanations, Ackerly's gut swelled with guilt. "I'm…sorry. I don't really know what that's like…"

"It's okay," she assured him, and he knew the kindness in her tone was sincere. "I'm glad you don't."

"Periculand is a safe place," he said, feeling almost like Fraco as the words spewed from his mouth. "We'll make sure you can stay. We'll make sure the Wackos never get you again." The guilt in his gut was assuaged with a flutter of lightness when Ashna's pale lips curved with appreciation.

"Thank you."

19

Escapees

Zeela knew why Naretha had wanted her to flee the scene rather than become a captive: so she would find a way to rescue them. It was what she should have done when the Reggs stormed Jamad's house, and the regret she harbored from that incident was the only reason she'd agreed to abandoning them this time. But, even though she'd been confident she would be able to track them with her restored eyesight, she had failed—again.

After catching up with Charlie in the woods and encouraging him to keep moving with the rest of the group, she'd sprinted back to where she'd left her friends, prepared to attack the Reggs with stealth—and a measly stick she'd picked up along the way. When she arrived, though, the Reggs had already hauled them off, Avner, Jamad, Naretha, and Meredith all captured and gone. She'd tracked their forms up the hill to the highway, but by the time she'd reached the road, the vehicle had disappeared even from her sight.

Frustrated and furious, she ran back down the hill, weaving

through the trees, which she saw clearly with her altered Affinity. They probably still appeared different in her eyes than anyone else's, but with the newfound ability to view organic matter with such clarity, trees and other vegetation were intricate and vibrant objects rather than the obscure blobs she was accustomed to. By the time she finally caught up with the group, they'd lagged to a dull trudge, hearts beating violently in their chests. A few screamed at the sight of her, perhaps fearful that she had been one of the Reggs, but after a moment the commotion died down.

It was impossible for her to discern which of this group might be the man with the magnetic Affinity, Charlie, given every human in her sight was merely a figure of heat, flesh, and bone with little to distinguish one from the other. With a sigh of defeat, she said to no one in particular, "The Reggs got away with four of our group members."

Saddened gasps filled her ears. A few of the whispers sounded relieved, though, as if they were grateful her friends had been captured instead of themselves. If she could tell which ones reacted in such a manner, she would have gladly speared them with her stick.

"Your friends?" a voice asked, and judging by the vocals, it was Charlie. He must have been the figure sidling next to her, though it was impossible to tell what feelings he bore at this news.

"Yes. I couldn't catch up in time. There's no telling where they'll take them." The weight of her words sunk in, as painful as the resumed throbbing of her right arm. The bullet grazing her skin had been initially jarring, but the haze of pain had rapidly been replaced with panic when the reality of the situation settled. Now the leaking gash was nothing more than an aching nuisance, the loss of blood so trivial compared to the loss of her friends.

Charlie placed a hand on her left shoulder. She couldn't see his aura, but she felt the soothing vibe he exuded. "I'm sorry. I'll help you look for them, but…we need to do something about these people first."

Zeela rubbed her forehead, resisting the urge to glare at these random strangers for whom she was now responsible. Why was it her duty to help these people? Some of them were *glad* Avner and Jamad had been taken. Her focus should have been on saving her friends, not these heaps of flesh and bone that meant nothing to her. But…if Avner were here, he'd want to help them. That had been his desire before he'd been apprehended, and if Zeela couldn't rescue him, she could at least do what he would have done.

"We'll travel to Periculand," she decided somewhat reluctantly. "Angor won't refuse innocent Affinities. You'll all be safe there." Pausing, she pivoted her head to Charlie and spoke in a quieter tone. "If Angor Periculy imprisons me, I need you to do all that you can to save Avner… Please."

His head bobbed in earnest agreement. "Of course. You and your friends are the only reason we made it out of that hellhole."

"Thank you," she whispered, returning his gesture of a pat on the shoulder. "We should get moving now, in case the Reggs come back. Plus, I want to make sure we have time to take a detour on the way."

"This van is dope," Jamad said, admiring the high-tech computers and gadgets that clung to the interior. There were no seats, so he, Avner, Naretha, and Meredith sat with their backs to the rear doors, Meredith gripping Jamad every time the van hit a pothole. Normally, such a clingy girl might have annoyed him, but there was something about the idea of Meredith thinking of him as her hero that Jamad was fond of.

"Much cooler than Periculand's vans," he continued, noting

Naretha's eye roll. "What, Salty? I'm appreciating *your* terrorist organization. You should be thrill—"

"Don't call her that," one of the Wackos snapped, glaring at Jamad with his tomato-red eyes. Seated cross-legged before one of the computer screens, he was the only one of the four who had opted to sit in the rear of the van with them, but Jamad doubted it was because he *wanted* to. There were only three spots on the front bench, after all, and this guy, with his pudgy fingers flying over the various keyboards, seemed to be the designated back-seater.

"What? Terrorist? I wasn't saying it like an insult, man. It's just a fact."

"No, *Salty*." He glanced briefly at Jamad in nervous offense. "You shouldn't call her names."

"It's an affectionate nickname."

"She doesn't seem to be very affectionate of you."

Naretha snickered from where she was wedged between the corner and Avner. "For a computer nerd, you can really read people, huh?"

The guy's cheeks burned as vibrantly red as his floppy hair. As he toggled through various windows on the computer screen, an image caught Jamad's eye that had him bolting upright.

"Go back," he commanded, crawling across the floor to get a closer look at the computer.

The guy shielded it with his body like a bear defending her cubs. "Get back in your spot. You're still a captive—"

"No, he's not," the woman intoned from the driver's seat. "Are you watching porn again, Kevin?"

"*No*! I-I—"

Too distracted by his own spluttering, the guy, Kevin, didn't notice when Jamad slipped beside him and tapped a few keys, bringing the screen back to the picture that had sparked his interest—the picture of *Naretha.* Her pale pink eyes were narrowed, as usual, but her pixie-cut hair was styled more fashionably than Jamad had ever seen, and she wore an elegant black gown.

"What are you—a Wacko celebrity? Princess of the Wackos?" Jamad joked before receiving a withering glare from Naretha.

"You took a picture of me at last year's gala?" Her raised eyebrows set Kevin into an embarrassed state of panic.

"I-I—well, I took pictures of everyone—"

"Even creepier," she noted, smirking faintly when he tried to stutter an explanation.

Jamad resumed his seat between Meredith and Avner. "What gala?"

"Ephraim liked to hold a gala every year at one of his mansions, where all of the Wackos—back then, Affinities for Freedom—could unite."

"Sounds a little reckless. Didn't the government ever find out?"

Naretha shrugged as she rotated a thick crystal of salt between her fingers. "Probably. There was never anything they could do about it, though, considering how easily we could annihilate them. Now, though, with those suits…"

"With what suits?" one of the men asked, rotating his head of sandy hair to face them. He clearly wasn't a natural blond, since his warm brown skin was nearly as dark as Jamad's. His equally beige eyes indicated his features had morphed with the development of his Affinity.

"The Reggs have Affinity-proof suits now," Naretha explained.

"Bullshit…"

"Don't accuse her of lying, Vishal," Kevin defended, though he immediately cowered when the guy in the front shot him a murderous scowl.

"There's no way the Reggs have that kind of technology," Vishal insisted. "Where did you hear of these suits?"

"I didn't *hear* of them; I saw them with my freakin' eyes, asshole. The Reggs have suits that can't be penetrated by my salt, or his ice"—she jabbed her thumb toward Jamad—"or his electricity"—she nodded toward Avner—"or any Affinity. We experienced this technology when we were *prisoners* of the Regg researchers—just a few hours ago, if you were looking for a specific time."

Kevin's eyes bulged. "You got stuck in one of the Reggs' labs—and you escaped?"

"No, I died there."

For a moment, the guy looked unsure as to whether her tone was sarcastic. Jamad would have laughed if the tension in the van weren't so severe. Vishal, despite Naretha's explanation, still eyed her skeptically.

"It's rare that anyone manages to escape a research facility, especially without outside help."

"Yeah, well, it's also rare that anyone manages to sleep with the leader of the Wackos, but here I am." Naretha's smile was so perfectly patronizing that Jamad had to chuckle now.

"Oh, pulling out the Wacko Princess card," he sang, clapping deliberately to agitate Vishal. "Do we *not* look like we could have just escaped from a research facility? I'm not wearing clothes, dude. Zeela's *eye*—" He paused, realizing Zeela wasn't here.

She'd managed to "escape," but now they weren't even captives. Part of him wanted to ask the woman to turn around, so they could retrieve the other Affinities, but Avner's strange silence stopped him. If he wanted Zeela in this van, he would have said something before it started moving. Even though Jamad thought his friend was being a self-righteous prick, he had to respect his wishes to keep Zeela out of trouble.

"We're all practically bald," Jamad decided to say, tapping his fuzzy head. "We didn't get buzz cuts to match."

"She has hair," Vishal huffed, nodding toward Meredith. She swallowed under his scrutiny, hugging her skinny legs.

"Because she was at the facility long enough for it to grow back," Jamad retorted. "We're Affinities just like you, man. Why don't you believe us?"

"Because we've had *Affinities just like you* sneak into our ranks as government spies. We can't blindly trust everyone."

"Drop it," Naretha warned Jamad, her jaw tight. "We'll clear this all up once we get to Headquarters. Have you alerted Danny of our impending arrival? He's not a fan of surprises."

"I don't think he'll really be a fan of *anything* right now," the woman muttered, shaking her head. "We're not going to Headquarters tonight. Best to let Danny's wrath settle—"

"What do you mean we aren't going to Headquarters tonight?" Naretha ground out, leaning forward aggressively.

"We told you there were three escapees." The driver twirled her dark green hair through her fingers with unease. "Danny is… not pleased. He blew up a police station."

"Mm, shame I missed it," Naretha hummed, tapping her fingers on her kneecap. "Danny will calm down if you bring me to him, so stop being babies and let's go."

Vishal ignored her demands and asked, "Where is the Reggs' research lab located?"

"I'll give the approximate location to Danny when we reach Headquarters."

The other guy in the front seat sighed and didn't even bother pivoting his purple-haired head when he said, "Headquarters is probably compromised." Though he'd been fairly chill about his near-death by ice, Jamad was still leery, waiting for the man to exact his retribution.

Judging by Naretha's harsh tone, she had no fear of enraging him. "Why would Headquarters be compromised?"

"Because three people escaped," Vishal snarled, as if he'd said it fifty times. To be fair, they had reiterated this fact quite a few times, but Naretha seemed convinced it was irrelevant.

"There's no way they would remember the exact location. Most of the houses on the lake look the sa—"

"These weren't ordinary prisoners. It's likely all of our Ohio locations—possibly even our locations in other states—will be compromised. We're headed back to our house now to purge it of any evidence."

"What prisoner would know all of our locations?" Naretha demanded. "Did Danny imprison Josh for leaving me behind? Good riddance if he did, but making Josh an enemy was a poor choice."

"We did hear that Josh was locked up, but he didn't escape," the woman said. Through the rearview mirror, Jamad saw the disquiet in her forest-green eyes.

"Then *who*?"

Exchanging a look, Vishal shook his head at the woman, but she bit her lip and then blurted out, "Ashna."

That one word drained all the fury building in Naretha. Her face blanched and she stared ahead with such stillness that Jamad worried she'd gone into shock.

"Who's Ashna?" he asked tentatively. Mostly, he posed the question to see if he could elicit a reaction from Naretha and break her out of her state of stupefaction.

It was obvious enough that this *Ashna* was an extremely powerful Affinity—one with vast knowledge of the Wackos' whereabouts—but the way Naretha answered sent an unsettling chill down Jamad's spine, a sensation that was becoming abominably familiar.

"Our doom."

20

New Acquaintances and Old Enemies

The first thing Seth noted when he awoke in a state of grogginess was that his sweatshirt reeked of vomit. The second thing he noted, through the hazy morning light of his dormitory's window, was a lump beneath the blankets of Hastings's bed.

For a moment, he was content, thinking everything was normal—that Hastings was sleeping late, as usual, and that he would get up and get ready without his roommate even stirring—but then the body in the bed did stir, and reality smacked Seth in the face. Hastings was dead, and someone was sleeping in his bed.

After scrambling out of his blankets, Seth found shoes on his feet. How had he gotten here? They'd visited Adara at the police station…and he had consumed quite a bit of alcohol in quite a short time… The rest was blurry. He did recall puking into a toilet with Ackerly, and he was fairly certain he'd revealed some outlandishly embarrassing details about Adara's childhood to the kid. After that…Wackos—they'd met three Wackos. One of them, he realized, as the sheets of Hastings's bed shifted, was in his room.

He shouldn't have been panicked. A *super strength* Affinity dwelled somewhere within him, after all, and if this Wacko attempted to murder him, he'd be ready. As the girl finally shimmied out of the blankets and squinted open her peachy eyes, though, he came to the conclusion that she was harmless—and hot.

In a weathered volleyball sweatshirt with her rosy-bronze hair contained in a chaotic bun, she looked like she'd climbed out of a garbage can. Everything about her was so far from Kiki's style and elegance. She reminded him of…Adara…but she wasn't Adara—she wasn't his sister. A grin spread across his lips.

"Good morning."

"Good morning," she mumbled, face scrunched in befuddlement. Rubbing her forehead, she stumbled out of bed, revealing that, beneath her baggy sweatshirt, her legs were bare. "Where's Cath? Did she go to breakfast?"

Seth averted his gaze and stared at the ceiling. "Uh…you're not wearing pants."

From the corner of his eye, he noticed her glance down and wince. "Oh. I'm not. I didn't think you would wake up."

"*Ever*?"

"Well, not for a *while*. You were *not* doing well last night, my friend… Damn, I forgot where I was. Can't believe we made it to Periculand." Her eyes cut toward him and she awkwardly said, "I'll put on my pants."

"Thank you," he sighed, rolling off his bed. "I mean, I have no *problem* with nude girls, but I don't want to be labeled a perv."

"Mm, how gentlemanly of you." After a few moments of shuffling, Seth spun around to see her wearing a pair of Hastings's purple cargo pants. "You are *skinny*. These fit me perfectly…" Her gaze flew up to him, and when she surveyed his legs, she frowned. "There's no way in hell you fit in these. Whose pants am I wearing?"

"My..." Seth scratched the back of his head. "Dead roommate's."

"Oh. Oh... Would it be offensive if I didn't take them off?"

Seth pondered a second and then shrugged. "As long as you don't tell Eliana where you got them, you should be good. Are you a Mental?"

"That's a rude question. Do I seem insane to you?"

"What? Oh—no, I meant are you in the Mental class...of Affinities?" he added, his eyebrows wrinkling when she continued staring at him. "You don't know about the three classes of Affinities? I don't pay attention in class and even I know that."

Her lips quirked as she crossed her arms. "Enlighten me."

"Well, uh, if you want the technicalities, you'll have to ask my brother, but basically there's Mental, Physical, and Natural. The Mentals wear purple"—he nodded toward her pants—"and the Physicals wear orange." He picked up a pair of his orange cargo pants. "I'm a Physical."

"And each represents a type of Affinity. I see... So, what's yours?"

"My..."

"Affinity."

"Oh." He shook out his hair, hoping his bedhead wasn't too atrocious. He'd never cared much about his appearance before, even around Kiki, but the way this girl examined him was nerve-wracking. "I...don't know."

She nodded, unsurprised by his answer, but *he* was surprised by his answer. He'd meant to tell her he had super strength, like he told everyone—like he told *himself*—but those three words had come out instead. Did he really not know his Affinity? He'd been so convinced he had super strength, but *Tray* was stronger than him.

"Don't tell my friends," he said, rather than retracting his previous statement. "They…believe I have super strength. They all probably think I'm incompetent. I don't want them to see me as *completely* useless."

"Well now, *completely* useless is a bit of an overstatement. You are particularly skilled at getting drunk, from what I saw last night."

Seth grimaced, glancing at her long enough to spot the cut on her cheek. Vaguely, he recollected noticing it last night. "Who's Danny?"

Her smile was humorless. "Ah, you remember that. You were very determined to receive a response. Danny's the leader of the Wackos."

"And you?"

"I…" She hesitated just long enough for Seth to wonder if the rest of her reply would be truthful. "I'm not a Wacko—definitely not. They're…awful. And if I'm not allowed to stay here, they'll find a way to kill me—and Cath and maybe Ashna." Slipping on her boots, she switched to a less dreary topic. "Is there a cafeteria at this school? I'm famished."

"You—like to eat?"

"Of course I like to eat. Those cheap Wackos were so conservative about rations… I need fuel if I'm expected to exert any physical energy."

"The Reggs recently cut back on our food, too," Seth admitted dejectedly, "but I'll take you down there. Just let me change out of this…pukey…thing."

Her returning giggle actually made Seth *blush*—so much that he had to turn around when undressing and wiggling into his school uniform. Though he couldn't see her, he was keenly aware of her eyes on his back; it made the immoral part of him wish he'd opted for being a pervert when she'd been unclothed—only so they would be even, of course.

"She wears the pants of the Mentals, yet she is not one."

Remaining neutral and not rolling his eyes proved an arduous task for Calder as his roommate pointed out irrelevant facts about every person who entered the cafeteria. When Calder had returned from his excursion to the police station the night before, Colton had been deep in the realms of sleep, unwilling to be bothered. As soon they'd awoken this morning, though, Calder immediately prompted him on what information needed to be discovered. Though he'd agreed, Colton, as usual, was obnoxiously difficult.

"What class is she in?" Calder droned, idly stirring his food around with a plastic fork. The portions had been noticeably smaller since the Reggs took over; luckily, they found his defensive capabilities useful enough that they didn't make him pay out of pocket for this unappetizing food.

"She is of the Natural class, but she is not aware this label has been placed on her," Colton narrated, his pine-colored eyes fixed on Naira, seeing more than an ordinary person ever would. "Within her dwells an Affinity for natural gases—and a budding attraction for Seth Stark."

"I know you're fond of romance, Col, but I've told you to leave it out of the reports. It's unnecessary and, frankly, obvious."

Colton didn't flinch at the harsh words; he simply continued staring ominously at Naira and Seth as they joined the other primaries. Tray was already seated at their typical table, his plain brown eyes darting back in Calder's direction every few minutes. Sometimes he wished he could throttle the kid or drown him again—this time long enough for the snooty know-it-all to start valuing his own life. If Nero saw them interacting...well, avoiding *that* was the reason Calder had decided to sit at a different table with Colton this morning. The few other secondaries at this table were quiet enough not to earn any negative attention from Big Boy.

Although, it wasn't like Nero was lucid enough to notice Calder's whereabouts, anyway. He probably could have started dancing atop the primaries' table, announcing his tentative alliance with them, and the brute would have been too dizzy to acknowledge it. To no one's surprise, Nero had utilized the confiscated alcohol for his own enjoyment last night, and now he sat beside Nixie, his face resting on the table as she lovingly rubbed his back.

"This romance would be insignificant, if not for the dire consequences it elicits," Colton continued in the voice that was the reason Calder was his only friend. Even his own cousin, Demira, could barely put up with his narration nonsense half the time. Over the past year, however, Calder had learned to admire his roommate's personality—and his Affinity for reading life like a book.

"Do these consequences have any effect on me or the fate of Affinities?" Calder questioned, studying Seth and Naira's interaction. Calder had kissed Naira in sixth grade. It wasn't an event that ever entered his consciousness, considering how many girls he'd kissed since then, and there wasn't a hint of emotion toward her lingering within him. Regardless, the way Colton met his eyes then made him wonder if one of his many childhood crushes could possibly influence his life now.

"The Demoness will awaken."

Calder stilled, clutching his plastic fork more intensely. Normally, he would have assumed the diction was merely part of Colton's theatrics, but the term was far too specific to be coincidental. "Repeat that again."

"Seth Stark's new infatuation with Naira Steele will spark the wick within Adara Stromer's chest. Her jealousy will consume her and all others with an eternal fire—"

"Okay, now I know you're being dramatic," Calder cut in, dropping his fork to cross his arms. "Why would Stromer even care?"

"Because Adara Stromer has been hopelessly in love with Seth Stark since the age of six. Even now, a small part of her wishes Seth would return her sentiments. His break up with Kiki Belven reignited that hope, but if he were to fall for—"

"How do you *know* all of this?" Calder's roommate's abilities had never shocked him before, but…this just couldn't be true. "How can you tell what Stromer feels from this distance?"

"Even if I could not view the Otherworld, I would know of Adara Stromer's obsession with Seth Stark. It's common knowledge."

Settling into a state of bitter chagrin, Calder decided he didn't want to know what else was considered common knowledge. "So, the Otherworld won't show you anything about Pericul y or Stromer from this distance? But…if you went to the police station…"

"The Otherworld would display all that is worthy," Colton affirmed with a nod.

Before Calder could inquire further, the cafeteria's doors opened again, this time for the ginormous girl who'd nearly demolished Nero. Puke-green hair flopped in jagged angles over her forehead, less messy than it had been at the police station last night but still considerably shorter than Calder's.

"Ah, Cath Clemens, commonly referred to as 'The Monster.' A body of steel but a heart as soft as freshly washed linens."

Calder rubbed his forehead in exasperation. "So, you're saying she's definitely not a Wacko?"

"The desire of her heart does not dwell with the Wackos."

"But whose *does*? Who here is conspiring with the Wackos? Who gave them Hastings's room number? You said you could figure it out."

"I could, yes, if that person were in this room."

"That's a start," Calder mumbled, surveying the cafeteria. Almost all the students were present, with the obvious exception of Adara, but none of the teachers had arrived yet.

"The deceiver draws near now…"

Calder straightened, searching frantically for anyone who could be the Wacko sympathizer. The doors hadn't opened, though, and no one had moved—except the girl sliding into the empty chair on his right.

"Pixie Prince," she greeted in a voice that wasn't quite right. Her hair was burgundy, but her face, though appealing, wasn't exactly Stromer's, and her orange cargo pants were a bit too baggy.

"The deceiver." Sighing, Calder shot Colton a wry glance. "You could have just said it was Dispus. Why are you here?" he added, turning back to Ruse, who grinned complacently. "And why do you have to look like an attractive female? It's disturbing."

"Oh, I'm not trying to look like an attractive female; I'm trying to perfect the Adara Stromer look. I have to keep it vague enough that no one *actually* thinks I'm her, of course—wouldn't want a repeat of last time. The Reggs still haven't sniffed me out."

"I'll make sure to tell them you're here if you don't tell me *why* you're here."

"Tray sent me. He wants an update on your progress."

"Hm, well, I want to drown him to death, but we can't all get what we want." Ruse blinked his reddish eyes, unsure of how to respond. Their hue was far less vibrant than Adara's, irritating Calder even further. "Tell Stark he needs to chill the hell out. That kid is so anal… No wonder he has no friends."

Calder glared at Tray, surrounded by the group of laughing primaries. The three new girls sat among them, and he noticed with a start that the small girl, Ashna, had *rainbow* hair that shimmered like a compact disc in sunlight. Calder was about to ask his roommate what such a unique color could imply, but Colton spoke first.

"Tray Stark actually has quite a few friends. More than you, if you'd like to compare…"

"Shut up," Calder grumbled, knowing it was true; Stark had a whole group of friends, but all he had was a group of asshole-ish allies he didn't even like. Calder might have been Colton's only friend, but Colton was also Calder's only friend. Shunning his self-pity, his gaze slid toward Ruse. "Tell Stark I'll find a way to communicate with him that doesn't involve you as a middleman."

"I'm actually a *wo*man right now, if you can't—"

"The sympathizer has entered," Colton intoned as the glass doors parted and admitted all of the teachers.

Calder swore loudly enough that the other secondaries at the table actually looked up at him. "Which one?" When Colton's brow furrowed, he urged, "Can you just show me?"

Though he was hesitant, he dipped his chin and then closed his eyes, transferring his sight to Calder's as they'd practiced for the past year. At first, Colton had been unable to show anyone the Otherworld, but now, for a few seconds, Calder could see what his friend saw.

Words and colors and *creatures* appeared throughout the cafeteria. "Ruse Dispus" was written above the shapeshifter's head, followed by a string of other titles and descriptions people had given him. A physical strain of green lingered between the Stark twins, even though their demeanors seemed otherwise affable. Above Nero floated a horde of grotesque winged creatures, their maws so close to Nixie that Calder would have jumped up to protect her if this weren't an illusion—a physical metaphor for the intangible secrets that drifted through reality.

When Calder finally composed himself, he honed in on the teachers now strolling to their usual table. He almost snickered when he saw the words "Mr. Grease" hovering above Fraco. Behind the vice principal, Aethelred chatted with Floretta, and Than walked between them. It was when Calder's vision locked onto the history teacher that something altered, jolting him out of the Otherworld.

Rearing back in his chair, he blinked and looked to Colton, who slowly pried his eyes open.

"Than," Calder breathed in disbelief.

His roommate nodded reluctantly, face contorted in a wince. "Than Floros, it appears, is an ally of the Wackos."

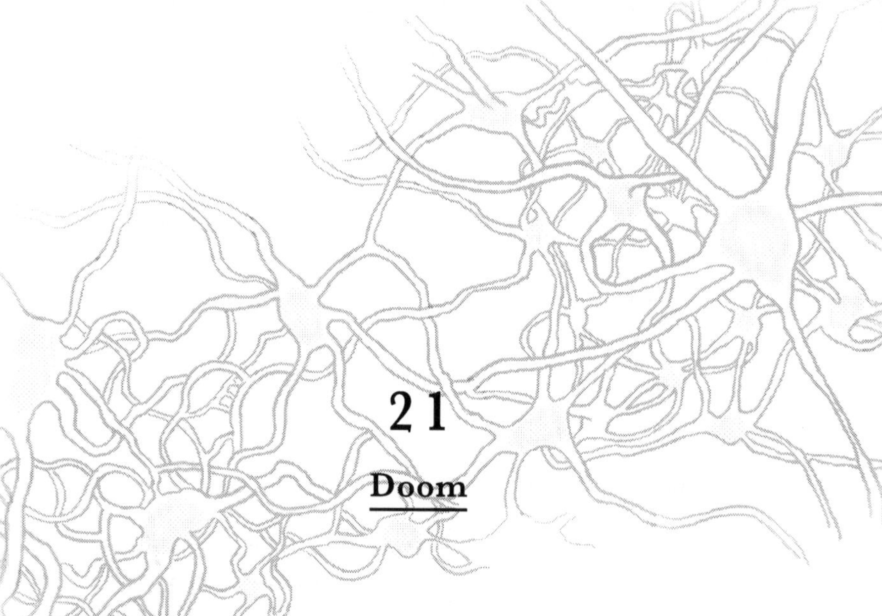

21

Doom

The sun rose as they arrived at the Wacko hideout, a small, ordinary house in the suburbs. Adults left for work, children hopped onto the school bus, and people jogged along the sidewalk, all completely unaware that a horde of Wackos dwelled in their neighborhood. Kevin, Vishal, and the other two, apparently named Devika and Nate, were skilled at keeping their identity a secret. They only exited the van once it was safely concealed within the garage and kept their blinds open enough not to draw suspicion but closed enough to hide their lives within. Danny would have approved.

What they were not so skilled at was efficiency, particularly in the area of packing their belongings under the pressure of possible compromise. An hour had passed since they'd pulled into the garage and they had yet to leave. Clearly, these four Wackos had a ton of shit to collect.

Naretha heard them banging things around in the upper level of the house, occasionally yelling obscenities at each other. None of that bothered her; what bothered her, as she slouched on one of the ratty old couches in the living room, was that Jamad wouldn't stop staring at her.

The kid had been gifted a hideous sweater of Kevin's, and Meredith wore some of Devika's clothing, so they weren't half-naked anymore, but Naretha would have rather endured Jamad's completely naked body than his cold, intrusive gaze for such a lengthy period of time.

"Our doom" hadn't been enough of an answer for the kid, unfortunately, but Naretha refused to divulge any details about Ashna beyond that. Jamad seemed enthusiastic about joining the Wackos, but he hadn't been initiated yet—he hadn't formally committed. Until then, he couldn't know the importance of that wretched girl.

The entire affair was still unfathomable to Naretha. Ashna had *escaped*. For Danny to let her out of his grasp—with all that she could do and all that she *knew*—something must have gone terribly wrong. It made sense that he would have dispatched every available Wacko to search for her, but Naretha knew it was futile. Ashna was too cunning to fall into his clutches now that she'd wiggled free.

Jamad couldn't know this, though—neither could Avner or creepy little Meredith, who was curled on the couch, dozing, as though they weren't on the brink of their demise. If Jamad knew the severity of this situation, he would never side with the Wackos—or Naretha. With Avner's incessant antagonism, she needed his best friend on her side.

That was why she'd remained silent over the last hour, enduring Jamad's relentless gaze from across the living room. Avner sat next to her, carefully positioned so he wouldn't come close to accidentally touching her. The kid rubbed his temples raw, likely thinking about Zeela. Naretha might have been concerned, as well, if they didn't have more pressing issues. She'd done her best to protect the girl, but now her own life was on the line, and her focus needed to be fixed on returning to Headquarters in one piece.

"If we're just going to sit here," Avner finally said, his voice barely a whisper, "can't we take the van and find Z?"

"You're into stealing cars *now*, are you?" Naretha mused. There was no humor left in the boy, though; his expression didn't change. "I was actually thinking the same—except I was thinking we take the van and boogie up to Cleveland instead of backtracking."

"And what—*leave Zeela*?" he snarled, inclining aggressively.

"A few hours ago, *you* were the one who didn't want her going to Headquarters."

"I didn't want *any* of us to go, but now, if we have to, we can at least go back for—"

"If we're going anywhere, I think we should go to a hospital," Jamad said, nodding toward the sleeping girl. "Her stomach is janked up."

"I would shoot salt up your nose if I wasn't aware that you don't realize how stupid you sound," Naretha said. "A hospital is the last place we should go. I suggested you treat the wound as soon as we got here."

"I don't know how to do that!"

"I'm not convinced there's anything you know how to do. When we arrive at Headquarters, a healer will fix her up. She's alive for now, so let it be."

"Fine...then we should go back and get Zeela," he concluded, and Naretha instinctively rolled her eyes.

"We don't even know where she is anymore. She could be halfway to Periculand by now—and we're not going anywhere near there. That place is a death trap. You heard what they said."

Avner sighed, this reminder certainly heightening his anxiety. The computer nerd, Kevin, had updated them about Periculand on the drive here: Hastings Lanio had been murdered by Angor Periculy; Periculy was in jail and the Regg ambassadors had taken over; Regg guards had infested the place; and Avner's little sister was a prisoner alongside Periculy for attacking people with her *fire Affinity*. If the kid weren't in such a rotten mood, Naretha would have given him an "I told you so."

"The fact that Periculand's a shithole only gives us more of a reason to retrieve Z." Jamad propped his legs up on the lopsided coffee table between the two couches. "If she goes in there, she's gonna end up in jail beside Angor and Adara."

Naretha jumped her eyebrows at Avner. "What a fun bonding experience that'll be for your girlfriend and your sister."

"This isn't *funny*."

"You don't have the right to tell Naretha what is and isn't funny," Kevin defended as he bumbled down the staircase against the left wall. Two backpacks were slung over his shoulders, and he clutched a heap of electronics in his arms. Naretha wasn't sure if they were gaming systems or equipment of actual use to the cause.

"I'm so glad to see you," she said, evoking an expression from him that crossed bewilderment and hopeless optimism. "Now I can threaten your life to get your companions to hurry the hell up."

"Uh...guys!" Kevin called up the stairwell as terror consumed his face. "Naretha's gonna kill me if you don't come down here!"

"Shut up, Kevin." Though the voice was muffled, Naretha was fairly sure it was sandy-haired Vishal—the one who was even more self-righteously pissy than Avner and acted like he owned the Wackos.

"They said they're on the way," Kevin lied, smiling like he

was holding in a turd. Naretha scowled at the peeling ceiling to prevent herself from assaulting him. "I'm—uh, gonna go put my stuff in the van…"

"Smart," was all she grunted before he scurried across the living room. Once he'd disappeared into the garage, Naretha nodded toward Meredith and said, "You should put her in the van, too."

"What are you gonna do?" Jamad asked when she stood from the couch and stretched her limbs. The numbness from the tranquilizer dart had worn off, and after so many weeks of motionlessness, she had a lot of energy to burn.

"I can't decide if I want to murder those fools upstairs or steal their van," Naretha contemplated as she lifted her hands above her head. Her nose scrunched as her own stench caught in her nostrils. "If I'd known those bastards were gonna take so freakin' long, I would have taken a shower."

"Yeah, I could really use a long, long bath," Jamad agreed, grimacing at his own armpits. Even though he was clothed, he hardly looked any less disheveled now than he had over the past few weeks. Stubble crusted his jaw as thick as the hair atop his head, and his blue eyes were drained. Arguably, Avner looked worse, given his yellow facial hair was pathetically patchy, but no one could beat Meredith with her grotesque wound that had already oozed blood onto her newly acquired garments.

"You could all use baths," the woman, Devika, chimed in as she sauntered down the stairs. Three bags were draped over her back, and she wielded a basket of files in her arms. "Why didn't you shower while you were waiting?"

Naretha had to remind herself that, technically, she didn't have the authority to harm other Wackos, otherwise these four would have received severe consequences. "We weren't aware we'd be sitting here for *an hour*. What the hell have you been doing? We need to *go*."

"My brother's being a prick up there. Vishal," she clarified as she strode through the living room. Naretha definitely believed they were siblings—the same brown skin tone, same athletic structure, and same place on her list of people she wished she could kill but couldn't.

"Well, he'd better get his act together before I rip his prick off. Snowman, take the girl out to the van," Naretha commanded before the Wacko could attempt to defend her brother. Wisely, Devika chose to escort Jamad to the garage as he hauled Meredith's frail form in his arms. Naretha spun toward Avner, who continuously massaged his temples. "Will you feel better if I let you electrocute that Vishal punk?"

"I'll feel better if you order these Wackos to help us find Zeela." His eyes lifted, the spark in them dead. He always tried to exude the maturity of an adult—and he *was* eighteen—but to Naretha he was still a kid, still naïve, and still under the impression that this world had something to offer him.

"I'll…see what I can do," she acquiesced. Avner's smile of relief had barely materialized when a bang reverberated from the front door.

The sound clearly dredged up the same memories for Avner that it did for Naretha, because the boy hopped up from the couch, primed for an attack. Although the door didn't fly off the hinges this time, the Reggs' entrance was as dramatic as it had been at Jamad's house with four soldiers stomping in, each wearing one of those goddamned suits. The moment the impenetrable obsidian material entered Naretha's sight, she knew they were screwed.

Without exchanging a word, she and Avner darted in the opposite direction, aimed for the garage. Bullets tore through the living room—real bullets that shredded the walls, exploded the couch's cushions, and ruptured the books on the shelves. By pure luck, neither Naretha's nor Avner's flesh ended up splattered among the ruins, and they rushed into the garage with only old wounds.

Naretha punched the button to open the garage door as soon as they entered. Jamad was nestled in the rear of the van with Meredith, and Devika hauled her belongings in beside them. There was no time to rearrange anyone's position.

"Start the car!" Naretha shouted as she slammed the door on Kevin, who was fiddling with something in the driver's seat. His jump of surprise was so delayed that she and Avner were already in the back of the van with the door shut when it happened.

"Wh-what?"

Patience abated, Naretha flopped over the seat to twist the key in the ignition. As she did, two guards bounded into the garage, guns spewing bullets at the van. Ephraim's preferred bulletproof design saved their asses.

"Oh-oh-oh!" Kevin spluttered, sounding like an averagely terrible pop song.

Knowing he would be useless, Naretha launched into the front seat and forced the car into reverse. The government vehicles parked in the short driveway, obstructing their path, should have deterred her, but they only heightened her zeal.

"*RAM THEM*!"

Without Kevin's foot on the brake or gas, the van crept out of the garage at a snail's pace, certainly not fast enough to inflict any damage. "I-I—don't know—They've never let me drive this thing before!"

"Really? *Really*? This bullshit again?"

Kevin could only gape, especially when she shimmied over

him, squeezing between his legs and the steering wheel, and then shoved him aside. Sprawled on the passenger's side, he slammed into the dashboard when she slammed on the gas pedal.

"Oh—oh my God—Naretha Salone was just in my lap..." Kevin was so close to swooning that he couldn't sit upright.

"What about Nate?" Devika demanded from the back. Naretha faced her direction but didn't acknowledge the other Wacko's expression of consternation as the van zoomed out of the garage, crashing into one of the government's cars. All six of them jolted with the impact, but Naretha plowed on, undeterred by the horde of soldiers falling into formation around them. "What about my brother? Are they—are they—"

"Shut *up!*" Naretha commanded, spinning the wheel to back around the cars blocking them. She smirked when a soldier's body thudded against the back door. And then she cursed when a few soldiers hopped onto the roof. "Is there *anything* any of you can do right now to improve our situation?"

"I-I—" Kevin screwed his eyes shut like he might let out the turd he'd been holding in earlier. Naretha was about to physically attack him for his incompetence when a clicking noise cut through the clamor, followed by shrieks from above.

"What the hell did you just do?" Naretha asked so quietly that she wasn't sure he'd heard.

"I activated the roof spikes," he breathed out as his red eyes flew open. "I've never gotten to use them before. That was fun."

Naretha had never heard of that feature on these vans, but she was definitely thankful for its existence. With newfound animation, she thrust the van backward again, plowing through bodies until it spun off the front lawn and onto the pavement. Her mirthful cackles overpowered the pinging of bullets against the vehicle's hull.

"K-Kevin," Devika prompted, rallying strength to her voice. "Detonate the bombs."

"B-but…Nate and Vishal…"

"*Do it*," she snarled, her voice wrought with remorse. As Kevin closed his eyes again, the house they'd spent an hour in erupted with deafening explosions of fire, sending the soldiers into a panic. It wasn't nearly as impressive as Danny's abilities, but it would erase the evidence and thwart these government hounds long enough for them to speed away.

Naretha paused for the briefest second when a wave of empathy overtook her. If confronted with the situation of killing those she considered family for the good of the Wackos, she would have done it as well, but it likely would have pained her as much as it did Kevin and Devika. They hid their tears well as the vehicle plunged forward.

"Here," Devika said from behind as Naretha wove through the neighborhood. Glancing back through the mirror, she saw the woman handing Avner what appeared to be a license plate. "We need to change the back plate so they can't track us."

"Me?" Avner said, incredulous. "You want *me* to do it?"

"No, I want you to hold my legs so I don't fly out of the van while *I* do it. I need you two to keep the doors propped open so they don't decapitate me."

Meredith made a pathetic little noise upon realizing the Wacko was addressing her, but Jamad eagerly scrambled to the back doors. Devika was about to open them when something landed on the roof with an abnormally gentle thump.

"That's either the biggest bird in history or a child," Naretha commented, beginning to cut the wheel hard to throw it off.

"Don't!" Devika exclaimed so abruptly that Naretha nearly drove them off the road. "Kev, pull up the roof cam."

With speedy fingers, he pried a computer screen out of the van's dashboard, which instantly displayed a view of the roof. Needle-sharp spikes blanketed the surface like a field of rigid grass, and two soldiers were skewered in them, droplets of blood flying in the wind. Perched on one of the men was a giant falcon, glowing like amethyst in the morning sunlight.

"What *is* that?" Avner peered over Naretha's shoulder to view the screen.

"Nate," Kevin breathed, eyes as wide as cherry tomatoes. Devika crawled toward the back doors, and before Naretha could protest, she thrust them open, permitting gusts of air and an oversized bird.

The wind drowned out Meredith's scream as the massive falcon landed in the rear of the van, its wingspan consuming half the space. All Naretha saw when she looked in the rearview mirror were purple feathers—until the feathers morphed, slowly shifting and dissolving until they were replaced with dark skin and the naked body of the Wacko they'd assumed dead.

"Well, shit, I didn't know he was a shapeshifter," Naretha said. "Why didn't you turn into a T-rex and devour all those Reggs?"

"Because—I've been shot," he coughed, and when Naretha squinted at the mirror, she saw that there was, indeed, blood gushing from his shoulder.

"Vishal..." Devika began, but Nate shook his head. "I'll...I'll change the plate...and then patch you—"

Avner must have picked up on the shakiness in her voice because he said, "I'll change the plate." Before he retreated to the back, Naretha grabbed his arm, careful to keep the van steady with her other hand.

"We can't go back for Zeela," she told him quietly. His yellow eyes remained calm and his mouth didn't open to object. "We'll go to Headquarters, regroup, get a new vehicle—and then we'll track her down."

"You…you'll help?"

Releasing his arm, she allowed her eyes to dart briefly from the road to his face. "You broke me out of Periculand…"

"For bargaining purposes."

"Yeah, well, I think we've both saved each other's asses enough times throughout this expedition that we can deem each other temporary allies. You've made it possible for me to return to my…boyfriend, so I'll make it possible for you to return to your girlfriend."

His bright yellow head nodded in the corner of her vision, and when she peeked at him, his caution had transformed into gratitude. Part of her wished she didn't have to lie—that she could help Avner seek out Zeela after they found safety—but she knew it couldn't happen. She was fond of Zeela, but there was too much at stake to worry about the fate of one girl. Plus, as proven when he willingly replaced the rear license plate, hopeful Avner would be more useful to the cause than satisfied Avner.

22

Deception and Perception

"Are you sure you're reading his brain right?" Seth asked, his knees digging into Tray's back as he leaned forward to look at Eliana. Since they'd entered the training gymnasium ten minutes ago, her focus had been fixed on Calder, who was apparently sending her mental messages. Tray couldn't believe the information Eliana had received, though—that Than Floros, the innocent history teacher, was a Wacko.

From where the primaries were clustered on the orange bleachers, they could see Than standing among the other teachers on the far side of the room, conversing amicably with Aethelred. Theoretically, it seemed plausible that Than was involved with the Wackos. He'd been alive for nearly three hundred years—there was no telling how many connections he could have made within the Affinity community. Considering he had hundreds of years left to live, he wouldn't want to spend them locked up by the government, which might have motivated him to join the terrorists.

Logically, though, it didn't add up. Than had never displayed any inclination toward violence; he didn't even seem to enjoy the new route training had taken with so much physical combat. Was that because he feared Periculand's Affinities would overthrow the Wackos, or was it because he feared the Wackos would demolish the students? The latter seemed to align with what Tray had observed thus far, but if they could verify this new evidence...

"Yes, I'm reading his brain right," Eliana mumbled, her voice nearly inaudible beneath Fraco's incessant snipping. With the principals absent from this morning's training, Fraco had been tasked with leading the exercise, which involved one partner ducking, rolling, and tackling the other partner's legs.

Nero and Calder demonstrated, as usual, and the bully was clearly hungover from the basket of booze the Rosses had unknowingly allowed him to consume the night before. Every time Nero attempted the tackle, Calder repeatedly drenched him, slowing him down and proving to everyone how futile these modes of combat were. Anyone with an Affinity that did not manifest physically, like many of the Mentals, would have no chance against someone with a power like Calder's. Even Nero, with his impressive super strength, couldn't thwart his smaller opponent.

Tray might have admired Calder's will to embarrass Nero so publicly if it didn't threaten to blow his cover. For weeks now, his mysterious resentment toward the brute had been apparent. If Nero discovered Calder held no loyalty for him, it would ruin their chances of him collecting information from the Rosses—as well as spark a civil war amongst the students. With the possibility of war outside of Periculand, they certainly didn't need one within.

"Are you sure his thoughts are clear?" Tray asked Eliana, glancing over his shoulder. She was wedged between Hartman and Kiki, brow scrunched as she employed her Affinity. The hue of her blue features had lightened considerably over the past few weeks, and with the way her Affinity had advanced, he didn't doubt her skills, but... *Than*? "He must be too focused on his demonstration with Nero to produce coherent thoughts."

Eliana bit her lip, briefly sliding her eyes toward Tray's. "Calder barely needs to focus to use his Affinity. If he weren't explaining this...situation to me, he'd probably be bored."

"I don't understand his roommate's Affinity." Tray stared at the mats as he contemplated. "How can this kid sense more than you?"

"His mind is...strange. He doesn't have any shields up, but I still can't read him. I can't read Than, either... He must have learned how to block mind readers over the past three hundred years."

"So, there's no way to confirm if it's true," Tray huffed, rubbing his forehead. They couldn't *ask* Than, and to inform the Rosses of their suspicion would mean jail time for Than whether he was guilty or not. He would end up in a cell with Angor, who Tray was progressively beginning to believe innocent, and Adara, which would be more like torture for the history teacher than punishment.

Adara... Tray had avoided any thoughts of her since their encounter the previous night. He'd almost admitted he *missed* her—but he didn't, not really. Everything had been miserable since her incarceration, but that had nothing to do with her absence; it had to do with Hastings's death and the Reggs' takeover and the fact that he didn't have any *homework* to fill his time. The only reason he wished Adara were here was because she was the only one who would be able to force the truth out of Calder—with her unruly fire Affinity, which would then destroy the whole town.

It was only a matter of time before she grew tired of imprisonment and burned her way out, Tray knew. Would Calder be powerful enough to douse her flames? He definitely seemed to have harnessed his Affinity well—better even than Nero, perhaps. Currently, Calder shoved a wave of water as the bully rolled, throwing his massive form across the mats until he lay flat on his back. Nero's ensuing snarl was intimidating enough that Ackerly actually jolted where he sat beside Tray.

"Mardurus." His growl rumbled through the gymnasium. Spitting, he pushed to his feet and slicked back his dripping gray hair. His white t-shirt was soaked through, clinging to the ridges of his bulging muscles in a way that almost made Tray fear for Calder's life.

The Pixie Prince, as Adara liked to call him, seemed entertained by Nero's wrath, though. With a flick of his wrist, he conjured all the water from the mats and from Nero, absorbing every droplet into his own skin. "Do you want our peers to think these lame moves are gonna save their asses from the Wackos?"

"Not everyone has an Affinity suited for combat, Mr. Mardurus!" Fraco shrilled, agreeing with Nero for once, albeit for different reasons. "Everyone must be trained to defend themselves!"

"Defend, sure," Calder said with a shrug, "but this is an offensive move. Why would we have Mentals jumping into battle when they're better suited for strategic positions?"

"Why would we have any teenagers fight in battles, is what he means to ask," Lavisa grumbled, her legs propped on the row of bleachers before them. Seated on Tray's left, he'd almost forgotten about her because she was so quiet. Today, she rubbed her forearms instead of picking her scabs, likely preparing for this drill. Tray agreed with her—and with Calder, for that matter—but the murderous gleam to Nero's eyes convinced him this little rebellion had to end.

"Can you tell Mardurus to quit it?" he asked Eliana. "He's drawing too much negative attention."

"Mind reading only works one way," was her cold reply.

"I'll handle this," Seth said before standing—and kneeing Tray's back in the process. "Hey, Fraco!" he called down to the vice principal, who bristled. Tray was almost certain he saw a vein bulge in the oily man's temple.

"Call me Mr.—"

"Yeah, okay, I know, but can we get this drill started? I'm dying to practice some Wacko-killing moves."

"Well, Mardurus, would you look at that?" Nero mused with a condescending smirk. "A normie wants to do this drill. If he can do it, anyone can."

"If your memory spans more than a minute, you'll remember you were the one who couldn't complete the drill, not me," Calder countered, his smile equally as patronizing.

"Oh *shit*!" Hartman blurted from his perch behind Tray. His stepbrother's nostrils flared as he prowled toward Calder. "They're about to throw down."

"Should I step in?" Seth asked, bouncing on his feet as Nero circled Calder.

Fraco shouted his typical, "Enough!" while all the other faculty members watched the scene with apprehensive eyes.

"No." Tray elbowed his brother's knee hard enough that Seth fell back onto the bleachers. "You'll get pulverized. Mardurus was foolish enough to bring this upon himself—he can deal with it."

Instead of dealing with it, though, Calder was spared from a beating when the gymnasium's doors opened.

"Ah, good, you're demonstrating," William said, observing his two student bodyguards with emotionless eyes. Miraculously, the Rosses' arrival had caused Nero to halt his predatory pacing and assume a docile demeanor. "Is the exercise nearly ready to be carried out, Fraco?"

"I-I—yes."

"Good," Artemis said, strutting in beside her husband. Though her enthusiasm was subdued, she actually seemed *gleeful.* Tray didn't have to wonder what could have ignited this kind of reaction from her, because the three new girls strolled in behind them, reminding him of their promise to divulge Wacko secrets.

Forming an opinion of these girls had proven a difficult task, given Tray didn't have much information to work with. Cath, the monster, was obviously the same person who had invaded Periculand two months ago, but although her footsteps vibrated the room, she'd displayed no signs of aggression. Not even her facial expressions were hostile.

The athletic one, Naira, was too much like Seth to be anything but authentic. Tray's brother wasn't capable of deception; if he said something, he believed it, even if it was false. If this girl claimed not to be a Wacko, she honestly believed she wasn't. The way she beamed at them as she approached was proof enough.

But Ashna... Tray had no idea what to think of Ashna. She'd slept in his dorm room last night, which had set him on edge... until she'd assuaged his pounding headache, unprompted. Could she really sense the activity of nociceptors with such ease? Headaches were even more complicated physiologically than other forms of pain, because there weren't any nociceptors directly in the brain and the source of the pain could form in multiple places—yet, she'd been able to decipher exactly what had caused his headache and had somehow prevented it. Would an untrustworthy person go through such trouble?

There was a sense of innocence about her but also a sense of shrewdness. She feigned timidity in large groups but then held an assertive air when necessary. Ackerly didn't see it—none of the others did—but Tray was determined to discover her ambitions.

"What's going on?" she asked as soon as she and her two companions reached the primaries' section of the bleachers. Subtle giddiness characterized them as Ashna slid next to Ackerly, Naira reclined next to Seth, and Cath plopped down beyond them, consuming two rows with her massive size.

"Nero and Calder are about to kill each other," Ackerly informed her, nodding to where the two boys still silently glared. The Rosses had assumed positions at the center of the mats, ending their demonstration so others could practice. "We're also worried that one of our teachers is a Wacko—"

"Ackerly," Tray hissed in immediate reprimand. "This can't be common knowledge."

"Which one?" Ashna asked, clearly alarmed. "Did you...overhear something?"

"No," Tray snapped before Ackerly could open his big mouth. Of course, now, when they had secrets to keep, the kid decided to stop being shy. "We're basing this knowledge off some freak who claims to see 'another world.' We can't come to any conclusions before we have solid evidence. Until then, we won't discuss it."

If Ashna was offended by his rudeness, she didn't show it—or perhaps she didn't have time to show it, because the teachers now rallied students onto the mats, and Than was the one ushering their group. All of them froze when the brown-eyed, brown-haired man stepped before them and awkwardly smiled.

"Break into pairs, if you will," he requested with a polite dip of his head. When he sauntered off to instruct another group of students, Ashna raised her iridescent eyebrows.

"That's the guy you think is a Wacko?"

"C-can you read minds?" Ackerly spluttered as pinkness crept into his cheeks.

"No..." she began, eyeing each of them warily, "but he didn't seem scary and you all seemed scared. I hope none of you plan to pursue a career in acting."

"I doubt any of us will have the opportunity to pursue a career at all," Kiki sighed, twirling her pinkish-blonde hair.

Since solidifying that her Affinity involved predicting the future, she'd been so ominously forlorn that Tray hardly recognized her personality anymore. She constantly stared into space not with blankness but with *pensiveness*, as if actual thoughts ran through her mind—deep, profound thoughts. Seemingly, she'd forfeited her quest for popularity, and Tray couldn't recall one nasty comment she'd directed toward him in over two weeks.

"Why is that?" Naira asked as she hopped down from bench to bench until she stood on the floor.

"Because we're not allowed to leave?" Kiki rolled her head until it faced her roommate. "Partners?"

"Sure," Eliana agreed as she stood, avoiding everyone's eyes.

"What does she mean you're not allowed to leave?" Ashna asked after the two girls had sauntered to the mats. The slow, clumsy pace at which Kiki now ducked and rolled made Tray snort.

"Uh..." Ackerly looked to Tray for help. He shrugged, unsure of how to tell these girls that they'd escaped one prison just to enter another. "W-wanna be partners?"

Ashna's brow furrowed, but after a moment she nodded. "Sure. I might have a hard time tackling you, though—you're bigger than me."

"Not by...that much," Ackerly said sheepishly, still glancing toward Tray for assistance.

With a dramatic exhale, he joined them in standing. "C'mon, Seth."

"Ooh, super strength versus super strength," his brother sang as he hopped down from the bleachers in the same manner Naira had.

The peachy-haired girl practiced the drill with Cath, though every time she collided with those trunk-like legs, the monster didn't even budge. Not far from them, Lavisa sparred with Hartman, who teleported away in fear every time she came close to knocking him down.

"You both have super strength?" Ashna asked the twins as they stationed themselves on the mats. Ackerly adjusted his glasses uneasily when he was forced to face her.

"Yeah, but mine is still developing," Seth explained as he cracked his knuckles. Tray didn't have the chance to comment before his brother ducked into a roll and exploded at his legs, knocking him onto the cushioned mat.

"Are you sure about that?" Ashna said with a giggle that Ackerly soon joined.

When Seth reached down to help Tray stand, he waved his hand away. "This is stupid," he grumbled, straightening his shirt as he straightened his body.

"Super strength must come in handy," Ashna commented, looking between both Starks. "My brother had super strength. I guess it's a common Affinity."

Ackerly must have noted that *had* as well, because he shuffled before saying, "Yeah…a few people here have it, like Nero."

They all glanced across the gym to where Nero aggressively tackled acid-spitter Dave, probably wishing it was Calder…who Tray now noticed was nowhere in sight. Had the Reggs punished him? All the teachers were here, but Calder was gone.

"He does seem like a bit of an ass," Ashna noted. "I thought he was going to hurt one of you last night… Luckily, I think the Rosses forgot about punishing you. We gave them some locations of the Wackos' hideouts and the president—er, soon-to-be president—is pleased. A government unit already invaded one of the hideouts and killed a few Wackos this morning."

"Damn, that was fast," Seth said with a whistle. "Did they kill any of the ones who captured you?"

Ashna dipped her head. "Yes, one—a guy named Vishal. He was…well, he always said he wanted to make me his bride once I was of age."

"His *bride*?" Ackerly's eyes widened. "That's—um…how old is he?"

"He *was* twenty-nine," Ashna said, wrinkling her nose. "But now he's gone, thank God… We told them where we think Headquarters is, too. Maybe they'll manage to catch some more."

Ackerly cocked his head at that, puzzled, but then a woman waltzed up to them, paralyzing him with her authority.

"O-Olalla Cosmos?" Ashna staggered back, as if stabbed. "You—you're…an Affinity *hero…*"

The Affinity ambassador chuckled, brushing her vibrant purple hair over her shoulder. "I'm not to be praised, dear. *You*, though—you must be the girl they're talking about, the one with the extraordinary hair." Ashna looked like she was ready to melt when Olalla ran a gentle hand over her rainbow locks. "So unique—but that isn't why I sought you out. I came to congratulate you on the recent triumph over the Wackos. It isn't often a hideout is raided, and with the coordinates for their headquarters…perhaps this whole issue will be resolved and we won't have to use Affinity children to fight this war."

"You think the Wackos can be defeated so easily?" Tray asked, drawing the woman's attention. When her eyes locked onto him, they lit with recognition.

"Ah, Tray, isn't it? And your brother, Seth. Have you any...news for me?" she inquired, likely referring to the Wacko sympathizer.

Seth immediately opened his mouth, but Tray cut in swiftly. "Not yet. We'll keep you updated."

"As I will keep you updated on my progress with the suits," she replied with a wink. "To answer your earlier question...I don't know how easily the Wackos can be defeated. I hate to think that the government will annihilate them all. They are terrorists, yes, but many are young, like yourselves. It seems...cruel not to give them a second chance. What are your sentiments?" she added, tilting her head toward Ashna. "You were among them as a prisoner. Do they all deserve death?"

Biting her lip, Ashna peeked around for prying ears. "No, not exactly. Many *are* evil, but some, like my friend, Naira, joined and then realized how corrupt it was. I imagine there have to be at least a few who can be redeemed."

"The problem lies in determining who is innocent and who is deceptive," Tray said, peering discreetly in Than's direction. If he was, indeed, a Wacko, maybe he was like Naira and had realized how evil the Wackos were. If he were still with them, wouldn't they have invaded Periculand again by now?

"Yes, it is a slippery slope," Olalla conceded with a solemn nod. Her gaze skipped around the room to Nero demolishing Dave, Kiki failing to roll, and the Rosses whispering to each other. "Be careful with whom you trust. Even mind readers can be deceived."

One of the Wacko hideouts had been exterminated—that much

Eliana gathered from William's elated thoughts. Although his mind was easier to read than Artemis's murky one, it was still slightly warped, like that of Aethelred, Fraco, and anyone else who might have known Angor's Affinity.

Since concluding that Artemis was the mind controller, Eliana couldn't stand in the same room as the woman without wanting to physically attack her. Her presence in the training gymnasium was enraging enough that, when it was her turn to practice the drill, Eliana actually ducked and rolled with force, slamming Kiki's legs and throwing her onto her back.

A high-pitched yelp escaped her roommate's throat, and Eliana almost mimicked it when she found herself caught within her lengthy legs, the two girls tangled on the orange mats. Peeking up, Eliana met Kiki's bulging eyes and was too mesmerized by her multi-hued irises to move.

"You knocked me over."

"I-I'm sorry." Eliana scrambled back and examined her limbs as if they were foreign. She'd never thought she would have any success in combat, but perhaps her festering aggressive thoughts had sparked physical capabilities she hadn't tapped into before.

"How did you do that?" Kiki demanded as she sat upright. "Why can't I do that?"

Though her initial reaction was to stutter a reply, Eliana paused and focused on her roommate's mind, sifting through her thoughts like an unorganized pile of papers. When she discovered the answer, it was impossible to keep her lips from inching into a shy grin. "I…think you're afraid of hurting me."

"Afraid…" Shaking her head, Kiki pushed to her feet and extended a hand toward Eliana. "Get up. I want to try again."

Placing her hand in Kiki's, she tried not to notice the softness of it by saying, "You want to try to hurt me?"

"I want to prove that I'm not afraid." With a grunt, she hoisted Eliana upright. Perhaps it was the rush of blood to her head, but Eliana felt suddenly dazed as she studied the features of the other girl's face. With the determination set in her jaw, it was hard to believe anything frightened her.

A bit dumbly, Eliana asked, "Afraid of what?"

Kiki blinked her long lashes. "Of—anything."

The memories running through her brain encompassed her dread for loneliness, the plague of her childhood. Much of it had been self-imposed—demeaning others, refusing to open up emotionally, and insisting all of it was acceptable—but Kiki saw her errors now, and Eliana empathized with her lack of human companionship. Everyone else would always look at her as the irredeemable bully, but with the way Eliana's own purview had altered over the past few weeks, she believed no one was beyond the scope of change.

"Okay," she said, stepping back. "Knock me down."

Swallowing, Kiki balled her fists and then ducked into a clumsy roll. Presumably, someone as popular as Kiki Belven would have had a cheerleader's grace, but athleticism had evaded her; the move was painfully slow. Still, Eliana braced for the tackle, only for a pair of massive hands to grab her arms and lift her. Squirming proved futile as the person deposited her on the floor a foot away, taking her place as Kiki's opponent. When she finally sprung out of her roll to attack, she met a wall of solid muscle.

"What the..." Kiki froze upon realizing the legs she hugged belonged to Nero Corvis. "Oh—oh." She staggered back and then fumbled into a standing position, fixing her wispy hair and ruffled shirt. "Hello, *Nero*."

Eliana cringed as a predatory grin spread across his lips. "Hello, Little Belven. Little Mensen," he added as an afterthought.

His slate-gray eyes landed back on Kiki with a flirtatious edge. "You're looking ravishing today."

Kiki batted her eyelashes and twirled her hair. Eliana waited for her to send some mental message confirming this was an act… but none came. Did she really think fawning over this bully would cure her loneliness? The girl's current thoughts answered that question. With a clenched jaw and curled firsts, Eliana watched the flirtation unfold.

"And aren't you looking hunky?" Kiki replied with an overdone smile. "It's nice to see you aren't drenched in that foul water anymore. Those Mardurus twins are despicable."

"I couldn't agree more."

Momentarily, Kiki's lips pursed with confusion, but she recovered with a swift, "So, you're done with that water bitch?"

Nero maintained his fiendish grin, and Eliana panicked at the thought of her roommate actually dating this jerk. She'd grown too much since her breakup with Seth to revert back to this life of seeking acceptance, relying on popularity, and engaging in shallow relationships. Part of Eliana wanted to intervene, but Kiki would hate her for it. Before, she wouldn't have cared about Kiki Belven's sentiments toward her, but the past two weeks had been…pleasant with her company. It was different than with Hastings, of course, but like Kiki had predicted, Eliana considered them friends.

Mustering the will, she prepared to interject, but then Nero covered his mouth in a girlish *giggle*. There was something unusual about his eyes, and Eliana guessed even before they transformed into a familiar bronze that this wasn't really Nero. Astonishment morphed Kiki's features almost as dramatically as Ruse's form shrinking from the mass of Nero to the size of Tray Stark.

"Water bitch? You'd better not let Nixie hear that one—she'll drown you." Ruse snickered, hand still covering his mouth. His hair was golden now, and Eliana thought him more handsome than Nero, but Kiki scowled like he was a worm that had snuck into her food.

"You—you cruel, heartless being!" she fumed, cheeks reddening beneath her makeup.

"Oh, c'mon. You didn't *actually* think I was Nero; he doesn't have that much charisma. His pick-up line is definitely something like, 'Bang me or I'll beat you.' Plus, I mean...he got with your *sister*. That doesn't deter you in the slightest?"

Kiki's exaggerated groan turned a few heads. Luckily, the Rosses were on the other side of the gymnasium and didn't notice her stomp away from Eliana to approach Hartman and Lavisa, who was leaping out of a roll. Her flawless execution of the drill was interrupted when Kiki seethed, "You and your brother!"

Pausing mid-tackle, Lavisa's dull eyes slid over to Ruse's shimmering ones. "I hope he did something worthy of this outburst."

Kiki groaned again and snagged Hartman's freckled arm. "I need you."

"Uh—"

"Don't question me!" The intensity of her tone almost distracted Eliana from the reasoning buried beneath this ostentatious show of outrage. As Kiki stalked through the exit with Hartman in tow, the mind reader was hollowed by the sad truth.

"Hopefully she doesn't need to make out with him, for his sake," Lavisa said to no one in particular. She strolled toward Eliana and Ruse as the Stark twins wandered over, Ackerly and Ashna at their heels.

"And for *your* sake," Tray huffed, rubbing his lower back. Based on his unvoiced complaints, he'd suffered quite the blow when his brother plowed through him during the drill. Eliana pried at Ashna's brain to see why she neglected to ameliorate his pain, but the walls around her mind were impressively thick.

Lavisa had no sympathy for Tray's physical pain and focused on the insinuation of his jab. "Hartman's a good kid. I empathize with him because his mother died when he was young."

"Does that mean *your* mother died when you were young?" Tray paused his back rubbing to really meet her eyes. Typically, his curiosity was born of the need to solve a larger puzzle or come to a concrete conclusion, but Eliana sensed he was genuinely intrigued by the intricacies of Lavisa's past simply for the sake of knowing her.

Her returning frown and her brother's unease confirmed the fact without Eliana peeping at either of their minds.

"I'm saying that just because I like him as a person doesn't mean I want to pin him against a wall and kiss his brains out," Lavisa stated much too nonchalantly.

"Is there anyone in this world you'd like to pin against a wall and kiss their brains out?" Seth inquired.

"No one I've met yet," she answered with a careless shrug. Eliana wondered if this statement internally miffed Tray because he had a crush on her or because the act of kissing one's brains out was physically impossible. The latter seemed the more accurate deduction, sadly.

"We're drawing attention," Tray snapped, brown eyes roving the room suspiciously. Indeed, a few other students stared at them, but on the other end of the gymnasium, the teachers and faculty remained ignorant to Kiki's theatrics—and her exit. "The adults already notice us enough. We need to stay under the radar until we can get this mess figured out."

"By 'this mess,' do you mean the fact that Than's a Wacko?" Lavisa asked flatly.

"It's not a *fact*—"

"And by 'adults,' do you mean Cosmos?" Seth added, nodding toward the unsuccessful vice-presidential candidate, who chatted cordially with Aethelred. "I don't see why we can't use her as an ally, bro. Seems like she's against the Rosses as much as we are. You don't trust her?"

"I'm…not sure," Tray admitted, his thoughts returning to the conversation he'd had with her a few minutes ago. It replayed with enough clarity that Eliana grasped Olalla's intrigue with the possible Wacko sympathizer…and Tray's suppression of their suspicions. "I don't think we should start rumors before they're confirmed, especially not to the people who can act on those rumors. We tread with caution. Anyone outside this group isn't to be trusted. Including you," he added to Ruse, who seemed unfazed by the accusation. "Still not sure what to think of someone who can become anyone so easily."

"You probably shouldn't tell me any secrets," Ruse agreed. "I'm a blabber-mouth."

With a faint smirk, Eliana eyed him sidelong, but then she heard a voice that drew her out of the external conversation and into a mental one

Ellie? Ellie? Is this thing on? Does it work?

Registering Seth's mental voice, Eliana looked to him with slightly raised eyebrows, and he sighed in relief.

I'm not good at this… What was I even thinking? Oh—oh, right. Is Kiks okay?

Eliana wasn't sure how to explain what she'd gleaned from Kiki's frenzied thoughts, and she wasn't sure she had the right to tell anyone. So, she nodded mutely to Seth and accepted his naïve gratitude while she recalled the thoughts whizzing through Kiki's mind upon her departure.

I need to stop being so gullible—I need to stop looking *so gullible. I need to see someone in a worse position than me, so I can stop feeling so bad about myself. I need to see Adara.*

"Stop telling me what I can and cannot do!" was the unpleasant whine Adara Stromer woke to that Monday morning. After her friends had so willingly abandoned her the previous night, she'd refused to engage in Angor's morning workout routine and intended to slumber her sorrows away—until she pried her eyes open to the sight of Kiki Belven storming into the hall beyond her cell. Sitting up slowly, Adara locked eyes with her nemesis and found they were nearly *pink.*

The color combination of Kiki's irises was so close to cotton candy that Adara almost began to salivate. When was the last time she'd eaten something sweet? Prison food was so *bland.* The rumble of her stomach distracted her until Kiki crossed her arms and spoke her name.

"Stromer. You smell like rotten garbage."

It was reminiscent of the insults Kiki had spewed at her for years, yet it had zero effect on Adara. She was in *jail,* but for some reason Kiki didn't have any power over her. Possibly, she lacked authority without her posse, though Adara doubted even Nero and his gang would have fazed her now. If anything, she would have basked in the negative attention of their derision.

That was why, instead of remaining quiet like her previous self would have, she decided to play the game.

"Funny, Belven. I was just about to say you *look* like rotten garbage. Telum," she prompted, eyes sliding to the officer standing awkwardly in the doorway. "Really? You can't bring me donuts, but you can let human trash in?"

"I couldn't *stop* her—"

"That's literally your job, Mitt." Adara hopped off her bed, body aching with stiffness, but kept her movements lithe as she approached the bars.

"He would have teleported her past me if I tried." Mitt jabbed his thumb over his shoulder. In response, an orange head of hair popped up beside him.

"Hey..." Hartman greeted weakly, freckles buzzing with his nerves.

Adara groaned. "Why would you help her, Ginger?"

"She said she would get Nero to beat me up if I didn't..."

"What sway does she have with Nero? In his eyes, she's an annoying little primie."

"Nero was just flirting with me at training," Kiki boasted, lifting her chin.

Adara's eyes narrowed. "Ah, good for you—your dreams finally came true, as they always do."

"Yeah, except it wasn't actually Nero." Hartman snickered but shrank when Kiki glared daggers in his direction.

"Shut *up*."

Adara glanced dully at Angor, who lounged on his metal slab, watching the scene unfold with intrigue. "This is the popular girl from my old school who rallied everyone else against me, if you were wondering. Really explains the unintelligence of today's youth. If it wasn't Nero, who was flirting with you? Someone unappealing, I hope."

"It—it *was* Nero—"

"It was Lavisa's brother, Ruse," Hartman answered. He proceeded to teleport out of the doorway and out of sight when Kiki glowered at him.

"Ha!" Adara clapped her hands together. "He was playing a prank on you."

The other girl's lips pouted slightly as she mumbled, "Yes…"

"This kid needs to be my best friend; his stunts are supreme. Tell him to come visit me."

"Ugh!" Kiki moaned at the ceiling. "You're not helping me!"

"Did you think I *would* help you?"

"I thought…" She sniffed, refusing to meet Adara's eyes. "I thought seeing you would make my life seem less pathetic. Instead, I just feel…silly."

Adara's eyebrows perked up slyly. "Finally realized I'm better than you, Belven? Only took you about ten—"

"You are not *better* than me," she sneered. Mitt had to hide his mouth behind his hand to conceal his amusement. "You are in *jail*. You're a criminal! You aren't cool, and no one likes you."

"No? That's odd—I've had quite a few people risk their asses to come visit me, including your ex-boyfriend. Seems *they* all like me. And I assume everyone knows I'm in jail and therefore knows of me, making me more popular than you." Adara's haughty eyebrow jump was enough to tighten Kiki's jaw. "I'd say life is going swimmingly for me—but I don't like the word *swimmingly*. Reminds me too much of the Pixie Prince, my natural enemy."

"Oh, Calder?" Kiki crooned, assuming a mischievous demeanor. "I hooked up with him after Hastings's funeral."

Adara's smugness plummeted as a sickeningly familiar sensation filled her gut. It was akin to when Seth had informed her of his first kiss with Kiki, except…almost *worse*.

"Don't look so suicidal, Stromer. She's obviously lying."

Blinking once, Adara snapped out of her momentary paralysis as the Pixie Prince shoved past Mitt and sauntered into the room, flashing a cocky smirk. At the intimidating gleam of his eyes, all witty quips died on her tongue. His deep blue hair was contained in a flawless knot, and perhaps she'd dwindled into insanity after almost three weeks in this cell, but she actually felt a bit self-conscious about how unruly and repulsive her hair had become.

"Obviously?" Kiki huffed, glancing at him with disdain. Standing beside one another, she was nearly his height, but he exuded far more maturity, especially now that her claim had been proven fraudulent. "Why wouldn't you want to hook up with me?"

Calder's eyes remained on Adara, tantalizing and calculating, as he said, "I don't think that requires explaining." Adara thought it required explanation, but he changed the subject. "We found out who the Wacko is—or, more accurately, Colton found out who the Wacko is."

The question on her tongue was answered a moment later when a boy wiggled between Mitt and the doorway. His skin was even darker than the police officer's, just as his forest-green hair and eyes were even darker than Calder's cargo pants. Adara recalled Calder mentioning his roommate's name was Colton, and though she'd never formally met the kid, she had seen him among Nero's group—always quiet, always at a distance. Now he gazed around the cells as if seeing mosaics on the plain white walls.

"Who's the Wacko?" Adara asked, rather than addressing Colton's weirdness.

"Not gonna tell you," Calder replied so swiftly that she barely processed his words. "Get up," he ordered, focus shifting to Angor. The King's face scrunched with bemusement, but he acquiesced and stood from his metal throne.

"Who is the Wacko?" Adara repeated, stepping toward the bars.

"Not gonna tell you. Don't stand so close to her," Calder

said to Angor, motioning with his hand for the man to move farther from Adara. Though Angor heeded these commands, Adara prowled forward until only the humming electric bars separated her from Calder. He frowned at the fact that she'd also closed her proximity with Angor.

"*Why* won't you tell me?"

"If I have to say I'm not going to tell you one more time, Stromer, I'll drown you where you stand."

The hint of sadism in his eyes made Adara shuffle backward, crossing her arms childishly. "Harsh..." she grumbled, hating the way all of his attention was now honed in on Angor—which was ridiculous. There was no way she'd grown so sensitive—no way she craved positive interaction so intensely that she cared if Calder was seriously rude to her, rather than playfully offensive. "Why would you even announce it if you're not gonna tell me?" she decided to ask, keeping her tone guarded.

"To get you fiery," he said with a wink.

To her dismay, his desired reaction actualized: A hot wave of fury coursed through her, irrational but instinctive, enveloping her like a second skin. It wasn't necessarily the wink that enraged her, but it had set her off, reminding her of the frustration building over these past weeks, the lingering sensation of warmth that had become as daunting as it was undesirable, and the reality of her situation—that none of her friends cared enough to save her from this prison. In fact, if she tallied up the statistics, the Pixie Prince had visited her more than anyone else. She'd never been one to give a damn about data or details, but to think that someone who was practically her enemy wanted to see her more than Seth...or...or even Tray...

"You need to say what you're seeing, Col, otherwise no one else knows what the hell is going on."

Calder's words yanked Adara out of her furious haze. Fortunately, no physical flames had seeped from her skin, but her flesh was sweltering, and she noticed Calder pointedly avoiding eye contact, as if something unusual had happened with her irises.

"Within the demoness dwells a volcano waiting to erupt," Colton said ominously. "An Affinity for fire is woven in her DNA, but she shuns her biology because of the mysterious way in which it manifested."

"Well, then it's confirmed." A presumptuous grin spread on Calder's face. "Your Affinity is fire, no matter how many times you attempt to deny it…Fire Demoness."

She was the one refusing to look at him now; all of her scrutiny aimed at Colton. "What exactly are you seeing?"

"The Otherworld shows me the necessary knowledge. For instance, Adara Stromer, a profound sense of jealousy overcame you upon hearing Kiki Belven had fallen into the physical realms of lust with Calder Mardurus."

"Okay, now I know you're full of shit," Adara said, disregarding the pompous curve of Calder's lips. "Nothing you've said so far has been remotely accurate."

"Colton's never wrong," the Pixie Prince sang in a way that made her squirm. "Now, I need you to tell me about Periculy. Innocent, or should I end him now?"

"You're gonna *kill* the King based on the strange assumptions of your roommate?" Adara questioned.

"If my facts are correct, *you* nearly killed him based on your own assumptions, which are far less educated than Colton's. If Colton is a god, you're a useless pile of ashes."

"Pile of ashes?"

"Pile of ashes," Calder repeated, eyeing the faint sheen of soot on her skin.

"Fine, Deranged Deity." Colton didn't flinch at her demeaning nickname. "Tell us what you *know* about Angor."

"And make it quick," Calder added with a cautious glance in Mitt's direction. "We need to get back to training before anyone notices we skipped out."

Weaponizer's hands flew up in innocence. "I won't tell on you. I'm trying to stay *off* the Rosses' radar after what went down last night."

"They got over the booze as soon as the freakin' *president-elect* praised them for discovering a Wacko hideout."

"Those girls actually gave up Wacko locations? They really *aren't* Wackos?" Adara asked. "Did the government find the headquarters?"

Calder pressed his lips together and shook his head. "Overheard them say the location the girls gave was empty. The Wackos must have known they were gonna get invaded and evacuated."

"I can't tell if this news pleases you or not," Adara mused, stroking her chin. "If the Wackos die, that means your enemy, Ventura, wins. But you've never seemed like an advocate for terrorism."

"I think we're screwed either way," he answered flatly, not bothering to entertain her speculations. "Colton, anything?"

"How did you two even get here?" Kiki piped up, finally over her earlier outrage. "I had to use the annoying teleporter to get past the guards, or they would have killed me."

"I don't think they've been sanctioned to kill," Calder said, watching his roommate watch Angor, "but we didn't want to get caught, either. Colton's Affinity includes the ability to show people the Otherworld. Those who haven't practiced with him just see blackness, like turning out the lights."

Adara cocked her head to the side. "You can blind people? That sounds evil. Maybe I should call you Satan's Seer instead."

Calder rolled his eyes, but Colton showed no emotion, his gaze still trained on Angor.

"This relates to the story of The Betrayer and The Betrayed," he said, his greenish eyebrows screwed in contemplation. "Angor Periculy was once a powerful man, but that power was stripped from him in more than one way—and all by the same person. The story has been skewed; an impenetrable drape has been placed over his memories, just as one has been placed over Adara's. Was this nefarious fabric sewn by the same hands?" Everyone stared at him, waiting for an answer. All he said was a rather anticlimactic, "I cannot say."

Adara's scowl deepened. "You can't say, or you don't know?"

"I cannot say. The words are embedded in my tongue with no hope of escape."

"And I thought *my* roommate was weird…"

"Eliana is not weird!" Kiki defended with far more vigor than Adara had expected. "She's my best friend, I'll have you know. Or…she will be, in the future."

Adara opened her mouth for a verbal jab, but Angor spoke first as he began to pace.

"Whoever has blocked the origin of your Affinity, Adara, is likely the person who led to its formation. This person must have been involved in your childhood, which leaves only two rational conclusions. This person who gave you your fire Affinity killed your parents, or…they are one of your parents."

Adara was smart enough to have guessed this much, at least, but to hear someone say it aloud, and given the assumptions they'd already deduced… "If Artemis is the one with the mind controlling Affinity—the one who erased *your* memories—could that mean she's also the one who killed my parents?"

Angor paused his strides, lips drooping into a frown. "Or

perhaps, with the physical traits you share, she could be your mother. It's too soon to come to such verdicts, but we need to consider the possibility."

Adara attempted to feign an aura of nonchalance, but she knew they all saw right through it. Tray had suspected the Rosses were her parents, but that had been more of a random, unlikely guess. All of the pieces fit together now.

"Inform Nerdworm." Adara barely had to look into Calder's eyes to know he understood her succinct command—or to know he was disgruntled that she was giving him commands at all. "And find a way to get Aethelred to touch Artemis. He's a single man; he can get creative."

Calder's eye roll evoked an actual laugh from Adara, and as he, Colton, and Kiki departed through the doorway, she swore she saw a laugh on his lips as well.

23

Family Friends

Due to helicopters scouting the area, Naretha had been forced to pull the van into various wooded areas for brief periods of time to avoid discovery. The group of Affinities used these breaks to remove the two Regg soldiers from the roof, as well as retract the flashy spikes that would surely draw attention to their vehicle. Judging by the redness around her eyes, the Wacko named Devika took these opportunities to remove herself from the group and shed a few tears over her fallen brother. By the time they arrived in Cleveland, she'd declared that Vishal had been an "asshole" and that "he was probably better off dead."

Avner wasn't quite sure what to think about that—or about any of these Wackos, for that matter. He'd expected all Wackos to be rough, nasty, heartless beings, and perhaps Devika's conclusion made her seem callous, but Avner knew it was merely a defense mechanism. Adara likely would have made the same claims about Avner if he died as a way to deflect her grief. After getting to know

Devika, Nate, and Kevin a little better throughout the prolonged ride to Cleveland, he had a hard time deeming them evil.

Devika proved to be a skilled medic, and after patching up Nate's gun wound, she moved onto Meredith's stomach, sewing together the flesh that had been too torn to heal on its own. Jamad offered to use his ice Affinity to numb her while Devika worked, but Meredith claimed it didn't hurt, and Avner wondered how much torture this poor girl had gone through to make her immune to pain.

After what felt like a lifetime of weaving through Cleveland, attempting to ensure they weren't being tracked, Naretha finally drove them out of the city toward Lake Erie, leaving the skyscrapers behind to enter a more residential area. Though Avner had lived in Ohio his whole life, he'd never visited the city or the lake. It was definitely ugly: a blanket of gray beneath the cloudy sky, so unlike the glorious pictures of sunny beaches and pristine blue water he'd assumed all lakes looked like. He still liked to watch the scenery pass through the tinted window, though, and given Meredith was the only one peering out with him, everyone else must have already seen these not-so-spectacular sights.

"How much farther?" Jamad groaned, resting his head back against the window of the van. Avner and Meredith knelt on either side of him, ogling the lakeside mansions.

Naretha threw her hand over her shoulder to pelt him with a pea-sized salt crystal. "Shut up."

Cursing, he rubbed his forehead and glared at her. "Have the rest of you been here before?" he asked the other Wackos. Nate was asleep, but Devika and Kevin both shook their heads.

"Vishal went a few times... Its location was always a secret to outside Wackos during Ephraim's rule," Devika explained, glancing cautiously at Naretha to see if she would rebuke her. "Danny's not as secretive."

"Because he knows he can incinerate anyone who tries to get near it," Naretha grunted, eyes on the road ahead. Avner noticed her normally outrageous driving speed had dwindled to a crawl, but he was still surprised when they turned into one of the mansions' driveways.

"This—*this* is Wacko Headquarters? A house—in plain sight?" Avner stammered, staring out the window as they crept past the side of the inconspicuous brick house. It was less showy than many of the others but still ginormous and clearly owned by someone with considerable wealth—or, apparently, a terrorist organization.

Naretha snorted. "This is the vacation home of a Wacko whose name I won't divulge. We don't just hang out on the back patio, Sparky. Be patient and you'll see."

Though he'd never admit it, Avner was as intrigued by the Wackos' main hideout as Jamad appeared to be, but he kept his mouth shut as Naretha parked the van in the small lot behind the house. A gaudy patio rested adjacent to the pavement, topped by an oversized balcony that must have extended off the master bedroom.

"It's a real shame you don't use the patio," Jamad crooned to Naretha, who ignored him as she turned off the engine.

Silence ensued. Even when they filed out of the van and regrouped on the pavement, the yard's ambience was so…peaceful. A flat plot of grass extended beyond the driveway and the patio, and though most of the shrubbery was dormant, a garden had been planted around the perimeter of what Avner realized was an in-ground pool.

"Damn, you Wackos are living in luxury," Jamad said with a whistle as he surveyed the backyard.

"We're not permitted to touch anything above ground," Naretha snapped as she slammed the van door shut. When she rounded the back to join them, she eyed the neighboring houses with suspicion.

"This pool looks like it's below ground to me," Jamad said. "Can I swim in it, or..."

"Only you would want to swim outdoors in November," she grumbled as she shoved past him. "Let's move."

Avner opened his mouth to ask if any of the neighbors would notice the vehicle, but then it began to *sink.* The entire block of pavement beneath the van descended, leaving a large chasm of darkness in the ground beside them.

Jamad pointed at the hole. "I assume that's supposed to be happening?"

Naretha grunted but didn't bother replying before stalking down the stone path that wound through the yard past the pool. The other three Wackos followed readily, but Avner and Jamad walked slower to help Meredith stagger along.

As they strolled through the yard, Avner absorbed every little detail, hoping he'd remember enough to expose the Wackos' location once they escaped it. The entire concept was crooked. He had witnessed what the government did to Wackos when they were discovered and should have been empathetic to them at this point. But even if they seemed innocent, he knew they were terrorists, and even if he didn't have a personal grudge against them, he knew their imprisonment would bring peace to American society. Plus, if he, Jamad, and Zeela were criminals now, perhaps this knowledge could buy them absolution.

Upon his first glance, Avner had been so distracted by the

pool that he hadn't noticed a small stone cabin lay at the edge of the property, right before the cliff that plummeted down to Lake Erie. Trees draped over the roof, nearly concealing it from view, and Avner wondered how a whole terrorist organization fit in its basement.

When Naretha reached the wooden door, she paused, spinning to face the rest of them with a grave gleam to her eyes. "This compound could be compromised. There's no way to know how many hideouts have been discovered. If this is a trap—if there are Reggs in this cabin—you all need to be ready to fight."

Her gaze slid pointedly in Meredith's direction. The girl hung between Avner and Jamad, her energy depleted from the short walk across the yard, but even in full health she wouldn't have been helpful. Naretha exchanged a glance with Jamad that Avner interpreted as, "Ditch her and save yourself." His friend's returning glare said, "No," but if faced with the choice of helping Meredith or surviving, would Jamad really sacrifice himself for her? The noble answer was yes, but the real answer… Avner didn't want to have to find out.

"If Headquarters hasn't been compromised, Danny will be here," Naretha continued, her tone too resentful for someone discussing their boyfriend they hadn't seen in months. "Which means *you two* need to keep your mouths shut while I convince him not to kill you."

"Kill us?" Avner repeated.

"I'm not very good at not talking," Jamad griped.

Naretha ran her fingers over her lips, as if to zip them shut. "Quiet, starting now." Pivoting, she faced the door again and punched in a few numbers on the handle's keypad. When it beeped and blinked red, she swore. "Danny must have changed the code… That little bastard thought I would give information to Periculy. Kevin."

"What—oh, me?" he stuttered as Naretha jabbed her finger toward the keypad. "Oh—uh—yeah, sure." Without touching the door, Kevin screwed his eyes shut and the lock clicked, permitting them entry.

Before pushing past him, Naretha grumbled, "Why do you have to be so annoyingly useful?"

"I-I don't know. I just…am."

Naretha paid him no mind, but Devika smirked as she shoved him through the doorway. Nate shuffled in next, one of his broad shoulders still sagging because of his bullet wound, and then Avner, Jamad, and Meredith brought up the rear, taking careful steps through the narrow kitchen that served as an entryway. After walking into a vast room lined with windows overlooking the lake, they skidded to a halt at the sight of a girl lounging on one of the brown leather couches.

Her hair, as yellow as Avner's, was arranged in a bun messier than Adara's on a Saturday morning, and bandages tinted pale pink from blood covered her nose and arms. With her black boots propped on a wooden coffee table, she idly watched a flatscreen television that hung from the ceiling. The news blared so loudly that she probably hadn't heard them enter.

"These three Wacko prisoners, who remain anonymous, have done a great service to this nation," the newscaster said. "After escaping the terrorists' clutches, they informed the government of two Wacko locations, one being the infamous headquarters of this nefarious organization. Teams of highly trained soldiers managed to purge both locations, and we wait now to see how this uprooting will affect their reign of terror.

"Meanwhile, in the city of Cleveland, three buildings have been partially destroyed with bombs. Footage of the events is being recovered, and local officials are looking into the cause of these explosions, which stole over a hundred lives. If any suspicious activity is noticed in the city, please contact local authorities. Anyone with oddly-colored hair is to be detained immediately, as they could be Wackos seeking revenge…"

"Hey, Wacko," Naretha called tantalizingly. The girl on the couch jumped, spilling her drink, and hopped to her feet in defense.

"Shit, why—" Yellow eyes locked on the group, the girl paused and blinked in disbelief. "Na-*Naretha*?"

"Alyssa," she greeted flatly. "Are you surprised to see me here?"

"Wh-who…" The girl glanced around at the group. "How are you *alive*?"

"How did you break your nose?" Naretha countered, appraising her multitude of bandages. "Should I assume these are all Danny-inflicted wounds?"

"The nose was Cath," Alyssa replied with a wince. "The rest was Danny, yeah…"

"Cath?" Naretha echoed, head tilting as if the name made no sense to her.

"She…escaped with Ashna."

"No," Naretha breathed, but when the expression on Alyssa's face didn't change, she seemed to accept the fact and swore. "And *you*—you were the one that let them out?"

"I-I didn't mean to! I was guarding that girl's room—the Periculand bitch Danny's been trying to trade for—"

"I hope you're not talking about Maddy." Jamad left Meredith against the wall to prowl toward the front of the group. "Because if you are, I'll gladly freeze the life out of—"

"Quiet." Naretha grabbed his ear before he could stalk past her. "You don't get to kill her. I do."

"Naretha, please," she begged, staggering around the couches to approach them. "I tried my best to stop them, but they overpowered me. Danny already punished me—he almost killed me!"

"He should have killed you," Naretha muttered, eyes still slivered. "I'd like to hear the story from someone else's mouth. Take us to Danny's office. *Now*."

Scurrying to the far right corner of the room, Alyssa fumbled with the lock of a door that looked like it should have led to a closet. When she finally opened it, Avner saw two silver doors on the other side—elevator doors.

The interior was large enough to fit all eight of them, but Alyssa opted not to join. Rather, she hastily closed the doors from the outside before Naretha could insist she accompany them for more punishment. That Danny physically punished his inferiors didn't surprise Avner, but it certainly didn't make him excited to meet the man, either.

Growing up in a suburban town without the luxury of vacations—or the misfortune of any severe injuries—Avner had never needed to use an elevator. The jolt and the stomach-flipping descent induced nausea, but he maintained neutrality throughout the full minute of the ride. When they reached the bottom, the doors they'd entered through didn't open; instead, a different set of doors at their backs did.

Naretha had expected this, and with none of the others' disorientation, she sauntered out of the elevator into the darkly-colored room awaiting them. Avner was far more tentative when exiting, his movements guarded as he walked beside Jamad and Meredith.

The office wasn't the underground lair Avner had anticipated. With another flatscreen television mounted on the right wall and a ginormous desk planted in the center, the setup was fairly modern. It reminded him more of Angor Periculy's quarters than an illicit hideout.

The evilness of this place, Avner realized, was not in the setting but in the man who sat at the desk, patiently waiting for their approach. Every aspect of him exuded deviance, from the way his feet rested on his desk to the tattoos of skulls and explosions splayed over his arms. His hair waved over his head like a field of flames, the bright orange hue inlaid with blazing reds and yellows. Though Avner recalled Naretha claiming Danny was younger than her, the Wacko leader, with his smug smirk and luminous eyes, seemed ages beyond the rest of them.

"My love," Danny greeted, his lustful gaze trained on Naretha. "Come closer."

With the gait of a soldier, Naretha stepped up to the desk and faced him stonily. The others followed suit, Devika and Nate standing at attention while Kevin performed a pathetic little bow. Avner remained behind them with Jamad and Meredith, hoping not to be noticed.

"No, no, come *closer.*" Danny motioned to the empty air beside his chair. Despite her obvious reluctance, Naretha rounded the desk and stopped at her boyfriend's side, bending to smash her lips against his in an intimate kiss. Either she was a spectacular actress or their relationship was ridiculously strange.

"Ah," Danny sighed when they finally broke apart, "I knew you would find your way back to me. I hope you didn't divulge any information to Angor during your time in Periculand?"

"Periculy's interrogation methods are lamer than you'd think."

"Good, good. I knew you'd hold up against him."

"Is that why you didn't send a rescue team?" she asked, her voice calm but laced with venom.

"Darling"—he stroked a finger down her arm—"I knew you didn't need it. Look at you—you made it back here in just under two months, *and* you brought a heap of new recruits. It would have been an insult to your ability if I'd sent some pathetic lackeys to your aid. Tell me about our new friends."

"These three are Wackos from the hideout that was recently exposed," she explained, motioning to Nate, Devika, and Kevin. "We were there with them when the Reggs invaded, and we just narrowly escaped. I assume that was Ashna's doing."

Danny's good humor faded as his smile turned vicious. "You've been informed then… Yes, you can imagine she and her companions are actively seeking to destroy us. Although, the location she gave the Reggs for Headquarters was our decoy. Thus, we are safe here…for now." Naretha's lips twitched the slightest bit, but she portrayed no other hint of emotion at this news. "We will seek out Ashna, and we will find her. Until then, today is a day for celebration. My love has returned to me." Danny smiled up at her, and she mirrored the expression flawlessly. Yet, after having known her a few weeks, Avner saw how fake it was. Naretha didn't *smile*—she smirked devilishly at other people's pain.

"Shall I assume the little ones in the back are Madella's friends?" Danny inquired as he stood from his seat and peered at them. Jamad's nostrils flared with the sound of Maddy's name on this lunatic's tongue, but luckily his expression resumed neutrality as Nate, Devika, and Kevin parted to display them to the Wacko leader.

"Yes," Naretha confirmed curtly, neglecting to mention that Meredith was not. Perhaps it was better that way; then, if Danny decided to kill them now, he wouldn't go after Maddy's third friend, Zeela.

"It appears you and the boys got matching haircuts, my dear," Danny mused.

Naretha's expression soured. "Unwillingly." The Wacko leader was too preoccupied with studying the three teens to care what she'd said. His gaze was currently fixed on Meredith, and for the first time since their parting, Avner was grateful Zeela wasn't present. "We experienced a minor detour on the way here…at a Regg research facility."

Tearing his eyes from Meredith, Danny pivoted toward his girlfriend and finally noticed her arm was bandaged. "Where is this facility?"

"We have a rough estimate of its location. This one burned it to the ground—"

"Fire Affinity?" Danny interjected, his cataclysmic eyes settling on Avner.

Though his gaze elevated Avner's heart rate with fear, he put on a façade of indifference. "Electricity."

"Ah." A grin curled along Danny's lips. "Avner Stromer."

His façade shattered at the utterance of his name. The Wacko leader knew his name based on his *Affinity*? Had Maddy told him all about her friends?

"Don't look so surprised," the man drawled, as if reading his thoughts. "Our parents once worked together, if you didn't know."

"My…*parents*?"

"Yes, yes, they were allies once upon a time," Danny droned. "But, of course, your parents chose to aid the government that detests us, while *my* father had a different vision."

"Who…" With Naretha's harsh glare, his questions died on his tongue. How could he *not* ask about his parents, though, if Danny knew who they *were*? Before a coherent string of words formed in his mind, Naretha spoke again.

"We killed all of the employees at the research facility, but… we believe there might be some survivors who will interest you." Avner's brow creased, his brain too preoccupied with his parents to process her implication.

"Affinities?" Danny asked.

When Naretha shook her head, it dawned on Avner. The realization came too late, though, because before he could stop her, she said, "No, the Starks."

"The Starks..." Slowly, Danny's eyes illuminated with manic delight. "But you were not able to apprehend them?"

"They were chained. We would have had to forfeit our lives to the Reggs to obtain them. But now, with the Reggs dead..." Naretha's eyebrows perked, and judging by the calculating look on Danny's face, he understood her suggestion.

"I...have a tracking Affinity," Devika piped up, her voice unsure in the presence of her leader. "I'll be able to find the research facility...with your permission."

"A tracking Affinity? That's quite useful... Why didn't my father recruit you for Headquarters?"

Devika licked her lips with discomfort. "Do you forget the terms you made with my brother?" Puzzled, the man studied her for any clue as to who her brother might be, but when it became clear he had no idea, she sighed. "Vishal."

"Ah!" Danny clapped his hands together. "That bastard. How could I forget? Of course, of course... Where is he?"

"Killed...by the Reggs."

Instead of condolences, the Wacko leader's enthusiasm multiplied. "Well, then it seems the deal worked out on my end. Not so well on his, though." A muscle flickered in Devika's jaw, but she made no comment. "Yes, you may lead the search for the Starks. Take whomever you need to accomplish the task. I want those two Reggs found—alive, if they aren't already dead. I have plans for them."

Devika dipped her chin. "And may I have your permission to track down the Regg soldiers afterward—the ones who destroyed our hideout? I would like to avenge my brother...and put a small dent in the Reggs' ranks, of course."

"I have no care for your brother, but any day a Regg dies at the hand of an Affinity is a splendid day, indeed. Track and kill as many as you'd like; you don't need my permission." With that, he waved her off, and Kevin and Nate followed her to the elevator, likely planning to join her murderous mission.

Avner's head reeled at the prospect. As much as he wanted to reunite with Zeela, he knew his main priority now needed to be finding a way to rescue the Starks—preferably before he had to go head-to-head with Nate and his animal-morphing Affinity.

"Now, you three," Danny purred as he waltzed around his desk. "Periculy's little pets... Though I suppose you no longer are, considering you defied him in order to bring Naretha to me. How should I repay you?"

Jamad opened his mouth, but Avner knew that, with the way his friend's morals had shifted over the past few weeks, whatever he said would ruin this for them. Before the other boy could say anything, he spoke first.

"We would like our friend, Maddy," Avner said. "We would like to leave here with her. We...don't plan to go back to Periculand—the Rosses would probably put us in jail if we did—and after what we experienced at the research facility, we have no intention of going to the Reggs with any information about...this place. We just want to be together and safe again."

"Such a sweet proposition," Danny mocked. "What, exactly, is *unsafe* about this place? Is there something to fear, Avner Stromer, in a place composed solely of Affinities? With the Wackos is the only place you *will* be safe. The government is after you—they know what you've done, how you've broken a Wacko out of jail. They will hunt you, and they will not spare you."

"I'm aware that the government is cruel to Affinities," Avner said, fighting to keep his voice even, "but I don't condone what the Wackos stand for. It doesn't have to make us enemies, but…I can't join you."

"Pity." Danny took a few methodical steps closer. When they were only inches apart, he narrowed his eyes and whispered, "Just like your father in spirit." It was nearly impossible for Avner to remain still as the man ran a finger along his jaw. His skin was uncomfortably hot and his proximity terrifyingly close. "And just like your father in irritatingly good looks."

Jamad snorted where he stood a few feet away, and Danny dropped his hand to whirl toward him. Sobering immediately, the other boy stammered, "I—It's just…I've never met anyone who finds Avner attractive, except his girlfriend, and she's blind."

That comment sparked amusement in Danny and, smirking faintly, he stepped back, distancing them to the point that Avner could actually breathe without fearing for his life. "I will give you what you want," Danny said after a moment, nodding to each of them. "Josh!"

Avner spun as a door behind him opened, admitting a man whose stature was oddly familiar. Fragile and gaunt, the guy's black- and blue-streaked eyes darted around nervously as he hobbled toward them. Dark makeup seemed to have once covered his eyelids, though now it had faded to a deathly sheen of gray that made him look like a decaying zombie. His hair, jet black fading into an electric blue, was overgrown, flopping to one side of his head, and the stench he brought with him was reminiscent of Avner's. That, coupled with the modern manacles constricting his ankles, confirmed that Josh was a prisoner.

Avner waited for Maddy to enter the room behind him, but

then Josh's apathetic eyes locked with Meredith's, and she toppled to the floor.

Instinctively, Jamad jumped into a defensive stance. "It's the Wacko from JAMZ!"

Avner recognized him now, recalling how bodies had fallen throughout the basement at this Wacko's will. Before Jamad could raise a hand to freeze him, however, his eyes drooped and his body wilted, falling on top of Meredith's with a thud.

Instead of electrocuting Josh and starting a brawl, Avner spun toward his only conscious ally with pleading eyes. "Naretha, please—" But no sympathy washed over her face before Josh stepped into his line of sight. His consciousness slipped from his grasp, and his freedom went with it.

Fury flared in Naretha's chest at the sight of the two boys and that pathetic girl being dragged away by a few of Danny's lackeys, who had entered the office upon his command. The Wacko leader didn't have to explain for her to know they were now his prisoners. Avner and his big mouth… Maybe it was best they remained out of the way until she figured out what had happened during her absence.

The real source of her rage, she decided, wasn't that Avner, Jamad, and Meredith were prisoners but that *Josh* had knocked them out.

"You little bitch," she snarled at him the moment the lackeys disappeared from the office. Stomping around the desk, she disregarded Danny's warning glare and snagged Josh by the collar of his greasy shirt. "You *left* me! You're the reason for all this shit! Did you know that he left me?" she asked, spinning toward their leader while maintaining her grip on Josh. "Did you know that your little boy-toy could have brought me back but *didn't*?"

A placid smile crept onto Danny's lips. "I'm aware." After pushing off his desk, he approached them, halting his strides at a safe distance. "That's why I placed Josh in a cell, where he's spent the last two months contemplating his mistakes."

"It wasn't a *mistake*—"

"Regardless," Danny interjected, harshness seeping into his tone, "neither of you completed the mission as tasked. Hastings Lanio was not retrieved, and it has negatively impacted our situation in a way I never could have anticipated."

"Did you tell him *why* we were unable to complete the mission?" Naretha asked Josh impatiently. "Did you tell him who intercepted us?" Shamefully, he bowed his head, and Danny looked to Naretha with arched eyebrows. "Nero Corvis and Adara Stromer—and some water-freak."

"Male?" he inquired, and Naretha nodded. "Calder Mardurus… They work together?"

"About as well as we do." She jerked her chin disdainfully in Josh's direction.

"And yet they managed to beat you—a bunch of little teenagers. Perhaps you should keep your mouth shut, Naretha, before you make yourself sound even more pitiful."

She did press her lips together, but only to contain the slew of curses resting on her tongue. "What is our punishment, then?"

With a sniff, Danny grimaced in distaste. "I believe justice has been served—but know that I won't be so forgiving next time. Wash up; our celebratory feast is scheduled one hour from now. Remember to smile, Naretha…and wear something sexy, so my eyes can be as satisfied as my stomach. Both of you." Licking his lips, he turned on his heel and padded back to his desk.

Naretha's gaze slid toward Josh, who, with Danny's back to them, actually had the courage to scowl at her. "Twat," she muttered before stalking across the office. Instead of entering the elevator, she slipped through the door that led to Danny's private bedroom, miffing Josh to the point that he grumbled to himself. It was the only reason Naretha was even remotely delighted to enter these living quarters again.

Danny's bedroom was as plain and dull as the other rooms in Headquarters, with pale gray walls and no windows. The massive bed, which had previously been his father's, rested against the right wall not far from the personal kitchenette snuggled in the far corner. Directly to her right dwelled the elevator, which also granted access to the bedroom via private code. Since Josh likely knew this code, she was surprised he hadn't entered the elevator through the office and exited on this side to reprimand her for destroying his reputation with Danny. Honestly, she wished he had.

Though she'd shared this room with Danny for a month, it felt far from home. Even as she opened one of the ornate dressers and saw her clothes within, the whole place seemed foreign. Why couldn't Danny have sent her on another mission? She would have rather been slipping on leathers to go fight the Reggs than picking out a scanty dress to wear to some dinner. Now that Naretha had failed Danny, though, she doubted he would allow her out of his sight for quite some time. She would become his little pet, especially now that Ashna was gone.

She had spent the past two months dreaming about her return, but now that she was back, all she wanted to do was escape—make her own plans, follow her own rules, find Zeela...

With the frustrated thoughts buzzing through her head, she almost didn't hear the elevator doors open behind her. Good—

Josh was here for an argument. She was in desperate need of someone upon which to release her aggravation. When she spun around, however, it wasn't Josh stepping into Danny's bedroom; it was Danny's brother, Zach.

Their demeanors were so incomparable that it was sometimes hard to remember they were brothers. Where Danny was confident and crass, Zach was cautious and courteous. Where Danny was compact, muscular, and athletic, Zach was tall, gangly, and awkward. Even their reactions to her presence were wildly different; upon witnessing her where she stood by the dresser, his steps out of the elevator were so slow and careful that she would have snapped at him to hurry up if she weren't paralyzed by the sight of him, as well.

"Is it really you?" he whispered, voice barely audible.

Swallowing, Naretha kept her posture rigid. "Am I really so unrecognizable without my hair?"

Zach closed his mouth, inhaling through his nostrils, and then frowned. "You're far less sanitary than usual."

"That's what happens when you're unable to shower for two months."

He scratched the back of his neck but refused to move any closer. His ashy hair was abnormally disheveled today, as if he'd recently awoken from his daily nap, but other than that, he looked as neat and fresh as always, unaltered even when everything else had changed.

"Prove to me who you are," he finally said, eyeing her timidly.

"*Prove* it? What, are you afraid I'm a shapeshifter in disguise? You want me to show you my tattoos? Are you trying to get me to remove my clothes, Zachary?"

Every muscle in his face twitched. "It's *Zacchaeus*."

"I know," she said flatly, crossing her arms. "I just like to watch you squirm, which is tempting me to take off my—"

"Don't," he interjected, glancing warily toward the door to the office. Naretha sobered at the thought of Danny and his possessiveness. "I should leave. I just…wanted to see that you're actually alive."

"Wait," she sighed before he could retreat to the elevator. "Where is Danny keeping the prisoner, Maddy? Her…friends are here."

Zach blinked, nonplussed. "Danny's letting her go?"

"No. I just…peeked at his computer when I was behind his desk and saw that only one of the cells was occupied—with Josh, meaning she's not locked away anymore."

"She's in…" Zach's grayish eyes darted around uneasily. "My room…"

Her insides curled with bitterness at his words. "Ah. Right. Eighteen-year-olds aren't too young for you?"

His discomfort morphed into chagrin. "Twenty-two-year-olds aren't too young for you?"

"That's *different*—I don't have a choice and you know it." Zach simply snorted, and she barely contained the urge to hurl an oversized salt crystal at his head. "Tell your child-girlfriend that her friends are here, unless you're too petty to relay information for me. They'll want to see her."

24

Different Breeds of Monsters

After less than twenty-four hours, Maddy already felt like Zach's bedroom was her home. She'd awoken to a tray full breakfast food waiting on the nightstand, accompanied by a stack of fiction novels and a note in an elegant scrawl that simply said, "*Enjoy.*" That Zach had actually succumbed to entering this side of the room—for *her*—was enough to bring a blush to her cheeks, even though he was nowhere in sight.

So far, she'd learned the Wackos' food rations were minimal, but Zach had managed to get her three whole plates—perhaps enough to make up for the malnourishment she'd suffered in that dark dungeon. After savoring the meal for a full hour, she picked up the first book atop the pile and spent the day in fictional bliss.

By the time the little window embedded in the wall darkened, Maddy took a break from reading to stretch on the floor. It was while she pressed her nose to her knee, extending her leg and trying to reach the same length with her fingertips, that Zach reentered the room. Immediately she retracted her elongated limbs, blinking up at him in embarrassment.

"Do you know how disgusting that floor is?" he demanded, wrinkling his nose at it.

"I—no." She hopped to her feet and wiped off her pants. "Sorry…"

His expression mollified, but he didn't acknowledge her apology as he scrutinized her with those dust-colored eyes. "Your friends arrived."

"My—what?"

"Your friends. Two boys and a girl."

"R-really? They came?" Everything around her swam in a blur. Zeela, Jamad, and Avner had traveled all the way from Periculand to wherever this hideout was to *save her*. Danny had told her weeks ago that they were on the way, but…she hadn't believed him. She trusted Zach, though; the expression on his face was too honest for this to be a fabrication.

"Yes," he confirmed uneasily. "They're…in the cells."

"Oh." Maddy's elation plummeted as she recalled the glass-paneled, closet-sized cubbies that had housed the Wacko, Josh, and which now housed her friends as well. "Oh…"

Awkwardness enveloped his posture and an apologetic gleam consumed his face. He probably felt guilty for his brother's actions, and she wanted to reassure him it wasn't his fault, but… *was* he completely blameless? He'd expressed vague contempt toward Danny, but if the Wacko leader hadn't locked him away, he obviously hadn't argued against her friends' imprisonment.

"I can bring you to see them when Danny goes out," Zach said. "It might be a few days… His trips are often sporadic."

"Yeah." She coughed. "Yeah, that would be great. Thank you."

He eyed the bare walls, and Maddy thought he might be looking for dirt or imperfections, but then, when he spoke, she realized he was avoiding her gaze. "Which one is your boyfriend?"

"My—oh. Oh, no. Neither." Her words were so choppy that it didn't sound convincing. "I—well—I used to have a crush on Jamad, with the light blue hair, but he's too much of a flirt. And Avner's dating Zeela...plus he's always been too friendly for me."

Zach's eyes flew to her, incredulous. "Too *friendly*?"

Warmth trickled into her cheeks as she stared down at her feet. "Yeah, I guess. It would be hard to look at him romantically. He's too open, too exposed. I prefer something...more mysterious." She peeked up at him, expecting confusion or disdain, but his face was wrought with contemplation. "It's probably weird—"

"No, it's not. I do, too."

Her lips curved faintly as his did. "Let me know when we can go see them."

"Are you hungry?" he asked before she could retreat to her bed.

"I'm still full from breakfast; you don't need to get me any—"

"Well," he interjected, clearing his throat, "there's actually a feast up in the cafeteria...to celebrate my...brother's girlfriend's return."

"The girl that traveled back here with my friends," Maddy recalled.

Zach's nod was strained. "Since you're officially a Wacko now, you're invited. You'll need to behave, though. Danny has your friends; he won't hesitate to use them against you."

"I know," she assured, smirking. "Despite my history as a prisoner, I'm not much of a rebel. I know how to stay out of trouble."

"Good..." he said, too deep in rumination to react to her joke. "You'll have to dress nicely. Danny likes to make a spectacle of these events."

Maddy glanced down at the plain sweatshirt and jeans

she'd been gifted upon her release from the dungeon. "This isn't good enough?"

His lips did quirk now, but only briefly before his expression dimmed. "My roommate won't care if you borrow some of her clothes." His nose twitched at the fishnet tights sprawled on the floor. "Good luck finding something that fits your style…"

It had become apparent to Zeela that the group of Affinities she traveled with was weak. Not physically—though, most of their muscles *were* atrophied—but mentally. After escaping the Reggs, the group had barely trudged through the woods for an hour when complaints halted their journey. These people were *tired* and they needed to *rest*.

Only because Avner would have permitted it did Zeela grant their wishes and allow them to take a short break. How any of them could sleep at a time like this was beyond her. They were in the middle of a forest, where Reggs might find them at any moment, and with those high-tech suits, they *must* have seen this massive group of Affinities sprinting away. The Reggs would come back, and the Affinities were simply going to lie around and wait for them.

By the time they all woke, the sun had risen, shifting the lens of Zeela's vision into a lighter tone. At a brisk pace, she led the pack out of the forest and into the fields—the same fields they'd run through after escaping the research facility. Due to fatigue, the length of their journey this time tripled that of the previous night, and when they arrived at the ruins of the barn, her vision had returned to a darker shade, signaling the sun's descent.

"Well, the fire's dead," Charlie huffed as the group halted a few paces from where the entrance once stood.

"And so is the barn." Her eye scanned their surroundings,

so altered since the day before. It was a miracle the fire hadn't consumed the whole field, but judging by the small amount of withered matter, only a few feet of grass had burned around the barn. The structure itself was barely distinguishable to Zeela now, likely just a heap of ash. Her vision did detect some heat lingering among the rubble, though—embers that had yet to cool.

Taking a few steps forward to inspect further, she said, "We'll need to be careful with the embers and our bare feet. I'll go first. Charlie, you follow," she added with a glance back in his direction.

"I'm Key Fingers," the mass of heat said, and Zeela swore internally at her mistake. Hadn't Charlie stood there a moment ago? With how similar everyone appeared, she would have to memorize how the bones and muscles of every person she knew differed.

"Let's go," Charlie prompted. His structure was taller than that of Key Fingers, she observed, and his muscles were denser with less atrophied. She could learn people's looks again—she would have to.

Nodding, Zeela strode into the mound of charred debris. The mixture of ash and rubble was slightly damp beneath her feet, but it hadn't rained. Although this struck her as odd, she continued onward, dodging the smoldering embers, while Charlie cautiously followed in her footsteps. As she moved, she searched for any hint of the staircase leading into the facility below. The earth didn't feel hot enough for the fire to have moved underground, so when she finally did spot the opening, obscured by two massive beams of charred wood, she didn't hesitate to approach it.

"I'll grab the other side," Charlie said. After surveying the path he'd have to take to get there, Zeela dipped her chin in agreement. It took them longer than she would have liked to remove the beams, and even from a distance she heard the other Affinities starting to complain about how cold, exhausted, and unhappy they were.

"Ignore them. They're ungrateful," Charlie grunted as they heaved the second beam onto the grass. The metal stairwell loomed below, likely dirtied with debris Zeela couldn't detect. "Do you want me—"

"No, I've got it." Before her brain could convince her not to, she plunged down the stairs. The ashes were less damp here, the scent of smoke less pungent. With her X-ray and heat visions, she couldn't perceive any traces of life on the first floor of the facility, but two definite forms lay motionless on the level beneath.

"They're in the experimentation room, I think," Zeela told Charlie, her voice echoing eerily off the corridor's walls.

As she slinked along, her foot hit something fleshy, and the stench that had been covered by the smoke hit her: deteriorating humans. Dead, the bodies were less noticeable in her heat vision, but she could now pick out the muscles and bones and *blood* of the Affinities the Reggs had shot and killed. Charlie must have noticed them a moment after, because he began gagging as they scurried through the hall, unable to avoid the corpses.

The door at the end of the corridor was still ajar, so they hurried through it and skipped down the second stairwell, immersing themselves in the hellhole to which Zeela had hoped never to return. Though it was difficult for her to see, she discerned that the wooden door to their little dungeon was open, excreting the two dead Reggs' decaying odors.

"Do you want me to extract the handle from the door?" Charlie asked, voice nasally as he held his nose between two fingers.

Zeela pushed on the metal door handle, and as Charlie had probably sensed, it was locked. Before she could give him consent to rip it off, movement sounded from within, paralyzing them.

"H-hello?" a weak voice croaked, followed by a cough and a stronger, "Hello? Is someone out there?"

Zeela realized then that she didn't even know their first names, so rather awkwardly, she called, "Mr. Stark?"

"Y-yes—yes!" he exclaimed, fiddling with the lock on the door until it opened. Even without the metal between them, the man looked the same to Zeela now as he had a moment ago: a compilation of bones and muscle that was a bit taller than Charlie, perhaps with more plaque buildup in his arteries. The hallway must have been illuminated well enough for him to absorb Zeela's appearance—her white eye, her missing eye—because his enthusiasm rapidly dwindled.

"Are you…"

"Wackos?" Charlie offered. "No. Affinities, yes. We were stuck in this facility until yesterday."

"We're friends of Avner Stromer," Zeela added, hoping this would assuage the tension. "I know your sons, Seth and Tray. I went to school with them in Periculand."

A faint sigh of relief escaped the man's throat. "They're doing all right?"

"They were when I left. Adara's fine, too."

The man snorted, shaking his head. "Adara… I'm surprised she hasn't landed herself in jail yet. Is she just as much of a troublemaker in Periculand?"

"I don't think she's done anything *illegal* yet…"

"Hm… Well, I'm Richard, and my wife, Linda, is sleeping back there. When that fire started, she broke her hand to free herself from her manacles. Either of you have a healing Affinity?" When they both shook their heads, he exhaled. "Well, we'll find a hospital soon enough… Once we were both free, we hurried down here to activate the outdoor sprinkler system. It put out the fire quick enough to save us, but the path up the steps was blocked. We've been sending out distress signals for hours. I guess you got one?"

"Distress signals?" Zeela repeated as panic crept in. "As in… people know you're here? As in…the government might know you're here?"

"You should wake your wife," Charlie urged, head turning toward the stairwell, as if Regg soldiers might charge through at any moment. "We should get going."

"We…wanted the government to know we're here," Richard insisted. He did react to their alarm, though, warily retreating to wake the woman named Linda. She slept atop one of the metal experimentation tables—probably the same one on which they'd carved out Zeela's eye. The thought spiked her surging adrenaline to the point that she considered leaving the Starks just to get away from this place.

"I don't think you want the government to find you, considering they're the ones who locked you up here in the first place," Zeela explained as calmly as she could. "I'm not sure what the Reggs have against—"

"The government doesn't run this place," Richard said, appalled that she would even imply such a thing. He sounded convinced of his own words, but Zeela knew they couldn't be true.

Who operated this place if not the government? Who would have the funds—and who would have such an interest in the abilities of Affinities other than the government that fought against them? But why *would* the government be after the Starks? Even if they had committed some crime, why place them *here* with Affinities, rather than in a real prison?

A memory surfaced in her mind—one of Naretha mentioning the Wacko leader sought to apprehend the Starks. That didn't make sense, though. The Wackos were terrorists, but their reason was to *stop* the government from running facilities like this. Why would Danny have one of his own? He had to be twisted, but Naretha, his girlfriend, had *been here*.

Shaking the wild thoughts from her head, Zeela trained her vision on the Starks, who now approached the doorway. There was no way to sort out Linda's features, but she was shorter than her husband, and Zeela picked out the broken bones in her hand and the weary sag of her shoulders. She didn't bother to introduce herself or imagine what kind of horrified expressions the woman might be making at her lack of an eye; with a curt nod toward the stairwell, she began her ascent from the depths of this hell.

Before they reached the second staircase leading to the ruins of the barn, however, Zeela sensed something was terribly wrong. Commotion sounded from above, and when she fixated her eye beyond the metal and dirt and rubble, she saw bodies running in chaos as a massive, bird-like creature swooped around in a vicious attack. Even after rubbing her eye in disbelief, she was met with the same outlandish reality.

"There is some shit going on up there," she said as Charlie stepped beside her. "I need you to peek up the stairwell and tell me what you see."

The man swallowed after a booming squawk reverberated through the earth. Tentatively, he mounted the stairs, and Zeela followed until they poked their heads above the barn's debris. Without any objects to interfere with her sight, the scene still appeared as bizarre as before: Affinities fled across the open plain as a bird the size of a car plucked them from the ground and launched them into the air. Some survived; some didn't. The violence was so distressing that she almost didn't notice two figures slowly trudging through the ashes, careful to avoid the embers.

One—a male, judging by his voice and body structure—swore when he stepped on a particularly large ember that melted some of the rubber sole of his shoe. The other, a female, snapped at him to be careful, and though neither of them sounded familiar, Zeela still whispered to Charlie, "Do you recognize them?"

At the shake of his head, she motioned back toward the Starks to follow. These two strangers were clearly searching for the underground lair, and without Zeela's more abstract sight capabilities, she couldn't determine if they were friendly. The only chance they had of escaping unseen would be now, and if these people controlled that unfathomable winged creature, Zeela did not want to be seen.

Unfortunately, it was hard for her to gauge how well the darkness of night veiled their appearance. She hoped that, as they gradually emerged from the stairwell, crouching low and using chunks of the fallen barn as cover, they would remain undiscovered. The strangers were so busy sifting through the debris that they probably wouldn't have glanced in their direction—until Richard tripped on the lip of the staircase, flopping into the ash with a thud.

Zeela and Charlie both froze at the unmistakable cocking of a gun.

"Stop—don't move!" the female's voice barked as the two figures stalked toward them, disregarding the embers. The gun was hazy in Zeela's vision, but she knew it wasn't loaded with tranquilizing darts; these were real bullets, and if she was shot, she would die. If these people planned to haul her off to another research facility, though, wouldn't death be better?

Thankfully, she didn't have to answer that morbid question, because Charlie wasn't ready to die today. Raising his hands as if in surrender, he summoned the gun, ripping it out of the woman's grasp. Once he had control of the weapon, Zeela didn't have to see the strangers' auras to feel the fear in the air.

"Don't make me shoot you," he warned, his voice steady even though his body trembled. "I've been told I have impeccable aim."

"We don't want violence," the woman said carefully. "We just want the Starks. Give them to us, and we can part ways peacefully."

"You don't want violence?" Zeela challenged, glimpsing past them at the carnage the monstrous bird was immersed in. "Is that not your pet?"

"We were attacked by that group first," she dismissed. "Didn't even get a word out before they charged at us. This is self-defense you're seeing."

"I wouldn't call it a fair fight," Zeela retorted dryly, examining the strangers' bodies for some hint of their allegiance. With the gun, it seemed unlikely they were Affinities, but they weren't wearing Affinity-proof suits. Could they be mercenaries hired by the government to track down the Starks—or hired by Danny to track down the Starks? None of it explained the supernatural bird.

"I wouldn't call thirty against three a fair fight, either. Give us the Starks and we'll leave you unharmed."

"You don't seem to be in a prime spot for negotiation," Charlie observed, shifting the gun in his hands. "How about you stand still, so I don't have to shoot you, and then we'll walk away with the Starks? Deal?"

The woman opened her mouth, but no noise emitted before Zeela's ears were filled with the rumbling of an engine. Pivoting to the right, she found a vehicle bumbling through the field, heading straight for them.

"No!" the unfamiliar man cried. "Someone's stealing it!"

"I told you, you should have stayed in the van," the woman growled at him as she broke into a sprint toward the vehicle. At the sudden movement, Charlie instinctively began shooting, and screams riddled the air—mostly from Richard and the unfamiliar man. As Charlie continued his assault, Zeela ushered the Starks away from the madness, but the vehicle had already drawn too close, wedging them between it and the strangers, who had taken cover behind a beam to avoid Charlie's bullets.

Given the driver was the sole occupant, Zeela was tempted to storm into the van and claim it as her own. When the driver rolled down the passenger's side window to shout for them to enter, though, Zeela's face broke into a grin. Even with the clamor erupting around her, she recognized that voice: Key Fingers.

"Get in," Zeela told the Starks after thrusting the van's door open.

Hesitantly, the couple approached, Richard helping his wife in even though he seemed to be the tenser of the two. Based on the way they both situated themselves as far from Key Fingers as possible, the crazy old woman didn't help mitigate their anxiety. For Zeela, the only person she might have been more relieved to see driving the van was Avner.

Yelling for Charlie to join them, she hopped into the passenger's seat. The jostling of the van signaled his entrance through the back door, prompting Key Fingers to slam her foot on the gas pedal. Another yelp escaped Richard's throat as the vehicle jolted forward, bumping and jerking along the uneven terrain.

As the back door shut, sealing them within, Zeela vaguely heard the two strangers shouting while they ran to chase down the van that had once been theirs. Even driving on the rough grass, the vehicle outpaced them, and Key Fingers plunged on until the strangers were two specks in the distance. That bird, though… It was as far away as the humans, yet Zeela could still see it clearly, as if it were an ordinary bird hovering directly behind them.

"Does anyone know what in the hell that *beast* was?" Key Fingers questioned.

"Some kind of genetically-modified monster?" Charlie guessed through panting breaths. "I've never seen a bird that size."

"What did it look like?" Zeela asked, feeling a bit worthless for having to ask at all. Her vision had always been different, but with so many of her sight's facets eliminated, along with one of her eyes, she felt as detached now as when she'd been blind.

"It was…purple, I think," Charlie said. "Must've been a falcon of some sort…"

"I'm assuming falcons aren't typically purple?"

"You'd be surprised, girl," Key Fingers said with a whimsical inflection. "I've seen plenty of purple animals while under the influence of drugs."

With raised eyebrows, Zeela peered back at Charlie and asked, "Do you think it could have been an Affinity shapeshifter?"

The graveness of his response chilled her. "I know those two I shot at were Affinities. Hard to tell in the dark, but I think they had red and green hair. I don't know how well you can see the details of this van, but…I'm pretty sure this thing belongs to the Wackos."

Zeela leaned her head against the back of her seat, absorbing the implication of his words. If the Wackos had known where the research facility was and that it had been destroyed, did that mean it belonged to them?

This mission had begun with the intention of saving Maddy, but somehow she'd arrived at the point at which she needed to run as far away from Maddy—and the Wackos—as possible. Selfishly, she wanted to abandon the Starks and search for her friends, but she'd made her choice when she hadn't been captured with Avner.

She would deliver the Starks to safety, wherever safety was, and she would hope she didn't fail them like she'd failed that ravaged group of Affinities.

When Zach had said he hoped Maddy would find clothes that fit her style, he should have said he hoped she would find clothes that fit her *at all.* Whoever Zach's old roommate had been was considerably thinner than Maddy, forcing her to mold her body into an unusual shape to slip on a dress. Even then she felt wildly uncomfortable, squirming and fidgeting as she exited Zach's private bathroom to reenter his bedroom. When she found him standing beside his bed, clothed in an elegant suit that matched the gray of his hair and eyes, she almost quite literally melted into a blob.

As he surveyed her, his lips curled in a way that implied he thought her just as unattractive as she felt. "I apologize that my… roommate doesn't have the finest taste in clothes." Gaze lingering on the black leather dress and knee-high boots, Zach cleared his throat and added, "You, uh, got taller."

Maddy peeked down at her lengthy legs, which she'd elongated so that she now stood nearly as tall as him. Since she didn't often assume this height, it was odd to look directly into his eyes when, minutes ago, she'd had to tilt her head up at him. "I… wasn't thin enough to fit otherwise."

Relief washed over Zach's face, and Maddy must have creased her brow in response, because he hastily explained, "I was worried you might have chosen this appearance because you thought people would like it better."

"Do you…not like it better?"

A smile trickled onto his lips, but he seemed to think whatever was on his mind was not worth voicing because, instead of answering, he motioned toward the door and mumbled, "Let's get this over with."

Zach held open the door for her, but Maddy knew he only did so because he didn't want her to infect the door handle. She nodded in gratitude nonetheless, sauntering into the hallway with her clunky boots. Most of the doors were wide open on this floor, permitting conversation between the Affinities flooding out of their bedrooms toward the elevator. A few dressed formally, like Zach, but the majority wore the same dark, punkish style as herself, alleviating her nerves. Maybe she'd actually blend in at this gathering of Wackos.

While living in Periculand during the past three years, she'd grown accustomed to brightly-colored hair clogging a corridor. What struck her as unusual about this sight was that these people all smiled and laughed and joked, as if it were *natural*. This was common in Periculand, but she hadn't expected it within a terrorist organization.

"Do you know everyone?" Maddy whispered to Zach as they submerged into the crowd.

"Most." The boisterous cackle of a teenage girl walking ahead of them nearly overpowered his voice. Many of the Wackos were young, she noted, though there were a few middle-aged and elderly people sprinkled throughout.

"The older members worked with my father for years," Zach explained, eyeing the mass clustered before them with pensive eyes. His gait was slow, purposely removing them from the others—probably because he couldn't handle standing so close to their germs. "The younger ones, for the most part, have joined over the past few years with the government's increasing hostility and our rising…popularity."

"The Wackos *have* become rather notorious on the news… Who pays for all of this, though—and what's the *goal*?"

Zach pressed his lips together, waiting until the other Affinities piled into the elevator, leaving the two alone. With only the cool metallic walls and the harsh fluorescent lights filling their surroundings, he puffed out a breath. "Danny's goal seems to be destruction—death, domination. Very different from the original objective, but…he has the support of the other…Wackos."

"Is that why he became leader instead of you at your father's death?"

His lips twitched, but no response emitted before the elevator doors parted, beckoning for their entry. Once sealed within, Maddy was convinced they would suffer the rest of the journey in silence, but then Zach, sounding as flustered as she'd ever heard him, said, "The position as leader was left to me upon my father's death, but…Danny didn't think I was fit for the role. He challenged me to a…physical duel, and clearly I had no chance. I failed…everyone."

Maddy was so distracted with sympathy that, when the elevator jolted upward, she stumbled into him, tripping over her dramatic boots and clinging to him for support. Disgusted by the physical contact, Zach shoved her off, and she slammed into the side of the elevator. Though her shoulder ached from the impact, the flame of humiliation rising in her cheeks was arguably more painful.

"I-I'm sorry." He reached out to right her but then recoiled. "I…didn't mean to hurt you. Are you all right?"

"I'm fine," she assured him, though she avoided his gaze as she hugged her torso and stared at the silver doors. "You didn't—I didn't—" Biting her lip, she peeked over at him and found his usually unreadable face riddled with self-loathing.

"I'm *not* fit to be a leader," he mumbled, mostly to himself it seemed. "I'm barely even capable of touching another human being… My Affinity is useless in combat; the Reggs wouldn't be threatened by the very notion of me as they are with Danny."

"Do you *want* the Reggs to fear you?"

He grimaced, hesitating long enough that they reached their destination before he replied. Once again left thinking her questions would remain unanswered, Maddy was baffled when he jabbed the button to keep the doors sealed.

"I want Affinities to be respected members of society," he said, his finger still pressed against the button. "I want the Reggs to treat us fairly, and I want justice, but I don't think violence is the way. We need diplomacy, and—and Danny's a fine negotiator, until he doesn't get his way. The Reggs have mistreated us too many times for him to end this in any way other than total domination. By the time he's through, all Reggs will be dead or slaves. Only one person could contain his anger, and that person is gone."

"Your father?" Maddy guessed as he removed his finger from the button, allowing the doors to peel apart.

"My father wouldn't have been pleased with the way things have gone," Zach conceded, his voice nearly drowned out by the commotion of the cafeteria. "But there's nothing we can do about it now. C'mon, and try to stay quiet, if you can." The warning was obvious as his gaze drifted across the room to where his brother sauntered around, laughing with other Wackos like a normal guy. "I can't believe he's actually wearing that ridiculous suit..."

Danny's bright red suit did look a little ridiculous surrounded by the neutral colors everyone else sported. On Aethelred, a red suit had always been charming and cordial, but Danny looked like Satan incarnate in his.

"He certainly likes to intimidate," Maddy commented under her breath.

Zach snorted. "He acquired that suit the day our father died."

It shouldn't have been a question, but the way he said *acquired* caused her to ask, "He...bought it?"

"He blew up the cashier and then he took it," he responded flatly, remorsefully. The suit's devilish quality elevated with that. Stepping out of the elevator felt like stepping into the lair of a monster.

The cafeteria, which Maddy hadn't entered before now, was twice as grand as Danny's office. Round tables littered the floor, but instead of the vibrant hues that characterized Periculand's, this cafeteria's color scheme didn't expand past the gray-scale; the tables were black, the walls gray, and the chairs a pristine white. Along the left and right walls were two kitchens where a few Affinities prepared food while another—a man likely in his thirties with sea foam green hair—levitated plates to each of the tables until every Wacko seated had a platter of various meats.

"We used to eat a lot of fruit when my father was in charge," Zach muttered to her as they wove through the cafeteria, dodging tables, chairs, and flying plates, "but I think Danny's trying to turn us all into carnivores."

"Why fruit?"

He coughed with an actual hint of humor. "It was his Affinity."

"His...what?" Maddy spluttered, but Zach's wariness of their surroundings had already resumed, leaving her to wonder how a man with an Affinity for *fruit* could have founded a terrorist organization.

Since she hadn't been allowed to interact with anyone until now, the only familiar faces in this sea of gathered Wackos were the girl with the bumblebee-yellow hair who'd guarded her door and Josh, finally free from his cell. With his dark suit and freshly-cut mohawk, she barely recognized him where he sat at a small rectangular table to the right of Danny's...*throne*.

It must have been a new addition to the cafeteria, because the black metal was shiny and polished without wear. Towering at least eight feet tall, the back of the throne was designed like a nuclear explosion—a mushroom plume of smoke and fire. Behind it, painted on the wall, was a mural of *Danny* walking out of a similar explosion, though this one popped with blinding color that matched his hair. His expression in the painting was as manic as his expression in this moment: that demonic grin accompanied by those feverish eyes. When his gaze landed on Maddy and Zach, who had almost reached the front of the room, his eyebrows jumped in a way that made her wish she could flatten to the floor and disappear under a table.

"The mural is really over the top," Zach muttered as they approached a second rectangular table at Danny's left. "My brother forced Josh to paint it while the poor kid was in chains—part of his punishment for leaving Naretha behind."

As Zach assumed the seat closest to the throne and Maddy hesitantly sat beside him, she wanted to ask which person Naretha was, but her question was satisfied a moment later when the elevator doors glided open and the hall fell to a hush.

"My beloved," Danny greeted from his throne, placing a hand over his heart. Naretha's lips formed a strained smile as everyone slowly stood and clapped, some looking genuinely pleased and others looking subtly terrified of what Danny might do if they didn't participate.

Based on the dark makeup and scornful eye rolls, Danny's girlfriend was just as nasty and daunting as Maddy had expected. Instead of wearing gothic attire, Naretha was adorned in a tight, sequined dress which matched her eyes perfectly with its pale pink pigment. Though Maddy assumed her hair would have been pink as well, Naretha was nearly completely bald, only a stubby layer of fuzz coating her scalp.

"This is new," Naretha observed, eyeing Danny's throne and mural appreciatively. "It suits you."

"As it suits you," Danny cooed, patting one of his thighs.

A naughty grin consumed Naretha's lips, but Maddy swore that, just before, she'd seen the woman's nose twitch. Whether she wanted to or not, Danny's girlfriend took her appointed seat on his lap, crossing her lengthy legs and facing the crowd like a queen. The instant her eyes landed upon the table to her left, where Maddy and Zach sat, all dignity and propriety fizzled into a black rage.

"As you all know," Danny began before Naretha's fury could physically manifest, "we've gathered here today to celebrate the return of my lovely girlfriend. Tortured by Angor Periculy for an entire month, she survived and prevailed, maintaining Wacko secrets and protecting this organization over her life." A few people hollered and clapped, but Zach frowned with disapproval. "Tortured by Reggs for weeks afterward, Naretha managed to escape a research facility and destroy it with the sheer power of her Affinity. She is an inspiration to—"

"Danny, dear," she interjected through gritted teeth, and all rustling and applause silenced at her voice. Perhaps Maddy hadn't been the only one in this room told to never interrupt Danny. Naretha must have known she treaded over unstable territory, because she plastered a loving smile that seemed foreign onto her face. "I believe you're giving me too much credit. I never would have escaped Periculand if a few rogue students hadn't freed me. I never would have escaped the Regg facility if those same kids hadn't fought by my side, all so they could come here and save their precious friend." Pausing, Naretha's eyes slid toward Maddy, petrifying her. "If she weren't so inherently skilled at being a damsel in distress, I wouldn't be here. So, the one we should really praise is her, Faddy."

A few muffled snickers wove through the audience as all gazes spun toward "Faddy." She wasn't sure she would have been any less mortified if Naretha had pronounced her name correctly. The rest of the Wackos hung in an awkward limbo, unsure of whether to applaud Maddy or scorn her.

"It's refreshing to see you haven't matured at all during this ordeal, Naretha," Zach finally sneered, breaking the silence. Her placidity faded with his comment, her nostrils flaring with such intensity that Maddy curled away. Danny would *definitely* react poorly to criticism toward his girlfriend; a brawl between the brothers was about to break out because of a stupid comment.

Feeling responsible, Maddy was about to speak up in a feeble attempt to alleviate the hostility, but then Danny chimed in, his words aimed at his girlfriend like a father scolding his child. "Now, Naretha, Madella is one of us—a Wacko. I assume that you're mispronouncing her name affectionately, hm?" The tone was almost too reasonable and calm to have flowed from Danny's mouth.

Naretha seemed beyond bewildered, but she covered it up with another complacent smirk. "Of course—so much affection," she crooned, shooting Maddy a glare that promised murder.

"Good," Danny said. "Now, let's dig into the feast, shall we, while I make a few announcements?"

Hesitantly, the Wackos nodded, gradually retrieving their forks. Judging by the way they eyed Danny with apprehension, none of them had a particularly large appetite, the reason for which was solidified when their leader continued his speech.

"At this point, I assume it's common knowledge that three very dangerous people have escaped this compound. Many of you knew of Naira and Cath, and I doubt any of you could forget

Ashna... All three have evaded us and run off to an unknown location. This has sparked fear among many of you, but...how could you even begin to fear when *I* am your leader?" All eyes bored into their plates at the aggressive accusation. Maddy avoided the Wacko leader's gaze as well, focusing intently on her mystery meat, until Danny's voice finally boomed throughout the cafeteria once more.

"The girls may divulge our location to the Reggs, but would the Reggs dare attack us? No, no, I don't believe they would. Nevertheless, I have been working tirelessly to discover the girls' whereabouts, and it's only a matter of time before they will be eliminated. So, worry not. Focus on the tasks at hand—the missions I've entrusted to each of you—and allow me to handle this catastrophe like the capable leader I am."

Heads bobbed throughout the crowd, many honestly relieved while others were still quietly skeptical. Maddy wasn't sure what opinion to have. The escape of these girls could mean the end of the Wackos, which would have been beneficial before, but now that she had tattoos like the rest of them, wouldn't she be placed in jail—or killed—like any other Wacko? Though she hardly knew him, she also couldn't help but wonder what might happen to Zach.

As conversations blossomed throughout the room and Danny lifted his chin in satisfaction, Zach inclined his head toward her and murmured, "He's not going to find them."

"Why do you think that?" she asked carefully, stabbing her fork into what appeared to be a piece of sausage.

"Danny has no idea where they are—he's bluffing. He put a tracking device in Ashna, but she managed to turn it off."

"The other two don't have tracking devices?"

"They didn't seem...likely to escape. Ashna did. She's...well, she's definitely surpassed the intellectual capacity of a fifteen-year-old." His smile was almost smug. Was it possible he'd *helped* her as a way to destroy his brother?

This wasn't a question Maddy could ask now—and she wasn't sure it was one she should ask *ever*. Being in such close proximity to the family that ran this terrorist organization seemed dangerous enough. If anything, she should have focused on contriving a way to escape this place, not trying to uncover the social undercurrents that could possibly get her killed.

"Well," Maddy said, aware that Naretha's venomous eyes lingered in her direction, "I hope everything works out for the best in the end."

Zach nodded stiffly, understanding her hidden meaning. Before his lips could part to comment, the elevator chimed open, admitting not a person but a *falcon*. On mauve wings, the falcon soared through the cafeteria, invoking yelps and screams of terror. Danny, however, was completely unfazed, and Naretha smirked brutishly, especially as the bird landed before the platform of the Wacko leader's throne and then morphed into a man—a naked man.

Maddy would have instinctively averted her eyes if not for the wounds marring his dark skin. None of them were particularly serious, but blood dripped down the muscles of his chest, and his hair, the same purple his feathers had been, was streaked red. Despite his injuries, Danny's lips curled with devious delight as he raked his eyes over the man.

"Well, isn't this a pleasant surprise?" Danny mused, though the man panted too hard to have heard. When someone handed him a towel, he barely breathed the word "thanks" before wrapping it around his hips. "I assume you came ahead of your friends to inform me that you've captured the Starks. Those two Reggs put up a fight, didn't they?"

"Not…the Starks," the man breathed as the heaviness of his pants finally subsided. "We made it back to the research facility, but there was a group of hostile Affinities there. They ambushed us, making it possible for some of them to escape with the Starks."

Danny's enthusiasm faded into a grotesque umbrage. Standing and causing Naretha to fumble off the throne, Danny towered above the man, who would have been taller than him without the platform, and quietly said, "You returned here empty-handed?"

"We wanted to update you on our progress," the man replied with growing unease.

"The progress you haven't made? Yes, I'm so grateful for the update."

Many of the Wackos chuckled, but Zach's posture was rigid beside Maddy, and she squirmed at the way Danny's bright eyes began to blaze.

"Devika and Kevin are still out there," the man said tightly. "We will find the Starks again. It's just going to take us longer than we antici—"

"The fact that two *Reggs* were able to escape you is pathetic in itself," Danny drawled, as if the man hadn't said a word. "If you can't complete such menial tasks, you're of no use to me."

Maddy expected the man to beg, but he kept his voice even as he said, "We won't fail again. Devika's on their trail, and once I get back to them—"

"Get back to them?" Danny repeated with a cruel laugh. "How will you get back to them if you don't have legs?"

The man's face slackened, as if his legs had already been dismembered, but as Danny stepped forward to exact what he perceived as justice, Naretha grabbed his arm and glared into his simmering eyes.

"Don't you think it'd be beneficial for Nate to keep his legs? How about, instead of ruining him, you save his punishment for the Starks when they arrive? Which they surely will," she added with a pointed look at the man, who nodded profusely. "The Starks are just measly Reggs, after all. Nate, though pathetic, is an Affinity with skills that can help our cause. But, of course, the choice is yours." This last addition to her speech seemed the most necessary part; Danny had looked thoroughly inclined to ignore her advice, until she gave him a choice in the matter.

After a minute of contemplation, he plopped back into his throne and narrowed his eyes at Nate. "You have one week to capture them. If you are unsuccessful, you will no longer be welcome at this establishment, and if we find you after that, we won't hesitate to hand you over to the Reggs. Be gone now, before I change my mind."

With a curt bow, Nate transformed back into a falcon, the process so swift that Maddy couldn't comprehend how it was physically possible.

"You make me so gracious, my love," Danny droned as the bird disappeared through the elevator. Reaching up, he pulled Naretha into a passionate kiss that had all, except a few horny teenagers, staring down at their plates to avoid awkwardly watching.

Maddy's instinct was to do the same, but then she noticed Naretha's eyes were open as she mashed her lips against Danny's—and she stared in their direction. Though her gaze was as intense as before, the severe loathing had diminished, leaving only drained, weary relief.

25

The Art of Awkwardness

Eliana had drawn the same image every day for the past week: Zeela surrounded by flames. Realistically, she wouldn't have survived such an inferno, but the scene became clearer in her mind every time she depicted it, and her sister, with her white eyes and determined expression, looked so fierce that she couldn't stop drawing it. The only strange part was that she couldn't draw Zeela's angelic hair. The pencil strokes never matched her memories, and for some reason it felt more natural to portray her sister with only short stubble atop her head.

It was this image that Eliana sketched in the library that Tuesday afternoon, the day after the three new girls had assimilated into Periculand Training School—the day after Kiki had stormed out of training because of Ruse's little prank.

Alone in their dormitory last night, Kiki hadn't verbally divulged any information about her encounter with Adara, but her thoughts had flowed freely, intentionally revealing her sentiments. As Eliana had anticipated, witnessing Adara in prison hadn't livened her spirits; if anything, seeing her again after so many weeks had made Kiki feel *guilty*—not about Adara's current situation but about how Kiki had treated her throughout their childhood. It was this budding remorse that Eliana's roommate had fallen asleep to, her dreams drifting into a realm where she'd decided to befriend Adara rather than bully her.

Now, in the library, with the pale afternoon light spilling onto the page before her, Kiki's brain was too distant for Eliana to sense. There were plenty of other minds to fill the library's silence, though—like Tray Stark's. Nestled in a secluded corner, he studied a book about Mental Affinities for clues as to how they could stop Artemis's mind controlling without the woman discovering they were aware of her abilities. Eliana should have been doing the same, but to consider there was a way to *thwart* Artemis—that there had been a way to prevent her from murdering Hastings but none of them had known… It was too much for her to handle. So instead, she drew abstract pictures of her sister amidst a world of flames to avoid the real world, which was likely to go down in flames around her.

Another mind that had pressed on hers over the past hour was that of one of the new girls, Cath. She sat at a table across the library, so far that Eliana barely distinguished her hulking form. Based on her thoughts, the girl was frustrated, but it was in such a pure, innocent way that Eliana was tempted to help her. A spike of alarm in the girl's brain finally gave her the courage to do so.

"*You,*" Eliana heard a nasty voice sneer through Cath's auditory system. The girl didn't fully recognize the speaker, but Eliana did. By his gruff tone and imposing structure as he towered over Cath's table, it was Nero. "*Finally caught you without your little friends,*" he continued as Cath peered up at him timidly. Eliana had already picked up her papers and drawing utensils to pace across the library and intercept the conversation. "*Not so tough without them, are you? Bet you never could've beaten me if you hadn't had that skinny guy and that stupid, salt-spewing—*"

"*Naretha isn't stupid,*" Cath defended, her voice nearly as deep as Nero's. Her thoughts flashed images of the Wacko with the pale pink hair, all memories affectionate. If Cath had been forced to work for the Wackos, though, why would she be so fond of Naretha?

"Regardless," Nero drawled, his voice now penetrating Eliana's own ears, "I think I owe you a few punches. I'd like to slam you into a metal door and see how you—"

"Nero," Eliana injected the moment she stopped beside him. She'd had more than a few insulting comebacks contrived, but now that his massive body loomed over her, all righteous rage fizzled.

"Ah, Little Mensen," he greeted as his gray eyes settled on her. "Should've known you'd be lurking around here with your… brain." He scrunched his nose at her forehead, where her mind reading capabilities lay, and then glared at the drawings hugged to her chest. "What is that? We don't have homework anymore."

"Oh—um—drawings." She produced a weak smile, fully prepared for him to yank them out of her grasp and tear them to shreds, but then he cocked his head, studying her with intrigue.

"You're an artist?"

"Y-yes."

His thick eyebrows furrowed as he snagged Cath's paper. When he shoved it in Eliana's face, she was bombarded with an assortment of colors that didn't amount to anything coherent. "Are you better than this?"

She swallowed, knowing he could uncover the truth simply by snatching her own papers. "Yes," she confirmed, avoiding Cath's eyes by fixing her focus on Nero's.

He slapped the girl's paper back on the table and crossed his arms. "All right, Little Mensen. If you're so good, I want you to draw a portrait of me—one worthy of being plastered around Periculand. I know I already look like a god, but feel free to exaggerate a bit. I want everyone to know I rule this place."

"A-a portrait?"

"Yeah," he said, almost *self-consciously*—as if he knew she thought the idea was ridiculous and now second-guessed himself. Unfortunately, his mind was too heavily guarded to validate this theory. "If you make me a portrait, I won't demolish this... beast," he added with a condescending sniff in Cath's direction. The dread in her moss-green eyes confirmed she had no interest in brawling with Nero, even if she had a decent chance of winning.

"Okay," Eliana finally said. "I'll draw...you."

"Good," Nero grunted with a hint of relief. "You have until my birthday, Mensen."

Eliana's eyes darted around awkwardly. "When's your birthday?"

Not knowing the date was apparently the most inconceivable notion, because Nero rolled his eyes dramatically. "One week from today, primie. I want to wake up to the sight of my face pasted on every wall of this campus."

"That's, um..." His vicious stare quelled her sarcastic remark. "Okay, sure. One week."

Nodding, Nero shot Cath a disgusted look before stomping off, his footsteps reverberating through the floor until he'd exited the library.

"I-I'm sorry," Eliana stammered, shuffling beside Cath's table. "I shouldn't have said my art was better than yours, because...it's not. Art is subjective. But...I knew that's what he wanted to hear."

Cath's large lips smiled softly. "You saved me from him."

"I, um—well, I don't know about that..."

"Sit," she commanded, motioning to the seat across from hers. Fumbling with her papers and pencils, Eliana plopped into the chair and dropped them on the table. As Cath surveyed her drawings of Zeela through her jagged green bangs, her face brightened with even more enthusiasm. "You are much better than me."

Biting her lip, Eliana examined Cath's pages, all strewn with bright colors etched with crayon. "What are you trying to draw?"

Redness seeped into her round cheeks. "You and your friends." With a dense finger, she pointed to one of the blobs of a medium blue hue. "That one's you, and that's your girlfriend." She then pointed to a pinkish figure: Kiki. With this information, Eliana saw the lines clearer, and it looked like she and Kiki were holding hands. "And that one's your boyfriend." Cath motioned toward a brown figure that also appeared to be holding Eliana's hand.

As soon as the facts registered in her head, Eliana let out a genuine giggle. "*Tray*? I have—a girlfriend *and* a boyfriend?"

"And I'm convinced your boyfriend might also be dating this one."

Eliana's smirk remained when Cath indicated a mustard-yellow depiction linked with Tray's. "Lavisa—and *Tray*? No, no... they don't get along very well."

"I know a lot of couples that don't get along." Cath shrugged her massive shoulders. "And a lot of people who can't pick just one person to date. Romance is confusing."

Eliana dipped her chin in agreement, still eyeing the drawing with faint amusement. "I'm...actually not dating anyone, though. I'm not sure...if I can let myself feel that way about someone again."

Cath nodded in sympathy. "The twitchy kid said you dated the boy the Wackos sent me to retrieve—the one who died..."

"Twitchy kid?" Eliana asked, rather than elaborating on the subject of Hastings. Cath pointed to the orange figure on her paper. "Oh, Hartman. Well, yeah...he's essentially right. We weren't officially together, but...technicalities don't make a difference. It hurt the same. I just wish..." Shaking her head to expel the thoughts, she refocused on the drawing. "Have you always liked to draw?"

Cath lifted the green crayon that matched her murky hair; it looked like a toothpick between her meaty fingers. "I never learned how to hold these—or those," she said, nodding toward Eliana's pencils. "My fingers have always been too big. But I'm trying to improve. I'm skilled with chaotic movements but not precise ones. I want to learn how to do more than just destroy."

Her thoughts were so genuine and desperate that Eliana had to close her eyes. It sounded so much like Hastings. But her optimism—her hope that people could be redeemed—had died with Hastings. How could she assure Cath that she had potential when, in this bleak world, it seemed so unlikely that she'd reach it?

"Everyone called you 'the monster' when you first came here," Eliana started slowly, "but you're not a monster. You have one of the sweetest minds I've ever encountered. I really admire you for your effort."

Cath's blush was even more profuse than it had been earlier. Before she could voice her gratitude, though, a person popped up beside their table with crossed arms and raised eyebrows.

"Here you are." Kiki glared down at Eliana with cotton candy eyes. "I've been looking all over for you. We—" Her voice came to an abrupt halt when her eyes locked onto the drawing sprawled on the table—not Cath's, but Eliana's. "I know that."

Eliana blinked and then glanced between her roommate and her depiction of Zeela. "Um...what?"

Kiki ignored her, grabbing the paper. "I've seen this before, but I didn't remember seeing it until I saw this just now."

"You *saw* this?" Eliana repeated, standing to peer over the image with her. "As...as in...the future?"

"I-I don't know." Tossing the paper back onto the table, she hugged her torso and peeked over at Eliana with uncertainty. "Now I can't stop thinking about it. How did you know to draw that?"

"I...don't know," Eliana echoed as uneasiness crept through her. "I've been drawing it for days. Maybe...maybe I've been reading your mind while we're both...asleep—like I must have on the night Ruse appeared at our door as Hastings."

Kiki's eyes narrowed. "Are you telling me...you've been stealing my dreams for a *month*?"

"Unintentionally," Eliana said with a wince.

Her roommate's nostrils flared, but she didn't voice her disgruntlement. "We'll figure this out later. Right now, we have work to do. Calder, whose attractiveness Adara *ruined* for me with the fact that he's actually *into* her, wants us to go dig up dirt about Than, who, even if he is a Wacko, is still the hottest three-hundred-year-old I've ever encountered."

"Calder...told you he wants us to investigate Than?"

"No, but he's about to—probably in a few seconds."

Eliana's brow wrinkled, but then she sensed Calder's consciousness slip into the library. As Kiki had predicted, he stalked toward them a few seconds later. "Nero sent me here to tell you he wants a 'manly crown' on his head in his portrait," he said to Eliana by way of greeting. His expression was dry and partially exasperated as he added, "Do I even want to know what that means?"

"*I* want to know what that means," Kiki demanded, arching her eyebrows at Eliana.

"I—never mind." Her gaze flashed briefly toward Cath. "Is there any other reason you're here?" she asked Calder, who was now bored enough to play with an orb of water he'd conjured from his hand.

"Keep up the sass, Mensen, and you won't live to hear the answer to that question." With a smug little grin, he flicked a few droplets of water at her face. "I think Belven here already knows I'm only talking to you because I want you both to sneak into Than's office and figure out if he's a Wacko."

"I *do* know," Kiki snapped, her chin held high, "but you weren't nearly this rude in my vision."

"Your brain just can't conceive how charming I am," he mused, lips stretching wider. As his gaze landed back on Eliana, he sobered from his egotistic high. "We need to determine if Than's a Wacko. I've been trying to find Periculy's folder in the Reggs' office whenever I'm up there, but they've hidden it well. If we can find some evidence on Than, then at least we know *one* of our enemies. Of all the primies, you seem the most capable of discovering that evidence."

Kiki flipped her pinkish-blonde hair over her shoulder. "You don't need to tell me I'm amazing."

"I wasn't. I was talking to Mensen." A pout immediately consumed Kiki's face, but Eliana couldn't suppress a smirk. "Let me know if you find anything—discreetly," Calder stressed with a pointed look in Kiki's direction. "I'm convinced my roommate knows all the answers to our questions, but he won't talk, and I doubt you can read his mind. Any luck with the librarian? She must know something, since she was banging Angor."

Eliana's eyes cut to the right, where the librarian sat behind the front desk. She'd never been much of a talker, but she'd been even more subdued over the past few weeks since Angor's incarceration.

Unfortunately, the former principal seemed to have trained her in the art of blocking mind readers, because most of her thoughts were shielded, and the few Eliana extracted were as foggy or blank as anyone who'd harbored information on Angor's Affinity.

"No, nothing from her," she said. "Her mind seems as wiped as the rest… Artemis must be exhausted from altering all of them."

"That's the problem," Calder grumbled. "She's been acting fine—maybe even more animated than before. Maybe using her Affinity gives her strength, rather than draining her."

"That would make her even more dangerous…"

"As Stromer so politely suggested"—Calder's languid eyes flickered toward Kiki—"I asked Aethelred to get…*creative* with her. He obviously refused—not just to get sexy with a married woman but to even accidentally touch Artemis at all. So, we still know nothing for certain."

Kiki threw her head back and groaned. "Can't you just drown the truth out of her or something? All of the training is making me *sore*, and I think I'm starting to gain *muscles*. I don't want muscles! Soon I'm going to look like stupid Lavisa!"

Calder eyed her drolly. "I don't think you have to worry about looking like Lavisa. And I don't think it'll be possible for Artemis to admit she's a mind controlling murderer if I'm drowning her. Even if it were, I don't want to land in jail if we're wrong about this. Just see what you can gather about Than. And you"—he looked past Eliana at Cath for the first time—"tell anyone you heard any of this, and I'll fill your lungs with water."

Cath glanced up from her newest illustration, drawn with a dark blue crayon. Judging by her flustered thoughts, she hadn't paid attention to any part of their conversation. "Here," she grunted, handing her artwork to Calder without meeting his gaze.

Yanking it from her grasp, he scrutinized it for a long minute and then said, "Thanks. I think I'm gonna go hang this on the ceiling above Stromer's metal slab, so she has to stare at me all day." With a nod of appreciation at Cath, he spun on his heel and sauntered out of the library, admiring the drawing the whole way.

"You impressed Calder. That's...impressive," Eliana remarked, mildly nonplussed. Cath beamed with such mirth that she couldn't stop her lips from curving as well. "Kiki and I have to go... Will you look after my drawings for me?"

"Of course." Cath gathered Eliana's papers behind the walls of her hefty arms. "I will guard them with my life."

She might have laughed if she hadn't known the girl was completely serious. With a nod of gratitude, she strolled away, sifting through every mind in the vicinity as Kiki scurried after her. "I don't sense Than in the building."

"Then let's go." Kiki seized Eliana's hand to drag her toward the stairwell, and the sensation of physical contact instantly made her want to pull away.

Other than during drills in training, the last person she'd actually touched had been Hastings. Feeling Kiki's hand in hers now dredged up memories of her and Hastings sharing intimate moments, but it didn't hollow her like recollections of him normally did. Kiki was so wildly different from Hastings that, as they ascended the stairs of the Mentals Building, Eliana began to welcome the touch of someone who didn't remind her of him—so much that, when they reached the second floor corridor and Kiki dropped her hand, Eliana wished she hadn't.

The door to Than's office was surprisingly unlocked, and Eliana wondered if Calder had something to do with it. If he'd taken the time to unlock Than's door, though, why wouldn't he have snooped around himself? He probably thought himself too important to waste time with such tedious tasks, Eliana concluded as she and Kiki snuck through the doorway.

Like Fraco's office, Than's consisted of a desk positioned before the glass wall at the back of the room and filing cabinets—though far less than the vice principal had. Most of the space was occupied by souvenirs from the various countries he'd visited over his nearly three hundred years of life, and three whole bookshelves of history volumes lined the left wall, at which Kiki rolled her eyes.

"Don't tell me we need to look through all of those for *evidence*."

Eliana pressed her lips together as she glanced between the bookshelves and the filing cabinets on either side of the room. "I'll search the books for any hidden clues if you want to check the cabinets?"

"That sounds even more boring," Kiki moaned as she trudged over to the shelves and yanked one of the books out. Eliana fought not to chuckle when its weight nearly pulled Kiki to her knees. "This is such a waste of paper! Anyone who reads clearly doesn't care about the environment." Slamming the book down on Than's desk, she scowled at it as if it had attacked her.

Eliana extracted an even thicker volume and set it on the floor. "You really don't like to read…at all?"

"Well, I did read a book *once*," she admitted with a coy smirk.

Crouched on the ground, Eliana began flipping through the book to distract herself from Kiki's mischievous expression. "Did you like it?"

"It was pretty smutty, so yeah. Don't tell Adara, or she'll start calling me Nerd-Bitch or something weird like that… I think I like your art better than books, anyway."

Eliana hoped the lighting was dim enough that her roommate couldn't see the heat surfacing in her cheeks. "You…do?"

"Yeah." Her tone was so casual that it barely sounded like

a compliment. "Your drawing of your sister was so…lifelike—almost exactly the same as the dream I forgot I had."

When Eliana peered over her shoulder, she found Kiki giving her a tight-lipped smile. "I…don't *try* to steal your dreams," she insisted, embarrassed. "I usually try not to read your mind at all. I don't want to be…invasive."

"Hm," was the girl's only response as she rifled through the book.

"Should we…talk about our…connection, or…what the dream of Zeela in the fire might mean?"

"It probably means your sister's gonna die in a fire," Kiki said with a careless wave. "I bet Stromer will be the one to cause it, too."

"Did you *see* that?"

"No." Her lips twitched as she peeked at Eliana from the corner of her eye. "I don't see anything particularly important, since *someone's* been stealing my dreams."

The heat rising in Eliana now was too intense to be bashfulness. All of the frustration buried in her heart gradually inched upward, threatening to explode over the pettiest accusation. She wasn't *really* angry with Kiki—she was angry that her Affinity was so useless; she was angry that her sister might be in danger and there was nothing she could do about it; and she was angry that Hastings was dead and that she didn't even know who killed him.

"Maybe," Eliana began quietly, "we shouldn't be roommates anymore."

The other girl's face drooped for a moment before she defaulted to defensiveness. "Why?"

"So I stop accidentally stealing your dreams."

"I don't want to be Lavisa's roommate—"

"I'll be Lavisa's roommate."

"I *want* to be *your* roommate!" Kiki's whole body had rotated toward Eliana by now, and she was almost seething. "You're the only person in this town who understands me! You're the only person who doesn't look at me like I'm some prissy bitch or some pathetic child! You're the only person who ever has—including Seth, including my sister, including my parents—" She cut herself short, running a hand through her curly locks as she glared up at the ceiling.

"It's…been bothering me that I haven't gotten many visions. I feel…worthless. But maybe this connection between us *isn't* a bad thing. Maybe you can decipher my dreams better than I can. The details you put into that drawing…I didn't notice them until they were on paper like that—Zeela's short hair, I mean. I'd just assumed her hair was long, like it was when she left, but you must have interpreted my vision better than I did. So, maybe… if we work together, what seems like a curse could prove useful."

The intelligence of her thought process was mildly dizzying to Eliana. She'd always known Kiki was smarter than she let on, but Eliana hadn't considered the implications of what this connection could mean in terms of practicality. Separate, their Affinities had been fairly volatile, but perhaps together they could reach their full potentials.

"We…need to find a way to maximize this connection then," Eliana decided, straightening to her feet. As she did, her vision caught the book Kiki had searched through—and she saw a note poking out of the pages. Stepping between her roommate and the desk, Eliana yanked out the letter and unfolded it.

The words were composed in a sloppy scrawl, and though Eliana had always known Than's handwriting to be neat, she imagined that, in haste, it could easily be this messy. With the fervor of the moment that had just passed between her and Kiki, she read:

Danny has been badgering me to tell him if Ashna is here, but I've been ignoring his messages. He's bound to come here and demolish the whole town either way, but at least I can buy her a little time to complete her mission first. I don't want to put you in danger by telling you this, but I don't know who else to trust. If you can in any way help me defer suspicion from Ashna, I would greatly appreciate it.

"Did you read it?" Eliana asked, her voice barely audible with the shock of this evidence. Kiki was just as speechless, nodding absently as she stared at the note. "He didn't address it to anyone. Who do you think he meant to give it to? Or—or means to give it to?"

"I…I didn't even think we'd find any real proof," she whispered incredulously. "Sexy Than is a *terrorist*. And we're—we're sneaking around his office!" Without warning, Kiki tore the note from Eliana's hand and shoved it back into the book. "This guy is probably a *murderer*! Imagine what he'll do to us when he finds out we were—"

"He's not going to find out," Eliana said, but as the words flowed from her mouth, a familiar consciousness entered her awareness—one that had the potential to ruin this whole operation. "Fraco is coming up the stairs."

Blanching, Kiki's protruding eyes snapped toward the door. "There's no reason he would come in here."

"We should still hide!"

"*Where*?" Kiki hissed, but Eliana didn't have the opportunity to consider her question before the door handle began to jangle. Fraco, for some horrible reason, *was* coming into Than's office.

There was no time to run or hide. Luckily the vice principal's hands were too slippery to effectively twist the knob, but Eliana sensed through his mind that he was close to opening it. Likewise, she sensed through Kiki's mind that she knew Fraco would go directly to the new principals and inform them not only that the girls had snuck into a teacher's office but also that one of the teachers was a Wacko. With the Reggs' potentially malicious intentions, the primaries couldn't afford to divulge any new information to them.

So, Kiki hastily performed the first action that whizzed through her brain: She shoved Eliana onto Than's desk and mounted her.

With Kiki's legs straddled over her, Eliana could barely manage to blink up at the veil of long hair that nearly obscured the other girl's face. Producing a coherent stream of words proved even more impossible. "What—you—why—"

"Just go with it," Kiki hissed as she lowered her face toward Eliana's, both of their heads shielded from view by a curtain of strawberry blonde hair. When Kiki's lips got close enough to graze Eliana's cheek, she instinctively shied away, her heart hammering much too rapidly for her to construct an opinion on this situation. "Stop squirming! I'm not even kissing you!"

"It—*seems* like you are."

"You would know if I was kissing you, Eliana," Kiki breathed against her skin, and the sensation of it silenced Eliana just as Fraco succeeded in opening the door.

Though she couldn't see him from her vantage point, she did hear him muse a little, "Ah, there we go," to himself as he stepped into the office. His footsteps halted a second later at the sight of two students sprawled atop Than's desk.

"Students—students are—no—no! I can't witness—" he stammered as if he were a malfunctioning computer. "Children should not be engaging in sexual relationships! And—and certainly not *here*—"

Kiki sprung up, face flushed and breaths heavy, as if she actually had been making out with Eliana. "Ugh, Fraco!" She threw her hair dramatically over her shoulder before hopping to the floor. "You *had* to interrupt us?"

"I—you—you're in a teacher's—it's *Mr. Leve*!" Oil flew from his pores with his indignation. Eliana's paralysis from being straddled by Kiki morphed into giddiness, provoking her to giggle. The sound only enraged Fraco further, and he was so disturbed that he had to step out of the room to pace about the corridor. This gave Eliana and Kiki a quick moment to shove the books back into the bookshelves and then scurry out into the hallway, grinning goofily.

"You—will—both receive detention for this!" Fraco fumed, pausing his strides to glower at the girls.

In her state of ecstasy, Eliana emitted another hiccupping laugh.

"Will we, Fraco?" Kiki challenged, tilting her head. "What did we do wrong?"

"You were—*kissing*—in a teacher's office!"

"Do you have proof?"

"Well—well—"

"See you around, *Mr. Leve*." Kiki shot him a wink before grabbing Eliana's hand again. Fraco continued spluttering and seething to himself, and even once they were submerged in the stairwell, Eliana could still hear his frantic, puzzled thoughts. Her elation remained—until Kiki released her hand and Eliana noticed her expression had sobered severely.

"Do you want to tell Calder, or should I?"

Eliana's lips parted; she wasn't quite sure where this coldness had derived from. Even Kiki's thoughts closed off, fortified behind a barrier stronger than she had ever procured. "I-I can… I can tell him."

Insecurity overcame her, especially when Kiki pivoted on her heel and departed with an icy, distant, "Good."

26

Rainbow Rose

Flowers and Plants was probably the least visited shop in Periculand. Ackerly had worked at the florist's for more than two weeks now, and within that time not a single customer entered. Perhaps it was because the town was essentially under martial law, or perhaps it was because the population was so small and, as much as Ackerly hated to admit it, not many people appreciated greenery as much as he did.

Either way, his afternoons spent at the shop usually consisted of working in the greenhouse and growing plants or sitting behind the checkout counter and reading about plants. His boss, whose Affinity was the ability to eat endlessly and never suffer the consequences, knew very little about any sort of vegetation, which was clear by the fact that he'd named the shop "Flowers and Plants," as if it didn't sound redundant.

Ackerly voiced none of these judgmental sentiments and maintained his status as a good employee. Even if he had despised his boss, he wouldn't have quit simply because the job provided quality time for practicing his Affinity, an opportunity he'd lacked in training over the past couple weeks. All the Rosses wanted to do was teach them how to fight, and all Ackerly had gained from it was a few bruises and sore muscles. At work, though, he'd improved his Affinity to an extent not even Tray was aware of.

That was why, when the door to the shop chimed open and a customer strolled in while he was performing one of his more advanced techniques, he actually toppled off his stool.

"Ow," he grunted, pain lacing up his arm at the impact of his elbow against the wooden floor.

His glasses had slipped off his face with the fall, and as he searched for them, he distinctly heard a female's voice blurt, "Oh my God!" before a figure hurried behind the checkout counter.

Squinting, he peered up to see an indistinguishable face hovering above him. He might not have recognized her if that rainbow hair wasn't so utterly unique. Cheeks aflame with humiliation, Ackerly finally recovered his glasses and fumbled to stick them on his face. Even in the dim lighting of the shop, her iridescent eyes glittered, and her appearance was even more stunning than the water lilies positioned behind her. Scrambling to his feet, he could only gawk.

Over the past two days, Ackerly had been in Ashna's presence more than anyone else's, but his shyness pervaded. She'd slept a few feet away from him and seen him in the morning when his hair looked like a bush, and she'd even tackled him in training yesterday, yet his hands wouldn't stop trembling. He hoped she couldn't see it—or feel it with her nerve-related Affinity.

"Are you okay?" she asked, examining him worriedly. "You didn't break your wrist again, did you? I sense pain in your arm—"

"No—no, I'm fine." As he said the words, he realized they were true. The sharp pangs in his arm had dissipated, and his lips quirked when he processed why. "Um, thanks…for taking the pain away. Are you here to buy some flowers?"

A soft smile materialized. "Oh, no. I'm here to see you. Tray told me you work here, so…I figured I'd come visit."

"Oh, that's…" He paused when his eyes locked onto what she wore—the familiar flimsy sweatshirt and green cargo pants. "Where did you get those clothes?"

"Oh…I found them in a box in the corner of our room. They're a little loose, but they fit well enough," she said as she toyed with the fabric. "Ex-girlfriend's stuff you're too afraid to give back?"

"What? No—" Her grin broadened, and he knew she was joking, but he still felt it was necessary to clarify he had no ex-girlfriends. "They're Adara's clothes. We've been keeping them in our dorm, since she's in jail. I'm not—I wasn't—Adara and I are just friends."

"Mm. She's very possessive of you for a friend."

"I-I told you she thinks of me like a brother." When Ashna maintained an unconvinced expression, he sighed, "She's…got a crush on Seth, actually."

"Ah," she said with a nod. "I'll tell Naira to stay away from him then. She's the type to fall instantly in love with a boy and then cry about it for months if it doesn't work out."

"Well…it *could* work out. Not to betray Adara"—he cringed at the thought of her wrath—"but I don't think Seth will ever return her feelings."

"Still, I wouldn't want Naira to cross paths with her and her fire Affinity."

Ackerly's eyebrows creased in puzzlement. "How do you know she has a fire Affinity?"

"I saw it flare in her eyes when we were at the police station.

She's not a very subtle person, is she? Besides, her shirt was burnt and she was covered in soot. Not sure how she managed to ruin this sweatshirt, though." Lifting her arms, Ashna exposed the item's ripped underarms and shrugged. "It doesn't look burnt…"

"That was Calder—uh, the blue-haired boy with the water powers. Cocky smirk, likes to drown people for fun, kind of a jerk…"

"Yes, I know who you're talking about," she affirmed with a light-hearted laugh. "The sweatshirt does smell a bit like water—like stagnant, rotten wa—" Her words halted when her eyes locked onto the counter at Ackerly's side and the plant he'd been experimenting on when she'd arrived. He'd completely forgotten about it, but now it was all she would look at, and there was no way for him to hide it. "How did you…"

Trailing off, she took a step closer to the counter and ran her hands along the massive plant. Flowers akin to the color of lilac budded from the lengthy purple vines; there were so many that the bean they'd sprouted from was nearly invisible. That Ackerly had grown this without the aid of dirt, sun, or water was apparent to Ashna, because after studying the plant in awe for a few moments, she raised her gaze to gape at him.

"How long did it take you?"

Ackerly scrunched his face as he recalled, "Twelve-point-six seconds, I believe. I'm trying to get below ten seconds, but it's a little tricky…"

"This—is *insane*. I didn't know it was possible to grow anything without soil… You could, hypothetically, hold a bean in your hand and it would just *sprout*."

"Well, yeah…that's what I did." He scratched the back of his head. "It's not really that impressive… You, uh—like plants, huh?"

"I love them. They're so fascinating." Gently, she cradled one of the flowers in her hands. "Hyacinth, right?"

"Y-yeah. You know it by name?"

"I know most flowers by name. Water lilies behind me, bloodflowers over there—hey, do you have any gazanias?"

Ackerly had to close his mouth before answering to stop himself from drooling. "Yeah—yeah. Up in the greenhouse." He nodded toward the ceiling. "I can take you up there…if you want."

"I'd love to," she breathed as she carefully placed the flower back on the countertop. "But…will you get in trouble?"

"Nah," he assured before guiding her through the shop. Hundreds of plants cluttered the back, many of which would never be purchased, and behind the forest of flowers was the door leading to the stairwell. "My boss isn't around, and no one ever comes in here."

"Oh, that's good," she said, causing Ackerly to pause at the bottom of the stairs and glance back at her. With heating cheeks, she amended, "I mean it's good that we'll be alone. You seem more comfortable when you're not in a crowd."

"Oh, yeah," he agreed as he began to climb the steps. "I'm an only child, so I never really got used to having a lot of people around—and I was homeschooled, too, so I never really had any friends until I came here."

"That sounds lonely," Ashna commented once they both stood on the second floor. A steel door awaited them at the top of the staircase, and Ackerly busied himself with unlocking it to avoid her eyes.

"I never really minded… It's been nice to make some friends, though, like Tray and Adara."

From the corner of his lenses he saw Ashna open her mouth to reply, but the creak of the door interrupted her. Once the greenhouse was in view, whatever she'd meant to say died on her tongue.

Resting on the roof of Flowers and Plants, the greenhouse was even more spectacular than the ground floor. Rows upon rows of different types of vegetation filled the narrow space, and through the glass that encased it, they could see the night sky, along with the entirety of Periculand. Ashna didn't seem too interested in the outside scenery, though; all of her attention was swiftly gobbled up by the gazanias, which she immediately spotted in the far corner.

As he followed her to them, Ackerly took a quick moment to remotely grow the flowers, causing them to sprout upward and outward with even more volume and vibrancy. Ashna, apparently, was too sharp not to notice, because she wryly said, "I saw that."

Thankfully, she was too focused on the plants to see how profusely he blushed. When he joined her, she lovingly brushed her fingers along the gazanias, pale skin against fiery petals. It churned a sense of passion in his gut that he'd never experienced before.

"I've always loved these."

"Me too," he said too eagerly. Toning it down a bit, he added, "They remind me of Adara, for some reason."

"You're telling me you don't have a crush on a girl you think of when you see these beauties?" Ashna teased, wiggling her eyebrows.

"I—well—it's only because they're the most difficult for me to grow. They're so stubborn…and Adara is, too."

"Fair enough." She removed her hand from the flowers to survey the rest of the greenhouse. "For the record, though, I've always found gazanias the easiest to grow."

"You grow flowers? You like to garden?"

Her smile faltered with that, and she eyed him with such

intensity that he knew he must have sounded far too desperate. "I...have a hard time being honest with people. I've never felt like I've had a family, and I've never felt there was anyone I could trust, except Naira and Cath. People like to...exploit me because I'm young and they think I'm naïve, but I'm not, and..." Puffing out a breath, she ran a hand through her shimmering hair. "You're the most genuine person here—I know you are. Tray has secrets, I can tell, and Seth talks too much, and the mind reader freaks me out a bit—"

"E-Eliana? Eliana freaks you out?" Ackerly injected, unsure if he was more baffled by this unexpected spin on their conversation or that someone thought innocent Eliana frightening.

"She's got this—this look in her eyes." Ashna made an explosive hand motion beside her own eyes. "Like, she's quiet, but she'd gladly kill someone if they crossed her path."

Ackerly snorted in an attempt to contain his chuckle. "*Eliana*? Well...it's clear *you're* not a mind reader."

After letting out a laugh, Ashna bit her lip. "What I'm getting at is that...I want to have faith in you. Can I have faith in you, Ackerly?"

"O-of course. If you have something you want to tell me...I won't say anything to anyone. I promise."

She nodded, inhaling a deep breath before her gaze fell to a bed of white chrysanthemums on Ackerly's left. "You know your teacher with the flower Affinity—er, Miss Smith, I think?"

"Oh, yeah, Floretta—that's what we call her, anyway... She's—um—a nice lady."

He expected her to make a jab about him having a crush on Floretta like practically everyone did, but Ashna's face remained pensive as she studied the chrysanthemums. For a long moment, he thought she was preparing to divulge her secrets, but then

Ackerly saw it and *felt* it at the same time: The thin white petals unfurled further, blooming to the perfect degree. It wasn't the sight of a rapidly-growing plant that bemused him but the fact that he hadn't been the one to do it.

"I have that Affinity too," she said quietly—so quietly Ackerly almost didn't catch her words. "A flower Affinity."

His eyebrows furrowed so severely that he was sure he'd give himself a headache. "This—this doesn't make sense. Plants don't have neurons like we do…and even if they did, you don't have the ability to make things grow in humans—"

"My Affinity isn't just the ability to inhibit nociceptors," she interrupted slowly, allowing the truth to sink in. "I've been lying to everyone—always. The Wackos, at first, thought my only Affinity was for flowers. My intention when coming here was to make everyone believe it was my only Affinity too, but…then you fell." She stared at his wrist as she continued. "I couldn't let you be in pain, so I gave away that I have a nociceptor Affinity, and now I can't let anyone know about my Affinity for flowers. The Wackos…were starting to discover the truth, which was why we were so desperate to escape."

"You—have two Affinities?" he questioned, nonplussed. "How…how is that even possible? They're not even in the same class—"

"I don't have two Affinities. I…think I have infinite Affinities."

Ackerly blinked. "What…does that mean?"

"It means that…I could probably do any of the things anyone in this town can do. If I practiced, I could probably grow all plants like you can. I probably *could* read minds, but…I just haven't unlocked that part of me yet. I-I'm not completely certain how it all works. I just know I can grow flowers and inhibit pain and climb walls—"

"*Climb walls*?"

With a sigh and a wince, Ashna padded over to the nearest wall. After placing both hands on the glass, she gradually propelled herself upward, her hands sticking perfectly to the surface as she kicked with her feet. Once she reached the angle where the wall met the roof, she continued, her hands walking along the slanted glass as the rest of her body dangled. Craning her neck, she peered down at Ackerly as her feet swayed inches above his head.

"Spider-Man," he blurted in shell-shocked awe.

Confused, she backtracked a few feet and then released her hands from the glass, plummeting to the ground. Paralyzed, Ackerly braced himself for the cracking of bones, but Ashna landed in a flawless crouch before standing.

"Who's Spider-Man?" she asked.

"Uh—a comic book character. I, um, used to like comics... when I was a kid, of course. I'm over it now...obviously..."

"Ah, a pop culture reference. I sometimes forget about the outside world, because I've spent so many years cooped up with the Wackos. I'm guessing Spider-Man can climb walls...like a spider?"

"Yeah. There's always controversy as to how he manages it with his suit on, but—um, I'm guessing, by scientific standards, you have similar properties to a spider?"

"Similar, yeah. Spiders have micro-hairs that allow them to adhere to things, while my skin is a little more sticky—when I want it to be," she added, coquettishly reaching for his forearm. Ackerly knew she was only demonstrating her ability, but still, when her skin made contact with his, a tingle spiked up his arm. "You feel it?"

Thinking she meant the involuntary spark, Ackerly nodded instinctively, but then he realized she was probably referring to the stickiness. Yanking back gently to test it, Ackerly found that her hand went with him—and so did the rest of her body.

When she crashed into him, her forehead hit his chin, and he was about to spew a million apologies before he noted the pain was absent, probably because they were still in physical contact. With her face only inches from his and her hand and his arm still intertwined, he glanced down at her and softly asked, "Do you ever feel pain?"

"Only if I want to," she whispered back, eyes bright and wide. At this proximity, he saw every hue in them—multiple shades of pink and orange and yellow and green and blue and purple. There wasn't any red in them, but her shallow breaths perfuming his skin were too distracting for him to form an intelligible inquiry. "Sometimes pain can be a reminder of how pleasant other sensations are."

Ackerly swallowed thickly. "Did…that hurt?"

At first, she seemed to think he meant their recent accident, but then she followed his gaze down to her throat. After relenting her grip on his arm and taking a step back, she touched the bruised ring around her neck. "The…collar that did this to me had the ability to obstruct my Affinities. So…yes, it hurt."

"They were…really cruel to you, huh? The Wackos, I mean."

"Not always, and not all of them. But generally, they… It doesn't matter anymore. I'm not a prisoner anymore—at least not the same type of prisoner. The Rosses might be…suspicious, but they haven't mistreated me the way the Wackos at—at the hideout did."

Ackerly gnawed at the inside of his cheek, conflicting information swirling through his brain. "I'm…a little confused. Naira said the Wacko leader's dog attacked her when you escaped, but…

you were at a hideout, not Headquarters. Wouldn't the leader's dog have been at Headquarters with its owner?"

Expelling a breath, Ashna scrubbed her forehead. "That's what—" She stopped when her vision landed on a point beyond Ackerly. "Are those...*rainbow roses*?" Spinning around, Ackerly indeed found a cluster of rainbow roses. Each flower harbored multiple colors, reflecting her hair perfectly. "I've never seen rainbow roses before. How did you grow them?" she questioned, entirely entranced.

"Well...there's no way to grow them naturally, so I had to grow white roses, and then I divided each stem into separate parts and placed them in different colored dyes... It wasn't too hard." She was in complete awe, though, now walking past him to examine them closely. "I...usually compare things to plants and flowers," he explained, joining her as she caressed the rainbow petals. "Like the gazanias remind me of Adara, blue hibiscuses remind me of Eliana, parsnips remind me of Tray—"

"Because they look bland and boring but they're secretly sweet?" Ashna guessed with a sly grin.

Ackerly let out an awkward laugh. "I don't even know if Tray's *secretly* sweet. I was thinking more because taproots are the strongest roots, and he's strong... But, anyway, I couldn't think of anything that reminded me of you, so...I decided to make rainbow roses."

Lashes low, Ashna glanced at him with a kittenish smirk. "You're a real flirt, Ackerly. You know roses are said to be the prettiest flowers? I'm flattered."

Even if she was the flattered one, Ackerly was far more flustered. His brain felt mushy; he could barely even remember the pressing questions on his mind.

"Ackerly, Ackerly!" His name jolted him out of his trance. So engrossed in ogling Ashna, he hadn't heard Tray rush up the stairs and burst into the greenhouse. "Ackerly, Ashna is—" Stopping dead in the open doorway, Tray's brown eyes traveled from Ackerly to Ashna and he blanched. "Here. I—was informed that Nero was beating you up," he explained choppily, casting an apologetic look at her as he straightened his gray sweater. "Apparently that was a lie."

"Someone told you Nero was beating me up?" Ashna repeated flatly. "So, rather than going to save me, you ran to tell Ackerly?"

Tray's mouth opened as he grimaced. "Yes? Look, Ackerly, I have something urgent to tell you—alone. Can you come talk to me outside?"

"I-I can't just leave work—"

"Your shift is over." Tray marched through the greenhouse, oblivious to the lively vegetation. Though he grabbed Ackerly's forearm in the same place Ashna had, the gesture was far less tender. "Let's go. *Urgent*."

"I-I'm sorry," he called to her over his shoulder as Tray hauled him away. "We'll see you in the room tonight. F-feel free to hang out here as long as you want!"

"Do you even have the authority to do that?" Tray griped, but Ackerly barely heard him; his attention was fixated on Ashna where she stood alone by the rainbow roses, abandoned. Even if she had a lot of secrets, Ackerly wanted to trust her. Tray never would, though, so he allowed his roommate to drag him out of the greenhouse and down the steps.

"Who told you Nero was beating up Ashna?" Ackerly asked as they stalked through the shop. He was supposed to lock the place up when leaving, but Tray had no intention of waiting that long.

"No one, Ackerly," he retorted impatiently, swinging the front door open with such force that it nearly flew off the hinges. "I just had to make up a lame excuse to cover up the fact that I came here to talk to you about *her*."

"Wh-what about her?" he spluttered, trailing after Tray as he stomped across the white cobblestone streets.

"Well," he began with a dark, foreboding gleam to his eyes, "no one told me she was being pulverized, but I did receive some even worse information—some incriminating information."

"It…can't be true."

"It can and it is," Tray said as he and Ackerly approached the police station's front entrance. The late November wind flapped the Stark twin's normally neat hair into his eyes, but his emotional stress prevented him from caring. "I just explained it to you: Eliana and Kiki found a note in Than's office that explicitly implicates her as a Wacko. She's here on an undercover *mission*, Ackerly, and once she completes it, the Wacko leader's going to come here and destroy Periculand."

Ackerly continued shaking his head, wrapped up in his illogical denial. "But…Ashna said—"

"She said what?" Tray demanded when he abruptly cut himself short.

"N-nothing."

The lie was so blatant that Tray couldn't repress his reaction of rage. "*Said what*?" he growled as he grabbed Ackerly's shirt.

Yelping at the aggression, he winced behind his glasses and squealed, "Please don't punch me!"

Tray instantly released him, internally fuming over his lack of self-control. He'd always been the stoic one—the rational one—but now that terrorists had infiltrated their town and potential murderers ruled it, he was breaking apart.

"Sorry," he muttered, mostly as a way to compose himself. With gentler force, Tray opened the police station's door and let trembling Ackerly scurry in. The air was substantially warmer within, but Tray didn't allow it to soothe his icy demeanor as he stomped up to the desk. "Officer Telum."

Mitt, reclining in his chair and playing handheld Yahtzee, languidly lifted his head. "Mr. Stark," he greeted, saluting in mock formality. "I believe it's been a whole two days since I last saw you."

"We don't have time for you to complain about our arrival," Tray snapped, and Ackerly recoiled. "We need to talk to Adara about the Wackos."

"I'm not sure I wanna let you do that." Mitt placed his game on his desk. "When Mardurus came in here yesterday, he refused to tell her who the Wacko is, and she's definitely been stewing about it. Giving her the details would ruin the fun."

"Trust me, I wouldn't be here if I had a choice." Tray's eyes narrowed on the door to Adara. "But—wait, why was *Calder* here yesterday?"

"To tantalize Adara?" Mitt offered with a shrug. "And use his creepy roommate to figure out if Periculy's innocent or not. As far as I'm aware, no conclusion was made. Oh—except that the Rosses might be Adara's parents."

"I've been saying that since they first showed up! Let me guess, Adara believed it the moment it spewed from her precious Pixie Prince's mouth?"

Hands splayed in innocence, Mitt stood. "Whoa, Stark. I'm sensing some jealousy."

"I'm *not*—I just—Can we see Adara…please?" he added in the calmest voice he could muster. The officer's expression remained wary, but after a moment of contemplation, he nodded and opened the door.

Puffing out an agitated breath, Tray stalked into the posterior chamber, Ackerly at his heels. In the cell to the right, Angor Periculy squatted repeatedly for his daily workout routine—a perturbing sight—while Adara seemed to have grown tired of physical exercise and was sprawled on her metal slab, looking as disgusting and lazy as she always had in Tray's eyes.

"Don't bother me today, Weaponizer." Massaging her temples, she screwed her eyes shut. "I feel like shit, okay?"

"You look it, too," Tray mumbled, apparently loud enough for her to have heard.

Eyes bursting open, she sprang upright and stared at him. "What was that, Nerdworm?" she prompted, a diabolical grin spreading on her lips. "What do I look like?"

"Don't make me regret coming here with your childishness, Stromer."

"I'm not the childish one." With a flippant wave, she hopped to her feet. "You're the one who isn't mature enough to say the word 'shit.'"

"I wouldn't call cussing mature—"

"Greenie," she interjected, face brightening as she noticed him for the first time. Ackerly smiled nervously as he stepped beside Tray, clearly maintaining some distance between them. "Didn't think you'd keep your promise to come back."

"It—it's only been two days. Less, if you count the hours."

"This isn't a social call." Crossing his arms, Tray glared at Adara through the bars. "We're here because we've confirmed that Than is the Wacko sympathizer."

Angor paused mid-squat. "Than Floros?"

"The *history* teacher?" Adara said with equal incredulity. "The ancient dude who's never even slept with a woman? You're telling me *he's* a Wacko? I don't think I'll believe it unless I hear it from his mouth."

"Essentially, we did," Tray confirmed grimly. Angor stood straight, his expression wrought with skepticism. "Eliana and Kiki found a note in his office that he wrote, referring to the Wacko leader as if he knew him personally—and admitting that he's helping the new girl, Ashna, with a mission for the Wackos."

"Ha!" Adara barked, throwing her head back. "The unicorn girl? She *is* a Wacko after all? Well, I don't see *that* as shocking news. What did I tell you, Greenie? Pretty girls can tell lies..."

"She isn't lying," Ackerly insisted with more zeal than he typically displayed. "Ashna gave up two Wacko locations. Why would she do that if she were one of them?"

"To defer suspicion?" Adara suggested.

"By getting her own people killed?"

"She is on a mission, Ackerly," Tray said, tapping his hands together for emphasis. "She is one of them."

"We don't *know* that."

"It's *confirmed*!" Tray ran a hand through his disheveled hair in frustration. "Stromer, this is why we came here. You need to convince him he's being irrational."

"Me?" Adara gasped, placing a hand on her chest as if she had won an award. "You want *me* to convince him he's being irrational?"

"I found him showing off his greenhouse to her. I think he's *infatuated*."

"N-no," Ackerly stuttered, cheeks reddening substantially. "I...was just being polite."

"You've fallen for the unicorn's shimmery façade already, have you, Greenie?" Adara crooned with devilish intrigue. "You've known her for, what, *two days*? Less, if you count the hours."

"Stromer," Tray exhaled as he pinched the bridge of his nose, "stop joking around. You're the only person he'll listen to."

"Well"—Adara's chest inflated with haughtiness—"in that case, follow your dreams, Greenie. Even if this rainbow girl is a Wacko, she'll probably be a good kisser—maybe an even *better* kisser if she's an edgy terrorist."

"I-I never said I wanted to kiss her," Ackerly stammered. Though Tray thought his roommate blind and illogical, he empathized with the intensity of his embarrassment. Not much rattled Tray Stark, but Adara Stromer's crude quips never failed to stir humiliation in his gut.

"You didn't have to say it," she said with a frisky wink. "It's written in your blush, my friend. If we're going to assume she's a Wacko, we should also assume she's been with a few guys, since, you know, anything's *rational* at this point." Tray rolled his eyes at the look she shot him, but he didn't get to voice his input before she continued. "Since you won't be her first kiss, you should probably practice first. As your best friend, I will sacrifice myself for your sake."

"Y-you want me to…to kiss you?" Ackerly questioned, dumbfounded.

"I wouldn't say *want* is the correct term…"

"Enough with your antics, Stromer."

"I'm helping a friend, Nerdworm. It's better than all the discouragement you've been giving him. Poor Greenie's probably never even had a crush before!"

"She is a *terrorist*—"

"You can really help me?" Ackerly asked timidly, taking a step closer to the bars. Tray gaped at how easily he'd conceded to this madness, but his roommate refused to glance back in his direction. "I mean…I don't *know* if I'll kiss her, or if she would even want to kiss me, but…I don't believe she's a Wacko, and if we ever did…I would want to be prepared."

"Telum"—Tray whipped toward the officer leaning in the doorway—"give me your baton."

Mitt made a show of patting his uniform before saying, "I don't have one, Stark, and even if I did, I wouldn't give it to you. Would bashing your friend's head in be better than letting him kiss Stromer?"

"*Yes*, but I wasn't planning to hit him, any—" Tray tore his eyes away from Mitt when a cry penetrated the air. In the time he'd argued with the officer, Adara had instructed Ackerly to approach the metal bars in order to kiss her through them. But, as everyone had so foolishly forgotten, the bars were electrified, so when Ackerly clumsily pressed his cheeks against the metal, a shock coursed through his skin, projecting him backward. The poor kid's back smacked against the tiled floor, his glasses flying from his face.

"Second time today…" Tray vaguely heard him mumble. He didn't help Ackerly retrieve his glasses or get up; his virulent attention was fixed on Adara, who cackled like a witch within her cell. Clearly someone had remembered the bars' electric properties.

"I'm sorry—Ackerly," Adara huffed through her cruel laughter. "When I get out of here—I'll buy you some ice cream with Tray's money."

Scowling, Tray finally bent down to hoist up Ackerly as the discombobulated boy fumbled to adjust his glasses. His cheeks were bright pink where they'd made contact with the bars, but luckily, the electrical current wasn't strong enough to severely burn him—or kill him.

"You're despicable," Tray snarled, despising the urge for violence swelling in him. He'd always combatted Adara with intelligence, but this time she'd managed to outsmart him. She'd been aware of a fact that he'd neglected, and now he wished he could break past the electric bars to punch that smug smile from her lips.

"It was a *prank*, Nerdworm. I knew he wouldn't get *too* hurt." She rolled her eyes to meet Ackerly's. "Are you okay, Greenie?" When he nodded, she added, "I hope that *sparked* some sense into you. Bet you don't have any desire to kiss Wacko terrorists now."

"I don't think I have the desire to kiss anyone now," he mumbled, fidgeting with his glasses.

"You've traumatized him—you could have seriously injured—"

"If you're so worried about him, Stark, why didn't *you* volunteer to give him kissing lessons?"

"I…wouldn't know how," he grumbled, avoiding her demonic eyes. He could still sense her wicked smirk permeating the room.

"Ah, right, I almost forgot we're *all* a bunch of prudes here. Why don't you go ask one of the Belvens for help, Greenie? I'm sure they've both had more than enough practice."

"Ackerly clearly doesn't care about what Kiki has to say," Tray scoffed, crossing his arms over his chest. "She found *evidence* that Ashna's a Wacko and he still won't hear it."

"That's because Ackerly learned from the best," Adara boasted, holding out her hands as if accepting praise. "My number one rule is 'Don't believe a word that flows from Kiki Belven's mouth.' Okay, maybe number two, after 'Donuts are sacred and should be treated as such.'"

"Do you have any inkling as to what this mission could be?" Angor inquired, breaking out of the ruminating trance he'd been engulfed in throughout this entire exchange. "With Daniel in charge of the Wackos now…I suspect it will be something terribly dire."

"This is why Ackerly's horniness will come in handy, all puns intended," Adara added with a bawdy grin. "If unicorn girl's got a thing for him, and she doesn't find him suspicious, he can use their budding romance to determine her motives."

"I-I don't want to *use* Ashna," Ackerly said, flabbergasted. "If anything, I'll just prove she's innocent."

"Good," Adara said, clapping her hands together. "And you"—she aimed her pointer fingers at Tray—"should do something about Mr. 'I Love Blenders More Than Sex.'"

Angor tilted his head contemplatively. "Mr. Floros always was a peculiar specimen…"

"You have super strength, Nerdworm. Use it to interrogate the shit out of Than and figure out what his plans are. Just because this town's fallen to psychotic Reggs doesn't mean I want to see it demolished. I do still live here, and with no hopes of escape."

"If there were a method of escape, though, you would have been gone by now," Tray said darkly.

"Oh, of course. I would have dug your graves for you first, though. It's only respectful."

Tray expelled a long breath, rubbing his face in exasperation. "Life with you in prison is exceedingly worse than I expected. Without you around to cause chaos, everyone else seems to have assumed the task. Artemis is a mind controlling murderer, Than's a Wacko who's working with three new Wackos to ruin our town, *Kiki* is somehow becoming a useful member of our investigative team, and to top it all off, I haven't heard from my parents in over a month."

"Aw," Adara cooed, "now we know what's got Trayby's diaper in a bunch: He misses Mama and Dada. Well, kiddo, get used to it. They abandoned you, and you'll probably never see them again. Unless, of course, they return in the form of villainous dictators and throw you in jail. That's a possibility."

"Someone's bitter," Mitt noted with raised eyebrows.

"Nah, I'd say the fantasies I have about slitting my parents' throats far surpass petty bitterness."

"I just don't get why they would have written to me earlier in the year but now I haven't received any letters since the election," Tray said, too consumed by his own worry to care about Adara's sadism.

Mitt cleared his throat, his previous nonchalance withering. "I…think I know why your parents haven't been writing to you."

Snapping his head in the officer's direction, Tray blinked. "Why?"

Mitt shifted against the doorframe and swallowed. "Well, back in September, before I came here, we got a call that some guys in masks were creeping around your neighborhood. When we arrived at your house, we found your parents gone, but a group of Wackos was invading the place…searching for them. That was when the Wacko leader shot me…and then I accidentally projected the bullet back at him…and killed him."

Adara's jaw dropped before Tray's. "The Wacko *leader*? You never said you killed the Wacko *leader*."

"It—isn't supposed to be public knowledge." With a cough, his silver eyes slid toward the former principal. Angor was unaffected by this news; it shouldn't have surprised Tray that the man knew these details, but why wouldn't he have been informed that Wackos had tried to break into his own home?

"Why would the Wackos be searching for my parents?" Tray asked, shocked by the deadly calm in his own voice.

Angor folded his hands and sighed. "You're likely aware that your father worked for a media company."

Tray's breath hitched at the word *worked*—past tense. "Y-yes, as an editor."

"Publicly. Secretly, he wrote articles on the Wackos under a pseudonym. Through these articles, he revealed the violence of the Wackos, some of which the late leader, Ephraim, wanted to keep secret. Your mother, you likely know, was a scientist."

Tray's mouth was so dry that he could only nod.

"Her work was classified…because she was studying Affinity genetics. She was the analyst that examined blood samples for Periculand to determine which teenagers should be sent here. I worked closely with her for years—until this September, around the time that you arrived in Periculand. At that point, she and your father went off-grid, probably because they suspected the Wackos had discovered their identities. Their whereabouts are now lost, even to me."

Though his knees wobbled, Tray fought to remain upright, fought to subdue the bile rising in his throat. "Th-that's why they didn't bother to say goodbye to us the day we left… They knew we'd end up safe in Periculand, so they were fleeing…from the Wackos."

"Guess they never saw Seth's note, even though it was written in permanent marker," Adara said, her inflection hollow despite the sassy remark.

"I saw it," Mitt chimed in weakly. "His handwriting is sad."

"They must be at a safe house," Ackerly encouraged. "With such dangerous professions…they must have had an escape plan."

Tray shook his head, jaw clenched. He wanted to blame Angor for this: his mother had been *working* for him; the Principal had put her in danger. If he hadn't required that Tray and

Seth come here, they could have been with their parents, ensuring their safety.

Even as Tray thought these accusations, though, he knew they were empty. His mother had chosen to be a scientist—had chosen to work for Angor, just like his father had chosen to write negative pieces about the Wackos. They'd brought this fate upon themselves. Angor wasn't to blame—nor was he to blame for Hastings's death. This now was certain in Tray's brain, and he knew he had two enemies he had to end: the Rosses and the Wackos.

The only problem was: how could he formulate strategies and accumulate data with this new weight bearing down on his mind—with the possibility that his parents could be *dead*?

Perhaps not for the first time, Tray Stark sincerely wished the demoness were free from her cage to endure this hell with him.

27

Rotten

Maddy was careful to avoid Danny's girlfriend over the next two days. The woman had made it abundantly clear that she disliked the girl at the feast, and given she had the power to sway Danny's actions, Maddy didn't wish to provoke her further.

After the feast had ended, however, when Maddy retreated to Zach's room, Naretha had attempted to corner her in the corridor and *talk* to her. Luckily, enough people clogged the hall that she'd been swept away with the crowd, but now, cooped up in Zach's chambers with only her books as company, Maddy wondered what the Wacko leader's girlfriend might have wanted to discuss.

Taking off that tight leather dress had been the most glorious sensation, and since the feast she'd happily sported a t-shirt and sweatpants that she'd unearthed from Zach's previous roommate's drawers. Although still a little snugger than Maddy would have preferred, she was certainly relieved to wear something comfortable as she practiced her backbend that Wednesday evening. She was so engrossed with the mechanics of the movement and the extent of which she elongated her limbs that she didn't notice Zach had slipped into the room until her eyes wandered toward his bed, against which he leaned.

Observing his form upside-down and sideways, it took her much longer than usual to absorb the classiness of his attire, the perfection of his dull gray hair, and the severe interest in his expression as he watched her slowly retract to her natural form. Pushing out of the arch and standing with grace, Maddy then pivoted to face him, her feet naturally poised in a finishing stance.

"Sorry." She brushed a few wisps of orange hair from her face. "I didn't realize you were in here. It must…disturb you."

"That your hands made contact with the rancid floor?" he questioned, eyeing her fingers as if they harbored a disease.

Her lips curved mildly as she shook her head. "No, that I can stretch and bend so…unnaturally."

Shrugging, Zach stood straight to tower over her stout height. "You can imagine I've seen plenty of odd Affinities, some much more unnatural than yours. One guy down the hall can grow ropes from his *skin.* Used to eat ropes as a kid and now he's practically made of them."

Maddy grimaced as she pictured someone peeling ropes from the fabric of their skin—or *eating* them. "That's…freaky."

"He's not right in the head," Zach said with an exasperated sigh. "A lot of the Wackos aren't. My father found many of them in research facilities, like that kid."

"Research facilities," she echoed, shuddering. "My friends got stuck at one on the way here, didn't they? They must be…"

She swallowed, trying not to think about how altered and affected Jamad, Zeela, and Avner must have been after such an experience—all endured in order to retrieve *her*. Now they were here but as prisoners, while she lounged in a comfy bed all day and read books.

"Is there any way we can release them from the cells?" she asked feebly, knowing the answer. Zach didn't have to shake his head.

"I came here to see if you wanted to visit them."

"O-of course," she stammered as hope surged through her gut. "Now?"

Nodding, he beckoned for her to follow him toward the bedroom's exit. "Danny's out, and I doubt he'll be back for quite some time. He went to visit one of our…sponsors, and I don't foresee it going well."

"Sponsors?" she repeated, stepping into the elevator when Zach opened the doors for her. Glancing over her shoulder, she saw he had paused in the threshold, scrutinizing her bare feet with distaste.

"Aren't you going to put shoes on?"

"Oh—um—no?" Her eyes darted toward her feet, and she gave him a wincing smile. "I prefer the dirt and germs of the floor to shoes. They're so constricting."

He huffed a disgruntled breath but didn't make any further comments before joining her in the elevator and sealing them within the silver walls. In such a confined space, she could smell his fresh, clean scent of lemongrass and lavender. It had been so poignant compared to her own odor when she'd been trapped in that little torture chamber, and though it had become familiar to her in harsh conditions, she'd learned to love the fragrance since she associated it with food and *him*—the only human she'd been granted access to for a month.

"The only reason we can afford to operate in this complex is because of our sponsors," Zach explained, his words jolting her more than the motion of the elevator. "My father managed to procure a decent amount of money in his youth, but it was only enough to buy his own estate. Once his organization gained popularity, wealthy people—many of them Affinities—began to support his cause. With the money, he built this complex as a refuge for Affinities years before Periculy built his town. You can imagine he wasn't too pleased when Periculand opened and Affinities became required to move there.

"My father was all about choice," he continued, staring at the metal doors before him as if he could see his father's image in the shimmery silver. "He didn't want Affinities to be forced to do anything, and he didn't want the government to regulate our existence. He gave Affinities a purpose here, and he paid them for their work. Danny still does, of course, but the tasks are far more…violent. Before, my father mostly worked on raiding research facilities and seeking out individual Affinities in need, but now…Danny's extended his missions to murdering innocent civilians and causing violent mayhem.

"Some of the sponsors are starting to catch on. Two have dropped us, and I'm assuming tonight's meeting will end in the same result—likely accompanied by the man or woman's death. We *have* received a new sponsor recently, though, our highest paying one yet. Whoever he is, he's thirsty for blood…"

The air chilled at the prospect of Danny *murdering* someone at this moment—and that there were people who supported his sadism. When the elevator doors parted to reveal the Wacko leader's office, Maddy felt even more repulsed—especially when her vision locked onto Danny's desk, upon which Naretha perched.

"Took you long enough," she drawled, lithely standing from the desk and sauntering toward them. Maddy felt inclined to retreat into the elevator, but she kept her chin high as she trailed

Zach to the center of the vast room. In the far corner, Danny's little white dog, Shards, slept on a plush red cushion, and Maddy hoped their footsteps wouldn't wake the nippy beast.

"Too busy banging to remember that I'm doing you a favor?" Naretha questioned once they stood before her. While Maddy's face flushed at the insinuation, Zach was utterly unfazed.

"Have some decency, Naretha," he snapped, wrinkling his nose at her outfit: a gray sports bra and black spandex shorts, similar attire to what Maddy would have worn to a gymnastics practice, though she highly doubted Naretha planned to engage in any acrobatics. Still, the woman pulled off the ensemble much better than Maddy ever would have; Naretha's past three months of hell must have shredded some of her muscle mass, but she was still lean and toned, her abs as strong and defined as a gymnast's.

"Is this bothering you, Zachary?" She motioned to her half-naked body.

"*Zacchaeus,* and obviously it's bothering me. Just because you're dating Danny doesn't mean you can stroll around here so inappropriately clothed."

"On the contrary, I think that's exactly what it means," she countered, her soft pink eyes flashing friskily. "Unless we have a dress code now?"

Zach's lips formed a thin line of irritation. "Just open the door, Naretha."

Gaze hardening, she stomped across the room to the door leading to the prison cells. After she belligerently punched a few numbers into the keypad, the threshold cleared, revealing the hall Maddy always encountered in her nightmares.

"Danny didn't give you the code?" Maddy whispered to Zach, who peeked down at her from the corner of his eye.

"He...changed it once he released you. And he claimed I'm

not trustworthy enough to know it now since I—since we—since I didn't show as much contempt toward his last prisoner as he would have—"

Naretha's aggressive cough cut off their conversation. "Here ya go." She gestured toward the prison cells, sarcastically dramatic. "Have fun witnessing your friends in a state of decay."

With apprehensive steps, Maddy approached her, mumbling a quiet "Thanks" as she passed. The woman's smirk was too sardonic for her to feel this was a favor. Maddy didn't miss the contemptuous glare Zach shot Naretha before they entered the dungeon corridor.

The lighting here was as bright as the upper levels, but the ambience was far darker, and Maddy couldn't stop her eyes from darting toward that door at the end of the corridor, the one to her chamber of solitude.

"Stop looking like a lost puppy, Faddy," Naretha barked from where she remained leaning in the doorway. "We're not gonna throw you in one of these cells. You're *one of us* now."

As Zach muttered reprimands to Naretha, Maddy forced herself to look through the glass panels, where her friends dwelled. In the first cell on the right—where Josh had once been -encased—sat Avner, head tilted against the concrete wall and eyes peacefully closed. The lines of exhaustion and worry were set deep in his features, so different from the affable, carefree boy who had led JAMZ a few months ago. His grimy, neon yellow hair was as short as Naretha's, and his body had thinned to the size he'd been when Maddy first met him at the age of fifteen.

"There isn't even a bed for him," Maddy breathed, mostly to herself.

The other two, who had been engaged in a nonverbal argument, heard, and Naretha added a rather scathing, "At least they have drains for their piss and shit to go down. We didn't get that luxury in the Regg research facility."

"Neither did I when I was in there," Maddy said before she could stop herself. Naretha followed her nod toward the ominous end of the corridor, and her animosity dwindled into incredulity.

"Danny put you in *there*? What the hell did you *do*?"

"She didn't do anything," Zach said with a tinge of spite. "Danny was just angry that she wasn't you."

Swearing, Naretha rubbed her forehead. "Why didn't he put Josh in there? Such a disappointment… At least Faddy's friends broke me out of Periculand. Josh *left me there*."

"Have you…" Zach coughed, "made him pay for that yet?"

"Don't tempt me," Naretha retorted blackly. "I'm behaving myself until I can determine where he stands with Danny now. Before these losers got thrown in prison"—she motioned toward the cells—"I planned to convince Snowman to freeze Josh's balls off. Now I have to think of a new tactic. There's not much I can do with my salt without killing—"

"Is Snowman…Jamad?" Maddy interjected, carefully surveying Naretha's reaction. Luckily, it wasn't nearly as negative as Danny's when he was interrupted.

"Obviously. He should be in the next window," she added gruffly. "It's such a freakin' shame he's stuck in here. Annoying personality, yeah, but his Affinity's useful. He froze a Regg to death when we were breaking out of that goddamn facility."

"He—*murdered* someone?"

"God, don't tell me you're Team Sparky when it comes to killing Reggs." Naretha groaned, rolling her eyes. "Blindie would be disappointed in you, Faddy."

"Blindie—*Zeela* was okay with murder?"

"Let's put it this way," Naretha began as she toyed with a

crystal of salt in her fingers, "if you had the chance to kill Danny, would you?"

"I—I don't—I don't think I should answer that. You'll tell Danny."

"I will not tell Danny. I can't believe—" Naretha paused abruptly, her gaze slivering on Zach. "Does she not know?"

He barely opened his mouth as he murmured, "I didn't think it was public knowledge."

Lips trickling into a frown, Naretha closed her fist around her salt crystal and then aimed her scowl at Maddy. "Well, aren't you going to check up on your precious Snowman? I heard you're basically his girlfriend."

Maddy's cheeks blazed as she inched toward the second cell, eyes darting around frantically. "Who said that?"

"Does it matter if it's true?"

"It's not..." Maddy started to say, but then her vision fell on the second prison cell, where Jamad paced, lips moving as if muttering to himself. So enthralled to see him awake and alive and *moving*—even if his dark skin was marred with cuts and his face had sprouted a bushy blue beard—she lunged toward the glass, throwing her hands against it to gain his attention. As expected, his pacing halted, and he whipped his icy blue eyes toward her, but they didn't quite fixate on her, and he looked more puzzled than excited.

"Hello?" she was certain his lips said, though she couldn't hear a thing.

Spinning her head toward Zach, she asked, "Can he see me? Can he hear us?"

He bit his lip. "Well, no. The glass is a one-way mirror. He probably felt the vibration when you hit it, but he can't see or hear anything outside of his cell. There's a way to turn it off, I think..."

Maddy peered back into Jamad's cell, where he'd resumed pacing and ranting, his slow decline into insanity. "But…there's no way to get them out right now, is there?"

"I know the code," Naretha said, "but I'm not dumb enough to set them free. Danny would murder all of us if we even tried."

Sighing, Maddy stepped away from the glass and met Zach's rueful gaze. "Then I don't want them to see me. I don't want them to know…how weak I am." Her eyes drifted to the orange swirls encasing her arms. She'd taken Danny's bargain—became a Wacko to evade imprisonment—but judging by the fact that her friends were locked away, they hadn't taken the bargain. They'd had the courage to rot away in these cells rather than join the terrorists.

"Thanks for letting me see them," Maddy said to Naretha, her words sincere, "but I think I want to leave now."

The dull expression on her face indicated that Naretha was unimpressed by Maddy's gratitude and propriety. "I warned you this was a poor idea."

"I know," Maddy acknowledged with one last forlorn glance at her friends, "and you were right."

"My love," Danny greeted without affection when Naretha entered his office on Friday afternoon. It had taken her nearly two whole days to muster the patience to approach him. He'd returned on Wednesday night from his meeting in a piss-poor mood, and since he hadn't shared any information with her, she couldn't decide if it was because he'd had to kill the sponsor or if it was because the sponsor had decided to not drop them and Danny *hadn't* been able to kill him. With her boyfriend's unpredictability, Naretha knew she would have to tread very carefully when discussing this proposition with him, and she didn't often have the tolerance for such ridiculous games.

After Faddy had visited her beloved friends, though, Naretha knew removing them from their cells was a priority—not because she *liked* Maddy or even because she felt bad for the girl, but because Jamad and Avner were useful allies, and if they were forced to become Wackos, perhaps Maddy would stop clinging to Zach like a leech.

Not that Naretha cared about the two of them spending time together, because she didn't.

Because she *couldn't.*

"Is something troubling you?" she inquired with as much compassion as she could summon. Even as she rounded the desk to stand by his side, Danny's radiant eyes remained fixed ahead pensively.

"What do you *think* is bothering me?" He glared up at her. "Ashna gave away our decoy Headquarters location instead of the real one. Why?"

Naretha pressed her lips together; she'd contemplated the same issue, but the more she thought about it the less it made sense. "Knowing Ashna, it wasn't a mistake."

"Nothing she does is a mistake," he conceded, rubbing his fingers together as he ruminated. "The little bitch is taunting us."

It was a struggle for Naretha not to smirk, knowing it was probably true. Instead of elaborating on that subject, she asked, "Why didn't you have Devika track her down instead of the Starks?"

"I can't let *her* take credit for tracking down Ashna. What kind of leader am I if I can't even find a runaway *child*? No, I have confidence she'll accidentally trigger her tracking mechanism soon, and when she does..."

The explosive motion he made with his hand was unnecessary for Naretha to know his plans. For the girl's sake, Naretha genuinely hoped that tracking device was eternally disengaged.

"And what of your three new prisoners?" she prompted casually. "Have they given you any useful information on Periculand?"

Danny snorted, absently shaking his head. "Haven't even given it a thought. At this point, I'm beginning to doubt Periculy will regain power over his own town. If he had any desire to, it would have been done by now, with an Affinity like his. The man's probably been debilitated by his own grief. With *Reggs* controlling the town, it'll crumble within a matter of months. Let it die on its own."

After gnawing on her lip in agitation for a moment, Naretha tried again. "Jamad expressed sentiments of vengeance. His parents are Reggs, and they were the ones to betray us to the government. If we give him a chance, I know he'll fight passionately. Avner is a stubborn little bastard, but he's powerful. He's got… people he cares for out in the world. After the past few days in that cell of solitude, he might take the offer of joining us if it means he'll be able to reunite with those people eventually."

Stroking his chin, Danny slowly and suspiciously squinted up at her. "What about the girl?"

Without thinking, Naretha barked out a laugh. "I barely like giving compliments when they're true. Don't ask me to contrive some lie about her secret value. The girl's pathetic."

His lips formed a wide, manic grin. "Don't turn me on too much with your ruthlessness, darling, or you might not be able to finish your little scheme before my mind wanders."

Mouth drooping, Naretha internally cursed herself for believing she could outwit this sly little psychopath. "Well, given that your mind hasn't completely wandered *yet*, are you considering it?"

"Am I considering giving the two boys a deal and allowing the pathetic girl to rot?"

Naretha clenched her jaw, knowing how obnoxious Jamad would be if she didn't at least try to free his pitiful pet. "She's been through hell, and it definitely screwed with her head, but...she's tough enough, and I bet we could harden her if anyone around here has some spare time to work on it. Still don't have a clue what her Affinity is, but judging by the fact that her hair's changed, she must be decent at it."

"And if I release them and they betray us?"

"Do you want me to say I'll take responsibility for it?"

"No, no," he assured her with a dismissive wave. "You're much too valuable to me to be wasted. *Someone* will need to be punished, though, and I feel I've been far too lenient with *Zach* lately."

A snarl rose in Naretha's throat, but she swallowed it, feigning indifference. "If those little twats betray us, you won't be the only enraged one. If they take the deal and just *one* of them betrays us, I'll slaughter them all. Is that fair?"

"Fair *enough*," Danny acquiesced through a dramatic sigh. "Though I do hope you won't be too quick about their deaths."

If those kids were dumb enough to cross her... "I'll be sure to make them suffer."

"All right, since I know *someone's* gotta be listening out there, I'll warn you in advance that this is a spoiler because I don't want to ruin a TV show as amazing as *Fate* for you, but..." Jamad paused, inhaling a heavy breath. "Hillary breaks up with Todd in season four. There, I've said it. And I know what you're thinking: 'We all knew it was coming. Hillary is hot and Todd is not.' Okay—*yes*, but were they not soulmates? I mean, does anyone believe in love anymore? If Hillary can't love Todd, then Orla Belven could never love me."

Halting his pacing, Jamad's eyes roved the walls of his prison cell, searching for some camera or auditory device. So far, he'd spotted neither, but he wouldn't have cared if the entire Wacko Headquarters could hear him. Honestly, he would have *preferred* if someone were sitting on the other side of the mirror, eating popcorn and chortling about his incessant ramblings. At least then his existence wouldn't feel like a complete waste.

Surveying his appearance in the mirror—the bushy, overgrown cloud of facial hair, the way his icy blue hair puffed into an afro, the cuts and bruises marring his otherwise smooth skin, this ugly sweater he'd borrowed from that tomato-headed Wacko…

"Okay, fine, Orla Belven could never love me no matter what," Jamad concluded, shoulders slumping. "But, just so it's known, she *did* say I'm the most attractive guy she's ever slept with, and that makes me better than Nero *and* Avner. I hope you can hear me, Avner!" he added in a shout. "I hope you can hear me, and I hope you know I hate you!"

With another sigh that sounded almost like a groan, Jamad banged his head against the glass and stared into his own eyes. This close, he could see all the white specks woven within the pale blue and a few faint remnants of the brown they'd once been.

"Avner's the reason I'm in here, you know. I was about to join the Wackos—and I *wanted* to join the Wackos—but then Avner opened his stupid, *goody-goody* mouth, and now I'm stuck in yet *another* prison. I have to shit into this tiny hole!" He threw his hand back toward the narrow tube in the concrete floor. "It's not easy shitting into a hole that small. It takes a lot of concentration and coordination. Whoever's watching me out there, you should have seen the ease with which I shit into that hole and said, 'Wow, we need this guy.'"

Removing his forehead from the mirror, Jamad shook his head at his reflection. "If Naretha were here, she'd say, 'Yeah, Snowman, because we definitely recruit people based on how efficient their shitting techniques are.'

"You know what, Salty—you *should* make that a standard by which you judge people.

"'Even if we did, you'd still be stuck in there,' she'd say—with that *dry, condescending* tone of hers, no doubt—"

"Mm, no doubt at all," a dry, condescending voice sounded—the first noise other than his own ranting that had penetrated his ears in what felt like weeks.

"Naretha?" Jamad pressed his hands and his nose to the mirror as if he could see through it. As he did, the glass began to *move*, sliding the mirror upward and replacing it with a transparent window that gave him a view of the corridor beyond. Other glass-paneled cells lined the wall across the hall, but between his cell and the empty ones stood Naretha, her arms folded and her appearance tidy for the first time since he'd met her.

"Snowman," she greeted, eyeing him dully. Her hair was much pinker and paler than he remembered, probably because it had actually been washed, and the black tank top and ripped jeans she wore made her look like a civilized person. The wound on her arm from the experimenters remained, but it appeared to be healing, and though her bones jutted out a little more than they should have, she seemed healthy and whole, which was more than Jamad could say for himself or his friends.

"You need to get me out of here," he hissed, his words forming condensation on the pristine glass. Her voice had sounded so close and crisp, but even though she stood mere feet away, there was more disconnecting them now than there ever had been. "C'mon, Salty. I thought we were gonna take down the Reggs together. I thought we were friends."

"Just because we traveled here together doesn't make us *friends,* kid."

"I'm not sure I'm fond of how fond this boy is of you," the Wacko leader stated as he stepped next to his girlfriend. From beneath the fabric of his burgundy t-shirt, pillars of flame, tendrils of smoke, and blasts of explosive light consumed his skin, creating a mosaic of death and destruction.

"I'm not in love with her, man," Jamad said, splaying his hands on the glass once more. "I just appreciate her life goals, which include getting revenge on the Reggs. I'm on the same side as you."

Danny's eyebrows shot upward. "Even if our side chooses to oppose Periculand?"

"*Reggs* rule Periculand—of course I'll oppose them. I don't care what Avner says about *morals.* Letting Reggs have control over us is immoral."

"I'm glad you think so," Danny drawled as he took a few calculated steps toward the glass, "because we just spoke with Avner and he says he still has no interest in joining us. If we can trust that you're no longer attached to your old friend..."

"I'm not." Jamad removed his hands from the glass and stood straight. "I've been done with Avner since the moment those asshole Reggs who tortured us stood before us and he didn't want them dead."

"Good." Pulling a remote from his pocket, Danny unlocked the cell, glass sliding upward to leave an open threshold. Just like that—just by choosing not to be a stubborn little saint like Avner—Jamad had won his freedom. "Naretha will show you your room. Wash up quick. I'd like to hold the initiation ceremony tonight."

"Ooh," Jamad enthused, rubbing his hands together, "sounds exciting. Do I get to show off my Affinity?"

Danny's lips quirked in amusement while Naretha simply rolled her eyes.

"All you need to worry about is what kinda tattoo you want," she informed him, eyes flitting over the artistic depictions woven into Danny's skin. "I'm thinking a snowman right on your forehead, carrot nose and all."

"Oh, yeah, that's sure to strike fear into the hearts of our enemies," Jamad droned. "Hey—did…did Meredith refuse your offer too?"

Gaze cutting to the left, Naretha said, "We were going to let that be your decision, actually. Do you want to babysit, or do you want to leave her safely in her crib?"

Jamad followed her line of vision to the cell beside his. Beyond the wall of glass, Meredith was curled in the far left corner, knees pressed against her chest and bright magenta eyes staring lifelessly at the one-way mirror. After years in that research facility, she probably looked like a stranger to herself. Perhaps it would have been better to leave her in there; though Jamad had a soft spot for her, the girl was clearly deranged, and she would be more of a liability than a help when fighting the Reggs. The thought of her alone in that cell, though…

"Do babysitters get a salary around here, or…"

"You get rewarded with your own internal satisfaction over what a wonderful person you are," Naretha assured him with a tight, sassy smirk.

Jamad shrugged. "I'll take it."

By pressing a few buttons on his remote, Danny unlocked

Meredith's cell, the glass sliding down instead of up this time. As it disappeared, the girl blinked and unfurled her legs, staggering to her feet. So weak from years of atrophy, her knees bent inward and her shoulders hunched forward as she crept out of her cell.

"Welcome to the Wackos," Naretha congratulated without any sort of celebratory glee.

"I-I'm free?" Meredith stuttered, her wide eyes darting from Naretha to Jamad and then, with a hint of trepidation, to Danny.

"Yeah," Jamad said, gently patting her bony shoulder. "We're free—and we're gonna make sure the Reggs never treat anyone else the way they treated you."

For the first time since he'd met her, a smile broke across her face, and rather unexpectedly, she lunged at him in a hug, wrapping her arms around his neck and burying her face in his shoulder. Naretha snickered mutely to herself, but Jamad shot her a wordless glare as he returned Meredith's gesture. Maybe his parents thought him some vile disgrace, but to this girl he was a savior.

"I feel...very great," Meredith said once she finally pulled away.

"Well, you smell really bad," Jamad commented, at which Naretha audibly snorted. "No offense... I think we both literally smell like human feces."

Meredith nodded in agreement, a small, shy smile lingering on her lips.

"Which room should I bring them to?" Naretha asked Danny.

"208," he called back as he sauntered out of the dungeon corridor.

Pure indignation morphed Naretha's features as she glowered after him. "That's Cath's room."

"That *was* Cath's room," Danny corrected, disappearing into his office only after gifting her with a smug grin.

Visibly seething, Naretha stalked after him, vaguely beckoning for Jamad and Meredith to follow. With her newfound freedom, Meredith's confidence had swelled, and her gait was much less feeble as they trekked through the corridor. Jamad hadn't given much thought to where Avner's cell might have been, so when they reached the one closest to the exit and he caught sight of his old friend, he had to force himself to keep moving—not to loiter and dredge up sentiments of regret. Avner had damned himself, and Jamad refused to be needlessly dragged down with him.

Surprisingly, Naretha didn't verbally assault Danny for whatever he'd said to irk her; she merely stalked through his office to the elevator, barely checking to see if Jamad and Meredith had joined her before jabbing the button to shut the doors. After ascending two stories, the elevator stopped and they exited into a narrow, metallic hallway, lined with numbered doors. As instructed, Naretha escorted them to dorm 208, a small, square, windowless room with two beds. The décor was distinctly female, pink accents inlaid with punk posters, and the two dressers brimmed with leather skirts and lacy undergarments. Jamad noticed quite a few articles of clothing that were large enough to fit someone Nero's size, but the rest seemed petite enough for frail Meredith.

"I'll see if I can scavenge some men's clothes for you," Naretha said tautly, a hint of longing in her eyes as she scrutinized the room. "Danny might have assigned you to this dorm, but if you ruin anything in here, I'll clog your ear canals with salt. Got it?"

Meredith nodded profusely while Jamad gave her a quick bow of his chin, wondering silently who this *Cath* person was and how Naretha actually had the capacity to care for her so ardently.

Since there were not yet any clean clothes for Jamad, he allowed Meredith to use their shower first. He was surprised when, a minute after she disappeared into the bathroom, she poked her head out and asked how to turn the water on. After being confined to that dungeon for so long, though, maybe Jamad shouldn't have been surprised that she would have to relearn common functions of life.

After spending nearly forty minutes scrubbing grime off his own skin, Jamad reentered his new dormitory to find Meredith dry and sanitary, smelling of berries and honey, her skin ghostly pale without the stains of dirt and her hair a vibrant, blinding magenta without years of built up grease. Instead of the raggedy undergarments or the blood-soiled clothes she'd borrowed from Devika, Meredith now adorned loose fitting navy blue pants and bra that actually fit her. Though he'd seen the girl practically nude before, he still felt a little uncomfortable about being in a bedroom alone with her while she was so scantily clothed—until he realized she'd only foregone a shirt in order to inspect her stomach wound.

"Doesn't look like it's healing." Jamad stopped by the bed closest to the bathroom, where Naretha had deposited a stack of darkly colored garments. Typically he preferred lighter clothing, but the Wackos did seem to have a darker color vibe that he would apparently have to grow accustomed to.

"Oh." Meredith hiccupped, nearly jumping when she saw he had emerged from the bathroom. "Um—no, it's not… I don't know if it will heal. It's old. I can barely remember a time when I didn't have it."

Jamad's lips parted, but he wasn't quite sure what to say to that. "The experimenters just…kept reopening it, huh?"

Biting her lip, she grimaced down at it, likely bombarded with the nightmarish memories. "Well…yeah… They—"

The doorknob abruptly turned, and Jamad tightened the towel around his hips, preparing for Naretha to barge in and berate him for not dressing quickly enough. When the door flew open, though, it was not Naretha that filled the doorway but—

"*Mads*," Jamad breathed the moment her burnt orange hair and eyes entered his view. She looked exactly as she had when she'd disappeared from Periculand months ago, the same bouncy curls, the same soft face, the same tan skin—except now that skin was woven with intricate orange designs that laced up her arms with delicate beauty: Wacko tattoos.

"Jamad!" She took two eager steps into the room and then stopped at the sight of his bare chest and towel. "I-I'm sorry—I'll—I'll let you get dressed—"

"No, no, stay—I-I don't want to let you out of my sight again," he insisted, his throat constricting with emotion. After a month of her absence in Periculand and a month of trudging through hell to find her, Madella Martinez was finally a few paces from where he stood—and she was a Wacko. He couldn't judge, since he was soon to be initiated as well, but… "You—aren't in prison. We thought—I just…thought you were being tortured all this time."

"I…was locked away until recently," she admitted, avoiding his gaze by staring ashamedly at her tattoos. "Danny said if I didn't join him he'd kill all of us once you arrived and—and I'm so sorry I doomed us—"

"Hey, hey, it's okay." Closing the gap between them, he rested his hands on her shoulders. At this proximity, he saw all the faint freckles decorating her cheeks, the same orange hue as her hair. "I'm glad you didn't get yourself killed. I'm glad you're safe—I'm glad we're together again. I agreed to join the Wackos, too."

"Oh, J," she moaned, her face wilting with despair.

"No—no, it's *good*. I want to join them. I want to dismantle the Reggs. Those research facilities, Mads… And my parents willingly sent us…" Trailing off, he closed his eyes, burying the grief welling within them. When he opened his eyelids again, a figure was positioned beyond Maddy, awkwardly shuffling in the doorway.

"Oh, um, this is Zach." Maddy stepped back from Jamad to give him a clearer view of this *Zach*. His instinct was to be defensive and antagonistic toward the tall, lanky man standing there with his finely combed hair and sharp features, but Maddy's next words quelled the glacier building in his gut. "He's Danny's brother. I'm, uh, not really trusted to roam the complex without a chaperon yet."

"Neither are we," Jamad said after giving a stiff nod of acknowledgement to Maddy's chaperon. Zach's demeanor was as dismal as his gray hair and eyes, so starkly different from the intensity of his brother. "Naretha brought us here just a bit ago."

"Are Av and Z—" Maddy paused when she spotted Meredith standing in the left corner, probing the gash on her stomach. "Oh—you have a roommate."

"Yeah, Meredith." Jamad peeked over his shoulder at the girl. Her head didn't even perk up at the sound of her name. "She's—ah…we kinda grouped up with her when we escaped the research facility. She was there for…a while."

"Is she okay?" Maddy hissed with genuine concern as she watched Meredith squeeze the sutured wound.

"Meredith, stop playing with it," Jamad commanded, jolting the girl out of her trance. Noticing the visitors in their dorm for the first time, she blanched. "Don't panic, Mer. These are our friends…sorta," he added with an uncomfortable glance in Zach's direction.

"Which room did they put Avner and Zeela in?" Maddy inquired, slicing through Jamad's good humor. Leaving Zeela behind in the woods and ditching Avner in the dungeons hadn't seemed like unforgivable crimes until now.

Scratching the back of his head, he opened and closed his mouth four times before finally saying, "They're not… Avner's still in a cell. He refused to join the Wackos, so he's a prisoner. And Zeela…well—it's such a long story, Mads, but she didn't make it here with us. She's safe—she's safe," he amended hastily when tears began to bulge in her eyes, "but I'm not sure exactly where she is. We'll find her, though, I promise."

"But," she started, looking frantically toward Zach, "you said my friends—two boys and a girl…"

"Meredith," Jamad confirmed when Maddy looked across the room to the girl who was a stranger to her—the girl who had, in her mind, replaced Zeela. "But we'll find Z, Mads. You know she's like a sister to me, and you know she's smart and tough—she'll survive."

"And—and Avner? We'll find a way to free him, too, won't we?"

Quenching the desperation in her watery eyes was a painful task, but he couldn't give her false hope and promises. "Avner chose his own fate. He'll stay a prisoner as long as he wants to. And if he never chooses to join the Wackos…" Jamad licked his lips, hating the truth even as he spewed it, "then I'm gonna let him rot in there."

28

The Fate of the Demoness

Since Tuesday evening, Tray Stark had been even more annoying than usual. Calder had tried holding a secret meeting with him in their joint bathroom to discuss the affirmation of Than's allegiance as well as the new knowledge of Ashna's Wacko mission, but the Stark twin merely grumbled, "Later," and then locked himself in his dorm room. As expected, "later" had never come, because for the remainder of the week, Tray pointedly ignored Calder, and none of the other primies knew what to do about his newfound attitude, either.

The sudden lack of assistance from his strategic ally was more disconcerting than Calder could have anticipated. It wasn't surprising that Ashna was a Wacko; she'd shown up in a Wacko van, and it was too convenient that the Headquarters location she'd given had been empty. Still, her motives remained unclear, and having grown accustomed to being on the inside with the Rosses, Calder loathed this sense of the unknown.

Therefore, he spent the majority of his days observing Than's and Ashna's movements, searching for some clue to what they planned. Why the history teacher neglected to tell the Wacko leader that Ashna had arrived here was still a mystery, but Calder assumed it meant that her task shouldn't have taken long—but it *was* taking long.

This alluded to endless possibilities, which he spent his nights brooding about. The plant-kid's unexpected friendship with Ashna should have harvested more information, but all it had sown was tension between Ackerly and the rest of his friends. While the other primies were rightfully suspicious, Ackerly believed the girl blameless, resulting in continuous scowls from Calder as he non-verbally warned the kid to stop being so ignorant.

The lack of sleep, combined with the constant glaring, turned Calder into a grump, and he was in desperate need of someone whose dark humor could brighten his mood.

For that reason, he was almost anxious to accompany Nero to the Rosses' office when they summoned him that following Sunday afternoon; surely they needed their bodyguards for a visit to their predecessor's cell. When they arrived, however, Calder's countenance soured at the sight of the Reggs seated firmly in their respective chairs behind their shared desk, implying this would be another boring meeting, not a field trip.

"Corvis, Mardurus, sit." William motioned to the two empty seats opposite them. The cushioned chair on the left was worn and frayed from the repeated strain of Nero's heavy form, but the one Calder always assumed on the right remained in pristine condition. Its cushiness didn't make him any more pleased to plop into it, though.

The Rosses ascension to principals hadn't invoked any serious changes in the office's décor: Adara's spot of discolored wood and Angor's wall of books hadn't been touched, but Periculy's plaques and awards had disappeared from the left wall, leaving a blank sheet of red paint with a new flatscreen television in the corner. Currently, the news played on the screen, highlighting Emmett Ventura's "Life Before Presidency."

Calder's eye roll was interrupted by Artemis asking, "Well, Nero, why have you called for this meeting?" at which he fought not to display his surprise. Consumed with his own air of diplomacy, Nero didn't notice Calder's newfound demeanor of dread.

"It's been almost a month since Periculy was jailed," the brute began, eyeing the two adults as if they were his equals, "but there are still some *rebels* in this school who defy your authority—namely, Tray Stark and his hooligans. They're pissed their precious Stromer's in jail, and I know they're plotting."

Though Calder maintained a neutral expression, his heart raced. Had he actually heard something about Tray's wealth of knowledge on the secrets of this town—or about Calder *working* with the primies?

Nero sat forward, oblivious to his ally's internal fretting. "If we have a trial and find both Periculy and Stromer guilty, their little supporters will be less likely to rebel. How could they possibly justify associating with *convicted* criminals?"

Calder was tempted to mention that Nero was once a convicted criminal, but Artemis would have disregarded the fact. Already, she'd folded her hands on the desk and contemplated the suggestion.

"To tell you the truth, we don't have any evidence against Adara Stromer. Legally, she hasn't done anything seriously incriminating. The most we can do is fine her for destroying school property, and even that would only entail community service, not further jail time. But, you know she's a dangerous girl—wild and vengeful. We've been pushing back the trial because we know this town will be in jeopardy with her freedom."

"Then don't free her," Nero concluded, shrugging his meaty shoulders as a devilish grin spread on his lips. "Find her guilty."

Serious intrigue broke across both of the Rosses faces. William leaned forward and said, "What do you propose?"

Reclining, Nero crossed his legs; the pale light seeping in through the back wall of glass made his dark eyes glimmer with depravity. "Convicting Periculy will be simple since he *is* guilty—just gotta ask a few of my allies to testify about how he tortured them with his mind controlling Affinity. Stromer will be trickier, but my allies are all skilled at blocking mind readers; the judge won't assume they're lying when they say they overheard Stromer conspiring with Periculy to burn you both to char if his plan failed. Mardurus will gladly be one of those witnesses."

The sound of his name nearly made Calder jump, but he maintained poise, plastering a lazy smile on his face. "You can imagine no one wants Stromer to stay in jail more than I do. I don't have the patience to waste my time extinguishing her fires."

"You two won't have to worry about any of the details, really—just compose your own testimonies and ensure that Stark and his gang can't get into the courthouse," Nero finished, nose twitching at the mention of Tray.

"Legally, we can't bar anyone from entering the courthouse," Artemis reminded him, her words spoken carefully. "Anyone who wants to testify has the right. However, I believe we can find a way to ensure that Tray Stark and his friends are indisposed at the time of the trial. We'll schedule it for this week."

"Gather your witnesses," William instructed as if *they* had been the ones to come up with Nero's devious ploy. "We'll inform the president-elect of the plan so he can secure a spot in federal prison for Angor Periculy and Adara Stromer."

"Stromer's not going to juvie?" Calder asked, feigning indifference.

"Ah—Affinity prisons aren't structured by age or gender." William conjured a taut smile. "You can leave those details to us, though. We will ensure that Periculy and Stromer get what they deserve."

"Have you been able to locate Ruse Dispus, the shapeshifter?" Artemis asked as Nero stood.

"No, he's probably still hiding somewhere…but I'll sniff him out soon enough."

"Deliver him to us when you do."

Nodding, Nero motioned toward the door, and Calder followed, refusing to even dip his chin in farewell to the Reggs. Once they were within the stairwell, the brute's aura of superiority amplified.

"Stromer's gonna owe me a few debts after this."

Pursing his lips, Calder glanced up at him. "You just gave her more jail time—in a real prison. If anything, it nullifies the debt."

"No, because when the trial comes around, I'm gonna testify on her behalf—against the Reggs."

Calder should have seen this coming, but it was impossible to subdue his bewilderment. Nero reveled in it.

"I'll expose them for lying in court, they'll be jailed, and Stromer will be free—and in my debt. *And*, given that I'm second-in-command now…"

"Fraco's the vice principal," Calder reminded him flatly.

"I know," Nero said, his self-importance radiating as they walked into the library, "and soon he's gonna be *my* vice principal."

Adara had ogled the Pixie Prince for days—or, more accurately, she'd glared at a crude drawing of him that he'd requested Mitt paste on the ceiling above her bed for days. Designed in a dark blue crayon, the stick figure barely resembled Calder at all, but the point of it, she knew, wasn't to impress her with his artistic skills but to taunt her with the fact that he was out of reach—and that he'd refused to deliver the masterpiece personally.

Calder wasn't the only one neglecting her existence, though. Not one visitor had appeared in almost five days. Since the night Tray had come to announce Ashna was a Wacko and Ackerly had come to proclaim his love for that Wacko, none of her friends had visited, and Mitt seemed equally as perturbed about it. Though the officer rolled his eyes and played authoritative cop, he enjoyed the presence of outsiders as much as she did, which was clear through his increasingly dejected posture whenever he brought her food.

Angor didn't give a damn either way. He was perfectly content to sit in silence and meditate over the conspiracies running rampant in his town. For all they knew, Periculand's problems could have been solved by now and everyone had simply forgotten about them. Or maybe the Reggs' façade of peacefulness had cracked and they'd killed all of Adara's friends—or, worse, Artemis had finally decided to use her Affinity, seizing the primaries' minds.

No matter the case, Adara was beyond relieved when Mitt opened the door with a sly smirk on his lips and a person at his back. When Weaponizer stepped to the side and the visitor became visible, Adara had to stifle the elation sparking in her core: Calder Mardurus sauntered into the corridor outside her cell, his grin even more complacent than Mitt's.

Wearing a dark blue button up and gray slacks, he exuded a

composed, collected appearance. His hair told otherwise: wisps of navy blue locks protruded from the knot in a much messier fashion than normal. With the rings of darkness around his eyes, he'd either taken a few light punches from Nero or he was severely over-tired.

"Pixie Prince." She swung her legs over the side of her metal slab to approach the bars. "Thank God you're here."

Dark eyes appraising her, he allowed his lips to curl. "Have you been hoping to see me?"

She splayed her arms out on either side of her. "I need you to hose me down."

"Is that some kind of sexual reference?"

"No, I need a shower, you dimwit," she snapped, mildly flustered.

"Oh, *now* you need a shower?" A small ball of water formed before him, which he mockingly juggled between his hands. "Last time, if I recall, you refused."

"It's been almost a month since I've bathed," she said through gritted teeth.

Calder shrugged, unfazed by her rising fury. "I'm sure they'll let you shower before your trial. Although, you can never be sure with those Reggs."

"Yeah, but who knows when the hell that'll be?"

"Well, I don't have a specific date yet, but I know it'll be this week."

"This week?" Mitt repeated, stepping farther into the hallway. Angor stood from his perch, but Adara was paralyzed by this unexpected information. For weeks she'd awaited the trial, knowing she was innocent enough to be released, but the fact that Calder had come here to tell her about it—to *warn* her about it—made her question what the outcome would be.

"The Reggs decided it'll happen within the next few days," Calder confirmed.

"Finally." Mitt ran a hand over his silver head. "I'm sick of being a babysitter."

"What makes you so sure we'll both walk out of here?" Adara questioned.

"Well, for one," Calder began with a condescending tilt of his head, "convicted criminals go to *real* prison, so even if you're both deemed guilty, you won't return to this cell. Second, I know for a fact that *you*, Demoness, won't find yourself behind physical bars again. Metaphorically, though, you'll enter an inescapable dungeon."

Frowning, Adara crossed her arms. "What is that supposed to mean?"

"It means Nero has plans to ensure your freedom—at the expense of you becoming his slave." His tone of resentment convinced her to believe him, but she still barked out a laugh, shaking her head.

"You're funny, Pixie Prince."

"I'm glad you think so, but I'm not joking. Nero's got a whole plot in place in which Angor's incriminated, the Rosses are jailed, you're freed, and then he's installed as Principal of Periculand. He'll have all his *allies* on his side, guaranteeing his success."

"Including you?"

The ball of water absorbed into his palm, leaving him motionless and contemplative. "I haven't decided."

Adara narrowed her eyes, but she didn't spew any profanities because she could see the layers of this predicament. Would the town be better off with Nero as its leader than these illusive Reggs? At least the big bully was honest about his malevolent motives.

"I won't sway you either way, Pixie Prince, but I will say I have no intention of being one of Nero's *allies*, even if he does free me from this hellhole."

Calder's mouth quirked upward. "I'm aware. But *I'll* say your little boyfriend Stark struck a deal with Nero weeks ago: if your primie friends could beat Nero and his allies in a brawl, Nero would have to break you out of jail. If your friends lost, *you* would owe Nero a debt. You can imagine how it went."

Adara swallowed the rage creeping up her throat. "I will *destroy* Tray."

His gaze darted toward her torso. "It wasn't Tray."

Air expelled from Adara's lungs, cooling her as his words sunk in. When she lowered her arms, she found the heat building in her hands had thinned the fabric of her shirt, leaving it threadbare below her breasts.

Calder jumped his eyebrows. "Too bad your hands weren't a little higher, Stromer."

"Too bad you're still Nero's little *lap-dog*, Mardurus. I bet you laughed when my friends lost and you realized I'd be indebted to that boar."

His expression had soured, but he kept his inflection blithe. "Aloud, sure, I snickered. Internally, though…I don't enjoy the idea of you incinerating this town under Nero's command."

"He won't have to command me to destroy anything," she snarled, feeling a flame flicker on her finger. Ironically, the heat chilled her, but Calder had seen the brief flare, and his chagrin showed. To deflect from the near-outburst, Adara crossed her arms again and said, "Tell me about Seth."

This increased the wrinkle in his brow. "What do you want me to tell you?"

"How he's doing? If his super strength has surfaced yet? I haven't seen him since the night he upchucked all over the floor."

She nodded toward the hall, and Calder glanced down at the tile, almost bored.

"I don't keep tabs on your boyfriend, Stromer. I have more important things to worry about, like the barbarian I work for and the mind controller he works for—and the fact that at least two Wackos have infiltrated this town. You might be relaxing in here, but out in the real world we have a heap of shit to deal with."

"*Two* Wackos?" she gasped with heightened theatrics. "Oh, please, Pixie Prince, tell me *more*. You're the only person on this planet who has the ability to give me information. I'll bow at your feet, oh Highness—"

Engulfed in her dramatic display, Adara didn't have time to react when Calder lifted his finger and shot a jet of water at her throat. The force of it provoked an involuntary gag, but what really peeved her was that the water now seeped down her neck, soaking her chest and making her shirt nearly transparent.

Seething, she picked at the fabric clinging to her skin. Falling on Fraco Leve's desk nude hadn't been an issue, but something about the prospect of Calder seeing the curves of her body made her feel jittery—perhaps not in a bad way.

"What the hell, dude—you made me wet!"

"I tend to have that effect on females," Calder drawled, waving his fingers in a way that caused the water droplets to creep back toward her throat and then evaporate completely. Adara hoped Mitt's chortles distracted the Pixie Prince from the instinctive shudder that ran down her spine.

While the officer coughed to cover up his amusement, the former principal paced closer to the bars, scrutinizing Calder with intrigue.

"I've been curious...how do you manage to shoot water through these bars without electrocuting yourself?"

"I've had more than a few painful encounters with Avner Stromer"—Calder shot a pointed glance in Adara's direction—"so I taught myself how to purify the water I emit. Without any ions for electricity to travel between, the water isn't a conductor—which means I'm free to soak the Demoness whenever I please."

"Fascinating," Angor breathed despite Calder's little quip at the end. Adara rolled her eyes when the Pixie Prince winked.

"You're not as clever as you think, your Highness," she said. "I know you're just trying to direct the conversation away from the Wackos. Are you really going to withhold that information from me forever?"

"I was planning to, yes, but *you're* not as clever as you think, underworldling." His eyes slivered like two dark ravines. "It's painfully obvious that you already know who the Wackos are."

"Fine, then let's discuss the fact that *Than* is one of them. Opinions, everyone?"

"Don't you have your own?" Calder challenged, eyebrows arched.

"Oh, I do, but it's so *underworldly* that I don't think your mortal ears can handle it."

"The news is astonishing to me," Angor said before Calder could further the banter. "That Than could be working for such an organization… I was in my early twenties when we met, and he appeared, at least, to be in his late twenties. I always looked up to him—an inspiring, knowledgeable man. In fact, he took my side in a dispute I had with Ephraim, who went on to become the leader of the Wackos… The whole ordeal is so hazy in my mind now, though—skewed by whoever's blocked my memories."

"What did you do to provoke Floros to betray you and side with the Wackos?" Calder asked, eyeing the former principal with disdain.

Angor let out a weary sigh. "The problem is that I don't know. I could have done something truly ghastly, but if it was related to my Affinity, I have no knowledge of it. If I truly did something to offend Than, then I despise the man I was."

"Now that's a notion we can all get behind," Adara said. "Than might be almost three hundred years old, but he is an innocent lamb, and even I know that innocent lambs shouldn't be maimed. The man's never had sex. Three hundred years and he could never manage to get laid."

"How do you even know that?" Calder demanded through a laugh.

"I made sure it was part of the history curriculum," she informed him, at which he shook his head in awe. "Hey, speaking of sex, did you ever ask Aethelred to get creative with my mom?"

"Your mom?"

"That murdering bitch, Artemis."

"Oh, right..." He studied her with uncertainty, as if her appearance alone could confirm or deny whether Artemis truly was her mother. "Yes, I asked him, and as expected, he said no."

"Mm, you wouldn't think I'd be disappointed to hear that some guy *isn't* seducing my mother, but oddly enough, I am." Calder raised his eyebrows in a way that implied he *had* predicted such insolence from her, but she plowed on before he could speak. "You know what's also surprisingly disappointing? Unicorn Fairy's a Wacko. It's really not as satisfying as I'd hoped—nor is it very shocking. I mean, I might be the only human intelligent enough to have seen it coming, but it's not really my fault the rest of you have subpar brains."

"Unicorn Fairy?" was the only part of her rant Calder seemed to have heard.

Adara shrugged. "Couldn't decide which one she reminded me of more, so now she's both."

"Sounds far too docile for someone who's a Wacko," he commented dryly, "but...Colton doesn't think she's a Wacko. He says there's nothing suspicious about her—that she has no bad intentions."

"Hm, well, we should definitely trust some freak that can see *another world*."

"Tray said a note was found, incriminating both Than and Ashna," Angor said, disregarding Adara's commentary. "Is it possible someone knew this note would be discovered—that, perhaps, someone planted it there as a decoy to distract us from what might really be going on?"

"Don't even *say* that," Calder groaned, his pretense of composure finally crumbling as he sunk against the wall and buried his face in his hands. "There's already enough I can't figure out—don't make it harder by suggesting all the clues we have are a hoax."

"All options should be considered," Angor stated as he stroked his chin.

"But the Pixie Prince doesn't *like* that," Adara mock whined. "In fact, he's going to *cry* about it."

"I'm not crying," Calder snapped, his face whipping upward to glower at her. His eyes, though not bloodshot, looked even more sunken than before, and for once, she wished she weren't so heartless. "I'm *thinking*. I know you've never had to do it before, but—"

"Lame insult, Pixie Prince. Try again."

"I'm not playing *games*. Not all of us can just sit around and stare at walls all day."

"Are you angry at me because I'm in *jail*? You've been on the other side of these bars; do you really wanna be here again? Do you want to feel trapped and neglected and *useless*?"

From the doorway, Mitt cleared his throat. "This is probably a good time for me to do some...paperwork. Don't tamper with the keypad, Mardurus," he added, motioning to the electronic screen beside the door. Awkwardly nodding, the officer slipped out, leaving Adara to glare at Calder with the full heat of animosity.

"I don't know why he would think I'd try to break you out," Calder mumbled, invoking a sense of dejection in Adara. If anyone she knew was rebellious enough to bust her out of jail, it was Calder. The fact that he wasn't even considering it left her feeling unwanted—abandoned.

"I'm not angry at you for being in jail," he finally said, interrupting the bitterness stewing within her. "I'm angry at you for *existing*. You and your stupid friends... They haven't proven to be very useful allies. If anything, I'm like their mother, ordering them around just to find they're more preoccupied with their romantic relationships than our objective. You know your plant friend's got a crush on Unicorn Fairy? He sleeps in the same room as the girl and refuses to do any type of spy work. I'm not accustomed to my allies being so incompetent. Nero's posse might be a bunch of assholes, but at least they're adept members of society."

His use of "Unicorn Fairy" softened her antagonistic resolve. Folding into a cross-legged sitting position on the floor, Adara met his gaze through the bars.

"Are you telling me," she began slowly, emphatically, "that my group of friends is collapsing without my leadership?"

"That is not what I'm telling you *at all*," he retorted, though her question had rekindled a hint of good humor in him. His lips twitched in the briefest of grins before he added, "They've always been incapable, with or without you. I will admit, though, that Ackerly would probably be less infatuated with Ashna if you were around."

"Are you implying Ackerly is infatuated with *me*?"

"No, I'm implying you demand so much attention that he wouldn't have time to be involved with anyone else." Adara scoffed, at which he let out a laugh. "Don't try to deny it, Stromer. It's like, now that you're gone, your friends have realized they can have a life outside of dealing with your chaos—and I know this'll probably boost your ego, but...it's awful."

Resting her elbow on her knee, Adara propped her chin on her fist and said, "Tell me more about the negative effects of my absence, Pixie Prince."

His face was caught between a wince and a chuckle. "Is it... turning you on or something?"

"Would it matter if it was?" she countered with a knowing look at the bars separating them. Calder didn't bother to acknowledge them; instead, his eyes cut toward Angor, now leaning on his metal slab, observing their conversation with creepy intensity. "Are you living vicariously through our youthful banter, or what, Majesty?"

"I was, actually. It's easy to forget the playful witticisms that teenagers are capable of. My relationship with...Miss Alberts has been much less frisky than...the romances of my youth," Angor explained, his brow creasing as if he couldn't quite remember the past. If his teenage years were characterized by his Affinity, then he probably couldn't recall much of it. "Don't mind me, though. Carry on."

"You want us to discuss the fact that I'm too attractive for Stromer to resist while you're plainly watching?" Calder questioned.

"Oh, you want to talk alone? I suppose I'll take a nap, then. I wouldn't advise trying to kiss her through the bars, though,"

Angor warned whimsically. "It didn't go well for the last boy who tried."

As the man closed his eyes to rest, Calder's wry blue gaze fell on Adara questioningly. "Who did you intentionally electrocute by seducing them into kissing you? If you tell me it was Tray Stark, I might not be able to keep it a secret."

"It was Ackerly, actually. Wanted some kissing lessons for *Ashna*. I'd probably feel guiltier if he wasn't enthralled with a freaking Wacko… How'd you know it was a trick?"

He licked his lips, eyes glinting in the fluorescent lights. "Because you're a demoness, not a princess. Plus, I don't see why anyone would want to kiss you even if the bars weren't electrified. You haven't seen yourself in weeks, but you should be at least vaguely aware of how repulsive you are."

A thirst for vengeance should have roiled through her gut since he refused to cleanse her yet had the audacity to ridicule her, but instead of feeling the embers surge within, her natural reaction was to laugh. "I think I'm rivaling Fraco for greasiness." She held out her arm to survey the sheen of soot embedded in her pores.

"You'll need more than a little hose-down to remove the grime." He leaned his head back against the wall and watched her through half-lidded eyes. "I'm not saying I'm unqualified to get the job done, but I will inform you that my skill is advanced enough that I can *feel* the water."

Adara rolled her eyes as she settled back onto her elbows. "I wasn't aware we put Angor down for a nap in order for you to conduct a brag-fest—"

"I don't think you're comprehending what I'm saying." His tone was too low and soft to be an insult. "I can feel…*as* the water—I can feel what the water feels, if I want. And if it's covering you…" Trailing off, he raked his vision over her body and then ended with his eyes trained on hers, eyebrows perked with the insinuation.

Even though her stomach flipped, she didn't dare flinch a muscle or acknowledge the blood that must have surfaced in her cheeks. "You say this as if I give a flaming shit."

His jaw dropped slightly, but then he blinked, lips spreading into a grin. "*Do* you shit fire, Demoness? I'm wondering for statistical purposes, obviously."

"And what kind of stats are you recording?"

"I'm keeping track of how many times you unintentionally confess you have a fire Affinity. The tally is so high that I'll need to consult my data before giving you an accurate number."

His inflection was casual, but his eyes probed her as if they could extract the truth she'd yet to accept. She'd spent weeks convincing herself it was a nightmare—that the flames had been a cruel illusion—but she'd burned all her clothes off, which was why she now wore prison garb, and then she'd burned the sides of *this* outfit as well, a constant reminder of her unwanted power. Not to mention she'd destroyed an entire *floor* and nearly *murdered* Angor in the process. Her Affinity had indeed manifested enough times for Calder to collect conclusive statistical data, but to admit it aloud…

Inhaling deeply, Adara threw her head back, glimpsing the childish portrait of Calder on the ceiling before closing her eyes. "I know I have a fire Affinity, okay?"

The ensuing silence stretched too long for her comfort. Gradually, she inclined her head to peek out at him. Instead of leaning his own head against the wall, he sat upright, staring at her. With his ocean blue hair unusually rumpled and his face vulnerably interested, she found herself straightening to study him, as well.

"That was an intentional confession."

She pressed her lips together before saying a curt, "Yes."

His face twitched, and she felt hers twitch also, and the movements seemed out of place—involuntary—but perhaps they were both so engrossed in this moment of epiphany that they couldn't quite control themselves.

"The next step, you know, is to intentionally *use* it," he said as if speaking to a child.

"You know I'm *lazy*. Even one step a day seems excessive to me."

He snorted, biting his lip as he shook his head. "You know, I was actually hoping—naively—that your Affinity really *was* plants, like you claimed it was back when the Wackos broke in. Plants need water to survive, so you'd be subjugated to my abilities. Water and fire, though…"

"We've always been enemies," she said with a dismissive wave. "Now there's just an innate reason behind it."

His jaw shifted, but he didn't express an opinion before unfolding his limbs and standing. "The way I see it, Stromer, there are three options for the trial. You go with the flow, let Nero free you, and then you become one of his minions when this town switches over to Nero's Dominion. Or you call *him* out for orchestrating the whole conspiracy at the trial, of which you have no concrete evidence, and then you and Periculy end up back in this cell with Nero and the Reggs as company across the hall."

He nodded toward the empty cell at his back, and Adara scrunched her nose at the thought of her three worst enemies occupying it.

"*Or* you can claim you're guilty, avoid Nero and the Reggs, and go to federal prison, which probably means experimentation," he finished on such a bright, cheery note.

"All of those sound horrible," Adara said blandly.

"Well, there's a fourth option."

"Which is..."

"You burn this building to the ground *now* and we siege the town."

Her eyebrows immediately shot up at his blunt offer. The building was concrete, of course, so literally burning it to the ground might prove impossible, but not every wall was impenetrable, and as shown with the two still-distorted bars of metal, she could melt them all if she desired—if she dared—if she mustered the *control* to destroy only inanimate objects and not accidentally tear through humans in the process.

"Together?" she prompted, unwilling to admit the improbability of his proposition. "If you have the ability to drown anyone at will, why not just kill the Reggs and Nero yourself?"

Irritation trickled onto his face. "I...don't think I'm powerful enough to accomplish it alone."

"*Oh*? Are you admitting you *need* me?"

Ignoring her inflated ego, Calder said, "Artemis hasn't used her mind controlling powers on me yet—that I know of, at least. I don't imagine if I tried to kill her she'd just *let* me. Drowning isn't instantaneous; she'll have time to fight back, and then *I'll* be the dead one. Besides, Nixie can stop my Affinity with ease, and if I tried to kill her precious Nero, she would stop me."

Adara drummed her fingers along her chin. "I'm sensing some sibling tension here, Pixie Prince. If your sister has no problem fighting you, who's to say she won't obliterate me if *I* try to burn Nero alive?"

"You..." He paused, expelling a bitter laugh. "I have a feeling no one can stop you if you create a fire big enough—not Nixie... not even me."

His acknowledgement should have swollen her pride, but the

notion of her Affinity—her *fire* Affinity—becoming that outrageously out of hand terrified her. "Are you proposing, then, that I should stop the Reggs and Nero and the Wackos from demolishing this town by demolishing it myself?"

"They destroy, they rebuild. *We* destroy, *we* rebuild. *We* need to be the ones in charge of this town—not the Wackos, not the Reggs, and sure as hell not Nero."

She pictured them lounging in Angor's office, Adara's feet propped on that glorious desk as she chomped on a donut, Calder sulking in some distant corner with a rain cloud over his head because she refused to share. It was, essentially, what she'd sought to attain since arriving at Periculand. Now she possessed the means to solidify that end, but…

"I…can't," she ground out in frustration.

"Because the thought of working alongside me is so repugnant?"

"No, because the thought of *fire* burning my skin makes me want to vomit." Untangling her legs, she stomped to her feet. "I don't *want* this power. It—scares me."

Sympathy flashed over his face—or maybe empathy—but how could he possibly understand that all of her worst nightmares ended with her drowning in a pit of flames?

"The fire can't harm you, Stromer. Once you realize that… it gets easier. It's just a matter of practice—and of knowing your abilities and your limits."

His eyes settled on a point beyond her, swirling with ideas. Without bothering to voice these plans, Calder flicked his hand upward, and from it spewed a generous amount of water, arching through the bars and landing flawlessly on Adara's metal slab. When he lowered his hand, the contained sheet of water burst, drenching the bed and dripping to the floor at her feet.

"Dry that with *control* and you won't have to burn your way out; I'll set you free right now."

The challenge—and his complacent little grin—made her want to riot, but seeing all that water and knowing she *could* evaporate it but *couldn't* left her feeling as hollow and pitiful as ever. "This is bullshit," she grumbled, slumping onto the wet slab and folding her hands over her chest like she was a corpse.

"You're giving up?" His disbelief, at least, restored a bit of her confidence.

"Obviously—but I *will* have my revenge, Mardurus."

He hummed in disappointment. "And I'll be waiting out here where you can't reach me."

As he turned to go, she called, "For the record, I haven't been staring at walls: I've been staring at *you*." She pointed toward the ceiling, and he craned his neck to see what was plastered there. At the sight of his stick-figure self, his lips cracked into a classic smirk. "Can we talk about your terrible drawing skills?"

"Oh," he began, standing straight and fixing his shirt, "that wasn't drawn by me. That masterpiece was a gift from Unicorn Fairy's monstrous sidekick. I knew you'd appreciate it."

She glared up at the drawing, refusing to fall prey to his smug expression. "I would have appreciated it more if you'd hand-delivered it. You came all the way here and didn't even say hello."

"I wasn't aware you were so desperate to see me," he said in a tone that implied he would have thought she was desperate to see him even if she weren't.

"You know I thrive off the mockery of others. Do you want me to rot in here?"

"Your fate's entirely in your hands, Stromer. See you in court."

Swallowing back the dissatisfaction of his parting words, Adara waited a full minute before peering at the doorway, wondering if he might still be there, watching her. But the door had shut, sealing her in this lonely chamber with only snoring Angor as company, and the unnatural heat of her skin had turned the water on her slab to steam, leaving the hideous drawing as the sole remnant of the Pixie Prince for her to cherish.

29

Truth-Tellers and Falsity-Feeders

LAIRTYADSEUTEBYDAER

That was the note Ackerly had discovered on the bathroom mirror Monday morning. Even in his groggy state, it had only taken a few seconds to decipher: *TRIAL TUESDAY BE READY.* He would have to teach Calder some trickier codes for the future.

There wasn't an opportunity for Ackerly or Tray to contact him that day; while the students and faculty engaged in the typical training session, Calder, Nero, and the Reggs buzzed around town, preparing for tomorrow's trial. They hadn't publicly announced it, but thanks to Calder's little note, Ackerly and the primaries were aware, and Tray believed the Rosses would do all they could to ensure none of Adara's friends attended.

The pessimistic Stark twin spent the entirety of training that day plotting how they would sneak into the courtroom, proof that he was stressed and that, despite his constant denial, he cared about Adara's freedom. Still, his redundant claim was that they needed to attend the trial not for his childhood friend but for *Angor.*

"If Artemis is the mind controller, she'll definitely use her Affinity to ensure Angor's found guilty," Tray had repeated so many times that it'd become his mantra. "We need to be there so we can finally establish the truth."

"And so we can ensure that Adara doesn't go to federal prison," Lavisa had added more than once. Each time she'd been dismissed by Tray, at which point she would slide his roommate a flat look of impatience.

Ackerly had chosen not to involve himself with the bickering; most of the day he'd listened to Seth and Naira debate about whether chocolate candies were better than fruity candies. Ashna had been on Seth's side, the fruity side, while Ackerly had been undecided. The conversation had really gone nowhere, even though they'd returned to it multiple times throughout the eight hours, but it had provided a distraction for Ackerly to avoid thinking about Adara and her impending doom.

It was with this fear in mind that he decided he would go visit her once training concluded for the day. Upon exiting the gymnasium, however, his plans dissolved into the back of his brain when Ashna popped up beside him with a mischievous grin.

"Ackerly," she prompted, slowing his pace as the sea of students parted around them. While the other primaries exited the Physicals Building, Tray leading the pack with his determined gait, Ackerly paused near the entrance, turning to Ashna and being stunned, as always, by the glistening quality of her hair.

"What's—um—What's up?" he asked, readjusting his glasses.

Her smile shifted into coyness as she checked for signs of listeners. "Are you working today?"

"N-no. Why?"

Bouncing on her toes, she glanced back toward the gymnasium and said, "Then...*lettuce* go on a date."

"Le—da—joke? That—was a joke?"

"The *lettuce* part was a lame pun, yes." She bit her lip to contain a giggle. "But the rest... I just mean we should do something fun—and afterward we can visit Adara, if you want. You've all been so worried today... I wish there was more I could do."

"No, you—it's Adara's fault she's in jail, kinda," he explained, unsure of how to process this proposition. "But—yeah, we can do something fun...and then we can visit her. We'll probably have to borrow Tray's device to get past the Regg guards...but what did you have in mind first?"

"I did some *exploring* the other day when I was supposed to be going to the 'bathroom.' C'mon, I'll show you."

Pacing back toward the now vacant gymnasium, Ashna beckoned for Ackerly to follow, and upon straightening his sweatshirt as much as possible, he scurried after her.

"Being confined to such a small place for so long makes this campus seem massive," Ashna said, admiring the plain white walls as they continued past the gymnasium doors. When they reached the end of the corridor, Ashna entered the stairwell leading to the basement where, once upon a time, JAMZ had been held.

"Yeah, I got lost a lot the first few weeks," he admitted as they descended the steps. Faint lights illuminated the gray concrete walls and dull metallic stairs, giving the hall a much gloomier tinge than the floor above. As they approached the warehouse-like basement below, Ackerly was reminded of how the girl with hair too turquoise to compare to any natural flower had chased him, wielding a deadly metal chain.

"I'd never been to a school before this one," he continued as

Ashna passed the entrance to the main room and opened the door to a storage closet. "It doesn't really compare to your situation, but..."

His words dissipated when she flipped the light-switch, brightening the room and revealing shelves stocked with various types of sports equipment: footballs, basketballs, roller skates—

"Have you ever ridden a skateboard before?" Ashna asked, retrieving one of the orange skateboards. She tossed it in his direction, and he fumbled to steady it in his hands.

"Uh...no...not really."

"Well"—she grabbed a skateboard of her own and shot him a playful smirk—"you're about to learn."

Gathering a long, thin rope, Ashna strolled past him and disappeared through the doorway before he could protest. With a wince at the skateboard, he turned off the lights and trailed behind her into the vast basement. The orange mats that students had brawled on lay at the center of the floor, so Ashna kicked them to the side, providing ample space for them to *skateboard*. Ackerly's gulp echoed throughout the empty room.

"C'mere." She summoned him forward with her hand, and with a shaky sigh, he joined her in the middle of the room. Repositioning the skateboard in his hands, she took the rope and looped it through the bottom, tying an intricate knot before tethering the same rope to her own board. "Just so you don't get lost."

He chuckled, nervously but genuinely, as she set the two skateboards onto the concrete and then wiggled her eyebrows at him. "All you need to worry about is balancing on the board. I'll deal with the rest. Okay?"

"O-okay," he said, stepping gingerly onto the board. In this lighting, it was a similar shade to orange alstroemeria, and comparing it to a flower was the only way to calm his jitters as he attempted to stabilize himself.

"Don't look so terrified. If you fall and crack your skull I'll make sure you don't feel it."

Blinking, he realized Ashna was now crouched on her own skateboard, her body angled toward his as she peered up at him. "That's…reassuring…"

"I'm joking, Ackerly. I won't let you fall again," she said with such sincerity and intensity that he almost toppled off the board even though it wasn't moving. "Are you ready?"

A mute nod was all the confirmation Ashna needed to set them into motion. Ackerly wasn't sure how she planned direct the boards while in a squat, but then she pivoted and held one hand toward her skateboard. Like magic, the wheels began to spin, propelling it forward and dragging Ackerly's along via the rope.

"H-how…?"

She glanced over her shoulder and squinted one eye up at him, her eyebrows set in concentration. "You've never heard of telekinesis?"

"I—have." He stared down at the concrete as it blurred by beneath his board. They were nearly to the doors now, and at this rapid pace, Ackerly was sure they'd collide with the metal. Just when he was about to open his mouth and suggest slowing down, Ashna twisted her outstretched hand and the wheels abruptly skidded to a stop.

"Balance, Ackerly!" she encouraged, but the words were as futile as his attempts to heed the command. The jerking halt wrecked his stability, and without any hope of regaining it, he plummeted forward, collapsing on top of Ashna and throwing them both to the floor, where they rolled and tumbled in a tangle of limbs. By the time they finally stilled, Ackerly was pinned under her body while one of his legs was somehow draped over her back.

Fidgeting to lower his leg, he looked up at her through his crookedly resting glasses. Her long hair obscured his vision from the rest of the gloomy basement, submerging him in a world of rainbow bliss. "I thought you said you wouldn't let me fall," he breathed, too shocked by his clumsy mishap—and the fact that she was pressed against him—to think through his words.

"I wanted to see if you could do it yourself," she answered, pushing upward to hover above him.

"Clearly, I couldn't," he said, unable to contain an elated laugh when she giggled. Though her cheeks had reddened, he knew she wasn't nearly as flustered to be in this position, because by her telekinetic powers, his glasses shifted back into place.

"Are you in pain?" she asked quietly, pulling some of her hair behind her ear.

"No—no, I'm fine. Are you?" His eyes locked onto her throat, that permanent bruise staining her delicate skin.

"I'm always fine," she assured him, her eyes harboring a sheen that was far too sad to accurately reflect her statement. Rolling gracefully to the side, she propped herself up on her elbow, their faces still as close but bodies no longer in contact. "We'll need to work on that, I guess. Sorry I didn't stop you from falling. I could have, but…I've always hated when people try to do things for me—when they treat me like a child. I didn't want you to feel that way."

"No, not at all." He scrambled into a sitting position. "I know I'm not nearly as coordinated as—as anyone, really… I don't mind a little help."

Smiling, she sat up to face him, crossing her legs so her knees grazed his. Since she'd arrived, she'd worn Adara's green cargo pants, but Ackerly knew she wasn't a Natural. He doubted she could be categorized into any class with the uniqueness of her abilities.

"So…telekinesis," he remarked through an impressed sigh. "That's pretty…intense. Is that how you learned to skateboard? I mean—it must make it easier to balance…"

"I learned to skateboard before I even knew I had a telekinetic Affinity." Her joviality faded slightly as she stared down at her hands. "My…brother taught me how—he loved to skateboard and do anything generally dangerous." A laugh escaped her throat but it was practically humorless. "We always used to skateboard together up and down our driveway, listening to our favorite band, Bleeding Brains."

"Bleeding Brains? That sounds…"

"They're hardcore, yeah," she confirmed, chuckling softly. "My brother and I were always into crazy stuff. We had a lot of fun as kids."

Based on the sparkle in her eye, the answer to Ackerly's next question was fairly obvious. "Where's…your brother now?"

"He…died." Even though he could see her composure crumbling, she tried to force a smile. "It was—he was young—too young—but I should have seen it coming. He always thought he was more powerful than he really was, and he never wanted anyone else's help. Kinda like me," she admitted with a trembling exhale. "His arrogance was really what killed him. I hope I don't make the same mistakes."

"I don't think you're arrogant. If you were, you'd be bragging about your infinite Affinities rather than trying to hide them. You're humble, and you know you aren't indestructible."

"Yeah, the Wackos certainly could have killed me… They killed my brother," she whispered as if they weren't the only two people in this giant room. A cool wrath settled over her features as she met Ackerly's eyes. "I *hate* them. I hate what they've done—I hate what they stand for. And I know…I know, Ackerly, that you think I'm one of them."

His lungs seized up as he gaped at her, petrified by the confession.

"I can't read minds, but I'm not oblivious. I see the way Tray watches me, the way all your friends tiptoe around me as if I'm some dangerous predator, the way you always want to say more to me but never do. I want you to be able to talk to me—I want you to trust me—but I don't know how to make you believe I'm not evil."

"I don't think you're evil. I've…I've never had any siblings, but if the Wackos killed your brother, I don't imagine you'd want to be part of them."

She buried her face in her hands. "I don't. My brother was all I had left and they stole him from me." When she looked up again, he saw how pink the whites of her eyes had become, how much despair seeped from her pores. "My—my mother died giving birth to me…"

Baffled, he stupidly blurted, "That's…kinda rare now, isn't it?"

"She was sick—some disease that weakened her. Giving birth to me was too much for her to handle. She died *because of me.*"

"That's—not true—"

"My father seemed to think it was." Bitterly, she glared into the distance. "He never talked about it much, but I knew he always blamed me—always resented me. The grief was too much for him to handle and…he killed himself."

Ackerly's chest felt heavy as he studied her, unsure of how to respond. So many people in Periculand had endured traumatic experiences, but his life had been fairly *good*—perfect, almost. His parents had been loving and kind; no illnesses or deaths had ever befallen their small family unit. He'd been granted endless hours to do what he loved, and he'd never suffered severe emotions like guilt and sorrow and rage. How could he even attempt to empathize with someone who'd undergone as much as Ashna? It seemed more insulting than humane to try to act like he had any inkling as to the mental agony that must have constantly torn at her brain.

"I-I'm sorry. I—my friends—they shouldn't have suspected you."

"No, no," she said, waving her hand dismissively, "they have the right to be suspicious. If I thought one of you was part of the Wackos, I don't think I'd even be able to stand in the same room. It's been a struggle not to confront that Floros guy, but... disobeying Tray's orders would be like committing a sin, right?"

He couldn't conjure a laugh at her joke. The note Kiki and Eliana had found gnawed at his mind. If they hadn't found it, he would have no doubts about Ashna's loyalty. Even with the note's existence, the possibility that it was some implanted distraction was viable. How could he validate this theory, though, when she'd revealed so much to confirm her innocence? To question her now would be uncouth.

"We'll find a way to discover the truth about Than," Ackerly promised, hoping she didn't sense the unspoken "and about you" that could have easily fit at the end of his sentence. Knowing what he knew now about her past, it didn't make sense that she would be here on a secret mission for the Wackos...but then what *was* her goal?

"I hope we do—before the Wackos ruin any more lives," she added, her shoulders slumping slightly. She forced her torso upright again and finally met his eyes. "I'm sorry to pile this on you. I don't want you to feel bad for me, really, but I just...it's nice to be able to open up about it—to express my feelings. I've gotten so used to bottling them up that it's…strange—but in a good way. I can't think of anyone else I'd rather talk to."

Ackerly's lips parted and his cheeks burned, but luckily, he didn't have to contrive some pathetic response before she stood and extended her hand toward him.

"Ready for another round on the skateboards? I swear I won't let you fall this time. My main priority will be keeping you upright. I will treat you like a child, if you so please."

"I do, yeah," he said, grinning goofily as he took her hand and allowed her to pull him to his feet. Her hand lingered in his for a few extra moments, the clean softness of hers encasing the perpetual dirtiness of his. "I'll try not to fall on you this time."

Barking out a light-hearted laugh, Ashna ambled toward the skateboards, both chaotically strewn on the floor amidst the rope. Before bending to correct them, she threw a frisky glance over her shoulder, irises popping like rainbow roses in a world of concrete. "Don't try too hard, Ackerly. I didn't mind."

Tray skipped work that afternoon, claiming he was sick. The excuse wasn't necessarily a lie: Since Ackerly had emerged from their bathroom that morning with the knowledge of Adara's trial, Tray's nausea had progressively increased. His friends were convinced it was because he feared Adara would end up in federal prison—or perhaps a research facility—and while that was certainly a matter of concern, his apprehension also lay in the prospect that she would somehow be *freed*. It seemed unlikely that the Rosses would allow her to assimilate back into Periculand, but if she did…with her *fire* Affinity…

He dispelled these conflicting sentiments by focusing solely on the issue of Angor, Artemis, and which one of the two might possess the mind controlling Affinity. All deceptions would disappear after the trial—unless the mind controller was skilled enough to persuade even Tray into misguided beliefs. What if Artemis revealed herself only to coax them all into thinking she was innocent? What if Angor proclaimed he'd lied for the past month but then erased any memory of his confession?

Tray despised the notion that anyone had the ability to block knowledge from his awareness. To think someone could inhibit the range of his cognizance was possibly more dreadful than death. His Affinity was *strength*, though—not mental strength but physical strength. How could that useless ability stand a chance against an intangible force?

A knock on his bedroom door extracted him from these pessimistic questions. For minutes—perhaps hours at this point—he'd paced throughout his dorm room, dodging Ashna's mattress on the floor and glaring when it reminded him that *she* was a problem, as well. Thankfully, when he opened the door, it wasn't anyone who could make his dreadful life even worse: just the Affinity ambassador, Olalla Cosmos, who seemed to be one of their few adult allies.

"Ah, Tray, I'm glad you're here," she greeted, her mood considerably brighter than it had been over the past few weeks. She wore a light purple suit today, but it wasn't the clothes on her body that caught his attention, for in her arms she held a stack of white, leathery fabric that looked strangely familiar to the anti-Affinity suit he'd studied over the past three weeks. "I've finally created what I promised you."

Tray appraised the pile of folded garments. "I don't remember you promising me anything."

"It was more of an indirect promise. I used the data you

collected on the Reggs' suits to compose some of my own. Each one is not completely Affinity-proof, but instead tailored to your unique abilities. I've only had time to work on a few, I confess, but here I have one for you and one for your brother, both designed to withstand a substantial amount of weight without tearing. I'm in the process of working on one for your friend Lavisa that will be easy for her to move and fight in. Unfortunately, I don't believe there's much we can do to enhance the Affinities of mind readers and oracles, like your two Mental friends. I've been looking into creating something that might further the effects of my peace Affinity, and that knowledge might transfer over to their Affinities, as well. As for Adara—"

"Don't bother with her," he said a bit too harshly. Composing himself, he amended, "I doubt she'll need any type of suit. It seems likely she'll be in jail forever, and if not, she's in denial about her Affinity, anyway. If anything, we should create a suit that'll *contain* her fire so she doesn't set the world ablaze."

Olalla smiled sympathetically. "Adara can be trained. Any Affinity can be malicious if used for evil, but I see goodness within her. I've been trying to convince the Rosses to release her, but... to no avail. I have hope it'll play out in her favor, though. Don't give up on her just yet."

Although Tray accepted the two suits as gifts, he didn't quite accept her *hope* for Adara. Stromer wasn't *evil*, but her nature wasn't exactly redeemable, either. "Why are you helping us?" he decided to ask, eyeing the woman dubiously. "You must know the Rosses hate me and my friends more than anyone in this school."

"That's exactly why I *am* helping you." Sighing wearily, she elaborated. "The Rosses aren't...what you think they are. I've never been suspicious of them before, but after spending all of my time in this town with them over the past month...I fear they're brainwashing the other students, and you and your friends seem to be the only ones who are immune."

Tray paused before placing the suits on his desk. "Brainwashing how?" Olalla knew of some of their suspicions, but he hadn't thought she believed them herself.

"I don't want to jump to any conclusions," she said carefully, "but there seems to be more at play here than I originally thought. There's certainly a lot of…tension on this campus, and I've been working hard to keep things peaceful, but…it's tiring. I fear the time will soon come when I'm no longer able to withhold the built up violence and aggression and it will all come crashing down."

His heart rate must have spiked from its normal seventy-one BPM to over a hundred. Tray wasn't typically one to cave into panic, but was it possible the Rosses hadn't completely overthrown Periculand yet only because Olalla suppressed their malevolent intentions with her peace Affinity? If this was the case and Olalla grew fatigued, what would happen when the mind controller gained full access to his or her abilities?

"D-do you think you can last until tomorrow?" Tray asked, swallowing back his alarm.

"You're worried about the trial, I presume? I do believe I can last through it, but…that doesn't guarantee the outcome will be to your liking. I can keep it cordial, but if the Rosses intend to find both Angor and Adara guilty…there's not much I can do to prevent it."

"*Legally* is there anything you can do?" he demanded, hating the desperation in his voice. "You're the Affinity ambassador. Shouldn't you have some say in this—at least as much as they do? Aren't you technically their equal?"

"Technically yes, but they've always ignored technicalities. Being that there are two of them, they've always overpowered me with their opinions. Now that they're the undisputed rulers of this town, I doubt that, even though I was there as a witness, I will be permitted to testify in court. The problem is that it's impossible, for even me, to discern who is telling the truth—Angor or the Rosses. If I knew for certain…well, I might even take *illegal* action to ensure whoever is guilty does not ascend."

"I'm considering taking illegal action just to figure out the truth," Tray muttered before adding an awkward, "That was a joke." She chuckled, but Tray could tell she knew he'd been serious. "What about Aethelred? If we can get him to touch them—even just one of them—he'll be able to decipher what's true."

Olalla's expression was polite, but he could see the irritation in her eyes. "Aethelred is a good man, an honest man, but he refuses to touch anyone without their consent. Even if he did, though, I'm afraid with this mind controlling collusion that even his perception will be distorted. Regardless, Aethelred has always been one to strive for peace… Perhaps he can be swayed into helping us. I'll discuss it with him."

"Right, thanks," Tray said, nodding absently as his brain swarmed with the endless, awful possibilities.

"The time may come soon, Tray, when we'll all be forced to choose sides. I hope that, no matter which one of them is proven the mind controller, we'll remain allies."

Tray glanced down at the Affinity-enhancing suits, the kindest gesture he'd received from any of the adults at this school over the past month. He'd always had his reservations about Olalla Cosmos's motives—anyone with a Mental Affinity was to be treated with caution—but her tone was so genuine now, and he saw his own strain and worry reflected in her eyes. If anyone would help him and his friends save this town, it would be her.

"We will," he assured her, his first statement as finite as his next. "See you at the trial tomorrow."

"If your sister doesn't give me a massage, I'm gonna pummel you to death," Nero grumbled to Calder as they approached the Residence Tower. The brute rubbed his over-sized muscles as the wintry wind cut at their backs, throwing the hoods of their dark sweatshirts over their heads. The sun had set hours ago, but the Rosses hadn't permitted them to return to campus until they'd acquired at least five citizens to testify against Angor in court tomorrow.

Too bad all of the citizens they'd recruited throughout the day were being paid off by Nero to testify against the Reggs instead.

It certainly hadn't taken much persuasion to gather twenty people who would speak against the Rosses. Since their hostile takeover, the economy in Periculand had plummeted while the tax rate had risen, creating animosity among the townsfolk. Although Calder had helped him throughout the day, he couldn't determine if Nero's dreams for the trial were better than the Rosses. It seemed unlikely the bully would be a more benevolent ruler, and yes, Adara would be free, but at the cost of endless debts and eternal servitude.

All Calder knew was that if Nero did succeed in his scheme, he'd have to ensure he remained eternally at the brute's side. And if Nero lost...he'd have to convince the Reggs he'd never truly been on his side at all.

The real problem lay in the fact that Adara Stromer was the sole determiner of the trial's result, and Adara Stromer was the least judicious, most impulsive person he'd ever known.

"I don't see how my sister's refusal to massage you has anything to do with me," Calder said in response to Nero's threat of death by pummeling.

"Well, I can't beat up a girl," he huffed, tilting his head to crack his neck, "and you're basically her but male."

"Your logic is irrefutable," Calder droned as they finally reached the tower's entrance.

Sensing the sarcasm, Nero glared at him before yanking the glass door open and stalking into the lounge, not bothering to lower his hood. Calder did slip his off and waltzed in with a high head and narrowed eyes, smirking when the other students shied away. His expression immediately soured as he noticed a horde of students clustered around one of the flatscreen televisions. The Rosses stood imperiously behind them, watching the news with manic glee.

"The deed is done," Nero said to his masters as he stepped beside them. Calder halted a few paces away, gaze flickering between the Reggs and the news that delighted them so: *WACKO MURDERS TEENAGE BOY.* "What's going on here?"

"We decided to release a statement to the press about Hastings's death," Artemis explained, dark eyes glowing in the reflection of the screen.

"We're about to bring you live footage from southern Ohio," the reporter on the television said, "where a Wacko terrorist named Angor Periculy will soon stand on trial for murdering a young, teenage boy. As witnesses have stated, the man used his blood-vessel-bursting superpowers to kill the boy without any clear motive. Be warned that this man is mentally unwell. The coming footage might be difficult to watch…"

"You told the public about the trial?" Calder asked before he could stop himself.

"We thought it would be beneficial to remind the American

people that the government is not the enemy, the Wackos are," William informed him coolly. "With Mr. Ventura's inauguration happening in a little over a month, he agreed it's a good idea to keep the public alert of the threat."

"By feeding them lies?" Calder questioned through gritted teeth.

Artemis finally pivoted her head toward him, her expression incredulous. "Do you deny that Angor killed Hastings?"

"Can't say; I didn't witness it. I *know* Angor didn't kill Hastings with his 'blood-vessel-bursting superpowers.'"

"He forced Hastings to use his own powers against himself," Artemis snapped. "With the ability to control minds, he might as well have every Affinity."

Calder snorted to himself but didn't bother to argue as the scene on the screen switched, bringing them live to Periculand's police station. The image was a little blurry at first, but the camera soon settled on a figure nestled beyond the metal bars, her body lounging across a metal slab in an almost seductive pose—not that Calder found it seductive, but based on the mischievousness in her red eyes, an alluring aura was what she aimed for.

"Hello," she purred with a tone of grandeur, "I am the King of Periculand, the famous Angor Periculy who you all now fear because of my 'blood-vessel-bursting Affinity.'"

"I think the guy said 'superpowers,'" a voice from behind the camera piped up, and Nero growled instinctively upon recognizing it as his stepbrother's. "I don't think most Reggs know what Affinities are."

Adara's face flashed in a scowl. "Fine, 'blood-vessel-bursting *superpowers*.' I murder children for no reason, so you all must bow before me. Bow, I say!"

"I don't know if I'm capable of bowing while keeping the

camera aimed at you," Hartman said, the screen wobbling as he attempted the feat. Calder had to feign a coughing fit to contain his laughter at the furious bewilderment consuming the Rosses' expressions.

"No, no, aim it away from her!" a snippy voice boomed through the television's speakers, and giggles of "Fraco" trailed through the lounge. "Give me the camera, Mr. Corvis! We don't have time for this nonsense!"

"You can't even hold it, Fraco," Hartman insisted, the image on the screen whizzing incoherently as the two grappled over the camera. "It'll slip right out of your hands!"

"Miss Stromer cannot be on television! This interview is for Mr. Periculy only!"

"What, Mr. Grease, you don't want the world to know the government has imprisoned an innocent girl in a cell with someone they believe to be a murderer?" Adara crooned as Hartman regained control over the camera. Finally landing on her again, it showed her hopping off the slab to approach the bars. From this angle, everyone could see the two she'd partially melted, now looking like distorted silver icicles.

"Hello, world. I bet all of you assholes from my old high school are looking at me now and saying, 'Damn, she's a badass criminal.' I won't confirm or deny this, obviously, but I would like it to be known that I'm not generally this freakin' repulsive. If I'd known I was going to be live on television today, I would have showered. Oh... *wait,* that's right—I've been prohibited from showering for the past *month* because the Rosses are *bitches*—"

"That—is—*enough*!" Fraco shrilled, jumping around in an attempt to obstruct the camera's view of Adara with his own shiny face.

"I think she might have managed to drop a curse in every

sentence just then," Calder mused, lips curving farther upward with every word. When Nero shot him a virulent glare, he quelled his amusement and added, "Just stating a fact."

"It's not even a fact," Nero muttered, arms now crossed over his chest. "She missed one in the second to last sentence. Was hoping she'd drop an f-bomb in there, too."

"Point the camera at Mr. Periculy, please, Mr. Corvis," Fraco prompted on the television, his tone substantially more relaxed.

"Go ahead, Ginger," Adara sighed as she retreated to her slab. "I've said all I need to say—not all I *want* to say, but I'm not greedy."

A loud snort emitted from within the lounge, and Calder followed the sound to the yellow couch where Lavisa Dispus sat, aggressively sharpening a stick with a knife. The Rosses were too tangled in their own dismay to notice the girl or her weapons.

"Okay…" Hartman mumbled as he readjusted the camera. "Fraco, don't stand so close, man—you're getting oil on the lens!"

"*Shush*!" the vice principal barked, positioning himself beside the bars, his body partially directed toward the cell and partially directed toward the camera. Beyond him, Angor relaxed in his corner, hands folded placidly in his lap. He looked considerably cleaner than he had yesterday, and Calder wondered, with a hint of acrimony, if the Rosses had allowed him to shower for this interview. It didn't seem to fit their agenda of making him look like some disgusting murderer, but if he'd appeared as unkempt as Adara, people would have suspected mistreatment—of which Adara had ensured public knowledge, anyway.

"Mr. Periculy"—Fraco's eyes darted between his clipboard and his former superior—"tell us: Why did you murder an innocent boy? Why are the Wackos targeting children? Should average Americans fear for their lives?"

"I'm not sure how to answer that," Angor replied frankly. "As far as I am aware, I did *not* murder an innocent boy—or any boy at all. Certainly not Hastings—"

"No, no, *no*," Fraco hissed, glancing nervously toward the camera. "Mr. Periculy—"

"I apologize, Fraco, but I'm afraid the script you've given me is too oily to read." Angor held up a yellowish piece of paper, and Fraco blanched, watery eyes popping in dismay.

"We should have known the script would be a bad idea," William whispered, just loud enough for Calder to hear.

"You should have known this whole thing would be a bad idea," he said, unable to keep the vindictive hilarity out of his inflection. "What made you think Angor would comply with incriminating himself as a murdering Wacko terrorist on national television?"

Artemis shifted awkwardly, avoiding his inquisitive gaze. "We gave him…an incentive—a lesser sentencing when he's found guilty tomorrow."

Not laughing proved a difficult task for Calder, but he managed to keep his mouth shut and swallow the demeaning insults on his tongue.

"We need to put an end to this before it gets out of hand," William said.

"We'll call the media station on the walk across town," Artemis agreed as the two stalked past Nero and Calder toward the exit. "We need them to cut the feed as soon as possible…"

Hurrying out of the lounge, destined for the police station, the Rosses left the students to watch the interview unfold with far less restraint. As Fraco repeated his questions and Angor refused to give the desired answers, the spectating students broke out into actual laughter, all reveling in the vice principal's misery.

"What a wonderful way to end this hellish day," Nero remarked, and for a moment, Calder thought the darkness in his tone indicated he was about to attack the giggling students. When he pivoted to face Nero, however, the big bully's lips formed a devious grin, those gray irises gleaming in a way that often invoked the slightest tinge of fear, even in Calder.

"Listen up," he bellowed, his deep voice silencing the entire lounge. The only noise that remained audible was Fraco's choppy, desperate gabbing on the television. "At midnight tonight, I'll be turning eighteen, and it appears Adara Stromer's given me a nice little gift: The Rosses are preoccupied, and it seems unlikely that they'll return here for a while."

Pausing, his gaze swept over the circular room, all heads turned toward him in apprehension. Calder had watched Nero beat up plenty of kids, but he wasn't sure how long he'd be able to stand around while the brute pulverized the entirety of Periculand. He was prepared to interject and insist that the Reggs could come at any moment, but then Nero's next words assuaged all dread with an unexpected thrill. "Let's have a party."

30

Fiery Fate

Arguably, Key Fingers was a more atrocious driver than Avner, who had never even acquired a learner's permit. Since her finger had been the key that powered the stolen van, she'd only used one hand to steer. Zeela had seen plenty of adults accomplish this with ease, but Key Fingers was old—perhaps borderline senile—and so her one-handed driving was a nauseating, death-defying experience. Naturally, everyone else in the vehicle had insisted they pull over as soon as they felt it was safer to stop and risk discovery than continue to allow her to drive.

Charlie had taken the wheel at that point, but his turn hadn't lasted long before he'd realized they were low on gas. Since they hadn't possessed any money—nor had they wanted to be caught driving a *Wacko* van—the only real option was to pull into a parking lot and steal another car. The last time Zeela committed theft had induced guilt, but there had been no remorse this time.

The night had cloaked their crime well: Without incident, they successfully claimed another car, this one much smaller, forcing Zeela to cram in the back with Tray and Seth's parents. From there, they'd driven north to where the Starks owned a small cabin in the woods, not far from Lake Erie—and Cleveland, she'd acknowledged with unease. She hadn't forgotten Naretha accidentally informing them that Wacko Headquarters was located near the city. Although it had been her goal to arrive at the hideout and retrieve Maddy all along, now that they knew Danny sought the Starks—and might have been linked to the research facility—Zeela wanted to flee far, far away.

Despite these persistent worries, she'd been securely snuggled in the Starks' cabin for almost a week now. No Wackos had ambushed them when they'd arrived at the tiny structure nestled in the woods, and they'd survived six peaceful days of freedom and tranquility.

Though they couldn't visit a hospital, Linda Stark was skilled enough with medicine to suture the bullet wound on Zeela's upper arm. It still ached, but she was profusely grateful the woman had been able to mend her—especially with her own broken hand, which, as Zeela's eyes detected, remained unhealed.

Richard constantly fretted over his wife's wellbeing, but Linda repeatedly assured him she was all right, even though Zeela saw the swollen nature of her hand and the building tension in her muscles. The woman masked her pain well, and she'd spent the past week patiently teaching Zeela anatomical terms. Learning the names of bones and muscles and even organs helped her immensely when trying to discern people and their feelings, and with her state of panic mitigating, she began to see shapes and objects with more clarity.

Still, auras were removed from her realm of perception, as were distinct physical features and anything with an artistic nature. Because of this, Zeela had been unable to observe the cabin's aesthetic, but the layout was clear in her mind. Currently, she sat on a soft couch in the living room, facing a television that she saw only as a blob of heat. Beyond the television lay a dining room, where Charlie read a book, and to the left of that room dwelled the kitchen, where Richard cooked soup. To the left of where Zeela sat was the cabin's sole bedroom, the bed of which Key Fingers napped in. She saw each of them with as much clarity as she saw Linda, who sat on the couch beside her, purposely warping the muscles of her face and prompting Zeela to recite them.

"Which muscle am I moving now?"

Banishing her heat vision and focusing solely her new ability to view human tissue, Zeela noticed the small muscles above either one of Linda's eyes pressing inward and downward, an expression Zeela recognized as the furrowing of her brow.

"The corrugator supercilii—and between them the procerus muscles are being utilized, too. Your eyebrows must be creased, perhaps in anger or frustration or confusion." She leaned back slightly when the muscles around Linda's mouth—particularly the zygomaticus major and minor in her cheeks—contracted to form what she perceived as a smile. It wasn't as reliable as her auras had been, but at least now she felt a little less disconnected from human emotions.

"It's so fascinating to me that you can see it all," Linda said, not for the first time. The woman, who had confessed to being a scientist, had been utterly enthralled with Zeela's Affinity since discovering it. This interest had disturbed Zeela at first, but the woman had proven docile and humane, never asking anything intrusive or touching her outside of the purposes of instruction.

"I'm still getting used to it. Organic, living matter is the easiest for me to detect now, but I'm slowly getting better with other elements and objects," Zeela explained, scratching the back of her scruffy head. Less than an inch of hair rested on her scalp, and now that she had the ability to use her limbs, it was strange not to run her fingers through her previously long locks.

Her lack of hair was the least of her concerns, but being cooped up in this small space for the past week had given her time to dwell on the abundance of awful aspects in her life. In any other circumstance, Zeela would have thought learning anatomy tedious and boring, but now the only alternative was to wonder what type of torture Avner and Jamad currently endured.

Clearing her throat, she pried her mind out of the hopeless thoughts and redirected her attention to Linda. "My sight was different before..." She motioned vaguely toward her missing left eye, and the woman dipped her chin in understanding. "I was born blind, but my Affinity gave me the ability to see things no one else can. I spent a lot of time perfecting my sight in Periculand, but it seems like it was a waste now."

The muscles near Linda's mouth moved in a way that Zeela assumed meant she pursed her lips in contemplation. After a moment, the woman quietly asked, "What was Periculand like?"

"I enjoyed it," Zeela said, attempting to breeze over the fond memories and avoid the heartache that now accompanied them. "Better than my parents' house, at least. Now, though, with Angor in jail...I can't imagine how different it could be."

Linda sighed and slumped back into the couch. They'd heard on the television not long ago that Angor Periculy had joined the Wackos and killed Hastings Lanio, prompting the Regg ambassadors to take charge of the town. Zeela's initial reaction had been one of deep despair. Her sister had never been one to gush about her feelings, but Eliana and Hastings had been a pair, and to think Angor had *murdered* him...

The very concept seemed outlandish to Zeela; she was convinced the Regg media twisted the story to make Affinities look dangerous. How convenient it would have been for them to label Angor a Wacko and then hostilely overthrow his leadership, claiming a town of Affinities as their own.

The news of the Reggs' hold on Periculand was the only reason they hadn't left the cabin for the town. On the first morning they'd been here, they'd heard mention of the Regg ambassadors' control, and from there they'd gathered bits of new information every day, like that terrorist explosions had erupted in Cleveland, and the government now detained any person with oddly-colored hair, and an oversized falcon had been spotted numerous times in central Ohio—all solidifying their decision to remain stagnant.

Zeela longed to reunite with Avner, Jamad, Maddy, and Eliana, too, but the risks and inevitable failures were too abundant to form a plan. The inaction ate at her insides, but whenever she thought of encountering the Wackos, that monstrous bird, or more Regg researchers, she really began to savor the softness of this sofa, the feeling of freedom.

"I'm worried about my son, Seth," Linda said, playing with what Zeela could vaguely detect as the hem of her shirt. "Tray has never been a rebellious type, always following the rules and striving to achieve, but Seth…I fear he might try to defy the Regg ambassadors—might get himself in trouble. He has a good heart, but…sometimes his common sense isn't there. And with Adara in jail, he must be reacting poorly."

Zeela hadn't known the Stark twins very well, but from how Tray had defied Nero in JAMZ, Linda's view of Seth as the assertive leader didn't seem to align.

"Seth always needed our guidance more than Tray," Linda

continued, head tilted toward the ceiling. "I felt so bad leaving them, but…we knew they would get taken to Periculand."

Zeela's eyebrows creased. "What…do you mean?"

Expelling a breath, Linda shifted where she sat and ran a hand over her head. "I was the analyst who examined the blood samples of teenagers in Ohio, determining whether they had an Affinity. I vaguely remember testing yours years ago, one of the first… When I realized this past summer that my sons both possessed the chromosome, I was obviously distraught because of how Affinities are treated in this country. Richard and I have always been involved with Affinities—him and his journalism, me and my research—but with our sons actually *having* the chromosome… we knew it was only a matter of time before the Wackos discovered our identities.

"So, even though we didn't want to see our sons go, we allowed Angor to have them. The day they were taken—also the day Adara got arrested," Linda added with exasperation, "we knew Fraco and Aethelred were coming. After we left the police station, we planned to go to my office and collect some files before heading back to our house to say goodbye, but when we arrived at my facility, there was a hooded man waiting there for us.

"Running was futile. He—he definitely had an Affinity, and I'm still not quite sure what he did to us, but we were captured, and all I remember was waking up in that little underground room, both Richard and I chained to beds. We assumed our captors were Wackos, but…now I don't know what to think."

"And I thought they were Reggs but…I don't know what to think, either. Why would the Reggs want you and why would the Wackos want us?"

Linda bit her lip, presumably in awkward reluctance. "The researchers *were* fairly intrigued by my knowledge. Numerous times they brought me down to their lab to help them with samples and data. I never saw any of the prisoners, but…the walls weren't thick enough to block out the screams. I knew what was going on. I wish there was something I could have done to stop it."

"At least they're all dead now," Zeela muttered, almost wishing they were alive again so she could kill them with her own two hands. Violence had never been in her nature, but as she pondered what they'd done to her and her friends, her fists curled with aggression.

Contemplating these murderous thoughts, her vision fixed on the opposite wall above the television, where a small insect crawled. The beetle moseyed downward, its pace steady as it disappeared behind the television screen. Squinting, she used her x-ray vision to see past the heat of the TV and focus on the bug again, but once she did, she noticed it had vanished.

Then, a moment later, a rat scurried across the floor.

Stilling, Zeela blinked and said, "Do you have a rat problem in this cabin?"

"No." Linda sat up with gradually growing alarm. "Did you—"

Her husband's scream interrupted her question.

Both Zeela and Linda jumped to their feet, and in the dining room Charlie scrambled out of his chair, grabbing it in his hands to wield it as a weapon. Honing in on the kitchen, Zeela found that, as Charlie charged in with his chair, a giant dog attacked Richard, biting at his leg in an attempt to drag the man down. Too focused on its task, the dog didn't realize Charlie's entrance, and so he thwacked the beast with his chair, releasing its grip on Richard as a yelp echoed through the cabin.

"I know Richard hid a gun in here somewhere…" Linda rummaged through drawers and clutter that Zeela could hardly see.

Her vision was trained on the kitchen, anyway, where the dog… *broadened*, its muscles and bones all elongating and widening until the animal had assumed the form of a bear.

The beast barely fit in the tiny kitchen, forcing Richard and Charlie against the walls. Though Zeela couldn't detect their emotions, she imagined they must have been as panicked as she was, especially when Richard yelled, "LINDA! BEAR! *RUN*!"

"*Bear*?" Linda repeated, whipping to face Zeela. "I thought it sounded like a dog!"

"Well, it's definitely a bear now," she said, her eye wide and posture paralyzed as she watched it prowl toward Richard. The Regg man was completely defenseless against the deadly beast, but Charlie, abandoning his useless chair, wasn't.

As the man crouched down beside the bear, close enough that the beast could have effortlessly ended him, items flew from the counters, cabinets, and drawers, all aimed for the human magnet. With the bear between Charlie and most of the kitchen appliances, they rained down on the animal instead.

Pure metal was easier for Zeela to discern than anything riddled with plastic, but she still recognized the toaster, bowls, and utensils crashing into the bear with a force that managed to delay its attack. As soon as the barrage of objects ceased, a roar ripped through the air, halting Linda, who had resumed searching for the gun.

"Oh God," she whispered, her body trembling as the bear's enraged breaths echoed from the kitchen.

Zeela was certain Richard and Charlie were about to be devoured when a bang sounded on the front door, accompanied by a familiar female voice. "NATE! YOU CAN'T KILL THEM!"

Silence ensued, and Zeela desperately wanted to watch how the bear reacted to this command—to see if the men would survive—but the two silhouettes of heat, muscle, and bone stationed beyond the front door captivated her attention.

"They're right outside," she murmured, loud enough for Linda to hear.

"They shouldn't be able to get in. Everything is electronically locked."

Just as Linda spoke, though, the lock clicked. The wooden front door swung open, granting access to the intruders, surely the same two people they'd escaped at the site of the burned barn. How they'd managed to unlock an electronic handle with such ease was beyond her, but it didn't matter now as they stalked into the cabin.

Though they were both roughly the same height, the one was clearly female while the other was clearly male with their differing organs and bone structures. The woman stood only a few inches taller than Zeela, but her athletic gait, thicker muscle mass, and higher fat composition affirmed that she would stand no chance against her in a physical brawl. The man's stature was rounder and his width was probably double Zeela's, but with his frailer muscles and clumsy movements, she *might* have been able to beat him... if she had weapons to match theirs.

Both intruders held dense wooden clubs, the material pure enough for Zeela to view with relative clarity. The woman also possessed a wooden spear, tipped with a firm, sharp stone. Apparently, they'd taken note of Charlie's magnetic Affinity and had come prepared this time.

"Who are you?" Linda demanded, voice wavering slightly. "What do you want with us?"

"I'm Kevin." The man waved his empty hand in greeting. The woman proceeded to smack his upper arm with her club, and he squeaked. "What? I was being polite."

"We aren't here to be polite," she muttered before redirecting her attention toward Zeela and Linda. "Surrender and we won't hurt you. We don't want violence."

"Tell that to your bear-friend." Zeela jerked her head toward the kitchen, from which a symphony of chaos still emanated.

"NATE!" the woman yelled, quelling all noise. "STOP BEING AGGRESSIVE FOR ONE GODDAMN MINUTE, WILL YOU?"

Evidently, he acquiesced, because the kitchen was peacefully quiet for the first time since the invasion began. The woman opened her mouth, probably to explain their purpose here, but then, to everyone's surprise, the door flew open behind Zeela.

A minute ago, she would have been relieved to see Key Fingers bounding out of the bedroom, fingers shaped into ten sharp drills, but now, when they'd been close to a real discussion, Zeela almost jumped in front of the old woman to thwart her. Sacrificing herself proved unnecessary, however, because the man named Kevin had taken the task upon himself, plowing through the living room and bashing his club over the woman's head.

Although tough, Key Fingers was no match for the solid club, and she toppled to the floor like a doll, consciousness lost. The only reason Zeela hadn't fallen into a frenzy was because she could still see the woman's heart beating, and the wound swelling atop her skull appeared superficial enough to heal.

"Kevin, you just killed an old lady," the female intruder said in disbelief.

"I-I—She was gonna murder us!"

Sighing, the woman said, "I'm sorry. My friend isn't suited for combat."

Linda seemed to have decided *she* was suited for combat, because while the female intruder apologized, Linda had rapidly retrieved a lamp from the end table. The object was hazy to Zeela, but she clearly saw the Stark mother lift it above her head and then hurl it at Kevin, the ceramic exploding into shards as it collided with the man's head.

Screaming, Kevin wobbled, on the verge of collapse. There was no way his female companion wouldn't retaliate with an attack now.

Using this moment of distraction to her advantage, Zeela whipped around and grabbed the television, its cord cleaving out of the wall as she launched it at the woman. The cooling blob of heat struck her left shoulder, thrusting her backward and forcing the club from her left hand.

Linda threw everything at Kevin: books, cushions, pens—none of which Zeela could fully distinguish. Still, she adopted the same method, scrambling to grab objects on the TV stand, but there was nothing of substantial weight or impact, and since she didn't have the strength to lift furniture, she was left unarmed. The woman possessed her spear, though, and she flung it through the air, the pointed stone aimed straight for Zeela's chest.

The spear's elements were detectable to her eye, but the weapon glided through the room with too much speed for her to do more than dodge to the side in an attempt to evade it. An involuntary cry escaped her mouth when the tip embedded below her left clavicle, not far above her lung. Her knees gave out with the dizziness, plummeting her body to the wooden floor.

Everything was a torrent of incoherency. Heat and flesh and metal swam through her vision, and *pain*—a stinging, throbbing ache so powerful it made her gag and writhe. The bullet wound she'd suffered had been wildly unpleasant, but this was unbearable. She couldn't suppress a moan as she stared up at the ceiling, seeing colors and shapes she'd never witnessed before. Blood seeped into her shirt, clinging to her skin in a way that induced nauseating claustrophobia.

In the lab, when they'd carved out her eye, she'd passed out from the trauma. She hadn't wanted to wake up—but she had because she'd known that when she did, Avner would be waiting there for her.

In the woods, when they'd shot her, she'd been disoriented to the point of debilitation. She'd wanted to collapse and cry—but she hadn't because she'd known that if she ran, she would have the opportunity to save Avner, Jamad, and Maddy.

Now...what awaited her if she gritted through the pain? How could this scenario end in any way other than her capture or her death? Wherever these Wackos took her wouldn't bring her back to Avner. Even if she managed to fight her way out and kill these assailants, she wouldn't have the strength to search for her friends; she'd be cooped up in this cabin for another week—and then another and another, while her friends were probed and maimed and tortured.

Better to let her uselessness kill her now than to let it gnaw at her for the rest of her miserable life.

"Please," Linda sobbed, distantly...so distantly... "Don't hurt her—don't kill us. She's just a child—we have families—*please*!"

The sound of bodies dragging across the floor reverberated in Zeela's ears, along with the pounding of bare footsteps.

"They aren't dead," a deep voice said somewhere to her left. "I merely knocked them out. Happy, Devika?"

"Overjoyed, Nate," the woman responded agitatedly.

"*Rich*," Linda moaned quietly, somewhere to Zeela's right.

"Throw those two in the van," Devika commanded. "Kevin, take her out with them."

"Wh-what about the other two?"

"The lady with the drill fingers could be useful, if she's breathing… I'll check. We'll leave the other one. Looks like she's blind—I doubt Danny'll want her. She'll probably bleed out soon, anyway…"

Various footsteps vibrated through the floor, a heavy pair exiting the cabin, dragging those bodies, and a clumsier pair following after alongside a staggering pair. The last set approached Zeela, pausing not far from her head. When she squinted her eye open, an ambiguous figure crouched beside her, examining unconscious Key Fingers. With a weary exhale, Devika hauled the elderly woman into her arms and stalked out the front door, leaving not a muscle or bone in sight.

Blood was everywhere, though—*Zeela's* blood.

Her veins would drain onto the floor, and no one would be here to watch her die. No one would even know she was dead. Avner, wherever he was, would always wonder, and if he ever escaped, he would always search.

As she closed her eye to accept her fate, a blip of heat flew through the open doorway, so small she barely noticed it. For a moment, she believed it was the shapeshifter named Nate, returning in the form of a bug, perhaps to save her. But as that heat expanded, Zeela realized that it was not the controlled morphing of one living creature into another: It was the building of a fire.

Flames latched onto the wooden structure of the cabin, consuming it inch by inch. They would eat her, too, and she would let them. She just hoped that someone would know of her fate—that Avner would learn of her fate. Because, even though she had failed him, he wouldn't settle for failing her. He would tear apart the Earth to find her, and if he survived, she didn't want his hopeless search to devour him in the way this inferno devoured her now.

She recalled the way he'd sacrificed himself for her in the barn, how he'd gone back to fight the Reggs even though it seemed futile. It had resulted in a fire like this one, but he hadn't succumbed to it; he hadn't died.

As she stared up at the heat licking the ceiling and inhaled the noxious smoke, she knew she would.

Kiki Belven hadn't made any efforts to maximize her connection with Eliana over the past week. Rather, she'd avoided her roommate as much as possible. She spent little time in their dorm room, sat on the opposite side of the table during meals, and forced Hartman to be her partner in training, leaving Eliana to work with ruthless Lavisa. If it had been anyone else she'd raided Than's office with—anyone else she'd mounted and practically made out with—she would have been entirely indifferent, but Eliana...innocent Eliana... She felt like she'd violated the girl.

At the same time, she wasn't sure if apologizing was appropriate. An apology would imply she regretted it—that she wouldn't do anything like that again—but was that true?

Kiki wasn't ready to answer that question, and considering Eliana had the ability to read her mind, she didn't even want to think about it. She knew how to build walls around her brain—to an extent—but it was an exhausting feat, and she simply didn't have the patience to exert herself. So she opted to focus on shallower things and remain out of Eliana's range whenever the deeper ponderings threatened to enter her consciousness.

For most of that Monday afternoon, Kiki had relaxed in the lounge, pretending to read magazines while discreetly eavesdropping on gossip. Drama was nearly nonexistent here compared to her old high school—probably because she hadn't bothered to provoke any herself—but it was still amusing to listen to a group of secondary girls gush over how *hunky* Tray Stark was. God, if they'd seen that kid before he hit puberty… It had proven difficult for her not to emit a snooty giggle.

Obviously, as soon as Nero had announced his party to the entire lounge, Kiki abandoned her magazines and hurried up the spiral staircase to fix her makeup and replace her skinny jeans with a mini skirt.

Upon approaching the door to room 305, she paused, sensing Eliana within. Of everyone at this school—perhaps of everyone everywhere—Eliana was the only person she had the capacity to mentally *feel.* She knew it was linked to their strange connection—Eliana's ability to decipher Kiki's hidden visions. Their brains could have been connected in numerous ways, and Kiki was tempted to explore it, but…Than's office…

Now, as she stood before their door, she knew she would have to confront Eliana. They'd been in the same room alone since the incident, but typically one of them was asleep—or pretending to be. With the fuzzy nature of Eliana's consciousness, she could have been asleep, but there was something foreign about the nature of this fuzziness.

Regardless, the need to beautify herself, coupled with the innate pull from Eliana's abnormal cognitive state, drew her into the room. Keeping her head high, she plunged through the doorway, refusing to give her roommate a substantial glance as she sauntered directly toward the closet. She'd noticed immediately that Eliana sat at her desk, drawing, but she hadn't bothered to acknowledge Kiki's presence, so Kiki wouldn't acknowledge hers.

As she searched through her copious amounts of clothing for the perfect skirt, she kept her movements quiet, listening intently to Eliana's pencil strokes. They were normally so soft and soothing, but today the sounds were aggressive, rushed, as if her arrival had deeply aggravated the artist.

Kiki couldn't dwell on it; Eliana would follow her thoughts unless she guarded them, a task that would be utterly impossible if she wished to focus on finding a skirt of party quality. Instead, she masked her concern with obnoxiousness.

"Can you *please* quiet down back there? I'm *trying* to concentrate."

Pausing for one moment to make a show of examining one of her skirts, she listened for any change in Eliana's behavior. She hadn't expected a response, but she had expected Eliana to at least slow her drawing pace, perhaps halt completely to scowl at the back of Kiki's head. There was absolutely no change, though. When Kiki finally grew impatient and whipped around to face her, she found her roommate hadn't flinched in the slightest. She was still hunched over her desk, scribbling furiously as if her life depended on it.

Kiki *should* have left her alone. She should have grabbed the skirt she'd chosen five minutes ago and retreated to the bathroom, but there was something almost *disturbing* about the fervor with which Eliana drew. In the three months she'd known the girl, she'd never witnessed her do anything with such haste and imprecision.

Gently removing her chosen skirt from her closet, Kiki hugged it to her chest and slunk across the room, sneaking behind Eliana's blue head to peer over her shoulder. In the pale tank top she wore, a few black dots poked out beneath the fabric—a tattoo on her left shoulder.

The unexpected revelation was rapidly disregarded when Kiki's vision landed on the desk. With the speed of Eliana's hand, the sketch should have been sloppy, but somehow, it was the most lifelike piece of art she'd ever crafted. When Kiki finally recognized what was strewn on the page, she nearly dropped her skirt at its eerie familiarity.

Reds, oranges, and yellows popped on the paper, composing a raging sea of fire. At the center dwelled a figure lying on her back, arms splayed lifelessly. Kiki's first instinct was to assume it was Adara, especially with the black t-shirt and jeans, but this girl's features were delicate, and her head was devoid of Adara's dark hair—or any hair at all. Unless Eliana had neglected the eyes, this girl only had one, and it was completely white.

A sickening feeling snaked through Kiki's core as she recalled the drawing Eliana had worked on in the library last week, so similar to this but with one major difference. In the first drawing, Zeela had been alive; in this drawing, she was dead.

Eliana's sister was dead—or she *would* be. How could Eliana draw this so emotionlessly? Why had she put so much precision into every line, every detail, as if the hue of a flame mattered more than the end of her sister's existence? Kiki hated her own sister, but if she saw Orla like this, she'd break.

Unable to quell her quaking limbs or repress her panic, Kiki fumbled to place her hand on Eliana's shoulder, right above that mysterious tattoo, and shook it as gingerly as she could.

"Eliana… Eliana."

Her red pencil continued stroking lines in the fire, inflating the inferno to the point that it nearly engulfed Zeela's body.

"Eliana," Kiki tried again, shoving her shoulder with more force. It didn't make a difference; she maintained her hurried drawing pace, not reacting when the momentum of the shaking resulted in a wayward stroke of red across the paper.

Unnerved, Kiki tossed her skirt onto her bed and then encased Eliana's eyes with her hands, essentially blinding her. She was certain this would deter the drawing, but it didn't. Even without her sight, Eliana persisted as if in a trance.

With a groan of frustration, Kiki ripped the pencil from her hand, leaving her without a drawing utensil. In response, Eliana simply retrieved the orange pencil, and then when Kiki extracted that, she retrieved the yellow, then the brown, then the blue, then the black—until Kiki had snagged every one of her pencils and hurled them at the wall, leaving marks of color.

She didn't care, because Eliana *still* tried to draw, her empty hand dragging across the paper, smudging it. The only way to stop her would be to extricate her from her desk.

Inhaling deeply, Kiki gripped her roommate's shoulders and, with a wince, yanked her from her chair, throwing her across the floor with more strength than she'd intended. Eliana's head collided with Kiki's bed frame, and her hand finally stopped moving.

Eyelids fluttering, her blue eyes squinted up as Kiki dropped to her knees, lifting Eliana's head beneath one hand and cupping her cheek with the other.

"Eliana?" she whispered, her voice high-pitched with worry. "*Eliana—*"

"Wh-what's going on?" she croaked, brow screwed in befuddlement.

"N-nothing." Kiki swallowed, attempting to relax her posture before she repeated a firmer, "Nothing."

Forehead still wrinkled, Eliana sat upright, disentangling from her roommate. With quivering fingers, she felt the back of her head and then slowly rotated toward Kiki in disbelief. "Did you just...assault me?"

"No—*no*—I would never—how could you think—"

"How could I think you have little regard for others' feelings when you've spent your entire life bullying Adara and Tray?" Kiki had never witnessed such a dark, cold expression on Eliana's face, and it scared her more than the crazed drawing had. "How could I think you have no problem with physical aggression when you *climbed on top of me* and then acted like—"

Although Kiki knew where this was going, she was unsatisfied when Eliana suddenly cut herself off, her vision suddenly fixing on a point in the distance. Following her gaze, Kiki found her staring at the fallen chair and the pencils splayed across the floor. Then Kiki's dissatisfaction shifted into anxiety.

"No—Eliana—" she pleaded as her roommate stood, padding toward the desk as if enveloped by another trance. Scrambling to her feet, Kiki attempted to wedge herself between Eliana and the desk, but her eyes were already locked on the drawing, her body rigid and paralyzed by the sight that lay before her.

"What is this?" she asked as she gradually registered the flames, the body, that one white eye.

"You…you drew it. You wouldn't stop drawing it. I had to… use force to…"

Eliana clearly wasn't listening; she merely gawked at the image of her sister dying in those flames. Then, as if the truth finally smacked her, she hiccupped and allowed the tears to flow. "*Zeela…*"

Kiki bit her lip, watching as Eliana hugged herself and breathed incoherent mumbles. Whenever Kiki was upset, she liked to isolate herself—to see if anyone cared enough to seek her out—but Eliana didn't need to be sought out: she was right here, and all Kiki had to do was reach out and comfort her. How could she justify touching her now, though, when their last physical encounter had led to uncertainty and disconnect?

Maybe none of the outside factors and previous problems really mattered now—the note they'd found in Than's office, the mind controlling witch ruling this town, the confusing *feelings* that had developed within Kiki... All of that seemed trivial when confronted with the fact that Zeela Mensen would die.

Extending a tentative hand, Kiki caressed her shoulder, brushing her fingers gently across the black dots. Despite Eliana's emotional coldness, her skin was warm, and Kiki was met with the urge to embrace her completely—to wrap her arms around her neck and hold her as she cried.

Eliana's urge was of a different nature; instead of leaning into Kiki's touch, she shied away, whirling around with violence in her eyes. The hue of the irises had faded even in the last week, now a pale cerulean instead of the brighter cobalt they had been. Kiki found herself utterly entranced by them, even with the flames of Zeela's death burning in the darkness of her pupils.

"*You* did this," Eliana said with creepy calmness. Kiki's brain didn't comprehend her words until she pointed aggressively at the drawing. "You gave me this knowledge of the future, and there's nothing I can do to erase it—nothing I can do to prevent it. My sister is going to *die*—she could already be dead! And now it's permanent because *you* predicted it!"

Kiki's heart pounded faster with every accusation, her defensiveness overthrowing all affection for this girl. "It's not my fault your sister will die! I can't control the future!"

Eliana sniffled—not pitifully but viciously, her eyes still slivered with animosity. "You can't control *anything*, not even yourself. I bet you *can* influence the future, and because you're a spiteful, selfish person, the world's going to crumble into chaos."

Ignoring the jab, Kiki tightened her jaw and ground out, "You drew Zeela *alive* in the fire before. How do we know this drawing is true instead of that one? We should explore this. We should try to figure this out."

"No!" Eliana snapped, oblivious to the water leaking from her eyes. "I don't want to be anywhere near you and your diseased mind. You're a plague to me—you're a plague to *everyone*! I want nothing to do with it."

Kiki felt as if a claw of truth had slashed through her chest, but she brushed off the pain, just as she'd brushed off every insult that had ever ripped through her. Spinning on her heel, she stalked to her bed, snatching her skirt from where she'd thrown it. Looking at the soft blue color only reminded her of Eliana, and the fabric now felt brittle between her fingers. Hating her Affinity—and hating *herself*—Kiki hurled the skirt toward the closet and then marched out of their room, leaving Eliana to mourn alone.

Her first instinct was to stomp to Seth's room and yell at him irrationally before kicking him out of his own dorm and claiming it as her own quiet spot. But Seth was her *ex*-boyfriend, a fact of which she constantly had to remind herself, and he had a roommate now who might not appreciate her barging in and barking orders.

Who else could she go to, though? Eliana was her only friend here, her only friend anywhere...and she had ruined that relationship. They were meant to be friends, Kiki thought, but maybe their brief time of companionship had already ended. Maybe Kiki *did* have a negative effect on the future simply by being a bitter, bitchy person.

Hearing the sounds of chatter below, Kiki decided she didn't want to be alone. The best way to cope with the emotional distress would be to distract herself. So, without her shimmery makeup or cute miniskirt, she waltzed down the spiral staircase to immerse herself in the clamor of Nero's birthday party.

Most of Periculand's students had gathered in the lounge. The handsome bully was nowhere to be seen, but Kiki did spot one of his groupies hauling a box of bottles across the room—the acid-spitter, Dave. He appeared to have climbed out of a hole in the floor that led to what Kiki assumed was the basement beneath the tower, the existence of which she hadn't been aware. Apparently, Nero and his gang knew of it, and they'd stored alcohol down there for quite some time, judging by the mountain of boxes now piled against the wall.

None of the other students dared approach the booze yet, and Dave was the only one moving boxes at the moment. As Kiki observed his neon green hair, she realized for the first time that he was actually mildly attractive. Nothing compared to Seth or Nero or Calder, but he was certainly better than that geeky green-haired boy, Ackerly, who now entered the lounge with rainbow princess Ashna at his side. Positioned at the bottom of the staircase, Kiki wondered if Dave's acid would burn her lips if she tried to kiss him. A twisted, broken part of her almost enjoyed the prospect that he could burn her—that he could match her emotional turmoil with something physical.

"Hey, Kiki," a nasally voice greeted, and Kiki blinked out of her aberrant thoughts to find the geeky green kid had approached her—and *talked* to her.

She gave an exaggerated eye roll. "What do you want?"

"I, um—Have you seen Tray around…anywhere?" Ackerly asked, eyes roving the lounge behind his glasses. Ashna stood at his side, studying the room with the smile of an innocent child but the gaze of a cunning adult.

"I don't keep tabs on that loser." Kiki flipped her hair over her shoulder. "Go find him yourself."

Ackerly didn't stutter at her harsh words; instead, his vision fixated on the boxes Dave stacked, and his brow furrowed. "What's…going on?"

"Nero's throwing a party since those Reggs left. I would advise you two children go hide away upstairs before it gets too intense," Kiki said, flicking her fingers toward the stairs. Ashna's demure demeanor soured into hostility at the word "children."

"The Rosses left?" Ackerly repeated. "Where'd they go?"

"To deal with Adara," Lavisa drawled as she approached their little huddle. As usual, her drab yellow hair was contained in two unflattering braids, and she wore a dark t-shirt and baggy pants that made her look like a five-year-old boy. With Kiki's building aggravation, she felt inclined to use one of the moves they'd learned in training on her—until she remembered Lavisa's Affinity was literally to annihilate people. She decided she would use her verbal skills of combat instead.

"God, *you're* here and you're talking about *Adara*." Lavisa simply arched her ugly yellow eyebrows, so Kiki added, "Can you go somewhere else?"

With a dismissive eyebrow jump, Lavisa turned to Ackerly. "The Rosses thought it would be a good idea to let Adara go on live television. You can imagine it went poorly. They're at the police station now, and Nero's taking the opportunity to throw a party for his own birthday, which, conveniently, is tomorrow."

"The Rosses are at the police station?" Ackerly's shoulders slumped. "Ashna and I were planning to visit Adara before her trial tomorrow."

Kiki gripped the stair railing. "Adara's trial is *tomorrow*?"

"Did you not hear Tray ranting about it all day today?" Lavisa asked flatly.

"I don't listen to anything that nerd says," Kiki sneered, lifting her chin. "I don't feel like listening to anything you have to say, either. If you're all gonna be a bunch of boring dweebs, don't bother hanging around and ruining this party for the cool people."

"You've really perfected the 'high school diva' act, haven't you?" Ashna quipped, causing Ackerly's eyes to bulge in fear.

A sly grin spread across Lavisa's lips. "Indeed she has."

Kiki emitted an affronted noise even though their comments had no real effect on her. Being a diva in these girls' opinions was nothing compared to being a spiteful, selfish person in Eliana's. Still, she'd had enough of these losers' presence; stomping her foot, she twirled around and stalked through the lounge, approaching the acid-spitter as he continued to arrange boxes.

"Hello, David," she purred as she stepped beside him and leaned against the stack of boxes, batting her eyelashes at him. Pausing his work, his lime green eyes shifted toward her and scowled.

"Little Belven," he greeted, his voice as acidic as his skin. The clear residue shone on his arm, prepared for an attack.

"Don't get so hostile with me, David. Stop acting like Nero's puppet and get your own personality."

His fists clenched around the box he held. "No one here calls me David. Only my mother calls me David."

"Aw, that's cute," Kiki crooned, running her finger down the sleeve of his white t-shirt, "but I'm not here to talk about your mom—"

"If you want the booze, you have to wait for Nero." He angled his head back toward the secret hole. "All this is his, and he's not just givin' it out to anyone."

"I don't want your stupid beer, David. I want *you*." Taking a step closer, she brought her lips toward his ear, hovering a centimeter away as he remained frozen. "I want to taste your acid—"

"You want to taste *acid*?" a voice rumbled, jolting Kiki away from Dave. When her eyes cut to the left, she found Nero ambling toward them, three boxes nestled effortlessly in his arms.

"I knew you were dumb, Little Belven, but I didn't know you were suicidal."

"I'm not suicidal," she defended instantly. "I wouldn't *swallow* it. I just want to experience everything I can, okay?"

"Be patient, Little Belven. This party will be an experience to remember." Nero dropped the boxes and unfolded the lid on the topmost one to rummage within. His affability swiftly dwindled as he pulled out his empty hands. "There're only two bottles in here. Someone's been stealing from my stash."

Slowly, his head pivoted toward Dave, whose face had paled nearly as white as his shirt.

"I-I don't know who would have done that."

"No?" Nero challenged. "You and Demira haven't been sneaking into the basement to get drunk and bang?"

"N-no—I haven't done anything with Demira in ages, I swear—"

Nero thrust his hand forward to wrap it around Dave's neck, but Kiki jumped in front of the acid-spitter first, crossing her arms and glaring at Nero's palm, suspended before her nose.

"I don't care if you beat this kid up," she said, peering through his fingers to meet his harsh eyes, "*but* I would like him to be capable of banging *me* afterward."

Nero's nose twitched as he glanced between them. "You... want to..."

"Just because *you* don't want to have sex with me doesn't mean everyone else doesn't. I'd venture to say that practically everyone else *does*."

Though Nero snorted, he did lower his hand, eyeing Kiki warily. "I don't want to display discord between me and my inferiors—it'll look bad. So have him. I'm sure I'll find your corpse afterward. The only reason Demira doesn't die after screwing him is because that girl's probably a freakin' robot."

"I think I can handle a little bit of acidity," Kiki assured him, cocking her head to the side.

"Someone deserves a fist to the face for this, though," Nero growled, his dark eyes sweeping the lounge. The first person they landed on stood a few paces away, still conversing with wretched Lavisa and judgmental Ashna.

With a maniacal grin spreading across his face, Nero prowled toward the staircase, his reverberating footsteps alerting Ackerly and the two girls of his approach. Guilt surged through Kiki's gut; she'd saved the acid-spitter by pretending to be infatuated with him, but in the process she'd doomed Ackerly to a ruthless flogging. Maybe Eliana was right; maybe Kiki altered everyone's fate for the worst.

"Plant kid."

"H-h-h-hi," Ackerly stuttered, already cowering.

"It appears there's a shortage of beer," Nero explained as he cracked his knuckles. "Someone needs to take the blame."

"Leave him alone, Nero," Lavisa cut in, slipping between the boys as she rolled her wrists.

The brute's sadistic smirk stretched wider, not at all intimidated by her threat. "Oh good, I get to beat up two primies tonight. What a wonderful birthday gift. Should I start with you, Little Dispus?"

Lavisa assumed a fighting stance. "As long as it's fair."

Fair definitely wasn't part of Nero's vocabulary; the sentence barely left her mouth before he swung at her temple. The agile girl dipped down and swept her leg in a horizontal arc toward his ankle. He stumbled with the impact but didn't relent, reaching down to grab her yellow braid. Heaving her up by her hair, Nero bared his teeth in a grin as Lavisa gritted her teeth in pain.

"Ready to fly across the lounge, Little Dispus?"

"No," she said, swiftly slamming her flattened hand into the side of his neck.

Even with the thickness of his muscles, he felt the blow, releasing her immediately and staggering back. After raising his fists as if to dole another punch, Nero tricked Lavisa by lunging to the left and wrapping his hand around Ackerly's throat, halting her mid-strike and invoking gasps from spectators.

Kiki was petrified where she stood, dread washing over her at the prospect that she'd unintentionally led to two deaths in one day. Ackerly wheezed and Lavisa gaped and Ashna—Ashna had clearly lost her mind. Because as Nero threatened to choke the life out of Ackerly, she placed a hand on his bulging forearm, drawing his animalistic attention toward her.

"Don't—don't hurt him," she pleaded breathlessly. "I can give you what you want. I-I have…an alcohol Affinity."

His hold on Ackerly's neck gradually loosened as he processed her words. "You…*what*?"

Swallowing, Ashna removed her hand from Nero's arm and stiffened her posture. "I have an alcohol Affinity. I can…produce alcoholic beverages. I can replenish your…stash," she added, eyes darting toward the numerous boxes lining the wall behind Kiki.

"Prove it," Nero huffed, maintaining his grasp on Ackerly.

Licking her lips, Ashna extended her arm and cupped her hand. As Kiki inched closer to the scene she realized a tiny pool of clear liquid had formed in the girl's palm. "Taste it."

"What if it's poison?"

"I'll try it," Lavisa sighed as she dipped her finger into the liquid. That Ashna hadn't stopped her should have been enough proof, but Nero wasn't convinced until Lavisa had tasted it without keeling over. "Vodka, I think. I've never been much of a drinker."

Freeing Ackerly, Nero took an assertive step toward Ashna and forcefully poked his finger into her palm. After tasting the substance, his lips curved upward, and somehow, standing only inches from him, the girl managed not to recoil.

"You do have an alcohol Affinity," he declared with satisfaction. His tone hadn't been particularly loud, but others had heard, and whispers trailed throughout the lounge. Kiki couldn't remember anyone mentioning to her specifically what Ashna's Affinity was, but she was baffled to discover it was the ability to produce *alcoholic drinks.* Why couldn't Kiki have gotten a useful Affinity like that rather than one that provoked disparity and death and destruction?

"Well then," Nero started, eyeing Ashna like she was his newest pet, "looks like we'll have a party after all. Mardurus, get up here!" he shouted toward the hole, resulting in Calder's head popping out of the floor. His expression remained languid, even when Nero's transformed with giddy delight. "Let's begin the festivities, shall we?"

31

Revelations

"Never have I ever…murdered a teenage boy," Adara stated, waving her hand in Angor's direction. "Put a finger down, Your Majesty. We all know you're a—what did they call you—a blood-vessel-bursting-beast?"

"I believe you're the first person to have called me that, actually," Angor said, refusing to lower a finger. Since Fraco's biased questions—all of which Adara knew had come straight from the Reggs' mouths—had failed, she'd sparked a game of Never Have I Ever with the former principal, alluding to the same accusations the media tried to pin on him.

Hartman continued filming, standing outside their cell with the video camera in his hands, teleporting from place to place to avoid Fraco. The vice principal had tried to pry the camera from the boy's grasp for at least twenty minutes, unsurprisingly to no avail since his greasiness inhibited him from gripping it. At one point he had succeeded in oiling the lens, no doubt resulting in poorer video quality, but as long as the public could hear how ridiculous the government's claims were, the visuals didn't matter. Whether or not the news station had cut them off was a mystery, but Adara sincerely hoped the world wasn't deprived of her sardonic sass.

"Mr. Corvis," Fraco pleaded, blinking profusely. For a while, he'd used the consequence tactic, but given Hartman, who had grown up with Nero for a stepbrother, wasn't even mildly intimidated, he'd resorted to the incentive approach. "If you give me the camera, I will pay for your meals."

"Indefinitely?" Hartman questioned, orange eyebrows rising with intrigue.

"Well—"

"If it's indefinite, I can't refuse." He gave Adara a pathetic shrug.

Dropping her hand, she groaned. "You are *weak*. If you give him that camera, Ginger, I will *make* you teleport in here and break me out."

"Oh, shit." His head pivoted frantically between Adara and Fraco. "I can't do that—I'll be a fugitive! Sorry, Frakes, but I can't take your—"

"Oh, don't believe her lies!" he cried, shooting a glare toward the jail cell. From the corner of her eye, Adara spied Angor's satisfied smirk spreading wider. "She can't *make* you do anything. Now, give me the camera before the Rosses—"

"Before we what, Fraco?" a stern voice interjected, drawing all attention toward the doorway. Previously, Mitt had leaned on the doorframe, watching this whole scene unfold with the utmost amusement, but now he'd been pushed aside completely, making way for the two enraged Reggs.

Artemis, who had been the one to speak, adorned her typical suit, her hair pulled into the tightest knot and her dark eyes boring into Fraco with contempt. William's appearance was equally as authoritative, though his antipathy was clearly aimed at Adara and Angor rather than his vice principal. Regardless, at the sight of them, Fraco staggered back, bowing his head submissively.

"I-I'm sorry—I—Mr. Corvis—the camera—"

"Enough, Fraco," William snapped, forcing the man to bolt upright in alarm. "The news shut this feed down before Stromer could spew more of her blasphemy."

"Dammit!" she swore as aggressively as she could. Unfortunately, the Rosses were not so easily frazzled, but Fraco jumped at the sound. "Now the world doesn't know all the things I've never done! I was hoping it'd spark some sympathy since I've never gotten the chance to murder anyone and now I probably never—"

"I don't believe anyone in America will be sympathetic to you with your attitude," Artemis interrupted, her inflection much less composed than usual. Even if the cussing didn't perturb her, Adara's display on the news had, and for that she allowed a devilish grin to consume her lips.

"So unloving, Mommy," she sang, provoking shock from the Rosses and tension from Angor. "No wonder you abandoned me and Av all those years—"

"I thought we agreed we were going to be discreet about our knowledge," Angor said through his teeth.

"Screw discreet," Adara droned, padding closer to the bars. The electricity was off today because of the interview, so she took this opportunity to stroke her fingers along the bars she'd melted, pretending to admire them. Really, the fact that she'd half *liquefied* this metal with heat terrified her, but she expelled the fearful thoughts as she met the Rosses' eyes. "I want to talk about how you two are my freaking *parents*—oh, and how you also have the mind controlling Affinity that killed Hastings."

Artemis's eyes slivered with the accusation. Adara heard Angor hastily removing himself from his metal slab behind her, but she kept her gaze locked with her mother's.

"She's joking," Angor said, positioning himself beside Adara as if his mere presence could undermine her.

"I'm not." She wrapped her hands around the melted bars and peered at the Reggs through them. "I want to let them know what we know so they can make an educated decision: let us go right now and we won't tell the world the truth, or ignore this warning and suffer our wrath in court tomorrow."

Artemis took a step forward, scrutinizing Adara with heartless eyes. "What exactly do you *know*?"

"Everything I just told you," she said, removing one hand from the bars to wave it around, "and more. We won't divulge *all* our information, of course. I can tell you two must be fond of surprises. It's your choice if you want your secrets revealed in public or not."

The way Artemis's gaze bored into her was unnatural. Adara's face scrunched as she strained to conceal her mind; Angor had taught her how over the past weeks, but she feared this woman could tear down those walls without Adara noticing. She definitely didn't *feel* anything, and she couldn't decide if this was a good or bad sign, especially when Artemis's face contorted into an ugly simper.

"Say what you want tomorrow. We have nothing to hide."

Adara's grip tightened around the bars. The Rosses *did* have something to hide—unless they no longer cared if it was hidden. For some reason, they would rather reveal their ability—and their wickedness—than allow Adara and Angor to walk free. Were the two prisoners really such a threat to someone who could *control minds*?

"We have much planning to do at the courthouse," Artemis announced to Mitt, who had reappeared in the doorway, looking sullen. "Please alert us if the prisoners try anything…shady."

Mitt nodded, but Adara could tell by the gleam in his silver eyes that he would have rather released the prisoners from jail than help these assholes.

"Come along, Fraco," Artemis said, prompting the vice principal to scurry after them.

As the woman exited the corridor, she reached over to the electronic panel on the wall, and before Adara could process what she was doing, the bars' electricity suddenly sparked to life, coursing through the metal and seeping into her skin.

Her muscles contracted, forcing her arms to push away from the bars. She landed on her back and stared at the crayon depiction of the Pixie Prince, unsure if she felt pain. Though the shock was mildly dazing, it didn't distort her thoughts enough to quench the fury budding in her chest.

"You *bitch*!" she shrieked after them, pushing upright and crawling toward the humming bars. The Rosses had already disappeared, not bothering to glance back at her as they departed the police station. "First you abandoned me and now you're damning me and you won't even let me take a freakin' *shower* even though Angor got one!"

Mitt grimaced in the doorway, shifting awkwardly in place. Hartman vibrated in the hallway, the camera now limp at his side. Angor stood only a few paces from her, his lips in a tight line. It wasn't until she staggered to her feet, taut and seething, that all three of their expressions twisted into dismay. Even in her blinding ire, Adara knew why: Her hands were aflame, blackening and hardening beneath the radiant fire.

Hartman vanished in an instant, and Mitt ran into the front

lobby, but Angor remained paralyzed within the range of her increasing inferno. She didn't *want* to burn him; she wanted to burn Artemis and William for putting her here—for leaving her here—for giving up on her now like they had when she'd been a child.

The ever-present ache of her worthlessness fueled this fire, feeding it to a point beyond control. Heat crept up her arms, morphing her flesh to simmering rock that threatened to light her clothes ablaze.

Through the undulating glow of reds and oranges and yellows, she met Angor's pink eyes, so dull compared to the colors bursting around her. The temperature wouldn't affect her, but she could see him sweating, his skin growing feverishly red. Soon the flames would lick him. He would blacken and harden like her, but he wouldn't survive it.

She'd been wrong before; she *would* get the chance to murder someone, and as with Hastings's death, it wouldn't be the person who deserved it.

Desperately, she fought against the bitterness that had gnawed at her for so many years. If only she had a docile Affinity like Ackerly's, something that nourished rather than destroyed. Instead, she'd been gifted with a connection to the one element she loathed—and the one element capable of morphing that loathing into something even more grotesque, something even more unstable than she was.

In her haze of suffering and turbulence, Adara abruptly stepped backward, her legs moving so mechanically that it confused her. Had she told herself to back away from Angor? It would have been logical, but she couldn't recall consciously contriving the thought. She kept retreating until she was pressed against the opposite wall, her arms still scorching despite this display of control. Even from afar, she could see that Angor's expression remained cool and collected, as if he'd expected her to back away—as if he'd forced her to back away.

"*You little—*" she began to snarl but then Mitt raced through the doorway, a silver fire extinguisher in his hands. Before she could speak another word, the nozzle spewed water, drenching her and snuffing the flames. As the liquid seeped through her clothes to fill the crevices of her rocky flesh, the hardened skin slowly disintegrated into a dark ash that mixed with the water and dripped onto the floor.

Still, her body remained rigid against the wall, all muscles frozen except those above her shoulders. She used the function of her face to spit into the puddles at her feet and then scowl at Angor.

"You *liar*! I defended you—I *believed* you! But you've been the mind controller all along. *You* killed Hastings—"

"What are you talking about, Stromer?" Mitt demanded through panting breaths.

"Don't you see what he's doing to me?" she questioned, attempting to move her body with no success. Since Mitt couldn't read her thought process, she jerked her head around, teetering her body but not softening any of her limbs in the slightest. "He is *controlling* me! He *paralyzed* me!"

Mitt's silver eyes bulged as they flew between Adara and Angor, the truth finally settling in. Dropping the fire extinguisher, he fumbled for a weapon but found he had none.

Angor sighed dramatically. "If you two will please calm down, I can explain—"

"To hell with your explanations, you deceitful douchebag! I should have killed you twice now!"

"And yet you have not, because you know I'm innocent."

"*No*, both times I failed to kill you were because of forces out of my control—such as *you* prohibiting my movements," she added, dipping her chin toward her petrified body. "Stop trying to convince me you're innocent with your mind manipulation!"

"Adara—"

"You are so far from innocent that you actually seem innocent!" she shrilled as if he hadn't said a word. "I don't know how you've done it, but you have, and you need to *die*!"

"Adara, if you would give me a moment—"

"You don't deserve a moment!" she barked, her thoughts so poignant, she could barely detect the exasperation on his face. "You don't deserve shit! If you fell into a sewer, it would spit you out—that's how disgusting you are!"

"I feel as if you're exaggerating now."

"I don't give a damn about how you feel! If I woke up as you tomorrow, I would kill myself to do this world a service."

"Yes, well, that was unnecessary to state since you never *will* wake up as me."

"Keep him distracted, Stromer," Mitt commanded as he started toward the door. "I need to alert the Rosses—"

"That seems like a bad idea, Officer Telum," Angor said, and the other man's motor functions ceased. "The last thing we need is for Hastings's true murderers to gather substantial evidence against me."

"*Mitt*!" Adara moaned, banging her head back against the wall. "Why would you *announce* you're going to get help?"

Rotating his head toward the cell, Mitt said, "I didn't think he could immobilize two people at once."

"Well, you thought wrong, imbecile, and now we're both stuck here with the most dangerous man on the planet," she huffed, wishing she could relax her muscles and melt onto her metal slab and *not* deal with the fact that this scumbag had duped her.

"I know you don't mean it as a compliment, but I do enjoy the prospect of being intimidating after so many weeks of squalor." Angor walked to his own bed and reclined on the metal. "Now, if you'll promise to be peaceful, I'll release you both and we can talk."

Adara plastered the fakest of smiles on her face. "And if *you* don't go to hell right now, I'll take you there myself."

"How, exactly, do you plan to do that?" Mitt asked, craning his neck as far back as he could to meet her eyes.

"Don't question me, Telum!"

"If neither of you will shut up long enough to allow me to speak, then we'll remain in this suspended state of uncertainty," Angor said through an exhale. Panic ignited within her as he closed his eyes and folded his arms over his chest but didn't bother to release her. "Wake me when you're ready to hear the truth."

There wasn't a set curfew in Periculand, but never had Tray, from his room on the third floor, heard such raucous noise emanating from the lounge after eleven.

Since Olalla had gifted him with the Affinity-enhancing suits that afternoon, Tray had studied and tested them with a researcher's precision. His and Seth's were identical except for size, his twin's a bit bigger than his own. Although Olalla had claimed they weren't Affinity-proof, Tray had yet to find anything that could penetrate the fabric; sharp objects couldn't tear it, water couldn't seep through it, and even his super strength couldn't pull it apart.

Wildly intrigued, he'd gone as far as to try on it on, discovering it was supple and comfortable, albeit a little too tight in the groin region. Adara would certainly make some comments if she ever saw him in it. He'd have to wear shorts over the spandex, he decided. And then Adara would mock him for being a *nerd*. There was truly no way to win with her.

It was as he was flexing in his new suit—not to admire his muscle mass, but to ensure the fabric was tough enough to handle his body in a state of flexion—when someone knocked on the door of his dormitory. Frazzled, he didn't bother to take it off; he simply threw on his sweater over the white material and jumped into his jeans, concealing the secret suit from view entirely.

Opening the door, he expected to find Ackerly and Ashna there, his roommate likely having lost his key in a pot of dirt or something of the sort, but instead, Lavisa Dispus leaned against the doorframe.

"Stark," she greeted blandly, surveying him with half-lidded yellow eyes. Despite the chilly weather, she wore a thin, black t-shirt, which made her skin look paler than usual by comparison, and he noted that her tattered wraps were secured around her hands, prepared for a fight.

"Is something wrong?"

Her lips twitched upward at his urgency. "Of course not. I only came up here to invite you to the party that's going on downstairs."

Tray peered over her shoulder as if he might physically see the clamor wafting up the spiral staircase. "I can't tell if you're being sarcastic or not."

"Of course you can't." Upon patting his shoulder patronizingly, her eyes narrowed, like she'd felt the skin-tight suit beneath his sweater, but she didn't comment on it before jerking her head toward the stairs. "Come see for yourself."

Glancing back at Seth's suit, which lay exposed on his desk,

Tray gritted his teeth and then hurried into the hall, closing the door behind him. "Is everyone downstairs?"

"Everyone except Eliana," Lavisa confirmed, strolling down the steps. "Kiki says she's sulking in her room."

Tray paused on the stairs, peeking at the door to room 305. "Is she okay?"

Lavisa shrugged. "Probably. I didn't ask what was wrong. I don't like to get involved in girl drama."

Resuming his pace, Tray caught up to her. "Aren't you a girl, and therefore a contributor to 'girl drama?'"

"Not when I can avoid it. Besides, this isn't *just* girl drama: it's *romantic* girl drama. Very sensitive territory."

"What, are Kiki and Eliana fighting over a boy now?"

Lavisa halted abruptly at the landing of the second floor and spun to face Tray, a whimsical expression dancing across her features. "You don't know, do you? You're *that* socially inept."

"Is it Nero?" Tray asked, his dread apparent in his tone. When she shook her head, he racked his brain—and then a nauseating thought dawned on him: Kiki, who had been his childhood bully, hadn't bothered to utter one nasty remark to him in weeks, and until now, he'd had no explanation as to why. "Is it—" He swallowed, lowering his voice to a whisper. "Is it *me*?"

Lavisa barked out laugh, the most jovial display of emotion he'd seen from her in weeks—or perhaps ever. Shaking her head once more, she began her descent again, musing to herself, "You're the most conceited geek I've ever come across."

"It's *not* me? Well, that's certainly a relief. Seth would've beaten me up if Kiki had a crush on me—not to mention my… feelings for Eliana are only in the realms of friendship."

"*Really*?" Lavisa challenged as they approached the first floor. "I thought you had a crush on her."

"*No*. She's too...quiet."

"Too quiet? And you're what, a social butterfly?"

"*No*, but if I'm going to bother with something as trivial as romance then I need someone who's...less ambiguous—easier to read—blunt. I don't have time to decipher silent cues and emotions."

"Ah, I see," Lavisa said, but he barely heard it, for they'd passed the first floor, and the lounge sprawled before them, booming with noise and crowded with students. The diversity of hair colors, all milling and bouncing about, was so jarring to Tray that, at first, he didn't quite notice what all the students had in common—that nearly every one of them held some kind of alcoholic beverage.

"This—this is—the Reggs are allowing this?"

"No," Lavisa answered, "the Reggs are busy dealing with Adara. *Nero's* running this event because—who would've guessed—it's the big brute's birthday tomorrow."

Tray could only gawk as he followed her to the ground floor, immersing them both in the torrent of tipsy teenagers. Many casually relaxed on the couches while others had formed clusters of animated conversation. As Tray studied the whole scene, however, it quickly became clear that Nero's version of a party wasn't as lax and easygoing as most people's. On the far side of the room, the couches had been displaced, making space for what was essentially a drunk version of Nero's Dominion.

Currently, the girl with the lethal metal chain was at the center of the ring, wielding it like a lasso. Tray had never personally encountered her, but he remembered how she'd tormented Ackerly at that session of Nero's Dominion weeks ago, and he was fairly certain her name was Demira. Turquoise eyes alight with bloodlust, she whipped her chain against her opponent's head, sending him to the ground.

"That's the fifth person she's beaten," Lavisa muttered to Tray as they wove through the lounge. "Unless I missed someone while I was upstairs."

"Have you challenged her? Other than Nero, you probably have the highest probability of defeating her," Tray said as he wiggled through a few tightly packed students.

"True, but Nero's forcing anyone who fights to take a shot of vodka first and I'm not interested."

"You don't drink?" Tray asked before tripping over someone's foot and colliding into her back. When she turned around, he knew it was more than agitation in those cold, yellow eyes.

"*No*," was all she said. The intensity demanded explanation, but then his attention caught onto a sight near the wall to his left: a hole in the floor, from which half of Calder Mardurus's body poked out as he drug boxes into its depths.

Tray would have changed his course to confront the boy if he and Lavisa hadn't reached their friends. It was hard to call them his *friends*, though, considering the group consisted of Seth, his brother, Ackerly, his roommate, and Ashna, Naira, and Cath, practically strangers.

Perched against the wall near the glass doors, far enough from the brawls to evade Nero's attention, Seth narrated a dramatic story to the others, his hand motions sloppy and uncoordinated. Tray had never been a fan of drunk Seth, and seeing his twin now, captivating an audience and receiving grins of appreciation, stirred that ancient bitterness in him—the same feeling of jealousy toward his brother that had probably imbued his strength Affinity after years of its lingering presence.

"...dunno *how* he didn't realize what she was doing." Seth took a theatrical swig of his beer, careening slightly toward Naira, who lounged on his left. "First Adara locks him in the closet and convinces him to pee in a cup, and then ten minutes after releasing him, she *happens* to give him a drink that looks like piss? Uncle Rob is stupid with a capital *SSST*, let me tell you."

The rest of the group chortled, Naira's guffaws the loudest as she gripped Seth's shoulder for support. None of them even noticed when Tray and Lavisa stepped behind Ackerly.

"I wasn't aware that '*st*' was one letter now."

Seth blinked twice and then slowly fixed his glossy eyes on his twin. "Oh, hey, bro. Didn't think you'd come down here for this. Doesn't seem like your type-a deal."

"It isn't," Tray confirmed flatly, eyeing their drinks with distaste. Ackerly was the only one who appeared to be empty-handed, though Cath, who held a cup in either hand, seemed to be distributing them to students rather than consuming the alcohol herself.

"And yet you seem like the one who needs to be inebriated most out of all of us," Naira sang, swirling her cup around tantalizingly. She propped her elbow on Seth's shoulder, the position lifting her shirt enough to expose a sliver of her stomach. Flustered by the sight, Tray hastily met her peachy eyes, and her eyebrows jumped in response. "Cath, give him a beer. Or, better yet, why don't we get our man Ackerly here to grow us some cannabis?"

The innocent boy stiffened at the request.

"Ignore her," Ashna advised with an eye roll. Like Ackerly, she still wore her green cargo pants—or rather, Adara's green cargo pants—and her vibrant hair was contained in a braid that merged all of the various colors in a mesmerizing way. "She asks me to grow weed for her all the time."

"Yeah, but you *refuse* since you don't want to try expanding your flower Affinity to all plants," Naira said before sipping on more of her drink. With her casual tone, Tray almost didn't catch the connotation. When he did, his eyes narrowed, but he didn't have time to open his mouth before Hartman appeared beside Lavisa, orange eyes drooping and freckles vibrating at a subdued rate.

"*Mmmore*?" he hummed, extending his empty cup toward Ashna. Lavisa's jaw was tight with that same rancor she'd expressed earlier, but Tray's jaw had fallen slack at the sight of Ashna hovering her finger above Hartman's cup and then, somehow, spouting alcohol from her flesh.

"What the—you just—you—you have—no—"

"I think your robot brother is malfunctioning," Naira observed, retrieving a drink from Cath and handing it to Tray. "Relax, temperamental twin."

"No—no—this is—*Ackerly*," Tray finally hissed, unable to organize his thoughts with everyone's eyes trained on him. "We need to talk about this! She has more than one Affinity—"

"I…know," Ackerly admitted with a wince. He peeked over at Ashna, as if for *permission*, and she nodded, avoiding Tray's incredulous gaze. "She has…infinite Affinities. We didn't want to tell you because we knew you would react…well, like this."

"She—has—" Tray ran a hand through his hair as he turned away from them. Ackerly was unfazed by this knowledge, still infatuated with this deceptive girl, but Tray's mind sifted through the disastrous implications. This girl—this *Wacko,* mostly likely—had *infinite Affinities*. She had the ability to do anything that anyone in this room could do and she worked for the *terrorists*. This multiplied the direness of their situation by…infinity.

"I didn't want to lie to you, Tray," Ashna's soft voice sounded from behind him, "but you can see how my Affinity makes me…a target."

"Why, then, have you exposed yourself to half of Periculand?" he growled, his body still aimed away from them.

"No one here knew what my Affinity was before—I didn't

announce it. Now they all think that I can only produce alcohol, and I wouldn't have made that known had Nero not threatened Ackerly."

Spinning around, Tray met her eyes and saw the honesty in them. He'd never been particularly skilled at decoding human emotions, but he was intelligent enough to detect a lie—most of the time. Still, he didn't fully trust her, certainly not enough to question her further and divulge the knowledge they possessed.

"Fine," he said through a sigh of defeat. "Show me your Affinities, then."

"A-all of them?"

"Obviously not."

"Show him how you can't get drunk, Ash," Naira encouraged.

"Well, I *can*, but it only lasts for ten minutes at a—"

Tray's yelp interrupted Ashna's retort. He didn't typically react so pitifully, but the sudden drenching of his back had caught him completely off guard. With the suit on beneath his sweater, the liquid hadn't seeped through to his skin, but the impact of the water had startled him. Peeking over his shoulder, he found his backside soaked and, as expected, Calder approaching.

Tray scoffed at his sopping wet clothes. "Was that necessary?"

"I'm not sure why you're asking me," Calder said, appraising the whole group with guileful eyes. "Little Corvis was the one who dumped his beer on you."

"What do you—" But then he followed Calder's gaze to where Hartman teleported around the room in rapid succession, stealing drinks from Cath and pouring the liquid on random students, causing mayhem that Nero was sure to notice.

"I told him to spark a bit of a distraction so we can discuss tomorrow's trial." Scrunching his nose at the others, Calder added, "Privately."

"Why bother with the secrecy?" Lavisa questioned. "You know Tray'll tell us what's going on as soon as your little discussion is over."

The secondary tilted his head mockingly. "Do I know that, Dispus?"

She shot a disbelieving scowl toward Tray, but all he did was give her a tight-lipped nod before saying, "I'll be back."

Seth didn't seem perturbed by this; he and Naira continued giggling to themselves, drinking as if the fate of this town wouldn't be determined in a matter of hours. Lavisa and Ackerly stared after him, though, the former with suspicion and the latter with curiosity—and then Ashna watched him with a combination of both. Tray wondered, as he wove through the lounge with Calder, if she had the ability to read his mind.

Hartman's little distraction *had* proven successful; the brawls on the far side of the lounge had broken up, now replaced with an even more entertaining show of Nero chasing his stepbrother around the circular room. The birthday boy was clearly already intoxicated, his movements disoriented and clumsy as he pushed through people and staggered into inanimate objects.

In all the commotion, Tray almost didn't see Kiki Belven sprawled on one of the couches, batting her eyelashes at Hartman's roommate, Carrick, as he massaged her bare feet. Was *that* who Kiki and Eliana fought over? Carrick, in Tray's eyes, had never proven to have much of a personality; he was like a brick, as Adara had dubbed him. Tray's…*feelings* for Eliana really were obsolete, but it still irritated him to think he was so oblivious that he hadn't noticed the two girls fall for this blob of a boy.

Calder guided Tray until they'd reached a more secluded section of the lounge. A multitude of students concealed the collection of couches, but they were all too preoccupied by Nero's chase to care when the boys joined two others for this private discussion.

"Tray Stark, though burdened with emotions he cannot comprehend and problems he cannot solve, has not succumbed to the temptations of alcohol like so many of his mindless peers. Instead, he continues on with a clear mind, refusing to haze his thoughts, even if a lower level of cognition might ameliorate his stress," said the boy seated on the bright blue couch against the wall, his voice suave and serene. Tray had never personally interacted with him, but he knew him to be Calder's roommate, Colton, the boy who could see this "Otherworld." Everything from the way he sat so perfectly straight to the crazed gleam in his evergreen eyes pointed to his insanity, yet…his speech had been entrancing, and his words had been eerily valid.

"Despite this," Colton went on, "he has not denied himself the pleasure of being externally doused in the substance that would internally soothe him—"

"Don't screw with him, Col," Calder chided as he approached the red couch adjacent to his roommate's. "You know better than anyone that Corvis dumped beer on—"

"Don't sit *there*," a girlish voice said. Tracing it, Tray finally trained his vision on the second unfamiliar person, who wasn't so unfamiliar at all. How he hadn't noticed her before was beyond him, but on the green couch lounged the girl who should have been in jail—the girl whose trial they were about to discuss.

Though she shared Adara's dark hair and impish demeanor, she was very plainly not Adara Stromer. Tray pinpointed about thirty-seven minute details that gave it away—from the too-short length of her hair to the too-long length of her nails to the fact that her face was almost…slightly…appealing. That almost-prettiness alone solidified the result of his assessment, deeming her—or *him*—as Ruse Dispus.

"Join *me*, Pixie Prince," he purred, imitating Adara as he caressed the empty cushion beside him. "I've warmed it for you."

"Can you stop pretending to be Stromer, please?" Plopping down on his own couch, Calder glanced around warily. "You're gonna attract attention."

"If you know me at all, you know I don't view attention as a negative thing," Ruse retorted, but he heeded the command, his hair shortening, his limbs lengthening, his muscles broadening.

Tray had seen the shapeshifter undergo these transformations with swiftness, but right now he took his time—probably to irk Calder. There was definitely a hint of impatience in his posture when Tray turned to him and asked, "Can you dry me before I sit?"

Calder's lips curled as he examined the beer coating Tray's back. "Do I have an Affinity for alcohol, Stark? No. So, no."

Huffing a sigh, Tray slumped onto his own yellow couch and appreciated the suit he wore. The liquid, which he assumed was cold and sticky, didn't have any affect on his skin—although, he didn't doubt it would probably ruin his clothes. He couldn't afford to buy a new favorite sweater and jeans, not since he had to pay for food, not since his parents were missing—

"Tray Stark worries for his parents," Colton narrated, jolting Tray with the mention of his name.

Cheeks heating, he avoided the other boys' stares. "Don't—say that."

"His parents have consumed his thoughts, the question of their safety eclipsing all other concerns—"

"Stark," Calder snapped, his voice nearly drowned out by a wave of clapping and cheering directed at whatever the Corvises were doing. "Focus. We have more important things to worry about."

"There is nothing in this world that is more important to Tray than his parents, and since their safety is unknown to him—"

"*You* know, don't you? Just tell him they're safe and let's move on, hm?"

"You always ask me to lie, Calder," Colton said, giving his roommate a quizzical look. "I don't like to lie."

"Wait." Tray leaned forward, mouth slightly ajar. "Are you saying…that my parents *aren't* safe?"

"It would be a lie if I said they were," Colton confirmed, sending Tray into a frenzy. Until now this *Otherworld* had seemed nonsense, but in the past few minutes this boy had managed to read all of his thoughts with absolute clarity.

"No—they can't—Tell me where they are."

"I will tell you, but you will not rejoice—"

"*Enough*." Throwing his hands up to either side, Calder formed two identical orbs of water. In his frazzled state, it took Tray a moment to process that one was around Colton's mouth and the other was around his own. Grudgingly, he kept his lips clamped shut and seethed inwardly as Calder seethed outwardly.

"Huh," Ruse mused, his light brown eyes darting between the two silenced boys. Thankfully, he'd nearly completed assuming a new body, and this one was male, with muscular arms, a stern face, and plain brown hair, almost as if…he'd decided to become *Tray*. Even though he had a twin, watching this kid's perky attitude emit from his body was disturbing, but there was no way to react that wouldn't result in drowning.

"For once," the shapeshifter continued with a self-satisfied expression that Tray had never seen on his own face, "I'm not the one you're telling to shut—"

Snapping his fingers, Calder summoned a third sphere of water that congealed around Ruse's mouth, causing him to cough and choke. Then, unfazed, he glanced around at the three of them. "I have no interest in spending more time with any of you than I have to—except you," he added to Colton, who nodded in understanding. "Periculy and Stromer's trial is happening tomorrow morning, and tonight…the Rosses are going to plaster the cafeteria's walls with Angor propaganda—"

Tray raised his hand, relishing in the movement he'd been deprived of performing for the past month. With an eye roll, Calder removed the water inhibiting his mouth, and he sucked in a deep breath. "Why?"

"Because, as a way to ensure you don't show up at the trial, they're gonna frame you and your friends for vandalizing the cafeteria, and then you'll receive a full day of detention, monitored by Fraco—"

"I think I can take Fraco, thanks," Tray grunted, wiping water from his chin.

"Fraco won't be the problem. The problem will be that they plan to lock you in the Mentals basement—chained to chairs." Calder flashed a grin that made Tray question their alliance. "Apparently you primies are a real threat to them. Anyway, you know if you try to hide or avoid the punishment, they'll end up postponing the trial until they can ensure you won't be there. So you'll need to get caught, and you'll need to pretend you know nothing about—"

"I can't just let Adara go to trial without us! I need to defend her!"

Calder's blue eyes glinted like a deadly river. "Do you, Stark?"

"I—just mean—that she shouldn't go to federal prison—and since I've deduced that Angor must be innocent, we need him to take his position back."

"Hm, yes," Calder said, still eyeing him with skepticism. "I agree. Which is why you *will* be at the trial. Dispus here is going to disguise himself as you"—Ruse waved merrily, as if Tray didn't know who he was—"and then he'll get caught and chained by the Reggs while *you* sneak into the courthouse with evidence."

"What evidence?"

"Well, Colton, for one." Calder pointed toward his roommate, evaporating the water from his face.

"The Otherworld has revealed all truths to me," Colton explained, "and though my tongue is tied for now, I believe the intensity of the trial will be the perfect climactic point for me to finally divulge all."

"No one's going to believe your freaky friend," Tray said flatly.

"I know." The devilish smirk spreading on Calder's lip, reminiscent of Adara, made Tray cringe. "Which is why I also have something a little more concrete in mind: Angor's file."

Tray sat upright, eyes bulging. "You found it."

"Oh yes, and it's incriminating," he confirmed, though his tone sounded far from relieved.

"It incriminates the Reggs, you mean?" When Calder didn't respond, he added, "Can I see it?"

"I don't have it on me. I'll give it to you tomorrow once we're certain you haven't ended up locked in a basement. If you can't make it to the courthouse to deliver the evidence, then I will."

Ruse was the one to raise his hand this time. When Calder popped the water around his mouth, he didn't bother to evaporate it, drenching the kid entirely. After hacking up liquid for a few moments, the shapeshifter finally cleared his throat. "Tell me again—why can't you do this on your own?"

"Because if this goes south, I don't want to end up in jail."

"But…you don't care if we do, you're saying?"

"That's exactly what I'm saying," Calder affirmed without hesitation. Standing, he scanned the area before locking eyes with Tray again. "Meet me here thirty minutes before the trial tomorrow. If I can't make it, I'll have hidden the file in one of these couches. I would advise lying low until—"

"Where is Tray Stark?" a deep voice bellowed throughout the lounge. All conversation lulled, leaving only Nero's violent footsteps booming through the room. "I want to fight Tray Stark!"

"Well, that either means his stepbrother's dead or has teleported away in fear," Calder muttered. "It's probably a good idea if you run, too, Stark. Drunk Nero is arguably worse than sober Nero, and I need you alive until the end of tomorrow."

Nodding, Tray pushed off the couch, and he was about to slink over to the spiral staircase when someone shouted, "There he is!"

Tray's head shot up in alarm, but no one looked at him; they all looked at the boy who shared his appearance. For a moment, he thought it was Ruse, somehow having crossed the room in a matter of seconds, but the shapeshifter still sat on his green couch, now in an unrecognizable form. That meant the one Nero now prowled toward was Seth.

Shoving through the crowd, Tray jogged toward the other end of the lounge. His brother leaned against the wall, sipping idly on beer, but when he noticed Nero stalking toward him, he dropped his drink and hunched into a defensive stance, his dumb bravery amplified with his intoxication. "Finally you wanna fight me!"

Naira, for once, was actually on alert, her drink discarded to assume a similar combative pose. Ashna ushered Ackerly aside, shielding him with her body, while Cath clenched her fists and glowered at Nero with venom in her murky green eyes.

"Hey!" someone shouted when the brute was only a few paces

away from greeting Seth with an unfriendly fist. A jet of water followed, smacking Nero's back. He whirled around in rage, but as soon as his eyes locked onto the perpetrator, his expression mollified, for his girlfriend waltzed through the crowd, blue eyebrows raised.

From within the cluster of spectators, Tray watched as Nixie, with her punkish style and horn-like pigtails, stepped before her boyfriend, fishnet covered arms crossed over her chest. "Don't waste your time on that normie." She jerked her chin toward Seth, and when Nero squinted at him, he blinked at the realization that he wasn't Tray. "How about you challenge someone new—like the rainbow beer girl?"

"M-me?" Ashna cowered beside Ackerly like a meek child. She *was* one of the smallest people here, and she was definitely the youngest, if only by a few months. Despite this, Tray knew she had mentally surpassed half of this population. He could smell her intelligence.

"Yeah..." Gradually, Nero's eyes brightened with the prospect of a new victim. "Let's see how your little booze powers hold up against my might. Get us two shots, girl, and then let's get this started."

"Ashna," Ackerly started to protest, but she patted him on the shoulder before walking to the center of the lounge. Nero waited for her near the staircase while his cronies hastily moved couches, tables, and chairs toward the walls to make space. When Nixie handed her two cups, she filled them wordlessly and handed one to her massive opponent.

"You *are* useful," he said, wiggling his thick eyebrows at her before downing the beverage in one swig. For Ashna it took five gulps, but she drank it all and didn't back down, even when Nero began to crack his knuckles. His hands could have easily wrapped all the way around her thin arms—maybe even all the way around her legs—but she didn't balk, not even when Nixie whistled, signaling the start of their brawl.

Nero, ever the aggressor, lunged toward Ashna, planning to tackle the poor girl. Wincing, Tray prepared for the blow that would likely break half her bones—but then she lifted a slender finger, and a deluge of amber-colored liquid spewed from her flesh. Nero spluttered and spat and reared back when the alcohol collided with his face, momentarily blinding him with its sting.

Whispers erupted throughout the room, some giggling or exchanging bets as if there was actually a chance she could win. With her *infinite Affinities*, Tray was certain she could, but she wanted to keep her true powers a secret. Everyone here thought she only had an alcohol Affinity, and to reveal otherwise might jeopardize her safety.

Tray recalled her saying alcohol could affect her for ten minutes at a time, though, and it appeared that in her tipsy state of mind, she didn't care which Affinities she displayed. When Nero finally recovered and charged toward her once more, Ashna extended that same finger, but instead of gushing alcohol, it caused the barbaric boy to cry out in pain before collapsing to the ground, clutching his calf.

"She activated his nociceptors," Tray whispered aloud, though none of the students around him seemed to have heard; they were all focused intently on the invisible pain—proof of Ashna's multiple Affinities.

Some murmured in confusion, while others cheered her on, so enthralled by the sight of Nero failing that they didn't care about the details.

"I'll—kill you," he snarled, staggering to his feet even though his left leg was limp. This time, his movements were much less explosive as he stumbled toward her, arms swinging wildly. Before he reached her, Ashna squatted and then launched into the air with more force and agility than Tray had ever seen from anyone. This girl—who was probably only five feet tall—managed to touch the *ceiling*, which was at least twelve feet high. She remained there, dangling a foot above Nero's head, her fingers glued to the surface.

"What the hell!" at least ten people shouted, some in bewilderment and others in awe. Tray, even though he'd known she could do practically anything, hadn't wrapped his head around it until now, and as he watched her swing in the air, he realized how absolutely doomed they were.

Grabbing the air where Ashna had been seconds ago, Nero whipped his head around, dazed and disoriented. "Where…?"

"Sorry," she called down to him, an apologetic smile on her lips.

"Sorry?"

In response, a plush green armchair zipped through the lounge, colliding with Nero's back and knocking him face-first onto the ground. His nose struck the thin gray carpet, echoing an unpleasant *crack* throughout the room.

"Nice one, Ash!" Naira cheered as the chair skidded to a halt before her. Beside her, Seth applauded and Ackerly nearly drooled, but Lavisa glared at Tray, her eyes reflecting the same anxiety he felt.

Dropping to the floor, Ashna landed with a wobble and then righted herself, gazing down at Nero with a hint of pity. "I'll relieve your pain, to be fair, but I hope you know now that you're not invincible." As she opened her hand toward him, his groans turned into a sigh of relief, and a bundle of pale purple flowers blossomed behind his ear. "Relent in peace."

The word *relent* triggered a new wave of fury in Nero; instantly, he pushed off the ground, springing up to attack Ashna. Her hand snapped into a fist, flourishing the flowers behind his ear at an impossible pace; one second they were tiny buds, and the next they were part of a full grown vine, snaking around Nero's neck and squeezing.

"Accept your defeat," she panted, her eyes protruding with panic at the prospect that she might have to strangle him.

"*Never*," he wheezed, yanking the vine and tearing it to shreds. Before Ashna could muster a counterattack, he grabbed her throat, hoisting her off the ground and displaying her like a flimsy doll. As before, her feet dangled, but there was nothing calm about the way she thrashed and clawed at his muscled arm. "*Relent in peace*," he mimicked.

She opened her mouth but couldn't produce a sound. He would murder her, and Tray could do something about it—he *should* do something about it—but if Ashna was a Wacko, sent here to destroy them, wouldn't it be ideal to let Nero kill her? It would eliminate two of their enemies at once: Ashna would be dead and Nero would return to prison.

Still, watching the poor girl struggle was unnerving. It pulled at that righteous part of Tray, the part that, despite logic, hated violence and injustice. Ashna deserved a trial, not death.

Weaving through the worthless bystanders, Tray prepared to give Nero the fight he'd initially wanted, but then Ashna worked up the courage to kick her opponent in the groin.

Even while losing oxygen, she delivered a powerful blow, one that instantly made him release her and stumble back in agony. Succumbing wasn't an option for Nero, so he shot back toward her, this time aiming for a punch. Right before his fist could smash her face, Ashna threw her hand up—and she stopped his fist.

The entire room went stagnant, not a word uttered or a muscle moved.

"What the…" Nero breathed after a moment of paralysis. He stared at her hand, her small fingers barely spanning his knuckles, until that tiny hand twisted his, spinning him around and thrusting his arm behind his back in an unnatural, uncomfortable position. Biting his lip, Nero withheld a moan of rage and pain.

With one hand maintaining this debilitating stance, Ashna telekinetically summoned an end table and jumped on it, pulling Nero's arm up even farther as she did. He grunted and attempted to unwind himself, but then his body went completely rigid when Ashna brought her lips toward his ear and muttered something so soft even Tray, only a few feet away, couldn't hear.

"Surrender," she said at a volume that boomed through the lounge.

After a few ragged breaths and the twitch of his nose, Nero hung his head. "Fine."

Weariness, not triumph, consumed Ashna's expression as she released his fist, freeing him. Grimacing, she touched her bicep on the arm that had exerted so much force, confusion in her eyes. Her examination ended the moment Nero rolled his strained shoulder and then rammed through her, flinging her off the table and cracking the plastic. Without even glancing toward the fallen girl, he marched across the lounge to where Ackerly quivered beside Seth, green eyes wide behind his glasses.

"*You.*" Clutching his collar, Nero dragged the boy back toward the demolished table and planted him at the center of the room for all to see. "Your little girlfriend needs to learn a lesson. Nixie, get him a drink."

"I, uh, don't drink," Ackerly stammered, cringing when Nixie forced a cup into his hands.

Tray was now fully willing to intervene, but then he remembered Calder's advice to lay low. If Nero injured him now, who would stand up for Angor and Adara in court? Calder was capable, but…Tray still didn't trust his motives.

"C'mon, Ashna, do something," he mumbled under his breath, watching helplessly as the girl struggled to untangle herself from a pile of couches and chairs.

"Ackerly," she gasped as if she were feeling pain—as if her Affinities weren't working. Surely, if she'd been able to outmatch *Nero*, she should have been able to *stand*, unless she was truly so disoriented that she couldn't summon any of her Affinities. "Don't… Don't do it…"

"Pick on someone your own size, Nero!" Naira said as she and Cath swaggered to the center. Lavisa snuck through the crowd, picking a perfect angle to strike the brute from behind.

"I-I can do it, guys," Ackerly insisted, the cup trembling in his hands. "I can…" But his words were lost as he peeked up at Nero, who grinned at him like he was a meal. Despite this, he brought the cup to his lips and chugged the beverage. His face was contorted with reluctance and dismay the entire time, but he swallowed it—just as the glass doors to the lounge burst open.

32

Cloudy Morals

Without windows, it was impossible to tell the time, but Naretha guessed it must have been the middle of the night, because she'd been in a deep sleep when Danny awoke beside her. In the groggy haze, she barely registered his movements, but when he slithered over, the heat of his skin nearly burning her, she felt as if she'd drifted into a nightmare.

"I told you her tracking device would reactivate," he breathed into Naretha's ear, the words chilling her core despite his scorching presence. "Open your eyes, my love. Carnage awaits us. It appears we'll visit Periculand after all."

Maddy had been staring at the ceiling when Naretha burst into Zach's bedroom.

The tiny window to her right was dark, but Maddy hadn't slept much in the four days since Jamad had been released and Avner had not. Every night she mulled over the same unfathomable question: What had happened during their journey here that had split her two friends in such an irreparable way?

The boys had been practically inseparable from the moment of their meeting; for Jamad to be completely content with allowing Avner to *rot* ripped the fabric of everything Maddy knew. Perhaps the Regg research facility had altered their brains in a way that ruined their relationship. Being trapped in that little torture chamber had broken parts of Maddy that she didn't care to dwell on, and she imagined her friends had endured much, much worse.

Her bubble of rumination shattered the moment Naretha stalked to her bedside. Through the light of the open elevator, Maddy saw Naretha wasn't in her pajamas. Tight, black, leathery material encased her entire body, leaving only her head and hands uncovered.

"Well, this is reassuring." The woman's eyes trailed between the two beds. "I was convinced you two *had* to be sleeping together."

"What do you want, Naretha?" Zach groaned, gradually pushing upright to glare across the room at their unexpected visitor.

"Relax, Zachary. I don't plan to enter your precious side of the room," Naretha said as she grabbed Maddy's blankets and yanked them off, exposing her limbs to the chilly air. "We *are* preparing for an attack, though."

Zach scrambled out of his bed. "Someone's attacking the complex?"

"No, *we're* attacking someone else—Periculand, if you really need me to be specific. If you don't want Danny to attack *you*, I would suggest getting up."

"Wh-why are you attacking Periculand?" Maddy questioned as she swung her legs over the side of the bed.

Naretha's normally sardonic demeanor mollified as she stared blankly ahead. "Because they have Ashna."

Zach swore vigorously before fumbling through his dressers in search of proper clothing. Recalling his old roommate's clothes, Maddy also rummaged through the messy drawers on her side of the room until she found a leather outfit similar to the one Naretha wore. It would definitely be snug, but disregarding propriety, she stripped down and then squeezed into it.

Instead of taking the elevator, Naretha led them through the door, into the corridor beyond. When they stopped at room 208, she didn't bother to knock; she simply jabbed her forearm with her finger until the door clicked open. Then she barged in.

"Whoa—what the—" Jamad jumped out of bed and threw shards of ice at them, but his aim was poor. The icicles impaled the wall beside the door instead of Naretha, who would have been unfazed either way, or Maddy, who had instinctively hunched over to protect herself.

Blinking profusely, Jamad's vision finally settled on them as Naretha strolled into the room, Maddy straightened in the doorway, and Zach snorted at her reaction from out in the hall. She threw him a playful glare before turning back to her friend, who now leaned against his nightstand for support.

"What are you guys doing here?"

"We're going to war, Snowman," Naretha said as she chucked folded leather garments at him. Maddy hadn't noticed her holding them before, but they were the same fabric as hers and Naretha's—and Zach's. The brightness of the corridor gave Maddy a better view of how the tough fighting attire outlined his thin form with much more precision than his typical preppy clothes. It was difficult not to stare, and thinking about it brought a blush to her cheeks.

"Cool," Jamad said, pulling his new pants over his blue underwear, the only article of clothing he wore. The pale beams flowing in from the open doorway illuminated his dark skin, gracing his pale blue tattoos with a glowing quality. Maddy had watched Josh etch the intricate rings of icicles that now wrapped around Jamad's upper arms, the symbol of his commitment to the Wackos. His initiation had certainly been more jubilant than hers, during which she'd cried quietly for two hours as Josh wove Danny's chosen design into her skin. It hadn't been the pain of the tattooing, but the permanence of her decision, the irrevocability of this fate.

"Who's our opposition?" Jamad asked eagerly as he slid his tattooed arms into the leather sleeves.

Naretha clucked her tongue. "Periculand."

His enthusiasm withered slightly as his eyes cut toward Maddy. Her lips remained tight, knowing he must have recalled their fond memories of the place—the people they'd befriended, whom they would now slaughter.

"Are we…*killing* them?"

Naretha shrugged as she admired the punk rock posters on the walls. "If we have to."

Swallowing, Jamad shot Maddy a weak smile. "Well, at least we finally have a decent reason to hurt Orla Belven, right?"

"We've always had a decent reason to hurt Orla Belven; you've just never been capable."

Jamad pulled his shirt over his head and ignored her comment, but she knew by the annoyance in those icy eyes that the truth of her words grated on his pride.

"Wha… What's happening?" Meredith's timid voice piped up as she yawned into an upright position. Her magenta hair was the brightest object in this room, and in her four days out of confinement, her bony structure had managed to retain a little substance.

"Don't bother getting up," Naretha snapped, jolting the frail girl. "This doesn't involve you."

"We're just going out for a bit, Mer," Jamad assured as he buckled his belt. "Go back to sleep."

"It appears you've adjusted to the babysitting role well, kid." With a condescending smirk, Naretha chucked a sleek black watch at him. "For communication purposes during the battle. We all have one."

Maddy waited a full minute, watching Jamad admire his new tech, before she said, "Don't I get one?"

"No." Naretha looked right through her as she marched out of the room. "Because you're not coming."

"Not—" Maddy spluttered, shaking her head as she followed Naretha down the hall. "But I—Why?"

"Yeah, why?" Jamad echoed, as he jogged to catch up with them.

After punching the elevator button, Naretha pivoted toward them. "One, Faddy hasn't been trained. We don't let recruits go to battle until they've been trained for at least a month, and as far as I'm aware, her training hasn't even begun." Her accusatory gaze rested on Zach where he idled uncomfortably at Maddy's side. "Two, Faddy might be 'one of us,' but she's still loyal to Periculand. We don't need her double-crossing us in the middle of a fight."

"I'm in the same situation as Mads," Jamad defended. "I'm from Periculand, and I haven't been trained here. Why let me come and not her?"

"Because *I* cleared you for battle. I've seen your abilities in action over the past month; I know you're ready, and I know we need you. Plus, you aren't deceptive enough to dupe us. *She* is. Now, let's go before Danny blows us into oblivion."

As the elevator doors parted, Jamad gave Maddy an apologetic wince. "I'll bring you back some Starbursts, I promise."

Maddy pressed her lips together, containing the anger swelling in her throat. "If they're not orange, I won't forgive you."

Mock gasping, Jamad placed an offended hand on his chest. "Are you *not* my best friend? Of course they'll be orange. Tell Mer I'll get her some pink ones. That should keep her calm."

"Keep her—" Maddy cut herself short and gaped at the three of them as they entered the elevator. Naretha's expression was bland, Jamad's was hopeful, and Zach's was unreadable, even after all the time she'd spent in his presence the past few weeks. "Are you expecting me to *babysit* Meredith while you're gone?"

"Can't hear you," Jamad called before the elevator doors blocked him from sight.

Puffing out a sigh, Maddy rubbed her forehead and then trudged back into room 208. Meredith was out of bed now, examining the swollen, sutured wound on her abdomen. Jamad claimed the girl didn't remember how the injury had happened, but even if she did, Maddy wasn't sure *she* wanted to know. Simply looking at it made her queasy.

"Put on a shirt," Maddy commanded, grabbing a stray, rosy pink backpack from the floor and slinging it over her shoulder. "Just because we aren't allowed to leave the complex doesn't mean we can't eat."

Having three much younger siblings, Maddy was accustomed to dealing with slow, difficult children, but Meredith's pace still managed to test her patience. By the time the girl had picked out a white blouse and put it on, at least ten minutes had passed, and the corridor was now packed with Affinities.

All adorning black leather, the Wackos were too distracted by their own various tasks and duties to notice Maddy and Meredith slip into the elevator and ascend one floor to the cafeteria. The grand room was desolate at this time of night, especially with everyone preparing for departure. Since the feast, Maddy had been up here a few times, but sitting at these plain gray tables was much less satisfying than eating, chatting, and laughing in Periculand's cafeteria. Without Avner and Zeela, she felt so empty. Perhaps if they'd been here with her, she wouldn't mind being a Wacko.

Padding to the nearest kitchenette, Maddy dispelled that notion from her mind. These terrorists—who had tortured her and murdered innocents—were now heading for her old home. The school's cafeteria would soon be rubble, the students would be ash, and Jamad would participate in the destruction.

As Maddy scavenged through the cabinets, discreetly storing canned goods in her pink bag, Meredith studied the dark countertop, running her fingers over the glossy granite.

"My old house had counters like these," the girl stated absently. "Mom used to make cookie dough on them."

Biting her lip, Maddy slowly lowered a can of peaches into her backpack. "That must have been nice."

"It was. My sister and I would always help her. Until the researchers killed my mom—and my sister—and my dad." Her ghostly, ominous eyes slid in Maddy's direction. "I was fifteen when they took me. It's hard sometimes to remember my life before...but this reminds me." She smiled lovingly at the counter, and Maddy found herself petrified, unable to smuggle more food.

"I...have a sister, too," she said quietly after a few moments of silence. "Cintia. She's eight years old now. I haven't talked to her in months because of..." She gestured half-heartedly toward the walls, this hideout, her prison. "It's not the same as your situation, but...sometimes I feel like she's gone, even though she's not dead.

To her, I'm dead." Sighing, she stared down at her arms, the tattoos concealed by the dark leather. "C'mon, we should get back."

"Aren't we going to eat?" Meredith asked, trailing after Maddy as she started toward the elevator. No one had entered the cafeteria yet, but the last thing she needed was to run into one of the Wackos while carrying a backpack of their precious food.

"We are once we get to your room," Maddy assured her as they stepped into the empty elevator. Once Meredith joined her, she pressed the button for the third floor with a shaky finger. As soon as the doors opened, it would be a quick walk through the hall to the opposite elevator—the elevator she would take down to Danny's office, the only means by which she could access the prison cells.

The worst way this plan could have failed would've been if she hadn't wasted enough time in the cafeteria, meaning Danny and his closest, strongest allies were still in his office. She was so busy fretting about all the ways they'd kill her that she hadn't considered the plan might fail five steps before she even reached her goal—that someone might intercept their elevator ride by beckoning for it to stop on the second floor.

Maddy braced for an onslaught of hostile Wackos when the silver doors glided open. Meredith would be useless in a fight, and if there were more than four, she wouldn't stand a—

"Zach?" she breathed the moment the doors parted to reveal his lanky form, waiting alone. Where there had been Affinities hustling and clamoring fifteen minutes before, there was now a deserted hallway, so quiet her voice bounced off the walls when she managed an awkward, "Hi."

"Hi," he huffed as if he'd just finished running. "I—checked the room for you... Where did you..." His dusty eyes landed on the backpack hanging over her shoulders. "Are you leaving?"

Lying had never been one of Maddy's strongest qualities, so with a grimace, she said, "I...have to. Avner's a *prisoner.* He came all this way to save me; now I need to save him. I don't belong here anyway, and...I don't want to be here."

She'd thought that would offend him, but his expression didn't change as he stared down at her, stern and unyielding.

"I'm...breaking out of here," she said with such calmness that her next movement almost surprised herself; swift enough that Zach didn't have time to flinch, Maddy threw one of her arms toward him, extending it to an unnatural length and wrapping it around his neck with the flexibility of a rope. "And you're going to help me."

The silent threat was suspended in the air, slowly gnawing away whatever trust and fondness had accumulated between them. When he glanced at her arm, though, there wasn't any apprehension there, just his typical dry emotionlessness.

"You don't have to threaten me, you know," he said, scrunching his nose. "And I would prefer it if you removed your flesh from mine, please."

Perplexed, Maddy slowly retracted her arm. "You—you want to *help* me?"

With a snort, Zach wiped his sleeve over his germ-infected neck. "Well, I definitely don't want to help Danny. He's being a prick down in his office. I'll..." Eyes darting around, he lowered his voice. "I'll help you escape. There's a secret hatch that leads into the cells in case of emergency. I...didn't want to use it to visit your friends last week because I didn't want Danny to find out I know about it. Now it seems he's too preoccupied to notice."

"You'll really do that?" she whispered, too shocked to raise her volume.

"Yes." He stepped into the elevator and willingly positioned himself closer to her than he ever had before. Even through the leather, she felt the heat of his body beside hers, his fresh scent permeating her nostrils. "Danny and his horde have already departed, but some have remained behind to watch over the complex, so we'll have to be stealthy. You can be our lookout," he added to Meredith, who perked up with the attention.

"Oh...okay." She smiled softly to herself. "I've never been given a job like that before. What am I looking out for?"

"Anything that moves," Zach said as the elevator doors parted once more. They'd descended to the third floor, as Maddy had originally intended, and this dormitory corridor was as vacant as the one above. Marching through it purposefully, Zach paused at the door labeled 318 and tapped his forearm in the same way Naretha had earlier.

"Is there technology in your suit?" Maddy asked as the door swung inward. The dormitory within was bare except for one bed on either side; even the sheets were plain white, impersonal and unused. An inconspicuous gray rug was draped over the floor, and as expected, when Zach pulled it back, a flat, metal hatch lay beneath.

"Someone with a tech Affinity rigged this whole complex after my father died," Zach explained, crouching to tamper with the door. "My father hated electronics, but... Danny enjoys the power. Only a select few can access every room: me, him, and Naretha."

"He...trusts you, then," Maddy concluded as Zach finally pried the door open. It flopped over, revealing a hole into one of the cells.

"He may find me pathetic and annoying," Zach said, unlatching a flimsy ladder that unraveled down into the cell, "but I am still his older brother. He harbors some respect for me. We were friends once, and...I think that no matter how evil he becomes, he'll always subconsciously strive for my approval. Plus, he knows some people here would have rather seen me take over than him."

"Really?" Maddy's voice echoed down the hole as Zach descended the ladder. "And they're not...dead?"

"The problem," he grunted as he landed on the floor below, "is that he doesn't know *who* they are or *how many* there are. As long as those facts remain unknown, I should be safe.... All clear down here."

With a nod at Meredith, Maddy inched into the hole and gripped the wooden rungs. Once only a few feet above the ground, she dropped into a flawless landing, her boots inches away from the tiny opening prisoners were subjected to excrete in.

"All right, let's be quick," Zach muttered as the cell's mirror slid downward, permitting them access to the dungeon corridor.

Suppressing a shudder at her former chamber, she followed Zach until they reached the opposite end of the hall, where Avner resided. He was awake today, indolently picking his fingernails as he stared at the wall. Seeing him in this tattered state tugged at her heart with sorrow, sympathy, and spite. He'd chosen this fate, but he'd also sacrificed his life to try to save her, and for that she owed him freedom.

Avner's expression didn't change as the glass wall sunk into the floor. It wasn't until he could fully see the outside corridor that his yellow eyes widened and he staggered to his feet.

"Mads?" he croaked.

"Avner," she rasped as he tripped through the dirty cell to meet her. Even though his stench was as rancid as a sewer, she didn't hesitate to envelop his withered body in an embrace. He wore soiled pajamas and his stubbly hair was the color of puke and a pathetically patchy beard coated his face—but he was alive, and soon he would be safe.

"I'm so sorry," Maddy choked, retreating to survey his appearance. "I have some clothes you can change—"

"Later," Zach interjected, earning Avner's attention for the first time.

The two of them surveyed each other for a few painfully uneasy seconds before Avner said through a gruff voice, "Danny's brother."

Maddy's head whipped frantically between them. "You've —met?"

"No, but they look exactly alike. Don't you see it?"

"N-*no*—"

"Zacchaeus, right? Angor mentioned your name to me once." Avner extended his hand for a shake. "Nice to meet you."

Zach's chin wrinkled, his throat emitting a repulsed, gurgling noise, but he did manage to briefly tap Avner's filthy hand before hastily retreating down the hall. "Let's go."

"He's…friendly," Avner mumbled to Maddy, clinging close to her side. Clearly he was attempting to hide his atrophy, but she saw how strained his movements were, how his face twitched in agony every few seconds.

"He thinks you're gross. It's nothing personal."

"Well, I do feel pretty disgusting." Avner cringed at his own grunge. "Hey—where's Jamad?" he added, peeking around at the empty cells. "Did you free him already?"

"No…" Maddy avoided Avner's bright, inquisitive eyes as she led him into that last cell on the left. "He took Danny's deal, Av. I'm sorry."

He halted his strides, eyebrows creasing. "Danny's deal?"

"He…offered to let you guys become Wackos," Maddy reminded him, trying not to panic at the prospect that his brain might have degenerated.

"Yeah…and Jamad and I both refused," Avner said as Zach ascended the ladder. "That's why Danny threw us in those cells…"

Zach disappeared through the hole, but Maddy was too paralyzed to move toward the ladder. "Danny…didn't come to your cell a few days ago and offer to free you?"

"No," Avner answered with enough clarity that she knew he wasn't confused. "I'm assuming he did present Jamad with that offer, though."

"Get up here," Zach hissed from above, his face nearly indistinguishable.

Befuddled, Avner stumbled toward the ladder to climb the rungs. Maddy was too infuriated to watch him. Danny had *lied*—and *Naretha* had lied. They hadn't given him a choice. It was impossible to say how he might have responded to the proposition, but he hadn't even been given the opportunity to—

A yelp broke her out of her piqued thoughts as Avner plummeted to the ground. In his weak state of decay, he hadn't made it very far up the ladder, but the sound of him hitting the concrete was still loud and unpleasant. Dazed, he attempted to stand, readily taking Maddy's hand when she reached for him.

"I'll—"

"No, don't try again," Maddy said before he could groggily fumble for the ladder. He shot her a quizzical look that she ignored as she squatted and then sprung into the air.

The leather outfit she wore didn't elongate with her limbs, but thankfully, it didn't inhibit her from reaching the hole in the ceiling. After hooking her fingers around the ledge, she pulled up with enough force that her rubbery limbs propelled her through the opening. Scrambling back in alarm, Zach moved just in time for her to shorten her limbs to a normal length and land lithely in the dorm room.

Without wasting a second, Maddy flattened onto her stomach and peered down through the hole at Avner as he squinted up at her. After stretching her arms again, she wrapped them securely around his waist and then, groaning, used her strength and her Affinity to slowly hoist him upward. He gripped her arms to remain upright while Zach held her legs to prevent her from falling. By the time Avner had joined them in the room, Maddy was panting, her limbs tangled between both boys.

"Thanks—Mads," he coughed, rubbing his ribs. "Where—Meredith?" he blurted the moment his eyes fell on her.

Sprawled against the door as if actively preventing someone from barging in, Meredith's frenzied gaze locked onto Avner and she smiled. "I'm the lookout."

He nodded, returning her expression. "I see that. So, where do we go now?"

"We can't take the elevator up to the cabin," Zach said as he pulled up the ladder and sealed the hatch. Maddy gradually retracted her arms and legs, massaging them gently as they ached with soreness. "There will be too many witnesses. In the weapons room there's a staircase that leads up to the cabin's basement. You should be able to sneak out through there."

"You're...not coming?" Maddy questioned. "You're staying here?"

"I have to. Danny might be crazy, but...not all of the Wackos are bad. I need to make sure this organization doesn't ruin them—and the world."

Maddy gnawed on the inside of her cheek but couldn't come up with a counterargument. His father had built the Wackos, albeit they'd gone by another name back then. She understood how Zach would view the organization as his responsibility, even though he wasn't the rightful leader.

As they exited room 318 and took the elevator up to the cafeteria, Maddy and Avner both moved sluggishly, her muscles fatigued and his muscles deteriorated. Zach propped her up whenever she needed it, carefully avoiding her skin and only making contact with her clothes, while Meredith, though as weak as Avner, held his hand in encouragement whenever his body threatened to collapse.

"Will you make sure Meredith gets back to her room safely after we leave?" Maddy whispered to Zach as they trailed through the empty cafeteria. His hand was at her elbow, but he had a difficult time grasping it since her bones felt mushy.

"You don't want to bring her with you?" he muttered through his teeth.

"I wouldn't know what to do with her," Maddy admitted shamefully. "She's probably safest here…with Jamad… Did you know that Danny didn't offer Avner freedom?"

"He—didn't?" Zach's footsteps faltered slightly as they passed Danny's throne.

"You didn't hear Avner down in the cells? Danny never came to ask him if he wanted to join the Wackos. He only asked Jamad."

"That bastard." He tightened his fingers around Maddy's arm and glared at the mural of his brother, splattered beautifully on the wall. "Probably because of his grudge against the Stromers…"

"Danny knows the Stromers? He knows who Avner's parents are?" Her heart beat incredibly fast as her brain worked through the possibility. Avner had never even known who his own parents were—but that hadn't stopped them from being the only two people in this world he absolutely loathed. Glancing up at Zach expectantly, she waited for his reply, but he didn't bother to give one before opening the white door that rested beside Josh's explosive artwork and guiding her into the weapons room.

Like the rest of Headquarters, the weapons room, with

unadorned walls and a concrete floor, was well lit, organized, and somewhat daunting. Given many Affinities were deadly on their own, Maddy hadn't considered that the Wackos would require a room brimming with Regg-like weapons, ranging from guns and bombs to swords and axes and shields. The labyrinth of inventory was even more impressive than Periculand's library, and at first, Maddy almost didn't notice the staircase on the other end of the room, nestled against the left wall, leading up to a metal door.

Wordlessly, Zach nodded to the left, where he proceeded to slink against the wall, keeping his head carefully ducked behind a line of shelves that housed various electronics. With Avner at her heels, Maddy followed, barely needing to bend to stay hidden. She thought they were hiding from cameras until she heard voices echoing against the bare walls.

"...can't believe I'm bringing Danny's little toy dog to a battle," a familiar voice grumbled, nearer than Maddy would have liked. "Agh! This nasty little rat is farting on me. Snowman, bring me an ax, will you? We can pretend it accidentally decapitated him while we were gathering—"

"We're not decapitating the dog," Jamad droned, his voice farther into the room but closer to their location. Behind Maddy, Avner seemed ready to lurch up in greeting, but she grabbed his hand and shook her head. She wished Jamad could join them, but Naretha definitely couldn't.

"You can't tell me what to do," she snapped, a disgusted scoff following shortly after. "I want this thing dead."

"But he's so cute—like a little snowball!"

"Yeah, until he bites you or impales you with glass..."

Zach paused abruptly, and Maddy almost bumped into him until she realized why they stopped: There was a gap in the shelving, a brief window in which Jamad might spot them.

Enthralled by his conversation with Naretha—and his examination of a massive gun—he faced the opposite direction, but Zach still moved with caution and stealth as he slipped past the gap, leaving only a few short paces between him and the staircase. Maddy was a little more hesitant, her eyes darting from the stairs to Jamad—until he suddenly spun around to study a different gun and found her directly in his line of sight.

Both utterly frozen, eyes locked and mouths agape, Maddy and Jamad stared at each other, processing their predicament, determining what to do with this divide between them. After a breathless moment, her eyes finally flitted toward the staircase, and then she beckoned with one hand for him to join them. Even if he hated his family—even if he hated all Reggs—he didn't hate her…did he?

"Ma—" he began, likely about to utter her name, but he covered his mistake with a cough.

"Do you want something, Snowman?" Naretha questioned, her voice farther than before.

"No…" Jamad said slowly, his jaw tight as his features morphed into a scowl, "but my friends want to escape."

Maddy had to cover her mouth with her hand to prevent herself from sucking in a loud breath. Deep within her heart she'd known Jamad would refuse her offer, but to *betray* them—

"Way to state the obvious," Naretha retorted, oblivious to his insinuation. Maddy should have taken this opportunity to dart after Zach, but she was too stricken by grief and indignation to move any of her floppy muscles. "We all know neither of your little friends want to be part of us. Why do you think Sparky's still in a cell?"

Jamad stepped toward Maddy, pausing only once his vision had fixated on Avner. Blue eyes chilling, he snarled, "Is he, though?"

This time, Naretha caught the indication in his inflection.

A little yip spiked through the air as she dropped Shards and dashed through the maze of weapons. Maddy and Avner darted for the stairs while Meredith lingered behind, screaming when Jamad threw arrows of ice that barely missed them before piercing the wall.

"*Meredith*?" he gasped. "You're *with* them?"

"I-I just thought we were going to eat food together!" she wailed, caving in on herself as she plopped to the floor. "I don't want to hurt you!"

It was sad, and Maddy almost wanted to retreat and comfort her, but she had to take this opportunity to escape. Mounting the steps two at a time, she lunged toward the door, just as a surge of salt crystals pelted it.

Maddy pivoted back and linked gazes with Naretha, who now stood at Jamad's side, both of their hands extended toward her. Avner was halfway up the stairs, body hunched and arm dragging him down since Jamad had encased his hand in a block of ice. Zach waited in the shadows between the staircase and the shelves, eyes flickering in all directions with uncertainty.

"Who's on the side of justice now, Stromer?" Jamad demanded, twisting his fingers in a way that provoked a cry of agony from Avner. He must have inwardly increased the ice, freezing and squeezing Avner's hand simultaneously. "Do you feel like a saint—breaking out of prison, dragging everyone around you into your little pit of self-righteousness? If you wanted out of that cell, you should have taken Danny's deal—"

"I wasn't offered Danny's deal!" he exclaimed through rasping breaths. "He never asked me to join him! He only asked you!"

Jamad blinked, his hand lowering slightly as he rotated toward Naretha, whose teeth were clenched with ire. "Is that true?" he whispered, unable to fully speak.

"Yes. What do you think he would have said if we'd asked him? Even if he agreed, he would have eventually betrayed us, just like Faddy is now. Your friends can't be trusted, Jamad. And I didn't want you going down with them."

"Is *that* true?" he repeated, elevating his voice as he directed the question to Avner. "Would you have betrayed us—betrayed *me*?"

Avner exhaled, staring at the ceiling in despair. "These people are terrorists, J. You're…" He trailed off, staring at that leather suit, at the way Jamad stood at Naretha's side with such confidence.

"I'm evil, aren't I?" He lifted his hand again. "I've never been as good as you, have I? As *perfect* and *selfless*—"

"*Jamad*," Maddy cut in, her voice half a sob, "you *know* Avner has flaws. You've seen him at his worst—we've all seen *each other* at our worsts. We're friends—we're *family*. This can't be our end!"

"It is," Jamad said frigidly, his words triggering an unrestrained assault.

Ice and salt and *glass* flew through the air, striking Maddy and Avner as they struggled to ascend the stairs. Most of the shards bounced off her thick leather, but his skin was exposed, resulting in various cuts and gashes. A few stabbed Maddy's face, and she squinted, shielding her eyes with her hand.

A column of ice coated her leg as she stepped on the highest stair, weighing her down and impeding further movement. With her Affinity, her only option of defense was to jump down there and physically attack with her limbs. Even without the ice constricting her leg, it would have been futile. The fact that Jamad had so easily debilitated her proved she was no match for them.

With his lightning, Avner would have been a threat. At maximum potential, he probably could have killed Jamad and Naretha instantly. His current capacity wasn't quite so deadly, but he did manage to muster a bit of his power, sending down a spark of electricity that zapped Danny's crazed little dog, halting the glass attack. Yelping, Shards fled the scene, leaving only salt and ice to barrage them with increased violence.

Since Jamad was accustomed to Avner's electricity and Naretha was so ruthlessly tough, his weakened Affinity would have little effect on them. Knowing this, Maddy extended her arm toward the door handle in one last attempt, but then salt consolidated around her flesh, tiny particles forming a cast around her hand. Simultaneously, ice crept up her leg, rooting her in place, and behind her, Avner met the same fate, his electricity failing to blast off the molds.

This really was the end for them.

Or, at least, it *would* have been, if they hadn't possessed a secret ally lurking in the shadows.

The moment Zach stood, Naretha and Jamad wavered as if he'd shot them. The former's initial reaction was the most dramatic display of emotion Maddy had ever seen from the woman. Her thin face drooped with disbelief, the spark of aggression waning in her eyes. As soon as Zach held out his hands, not in offense but in surrender, her hostility instantly resumed.

"What the *hell* are you doing?" she barked, aiming one hand at him and the other toward the stairs. "Did you *help* this kid break out of his cell? Danny will slaughter you!"

"He won't if you don't tell him."

"Don't tell him?" She released a vindictive laugh. "You want me to *lie* to Danny? Do you want *me* to die? This is some screwed up shit you've done, Zach. We need to put him back *now*!"

"He doesn't deserve to be a prisoner, and you know it. Once this business with Ashna dies down, you know Danny will get bored, and who'll be his new toy then? Avner doesn't deserve—that fate."

A cruel smile slid onto Naretha's lips as she shook her head. "You were going to say 'your fate,' weren't you? You don't want Avner to end up as one of Danny's possessions like I am, hm? Well, that's so *virtuous* of you, Zachary. Save this complete stranger, why don't you—but when Danny claims *me*, you do absolutely nothing!"

"The scenarios are incomparable!" he shot back, his voice laced with actual emotion, actual despair. "This kid has the chance to get away, Naretha. You and I—we never had that chance. We've been tangled up in this web since we were kids, and we will *die* here. Don't subject everyone else to our misery."

She snorted, eyes shimmering with rage. "You're *pathetic*. No wonder Danny's leader instead of you. Do you know what these two will do if we let them go? They'll report us to the government; they will give the Reggs all the information they need to sneak in here and *destroy us*. And I know—I *know* you're gonna say, 'Well, maybe it'd be better that way,' but it *wouldn't be*. Let's just settle this argument now, shall we?"

Zach opened his mouth, but not a word escaped before Naretha threw both hands in Maddy's direction, spraying a torrent of thick salt crystals. With protuberant eyes, she watched the sharp spears soar toward her face, guaranteed to tear through her flesh, perhaps with enough force to shatter even the density of her bones.

With the imminent collision, she whirled to face Zach, hoping to convey some kind of goodbye with the briefest of looks. He wasn't focused on her, though; his attention was trained on Naretha, because through an assortment of wizardly hand gestures, he formed a *dust cloud* around her.

Particles streamed from every surface, emerging from every hole and crack to bend to Zach's will. The tornado whipped violently at Naretha, turning her salt to dust at Maddy's feet before joining the whirlwind, her own element working against her. Jamad, whose jaw had slackened, hacked up the dust clogging his lungs, closing his eyes to ward off stinging blindness.

"Why doesn't anyone clean the dust in here?" Zach shouted as he continued gathering minuscule debris from every corner of the room.

"Because you're the only person who cares about *dust*!" Naretha screamed from within the cloud. Maddy took the opportunity of her distraction to bang her encrusted hands against the wall, beating off the salt until her fingers were unrestrained. "ZACH!"

"Go," he urged, nodding for Maddy to continue up the stairs. She could have; the ice on her legs was melting, and Avner was free from his own salt and ice confines after copying her method of destruction, but *Zach*... How could she leave him after he'd sacrificed himself in this way? If Danny returned from Periculand, he would annihilate his brother for this act of betrayal.

Perhaps he would hate her for this, perhaps he would only return here to face his brutal fate, but Maddy wanted to give him that choice, like he'd given her and Avner this one.

Extending her arm to fling open the metal door, Maddy ushered Avner up and then twirled toward the chaos. The dust didn't *harm* them, but Naretha and Jamad fought hard to extricate themselves from the haze. Maddy hoped that, even after the swirl ceased, they would remain disoriented enough not to thwart her plan.

The ice cast had hindered her before, but now she used it as an anchor, placing as much of her weight on that leg as she could. Then she lobbed her stretchy arms over the stairs' railing and embraced Zach for the first time.

He was certainly caught off guard, but he processed her intentions. Abandoning his assault, he used the assistance of her arms to launch himself up to the railing and then leap onto the stairs. She didn't bother to fully remove herself from him before hurrying up the steps, his body right beside her.

As they passed through the doorway at the top of the stairs, it dawned on her that Zach could have refused her embrace—could have shunned her even now—but he wanted to come with her. He'd made his choice even though, as he peered down the stairs, it seemed to pain him.

With the storm waning, Jamad and Naretha squinted their dust-crusted eyes at the open doorway and the escapees beyond.

"You *traitor*!" she shrieked at Zach, her voice more violent than any of the weapons in the room around her. Her hands burst with salt crystals and her pale pink eyes simmered with wrath, but she didn't aim at him—she didn't even aim at *Maddy*. Whatever Zach had once been to her, Naretha accepted his choice to reject her now, even if she abhorred him for it.

As Maddy scrambled to close the metal door and caught a glimpse of Jamad's remorseful blue eyes, she realized the same could be said for them.

33

Identities

Ackerly had never consumed a sip of alcohol, so to chug half a cup had him gagging on the verge of puking. Ashna had defeated *Nero*, though; she'd *humiliated* him. If Ackerly didn't accept this challenge, she would never respect him.

Watching her nearly strangle Nero with that vine—well, Ackerly's first thought had been a silent prayer for that mutilated plant, wishing it a happy afterlife. His second response had been to wonder *how* Ashna conjured those flowers and then a whole vine from absolutely nothing. Unless she had seeds hidden in her pockets, the flowers—Japanese wisteria, if he wasn't mistaken—had bloomed almost magically.

With the advanced and near supernatural abilities some Affinities had, Ackerly shouldn't have been surprised, but…he hadn't forgotten her incredulity upon discovering he had the ability to sprout beans without sun, soil, or water. He didn't want to believe it had been an act, but if she could summon flowers from nothing, his capabilities seemed pathetic.

After dwelling on this conundrum, his third thought had been to use his plant Affinity in the same way Ashna had used her flower powers—in an aggressive way. The prospect of sacrificing plants was unpleasant, but if he could procure vines thick enough to ensnare Nero—like ivy—then perhaps he'd be willing to engage in a little plant cruelty.

All of these plans had vanished with the consumption of that alcohol. Not because the liquid had distorted his thoughts but because, as he lowered his head and threw the cup on the floor, he found himself staring into the slivered eyes of Artemis and William Ross.

Jolting back, Ackerly gawked at them, unable to stutter a word. The lounge had grown eerily quiet, all mouths sealed and all movement abated. Even Nero, positioned beside the Reggs, was no longer the boisterous, cocky boy who'd challenged Ackerly mere seconds ago. His arms were crossed toughly, and his tight lips displayed no sign of shock, but Ackerly saw the unease in his eyes.

"Mr. Terrier," Artemis greeted tersely. Ackerly knew her features must have been rigid, but they seemed hazy in his vision, as if he had the wrong lenses in his glasses.

"H-hi," he stammered, swaying slightly.

"Sixteen, aren't you?" William prompted, his eyes flickering from the discarded cup to Ackerly's face.

"Fif...teen..."

"It's all the same." Artemis's gaze swept the lounge. "Everyone in here has been drinking underage, and it appears that the people we've put our faith in have allowed it—if not participated in it."

Ackerly was certain her attention fixed on the cup in Nero's hand, but his head pounded too much to concentrate. All he could focus on over the next few seconds was Ashna, where she lay perfectly still, chest to the ground and legs tangled in a chair. Her rainbow eyes were wide, but he couldn't tell what kind of message they conveyed.

He wouldn't have the opportunity to decode it, he realized, for the Rosses had deemed Nero the guilty host of this party, and for some horrible reason, Ackerly was dragged along for the punishment.

When they departed the Residence Tower, the frigid air smacked his senses back into place, clearing his mind, heightening the burn in his throat, and alerting him that two Regg guards, in their dark suits, escorted him toward the Mentals Building.

Four had a hold on Nero, probably because no suit was immune to being picked up and thrown across campus. The Rosses led the pack, and then, when Ackerly peered over his shoulder at the tower, he found Calder bringing up the rear, a guard at either of his elbows.

"Lost, primie?" he quipped, his smirk radiating even as the guards jerked him along. For someone who was about to be reamed out by the principals, he seemed fairly chipper.

By the time they reached the Rosses' office, Ackerly's initial headache had faded into a fuzzy high. Without this lighter state of mind, he probably would have been apprehensive to enter the room Hastings had died in for the first time since that morose afternoon. Instead, he waltzed in with curiosity, naively wondering how this meeting might play out.

"Sit," Artemis commanded the teens once she and her husband stood behind their desk. The eight guards remained stationed by the doors, quashing any hopes of escape—unless Nero decided to smash the office's back wall of glass, of course. Ackerly wouldn't have been surprised if he did.

As the big bully assumed the worn chair on the left and Calder plopped into the pristine one on the right, Ackerly blinked and scanned the room, befuddled. "There are...only two chairs."

"Tough luck, primie." Calder inclined his head toward the patch of discolored wood on the floor. "Looks like you're stuck standing in the circle of shame."

"Adara's circle?" Ackerly squinted down at the spot she'd plummeted through a few weeks ago.

"Do you doubt she'd be mocking you right now for getting caught?"

Positioning his feet at the center of the circle, Ackerly was about to reply, but William spoke first, his tone indicating he'd had enough of the banter.

"Do you understand the severity of what you've done?"

Ackerly's eyes darted between Nero and Calder; the former glared at the desk, refusing to meet his masters' eyes, while the latter drawled, "Is there some sort of number scale you're referring to? I'd put this at a seven out of ten. You have to admit it could have been worse. No one *died*—"

"But many were injured while engaging in your little brawls," Artemis interjected coldly. "The injuries are the least of our worries, though. The *problem* is that you've directly broken a law—and in front of the entire school. How can we permit you to enforce rules when you can't follow them yourselves? How can we endorse a student who has publicly committed a crime?"

"Is this the wrong time to point out this isn't the first time Nero's gotten in trouble with the law?" Calder asked, eyebrows arching.

"Cheeky today, Mardurus." Nero's gray eyes narrowed threateningly. "Almost like you don't care that we've gotten caught."

"You're the only one who's gotten caught, Nero," Artemis cut in. "Every other student in this school might have been drinking, but we put *you* in charge of the students, and given you're not a minor anymore, this is a serious offense."

Nero puffed up his muscles defensively. "I don't turn eighteen 'til tomorrow."

"No," William said, consulting his watch, "you turned eighteen thirty minutes ago. It's half past midnight."

For the first time Ackerly had ever witnessed, Nero blanched.

"Which means," the man continued, "that not only are you in trouble within this town, but also with the state of Ohio."

Clutching the arms of his chair, he leaned forward, seething. "I wasn't the only one over eighteen drinking."

"We know, and we plan to punish all of them, but, Nero..." Artemis trailed off, staring down at her hands, folded neatly on her desk. "We're disappointed in you. We had such hope for you. We don't plan to stay in Periculand forever. Once this business with Angor is settled and the town is to Mr. Ventura's liking, we plan to leave—and we planned, at that point, once you'd graduated, to bestow power on you—to, perhaps, give you the title of principal. Now, that notion has withered, all because of a stupid mistake on your part. A *stupid mistake*, but a public one, one we cannot brush under the rug."

Calder leaned into his hand, covering his mouth as if in grief, but Ackerly saw the light sparkling in his eyes, the sadistic triumph of vengeance. Maybe he *was* happy about Nero's harsh demotion. The brute wouldn't have noticed either way; his previously white face now filled with blood as wrath boiled in his veins.

"You're *joking*."

"Unfortunately, no," William sighed, folding his hands like his wife's. "The punishment won't be unjust—likely just a few hours of community service—but you won't be able to lead training anymore; you'll have no more sway over anyone than this green kid does."

Ackerly raised one hand in a trembling wave. "A-Ackerly—hi."

Rolling her eyes, Artemis chewed on the inside of her cheek, studying Nero solemnly. It took her so long to say anything to him that Ackerly grew distracted, his vision settling on a television against the wall, displaying the news. The volume was muted, but the headlines were loud enough to stop his heart: *WACKOS BLOW UP CLEVELAND APARTMENTS, OVER 300 INJURED, 100 DEAD.*

"Um—guys," he croaked, interrupting an emotional speech from Artemis. They all stared at him, he knew, but his eyes were glued to the television. "The...Wackos..."

Artemis whipped her gaze around and then scoffed dismissively. "Not uncommon. They pull these stunts at least once a week—which is *why* we are so adamant about training other Affinities to combat them. Don't you agree the Wackos are to be annihilated, Terrier?"

Seeing that the Wackos had killed so many people with such ease—and that they did it so frequently—Ackerly couldn't *not* agree. Risking a few hundred teenagers to prevent thousands of deaths seemed logical, but before he could say so, the telephone on the Rosses' desk began to ring.

Artemis's eyes continued boring into his, ignoring the obnoxious chimes and prompting him to respond to her inquiry.

"Aren't you...gonna answer that?"

"I want *you* to answer *me*," she insisted, and when the ringing ceased, he had no choice—until the caller's message permeated the office.

"Hello, rulers of Periculand," the unctuous voice cooed, and though Ackerly didn't recognize it, he knew with sickening clarity that it had to be the leader of the Wackos: the man named Danny. "My spies haven't seen Angor released from prison yet, so I assume it's still the Reggs: Artemis and William Ross."

The latter swallowed with trepidation, but the former remained stony, glaring at the phone like it was a disease.

"That it took me an entire week is really an embarrassment on my part," Danny mused without any hint of shame, "but I've finally discovered that those who escaped me are in Periculand. I didn't think my little Ashna would be stupid enough to trigger her tracking device. She figured out what points of pressure were necessary to turn it off; surely she'd also discovered that the use of her super strength would turn it back on."

The Rosses exchanged a confused look, probably because they were of the few at this school who still didn't know of Ashna's infinite Affinities. To Ackerly, it made sense; Ashna had appeared discombobulated after using her super strength, rubbing her arm as if something had changed there. It had probably been the tracking device, somehow turned on by the abnormal strength of her bicep.

"Nevertheless, we'll be there shortly to retrieve what is ours. This is a prerecorded message that I have set to send a half hour after we depart, so we should arrive an hour or two after you receive it. I hope you see my destruction on the television. Periculand isn't the only place I plan to raze tonight."

Ackerly heard the vicious grin in his voice, and he shuddered at the thought that this man would be here within a matter of hours. The prospect of fighting Nero had been daunting enough; how was he supposed to save Ashna from the Wacko *leader*?

"It's morning, technically," a dry voice droned, the sound muffled since he was likely farther away from the receiver.

"Shut *up*," Danny snarled, the aggression making both Ackerly and William jump. "I am *this* far from throwing you in a cell, *Zacchaeus.*" Clearing his throat, the man put on a pleasanter tone as he said, "Don't fret, Periculand. My brother will not accompany us on our mission tonight. You won't have to suffer the might of his *cleaning Affinity*. Now—"

They didn't get to hear what would happen *now*, for a commotion of shuffling interrupted his words, followed by a piqued, "*Shards*!"

Then guttural screaming, mixed with a dark blend of instruments, flowed from the phone, causing Ackerly to smack his hands on either side of his head. It was clearly intended to be music, but his ears had never endured anything so grotesque.

"Your dog broke the remote, Danny," the other man, Zacchaeus, said faintly, his voice overpowered by the screaming music.

The Rosses looked as disturbed as Ackerly felt, but Calder listened intently, his fingers stroking his chin until he abruptly bolted upright. "Pause it."

"Pause…?" William echoed, but Artemis fumbled with the phone until she'd halted the message.

"Bleeding Brains," Calder said, his eyes protruding in disbelief. "This guy likes Bleeding Brains."

Ackerly scratched the back of his head. "Well…I feel like most terrorists like bleeding brains."

"No—no, it's a band," Calder corrected, sparking a memory in Ackerly's mind. "They're too intense even for me, and I like that kinda stuff… Not even *Nixie* likes—"

"Holy seeds—that's Ashna's favorite band," Ackerly blurted out, recalling their conversation in the Naturals Building's basement earlier that afternoon. "She said she always used to listen to them with her…brother…"

Calder slowly pivoted toward Ackerly, who couldn't stop gawking at the phone.

"No, no—it's not possible—Ashna said—she said that her brother's dead—that the Wackos killed him—"

"Metaphorically, I'm sure they did kill the boy he once was," Calder said through gritted teeth. "Did she ever say exactly how her brother died? Ever say what his name was—or what her *last name is*?"

"N-no…I never thought to ask!"

Groaning, Calder rubbed his forehead and spun back toward the Rosses. "We need to find Ashna. If she's the Wacko leader's sister, she definitely knows his weaknesses."

"It also seems likely that she would know his exact plans…" Artemis tapped her fingers on the desk, contemplating. "Perhaps—perhaps she was sent here on a secret mission to infiltrate the town and give her brother *our* secrets. He said he had spies in Periculand, did he not?"

The note Kiki and Eliana had found pressed on Ackerly's mind, but he still couldn't believe Ashna was a Wacko spy—that she'd lied to him so intensely. "The Wacko leader also said he was coming here to retrieve Ashna and her friends because they *escaped*."

"Do you believe every word this psychopath says?" William demanded, pushing out of his chair to pace about the office. "He's clearly trying to distract us—to make us think Ashna and her friends are innocent when they're not. She gave us one hideout location that we raided, but you know as well as I do that they were only able to apprehend one Wacko—"

"Only one?" Calder injected, even though William's words had been intended for his wife. "I thought you said they got a bunch of Wackos."

"Sometimes the facts have to be skewed to appease the public," Artemis said tartly. "The Wacko Headquarters location Ashna gave us was also fraudulent. We assumed it was simply abandoned, but now…it sounds like she gave us a decoy location instead of the real one, saving her precious Wackos—her precious brothers."

Ackerly's head spun, but it wasn't the alcohol anymore; it was Ashna. The Wacko leader was her *brother*, and she'd come here not to destroy the Wackos but to destroy Periculand—to destroy *Ackerly*. He'd thought for the past week that she might actually care about him, that she might actually *like* him, but instead, she'd fed him nothing but lies, making him vulnerable for the slaughter that was sure to unfold.

"Play the rest of the message," Ackerly commanded, his voice calm but infused with venom. Artemis didn't question him before pressing the button.

The noisy music resumed, but this time Ackerly let it fill his core with rage—an emotion he'd never experienced before. This must have been the heat that built in Adara's gut every time someone made a snide comment, every time her red eyes flared with fire. He'd never succumbed to it before, but now, if Ashna were in this room, he would have sacrificed a hundred plants to make her suffer.

He really should have believed Tray.

After a few moments, the screams and clamorous instruments came to a halt, and Ackerly's anger dimmed with it. A deafening silence ensued, only to be ended with a familiar voice saying, "Well, that's one way to do it. Just blow up the speaker, yeah?"

It didn't add up, but Ackerly was fairly certain the voice had been Jamad's—Avner's friend.

Danny disregarded his comment and went on to say, "Periculand, surrender and open your gates to me, or we will ravish you."

"Are you threatening to rape someone or demolish a city?" a sardonic female voice intoned from afar. Ackerly didn't recognize this one either, but he was sure he heard Nero grumble, "Salt bitch."

"I'm metaphorically threatening to rape a city," Danny replied to the woman before redirecting his attention to the receivers of his message. "See you soon," he sang tauntingly, ending the recording.

The Rosses' office remained suspended in time for a few brief seconds before Artemis finally stood from her chair and addressed everyone in the room. "Ashna must be found and detained. Guards, signal the others—tell them to search for a girl with rainbow hair. Terrier, you'll find Fraco and inform him of what we learned here. Mr. Ross and I will gather the other students. Drunk or not, they will engage in a fight tonight. We haven't trained them for the past month for nothing."

Ackerly cringed, but he couldn't see any other option; if the Wackos were truly coming, everyone in this town would need to defend it.

"Hopefully, since Daniel will be here, we can finally put an end to the entire terrorist organization... Oh, and, guards," Artemis added, glancing at the men whispering into their communication devices, "I need six of you to escort Mr. Corvis and Mr. Mardurus to the police station."

Nero's eyebrows shot upward. "You want to let Periculy and Stromer fight?"

"No, I want both of you in cells until this is over. After what you pulled tonight, I cannot allow you to lead the student army. If we survive the night, the students of this town cannot be disillusioned into thinking underage drinking is acceptable—"

Nero and Calder both jumped up from their seats in unison.

"A horde of Wackos is about to invade our town and you want to put two of your best fighters in *jail* because of *underage drinking*?" Calder questioned.

"You can't put me in *jail*!" Nero roared, not at all miffed by the group of soldiers closing in on them. Ackerly scurried out of the way, knowing he should leave before the impending violence but finding himself too intrigued to depart. "You two are *Reggs—normies.* You don't stand a chance against the Wackos. *I'm* the one who's been training the students—*I'm* the one who should command—"

"You lost that privilege when you decided to throw a party in our absence," William stated as he padded back to his desk. "If we can't trust you during times of peace, how can we trust you during times of war? We will command the students. Guards."

The six Regg soldiers grasped the two boys, four on Nero and two on Calder. Nero thrashed and swung his big arms around, but the Reggs took the blows like a docile summer breeze—until one particularly impatient Regg smashed a fist against Nero's thick skull, actually dazing him. Calder didn't bother resisting; he simply glared at the Rosses and then at Ackerly, as if this were somehow his fault, too.

Despite his animosity, Ackerly swore he saw a tinge of relief on his face as the guards dragged them out—or perhaps it was excitement, because they wouldn't just go to jail: They would go to Adara.

The lounge erupted in chaos the moment the Reggs hauled Nero, Calder, and Ackerly away. Students scrambled to clean up the cups littering the floor and correct the furniture strewn out of place. A large group staggered outside in a lame attempt to puke up whatever alcohol they'd consumed, lest the Rosses returned to exact punishments.

Perched on the spiral staircase, Tray watched it all with an air of smugness.

This was what they deserved for hosting an underage drinking party in a town occupied by Regg soldiers. He was content with the knowledge that these rebellious teenagers would finally learn about consequences. The only aspect that bothered him was that *Ackerly* had been dragged off as well. Yes, he was the only student the Rosses had seen physically drinking, but still, he shouldn't have received the same treatment as a menace like Nero.

Tray had decided that if Ackerly didn't return after an hour, he would confront the Rosses and testify on his roommate's behalf. Even if the kid had plummeted to Adara levels of stupidity with his adamant belief of Ashna's innocence, he was still Tray's… friend—perhaps the first person he'd ever willingly called a friend.

Ashna, the object of Ackerly's irrationality, was a whole other problem entirely. The girl had recovered from her Nero-induced flight across the room, and half the students now fawned over her, admiring her super strength as she moved massive couches with those skinny limbs. Tray probably should have done the same, but he couldn't organize his thoughts when in motion, and he had a lot of thoughts to organize.

Like the question of how this incident would affect tomorrow's trial—and if the public knowledge of Ashna's multiple Affinities would result in her detainment and, consequently, thwart her Wacko-related plans—or if, with her newfound popularity, she would gather the other students onto her side: the Wackos' side.

Considering all the terrible turns this town could take, Tray soon became restless. That was why, when Eliana bumbled down the stairs and crashed into him, a piece of paper in her hands and a grave expression on her face, his lips broke into a genuine grin.

"Eliana, hey," he greeted, straightening to his feet as she fought to right herself. With her blue hair in a messy ponytail and the whites of her eyes tinted pink, Tray discerned that she'd either just awoken from sleep or was in a severely distressed mental state. Given his inexperience with emotional consolation, he convinced himself she was sleepy, even though the hollow grief was prominent in her glossy gaze.

"We have a problem," she said, her voice firm despite its brokenness. "I just drew this."

With the depiction thrust suddenly into his view, Tray had to blink a few times to fully focus. When he did, his brow crinkled at the bedlam and violence: Drawn with bright pencils, Eliana had crafted a scene of fire and destruction, and Periculand was its setting.

The front gate was wide open, permitting a horde of Affinities clad in black to attack the young students of Periculand, many falling or fallen under the assault. The Physicals Building was half-collapsed, the Naturals Building burned, and he saw himself among the fray, a head of brown hair fighting off a much larger opponent.

"Well," Tray said through a gruff cough, "I'm not really an artist, so if you're looking for a critic—"

"This isn't *art*." The tight clutch of her fingers formed indents on the paper as she waved it in his face. "This is the *future*. Tray…" She trailed off, her normal reticence resuming. "The Wackos are coming for us. They're going to destroy us."

"Are you sure?" Lavisa asked as she approached the bottom of the stairs, scowling up at the drawing. "How did you know to draw this?"

Lowering the paper, Eliana swallowed. "Kiki and I have…a connection. *Somehow* I read her predictions—er, steal them…"

"Well, where is Kiki?" Tray demanded, scanning the lounge for any sign of her pinkish hair. "If she knows what's going to happen, we need to talk to—"

"It doesn't matter where she is," Lavisa said, tightening her hand wraps, "but we do need to figure out when the Wackos will arrive and what their goal is so we can organize a proper defense strategy. I would say we could interrogate Ashna and her friends…" She peered over her shoulder at Ashna lifting a bright green table. Cath wasn't far from her, hefting a red couch, but Naira had disappeared, probably to puke outside with Seth. "But with her infinite Affinities, I think Than is a safer bet. Unless he's been lying, his Affinity is just living a long time. He won't be a physical threat against me or Tray."

"Wait…" Eliana's features warped with confusion. "Infinite Affinities? What do you—"

Before her question could fully develop, Hartman appeared on the step beside her, orange hair in disarray and chocolate nestled in the corners of his smirk. Knowing no one other than the teleporter would have an opportunity to say much now that he was here, Tray sent a mental image to Eliana of what Ashna had done to Nero, and her eyes protruded.

"Hey, guys," Hartman huffed, swaying into Eliana, who was too baffled to react. "Is Nero gone?"

Lavisa's lips curled wryly. "He's been gone for at least twenty minutes."

"Oh, sweet." He nodded around to the group. Recovered from the shock of Ashna's secret, Eliana awkwardly touched the corners of her own lips to alert him of his messiness, but he didn't notice. "I was distracting him for you," he added to Tray, "but then I ended up all the way across town inside someone's freezer. Longest distance I've ever teleported, I think. It had to have been a few hundred feet, if not a few *thousand*—or a few *hundred thousand*—"

"Sounds like a fluke," Lavisa commented as she finished securing her hand wraps.

"Even if it was, I didn't hesitate to reward myself by eating all of the ice cream in that freezer."

Eliana exchanged a mildly amused look with Lavisa. "We can tell."

"If you're so proficient now, why don't you teleport us over to the Mentals Building?" Tray suggested. "We have an emergency."

"Don't say *emergency*. I can't work under pressure, man. If you tell me there'll be more ice cream, though—"

"I'll buy you ice cream later," Eliana assured him as she looped her arm through his. She didn't add the silent "if we survive" that Tray saw written in her eyes.

Enthused by her promise, Hartman hastily waved at Tray and Lavisa before vanishing from the room. That he'd teleported out of the lounge in one go shouldn't have been impressive, but for Hartman it was.

"You know where Kiki is, don't you?" was the first thing Tray asked once the other two had disappeared.

Lavisa glanced forlornly up the stairwell. "I saw her go… upstairs with the acid-spitter."

"Up…oh—oh. I see." Tray stared at the ground, as if he might witness the two of them by merely looking toward the upper floors. He knew Kiki was…experienced, mostly because Seth had always tried to discuss it with him—even though Tray had explicitly expressed his disinterest—but to consider she currently engaged in such activities, with Wacko invasion impending, outraged him.

"Don't tell Eliana," Lavisa added, her yellow eyes harboring a threat.

"Is—*that* who they both have a crush on? The *acid-spitter*? Does he even have a name?"

Rolling her eyes, Lavisa leaned against the railing. "Yes, he has a name. But no, they don't like him, you blind idiot. They're into *each other*, but they're clearly in a fight. I told you, girl drama. Stay out of it."

"Kiki and Eliana are into each other..." Tray whispered to himself. For some reason, he couldn't wrap his mind around quiet, innocent Eliana being infatuated with obnoxious, heartless Kiki—nor could he imagine Kiki settling for anyone who wasn't the pinnacle of popularity. The entire concept was as insane as Ackerly liking Ashna. With all of these ridiculous romances budding, Tray was sure this town would implode on itself before the Wackos even arrived.

The subject was dropped when his entire surroundings unexpectedly changed. In a matter of seconds, Hartman had teleported back into the lounge, grasped Tray's arm, and then teleported them both into the library. In the middle of the night—or morning, technically—the ground floor of the Mentals Building was absent of life and light; only the glow of the half moon shimmering in from the wall of glass illuminated the tables, chairs, and rows of books.

"That had to have been a hundred feet!" Hartman exclaimed, his enthusiasm reverberating through the empty room. "You can't tell me that wasn't a hundred feet!"

"I'm almost inclined to believe in a god," Tray stated dryly. "Where'd Eliana go?"

"Upstairs!" he shouted, his voice carrying through the air even after he departed.

Grumbling to himself, Tray stalked toward the stairwell embedded in the left wall. As soon as he passed through the door, he sealed his lips, because hushed voices emanated from above. Fearing it might be the Rosses, his eyes darted frantically for a place to hide, but then Eliana's voice hissed, "Tray, get up here."

Jogging up the stairs, he halted on the landing to the third floor when he found Ackerly standing next to Eliana, cheeks red and face contorted with…annoyance. Tray had never seen Ackerly *annoyed.* This was the kid who would gladly spend any length of time with Adara Stromer; Tray had thought his patience unlimited.

"Have you seen Fraco?" Ackerly asked, his tone indicating he'd already asked Eliana and received a negative response.

Since Tray couldn't give him a positive one, he countered with, "What happened with the Rosses? They let you off the hook?"

"Oh, um, yeah," he affirmed, glancing up toward the fourth floor, "but the Wackos are on their way to raid the town. I'm supposed to tell Fraco."

Eliana grimaced in concentration. "I don't sense him in this building… Do you know when the Wackos will get here?"

"Probably an hour." Ackerly's lips scrunched as he glared between them. "Ashna's…a Wacko. She's been plotting against us this whole time. You were right."

The confession startled Tray, and he felt much less satisfied than he thought he would. "Who…finally convinced you?"

"Bleeding Brains," Ackerly sighed as his shoulders slumped. Tray shot Eliana a quizzical look, but even she seemed puzzled by his statement. "The Wackos called, and the leader accidentally started playing some music, Calder told me it was Bleeding Brains—he and Nero got thrown in jail, by the way."

"*What*?" Tray's body tensed as if he could physically attack this news. "They can't be in jail! The Wackos are about to demolish us! Nero and Calder are the strongest defense we—"

"I'm sure the two of them will piss off Adara and they'll all bust out after she burns the place down." Lavisa's voice echoed through the stairwell as she and Hartman ascended from below. "Don't be so worried, Stark."

"Adara breaking out of prison only heightens my worry," he griped, running a hand carelessly through his hair. "The last thing we need is her adding to the Wackos' demolition with her irrational, impulsive, irrepressible—"

"All right"—Lavisa nudged past him toward the door—"we could stand here all day and come up with I words that describe Adara, or we could go interrogate Than and figure out why the hell the Wackos are coming here."

"I already know why they're coming." Ackerly's expression darkened back into that unfamiliar irritation. "They're coming for Ashna. They're coming because she led them here. They're coming because...she's Danny's sister."

Everyone stilled. Even Hartman, who almost always vibrated, had petrified with this revelation. Tray had been certain Ashna was a Wacko, but he'd never considered the possibility that she was the leader's *sister*. This made her more than a replaceable soldier of theirs; this made her untouchable. If they hurt the insane terrorist's sister, the consequences would be cataclysmic.

"We should capture her as leverage against Danny," Ackerly continued. "We should...threaten her safety until he calls off the attack. I want to go find her."

Pushing open the door to the third floor open, Lavisa gave him an unconvinced look. "I don't think *you* going to obtain Ashna is the best plan, given your history of being in love with her and all."

"I-I wasn't in love with her!"

"Either way, Lavisa's right," Tray said, earning a bemused eyebrow raise from her. "Ashna's hostile, and she has too many abilities for any one of us to fight her alone. We should apprehend her as a group—but first, we need to know what Than knows. He could have secrets about the Wackos' fighting tactics that can help us."

"I sense him in his office," Eliana said as they slipped into the corridor. Tray led the group—until Hartman teleported in front of him.

"I'll jump in there and sneak attack him," Hartman whispered, flashing an impish grin before he evaporated from sight. A moment later, a few yelps emanated from the door labeled "T. Floros," and Tray quickened his pace to reach it. Before he grabbed the handle, though, Hartman reappeared beside him, eyes as round as clementines. "You do *not* wanna go in there."

"Yes, we do." Shoving Hartman aside, Tray thrust the door open. He'd expected Than to have abandoned his character of innocence—to be a nasty, snarling Wacko, wielding some deadly weapon. He hadn't expected Than to have Floretta pinned to a wall, the woman's lilac eyes wide with alarm.

Tray's instinct was to react in a defensive form of rage. Gathering the strength of his Affinity, he pointed his finger toward Than and exclaimed, "Get your villainous hands off her, Floros!"

Instead of responding with a wicked smirk, Than's jaw dropped in bafflement. "V-villainous?"

Hartman intercepted Tray's threatening approach by teleporting in front of the Wacko. "No, no, he's not hurting her. They were…*making out.*"

Tray paused, quickly reassessing the situation. Now that he took a moment to truly study them, Than's arms were clearly wrapped around Floretta's waist in a romantic embrace, her face flushed not with fear but with embarrassment.

From the doorway, Lavisa chuckled. "For once, I really wish Adara were here to make fun of you, Stark."

"You two are—" Ackerly began, unable to finish his sentence as he stared at the teachers. Discovering Ashna was a Wacko had certainly infuriated the boy, but to find out his teacher-crush, Floretta, was romantically involved with someone who was literally centuries beyond him appeared to have broken him. "No…*no*…"

"Hey," Hartman said, spinning toward the intertwined adults, "if you two get married, you'll be *Floretta Floros*. Wouldn't that be funny?"

"Her real name isn't Floretta, and that's irrelevant right now," Tray snapped, taking a step closer to the teachers as they scrambled to disentangle themselves. "We know your secret, Floros."

Than's tan face paled considerably as his brown eyes scanned the group of primaries. "How did you find out?"

Tray kept his posture stiff and his chest puffed, mostly to remind himself that, though this man was physically bigger than him, Tray could easily defeat him in a fight. "Our spies found a note in here."

"Ah." Than glanced reminiscently toward his bookcase. "The note from Axelia. You didn't take it, did you? It is quite old and fragile, you can imagine… You were able to translate the ancient Greek, then?"

Slowly rotating his head, Tray found Eliana standing in the doorway, looking as confounded as he felt. "No…" she said warily, "we found a note that *you* wrote…to someone… You mentioned Danny—how you were keeping Ashna's presence here a secret from him for now—until she could complete her mission. We… know you're a Wacko."

Than's eyebrows crinkled in deep rumination, but then realization flickered across his features, as if he'd just remembered his own affiliation. "Oh…that note…yes…"

"So, what is Ashna's mission?" Tray prompted impatiently. "She must have done more than tell Danny about Periculand's secrets, considering that's been *your* job."

"Erm, yes, my job…" Than agreed with an awkward glance

down at his hands. "To tell you the truth, I don't know exactly what Ashna's purpose here has been. All I know is that her whereabouts were to be protected from Daniel's knowledge. If he were to discover her location, he would most certainly come here and execute her, as well as trounce the town—"

"Execute her?" Ackerly repeated. "But…she's his sister!"

"God, I told her not to tell anyone," Floretta sighed, massaging her forehead in exasperation. It wasn't her physical movements that caught Tray's attention, though; it was her unintended confession.

"Than didn't write the letter that Eliana found," he said. "*You* did—and you gave it to him. *You're* the Wacko! You're the one who's been feeding them information—who gave them Hastings's room number and the town's location and—and the one who's helping Ashna with her—"

"Yes, yes." By pulling up the sleeves of her pale purple dress, Floretta displayed the flower tattoos wending up her arms, the ones Tray had seen so many times and had thought nothing of. "These are my Wacko tattoos. I was a Wacko. I fed Ephraim information about Periculand for years. I gave the Wackos Hastings's room number—but that was before I realized Danny had taken charge, before I even knew Ephraim had died. I've defected since then. I don't want any part of them. They're just as much my enemy as they are yours."

"Eliana?" Tray beckoned without glancing back at her.

Floretta's expression mollified, and then Eliana's soft voice said, "She's telling the truth. I can't find any deception, but…you knew she was a Wacko and you were okay with it?"

This question was directed at Than, who exhaled a breath and shook his head. "The Wackos…were not always truly evil. I never joined, and I always sided with Angor against them, but they have saved many Affinities, like they saved Julie." He gestured toward Floretta, who squirmed either at his use of her real name or his mention of her past. "I understand why she chose to join them."

"I was kidnapped at my high school graduation," she explained reluctantly. Tray was tempted not to believe her, but a ghostly quality entered her eyes, unlike he'd ever seen on her typically cheery face. "I was…experimented on for years until the Wackos broke me out. Their morals might be skewed, but I will always be indebted to them. I will always choose them over the Reggs, even with Danny as their leader."

Tray and his friends all exchanged awkward glances—except for Hartman, who had raised his hand as if they were in the middle of class.

"Hold up…" he said, eyes narrowed. "Not to interrupt this depressing backstory, but if Floretta's the Wacko…then what's *your* secret, Than?"

"Oh." The history teacher cleared his throat and straightened his tie. "Well, I've lied to this entire school…about most of my history, in fact. I won't be turning three hundred on my next birthday, as I've led you all to believe. The date might be inaccurate, but if my knowledge is correct, I'll be turning two thousand five hundred and twelve. Roughly."

Tray choked at the unfathomable number. "That means you were born in BC times—that's impossible!"

"Not any more impossible than living to be three hundred. I age one year every one hundred years, rather than one year every ten, as I previously told you. Oh, I have lied to you students about so many things, but no one would believe the things I have seen, the things I have done! For one, I lied about my religion. I've always believed in the Greek gods, because I've witnessed them with my own eyes."

"Okay, so Than might not be a Wack*o* but he's definitely *wack*," Hartman said, and Tray couldn't say he disagreed.

"I also have a degree in philosophy, but I don't like to mention it because modern day humans have twisted many of the details about my old pals—"

"*Pals*?" Ackerly said. "You were *friends* with *philosophers*?"

Tray lightly backhanded his roommate's arm. "Don't promote his insanity. He's just trying to distract us so Floretta doesn't have to expose Ashna's plans."

"If I tell you what she's up to, you'll want to help her," Floretta said without a hint of doubt. "I may have pledged myself to the Affinities for Freedom, but I hold no allegiance to Danny. In truth, I've betrayed him, and if he discovers Ashna's here—if he comes here—he'll kill me as fast as he'll kill her."

"Well, he's on the way, so you'd better stop being ambiguous and just explain the plan."

"Danny—is coming here?" Floretta practically retched the words.

"That is the rumor I've been hearing," a smooth voice chimed in. Then, before he could turn, an orb of water covered Tray's mouth and nose, rendering him breathless. Everyone else in the room soon had a glob of water around their faces as well—except for Nixie, who stood between Eliana and Lavisa in the doorway, hands twirling maliciously.

"This town barely survived three of those Wackos; I doubt we could survive more," she said, entering the room with gradual, calculating steps. "So, if you've betrayed the Wackos, Floretta dear, I assume you'll be the perfect peace offering for them. Let them kill you instead of all of us—a noble sacrifice, wouldn't you say?"

Floretta's expression was nonplussed, but with the water surrounding her mouth, there was nothing she *could* say.

"Come along," Nixie beckoned, retreating into the doorway once more. Lavisa's fists clenched, barely suppressing a punch. "We'll want to meet them at the front gates. And you primies ought to come as well. I've been instructed by the Rosses not to let you out of my sight, just in case you get any wild ideas to free Stromer and Periculy from jail."

Tray tried to speak, allowing water into his mouth, at which he gagged and flailed. Rolling her eyes, Nixie moved the orb of water an inch away from his face. "Make it quick, Stark."

"Calder and Nero," Tray wheezed, hacking up water. "They're in jail, too."

"I *know*," she snapped, smothering his airways with the water once more, "and I don't care. My brother and my boyfriend are idiots. I won't let them stay in jail *forever*, but they at least need to be locked up long enough for me to save this town without any of their stupid help. I don't intend to be Nero's bitch forever. Now, let's move, shall we? Oh, and don't try to fight back. I won't hesitate to drown every one of you."

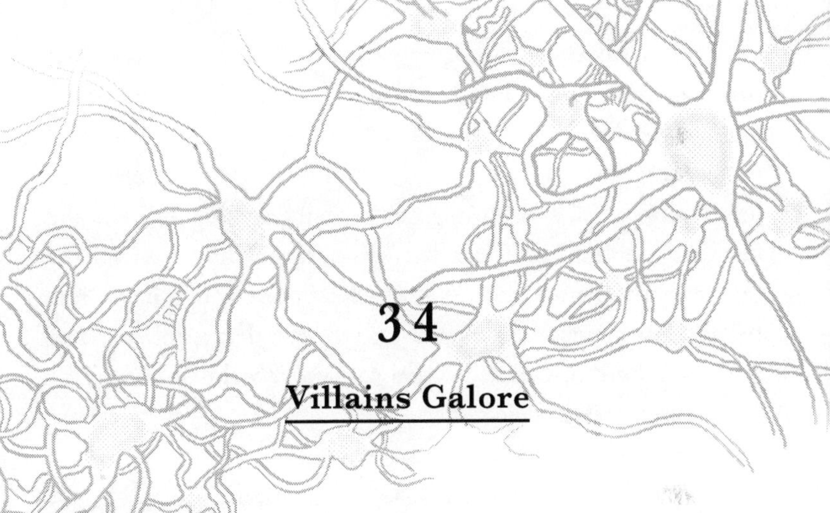

34

Villains Galore

Hours had passed since Angor froze Adara and Mitt in place. Even though she wasn't commanding her muscles, her body ached with soreness from hours of standing, and all she wanted was to drop onto her metal slab and take a glorious nap.

"How is it fair, Majesty, that *you* get to sleep all night and Mitt and I have to stand here like statues?" Adara prompted, not for the first time. The officer's head was tilted as if he'd fallen asleep standing, but Angor, though his eyes were closed, had the audacity to smirk.

"I don't believe it's fair, Adara, but as I've reiterated, the choice is yours."

She gritted her teeth, wishing he could see her venomous scowl. The stubborn side of her never wanted to give up, never wanted to cave to his manipulation, but the lazy side… "Fine. My ears are open. Tell us, exactly, how you can control minds but you're *not* the one who killed Hastings. This should be a real test of your lying abilities."

"Unfortunately"—Angor yawned into a sitting position—"Officer Telum has drifted into the land of dreams, so he will not be able to hear."

"Okay, then screw Mitt and tell *me*. He doesn't deserve to know anyway. *I* do. We're—" Internally cursing herself, she clamped her mouth shut. The small smile that materialized on Angor's lips implied he knew what she'd been about to say: friends. His soft expression reinforced the fact that, somehow, over the past month, Adara had actual come to *like* this strange man, as if he were a fun uncle of hers. She only had to try to move her limbs to know that *fun* had become *evil.*

"Well, spit it out before I make you," she demanded. "I might not be able to move, but I think we all know what happens when someone pisses me off."

With a brief chuckle, Angor stood from his slab and fixed his attention on Mitt. Before Adara could conjure a quip about how creepy he looked, the former principal mentally forced the officer to walk into the front lobby. The movements were so fluid that it almost seemed like Mitt controlled himself—except his head still lolled to the side.

"I'll allow Officer Telum to take a nap on his cot. Is that kind enough for you?" Angor questioned, pink eyebrows perking.

"I think that's the first time anyone's ever asked for *my* judgment on kindness. If I ever see Tray again I'll have to rub it in his face that someone actually values my opinion on morality."

"You'll see the Starks again. I'm not going to kill you, Adara." Sighing, he plopped onto her metal slab and then used his mind controlling powers to walk her over and seat her beside him.

"Ew, this is weird…" Scrunching her nose, she pointedly swiveled her face away from him. "What, are you going to tell me a bedtime story?"

"This would be a rather lame bedtime story," he said, staring at the ground, "considering all of the holes in my mind... I will force you to sit here, but I will not force you to look at me—mostly because I fear that controlling the muscles close to your head will interfere with your brain to a debilitating extent."

"How merciful of you... Okay. Talk. I'll try not to interrupt."

From the corner of her eye, he appeared unconvinced, but he plunged on regardless. "This...ability feels very new to me. I've been practicing over the past few weeks, and I have become quite proficient, but it does not feel like an Affinity I am rediscovering. I don't think I had this Affinity before we were imprisoned—"

"If I was going to interrupt, I'd say it's awfully convenient that you just *happened* to acquire this Affinity after the death that was caused by this Affinity—but I'm not interrupting."

To his credit, Angor actually continued without any hint of annoyance. "Since I lack the proper materials to research, I haven't been able to deduce the full scientific analysis of this ability, but with my previous knowledge, I can conclude that I must have a connection to people's upper motor neurons."

Adara blinked, finally meeting his eyes, just to give him the driest, cheekiest expression she could muster. "Are you *trying* to make me hate you, or are you naturally as irritating as Nerdworm?"

"I can control nerve cells in the brain," he explained patiently. "Nerve cells that can force your muscles to start or stop moving. However, I don't harness the ability to trigger your Affinity. I have tried, I admit, to no avail. When I first discovered that I could force your muscles to move, I feared I had actually been the cause of Hastings's death, but I cannot control minds, Adara, only bodies. If I did command Hastings to kill the Rosses, he used his Affinity of his own volition—which, of course, seems unlikely."

"Mm, an interesting story, Periculy," she hummed, studying

him through slivered eyes. "You could easily be lying about your ability to control minds, though. And your whole, 'I didn't have this Affinity until a few weeks ago' claim sounds like bullshit. You knew your Affinity before the incident. Unless your Affinity changed, you had to have known."

After a long minute of pensiveness, Angor said, "The science of Affinities is not stagnant. We are constantly discovering new knowledge pertaining to the properties of our chromosomes, the range of our powers. Though I have never heard of such a case, it does seem…possible that my Affinity might have morphed during a traumatic situation.

"Let's say, for instance, that my Mental Affinity before was related to nerve cells in some fashion. Then my son, Hastings, finds himself in a predicament where he cannot control his mind, and therefore cannot control his body. In my desperation, I try to coax him to stop what he's doing, but my Affinity doesn't extend that far. Wouldn't a chromosome that exists to adapt to harmful stimuli then give me the ability to control nerve cells in a way that I never had before? Couldn't my Affinity evolve into something greater?"

Adara's lips curled churlishly. "I don't know why you're asking me, man. I have no freakin' clue."

Exhaling, he leaned back against the wall. "It's just something to think about. I have to consider all options at this point, since so much is still unknown to me… Should I expect you to betray me in court tomorrow?"

"I don't think you should expect anything from me ever," she countered, but her hostility quickly withered as she loosed a breath and shook her head. "I won't betray you, okay? If you go down, I'll probably go down with you, whether I want to or not. Being on your side is the only thing I'm certain of in this whole shitstorm. The rest—the Rosses, Nero, the Pixie Prince—"

"Talking about me as usual, Stromer?"

Adara whipped her head—the only mobile part of her body—toward the doorway, through which Calder and Nero now entered. Donning dark sweatshirts and jeans, the duo looked as intimidating as always. The complacent edge to his expression made Adara wonder if he'd come to drown her. On his own he wouldn't have, but with Nero, his morals were not his own.

The boys didn't saunter in with their typical swagger, though; instead, they were constricted by handcuffs.

Adara found it difficult not to let the pure elation swelling in her show—and the pure dread. What would happen at the trial if Nero wasn't there to oppose the Reggs? What would happen if Calder wasn't there to support her? Not that she expected him to, but the prospect of enduring the trial without him—especially if none of her friends were allowed to attend—was daunting.

"We were just making a list of the people we're gonna kill when we win tomorrow's trial." Adara gifted Calder with a maniacal smirk that didn't reflect her conflicted mood. As she spoke, Angor silently released her tensed muscles; she tried not to look surprised as she hopped off the metal slab and stretched out the stiffness. When she peered back in Angor's direction, there was a warning in his eyes. Though she was tempted to divulge his incriminating Affinity to the three new arrivals, she knew Nero would be a potential enemy in court—and Calder might be, too.

"What are *you* doing, Weaponizer?" Adara asked, noting that Mitt, as he escorted the boys, used Nero as a human shield. Upon their arrival, the officer must have awoken from his nap, and though Angor had relented his hold on his muscles, he obviously hadn't forgotten. He now poked his head out from behind Nero's massive body, eyes flashing fearfully, as if the man would start controlling his neurons as soon as Nero wasn't in the way.

"Just—bringing in some new prisoners," Mitt coughed, his hands shaking when he unlocked the cell across the hall.

"Ah, finally," Adara crooned, eyeing the manacles on the boys' wrists like they were delectable donuts. "The day has finally come—or night, technically."

She assumed Calder would be chagrined by this situation, but his demeanor remained fairly mild, a secret smirk on his lips even as he was ushered behind bars.

"You're pretty wet, aren't you, Demoness?" he mused, eyes roving her body, then the puddle in the corner from the fire extinguisher. She should have expected him to notice the water—to sense it or *feel* it. Without control over her body, the warmth of her Affinity had failed to dry it over the past few hours, and so she'd remained soggy and wet, to Calder's delight. "You must have been thinking about me a little too long, hm?"

Nero's jaw clenched at the blatant flirtation, but Adara barked out a laugh, playing it off as meaningless banter even though it roused the embers in her core.

"What'd you two idiots do to get thrown in here? Did the Rosses discover your treacherous plan?"

Nero's eyes narrowed, his big head swiveling toward his cellmate, his ally. "What *plan*?"

For the first time, perhaps ever, Adara wished she had the ability to think before she spoke.

"I don't know, Stromer," Calder said, cool and smooth. "What plan?"

"Seth said I'm indebted to you because he's an idiot," Adara explained as flatly as she could. "I assume this means you don't want me going to federal prison, and therefore wouldn't agree with the Rosses' plot to incriminate me. I am capable of gathering information from people other than Mardurus, you know. Your asshole of an ally doesn't even deign to visit me."

Calder's lips slid upward, perhaps at how easily the lies rolled off her tongue, or perhaps in gratitude for not ratting him out. Or perhaps because he'd been the one to visit her most, and he knew it.

"Ah," Nero said, relaxing into her lie, "you've heard about the debt, then? Oh, do I have plans for you, Stromer—glorious plans. *This* is a bit of a setback, though." Nose twitching in displeasure, he nodded around the cell. "But I'll figure it out."

"Huh. Well, for your sake I hope you do. For *my* sake...I don't really care. Your plans won't interfere with mine." Adara shot a conspiratorial glance back at her cellmate. Angor, of course, was bemused, but she would explain soon.

"I don't think anyone's plans for the trial will matter considering the courthouse will probably be ash in the morning," Calder said. "The Wackos are on their way here as we speak. Turns out Unicorn Fairy's the leader's sister. Your plant friend was pathetically heartbroken. Suppose it won't matter how he feels if Ashna kills him, though."

"Ashna *is* a Wacko?" The revelation opened a dark chamber of vengeance within her. "She *lied* to Greenie? She actually—ha!" Calder blinked his lazy eyes as she erupted into a fit of angry laughter. Ackerly might have been a naive fool, but he was Adara's naive fool, and for someone to have taken advantage of him... "I will devour her like a rainbow sprinkled donut."

Calder's face twisted into about ten different expressions before he finally said, "Sounds entertaining for me."

"There will not be one sprinkle left once I'm done with her—not even a lick of icing."

"I can't tell if she's making death threats or sexual innuendos,"

Nero commented, at which Calder tilted his chin in contemplative agreement.

Mitt's silver eyes popped like coins. "Definitely death threats." Her hands hadn't exploded with flames, but the water logged in her clothes now steamed off her. The Pixie Prince beamed greedily.

"I will *burn* her for hurting Greenie," Adara growled, and she meant it. She hated fire—she hated her Affinity—but she would gladly use it to avenge Ackerly.

"Cool the rage, Stromer," Nero huffed, glowering at her through the bars. "Save it for later—once you're under my authority. I'll make sure your wrath isn't misplaced."

"I think she should keep channeling the anger," Calder said, disregarding his master's bristling incredulity. "Burn us out of here, Stromer. You know you want to."

"No one's burning anything." Mitt gave Adara a hard glare. Normally, it wouldn't have quelled her emotions, but she knew the dangers of her own power—and the dangers of Angor's. In a room with this many volatile Affinities, she knew it was best not to act *too* impulsively, however boring the inaction seemed.

"Nixie will free us," Nero insisted. "She'll come as soon as the Rosses tell her where we are. She knows this town will be doomed without us."

Angor slid off Adara's metal slab and joined her near the bars. Mitt shrunk back as far as he could without leaving the hall completely. "You were serious about the Wackos invading? They're truly on the way? With what purpose?"

"The leader thinks we stole Ashna or something." Calder shrugged. "He seemed pissed about it."

"Daniel's fury is never a positive thing," Angor muttered, stroking his chin as he ruminated. "The boy has a reactive Affinity.

Essentially, he's a bomb. Some say his abilities include nuclear reactions, but I can't recall if that's true…"

Adara's lips pursed. "He's a terrorist with a bomb Affinity? How fitting."

"You can imagine why the Wackos are so revered…" Angor stared between the bars as if he could see the world's mysteries unfolding between the metal. "And Ashna… I can't seem to remember Zacchaeus and Daniel having a sister, but it's quite possible her existence has been blocked with my other memories… So then, Ashna came here with the intention of luring her brother for destructive purposes—why? What does she have against this town? What are her motives?"

"How are we supposed to know?" Nero's aggression wavered slightly at Angor's stern gaze. Adara wondered what the hell the man had done with his weird muscle controlling Affinity to scare *Nero*. "All I know is that we got thrown in jail when the town's about to be attacked because I threw a *party*."

Adara covered the lower half of her face with her hand as she snorted through her nose. "*That's* why you're here? Well, the Rosses are certainly notorious for overreacting. All I did was almost burn a few people to ash and look where they put me. But, hey—how come you never threw parties when I was around? I'd be the life of the party—probably."

Calder's eyebrows shot up. "You've never been to a party?"

"I've never been *invited* to a party, though I have been to several—at Kiki's house, of course. Dumped chili powder into the drinks one time, which was fun."

"I wonder why they all hated you," Mitt mumbled. Adara's temper flared, but she didn't reply before the officer's radio beeped.

"Mitt—we need you out here by the gate," a woman's voice crackled through the speaker. It was probably the security officer,

Ira, who Adara still teased Mitt about on a regular basis. She would have cracked a joke now if the lady didn't sound so frazzled. "I see the Wackos' vans coming. There's gotta be twenty of them—we don't stand a chance. The Rosses are assembling the students, but they look weak, and I doubt any of the families in town will be much help. I tried to get that water girl—Nixie—to gather some of the stronger kids for me, but then she ran off claiming she has an idea to save the town—"

"Breaking me out, obviously," Nero said, mostly to himself, as he stretched his burly shoulders.

"—something about taking all the glory for herself and overthrowing the Rosses? I dunno, Mitt, she sounded insane. I need you over here so I'm not the only level-headed person defending this place." Ira concluded her rant with a hopeful sigh, but it was nearly drowned out by Nero's increasingly vociferous growls.

"I'm on my way," Mitt assured her through the radio before glancing around to his four prisoners, eyes gleaming like silver caskets. "Just don't—" He shook his head. "I'll be back—I hope."

His departure wasn't met with comfort or well wishes, only agitation because he hadn't offered to free them. Angor didn't bother to stop him, though; perhaps the former principal knew there wasn't much time to waste convincing Mitt to help them—or perhaps he knew Periculand was sure to burn if Adara was free to contribute to the chaos. She spat indignantly at the thought.

No one in this room was as enraged as Nero, though.

He seethed and simmered with enough intensity that Calder slipped to the opposite side of the cell to avoid him. When Nero ripped apart his handcuffs, the metal shards blasted in all directions, a few barely missing his ally's eyes.

"Your sister." Chest heaving, Nero towered over Calder, but the Pixie Prince didn't display a hint of fear. Adara quickly realized it was because he already had his defenses in place: His cuffed hands didn't stop him from conjuring water that eddied along the ground, preparing to merge and obstruct Nero's airways if he turned violent.

Adara was sure he would, especially when his hands formed fists the size of footballs. He'd managed to break her nose with minimal effort, and now, at the height of his furor, he would pulverize Calder.

Three months ago, she wouldn't have minded. Nero had punched her; she would have let him punch Calder. Even two months ago she would have rejoiced to see him demolished after he'd nearly drowned her in the training gymnasium.

But now—now she wasn't sure she was ready for Calder to die. She hadn't mocked the Pixie Prince nearly enough for him to leave this world, and he certainly couldn't perish before witnessing her break out of this wretched cell. What would be the point of freedom if she couldn't rub it in his face?

She was ready to do something—she wasn't sure *what* she was ready to do, and interfering with a quarrel between her two rivals seemed to counteract her goals, but she was ready when Nero lifted his fists. Instead of striking Calder with the full brunt of his strength, though, he reeled and slammed into the concrete wall at the back of their cell, plowing through it like a sheet of fabric.

Rubble shattered and dust plumed at the crack of Nero's body colliding with the wall. He tore through it with ease, plunging onward and fleeing through the alley between the police station and the firehouse before Adara could process what had happened.

Coughing and sprawled against the wall in shock, Calder stared at the crumbling doorway to freedom Nero had carved for them. He hadn't looked back to see if his minion followed; he expected it enough not to wonder if Calder would obey his lead.

The Pixie Prince had every reason to leave. Periculand was soon to be under attack by terrorists, and he was one of the few who stood a chance against them. On top of that, he'd just discovered his sister had betrayed him, content to let him waste away in prison while she sieged the town as her own.

He might have been confined in handcuffs, but he'd proven he didn't need any of his extremities to produce a storm. His eyes darted toward the hole, still showering dust and debris, and though Adara had seen it coming, a crevice of vehemence split within her when he marched through it.

"*Don't you dare, Pixie Prince*!" she shrieked, all inhibition abandoned as she launched at the bars of her cell, wrapping her fingers around the electrified metal. In her red haze, she barely felt the current course through her. If anything, it fueled her more, especially as she was zapped backward, her body skidding across the concrete floor, probably giving her another bout of road rash. She welcomed the injuries, because once she was liberated from this cell, those scars would remind her of who her natural enemy was—of who she needed to scorch the life from.

"Don't I dare what, Stromer?" The sly voice snapped her out of her murderous thoughts. Blinking, she finally focused beyond her cell again, where Calder stood, staring down at her with cynical amusement. "Did you think I was gonna leave you here? If you were a normie, I would have, but even I'm not proud enough to deny we need your talents tonight, however *untalented* you are with your Affinity."

"You—you—" She scrambled to her feet as his smirk broadened.

"I don't have an Affinity for walking through walls. I had to go around." He nodded toward the gradually closing door to the lobby, the one he'd walked through to *retrieve* her—to finally release her from this cell.

"I understand that taunting Adara is your favorite hobby," Angor said calmly, "but it would be ideal if you unlocked the gate."

Calder strolled to the electric panel on the wall. "I'm inclined not to let *you* out at all—but you created this town. You deserve to defend it. So, what's the code?"

"The code?" Angor echoed, befuddled.

"To unlock your cell." He glanced over his shoulder quizzically. "Neither of you know?" Adara and Angor exchanged a stupid look that had him rolling his eyes. "Of course, you two are incompetent…" he grumbled as he tampered with the screen, both hands raised because of the cuffs. "I should've just gone with Nero…"

"It's strange that you didn't," Adara pondered aloud. "I thought you were his loyal little dog, Mardurus, but here you are, stealing Nero's slave as your own. Finally decided to snap the leash, did you?"

From this angle, she just barely saw a muscle bulge in his jaw, but he didn't retort.

"The leash comment really gets under your skin, doesn't it?" she observed, pacing across the cell to lean casually against the same wall the control panel rested on. Calder refused to look at her as his eyes glossed over the glowing screen. "Really pollutes your waters, huh?"

Now his eyes slid toward her, eyebrows raised. "I guess that's one way to put it."

Humming, she tapped her fingers on her lips. "I'll remember that for future torture purposes."

His frown intensified as he motioned toward the control panel. "I'm trying to help you escape, if you're unaware."

"True, but I think we all know any alliance we form in here won't last long—and that anything you do for me can't come without a price." Even though she'd been the one to voice the words, she had to force herself to remain nonchalant when a devious little smirk surfaced on Calder's lips.

"Perceptive, Demoness."

"The devil whispers in my ear," she hissed with comedic eeriness. Angor, hovering only a few steps away, shifted uncomfortably, but Calder huffed a humorless laugh. "You weren't going to discuss this bargain with me before freeing me, then?"

"I'm surprised you find me decent enough to give you a choice. Everyone wears a leash, Stromer, even those wild enough to be strays." His blue eyes raked up and down her body, pausing on the burned portions of her shirt. "Someone will pick yours up eventually, and I'd like it to be me."

Adara succumbed to a sour expression. "I'm beginning to see why you don't like the leash comment."

"I don't think anyone likes the leash comment," he said darkly. "You agreed with me before—that freedom is an illusion. Has being *imprisoned* changed your mind?"

"I don't want to leave this cage for another one. Even if it's in your *majestic* company."

Ignoring her jibe, he dropped his hands from the control panel. "Well, luckily for you, you won't be leaving this cell any time soon. I guessed the password wrong so many times it locked me out of the system."

"*What*?" Adara lunged toward the bars but then thought better of it. "I thought you were hacking the system—not just putting in random codes!"

"I'm not a computer whiz." He paused as his eyes illuminated with an idea. Taking a step back from the wall, he lifted his bound hands and snaked a stream of water into the control panel. The screen fizzled and sparked before going black, the ever-present buzzing of the bars dying with it.

Sprinting across the cell, Adara pushed on the gate, but it didn't budge. The control system was down but the cell hadn't unlocked. Fuming, she shook and kicked the bars, as if her meager strength could break the metal.

"I've done my part, Stromer," Calder sang as he waltzed along the outside of the cell. He stopped inches away from her, with only these aggravating bars parting them. "I was hoping to do *all* the work so you'd be eternally indebted to me, but…I have been itching to see you melt your way out of here. And now you have the chance."

His gaze slid from her fingers, growing white from gripping the bars so tightly, to her eyes. She wondered how red they truly were—how demonic she looked now, trapped behind these bars, clutching them like some feral beast.

Where she was a monster of rage, Calder was a monster of mischief, his expression smug as he watched her struggle. A true Pixie Prince. "I never gave you a second chance to take that shower you refused. Now I've handed you a second chance to burn your way out; will you really refuse it?"

"Can't you use your water to unlock it or something?"

Instead of attempting the challenge, Calder took a step closer to the bars, so close she felt his breath on her face—cool, almost cold compared to her natural heat. "Afraid, Stromer?"

She didn't think before grounding out a pathetic, "No."

"You seem afraid—and *weak*," he taunted, his tone slow and deliberate. She was very conscious of the droplet of water now running through the creases of her fingers, emerging on the back of her hand and sliding down her wrist, but she refused to acknowledge it with a look—refused to break his unrelenting gaze. "Maybe that's why none of your friends bothered to come here and free you, even when this town is on the brink of destruction. You're not good enough for them anymore."

"I know what you're doing," she said through gritted teeth. Knowing what he was doing didn't stop it from irking her, though. The heat still rose to the surface, threatening to materialize. That droplet of water steamed, but Calder ensured that new particles appeared, allowing it to climb steadily up her arm. When it slipped beneath the sleeve of her prison garb, she stifled a shudder.

"Is it working?" He flashed a grin, as if he hadn't dug into the most sensitive parts of her heart. She was so focused on ignoring his jabs that she almost didn't notice the little water droplet seep out from the collar of her shirt—and then expand into a spiral that soaked her entirely.

Despite the *no* on Adara's tongue, her answer was very clearly a *yes*. The water he'd drenched her with evaporated, her skin, hair, and clothes drying as quickly as they'd dampened. That he thought he had so much power over her—that he *did* have so much power over her—was frustrating enough to melt the metaphorical cage around her Affinity.

Her hands charred as flames erupted. Instead of worrying about the effects of the blaze, she reveled in the heat, in the dawn of her destructive capabilities—in the sight of Calder stumbling away from the bars. He'd wanted to leash her, but he'd unleashed her, and not even she could harness herself.

Especially when the door to the hallway burst open, presenting her with the person who had led to all this, the person who had recently become the target of her anger. Past the blurry flames climbing up her arms, past those goddamn bars, and past Calder's horror-stricken face, stood Unicorn Fairy. At Adara's vindictive grin, the girl balked, cheeks paling beneath that rainbow curtain of hair.

"What a pleasant surprise," Adara intoned, wrapping her fingers around the bars once more. The metal melted within her grasp, but her fear was as hardened as her skin, her mind as unfeeling as her body had become. "I've been craving a midnight snack."

Eliana hadn't realized how terrified she was of Nero until she'd found herself at the mercy of his crazed girlfriend.

Directly ahead, Nixie walked backward, her hands dancing in the air as she threatened to drown them all. Though her dark blue eyes were identical to Calder's, there was something inherently different about them. Looking into Calder's irises was like squinting up from the depths of the ocean, where warmer, sunnier air awaited; looking into Nixie's irises was like gawking down into the depths of the ocean, where deadly, monstrous creatures festered.

Even though the orbs of water remained over their airways, ready to strike at any moment, Nixie had been gracious enough to permit them each a small breathing hole, which was the only reason none of the primaries had drowned on their trek from the Mentals Building. The only reason Eliana wasn't panicking was because of the various thoughts her friends unintentionally threw her way, Tray's being of the utmost hilarity. He kept fretting over how unreasonable Nixie's fishnet top and miniskirt were in this frigid weather, as if not wearing a coat was the worst crime she'd committed.

Now walking toward the Residence Tower, Nixie led the group with her backward stride while her turquoise-haired friend brought up the rear, smacking a long metal chain on the ground like a whip. Eliana knew her name was Demira, and she also knew the girl wouldn't hesitate to beat any one of them with her metal chain if they retaliated. Ackerly seemed to be her target, as he had been during Nero's Dominion all those weeks ago, and the poor kid had gone from being distraught over Ashna's true identity to being terrified for his life.

"Oh, don't look so glum, Dispus," Nixie said to Lavisa as they approached the Residence Tower. Lavisa's mind swarmed with an assortment of lethal moves she wished to execute, but she masked her defiance with an air of indifference. "Once I save Periculand, the Reggs will surely gift this town to me, and you would make a formidable ally. What do you think, Demira?"

"I think her brother's a useless twat, but I'd take her over the rest of these primies."

Hartman raised his hands, as if they were in a position to ask questions. With a weary exhale, Nixie dropped the orb around his face, drenching his white sweatshirt as he gasped for air.

"What, Corvis?"

"If you're betraying Nero, does that mean we can be friends now? I've always found you attractive in a really scary way, to be honest."

"We're not betraying Nero," she said, almost as if trying to convince herself of the fact. "We're simply proving our worth in this town—our power. I don't want to rule beside Nero as some second-in-command girlfriend—I want to rule as his equal."

"Oh..." Hartman nodded, lips twisting awkwardly. "I take back what I said about the attractiveness, then—totally a joke. I hope we can still be loving stepsibling-in-laws—"

Another mass of water consolidated around his face, choking him as he stumbled forward into Lavisa's back. Eliana wasn't sure if Nixie gave him a breathing hole this time. From the corner of her eye, she spotted the dark gleam in Tray's eyes, an entirely different species than his typically frustrated scowl.

"We suspected Than was a Wacko," Nixie informed them superiorly. "You primies aren't nearly as good at guarding your minds as you'd like us to believe. It wasn't hard for Watkins to discover your suspicions. We told the Rosses, and they even had Fraco investigate, obviously to no avail..."

That was why Fraco went into Than's office the night she and Kiki had. Eliana couldn't decide if she was more embarrassed about the recollection of that night or that the Rosses and their minions had leeched information from them for weeks and she hadn't noticed.

"It was a nice little treat for you primies to uncover that Floretta is a Wacko as well. You two will be the perfect sacrificial offerings," Nixie called to where the teachers trudged along beside one another.

Demira emitted a cackle from behind, but the noise went right through Eliana's ears. Her focus was trained acutely on the front of the Residence Tower, where the Regg ambassadors assembled students in a battle formation. Many of the older teens with powerful Affinities were positioned at the front, while the younger, less aggressive Affinities lingered near the rear. Seth, Naira, Ashna, and Cath were all absent, which wasn't wholly surprising. What really disconcerted Eliana was that Kiki was nowhere to be seen, either.

Their argument seemed so petty now that Eliana thought about it. She shouldn't have taken her grief over Zeela out on Kiki; it wasn't even confirmed that her sister was injured at all. She ached to discuss it with Kiki—to apologize for her absurd outburst—but even though Orla was stationed at the center of the throng, as if she could defeat the Wackos with her good looks alone, the younger Belven was out of Eliana's range of sight and mind.

Eliana, an unpracticed mental voice beckoned, and it took all of her will not to glance in Lavisa's direction. Although she'd accidentally pried through the girl's mind a few times, Lavisa had never intentionally sent thoughts, and her face contorted with the effort. *I'm going to attack Nixie before the Reggs apprehend Floretta. We can't just offer her as a* sacrifice, *even if she used to be a Wacko. Tray and Hartman will help me. I need you to get Ackerly out of the way. I don't like the way that metal-wielder's eyeing him...*

Bowing her head in the slightest nod, Eliana braced herself for action—but then the Rosses noticed them, thwarting Lavisa's assault.

"Ah, Nixie," Artemis greeted pleasantly, leaving her husband to corral the students on his own. "I knew you'd find Stark and his rebellious friends." Her dark gaze bored into each of them with contempt. "I shouldn't be surprised Mr. Terrier opted not to inform Fraco of the impending invasion. You've probably been in league with your little Wacko girlfriend all along, haven't you?"

Ackerly shook his head violently, but when Nixie snapped her fingers, diminishing his airways, he instantly froze.

"I also have Smith and Floros here for you." Nixie gestured grandly toward the teachers. "Both ex-Wackos—perfect bargaining material."

"Wonderful," Artemis cooed, admiring Nixie as if she were her new favorite daughter. For once, Eliana actually wished Nero were here. His girlfriend sucking up to this evil witch and betraying him in the process almost made her sympathize with the big brute. "Let's bring the Wackos toward the gates to meet their old companions. Demira, if you would escort these primaries.

William and I have a special place for them amongst the student army."

Engrossed in their own haughtiness, Artemis and Nixie hadn't noticed Lavisa take a step toward them. As they turned to face the Residence Tower, the yellow-haired girl hooked her foot around Nixie's ankle, tripping her. When the Pixie Princess fell forward, Lavisa's fist was there to greet her with an uppercut to the chin, flinging her body backward.

The orb around Eliana's face dropped, drenching her in water that felt like ice seeping through her clothes with the midnight chill. All her friends had been liberated with Lavisa's expert blows, and while Artemis could only splutter, Demira was actively livid.

Her metal links flew through the air, weaving within the crowd of soaked primaries like a flying snake. Lavisa ducked, avoiding a strike to the throat, but the chain wound back at her again, this time coiling around her wrist and yanking her forward. Lavisa used the momentum to roll on the pavement and then spring at Demira, tackling her to the ground.

Nixie had recovered by now, rubbing her jaw and struggling to adjust her vision as she staggered toward the brawling girls. Extending her hands, she discharged a stream of water, but her aim was awry, slamming Demira instead of Lavisa. The metal chain slipped off Lavisa's wrist, clanking to the ground, as the turquoise-haired girl scrambled to her feet and wiped her wet face.

Using this mishap to her advantage, Lavisa side-kicked Demira in the stomach and then rounded toward Nixie, slapping her hands and kneeing her in the gut. With both girls doubled over and Artemis slipping back toward her husband for protection, Eliana scurried to Ackerly, silently ushering him away.

Not two steps were taken from the scene before his knees buckled and his hands flew to either side of his head as he groaned. His rattled thoughts flowed through her mind a moment before her eyes registered what was happening: Demira, though wounded, used her Affinity to bend the metal of his glasses inward, pressing on the sides of his head and piercing his temples.

Eliana instantly whirled around. Nixie and Lavisa fought fist to fist, the former using spurts of water to her advantage while the latter used her unnatural agility and speed. This left Demira unattended, teal eyes sparkling with malice at her target, unaware of the primary who proceeded to deck her from behind.

With Ackerly moaning and bleeding beside her, Eliana didn't have time to watch Tray and Demira wrestle. Based on her yelps and his constant worries over accidentally killing the girl, he would have no problem winning this fight. Instead, Eliana propped Ackerly up with her arms, examining the holes that the sharply bowed metal of his glasses had produced. Blood trickled down his face, mixing with the remnants of Nixie's water and dripping off his chin.

"I-I'm afraid to take the glasses off," Eliana admitted, wincing apologetically when his weary green eyes peeked over at her. "I don't want to make it worse."

"Let me help him," Floretta said as she and Than approached. Lavisa now had Nixie in a headlock, but Nixie had Lavisa's whole head encased in water, and Tray had Demira pinned to the ground, but Demira had her chain looped tightly around Tray's throat. The only reason both duels hadn't come to a stalemate was because Hartman teleported around rapidly, kicking and punching the secondary girls with an "Ah—sorry!" every time. They grunted as their Affinities waned, neither able to counteract Hartman's attacks with his unpredictable disappearances.

Artemis, Eliana realized, had vanished entirely. She wasn't even by her husband and the army of students. If Artemis had a mind controlling Affinity, why hadn't she interfered with Lavisa's outburst? Was she saving her strength for the Wackos, or had they been wrong about her abilities?

"This isn't the first time we've had an incident like this," Floretta grumbled as she carefully pried Ackerly's glasses from his face. Once they'd been removed, she shot a scowl in Demira's direction. The girl had finally been subdued, her aqua hair splayed around her dazed face like a blanket of exotic waters. Tray stood above her, huffing and rubbing his throat, which bloomed with bruises from the force of her metal chain.

"Probably why she's been eyeing me with bloodlust for weeks," Ackerly mumbled, bringing his fingers to his bleeding forehead and grimacing. "Not a lot of people have glasses for her to bend like that..."

Panting, Tray ambled over to them, and Lavisa and Hartman appeared a moment later, having teleported from somewhere. When Eliana glanced beyond them, Demira and Nixie were gone.

"Teleported them up to their room," Hartman assured her with a wink. "They'll have a nice, long slumber in their beds while the rest of us fight the terrorists."

Sensing Eliana's puzzlement, Tray sent her a fuzzy mental recap of Hartman "sorry"-punching Nixie and then Lavisa elbowing her face in a way that stole her consciousness.

"I don't want any of you to have to fight the Wackos." Floretta's lavender eyes flashed worriedly at the assembling students. "If I thought Danny would actually give up, I'd sacrifice myself to them, but...he won't relent until he has Ashna."

Even though he was half-blind, Eliana felt Ackerly plotting how he could find Ashna—how he could betray her in the same way she'd betrayed him.

"We need to find Ashna, then," Tray concluded, ignoring Floretta's look of protest. "Eliana, do you sense her anywhere?"

Eliana closed her eyes, probing the area for any signs of the glittering, rainbow wall that characterized Ashna's mind. As she expanded the range of her search, though, she was met with the harrowing reality of their predicament, the sheer mass of it.

"The Wackos—they're almost here. I-I feel them—so many—"

"They're here already?" Tray demanded, scanning the gates beyond the Naturals Building. When Eliana followed his gaze, she was met with the physical sight of what her Affinity had sensed: lights materializing in the distance, a constellation far brighter than the stars.

"Danny's never been one to follow traffic laws. He always has liked to speed… We need to buy some time," Floretta said, marching toward the gates. Tray was at her heels, and Eliana followed with her friends, passing the gathered students and horror-struck William. He'd noticed the bright white death sentence, growing closer by the second, and his thoughts were plainly panicked. There was no trace of the man who had preached about how easily Periculand could defeat the Wackos.

"Danny won't back down," Floretta said as they passed the Naturals Building. The Regg soldiers formed a defensive wall behind the gate while the security officer, Ira Wright, barked orders to them from her post atop the fence. "He has an…*explosive* Affinity, and he thrives off its use. But if we can distract him long enough for Ashna to get into position, we might stand a chance."

"We aren't letting Ashna complete her mission," Tray retorted stubbornly. Eliana understood his distrust, but if the girl wanted to thwart her brother and save Periculand, shouldn't they let her? Adamant in his caution, Tray added, "I don't trust any of you Wackos."

"This is the only way," Floretta said in her teacher's voice. Tray was taller than her, but the reproach of an authority figure shrunk him to the size of a boy. "You have to trust us. We won't let Periculand burn."

Right after the words left her mouth, an explosion rocked the earth, throwing them asunder. Tray, Lavisa, and Floretta maintained their balance, but Eliana toppled over, her head, thankfully, collapsing on Than's torso instead of the pavement. As the man politely assisted her into an upright position, Eliana saw an inferno had consumed the front gate of Periculand, knocking many of the soldiers to the ground. It blazed three stories high, and none of the Reggs' extinguishers came close to quenching it.

"We really shouldn't have knocked out Nixie," Hartman said after teleporting to Eliana's side. He must have instinctively disappeared at the shock of the explosion, but now he was here, reaching down to help her up.

She examined the scene of destruction, so heart-wrenchingly similar to the drawing she'd involuntarily scribbled. Reggs were strewn dead on the ground, and the young Affinities would be next. *They* would be next. Even once Eliana was fully upright, she couldn't stop herself from clenching tightly to Hartman's hand.

As the smoke and flames began to decrease, Lavisa and Tray assumed defensive positions. It was impossible to tell how close the vans were now, and Ira's station above the fence had been destroyed, the poor woman either lying dead or severely injured in the grass. Tears rose in Eliana's eyes, not just with her own emotions but also with the sorrow and dread that seeped from every soul around her.

The only relief from the heavily negative ambience was an increasingly palpable sense of giddiness, foreign to her mind and inappropriate for this situation. Its origin emerged from within the crackling fire: a man clothed in sleek black leather, his hair waving over his head with the same intensity as the conflagration at his back.

The mere sight of him caused Eliana's knees buckled, and she had to cling to quivering Hartman for support.

His mind was as chaotic as the destruction he'd left in his wake. His eyes were two glowing orbs, full of wicked delight. His grin was even more terrifying than Nero's—even more terrifying than Artemis's or Angor's or even *Adara's*. He was worse than anything she'd ever drawn, and she had a feeling that if she tried to depict him on a page her hand would go straight to hell.

This was Danny. This was the Wacko leader. This was the man—the *young* man—who had extinguished lives with his explosive Affinity for the past few years.

"I know what you're thinking," he drawled, swaggering toward them, head held high. He was barely taller than Tray, barely taller than Floretta, but he exuded such might and authority that Eliana almost felt inclined to bow. "'Why didn't Danny incinerate this whole town with one flick of his finger?' Or, 'Why aren't we withering from nuclear radiation?'

"Well, I won't get into the specifics of it, but there *are* people I care about in this town, albeit few. I *could* eviscerate this entire town, and I *could* expose you all to nuclear radiation—I could bathe this whole world in it. But that isn't my goal—no, no. Not unless you force it to be."

He stalked closer, stopping once his face was clear to them and theirs to him. Eliana tried her hardest to remain still and confident, even when his blazing eyes studied her with intrigue. They were more beautiful than any piece of art—and far, far more deadly.

"But, I suppose my decisions rest in your hands now," Danny mused, his gaze finally settling on the ex-Wacko, "my lovely Floretta."

35

Wacko Attacko Pt. 2

"I'm not understanding why we have to make out *hhhere*," Seth slurred as he followed Naira through the empty streets of Periculand. He wasn't *that* drunk. He'd only drank Ashna's magical alcohol nonstop for the past…three hours…or maybe four…

Regardless, he was a big boy; he could handle a little poison, even if it made his head pound and his legs wobble and his sight blur when he tried to glance over at Naira's luscious bronze hair. She was like a rosy princess with those furrowed pinkish eyebrows and worried peachy eyes. Her princess dress might have been Seth's dead roommate's t-shirt and cargo pants, but she could make anything look beautiful.

Beautiful? When had he started thinking Naira was beautiful? When had he started thinking *anyone* was *beautiful*? He'd always considered Kiki "hot" and even Adara—his sister—wasn't bad to look at, but neither was *beautiful* in his eyes.

Maybe it was his inebriated state of mind, or maybe it was

her enticing nature—the open but mysterious way about her. Naira had proven to possess a much deeper personality than Kiki; in the past week he'd known her, he felt like he'd learned a new component of her character every moment. While his ex-girlfriend only liked popularity and prettiness, Naira liked volleyball and bacon and karaoke and sleeping without her pants on and reading comic books and—and, well, a lot of other stuff. They hadn't talked about anything personal, of course; he didn't know anything about her childhood or her family or what her life goals were, but he knew she was capable of tackling him in training, and for that he was certain he adored her—in a "you're a stranger but we should be friends" kind of way.

Although, based on the fact that she currently held his hand, guiding him to a secluded alley in town, maybe it was more of a "you're a stranger but we should date" kind of way.

He was probably moving too fast, though; Naira *had* whispered some rather seductive words in his ear after the Rosses broke up the party, and she *had* made it clear this venture was of the physically frisky kind, but they were barely acquaintances. Seth definitely didn't have a *problem* with a casual hookup, but part of him had always wanted a *real* relationship, one rooted deeper than physical attraction. He wanted someone who would join him in his stupidity but then also listen seriously to his problems—and someone who he could do the same for in return.

Kiki hadn't been that type of person. And Adara—not that he'd ever seriously considered *dating* Adara, but…she would easily engage in his stupidity but never put herself in a position vulnerable enough to be emotionally intimate. Even when she was irked she would never say *why*, and perhaps that remoteness was the only reason he'd never bothered to think of her as anything *more*.

Rambling drunken thoughts aside, Seth was intrigued to see

where his excursion with Naira would lead. He just couldn't determine why, exactly, she'd chosen to stop them in the road beside Periculand's police station.

"Well, we couldn't go up to our dorm," she said, pushing him lightly against the white concrete building. His senses were duller than usual, but he really liked the way her hair glistened in the rays of the streetlight on the corner, even if it was a bit blinding. He also felt as though he should have been aware of something… like the fact that Adara was probably directly on the other side of this wall, but—no, that couldn't have meant anything.

"The Rosses are bound to sweep the entire tower once they're done punishing Nero." Naira twirled a finger though his unkempt hair. "I think we've both been drinking a bit too much to pass a sobriety test."

"Oh…true…" His sight swam in and out of focus, trying to hone in on her face and the cloudy night sky all at once. Pale freckles dotted her cheeks, and there were a few flecks of brown in her irises, remnants of their former, darker color. "So…are you gonna kiss me?"

Any enthusiasm lingering on her face dwindled into uncertainty as she stroked her hand along his jaw. "I should…but I don't know if I want to."

His brow wrinkled as he shifted his back against the wall. "Oh…I—"

"No, I don't mean that." Bristling slightly, she disentangled her hands from his head. "I *do* want to… I just want it to be real."

"I-I-I can sober up." Seth blinked rapidly, as if the alcohol in his system could simply excrete from his eyeballs. "I want it to be real, too."

"No, it—wouldn't matter if you were sober, Seth." With a

sigh, she raked a hand through her hair. "I would have to kiss you like this either way."

His absolute confusion slowly cleared the haziness of his mind. He was suddenly very conscious of how close her body was to his, of the glimmer of remorse in her eyes. She appeared far too lucid for someone who'd drunk the night away alongside him. He wracked his brain, attempting to remember if she'd *actually* guzzled down drinks or if he'd simply assumed she had.

"Why…do you *have* to kiss me?"

Exhaling again, she stepped back and glanced above his head to where a small, barred window resided: the window to Adara's cell. "I guess if I tell you now you won't remember tomorrow anyway…"

"Tell me what?" he asked, straightening with apprehension.

Guiltily, she peeked over at him and bit her lip. "That I've been lying to you for the past eight days."

"A-about everything?"

"No, no, not about everything. Most of it was real, but…I was never a prisoner of the Wackos, Seth. I…*am* a Wacko. I'll always be a Wacko, just not in the way you think."

"You're…a Wacko…" he repeated quietly, his brain feeling mushy again. He stumbled forward with the shock of it, and she swiftly grabbed his shoulders to prop him upright.

"Seth." She moved her head into his line of sight. "I'm not evil, I swear. I want us to be on the same side. I want us to be friends. I was starting to think we were—or that we could be."

"You're a *Wack—*" A series of explosions overpowered his voice. One originated near Periculand's front gate, and when Seth staggered away from the police station, he saw plumes of smoke wafting into the night sky, illuminated by a bright source of light beyond the shops.

The other had been the reason he staggered away from the police station—the reason the ground had shaken beneath his feet. *Something* had erupted on the opposite side of the police station, and when Seth peered out onto Periculand's main street, he witnessed a hulking figure sprinting away from town toward campus. Even from this distance, he distinguished students, congregating at the base of the Residence Tower. While it could have been part of the Rosses' punishment, Seth had a horrible feeling it was related to something much more dire.

"Balls," Naira swore, her face wrought with alarm as she hopped on her toes to see what might have befallen the front entrance of the town. "Ashna knew her tracking device reactivated, but I didn't think they'd get here so fast."

"*Who*?" Seth demanded, whirling around to face her and then nearly toppling to the ground.

"The Wackos."

"But—aren't *you* a Wacko? Shouldn't you be—I dunno—*happy*?"

"No," Naira said gravely, shaking her head at the billowing smoke. "I don't think I can ever really be happy, not when Danny's breathing."

"Danny…the Wacko leader!"

"Hopefully not for long," she muttered with a glance toward the police station. "C'mon. If the Wackos are invading, I think this town's gonna need your super strength."

Succumbing to emotions was a rare occurrence for Tray, but with the Wacko leader standing two feet in front of him, it was impossible to suppress the terror permeating his thoughts. Never had he imagined there was a person more demonic than Adara Stromer.

Then again, Tray wasn't known for his imagination; he was known for his dedication to facts, and he was currently drowning in the fact that Danny was about to incinerate them all.

With the conflagration blazing at the town's entrance, Tray wished his Affinity-enhancing suit hadn't inhibited Nixie's water from seeping onto his skin. He needed something to cool his flesh; he needed something to physically quench his mental turmoil. His brain was such a mess that he could barely comprehend why Danny had addressed Floretta almost romantically—or possessively.

"So, my darling Floretta," he prompted, those fiery eyes trained on the woman to Tray's left. "You've been neglecting my messages. Now you have no choice but to answer my inquiries. Where is my traitorous pet you've been hiding from me?"

"Darling?" Hartman piped up. Tray was too wary of Danny to glance back, but the teleporter was close enough for him to feel his vibrations. "*Lovely*? Where's Ackerly? He'd be so jealous right now."

Tray was about to scour the scene for Ackerly, who had mysteriously disappeared, but then he noticed the briefest bit of panic settle in Danny's eyes when they landed on Hartman. It vanished as quickly as it had appeared, leaving Tray to wonder if something horrific arose behind him.

"You're right—perhaps I shouldn't be so affectionate toward someone so weak." Danny's nose twitched disdainfully in Floretta's direction. "Julie, Julie, Julie… Abandoning the most intimidating organization in the world for *this* place. You're only as strong as your leader, and if I'm not mistaken, Periculy's still in jail—his own jail, that he built!" He barked out a laugh. "Pathetic. And now you're going to die defending my little sister… If you cared for her so, I don't see why you would have ditched her in the first place. Oh, the poor girl was so distraught when her beloved Floretta left. Cried about it for *months*—"

"We'll give you Ashna," Tray interjected, causing Danny's face to morph into a sickeningly befuddled expression. "We just need to figure out where she is."

The man studied him thoroughly, a sadistic grin inching onto his lips. "Tray Stark. Well, if this isn't a pleasant surprise. This is going to be more enjoyable than I thought."

It took all of Tray's effort to keep his jaw from dropping. Unfathomably, the Wacko leader knew his name.

The information he'd learned from Officer Telum flashed in his head—that his parents were wanted by the Wackos and had, perhaps, been taken by the Wackos. Then the pieces slipped into place: Danny had either captured or killed his parents—and the twins would be next.

His muscles constricted, attempting to contain the physical symptoms of anger swelling within him. All he could think of was how satisfying it would be to crush this man's skull with his fist. Danny could explode matter with his Affinity, but there was nothing he could do if Tray decided to crush his head between his fingers.

Self-disgust swiftly nullified that fantasy. Where was this viciousness *coming* from? Since when did Tray consider defeating people physically rather than with knowledge? Either way, he was sure he could have beaten Danny in a duel, but…he had to compose himself. He couldn't risk dying just because he was unreasonably hormonal.

"I think," Tray finally said, snuffing his rage and attempting to remain diplomatic, "I saw Ashna sneaking toward the center of town."

He nodded toward the heart of Periculand, and Danny surveyed the landscape without any indication that he'd detected the lie. Other than the police station, the shops would be mostly empty tonight, and if Tray could lead the Wackos away from campus, maybe the Rosses could actually formulate a decent strategy on how to save this town from demolition.

"Interesting." Stroking his chin, he studied Tray. "Your parents have been so *difficult*, but you—you're compliant. I certainly wasn't expecting to *like* you. Perhaps my ideas for your future will have to be rearranged…"

Tray wasn't sure what to make of this, but he felt his friends' unease, mirror to his own unease.

"All right"—Danny snapped his fingers, creating a thin tunnel in the inferno behind him—"since you're all being so obedient, here's how it's going to go: Tray Stark will escort me into town, where we'll apprehend Ashna. You'll give her a bit of a beating with your super strength"—his eyebrows jumped, and Tray fought to keep his expression neutral—"and then you'll accompany us when we leave with her. I'd also like…you," he said to Lavisa, who stiffened with animosity. "I have no idea who you are, but you look like you'd readily eat me alive, and I enjoy that kind of—"

"Have you found willing recruits, or are you bullying these children into joining us?"

Tray had definitely heard that voice before, and when the woman stepped on Danny's right, he realized where: This was the Wacko Periculand had detained a few months ago, the one Avner and his friends had fled with. That she was here now could only mean Adara's brother succeeded with his mission…or he was dead.

"These children don't know what they want, Naretha. I have to *tell* them they want to join us, not force them into it. The desire's already there; I'm simply bringing it into the light."

Another figure stepped beside Danny, and Tray almost

jumped into a fighting stance at the sight. Although he'd never seen this Wacko with his own eyes, the others had told him of the guy who'd knocked out numerous students with his sleep-inducing Affinity during the first Wacko infiltration. His midnight black and electric blue eyes were unmistakably the same as the ones Eliana had described, and if Tray couldn't remain in Danny's favor, he'd be passed out on the pavement in a matter of seconds.

"Ah, I forgot you've all been acquainted with Naretha and Josh, my most trusted allies." Danny motioned between the two Wackos. Both remained stony, though Tray did notice their scowls when they peered at each other. "It is a shame Periculand didn't get along better with them during their last visit…but, the past *can* be forgiven, can't it, Floretta?"

Naretha started at that, her head whipping toward the woman she hadn't deigned to look at before. Her pale eyes narrowed as they soaked in Floretta's appearance. "Guess I shouldn't be surprised to see you, Smith. I'm only surprised you're in Danny's presence and still breathing."

"Let's not be hostile, darling," the Wacko leader chided with a patronizing smirk.

"*Another* darling?" Hartman asked. "How many darlings do you *have*?"

"As many as I please," Danny dismissed without bothering to glance in the boy's direction. "Now, let's get back to business. I have no interest in returning here if I don't have to, so I want to make sure I kill everyone I want to kill while I'm here. The list includes: Angor Periculy, Mitt Telum, Artemis and William Ro—oh—oh, would you look at this."

Pivoting, Tray followed the man's suddenly intrigued gaze toward the Naturals Building, beside which a horde of students approached.

"William appears to be coming right to me! This makes things *far* less complicated. Naretha, dear, if you would go secure Telum for me—perhaps preserve Periculy in a casket of salt while you're at it. I'll meet you at the police station as soon as I've caused a little—"

"Don't attack them," Eliana pleaded, breaking through Tray and Floretta to address Danny directly. "They—they're just kids. We'll find Ashna—I think I already know where she is."

"Hm," Danny hummed mock pensively. "No. You're interrupting my fun, and I don't like to be interrupted."

With that, the ground beneath Eliana's feet erupted, launching her, Floretta, and Tray in opposite directions. Tray's initial alarm over the females' safety was quenched the moment his shoulder collided with the unforgiving pavement, his head crashing down immediately after.

Ears ringing and body aching, he pushed off the ground and blinked around. Eliana lay not far from him, equally as dazed, but Danny had moved past them, strolling toward the student army like they were his old friends. Josh followed, but Naretha stalked through the grass toward the center of town, disregarding the destruction her leader was about to engage in.

"Naretha, acquire my targets," he called after her, his tone cool despite the heat wafting from the crater he'd exploded in the ground. "And if you see Ashna, I want her alive. Josh, summon the others. We're going to feast on violence tonight."

While Tray struggled to sit up, a series of booms overpowered his groans. Danny, as he strolled toward the students, blew up small chunks of earth as if land mines riddled Periculand's soil. None of the students stood directly above these explosions, but many screamed and retreated, leaving William frazzled as he barked orders for the lines to reform.

After only five minutes of knowing the Wacko leader, Tray understood Danny was merely tantalizing them. He could have turned this whole town into a crater in a matter of seconds if he wished, and he probably would once the thrill of their fear waned. Tray had tried to be passive, helpful, reasonable, but there was no way to rationalize with irrational people.

Warding off the pain that creaked through his limbs, he stood and faced Danny. The Wacko leader's back was to him, but that was his advantage. He'd succumbed to his fear before; now it was time to succumb to his rage.

Utter control over his body had been a foreign concept to him months ago, but he'd practiced. He made enough of a show in training of being peeved and uninterested that his friends didn't know it, but he'd worked to harness his Affinity, infusing his brain with movement patterns that would inflict damage. The suit he wore must have had some type of compressive or adhesive properties because he felt the ease of his blood flow and the suppleness of his muscles, enhancing his Affinity, as promised.

Ignoring fallen Eliana, quivering Hartman, and riotous Lavisa, Tray assumed an athletic stance. Then he surrendered himself to the instinctive impulses of his amygdala.

The "fight or flight" response was a psychological reaction Tray had learned about but had rarely experienced. He had felt anger threatening to overcome his brain before—when he had first discovered his super strength or whenever Adara said something particularly idiotic or even five minutes ago when he'd remembered what Danny had done to his parents—but he had never allowed those hormones to manifest.

Now the buildup of chemicals had finally overflowed, resulting in a surge of energy that Tray used to launch forward and tackle Danny from behind.

Surprised, the Wacko leader lurched toward the ground, the two of them rolling and grappling. Tray was stronger, but Danny was a natural fighter—and a bomb. In a fist-to-fist fight, Tray would have won, but as they wrestled on the pavement, the Wacko used his explosive Affinity to throw a detonating pulse off his own skin. No amount of super strength could combat a blast of that magnitude. It hurled Tray through the air until he tumbled along the pavement, his sight discombobulated and his brain wrecked.

The adrenaline pumping within him blocked the pain of the impact, but there was no point in challenging Danny again. He expected it now, and Tray stood no chance against him anyway. The leader would murder half the town, and there was nothing Tray could do about it. This fate was confirmed when, through the gate of flames, a horde of Wackos appeared, all dressed in black, all promising death.

"Stark, can you stand?" Lavisa asked, hovering above him. Squinting, he saw the outline of her yellow hair, illuminated in the reflection of the fire. "They're coming in hot, and I don't think I can hold off more than a few at a time."

"I'll help," Floretta offered as she staggered to her feet. Soot and dirt now covered her pale purple dress. Tray hadn't thought about how disheveled he probably looked, and when he peered down he found half of his sweater burnt off. The white suit beneath was unscathed, and although it was clearly visible to Lavisa, she made no comment on it. Perhaps she *had* felt it when she'd patted his shoulder earlier.

"Where did Danny go?" Tray asked, eyes darting around the scene. William had withdrawn back toward the tower, while Josh knocked out fleeing students at random. Even among the array of oddly-colored hair, Danny's stuck out, and it was apparent his destination was the Physicals Building, where many of the students had retreated.

"Tray," Eliana moaned, crawling across the ground toward him. Blood stained her left calf, but she moved swift enough that he knew she hadn't been seriously wounded. "In my drawing—the Physicals Building—he's going to demolish it—"

At her words, Tray recalled her depiction of this very battle, how fire had been speckled throughout the campus, but the Physicals Building burned the brightest. The image hadn't shown the abundance of hiding students who would now burn in it.

"Lavisa, try to hold off the horde with Floretta and Than," Tray commanded, and though the teachers looked wary, she nodded without question. After extending to his feet, he reached a hand down toward Eliana. "Can you stand?"

Nodding, she took his assistance and pushed upright, clearly favoring her right side. "We need to distract Danny long enough to get the students out. It's inevitable that it'll blow, but if we can save—"

"I'll go warn them," Hartman announced, and before anyone could protest, the teleporter disappeared from sight. Worry flickered on Lavisa's face, but she focused on tightening her hand wraps, honing her vision on the approaching enemy, soon to be upon them.

Tray knew he had to thwart Danny again—he had to sacrifice himself, even if it resulted in a worse reaction than last time. He and Eliana should have sprinted across campus to intercept him—not that Eliana could exactly *sprint* in her condition—but Tray hesitated a moment, suddenly more concerned about Lavisa's well-being than that of all the students.

Logically, it made sense, he supposed. Lavisa, though disagreeable, was a more influential acquaintance to him than most students here. But for him to place her life—one life—over the lives of tens, perhaps hundreds of others, was foolish and unreasonable. He *had* to abandon her here at the front lines, and he didn't have time to be emotional about it.

"Stay with her," Eliana urged, obviously having read his mind. He chided himself for being so open, but now wasn't the time to practice mental shields. The first aggressive Wacko had just come into contact with Lavisa, and Floretta advanced on them with thick, flowered vines while Than combated with intense martial arts. "I'll find a way to distract Danny. You're needed here—"

Her pleading was useless, though. There was no point in leaving the front lines now, for Danny had already staged his grandest explosion. The right half of the Physicals Building erupted, burgeoning with flames and smoke, spitting concrete and rubble. From a distance, Tray saw many students had managed to escape in time, likely with Hartman's warning.

But…the teleporter hadn't returned to them, and his head of bright orange hair was nowhere in sight. Based on Tray's conclusions and the despair morphing Eliana's face, they both knew where Hartman Corvis was—or where he had been.

After leaving Headquarters a little later than planned, Naretha, Jamad, and Danny's freaking *dog* had caught up with the rest of the Wackos at the site of an abandoned building in the outskirts of Cleveland—or what had been an abandoned building until Danny, in his frenzied anticipation, leveled it.

The media had probably already exaggerated it out of proportion, claiming he'd killed hundreds of innocents when he'd only murdered a decaying heap of rubble. He'd built up so much excitement and aggression that if he hadn't let it loose there, he would have demolished their own vans on the drive to Periculand in the same way he demolished the school now.

As she jogged toward the center of town, Naretha heard the periodic booms of his destruction and saw the reflection of the flames alighting the white buildings of Periculand. They should have recruited these kids, not physically and mentally scarred them to the point of uselessness. Most of them hadn't chosen Periculand. Most of them had been brainwashed into thinking the Wackos were purely evil. With the way Danny acted, Naretha couldn't blame them for believing it.

Considering the Wackos' morality reminded her of the not-so-pleasant interaction that had occurred two hours prior. It was hard to forget her little skirmish with Zach since her black uniform was still coated in his dust, a reminder that he'd abandoned the Wackos—that he'd chosen *Faddy* over her.

She should have seen it coming. Danny had been unnecessarily rude to his brother during the little conference in his office before their departure. Not to mention Danny had rubbed his leadership in his older brother's face for months. Naretha's prolonged absence from Headquarters had probably made Zach question why he stuck around at all.

Or perhaps it had been his father's death and his sister's disappearance. There was no reason for Naretha to fool herself into believing Zach still cared about her existence, not when he'd made it painfully clear he didn't.

She'd had the entire van ride to let the indignation fester, but the worst part was that she couldn't feel truly vehement about it. To say she'd *hoped* Faddy would break Sparky out of his cell would've been an exaggeration, but Naretha had left the girl behind knowing she would at least attempt it. Despite her efforts to vouch for Avner, Danny had ultimately decided not to give him the option of freedom, and it would have been vindictively hilarious to see her leader's reaction to the kid's empty cell upon their return.

Of course, that fantasy of hers involved a few deadly consequences, such as the entire complex exploding with his fury—or with a Regg attack.

If only Avner and Maddy had escaped, Naretha wouldn't have been too concerned. They could have divulged the location of Headquarters, but there were still so many other hideouts throughout the country, so many Wackos that would have been unaffected. Ephraim, despite his aversion to technology, had implanted a kill switch in the compound; if the Reggs infiltrated, the place would blow as if Danny had erupted it himself, erasing all information regarding the organization. The Reggs wouldn't have been able to truly infest the Wackos with just Avner and Maddy.

But with Zach, they would.

Zach knew every facet of the Wackos—every facet of Danny and even Naretha. If he wanted the government to quash the Wackos, they would succeed. That was what worried her most, even as she trekked through a foreign town to confront one of the most powerful Affinities alive. Ashna had escaped Headquarters and she hadn't compromised it, but with Avner's influence, Naretha had no doubt that Zach would.

With their leader's current attitude, perhaps he deserved to be defeated. Naretha would never side with the Reggs, but standing beside Danny's ethics became increasingly more difficult. Part of her wanted to run back to campus and intercept him, but she knew the swiftest way to end this bloodshed would be to detain Ashna. The girl had led them here; if her life was forfeited for the sake of these innocent Affinity kids, Naretha would feel no sympathy.

When she emerged from the wooded area onto the pavement, a massive figure zipped past, headed for the school. She didn't pause to really study him, but with his dark hair and unnaturally immense form, it must have been Nero, the asshole who had played a part in her capture here—which had led to the research facility and the torture and the nightmares that now plagued her sleep. It was tempting to clog his airways with salt, but…she would come back for him later.

Even if she hadn't been a prisoner here before, finding the police station would have been a simple task. It sat on Periculand's main road, tucked beside the considerably larger firehouse. As she approached, she noticed a giant hole had been carved into the left wall—and not neatly. Almost as if something had barged through the concrete…

Brow furrowed curiously, she meant to look back toward fleeing Nero, but then her eyes caught onto an equally enormous person huddled beside the police station's entrance.

At first, she was convinced it was a hallucination, her mind cruelly showing her what she desired most. But Cath Clemens really stood there, staring at her with those big, green, tear-filled eyes. As usual, the clothes she wore were a bit too tight for her thick limbs, and after not seeing her for so many weeks, Naretha was stricken by how much this girl had grown since they'd first met eight years ago. Even through the intimidating exterior, the same gentleness of her youth radiated, her motions cautious and timid as she stepped forward.

The urge to hug her nearly clouded Naretha's judgment—nearly made her forget all the ways in which Cath had betrayed her. Then her gaze drifted to the police station she'd been trapped in for a month, and she was reminded of the hellish weeks that had ensued, the blame for which could rooted back to Josh…and Cath.

"Don't come any closer," Naretha warned, hating herself as the words flowed from her mouth. Cath heeded them instantly, planting herself on the pavement a few feet away.

"Na-Naretha?"

"Am I hard to recognize with the haircut?" She meant to sneer it, but the poison in her tone was weak.

"Y-you're alive. I thought you were…" Trailing off, Cath stared down at her feet. "I didn't want to leave you here, but Josh made me. I…didn't want to get in trouble. When Ashna said she was coming here, I knew I had to come back to save you…but you weren't here."

Danny hadn't told Cath that Naretha escaped Periculand? He'd made it abundantly clear that he'd expected her to return, but he hadn't informed *Cath*, who he knew would be the most distraught over Naretha's absence. Her rage was aimed at a new target now, a target at which she would never be able to shoot.

"I made it back to Headquarters, but *you* weren't there. You abandoned us to join Ashna on her little *quest*."

"I did it for you!"

"Stop—*stop*," Naretha commanded, unable to meet the girl's eyes as she held up her hand. Cath's face drooped at the threat, knowing very well what Naretha could do with the flick of her fingers. "Just tell me where Ashna is."

Cath jerked her head half-heartedly toward the police station. "In there."

"As a prisoner?"

"No…"

After a moment of impatiently waiting, Naretha sighed, "Then *why*, Cath?"

She shuffled, peeking up at the stars. "Ashna needs her."

"Needs *who*?"

"I can't tell you."

"My *God*, Cath." Naretha groaned, throwing her head back. "You know I'm about to barge in there and apprehend Ashna, don't you? I'm going to constrict her in a mold of salt until she tells me exactly what the hell she's up to. You *know* I don't want to hurt her, and you *know* I don't want to hurt you. Just tell me what I need to know."

Cath's hands formed fists, her feet repositioning into a defensive stance. "Ashna said I have to attack anyone who tries to thwart her."

"Oh, and you obey Ashna now? Have you *forgotten*, Cath, *why* you ended up with the Wackos in the first place? Have you forgotten why you're not *dead*?"

Swallowing, her expression shifted with conflict, but Naretha could tell by her body language that she wouldn't back down. She would *actually* take a swing at Naretha because of *Ashna*. It would have been appalling if Naretha weren't *actually* planning to take a shot at Cath because of *Danny*. Oh, those manipulative Mayers. Even Zach, the docile one, had a habit of stirring mayhem.

Thinking of the eldest Mayer dredged up too many fond memories, especially of the time the two of them had spent with Cath, which was the last thing she needed in this moment. Luckily, all thoughts and forthcoming actions were discarded when a bright light flared through the hole in the police station's side, diverting Naretha's attention and Cath's with it.

"What the hell is Ashna *doing* in there?" She stalked toward the entrance, and Cath was about to stop her when melodic voice halted them both.

"I'm on my way to the police station, Naretha," Danny sang, the words emanating from the black watch on her wrist. "I hope you've apprehended our prey."

Cath's face scrunched with distaste. "I forgot how *creepy* he is."

"Lucky you," Naretha snorted. In looking back at the girl, her gaze darted toward the campus, from which a silhouette approached—a Danny-shaped silhouette. If he saw her wasting precious time talking to Cath, who had betrayed them—

"*Run*," she hissed, and the girl didn't question her. Footsteps reverberating through the pavement, she disappeared around the far side of the police station into an alleyway that Naretha hoped led far away from here. Danny would be too drunk from the use of his Affinity to have seen her, but once Ashna was in his grasp, he would raze the town to find the other two escapees.

The reminder of the second escapee, Naira, had Naretha on high alert as she slunk into the police station. It wouldn't have surprised her if the girl waited in the shadows of the dark room, ready to douse intruders with poisonous gases.

As she quickly scanned the filing cabinets, the desk, and the cot, she was reassured that the room was empty—but the open doorway leading to the back hall of cells was not.

Standing before the blazing light was Ashna, her wavy hair glowing like a sun-drenched rainbow. Normally, having her back to the salt-wielder would have been a dangerous position, but when Naretha drew nearer to the threshold, she realized something much worse dwelled on the other side.

Behind the bars of the cell to the right, a demon was aflame, its eyes as bright and red as freshly drawn blood, its arms as fiery and blinding as torches, its skin as jagged and dark as volcanic rock. The smile curling onto its lips was so sadistic that even Naretha balked; when it wrapped its pointed fingers around the metal bars and they began to melt, Naretha was slammed with the daunting realization that she would be no match for this creature. The only other person she had ever thought that of was Danny.

"What a pleasant surprise," the demon sang, its voice crackly but…familiar. Naretha realized why the instant her vision locked onto the boy standing in the hallway, his dark blue eyes sparkling with terrified delight. It was impossible for her to forget these two petulant children: the boy who had bested her and the girl who had been utterly useless.

She wasn't so inept anymore. No, in the past month Adara Stromer had become more deadly than her brother, and she would employ her Affinity in a way Sparky would never dare. Avner was an angel, a suppressant of violence and fun, but Adara was a demoness, an invoker of violence for the sake of fun.

Her head tilted greedily as she surveyed Ashna. Naretha stood carefully out of view, concealed by darkness, but she still didn't like Adara's eyes roving in her direction. "I've been craving a midnight snack."

"A-Adara." Ashna took a gradual step closer to the bars liquefying in the demoness's grasp. "Let me explain—"

"Explain how you betrayed Ackerly and plan to destroy this town, you mean?" She cackled, her head spewing embers as she shook it. "I'm not a fan of the part where the villain explains how *ingenious* their plan was. Let's skip to the fun."

"But I—"

Bullets of fire ripped through the air before Naretha could properly react. She did duck on instinct, but that shouldn't have stopped the flames from igniting her clothing or burning her skin. When neither occurred, she rose from her crouch and found Ashna's hands had flown up, creating one of her flawless force fields.

"Show off," Naretha grumbled, but Ashna was panting too hard to hear. Adara's rain of fire ceased, but the girl's arms continued burning like dueling bonfires, her clothes now singed from the fiery pellets. The boy, who Naretha recalled was named Calder, hastily quenched the flames eating away at his sweatshirt. With his water Affinity, the job was swift, but he still seethed upon its completion, his narrowed eyes darting between the girls.

"What the hell?" he snapped, motioning with his cuffed hands toward the simmering holes in his sweatshirt and jeans. "You could have shielded me—and *you* could have not thrown fire at me."

"True," Adara conceded with a simper.

Calder ignored her as he turned back to Ashna, who had lowered her defenses. "Keep her fiery," he encouraged through a whisper, gesturing with his eyes toward the half-melted bars. "Enough that she can create a hole to escape."

Adara rolled her eyes. "I can hear you."

Ashna acted as though she'd said nothing as she hissed, "That's what I'm trying to do."

There was a brief millisecond in which Calder looked satisfied, but his face rapidly morphed into suspicion. "You *want* Adara out of her cell?"

Even from behind, Naretha saw how tight Ashna's jaw was. "Yes."

"This is unfortunate." Calder sounded more annoyed than alarmed. Whipping his hands upward, he streamed a jet of water directly at Adara, drenching her rocky form and smothering her flames. As she blinked and spat and snarled, he glanced at Ashna and said, "I *was* going to let Stromer quench the fires that are likely burning this town, but if you *want* her out, that must mean your leader has some other plans for her. Sorry, Demoness, but your incarceration must continue. And you—" Calder's grin turned savage as he focused on Ashna. "I can't say I'm sorry that I'm going to end you."

It had taken the kid's speech for the truth to dawn on Naretha. Ashna wasn't working for Danny, like Calder thought; she worked for herself, meaning her reason for freeing Adara was self-centered. With that knowledge, the pieces of her plan merged, and Naretha swore aloud—consequently, notifying the others of her presence.

Ashna twirled, hands raised for combat. Naretha's were, too, and the two stood frozen, staring at each other warily, as Calder watched with arched eyebrows.

"Ah, the salt Wacko," he mused, now playing with an orb of water that hovered above his bound hands. "Came back to redeem yourself, did you?"

"I'm only here for *her*," Naretha sneered, not even deigning to look past Ashna at the boy, "but if you force me to prove myself, don't be shocked when you're dead."

"You!" Adara shouted, her voice wrought with rage.

Naretha exhaled wearily. "Yes, hello. It's me."

Steam wafted from her hardened flesh as the darkness flaked off, forming a pool of ashes around her. She clutched the bars she'd disfigured, but her heat had dwindled. The only flare left was in those demonic eyes. "Where the hell is Avner?"

This girl's dissimilarity to her brother was refreshing, but if Ashna's plans for her were what Naretha thought, then perhaps it was wisest to kill her off now. The death of his sister might be enough to make Avner crack, which Naretha would have wanted to see if she weren't the target of his vengeance...which she would be if she murdered Adara—

"Your brother is safely secured," a voice said, snatching the tricky decision from Naretha's hands. Danny appeared beside her, and if anyone died now, it would be at his hand.

The front room was dimly lit compared to the corridor of cells, but his eyes glowed as if reflecting the sun. There was something inherently enticing about him, even now, knowing he'd probably incinerated half a town, but Naretha couldn't say she was thrilled to see him. Nor did she particularly enjoy the way he sized up his sister like a prize he would claim and then crush, just so no one else could.

"Avner's behind a glass wall, though, not bars." Danny eyed Ashna's outstretched hands without a hint of fear before glancing past her at Adara. "The Wackos are far more high-class than *Periculand*."

"Hello, Daniel," a male voice called from beyond the bars. From this vantage point, Naretha couldn't see him, but she knew who it was.

"Principal Periculy," Danny greeted, his excitement doubling with the presence of another one of his targets. "Or should I say *ex*-Principal Periculy? Oh, the irony of being locked in your own jail. I am impressed that you've kept your sass, though. Watching you on the news earlier was quite entertaining. I can't say I'm necessarily a fan of the Reggs associating you with our movement, but I do hope it's finally opened your eyes to our common enemy."

"I've always known they were our enemy," Angor said, almost smugly. "I just have a habit of using my enemies against themselves rather than turning them to useless ash."

That wiped the grin off Danny's face. Adara, somehow, was smart enough not to snicker. Naretha couldn't breathe until his complacency finally resumed.

"I'd love to chat more, Periculy, but I have a sister to discipline." His eyes settled hungrily on Ashna, reveling in the way she trembled under his glare. "You understand what it's like to deal with unruly children. Can't say that I've *killed* any under my watch, but they can be so difficult to tame."

"Too bad you haven't tamed me yet," Ashna said. Naretha sharpened her focus, preparing for an onslaught of multiple Affinities, but then, unexpectedly, the girl vanished, leaving an empty spot within the doorway.

"Since when can she *teleport*?" Naretha blurted, her inhibition as absent as Ashna. This shift of events was sure to set Danny on edge; outbursts of disbelief would not be welcomed.

Unfortunately, Adara didn't seem to recognize this because, regardless of the smoke seeping from Danny's skin, the girl exclaimed, "I thought she had a *nerve* Affinity! Did she kill Ginger and steal his power or what?"

"Oh, yeah, you missed that," Calder said with far too much nonchalance. "Not that Little Corvis died, but that Unicorn Fairy's got multiple Affinities. Infinite, if I heard the rumor right."

"*Infinite* Affinities?" Adara repeated in bewilderment. "That's a thing?"

"Fascinating," Angor chimed in. "This could support my theory…"

"Tell me," Danny growled, gradually glancing at Naretha, "that you've at least apprehended Telum."

The murderous quality of his glare was enough to open an unpleasant sensation of apprehension in Naretha. If Danny wanted to blow them all to hell, there was nothing her meager salt could do to stop him. "He wasn't here when I arrived. I haven't seen—"

"He left to deal with your little invasion a while ago," Calder cut in, swirling an orb of water lazily in the air. "Not sure why you'd fear him over anyone else. He's definitely one of the least intimidating cops I've encountered."

"It *probably* has something to do with the fact that Weaponizer killed his father." Adara arched her eyebrows in Danny's direction. "If you're pissed because you wanted to kill him yourself, I think I can empathize. My father's currently near the top of my 'To Kill' list—"

"As are all three of you," Danny said tonelessly. It took Adara a moment to close her mouth and look rightly confused, but Calder was quick to dissolve his orb of water and meet the Wacko leader's gaze.

"And why would that be?"

"I'm guessing Avner did something annoyingly perfect that offended you and it's now being blamed on me?" Adara offered.

"Your brother refused to join me—and *you're* the one who knocked out my beloved Naretha, subjecting her to months of imprisonment," he added to Calder. Naretha didn't remember Danny caring nearly this much about that fact, but perhaps Ashna's disappearance heightened his level of peevishness.

"And you—" He stepped into the threshold to see Angor clearly. "You were a thorn in my father's side for decades. I won't let you ruin my organization with your blasphemy. I won't be as tolerant as my father was."

Naretha had anticipated what happened next, but she had thought the conversation would draw out longer, that she would have an adequate amount of time to formulate some plan as to how she could convince Danny to leave these Affinities unscathed. She hadn't thought he would erupt the very building they stood in.

The explosion detonated the ceiling, caving the concrete inward. Chunks of rock and rubble rained down, but Naretha sprinted to the exit swiftly, avoiding anything more serious than a few scratches. Once out on the street, she saw the back half of the building had collapsed, burning as brilliantly as the front gate had.

Danny walked through the still-standing front door as if he'd just signed a business deal. There was no hint of remorse, no trace of what he'd done in his expression. It was as if those three people had never existed at all.

Naretha didn't give a damn about Calder; that cocky kid could rot beneath the wreckage, and she was pleased Angor Periculy had finally met his end. His existence *had* been detrimental to Affinities for Freedom for many years, and she was glad to know it wouldn't continue on with the Wackos.

Adara was the issue. Naretha didn't know the girl personally, but she did know Avner, and she knew how ardently he cared for his sister. He wasn't really Naretha's problem anymore, but to think he was out in the world somewhere, soon to discover the death of his sister, reminded her too much of her own brother's death, the pain, despair, and wrath that had followed.

As a result, she'd served Ephraim with a new thirst for violence, vowing to eradicate the type of Reggs who'd been heartless enough to murder an innocent boy. Although Avner had been inclined toward passivity for now, this would unlock a vicious section of his personality, one that would prompt him to seek out and annihilate those who had stolen his sister's life.

For once, Naretha didn't look forward to the slaughter.

36

Unnecessary Deaths

"Hold on," Seth coughed before pivoting to the left and vomiting at the doorstep of a shop. When he slowly raised his head, he was met with the sight of the dry cleaner's he'd worked at for the past few weeks. His boss would *not* be happy—if he survived the bedlam scourging Periculand, that was.

"All right," he said, his lips and tongue contorting as he gagged. The puke was mostly liquid, but it still left a putrid tang lingering in his mouth. Recomposing himself, he spun back toward Naira, who stood at the center of the semi-circle alleyway, arms crossed. "I'm good."

"You keep saying that and then you keep barfing ten seconds later." She scrunched her nose. "It's taken us nearly ten minutes just to walk halfway around this bend."

"That's because…the ground is moving," he insisted as he stumbled across the cobblestone toward her. "Like a treadmill."

Normally, she would have laughed, but now her expression

was humorless as she grabbed his shoulders to steady him. "I'm gonna find somewhere for you to hide while I go deal with the invasion, 'kay?"

"No-no—I wanna come," he said, unable to keep the whine out of his voice. "I just can't *run*—the headaches, the stomachaches—"

She puffed out a sigh before glancing at the night sky. "If you were sober, I'd let you join me, but you're a liability at this point."

Seth never thought he would live to see a day where he regretted getting drunk, but that day had come, and he was really, really pissed at himself. The urgency of the Wacko attack had sobered him a bit, but the physiological effects that resulted from his over-consumption of alcohol were inescapable. If he accompanied Naira now, he *would* be a liability. She'd have to worry more about keeping him safe than saving others. As much as he wanted to join the action—to finally engage in a fight that would draw out his super strength—his twin's voice barked at him in his head, telling him it would be irrational.

Rummaging through his pocket, Seth extracted the key to the cleaner's. "I'll go sit in there and ride this out… The moment I'm better, though, I'm gonna super strength my way to campus and help you—*but*…only if you kiss me."

A laugh escaped her mouth as she planted her hands on her hips. "Really? Now or later, Stark?"

"Both? All? Always?" Another giggle from her. "Oh, and you also need to explain to me why you had to kiss me outside of Adara's jail cell but didn't…and probably the whole 'you're a Wacko' situation."

Any enthusiasm in Naira's demeanor deflated as she shuffled in place. "It's…a long story, Seth—one that I *will* tell you eventually, but we don't have time now. All I can really say is…I was instructed to kiss you by Ashna, but I didn't because…because I *did* want it to be real—I still *do*, actually. She had this plan—well, she's had a lot of plans, but they've all fallen through now… Basically, I was supposed to lure you into the alley and kiss you outside of Adara's cell to make her jealous—to get her angry—to provoke her fire Affinity. Adara's the only one in this town who could even start to stand a chance against Danny. Even Ashna, with all the Affinities she's harnessed, can't thwart him. With Danny, you have to fight fire with fire, and Adara's the only one who can."

"Danny has…a fire Affinity?" was all Seth could think to ask. His mind reeled—mostly because she'd said Adara would be *jealous* to see him making out with someone else. Why would Adara be *jealous*? Unless…unless…

"Mm, more like a…*nuclear* Affinity," Naira corrected through a wince. The word *nuclear* was enough to snap him out of his ridiculous thoughts.

"*Nuclear*? Are we all being exposed to radiation?"

"Probably not…" Naira said, though it didn't sound very reassuring. "He *could* expose everyone to radiation, but even *he's* not that cruel. As far as I know, he's learned to contain the nuclear part pretty well, so he just explodes things. Sometimes for fun. Sometimes to make his sister come out of hiding and surrender, like now."

Seth's rapid blinking increased his headache to the point that he was convinced he'd heard Naira say *sister*. Before he could question it, though, a figure materialized from around the bend of the alleyway. Eyes widening, Naira hastily shoved Seth into the small crevice between the cleaner's and the adjacent building.

With their backs both pressed against the brick wall, he opened his mouth to speak, but she instantly clapped her hand over it, silencing him as footsteps approached. They both held their breaths as a man passed their dark alley, his greedy eyes scanning the street for signs of life. His hair was a creamy white, like the exterior of Periculand's shops, but he appeared not much older than them, maybe twenty at most.

Once he was safely past, Naira sighed quietly and scrubbed her forehead. "That was a Wacko—Jez. He's insane."

"Aren't all Wackos insane?" Seth whispered, earning a wry glance.

"Not like Jez. If he finds us, he'll hang us."

"*Hang* us? Like—with a rope?"

"That's his Affinity," she informed him ruefully. "Ropes. And he's sadistic with them, that's for sure. I always avoided him, but Ashna got into a fight with him once and he nearly choked her to death." Seth gaped as he attempted to process her words, but a new wave of dread had already consumed her face. "He's headed for the police station—dammit. I'm gonna have to stop him. I can't let him get to Ashna—or Adara. I didn't want to involve you, but…can you back me up if it goes poorly?"

"Of course." He attempted an awkward stretch in the crammed space. "What should the code word be?"

"Code word?"

"Like—if you're dying and you need help, you'll say a code word and I'll know to jump out and save you."

Naira's peachy eyebrows creased. "You won't be able to tell if I'm *dying*? How will I be able to speak if he's choking me with ropes? You know, never mind. Don't save me. But if I become incapacitated, I need you to sneak around the opposite side of this semi-circle and go to the police station and—"

A white rope snapped through the mouth of the alley, wrapping around her wrist and yanking her into the street with enough force to throw her to the ground. The Wacko named Jez sauntered toward her, his hands walking along the rope to keep it taut.

"Oh, hello, Naira," he said roughly, tugging on the rope and pulling her arm in a way that made her yelp. "I thought I smelled a traitor."

"Jez," she greeted through gritted teeth. "Was hoping I'd never have to see *you* again."

"Oh, I know. That's why, when I heard you and the little runt ran to Periculand, I knew I needed to pay you a visit."

The only movement Naira made was the clenching and unclenching of her hand, probably because the rope seemed to be cutting off her circulation. "I assume by *runt* you're not referring to Cath."

Jez stiffened, his white-irised eyes scanning the area for her monstrous ally. Seth was her only backup, and while he'd initially been shocked, he now slowly formulated a plan. This Wacko seemed as well trained as Naira, Cath, and Ashna, so Seth would have to catch him off guard.

"Neither of them are here," Naira said, likely to divert Jez's attention from where Seth prepped himself in the hidden gap. "I'm alone."

"Well, that's unfortunate." Jez's smirk returned. "Danny will be disappointed I didn't acquire his little sister for him. Though, I suppose it also means no one's around to hear you scream—or choke—or die."

Seth was tempted to say something super cool and witty like, "You're the one that's gonna die," but stealth was of the utmost importance. So, shaking out his limbs one last time, he withheld his courageous proclamation and launched out from between the buildings.

To his surprise, *Jez* was actually surprised. The Wacko didn't even have a moment to react before he'd been tackled to the ground.

"*Seth*! I didn't say the code word!"

"We didn't agree on a code word!" he shouted back at Naira as he grappled with Jez. Super strength or not, Seth was *definitely* stronger than this guy. Pinning him to the ground was laughably easy. Keeping him there was the hard part, because even though Jez's squirming was futile, he still had the ability to utilize his ropes, which literally *grew out of his skin.*

The white chord projected from his flesh like a rapidly sprouting and grossly oversized hair, extending from his forearm and snaking toward Seth's neck. Knowing what fate awaited him if this guy managed to tie a noose around him, Seth scrambled off and retreated toward Naira. By now she'd disentangled the rope from her wrist, which was rubbed raw from the friction, but her hand continued opening and closing.

"I told you not to help me. You shouldn't be out here."

Seth wobbled, feeling suddenly dizzy, but he still flashed her a cocky grin. "I *was* helpful, though, wasn't I?"

"Yes, but—"

A prickly substance suddenly looped around Seth's wrists, drawing his hands together and immobilizing them. He shouldn't have been startled when Jez used the lasso to jerk him forward, but he still did yelp when he plummeted face-first onto the cobblestone.

Luckily, his extended arms lessened the impact to his chin, but his whole body felt the ache of the collision. The intensity of his headache magnified, and he was so disoriented that it took him a moment to register what was happening when Jez's rope hauled him to his feet, his arms now suspended above his head.

"*You*." A sadistic shimmer entered the guy's eyes. "You're on Danny's wanted list."

"Why?" Seth asked as he kneed him in the gut. Howling, the

Wacko hunched over, seething and clutching his stomach. The rope holding Seth's hands in the air slackened, and he shucked it off before grabbing Jez's white hair and yanking his head up. "Why?"

The Wacko smiled through his grimace. "Danny's a fan of family reunions."

Seth blinked. Then he released Jez's hair, staggering back and nearly tripping over the fallen rope. His parents—

Another rope flew from Jez's arm. There was no time to react—no time to duck or dodge or even grab it before it secured itself around Seth's neck.

"Jez—*don't*!" Naira pleaded, but her voice sounded distant in Seth's ears. Everything was hazy—similar to the way in which the world had appeared through his drunken eyes. Perhaps all the movement had brought back the negative effects of his alcohol consumption—or maybe the rope tightening around his throat prohibited blood from properly flowing to his brain. He felt the pain—the pressure of the rope, the lack of oxygen in his lungs, the pounding beneath his skull—but he also felt disconnected from it, his consciousness evading him.

Naira stepped behind him. He sensed her rather than saw her. The world was a blob of white, Jez's crazed eyes the only distinguishable feature amidst the cloudiness.

"I told you not to come out, Seth," Naira said, her voice like a fading song in his ears. He swore he saw Jez swaying, his menacing eyes drooping, though it could have been his imagination projecting his own motions onto those around him.

Naira, now standing at his side, remained steady, her expression as apologetic as her tone. With her next words, his awareness finally fled, bringing with it the pain, the nausea, and the sensation of the rope ringing his neck. "I'm sorry."

Nero would have gladly admitted he looked like a Greek god as he ran down Periculand's main street, black sweatshirt abandoned and bare muscles swelling to an unnatural girth. He'd made the mistake of idling in a cage once, but he'd vowed never to sit behind bars again. Especially not when *Reggs* had put him there, as if they had any real influence over him. Especially not when he had the opportunity to prove his power, to win his leadership through might. Especially not when his girlfriend had *betrayed* him by overthrowing his authority and claiming his minions as her own.

What agitated him the most was that Nixie *could* easily rally his forces behind her. All of Nero's allies respected and feared her as much as they did him. If she ordered them to turn their backs on him and follow her when he wasn't around, they would scamper after her like lost sheep.

That was why Nero had to ensure he *was* there. No one would question his rule over Nixie's if he was physically present. At least, that was his belief, and he would guarantee that his beliefs became reality.

Challenging her might have proven less difficult if her brother had decided to follow him out of the police station. Nero could beat her to bits if he wanted to, but…he didn't really want to. She'd been his girlfriend for the past year, and despite his antipathy for most people, he didn't hate Nixie; he almost actually *loved* her. The concept was so foreign to him that he didn't like to consider it, but her betrayal fractured more than his pride.

That was why he would have preferred to threaten Calder in order to win her back. Nero didn't want to physically harm Nixie, but he wouldn't have minded giving Calder a few bruises, especially now that the kid had essentially betrayed him as well.

Nero shouldn't have been surprised that Mardurus stuck behind with Stromer. Over the past few weeks, their little *connection* had become increasingly conspicuous. His plans for that *connection*... Well, he would brood on that later.

The Wackos must have blown their way into town in the same instant Nero smashed his way out of jail, because the school's campus was bathed in flames but he hadn't heard the initial explosion. He did hear the booms that followed, though. None were dramatic enough to stop his strides toward the school—until the Physicals Building erupted, dragging the sounds of screams and cries with it.

At that, his pace faltered. Nero wasn't one to balk at destruction, but to see a building that had seemed so permanent crumble with such ease... He definitely didn't want to find out what these explosions could do to *him.*

Scanning the crowd of young Periculand Affinities, pathetically attempting to ward off the Wackos, Nero was pleased to see Tray Stark running *away* from the battle like a scared little girl. The urge to gloat immediately changed his trajectory; instead of joining the struggling students at the front lines, he hurried after Stark, weaving through the smoking holes in the earth and the battling Affinities until he caught up.

As he grabbed Stark by the back of the neck, it became apparent to Nero that the kid hadn't been running *away* from the battle but *toward* the Physicals Building. The heat of the burning building was nearly unbearable, even at a distance of at least thirty feet. Nero ignored the discomfort—and the fact that Stark had probably planned to dart bravely into the fire and save any trapped survivors—as he spun the little prick around and tightened his grip on his throat.

"H-hi," Stark choked out, eyes twitching from the pain of

Nero's grasp. Still, the brown was visible, confirming this wasn't the normie Stark twin. Good. Nero longed to pulverize Tray Stark in a fight that could result in death.

Punching him in the gut, he released Stark and chuckled as the kid doubled over, coughing and groaning.

"Stand," Nero barked, yanking him up by the hair. Stark's face twisted, and with the flickering of the flames, his irises looked gray. Disregarding the strange lighting, he thrust his fist into the kid's cheek, forcing out a grunt.

"Fight me, Stark." Nero circled him as the boy rubbed his bruised jaw. "Let's see who's really the strongest in Periculand."

"This—doesn't really seem like a good time. You know we're being invaded, right?"

"*Obviously.*" Nero swung for his head, but then the head wasn't there. It had lowered a few inches, just enough to evade his fist. For a moment, he thought Stark had merely ducked, but when his eyes settled on the person standing before him, it wasn't Tray Stark. "Little Dispus?" Surveying her hay-like hair, Nero wondered how she'd switched places with Stark so rapidly. He whipped around, searching for Stark, but he was nowhere in sight, which meant—

"Big Dispus, actually," the little sack of shit said, his grin remaining even when he morphed out of his sister's body and took the shape of a random boy Nero didn't recognize through the haze of red ire clouding his vision. "My sister's fighting to save this town, like you *should* be."

"Oh yeah?" Grabbing a fistful of Dispus's pale gray hair, Nero tilted his head up and spat in his face. "And what are *you* doing?"

The shapeshifter cringed at the saliva slipping down his cheek. "I was going to go help Eliana—Mensen, you know. She ran into the Physicals Building to see if anyone survived."

"She went in *there*?" he questioned, jerking his chin toward the flaming, crumbling building. "Why the hell would you let her go in there?"

"I-I didn't. She ran off before anyone could stop her, and Tray told me to go after her since he's busy fighting off Wackos—"

"Is that why you looked like him?"

"Well—no. I was practicing my Tray Stark look, but then the Wackos broke in and I forgot to change—"

"Your Affinity is useless," Nero snapped, thrusting his head back with enough force that he crumpled onto the walkway. "Let a real man handle this."

"I don't see any real men around here!" Dispus called after him as he stalked toward the Physicals Building. For the first time, maybe ever, Nero blatantly ignored a provocative taunt. Normally he would have taken it as an excuse to give a beating, but knowing Little Mensen was within this inferno canceled out his bloodlust.

After passing through the glass doors, which were still intact, Nero discovered the left half of the building remained untouched. The gymnasium was in pristine condition, and from this angle he spotted a few students huddled on the bleachers, crying to themselves. Wimps.

The right half had not been so fortunate. Walking down the hall toward the nurse's office was like walking through hell. Massive chunks of concrete had caved in from the upper floors, and desks and chairs from the classrooms had rained down from above. Most of the furniture was aflame, and with some of the walls undamaged, the accumulation of smoke was so thick that Nero wished he wore a shirt he could use to shield his airways.

Suppressing a gag, he shoved slabs of concrete aside like pieces of paper and wondered how Little Mensen had managed to get past all this wreckage. She was tiny, he supposed—tiny enough to squeeze between the gaps he could only fit an arm through. How far had she gotten? Was it possible she was already dead, suffocated by the smoke his gigantic lungs could barely handle?

Then he heard a cough—a girlish cough.

Heaving aside the half-charred door to the nurse's office, he was greeted with the devastation of a collapsed room. The two white beds that injured students—mostly Nero's victims—would lie on to wait for the nurse's healing touch had been crushed by the ceiling, as had the desk. When he carefully rounded it, he balked as a strange sensation of grief overcame him. A man lay dead beneath the rubble: Jason Pane.

His bruise-purple eyes stared flatly upward, devoid of their typical nurturing quality. With the dust and ash draped over his sallow skin and orange scrubs, he looked like an old statue that had been neglected for years.

Nero had never really liked the nurse. The man always healed his victims when the purpose of his viciousness was to inflict long-lasting suffering. Pane had helped his allies on numerous occasions, though, as well as himself, and it was odd to think someone with an Affinity for healing could have died with such ease. The blow must have killed him too instantaneously for healing.

Another cough drew him away from the nurse's corpse. Turning toward the opposite corner of the room, Nero's eyes fixated on the girl crouching beside a mound of concrete. Her hair, strewn chaotically over her back, glowed an iridescent shade of blue in the light of the fire. With the smoke hazing his vision, he almost didn't notice her clothes were singed in various places while her left leg oozed a slow stream of blood from beneath her jeans.

When Nero took one step toward her, she hastily rotated, revealing that she covered her mouth with the fabric of her cardigan—and that a person lay on the ground beside her.

His face was doused in perspiration and contorted with hysteria, his freckles vibrating so quickly they were almost invisible. Debris coated his entire body, but only his right leg was pinned underneath the concrete, hindering him from escape. A long-brewing sense of malice spread a grin across Nero's lips.

"Nero," Little Mensen breathed, and his chest instinctively puffed at the sound of his name. Sweat and tears had mixed on her ashy face, masking her fair skin, but the raw terror was clear in her eyes. "H-he's stuck. I tried to lift the concrete but I-I'm not strong enough."

The reverence with which she regarded him welled his pride. Crossing his arms over his chest, Nero said, "Only a few have been graced with the strength to save lives—but this one's isn't worth the effort."

"*Please*!" the little worm moaned, shifting and then emitting a piercing cry. After all the years of being pummeled, Nero thought this kid would have been immune to pain, but he *still* hadn't toughened up. His softness would be his demise.

"Nero," Little Mensen repeated quietly, her voice cracking this time. She gazed up at him with dejection now, as if she'd expected him to act this way but still felt the need to try. The look thawed his resolve—but he couldn't show it. He had to maintain an aura of stubbornness. "Please, Nero—he's your *brother*."

That hardened him again, and when he scowled down at her, he didn't have to fake it. "He's no brother of mine. If he deserves to live, why doesn't he teleport himself out of there? All he's ever been good at is disappearing like a weakling."

"I-I *can't*!" he groaned through hyperventilating breaths. "I tried—and I can't focus—the pain—*agh*!"

Little Mensen rushed back toward him to stroke his forehead soothingly, to push his unkempt orange hair to the side. Nero rolled his eyes. Always so dramatic, this runt. Just seeing how much compassion this girl had for him made Nero loathe her.

At the same time, he'd never been drawn to others' capacity for sympathy the way he was with Eliana. Usually he saw emotion as a weakness, but for her it was a strength, a weapon she wielded with consequence. Even if she couldn't read the explicit thoughts running through his mind because of his impressive mental shields, she knew exactly how she had to act in order to reach him. She knew he liked to have dominance over his own decisions; she knew he basked in the satisfaction of others being at his mercy. Perhaps she really was distraught over his stepbrother's predicament, but she played it to her advantage.

Even though he recognized her shrewd ploy, he succumbed to it. Little Mensen wouldn't be nearly as useful as Adara Stromer, but he did smirk a little at the prospect of Eliana being indebted to him.

"Do you have my portrait ready?" Nero questioned in his deepest voice.

"Your—your what?"

"My portrait—the one I ordered you to draw. It's my birthday, Little Mensen. Your deadline has come."

"I-I—yes." With a sniffle, she nodded. "It's in my dorm—"

"Excellent. I expect it in my hands as soon as this battle business is finished."

Her shock at his nonchalance was evident, but she couldn't manage to utter a word. All she did was scramble out of the way as he marched toward them. Nero towered above his stepbrother, the bane of his existence. How effortless it would have been to crush his skull with the heel of his shoe. There were worse fates than death, though, and at Nero's hand, Hartman would suffer them.

Without any gentleness, he lifted the concrete slab, inducing a sob from the little twat. Nero snorted when the kid tried to move on his own and failed, prompting Eliana to rush over and haul him out with what little physical strength she possessed.

"You'd better not make me regret this," Nero growled, dropping the concrete carelessly. Dust wafted with the smoke, causing the primaries to hack dramatically as they slumped onto a clean patch of the room. "Just because you didn't die today doesn't mean you won't die tomorrow."

"Th-thank you," Hartman stammered with a wince of gratitude. Nero didn't deign to give him a grunt of acknowledgement.

"We need to get you to safety." Little Mensen pushed to her feet. "I can try to help you limp out of—"

"Shut up," Nero snarled, stalking past her to scoop up his incompetent stepbrother. Hartman looked arguably more terrified in Nero's arms than he had under that deadly slab. "Just so everyone in Periculand knows how much of a baby you are."

"I-I-I am a baby," Hartman agreed, nodding vigorously. "Very—big—baby."

Humorous relief flashed across Eliana's features, and Nero felt inclined to smile with her, but he swiftly stifled the desire.

"Any other pathetic people that need saving?" he asked gruffly.

"There was, um, a girl." Hartman glanced somberly toward the heap of debris he'd been pinned under. "I was trying to teleport her out of here when the building blew. She died almost instantly…and so did Dr. Pain."

Eliana pressed her lips together in silent mourning, but none of them had much to say. It was fortunate, really, that the Wackos hadn't extinguished the entire town yet. The calamity should have felt tragic, but to Nero it didn't. The whole event would have been avoided if he hadn't been jailed, if he'd been there to ward off the Wackos upon their arrival.

As they trekked out of the Physicals Building, Hartman in his grasp and Eliana at his heels, Nero smiled vindictively at how much he would rub this whole catastrophe in the Rosses faces—and how glorious it would feel to squish their skulls into their brains.

37

Physical Limitations

Ackerly felt like he was in one of those cheesy horror films when the protagonist dramatically loses his glasses and then fumbles around for them until the monster sneaks up on him and kills him. Except he had somehow managed to stumble all the way into the center of town half-blind without being attacked.

Currently, he was ransacking Louie's Lenses, searching for a pair of glasses that could improve his sight so he didn't have to hide from the battle in blindness. He would never forgive himself if he didn't fight. The blame for this invasion could be attributed to him more than anyone else. If he had listened to Tray, perhaps they would have thwarted Ashna long before she led the Wackos here.

Muffled booms had quaked through Periculand for the past twenty minutes, probably. Ackerly didn't have a watch, nor could he have read the time even if he did have one. He guessed based on the amount of time it usually took to trek from campus to town, along with the thirty seconds he gave his eyes to adjust to each pair of glasses he tried on. None had been particularly helpful, and his eyes burned from the strain of looking through so many different lenses.

The franticness should have distracted him from all that had been unveiled within the past few hours, but it only added to his agitation over the circumstances. Floretta, his favorite teacher and essentially his idol, had been a terrorist, and despite her claims of deflection, she was still adamant about helping Ashna, another Wacko—the leader's *sister*.

It was difficult for him to think about Ashna without wanting to crack every pair of glasses in this shop and hurl the remnants at the wall of contact lenses—or ditch his quest and curl up in a corner and be sad.

Mostly, he wished to talk to her. He'd been ignorant about her—perhaps he'd always been ignorant about a lot of things—but even though his physical vision had been distorted by the loss of his glasses, his intellectual eyes had been cleared. Skepticism had replaced his gullibility. All the open doors in his heart had been slammed shut. He should have never trusted Ashna, and now he would never trust anyone at all.

Wallowing in his emotional anguish would have to wait. The vibrations shaking the earth indicated the Wackos had succeeded in infiltrating the town. He'd never learned explicitly what Danny's Affinity was, but based on the type of destruction he'd alluded to in his voicemail, coupled with the email Ackerly had come across a few months ago regarding a Wacko with a nuclear Affinity, he could safely assume Danny's Affinity was of an explosive nature. His plants wouldn't be able to combat *that*, but…he had to try to help his friends in any way possible.

He'd finally found a somewhat effective pair of glasses when movement suddenly flashed through the dimly lit shop. Spinning around, he discovered a person had appeared, and he didn't need full functionality of his vision to distinguish who it was.

Her hair was as colorful as the array of contact lenses spread across the wall at her back. The breaths that flowed from her mouth were ragged, as if she'd recently ran, but Ackerly hadn't heard the front door open. It was almost as if she'd…teleported. He decided right then that he wouldn't be surprised if she had.

"A-Ackerly?" For the first time, Ashna seemed genuinely flustered—but she was a good actress. Ackerly didn't need to see her mask of deception to know she would use her charm to entice him. "What are you… Is this… We're still in Periculand, right?"

She really had teleported, then. Just another one of the infinite secrets she'd withheld from him.

"Ackerly," she repeated, weaving through the displays of glasses to approach him. He noticed her pause a few times, likely to avoid the frames he'd littered on the floor. Once she stood a foot before him, she grabbed his hand. "You need to help me—"

Ripping his hand from her grasp, he met her eyes, those two hazy splotches of color. "I'm not helping you, Ashna. You're…a *weed*."

He'd tried to say the words with enough aggression to affect her, but she remained where she stood, unfazed. From what he could tell, she'd pressed her lips together, as if trying to summon patience. "We don't have time for this discussion now, but I swear we will talk about—"

"I don't want to talk about it. You are a *weed*."

"Any plant can be a weed. It's just a matter of perception."

She was right, but he couldn't *say* that. Instead, he said what had swirled through his mind throughout the past twenty minutes. "I saw you as a rainbow rose…and you are. Pretty on the outside but fake. All you've ever done is lie to me."

"You act like we've known each other for years!"

"I know, but I just—I feel like—You're the only girl—" He cut himself off, staring down at his shaky hands. "I've never really… liked a girl before. Unless you count Poison Ivy, but she's a comic book character… I just thought we might make a good match eventually. I thought you were actually interested in me—but you were using me, and I still don't even know why."

With his improper glasses and the tears burning in his eyes, it was hard to know exactly how she'd reacted to his confession. Her tone was gentler, though, and he had to fight not to be soothed by her words.

"I've hated lying to you, Ackerly—hated using you—but it's been necessary. I needed you and your connections to complete my goal. I thought I would have more time to explain it all to you, but I messed up. Horribly."

Ackerly bit the inside of his lip, eyebrows set in defiance. "You triggered your tracking device, didn't you? You're the reason the Wackos are here."

"It was unintentional, but yes, it's my fault," she admitted with a sigh. "Because of my alcohol Affinity, I can't get drunk for very long, but being so small, the few minutes after I've had a drink can really disorientate my rational thinking. The reason I didn't step in and fight Nero initially—when he threatened you and Lavisa challenged him—was because I knew I couldn't use my strength Affinity. But after the alcohol, in the midst of the brawl, I didn't care that my strength would reactivate the device. Once Nero threw me across the room, I managed to turn it off—that was why I couldn't defend you; I was trying really hard to concentrate on deactivating it. I wasn't quick enough, and now Danny's—"

"Your brother," Ackerly injected, startling her. "I know he's your brother. That's why I know you're working for them. You... made up that whole story about your brother—about how he had a strength Affinity, how he died—"

"He *is* dead—dead to *me*. He's not the same brother I once knew. Working for the Wackos killed that part of him. I don't consider him to be the same person, even. I never would have hurt the old Danny, but this Danny... I want to end him, Ackerly. He's hurting people—he always hurts people—and now I feel like it's all my fault. I want to fix this, but I can't do it alone. I told you about my Affinities, and that was true. Can you have faith in me now when I say I want to save this town—this country?"

Ackerly was inclined to believe this was a trap, but...the way Danny had talked about her in that message didn't make it *seem* like they were allies...and if the Wackos were *here* and she still hadn't admitted to being one, what else could she possibly have planned? What could she do to make this situation worse than it already was?

"I...want a very specific description of your plan," he finally said, even though he heard Tray's voice in his head telling him not to. "I'm not putting my faith in you anymore, but...I will put my faith in your plan if it'll help Periculand."

Even through his slightly obscured vision, he saw the ripple of disappointment in her expression. But then she composed herself, inhaling deeply before saying, "Fine, I'll explain what you need to know, but we don't have time for you to be shocked or angry. Every second—"

A deafening bang tore through the air, far too loud to have come all the way from campus. Danny must have been in town, exploding shops...like the one they were in.

Swearing, Ashna darted out of Louie's Lenses, and Ackerly scrambled after her, tripping over the discarded frames and bumping into about five different displays. The cold air slapped his skin as he darted onto the road, but the frigid air was soon forgotten when he turned around and saw smoke ballooning above the roofs…specifically above the police station.

"Adara," he breathed as confusion and panic paralyzed him. Had *she* exploded her way out of jail or had Danny? The virulence in Ashna's glower implied the latter, but Ackerly didn't have the opportunity to inquire about it before his fuzzy vision settled on a person approaching them.

At first, he feared it was Danny, but Ashna's posture was too lax. With the female silhouette and peachy hair, Ackerly was certain it was Naira even before she spoke.

"Ashna!" With a few worried glances back at the police station, she ran toward them. "I'm sorry—I tried—but I felt like too much of a bitch kissing drunk Seth, and now he's passed out—I had to lock him up in the cleaner's—"

"Naira"—Ashna gripped her shoulders—"relax. Adara didn't need to know you were kissing Seth to get pissed. Apparently, all she needed was to see me."

"So…" Naira's eyes darted to Ashna's hands, then over to Ackerly, then back to Ashna's face. "So you succeeded?"

"No," she huffed, dropping her hands to rub her temples. "I… got scared. I feel so pathetic, but…she's as terrifying as Danny. What happened with Seth?"

A dark edge entered Naira's voice. "Jez happened. I was poisoning the air with carbon monoxide to knock him out, but then Seth jumped in, hell-bent on saving me, and I couldn't manage to subdue Jez without Seth joining him. Seth's locked in the cleaner's. I threw Jez in a dumpster."

"Locked in the cleaner's is probably the best place for Seth right now… Is Jez dead?"

"Probably not, although I wouldn't really care if he was." Naira shrugged and then glanced at Ackerly. "Have you told him yet? Please tell me you have. I can't keep up this 'we were pathetic prisoners' act anymore. Nor can I watch you break poor Ackerly's heart anymore."

"I don't—I wasn't—" He shook his head and started again. "I want to know what's really going on. And…shouldn't we check the police station for Adara? I want to make sure she's all right."

"She's fine," Ashna said swiftly. "I can sense she's not in pain. Danny, though…he's headed back toward campus."

Naira gnawed on her lip. "You want to resort to Plan B, don't you?"

"We don't have much of a choice. I was a coward before; I'll need to suffer the consequences now."

Ashna's suffering shouldn't have miffed Ackerly in the slightest, but the thought of her in pain tugged at his heart. He supposed she never *really* felt pain because of her nociceptor Affinity, but then he remembered the agony on her face back in the lounge, when she'd been tangled beneath the chairs. Perhaps that had been emotional turmoil—fear for Ackerly's safety as he faced off Nero—and perhaps this would be an emotional consequence as well, something that would affect her with more severity than anything physical could.

"He still looks perplexed, Ash," Naira sang. "I think it's time…"

Ashna bit her lip now, but after a moment she gazed into Ackerly's eyes—and then her brow furrowed. "Those aren't your glasses. Ackerly—you're bleeding!"

"Oh." He touched his temples, where blood was crusted down the sides of his face. "Yeah, kinda. The metal girl bent mine… It doesn't matter—"

"What's your prescription?" She stomped past him toward Louie's Lenses. "I'll go find an adequate pair for—"

"Wait," he called, but she kept walking, dodging the truth—again.

He could have chased after her, but the thought of touching his skin to hers made him nervous in a way he didn't care to explore. Instead, he fished for a bean in his pocket, and then, so rapidly he impressed himself, he forced the roots out of the bean, extending the vine-like stem toward her until it wrapped around her wrist. The tether halted her, and she stared back at the string of flowers between them with trepidation.

"You…did it without even a seed," he recalled, thinking back to the Japanese wisteria she'd conjured during her duel with Nero. "You were so impressed when you came into the shop that day and saw the hyacinth…but that was a lie, too, wasn't it?"

The guilt was audible in her tone. "I didn't want you to know how…advanced my Affinities are. I was worried you might realize who I am and assume the worst."

"I…don't want to assume anything," Ackerly said softly. He'd assumed she was innocent, and that had been false. All he wanted now were the facts. "Just…tell me, please."

To a command, she would have stubbornly yanked her hand free, but to a plea she caved, retreating to him until the hyacinth vine was a limp decoration between them.

"My father," she said, eyes fixed on the purple flowers, "was not a good man—or maybe he was, but never when I was alive. I told you my mom died during childbirth, and…she did. My father always blamed it on me, but he took his initial rage out on Danny, by exposing him to an…explosion.

"It should have killed him, and I don't know if my father would have cared if it did. Instead, he developed an explosive

Affinity, including the ability to generate nuclear reactions. My brother avoids it when he can, but a few times it's slipped out..."

"But...nuclear explosions are *huge*! He must have killed thousands—"

"His are not as big as typical nuclear explosions, but...they could be, and he *has* killed people, accidentally and...purposely. He hasn't killed as many as the media claims, but...he isn't a good man, either. He *was*, though," she implored, toying with the vine around her wrist. "He was my best friend. My father favored Zach, my eldest brother, over either of us, so we always banded together...until my father got sick of our shenanigans and revealed to us the reason he exposed Danny to that first explosion—me.

"I had no choice in the matter of my mother's death and my father's harsh reaction—I was an *infant*—but Danny hated me for it. He went insane not long after that, killing random Reggs and torturing anyone in any way he could. My father wasn't one to engage in violence himself, but...he never stopped my brother. He let Danny become a monster; he *made* Danny a monster. I don't mourn my father's death, but Danny will seek vengeance against anyone who ever wronged him—likely as an excuse for bloodshed.

"Danny put an electric collar on me as soon as he became leader and renamed us the Wackos." With a bitter expression, she touched the ring of purple around her throat. "I've never...harnessed electricity, so it kept me docile. I knew I couldn't let Danny continue to lead, though. Zach deserves to be the leader; he would be diplomatic—he would actually *help* Affinities rather than just harm Reggs.

"So, I conferred with Naira and Cath, who both agreed that Danny couldn't remain in power. We planned an escape, and we succeeded. Then...we came here, because I'd heard a rumor that there was a girl here with a fire Affinity, and I knew she would be our only hope of matching Danny."

Glancing forlornly toward the police station, Ashna puffed out a breath. "That's why I needed *you.* As soon as I saw how much Adara cared for you, I knew I'd need to befriend you in order to get closer to her. It was so hard to visit her while she was in jail, though, and Tray was too suspicious for me to make any moves. I was planning to divulge all of this to you when we went to visit her at the police station tonight, but…then the party happened, and then this happened."

She gestured lamely toward the town. "Adara won't be able to stop this. She isn't trained well enough. I saw her aflame, and she has no control over it. She's a slave to her emotions, and so is her ability."

At least there was one point of her story Ackerly could verify—that Adara was wild.

There had been distress in Ashna's inflection when she'd recounted her family history, but it wasn't any different from the way she'd told her initial fabrication in the Physicals Building's basement. This could have easily been a deception as well, another lie to provoke sympathy from gullible Ackerly. But with what purpose? What did she have to hide now—and what could she possibly do that would be worse than blowing up Periculand? If Ashna was against Danny, then Ackerly would have to be with her, whether he believed her or not.

"So…" he began, scratching his hairline, "if Adara can't stop Danny…what's Plan B?"

"I have to fight Danny," Ashna said hollowly, staring beyond him.

"Do you…have a fire Affinity?"

She closed her eyes, face scrunching with remorse. "No, I don't. If I do, it hasn't surfaced yet. I just recently discovered my teleportation abilities. That's why I was only able to jump from the police station to here, probably a few hundred feet."

"That's still better than Hartman," Ackerly said weakly, at which both girls snorted.

Any amusement was quenched with Naira's whispered question. "Can you sense Danny?"

"He's close to campus now. We need to intercept him before he hurts anyone else. I'll need you two to move people as far away from the school grounds as possible." Ashna looked between them grimly. "But if this doesn't go well...maybe nowhere in Periculand will be exempt from demolition."

"Are any of our allies here?" Naira noticed Ackerly's puzzled expression and added, "We have a large group of Wackos who are loyal to Ashna—and Zach, consequently."

Ackerly blinked in disbelief—and then wondered if he *should* believe it. Ashna's story was convincing, but there was a barrier between them now, one that would endlessly question every word she said.

"A few of them are here, but they won't act until I tell them to," Ashna explained as she disentangled her wrist from the vines. "I don't want them getting killed if I fail. Just because I'm dead doesn't mean Zach is. There's still a chance he can rise up from within the compound and overthrow Danny even if I'm gone. Honestly, I hope he's doing that now, since he's not here. I instructed enough of our allies to hang behind that they could easily form a coup."

"Knowing Zach, he'll chicken out," Naira retorted dryly. "He's always wanted to get on Danny's good side—and never has."

"I'm aware," Ashna replied with years of pent-up resentment. "We need to get going. A sneak attack will work best, so stay stealthy. Oh, and we should really get you a new pair of glasses,

Ackerly. You've been staring at my forehead instead of my eyes this whole time and it's starting to freak me out."

In reality, he'd purposely stared at her forehead to avoid the attractive quality of her eyes, but he couldn't tell *her* that, nor could he refuse a better pair of glasses. This time he would have to ensure they weren't made of metal.

"So, Stark," Lavisa mused as she punched a Wacko in the face, "what's that secret suit about?"

From the corner of her eye, she saw him splutter, but then a Wacko charged toward him, and his seriousness resumed. "It's just an extra layer of fleece," he grunted as he hurled the Wacko to the side. Lavisa rolled her eyes as she grabbed her opponent's shoulders and kneed him in the stomach.

For how long they'd fended off incoming Wackos, Lavisa didn't know. There seemed to be an endless supply of them, and with her focus on the fight, everything else had drifted into the distant corners of her mind. Like the fact that her brother was somewhere within the pandemonium, likely doing something stupid to get himself hurt. Or the fact that, though Floretta had claimed Ashna would save them all, the mysterious girl was nowhere in sight. Or the fact that Hartman's last known location was the Physicals Building, which now resembled a graveyard of blazing rubble.

Eliana had immediately sprinted toward the building upon its detonation, insisting she would be able to detect him with her mind. Lavisa didn't really enjoy the thought of her plunging into a burning building, but there was no one else to volunteer. Any able fighters were needed at the front of the battle, especially since that Wacko Josh had subdued so many with his sleep-inducing Affinity.

Than had fallen prey to it a few minutes ago, and Floretta struggled to combat Wackos with her flowering vines. Officer Telum had joined the fray soon after the invasion began, and his ability to absorb and then project whatever penetrated his skin proved useful against the Wackos who had brought guns instead of superpowers. The ammo was tranquilizer darts, meaning Danny didn't want *all* of Periculand's Affinities dying tonight, but the Regg soldiers had perished.

Apparently those Affinity-proof suits weren't completely immune to damage.

Even though she'd never known any of the Reggs personally, it was still difficult for Lavisa to go on knowing someone in the vicinity had just breathed their last breath.

Many of the adults who lived in the town's neighborhoods had come to the school's campus to defend their homes and families, but the Periculanders were poorly trained compared to the Wackos. Every one of the terrorists was also a soldier. There were many who even Lavisa knew she couldn't beat.

Then there were others who didn't need to lift a finger to be effective—like Josh, or the green-haired man sauntering through the crowd, simply telling students to "halt" and they would instantly freeze. Lavisa avoided those two more than anyone. The last thing she needed was to be stupidly incapacitated by those with unfair Affinities.

Surprisingly, many students *had* returned from their hiding places to help. Once Danny had stalked away from campus, the severity of the mayhem decreased, and the teenagers clearly felt more comfortable without the fear that the ground would suddenly erupt beneath their feet. Lavisa wished Nero and Calder were here, and maybe even Adara and Angor. None were particularly trustworthy, but she would have accepted any form of aid at this point.

That was why she actually cracked a grin at the sight of Nixie, Demira, boulder-boy, and the acid-spitter strolling out of the Residence Tower.

Nixie swiftly formed orbs of water around five different Wackos' faces, while Demira wielded an even more lethal chain than before, choking and whipping any Wacko within range. Dave was doused in acid, his own clothes sizzling as he spewed the harmful liquid in every direction. Then the humanoid rock, Haldor, hurled stones at Wackos' heads, knocking them unconscious before they could process what had happened. Lavisa actually let out a triumphant laugh when boulder-boy managed to immobilize the green-haired paralyzer, at which Tray gaped at her.

"I thought you were only a fan of self-defense," he said, his disbelief unwavering even when a gust of supernatural air nearly swept him off his feet. A girl with a wind Affinity approached them, but Tray was too flabbergasted to care.

"I don't think any amount of force seems unnecessary right now." Lavisa ducked as a dart whizzed past her head. When she stood straight again, there weren't any Wackos traveling directly for her, but a person stood at her left, her pigtails perfectly preserved despite the blood caking her face.

Nixie's eyebrows jumped spitefully, and even as she thwarted Wackos with forceful jets of water, she maintained eye contact with Lavisa. "I should drown you for knocking me out."

"Can't say I would blame you." Cutting toward the right, Lavisa tripped the girl with the wind Affinity. The Wacko had managed to throw Tray a few yards back, but now she plummeted to the pavement, her head of bluish-white hair going limp when her face collided with the ground. "Although, now seems like a bad time."

"I think any time seems like a bad time," Nixie countered, snapping her fingers and drenching a man dashing toward them. Water must have flooded his lungs, because he collapsed to his knees and retched fluid into the grass. "You're skilled, Dispus, and I need talented people at my back when I declare Periculand as my own."

"You really wanna be the one in charge during the aftermath of this—*if* there's anything left to be in charge of?"

"None of this would have happened if the *Rosses* hadn't been in charge. Why didn't the Wackos host an invasion of this scale before now? Because Periculy had a strong hold of this town, and the Wackos were smart enough to fear him. Someone with power needs to rule this town, and I think after tonight, the Wackos will have a healthy amount of apprehension for me."

With a wild smile, Nixie waltzed away, making a show of torturing any Wacko who crossed her path. She might have been crazy, but Lavisa couldn't say that she was wholly wrong.

"I never thought we'd find ourselves fighting on the same side as Nixie," Tray said as he dusted off that strange, white suit. The fabric looked like miniscule scales, and it clung to his muscles in a way that made Lavisa feel awkward about observing it for too long. She'd felt it resting beneath his sweater when she'd patted his shoulder earlier, and even then she'd known it was more than a fleece undergarment. It made his muscles pulse with energy, poised for action.

"I never thought I'd find *you* brawling with such ease." A wry smirk inched onto her face. "You've improved, Stark. Now you've got brains *and* brawn."

To anyone else, it would have been a compliment, but Tray's lips curled with distaste at the notion, which was exactly why Lavisa had said it.

Straightening his posture, he glanced around at the bedlam and shook his head. Various scratches speckled his face, and his normally neat hair was an utter disaster, but somehow he'd remained relatively calm throughout this entire ordeal. Lavisa actually *was* a little impressed.

"We need to find Ashna. Guilty or not, we need to hand her over to the Wackos. Too many people are getting hurt. I wouldn't even be opposed to sacrificing Floretta if I thought it would end—What the..."

As Tray trailed off, Lavisa followed his line of vision to a small white *dog* darting through the crowd, dodging exploded mounds of dirt and feet that could have easily crushed his tiny body. Lavisa did have a soft spot for animals, but she soon realized there would be no mercy for this creature when shards of glass started shooting from its fur, targeting only the Periculanders.

"God, what the hell is this?" Nixie exclaimed from ahead as she pried splinters from the netting of her sleeves. "You Wackos are sick! You're gonna force me to drown a freakin' puppy?"

"Looks like you're on the wrong side, Nixie!" a familiar voice sang. Lavisa didn't believe it until she spotted Jamad Solberg sprinting after the dog, throwing casts of ice around his former peers' feet...in order to *help* the Wackos.

"Join the Wackos, everyone!" he beckoned whimsically, even as he attacked his old acquaintances with ice. "We have adorably evil dogs!"

He wasn't *killing* anyone, but Lavisa's blood still boiled at the knowledge that he'd betrayed Periculand—that he'd joined the *terrorists*.

Knowing she wouldn't stand a chance if he managed to sheathe any of her limbs in ice, Lavisa crouched and then wove through the crowd of clustered Affinities, a small knife now in either hand. No one had mustered the courage to challenge him, so he slowed his pace, projecting sheets of ice onto the ground around him, forming a slippery moat.

A crafty grin tugged at Lavisa's lips. Before Jamad could complete his moat, she sprung out of the throng, landing lightly and gliding across the ice. By the time she'd reached Jamad, he'd noticed her, but there wasn't enough time for him to turn and fight her; Lavisa's blade had already sliced through his calf, provoking an enraged cry.

The tough black leather he wore prevented the knife from cutting deep, but blood dripped onto the ice at his feet—and blood swelled in his face, a sign of his fury. He would pelt her with a torrent of ice crystals, and the little dog, positioned beyond the frozen moat, would shower her in shards of glass.

Except Lavisa hadn't slowed down. With her momentum and her skating strides, she slammed her foot into the dog's side before it could generate an attack. The animal whizzed through the air, yelping in a way that made her feel a little guilty—until she glanced around at all the people extracting glass from their flesh.

Now planted on the pavement, she rotated back toward where Jamad stood at the center of the icy surface. In the few seconds she'd taken to survey the crowd, he'd conjured a fleet of icicles, and Lavisa was their target.

Her body tensed, preparing to duck, dodge, and deflect. It seemed unlikely she'd evade all impalement, but she'd taken stab wounds in the past. She would simply have to make sure they hit spots that would inflict the least injury. There were only seconds to consider how she would have to move, but her brain in battle was as swift as her body. As long as she could predict the outcomes of outside forces, she could react adequately.

She hadn't expected Tray to *jump in front of her*, though.

There wasn't time to shove him out of the way. The storm of ice was upon them, and all Tray did to defend himself was shield his face with his arms.

Icicles overwhelmed them—or *him*, more accurately. Being larger than her, Tray took on the full brunt of the assault. Not even the smallest splinter grazed her.

The impact of the blows knocked him back into her, and she hastily caught him, her arms wedged beneath his armpits. Peering over his shoulder, half in a daze, Lavisa expected to see his white suit stained red, but the ice hadn't left a mark on the fabric. The icicles lay on the ground at his feet, as if the needle-sharp spikes had *bounced* off his body.

"That's some heavy-duty fleece you've got there, Stark," she remarked with much less sarcasm than she'd intended. The absolute impossibility of it had set her into a state of shock. She'd known his suit wasn't ordinary, but she hadn't thought it was *Affinity-proof.* That he'd protected her with such confidence and knew to shield his face implied *he* had been very well aware.

Scrambling out of her grasp, Tray stood and straightened his half-burnt sweater indignantly. "Don't get sassy with me—I saved you!"

"You also lied to me," she said, but the accusation was half-hearted. Fighting had resumed all around campus, and Jamad skated toward them as the dog closed in from behind.

"I want to kick it but I don't," Tray griped as they assumed a back-to-back position, leaving him to fight the dog while Lavisa faced Jamad.

"Mm, I know the feeling," she hummed, raising her knives. After his failure with the long-range attack, Jamad had produced two picks of ice that he wielded in either hand, perfect for close combat—Lavisa's favorite.

Tray seemingly succumbed to kicking the little beast, because Lavisa heard its familiar yelp as her opponent stepped into her proximity. She knew the magic-like properties of Jamad's Affinity would make this a tricky fight, so she aimed to distract him by exacting quick, unpredictable swings. Preoccupied with her relentless assault, he wouldn't be able to procure a sneak attack of ice.

Something else stole his focus as Lavisa slashed at his leather and jabbed her limbs into his. His pale blue eyes kept scanning the area as if waiting for something…or looking for someone. It continued to the point that she was *annoyed* he wasn't giving his full attention to the scuffle. She could have easily killed him. She could have stabbed him in the heart ten times throughout the brawl. But she didn't *want* to kill him, and she almost felt *silly* about fighting with such intensity while he lazed through it.

"Is Avner here?" he finally asked, the casualness of his tone jolting her backward.

"Is—" She halted her speech and movements, only able to blink as he met her eyes with an innocence that hadn't previously been there. "I thought Avner was with you."

"He was, but…" Jamad discarded one of his icicles to rub his forehead in exasperation. "I figured he would come here to try and thwart all this, but…he's not here. Is Zeela here, at least?"

Lavisa's eyebrows shot up. "I thought Zeela was also with you. So, you joined the Wackos but they didn't."

"The Wackos aren't as bad as everyone claims," Jamad began to say, but then he noticed the way Lavisa's eyes swept the scene with dry disbelief.

"No? That's funny, because it looks like the Wackos are hurting innocent people just to apprehend *one person*." She stashed her knives and crossed her arms, knowing that even if Jamad tried to hurt her he would fail. For once, Lavisa actually wanted to talk more than she wanted to fight, and she knew he would be more truthful if she gave the impression of surrender. "Why are you fighting for them? This is your *home*. How can you watch it burn?"

There *was* pain on his face when he glanced sidelong at the Physicals Building, but the stiffness of his stance indicated he hadn't quite yielded. "I just thought that...if I could turn my back on Periculand, it'd be easier to turn my back on my parents, when the time comes—Another long story," he added when he saw the befuddlement written on her face. "But then Danny blew up the gate and—and I knew I couldn't do it. So I tried staying in the van, but then Shards got loose and I had to chase him—that little monster has some serious bloodlust—"

"AGH! For the love of knowledge!" Tray swore from behind. More intrigued than panicked, Lavisa spun around to find he had a shard of glass wedged in his forehead, oozing blood into his eyes. "I'm bleeding!"

"Clearly," Lavisa intoned as she stepped toward him and plucked the fragment from his skin. He groaned in agony and she rolled her eyes. "It's a superficial wound, Stark. Get over it."

Tray continued grumbling, but the dog seemed not to think it had hurt him enough. Sharp slivers ejected from its fur, embedding in Lavisa's and even Jamad's skin now. Sighing, she took a second reluctant strike at the dog, punting him with enough force that he didn't rise when he landed.

"Whose dog is that and why does it have an Affinity?" she demanded.

Jamad grimaced. "Danny's."

"You killed the psychopath's dog!" Tray exclaimed in horror. "He's going to level this place now—*ow*!"

"Are you stuttering? Compose yourself before you—"

"No—I just got *stung*," he moaned, tilting his head to show a massive stinger had pierced the side of his throat. It looked like a *bee* stinger—but from a bee larger than that dog.

Lavisa grunted, clutching her arm, only to find she'd been gifted with her very own stinger. With only a t-shirt on her torso, her arms were exposed, and the stinger had rooted deep into her flesh, morphing it into a dark, angry, red welt.

That alone might have induced an involuntary sense of nausea, but what really overpowered Lavisa's brain with dizziness was the little red bumps popping on her arm, spreading to her torso and then, within a few seconds, her entire body. Even with the stinger in Tray's neck, such a sensitive spot, he didn't have this severe of a reaction.

"You were supposed to make sure Shards didn't get hurt, you noob!" a female voice shouted, but Lavisa couldn't locate its origin. The pounding in her head impaired her vision, and the swelling of her limbs made her joints buckle in a way that was unnatural for her.

"I'm not a noob!" Jamad yelled back from somewhere to Lavisa's left. "And you shouldn't have stung them!"

"We are in a battle!" the unfamiliar girl retorted, her voice growing closer. All Lavisa could see was an array of moving blobs. "If Shards is dead, Danny's gonna *murder* us!"

"That dog is invincible," Jamad insisted.

"He's the size of a large *rat*!"

"Hey!" a voice barked, and Lavisa was surprised to recognize it as Tray's. Never had he sounded so aggressive. He yanked the stinger out of his throat and hurling it at the person who had just joined them—a girl with bright yellow hair. Her features were indistinguishable, but Lavisa was still lucid enough to witness Tray wrap his fingers around her neck. "Look at what you did to her!"

It took Lavisa a moment to realize he was referring to *her*. "She's going into anaphylactic shock! *Fix her*!"

"Your girlfriend will be fine," the girl dismissed. "I used to be severely allergic to bees and look at me now: I can shoot stingers out of my skin. Maybe she'll end up with the same Affinity as—"

"She already has an Affinity," Tray snarled, and he must have tightened his clutch on her throat because a little yip emitted from her mouth.

"Oh, well, then, that's unfortunate for—"

A choking sound ensued—just as Lavisa dropped to her knees, the pounding in her skull too intense for her to remain upright. Bile rose in her throat and every part of her body felt like it was on fire, but she had to get up—Tray was about to murder this girl.

"Alyssa!" That must have been Jamad, but he sounded more agitated than alarmed. "Just extract the venom already, will you? Stark's got a super strength Affinity. He'll crush—"

"Stark?" the girl repeated, her volume rising with excitement even though it was strained. "You're one of the Starks? Oh, Danny will want you."

"Speaking of what Danny wants," a smooth voice interjected as a new member joined their strange circle. Lavisa inclined her head as much as she could and tried to discern the man's features. Black hair…with some blue…thin stature, bored expression—and then Tray plummeted to the ground, landing beside her, unconscious. Josh, then. "He's on the way back from the police station. We're to cease fighting and start grabbing hostages. We'll see if Ashna wants this entire town to go extinct. Killing is now permitted."

"Oh, and it wasn't permitted before?" Alyssa questioned.

Even with her blurry vision, Lavisa saw how piqued Josh was. After a moment of silence, he looked away from Alyssa like she was some inconsequential insect. "Spread the word. Everything needs to be in place once Danny returns to campus."

His eyes cut to Lavisa then, the black and blue irises as clear as if she stood directly in front of him. There wasn't kindness in them, but there wasn't cruelty either, only mercy, as was reflected in his next action. Because, even though she'd avoided him earlier, the numbness of Josh's incapacitating Affinity—an exemption from the physical and emotional pain that was sure to increase—was a gracious gift she gladly gave in to.

38

Manipulation and Control Pt. 2

"Your girlfriend's a bitch, you know," Hartman said as he stared up at his stepbrother. "I offered her my friendship and she declined. Guess I can't expect *you* to have a decent taste in—"

"One more word," Nero grunted as he climbed a mound of wreckage, "and I'll pull your larynx out of your throat."

"You know what a larynx is?" Hartman thought to Eliana in a theatrical mental voice. *That's what I'd ask him if he wasn't being so moody.*

She wondered if there was ever a time when Nero *wasn't* being moody. Luckily, he plunged onward ahead of her, oblivious to the faint smirk on her lips and the mental quips Hartman had sent her throughout their trek across the ruined Physicals Building. Hartman was one comment away from his death, and Eliana definitely didn't want to add to Nero's agitation.

The moment she'd seen the building blow, there hadn't been any hesitation in running to search for Hartman. *Running* was probably a generous term; it'd been more like a quick hobble because of the wound in her calf, soaking the bottom half of her jeans in blood. The throbbing had been unpleasant, but she couldn't fathom Hartman's death. He wasn't her favorite person in Periculand, but after spending time with him over the past few months, she'd developed an odd sort of fondness for him.

Now, as they neared the exit, rubble continued to shower from above in random increments, some partially obstructing their path. Eliana welcomed any delay in their departure from the building—their submersion in the battle. She'd blocked out the emotional anguish pressing on her mind, but it was impossible to close her ears to the sounds of destruction and death weaving through Periculand. By Nero's unexpected mercy, Hartman had survived, but what if Tray, Lavisa, or Ackerly had died? Or…Kiki? She'd barely had enough time to cope with the reality of Hastings's death; she couldn't endure another tragedy.

Struggling to hide her limp, Eliana followed Nero through the glass doors, immersing them in a town glimmering with various shades of flame. The Naturals Building was partially ablaze, and beyond that, the front gate retained remnants of its initial inferno. Somehow, the Residence Tower had remained unscathed, and Eliana hoped Kiki was secured safely behind its walls, especially when she saw the campus's courtyard was strewn with bodies. Many of the students had fought, and many had fallen. A few still stood, but the ratio between mobile Wackos and mobile students was not in Periculand's favor.

As they neared the dwindling action, Eliana noticed Nixie leading the Periculand force, and she sensed Nero's displeasure at the sight. Before she could trace the origin of his irritation, a dark arrow shot through the air, wedging deep in the muscles of his right arm.

At the unanticipated pain, he dropped Hartman, causing the younger Corvis to smack the pavement and then bellow about the agony his rear end now experienced. Eliana's brain ran through various plans of escape, but three Wackos had already rushed to detain them. A girl with sunflower yellow hair grabbed her upper arm, equally bright eyes surveying Nero with satisfaction.

"I must say, that was a damn good shot," the girl mused. As the three Wackos dragged—literally, in Hartman's case—them toward the center of the dying battle, Eliana realized it wasn't an arrow the girl had attacked with: It was an abnormally giant bee stinger, and Nero's footsteps had turned lethargic as a result.

"Wh-what's going on?" Eliana asked, infusing her tone with feeble innocence, which wasn't particularly difficult.

"Danny's on his way here, and you guys are his hostages," the yellow-haired Wacko told her, almost bitterly. "I would refrain from talking unless you want one of these." With her free hand, she motioned toward her swollen and purple nose. For some reason, Eliana feared a broken nose was Danny's most humane form of punishment.

Once all conscious Affinities were stationed in a circle near the base of the Residence Tower, Eliana noticed with relief that none of her friends were present. If Danny planned to use Periculand's citizens as collateral, she didn't want any of her friends to become a disposable means to the Wacko leader's desired end.

"Josh," Danny snapped as he stalked into the circle, his previous charm abandoned. Naretha followed him like a soldier, emotionless and numb despite the scratches on her face and the thick sheet of dust coating her leather garments. "Where's Smith?"

"Unconscious. Over there." Josh's blue-tipped mohawk bobbed when he jerked his chin toward the Naturals Building.

Danny's mouth settled in a tight line, but an outburst didn't ensue. "Who else's screams will draw my sister out of hiding?" This was more of a question for himself, one he posed as his gaze swept the crowd. It was a miracle he didn't spot the three people sleuthing around the outskirts.

Granted, the only reason Eliana knew they were present was because she sensed their consciousnesses. Josh should have been able to as well, but perhaps without the emotion-detecting aspect Eliana possessed, he couldn't discern one mind from another. To him, the three brains could have easily belonged to Wackos. To Eliana, they very clearly belonged to Ackerly, Ashna, and Naira.

Was this why Ackerly had disappeared earlier—to help with the girls' mysterious mission? The Wackos were too absorbed in their leader to notice him awkwardly scouting the assembly, which would have relieved Eliana if he weren't working for Ashna. Through his open mind, she detected him formulating a plan to rescue Periculanders, but why? Did Ashna hope to apprehend the students for her own leverage purposes? Or did she hope to remove the innocent Affinities and unleash her multiple Affinities on the Wackos?

"We'll start with the cripple," Danny announced, stalking to where Hartman slumped on the ground. "I know how my sister adores the weak."

His orange eyes flew wide, but when he squeezed them shut and tried to teleport, nothing happened; instead, he was whisked violently to his feet and yanked toward the center, repeatedly moaning "ow" until they stagnated. Josh and Naretha had retreated into the crowd, the former looking bored and the latter looking almost *aggravated*, as if Danny's actions pissed her off.

"Where should we begin with the weakling?" the leader jeered, receiving various responses from his followers. Many were silent, uncomfortable, but others, like the girl holding Eliana, were adamant about Hartman's torment, the apparent key to Ashna's capture. Either they delighted in the pain of others or they had some severe grudges against the Wacko leader's sister—or both.

Desperation coursed through Eliana as she peeked at Nero, swaying beside her, his face a dazed mask, his mind in a sluggish stupor. Nixie stood across the circle, watching with a clenched jaw, but she didn't seem inclined to intervene either. They were all going to let Hartman suffer.

This couldn't happen—not after he'd been saved from death—not when Kiki, Tray, Seth, Lavisa, and Adara might have been injured or killed—not when Zeela, her only real family, might have been gone, too—not when Ashna, the solution, lurked within the crowd.

Why did she continue hiding when Hartman's life was on the line? By now, it had become obvious that she and her brother were not on good terms, but just because he was evil didn't mean she was good. Judging by her passivity in this moment of peril, she was as heartless as the monster who'd vanquished half the town.

Eliana had no problem with sacrificing those willing to sacrifice others.

"I know where Ashna is." She stepped forward, only to be hauled back by the yellow-haired girl. Even as she blended into the crowd, Danny's eyes fixated on her, brimming with greed.

No! a voice squeaked in her head. It took all her will not to cut her gaze toward Ackerly, peering through the masses, pleading with those innocent green eyes. *We have a plan to defeat Danny! Just give us some—*

"Mind reader?" Danny inquired, his vocal voice overpowering Ackerly's mental one. Eliana nodded, and his lips curled hungrily. "I've always wanted one of you... Well, where is the little beast?"

Her jaw fell slack, her mouth too dry to speak, even though

the answer was on her tongue. Ackerly's plea kept playing in her mind, either because he repeated it or because it seemed too sincere to be false. What if he and Ashna really did have a plan that could thwart Danny but Eliana ruined it by revealing their location? It was such a gamble, and even if she trusted Ackerly, there was still a chance they wouldn't succeed.

"She's—" Eliana started, but then her mind was slammed with a memory so strong that she was transported from reality completely.

At first, it was entirely disorienting. Her awareness was thrust from Periculand into a foreign setting, one composed of gray walls and metal doors and no windows. After a few moments, another's thoughts and perceptions trickled into her brain, allowing her to see this scene from someone else's point-of-view: Ashna's.

None of the doors dared to open as Ashna stormed through the hallway of what Eliana now recognized as Wacko Headquarters. Her rage pulsed throughout the underground fortress, as bright as the red light blinking in the corner of her eye. Eliana felt its source rather than saw it: the cool electric collar ringing her throat, the reason the girl had arrived at Periculand with a necklace of bruises.

When she stepped up to the silver doors of the elevator at the end of the corridor, her reflection revealed black, punkish attire, so unlike anything she'd ever worn in Periculand. The aggression with which she marched into the elevator was also foreign to Eliana; never had she seen this reserved girl show such emotion, nor had she ever experienced anything like it herself.

The elevator descended two floors, but the doors refused to part, invoking a groan from Ashna as she banged on the metal. "Let me in!" She glared up at the corner, where Eliana spotted a tiny camera.

"*Please* goes a long way, sister," Danny's voice taunted.

"Not with you," she snarled, at which his laughter permeated the elevator. When the doors parted, granting her access to his office, he sat behind his desk, smirking.

"What the *hell*, Danny?" Her voice echoed through the grand room as she stalked in and slammed her hands on the wooden surface. His little white dog, which Ashna's brain referred to as Shards, lounged in his lap, and the tiny creature barked at the sudden noise.

"What have I done to rattle you this time, little sister?" Danny droned, slipping on a mask of boredom. Their favorite band, Bleeding Brains, played softly in the background, but it did nothing to mitigate Ashna's fury.

"There's always an ongoing list, isn't there? How about, for today, we focus on the issue of how poorly you've been treating Madella?"

His gaze flickered to hers, inquisitive. Even knowing she was in Ashna's mind, Eliana felt the urge to shudder at his unnerving attention. "Madella was brought here as a hostage," he said. "I wasn't under the impression I was obligated to treat her with any decency. As long as she's alive, she's a valid bargaining chip. The fact that I've removed her from that cell and given her a room is courteous."

"You've removed her from a cell and placed her in a new one. She's *locked* in her room and you have Alyssa guarding the door. Is she that much of a threat?"

"No," Danny conceded as he resumed petting Shards, "but you and Zach are."

Ashna snorted, standing straight to cross her arms. "That's why you gave Alyssa her very own remote, hm?"

Danny's eyebrows jumped as she nodded toward the handheld

device on his desk, which controlled her electric collar. Eliana sensed her recalling the numerous opportunities in which she could have stolen the remote, but she never would, because the moment she defied Danny would be the moment of her death—and possibly everyone else's.

"Alyssa is trustworthy; you are not," he replied, lips spreading into a spiteful grin. "Why do you fret for Madella so? Has Zach brainwashed you with his sentiments of mercy? The girl is from Periculand. She will hate us as all from Periculand do. If given any freedom, she will escape."

"She wouldn't *want* to escape if we convinced her that what we stand for is good. Instead, you scare her with threats and display us as a group of vengeful monsters. If we allowed her to assimilate with the group, she would realize the mission of Affinities for Freedom is in favor of *all* Aff—"

"That name," Danny interrupted, his demeanor glacial, "died with our father. We *are* the Wackos, whether you like it or not. Our mission is not for *all* Affinities. If there are Affinities who don't agree with our ideology, our methods, they're as pathetic as Reggs, and should be treated as such."

"That's not what Dad would have wanted. He wasn't a saint, but he did want to help *all* Affinities. He wouldn't have let Madella rot in her room. He would have introduced her to everyone, treated her as a guest, let her decide for herself if this is a movement she wants to—"

"Your opinion of our father is much too generous, sister. Regardless, there is no *decision* to be made. Madella was born an Affinity. It's only logical—only moral—that she agree with our views. Since she does not, she should be punished."

"She let Josh give her the freakin' tattoos—she said she wouldn't run away because she wants to see her friends. What more do you want, Danny? Want her to bow down to you like you're some god? You don't give a damn about other Affinities. You just care about power. If you want to win this war against the Reggs, we need all the support we can get. We need people like Madella. Hell, we *should* form an alliance with Periculand—with Angor—but you're too much of a pussy to consider—"

"Watch," he snapped, retrieving the remote, "your tongue."

Ashna stiffened, but she didn't apologize or back down. Eliana would have. That's what she'd been about to do before this vision was thrust on her: give into Danny's demands out of fear. Ashna was willing to risk her own safety for what she believed was right, and as much as Eliana hated to admit it, her views on morality seemed…moral. She didn't support Danny's cruelty, like Eliana and the others had assumed; she didn't want the Wackos to be terrorists. And if Danny found her threatening enough to put an electric collar around her neck, maybe she actually had the ability to overthrow him.

"Angor Periculy shows no interest in allying himself with me," Danny explained, toying with the remote in one hand while petting Shards with the other. "I sent him a letter about negotiating terms to exchange Madella for Naretha, and he refused. He stole her and he kept her from me."

Ashna didn't react to his strained words; there was no sympathy in her heart. To her, Danny's anguish was fair and deserved.

"You of all people know what Angor is capable of," he continued. "Do you not think he tortured her?"

Ashna's resolve crumbled with that. Biting her lip, she tentatively said, "Look, Danny…I want her back here as much as you do. We all miss her, and we're all worried about her, but… she volunteered for the mission. She knew the consequences. You were the one who refused to give her the pill."

"Would you rather her *dead*?"

"If Angor tortured her… Well, it doesn't matter now. You said she's on her way back, and given that, I'm grateful for your decision. I want to support your authority here, Danny, I really do, but…I can't support all your ideas. Like this." She touched the collar on her neck, the metal cool against her fingertips. "I never wanted Dad's position—your position. What he did to you…" She eyed the tattoos painting his skin, the fire and explosions and death that mirrored his Affinity—the Affinity his father had willingly subjected him to. "I'm sorry, but it wasn't my fault—not really. I don't want to be your enemy. All I've ever wanted was to help. Why can't you have faith in me?"

"There is no faith for thieves," he said quietly, unable to meet her eyes. Despite not knowing what Ashna had stolen, Eliana knew she was the thief. Ashna knew it, too, but she had never believed her brother thought so little of her.

"Fine," she said, spinning on her heel to depart.

"Sister," he called, pausing her in the elevator's entrance. When she turned her head to glare at him, the wrath pouring from that gaze must have discouraged him from speaking his original statement, for he simply said, "See you at breakfast tomorrow."

Eliana knew he didn't, though. This was the night Ashna had escaped the Wackos to flee for Periculand. It was during this conversation that she lost faith in her brother, that she decided she had to betray him.

I came here for Adara, Ashna thought as Eliana's vision returned to the present. Her brain had processed the memory in only a few short seconds. Danny still clutched Hartman by his ash-laden sweatshirt, staring at her expectantly, unaware of the information she'd been gifted.

Adara was the only person I've ever heard about who has an

Affinity so similar to Danny's, Ashna continued urgently. *She was the only one who might have been able to quench his explosions. I didn't want to lead the Wackos here, nor did I think Danny would come here with Periculy in charge. But then…he wasn't; Danny never told me Angor was imprisoned.*

Once I got here, I knew I had to work fast, but Adara was in jail, making it too complex. Now she's…well…I think she might be dead. Danny exploded the police station a few minutes ago and…and her nociceptors weren't receiving any stimuli, meaning she's either passed out or…passed away. I don't know if she made it. So I have to attack him on my own. I think I can contain his explosion with my force field Affinity—enough that no one will get severely injured. But we'll need to get Hartman away from him. And then…I need you to piss him off. I need him to explode.

Eliana wanted to ask why, but she knew Ashna wouldn't hear her mental message. Why would she *want* him to explode? Did she think containing the explosion within a force field would cause Danny to implode? It seemed unlikely that he could die by his own Affinity, but Ashna's rainbow eyes, peeking through the crowd, were full of determination.

"She's…in this town," Eliana stated, meeting Danny's gaze steadily even though her hands trembled. "But I won't tell you where until you let Hartman go."

There was a flicker of impatience in his expression, but then a smile snaked across his lips. "Sure, I'll let him go."

Eliana predicted it, but her jaw still dropped when Danny flung Hartman to the side. His cry as he smashed onto the ground summoned the same wrath in Eliana that she'd experienced through Ashna. Danny knew how to provoke explosions of various kinds, it seemed.

Wrenching her arm free from the Wacko girl's grasp, she hissed, "*That's not what I meant.*"

"No?" Danny sauntered toward her as the Wacko girl scrambled to reassert her dominance. Eliana let the girl grab her arms behind her back, mostly because she had no idea what she would *do* with her hands if they were free. She wasn't a fighter, and her Mental Affinity didn't give her the ability to inflict damage like Hastings's had. With the shields guarding Danny's mind, she had no power over him. She was as weak as a Regg.

"Do tell me what you meant," Danny prompted, now standing before her. He was too close. If he detonated now, Eliana would go down with him, even with Ashna's shields. But Hastings had been a martyr. He'd willingly died to save one person. Shouldn't Eliana have been more ready to sacrifice her life for the population of Periculand?

To fluster Danny, she would need Adara levels of sass. Boldness had never been in her nature, but the Wacko leader reminded her of everyone and everything she'd always been too scared to rebel against: Her parents, who had always been disappointed in her, who had always treated her like a disease; those therapists, who had prodded her with questions, who had observed her like she was an alien; the Rosses, who had, in one way or another, led to Hastings's death, who had allowed terrorists to siege Periculand.

If she'd had the courage to question any of them, perhaps things would be different. Perhaps *she* would be different. Now she would have to make up for her inaction, even if her survival instincts reared against it.

"You know what I meant. I wanted a fair exchange. But… all you want is to hide behind other people's lives because you're too afraid to lose your own. You instill fear in others to hide the fear within yourself. You'll never get respect because you don't give respect."

Due to his mental shields, these secret sentiments of his were mostly guesses, but he was easy to read, a fact magnified by the fury washing over his features. Her assumptions had been correct, and he did not want to hear the truth.

With the snap of his finger, the air beside her left ear erupted.

The Wacko girl staggered back, her swears muffled in Eliana's throbbing ear. Teetering, she struggled to balance, struggled to listen, struggled to hone in on Danny as he closed the distance between them and wrapped his sweltering fingers around her delicate throat.

"It's cute, mind reader, how you spit lies and expect everyone to believe them." His tone held too much passion to mark her statement as a lie. "Who here thinks a word she said is true—that I'm *afraid*—that I don't deserve respect?"

The Wackos remained silent, even though Eliana felt their collective unease. Hartman, who had crawled toward the edge of the circle, kept his mouth shut, even though Eliana saw the tears in his eyes. Nero, warding off the stinger's venom, didn't budge, even though Eliana sensed his thirst for vengeance. The apprehension permeating the air proved her point further.

"Who here thinks this girl deserves to live?" Danny demanded, eyes igniting when he received the same reaction. This time, Eliana knew Ashna moved into position. When Danny destroyed her, his sister would ensure he also destroyed himself.

The saddest part of it all, Eliana thought, was that there probably wouldn't be enough of her body left to bury beside Hastings's.

"Does murdering her seem like the best option, honey?" Naretha finally piped up. There was no affection in her tone, despite the affectionate term she'd added at the end. "You've always wanted a mind reader of your own. Her death would be a waste."

"I'm the one who determines that," he snapped, his fingers now scorching the flesh of Eliana's throat. She tried to stay tough, but an involuntary squeak escaped her mouth, widening Danny's grin. "And I've determined I don't like mind readers very much. Therefore, sister," he called out at a higher volume, "the mind reader's death will be the first on your conscience. Unless, of course, you count all of the lives spent here tonight in your honor. Then you have a long—"

"What—what is going on here?" a familiar voice questioned, parting the mass closest to the Residence Tower. Eliana was almost relieved to see William Ross stumbling out through the glass doors. Surely, the Regg would distract the Wacko leader long enough that Eliana could scurry away. Then she saw who the man dragged by the hair, and any concept of movement bled out of her awareness.

"*Kiki*," she breathed as pink eyes came into view. Glimpsing her now—clothes hastily thrown on, hair a bedraggled mess, face streaked with glittery tears—stirred deep sorrow in Eliana. A moment ago, she'd been prepared to die; now she remembered she had something to live for. She couldn't leave this world without apologizing for her absurd outburst, and she certainly couldn't allow *Kiki* to leave this world—not under any circumstances.

Both of their deaths seemed imminent, however, for while Danny held a hand to Eliana's neck, William held a gun to Kiki's temple.

"You little bitch," Nero snarled at the Regg, but his voice was breathy, weak. He tried to wrench away from the Wacko holding him, but he'd been too destabilized by the bee stinger to muster the strength. "You threw me in jail… I'll…kill you…"

William refused to acknowledge the brute, but he did react

to the threat by digging the gun's muzzle deeper into Kiki's flesh. A sob escaped her lips, and Eliana tried desperately to send her a comforting glance, a wordless apology, but her eyes were too clouded with tears to notice. "Why has the fighting ceased?" the man demanded.

"Oh, don't worry, the trauma isn't over yet," Danny crooned, tightening his grip on Eliana. "You've arrived just in time for the second act of the show to begin."

"The b-battle should not be *over*," William stuttered like a malfunctioning robot. "If the fighting doesn't resume, I'll—I'll shoot this girl!"

Eliana didn't even process the ridiculousness of his statement. All she comprehended was the anguish in Kiki's expression and the fact that this Regg threatened her life. Yet again, someone she cared for would die before her eyes. With Hastings, she had done nothing. She had watched in terror, too shocked to intervene. She could not make that mistake again.

"You *want* the fighting to resume?" Danny's eyebrows perked as if he'd been presented with a platter of his favorite food. "How incriminating. This must mean the government plans to watch us kill each other off—eliminating a mass of Affinities all at once."

"I-I will shoot her," William stammered so unconvincingly that Danny laughed, "and then I'll shoot you all!"

The man had lost his mind. Eliana wasn't at all mournful about his sudden insanity, but his volatility increased the chances of Kiki's death. If their theory was correct, he'd played a part in Angor's attempted assassination—Hastings's death. He had no problem with using children for his own agenda.

Why did he even *need* to at this point, though? If Artemis was the mind controller, she could have forced the Affinities back into battle, but why would she want them dead if she was one herself?

None of it made sense. All she knew was that she had to remove Kiki from William's clutches, and she couldn't startle the man in the process. She would have to be discreet. She would have to use her Affinity in reverse. She would have to become the very thing she loathed: a mind controller.

Tray would have laughed at this plan. It was ludicrous, really, a futile hope that defied logic. Eliana had the ability to decipher others' thoughts, but she had never managed to project her own, not even on the few occasions she'd tried. Failure was imminent, but in this moment, with Hartman injured and Nero half-sedated and any of her other potential allies detained or absent, she would have to turn her Affinity into a weapon.

"This is *proof*," Danny said, his voice a distant echo in her hazy ears, "that all of you should be on our side."

He spoke to the Periculanders, even Eliana, but she didn't listen. Her attention was trained on William's brain. His thoughts were sporadic and panicked, but she had to hope she could slip one of her own in there, a very specific command: *Drop the gun.*

"The Reggs want to annihilate us all," Danny went on, his outer voice matching the passion of her inner one.

Drop. The. Gun.

"Just because they haven't labeled you a 'terrorist' doesn't mean they don't see every single one of us as a threat—as the enemy. They've groomed you for death. You're like a bunch of innocent chickens they've prepared for the slaughter."

"This is why we should all be vegetarians!" Nixie cheered from across the circle, receiving a few chuckles from the tense audience.

"Let's not be rash here, Mardurus," Danny retorted, quenching Nixie's grin. Whether it was his rebuttal or the use of her last name that perturbed her, Eliana didn't care. Her concentration rested in repeating the same mental command over and over—to no avail. "The slaughter of animals is not the problem. Animals are beneath humans, and the problem is that Reggs see *us* in the same light. They believe Affinities to be a lesser species—one they can control—when in reality, we are the ones who can control them.

"Let's put aside all this bullshit," he proclaimed, releasing his grip on Eliana's throat. The heat of his fingers lingered there, and when she brought her hand to it, she found the skin was raw and sticky. "Let's forget this battle, the past, our differences. It's time to join forces, to end the Reggs once and for all. Do you think, Affinities of Periculand, that people like this Regg deserve to be in charge—deserve to *live*? He's threatening to murder this little girl in a lame attempt to get us to murder each other!"

"You've threatened to murder a lot of little girls," Tray huffed as he materialized from the throng, Lavisa at his side. Based on the cuts and bruises marring their skin—and the abnormal swelling of Lavisa's entire body—they had endured a rough evening, but they were present now, and all of Danny's attention had averted to them, giving Eliana the opportunity to divert all of *her* attention to William.

The female Wacko hadn't resumed her hold on Eliana, so she used the distraction of Tray's appearance to inch closer to William, hoping the proximity would magnify her efforts at mind control. Until now, she'd tried very simple, half-hearted orders, so she exerted all her effort this time and thought a specific demand: *Remove your gun from Kiki's head, William. Now.*

She hadn't expected anything to happen. Which was why, when William rotated his head away from Danny and toward her with absolute bewilderment, she instinctively mirrored his expression. He had *heard* her. As a result, the gun slowly descended from Kiki's brow, freeing her from danger, even though the man seemed not to be acting of his own volition.

"Threatening little girls does seem to be the trend these days." At that melodic voice, every head whipped toward the center of town. The crowd parted, revealing Olalla Cosmos, strolling down the path to Town Hall with Fraco and Aethelred on either side.

"Cosmos," Danny greeted, lips pursing tartly. "Finally decided to grace us with your presence, did you?"

Throughout this entire battle, the Affinity ambassador hadn't crossed Eliana's mind once. Why hadn't she been here to quell the bloodshed with her peace Affinity? Curious, the mind reader prodded at the woman's thoughts, but her brain was as elusive as ever. The murkiness of Olalla's mind had always seemed a little suspicious, but it was the patronizing smirk on her lips now that made Eliana wonder what her true motives were.

"Who am I to stop you from your goals, Daniel?" Olalla countered, joining him in the center. Tonight she wore a floor-length dress, the same plum purple as her glossy hair. With the matching shawl draped over her shoulders, she looked even more professional than the men in their suits or the Wackos in their leather. When she paused her strides, Aethelred and Fraco halted, as well. "Isn't it also a trend these days to give children whatever they desire?"

Danny's eyes slivered. "You're forgetting I'm not a child."

"Oh, no, I think you're forgetting you *are*." Her following smile was tight-lipped, but it irked the Wacko leader more than any toothy grin would have. His irises flared, but Olalla continued before a full reaction could form. "I think you've done enough damage here tonight. Ephraim would be proud to know he's finally had his revenge on Angor, but…Angor doesn't rule this town anymore."

"Ah, yes, the pathetic Rosses do." He cast a glance in William's direction. The Regg hadn't raised his gun since Eliana told him to lower it, but his hand was tangled in Kiki's hair, and Eliana knew her heart wouldn't calm until her roommate was completely liberated. "Even more of a reason for me to level it. The Reggs have shunned you, Cosmos. They didn't want you as vice president because they don't even want you *alive*. They want all of us dead. When will you admit my father was right?"

Olalla opened her mouth for a response, but it was William's voice that penetrated the frigid air.

"Fraco, what are you doing! I instructed you to find shelter for my wife!"

Eliana's gaze cut straight to Tray. His jaw was slack, his mind spinning with the same question as hers: Why would Artemis, the mind controller, need *shelter* during this battle? In a few seconds, Tray had conjured a dozen answers, but none aligned with the details they'd uncovered.

"Yes," Fraco acknowledged, sounding bolder than Eliana had ever witnessed, "but it's not *your* instructions I heed; it is Ms. Cosmos's. Ever since you framed Mr. Periculy for your own crimes and overthrew his leadership, I've been following Ms. Cosmos's directions with the hope that we can free this town's true principal from imprisonment."

This confession instilled shock amongst the Periculanders. Eliana had never seen Fraco as anything more than the vice principal, a man whose duty was to whoever governed the town, but his loyalty had always aligned with Angor.

"You don't deserve to control this town. You and your wife tried to kill Mr. Periculy!" he exclaimed as if scolding one of the students.

"No." William shook his head relentlessly. "Periculy tried to murder my wife! Where is she now? What have you done with her?"

"Your wife is safely underground." Olalla's tone was so casual that Eliana didn't catch the connotation at first, but then she *felt* the incredulity clanging through the crowd, the hundreds of minds all processing her confession to murder.

"Y-you killed her?" Tray questioned, swaying. "But—you're a woman of the government—the justice system—"

"I've done what is just," Olalla assured him with a sad smile. "She is at peace now, and that's another step toward what I've always strived for: peace for all."

"*No*," William moaned, finally releasing Kiki's hair as he staggered forward. She scampered away, dissolving into the crowd until Eliana could only sense her frazzled consciousness rather than see her physical form. "Artemis can't—she *can't*—"

"Oh, William," Olalla cooed as if speaking to a child who had lost his favorite toy. "What will you do without your precious wife? What will you be without her? What is the point of your life if you're alone?"

These words sunk into him with an unnatural impact, his thoughts immediately mimicked them. *What am I without Artemis? She was my best friend, my closest ally, the only person with whom I could confide anything. I can't go on without her—I can't go on—*

Despair and self-loathing oozed from him. Eliana should have felt vindicated that Artemis was dead and William now suffered—Hastings's murderers finally subjected to consequence—but the man's lament reflected her own grief upon Hastings's demise.

This was not peace for *all*. There could never be peace for *all*, because what brought one person joy brought another anguish. Peace was subjective. Peace was relative. Peace was an illusion.

A manipulation.

The gunshot made Eliana jump, Fraco squeak, Kiki scream, Ackerly gasp, Tray shout.

It was as deafening as Danny's explosions. Eliana couldn't distinguish what anyone said or thought or *did.* All she perceived were the droplets of blood sprayed on her face, the splintering of sanity within the frantic crowd, the *thud* reverberating through the ground with William Ross's collapse.

"Peace," Olalla stated, her soothing voice ringing through the pandemonium, "for all."

It should have been clear before now. It should have been clear when Olalla first came to Periculand and wooed the entire town onto her side with a single speech, but Eliana had been too naive. It should have been clear when Hastings had died, but Eliana had been too convinced Angor was the villain to detect it. It should have been clear during their entire investigation, but Olalla had blocked suspicion from their minds.

With her mind controlling Affinity.

"You made him kill himself," Eliana blurted out. The commotion faltered as she met Olalla's bottomless purple eyes, deep with deception. The Wackos had been unfazed by a Regg's death, but this accusation startled them. The only person who seemed unsurprised now was Danny. "You're the mind controller."

From where he lay on the ground, Hartman groaned, "Why do all the attractive females have to be evil! First Nixie, now Olalla—"

"Maybe you just have bad taste," Lavisa interjected. A few paces away, Nixie rolled her eyes, but Tray, at Lavisa's side, was too absorbed in the revelation of Olalla's abilities to acknowledge the banter.

"No—but—you—" Every sentence he started soon became nonsensical to his fast-working rationalization. Olalla could instill peace as effortlessly as she could instill discord. Olalla could have convinced them she wanted to help them when all she'd really wanted was to help herself. Olalla could have mourned Hastings's death as easily as she could have killed him—and she had.

"Controller, or manipulator?" the woman questioned, her gaze sweeping across the crowd. "Or…neither? My Affinity is to implant beliefs in people's heads. I made William believe his wife was dead. Whatever he did after that was of his own free will. Mostly. Perhaps he wouldn't have been *so* distraught if I hadn't made him believe his existence relied on her so heavily, but… we'll never know."

"You *murdered* Hastings," Eliana snarled, "and you made us believe it was anyone *but* you. We blamed Angor, then Artemis—is she really even *dead*?"

"I said she was underground; I never said she was *dead*. Her idiot husband only thought so."

"Because you *made* him think that," Tray snapped, looking equally as uncomfortable as he did enraged. It was then that Eliana noticed the strange white fabric clinging to his torso—and the claustrophobia he experienced because of it.

"It'll be true soon enough," Olalla dismissed with a wave. "Although, her death won't be quite as quick. William's was far too merciful to atone for all the Reggs have done to us."

"Why use Hastings to kill them when you could have done it yourself?" Tray demanded, practically spitting the words. "Obviously, you're capable."

"And I thought you were the smart one, Tray." Olalla tsked as she took a few languid steps in his direction. "I've been waiting for you to piece it all together. Why do you think Fraco told the Rosses you're the smartest student at this school? Because I told him to. I wanted to see how capable you were—not of hacking into Angor's office, but of turning against the Reggs. You passed that test, just as you passed the suit test."

Tray covered his mouth to withhold his nausea. "Wh…what?"

Olalla cocked her head, simpering. "Why do you think you

had such a sudden interest in the Reggs' suits? Because I planted it in your mind. I wanted to see what lengths you would go to for the sake of science. You banished your morals for it, stealing that suit and then examining it when you knew that you shouldn't have. True lovers of knowledge don't comply to the limitations of ethics."

"I—follow—ethics," Tray coughed as if each word were a wad of bile.

"When you can, sure. There's no need to be *unnecessarily* immoral, but it's reassuring to know your priorities are in check. It's also reassuring to see how eager you are to participate in my experiments."

Based on his thoughts—and his squirming—Tray's strange white suit had been a gift from Olalla, a gift that now seemed more like a garment of unwanted bondage.

"Why do you think I gave you the suit, Tray? To see if you'd be willing to risk *yourself* for the sake of science."

Panic spiked through Eliana in the same instant it spiked through Tray. Olalla must have detected his reaction, because her grin widened. "You aren't in danger; the suit is perfectly safe. Don't you trust me?"

"I'll trust you when you stop breathing," he grumbled, earning a chuckle from Danny.

"Sounds like we might have to fight for Stark." The Wacko leader's eyebrows arched at Olalla, and her humor didn't waver.

"You know it wouldn't be much of a fight, Daniel. Your mind could be mine in a matter of seconds, just as Tray's could. I like to keep the game fair, though, so I won't infect your thoughts...yet."

Eliana almost wished she would take hold of Danny's mind just to prevent his impending destruction. Her jabs seeped into him the same way her Affinity would. Perhaps Olalla's ability to read people so well—to elicit desired responses from them—was the origin of her Affinity.

"I want you to deduce with a clear mind what my motives are," she continued, eyes boring into Tray. She didn't invade his mind, though; his mental processing remained untainted by any outside forces. She really did want him to finish this failed investigation. "What could have provoked me to kill the Rosses a month ago when I'd worked civilly with them for years?"

"You...lost the election." His eyes flitted toward Eliana for some kind of confirmation, but Olalla's mind was too swampy to discern anything of value. "It made you hate the Reggs. Like... Danny said...they turned their back on you...and now you want to kill them all."

Olalla emitted a high-pitched laugh that had half the crowd cringing. "Killing them *all* seems a little extreme. If I wanted that, I would have simply joined Daniel—or sat back and watched him do all the work."

"My father always said you had a habit of letting others do your dirty work," Danny countered, but Olalla ignored him.

"I will admit, the election left me in a sour mood." She fidgeted with her shawl—the first sign of discomfort. "Perhaps the plan would have gone smoother if I hadn't been in such a peeved state of mind. But Harold and I had anticipated the loss. There was no fair way we could have won—"

"I wasn't aware *fair* was a part of your vocabulary," Danny injected, and Eliana sensed Naretha considering echoing the statement right back at him. It would have sparked a cycle of bad people incriminating worse people—an endless cycle in a crowd such as this.

"I had no interest in winning the election unfairly," Olalla said. "It would have been exhausting—and, frankly, impossible.

My powers only extend so far. I have limits, like any other Affinity. But I am capable of murder, with or without my Affinity. So then, Tray, why did I need Hastings—or rather, why did I *want* Hastings?"

The boy bit his lip, refusing to meet anyone's eyes. He didn't want any clues. Figuring out this puzzle wasn't merely an option anymore. "You didn't want to be linked to the murders. Hastings was Angor's son. If he killed the Reggs, it would have been traced back to Angor, not you."

"Closer," was all Olalla gave him.

"That's why you worked with them for years—why you didn't kill them sooner. You were waiting for Hastings to arrive here so you could use him to incriminate Angor."

She snorted humorlessly. "I'm beginning to think you insist on embarrassing me, Tray. I had no idea Angor even had a son—but discovering that fact *was* what set my plan into motion. I'd waited for the best method of execution for years—there were just so many options. As soon as I met Hastings, though, I knew he had to be Angor's son, and I knew he had to be the one, no matter what his Affinity was. After convincing Aethelred to let me search through Fraco's precious files, I discovered Hastings's Affinity and felt as if I'd been blessed. The perfect Affinity for an assassination."

That's why his file looked like it had been tampered with! Ackerly thought with enough volume to overpower everyone else's mental voices. Eliana remembered he and Adara had sifted through Hastings's file a few months ago, and as the memory replayed in Ackerly's mind, she also recalled the day she and Hastings had personally met Olalla.

Eliana had never seen the resemblance, but as someone who had worked with Angor for years, Olalla must have recognized Hastings's similarity right away. After briefly meeting them, she had departed with Aethelred for a discussion that had probably led to her forcing him to believe he wanted to let her snoop through Fraco's files. In a few short weeks, her plan had formed, and the devastation of the election had set it into motion.

"Some minds are harder to dupe than others," Olalla explained wistfully. "It took me longer than it should have to harness Hastings's beliefs. His mental abilities were so strong—I could only manage to infiltrate his thoughts when we were within a very close proximity.

"I was lucky that Angor summoned Hastings to his office that day. I'd been able to sneak into his mind from afar when he'd been out in the field with you all, his friends"—Olalla gestured toward Tray, Lavisa, Eliana, and Hartman—"but the force of my Affinity was so weak from that distance. If Hastings had not already been bound for Angor's office that afternoon, he might have ignored my nagging little voice. It is easy for me to block thoughts and memories and emotions, but planting new ones is trickier. Some people are not susceptible to persuasion, especially when their beliefs are already so firm.

"Thankfully, Hastings was always suspicious of Angor, and he had no clue the man was his father. It was not a far leap for him to conclude the mysterious principal was secretly an *evil Wacko* who needed to be eliminated," Olalla finished, a wicked smirk curling onto her lips.

"Oh shit." Hartman scrambled to sit upright, despite his injured leg. "You wanted to kill *Angor*? And you wanted to use his son to do it? That's *sick*—the bad kinda sick."

"Angor deserved to die by his son's hand," Olalla stated, not with any bitterness or passion, but as though it was an irrefutable fact. "He deserved to die looking into his son's eyes, knowing his son *wanted* to kill him—"

"Except he didn't," Eliana cut in, shaking her head. "He didn't want to kill Angor, and he killed himself instead. You *failed*."

Olalla rotated slightly but refused to turn her back to Danny—or even Tray. She was powerful mentally, but either of them could have demolished her physically. Half of the Affinities here could have defeated her with little effort. If they all banded together against her…

Even Olalla had said her Affinity had limits. There was no way she could slip her outlandish beliefs into hundreds of minds at once without anyone questioning it. The issue was coordinating an assault of that magnitude without Olalla foreseeing it. Eliana had spoken into William's mind, but it seemed unlikely that she could project her thoughts onto the entire mass of people, especially when the ability was so new…

…or maybe not an ability of hers at all. Yes, William had looked directly at her, and yes, he had lowered the gun when she'd commanded him to, but Olalla had walked over at that exact moment—with the intent of making William kill himself. What if he'd *happened* to look at her when it had really been Olalla speaking into his mind?

Frustrated and depleted, Eliana reluctantly refocused on the mind controller. She certainly didn't wear the face of someone who had failed. There was too much confidence etched in her features and laced in her voice.

"Did I fail?" Olalla challenged, mimicking Eliana's dejected thoughts. "Angor isn't dead, but he watched his son die, and now he's watching his beloved city burn. He was imprisoned within his own jail, betrayed by the Reggs he always trusted. Over the past few weeks, I've realized his death would have been much less satisfying than his continual suffering."

"You wanted to kill and now torture this man because—

because you're pissed he made a deal with the Reggs?" Tray demanded, his tone turning aggressive as he took a few steps toward her. Eliana swore she saw the woman flinch. "You're pissed he created this town for Affinities under the only conditions he could—by agreeing to train us for war? Children shouldn't be soldiers, but Angor isn't *evil.* He was willing to sacrifice his son to save the rest of us. You can't pretend he's wrong for that when *you* were the one that led to Hastings's death."

"So much drama here in Periculand," Danny enthused. "I would end it all now if I weren't so utterly entertained. And here I thought Angor had gone rogue, attempting to kill some Reggs. This is devious, Cosmos, even for you." His tone was more fervent than admonishing. There was no remorse when his vision trained on William's corpse. "I assume you'll seize Periculand as your own?"

Her lips curved shrewdly. "Periculand's always been mine. The Rosses were too incompetent to notice my influence, and I've always had a way of making Angor forget about our disagreements. I won't discredit him too much—there were many times his mental shields were too intense for me to fully penetrate, but he would be nothing without my charisma and diplomacy. There would be much less peace between Affinities and Reggs without my role as ambassador these past few years."

"Peace?" Naretha spat, stepping out from the crowd. "Do you call the research facilities *peace*? They *torture* Affinities. The Reggs don't deserve peace. They deserve war. We can't just stand aside—"

"Nor can we defeat them by brute force. We have powers, but they have numbers."

"Yeah, and we have Danny. If you didn't notice, he just destroyed half of *your* town without breaking a sweat. This was a fun little warm up for him. We can *easily* overthrow the Regg—"

"Naretha, dear," Danny interjected, stroking a finger down her cheek, as if that would calm her. Eliana felt the woman's temper flare even brighter. "Let's not argue. We came here for Ashna. All other issues can be discussed in a more formal meeting. Though, I can't guarantee it won't end with similar results..."

Flashing a grin, he gestured toward the flaming Physicals Building, and Eliana's jaw clenched at Olalla's careless smile.

"We had our differences in the past—your father and I—but I hope we can begin on a new slate, Daniel. Periculand and the Wackos need not be enemies any longer. You may have ruined this town, but from the ashes we'll be reborn under new leadership."

"Yeah," a gruff voice sounded, jolting Eliana where she stood. She'd forgotten Nero lingered beside her, hunched over and clutching his wounded arm. Even though his gait was clumsy, he shuffled toward the center of the circle, declaring, "*My* leadership."

The challenge hung in the air for only a few seconds before Olalla released a snicker. "You believe you have more influence in this town than I do, Nero? Well, you don't need my Affinity to determine that. Just look around—who here would follow *Nero's* leadership?"

His instability didn't stop him from glaring around at his peers, forcing them into submission with those stern eyes. Many of his followers slipped forward, the acid-spitter and Jerry Watkins sticking out conspicuously with their unwavering loyalty. But even though Demira asserted her allegiance, Nixie didn't move. She gnawed on her lip, wondering how to proceed with Nero's imminent loss. With a normally functioning body, he could have crushed half of Olalla's bones with one blow, but the bee stinger had weakened him.

"The Rosses let you play, Nero, but you aren't cunning enough for a position of real power." Gazing around the throng, Olalla elevated her volume to say, "Nero was the only student in Periculand who knew Angor's Affinity, but he never divulged the information. He was the only one who could have freed Periculy from jail, but he didn't because the Rosses gave him authority—and Angor *scares* him."

"N-*no*," Nero sneered as his friends gaped. "Nothing scares me—I don't know Periculy's Affinity!"

"You *did*, until my useful little primaries alerted me of the fact that you knew it." Olalla shot Tray a smirk. "I thought I'd covered everyone—blocking all memories regarding Angor's Affinity. He was always secretive, as I've said, so it wasn't a hard task...until I realized he'd used his Affinity on a student, during our little visit to the police station. If you hadn't let me tag along, Tray, you might've been able to weasel it out of Nero—*you* might have, at least," she amended with a sly glance in Eliana's direction. "Nero was too stupid to realize the weight of the knowledge he bore—the way in which he could have used it to his advantage. He possesses the strength of a leader but lacks the wit."

"And you have both?" Tray questioned dryly.

"You tell me." She didn't even have to lock eyes with him for her Affinity to begin its work. The warping of Tray's mind was no different than the simple change of an opinion, so subtle Eliana wouldn't have recognized it elsewhere. One moment he leaned toward Nero's side, and the next he saw "reason" and realized Olalla was the better choice.

"Do I possess the strength and wit to rule this town?" she prompted, tilting her head in mock wonder.

"Y-yes," Tray answered as his furrowed brows leveled out. "You'd make a better leader than Angor or the Rosses—or Nero."

"You little piece of—" The brute began to snarl, but then his beliefs abruptly morphed as well. With a muted expression, he said, "I think you'd make a great leader as well."

"Well then, it seems unanimous," Olalla announced, looking toward Danny, as if his word would be the deciding factor. Eliana knew otherwise. If Danny voiced dissent, he'd be quieted as quickly as the two boys. The Wacko leader sensed it, too, because for once, his lips remained sealed. "As the official Principal of Periculand, I'd like to thank you, Daniel Mayer, for the little distraction you caused here tonight."

As she indicated to the outcome of the explosions, the Wackos' faces all scrunched with confusion. Danny schooled his features into neutral acceptance of the praise, but Eliana felt his unease over her unexpected gratitude.

"The little battle gave me the bit of time I needed to finish up a project I've been working on. Fraco," she beckoned, and he scurried into the center. "My crown."

"Crown?" Apparently, this was bizarre enough to break through whatever beliefs Olalla had planted in Tray's mind.

"Damn, she's gonna be a queen." Hartman practically drooled as Fraco handed her the crown. From afar, it looked like a simple, silver tiara, but when Eliana squinted, she saw it was truly a compilation of wires and antennae, disguised to be beautiful.

Its appearance was inconsequential; it was the crown's function that mattered. For as soon as she placed it on her sheen of purple hair, the very fabric of the air changed. Eliana felt the toxic waves leaking into her brain, echoing through the minds around her in a deafening chorus.

Much of this night will be forgotten to you, Olalla's voice careened through every present consciousness, the words a lullaby to influence this nightmarish fate. *But I want each of you to remember my* power*—not my Affinity, per se, but the consequences I* *am capable of inflicting. To you all, I will have my peace Affinity, but you'll be wise not to test me.*

William Ross committed suicide tonight, not because I killed his wife, but because he knew he failed in his mission to eliminate all Affinities. The citizens of Periculand and the Wackos are still alive, and they are allies now, a force the Reggs will fear above any other.

Students in Periculand will continue their training, not to fight the Wackos, but to annihilate the Reggs. We will train ruthlessly, and we will not stop until every Regg is in chains or in the ground.

Angor Periculy is evil. The man tried to make his son murder me, Olalla Cosmos, with his Affinity that mentally forces others' muscles to move. His legacy will be one of shame and contempt, and anyone found conspiring with the man—or attempting to free him from the confines I plan to ensnare him in—will endure the same level of torture as he. Be wise.

The command tugged at Eliana's mind, but as the speech ended, she didn't feel particularly compelled to believe any of it. She still glared at Olalla with hatred. She still saw her as the woman who'd murdered Hastings—the woman who now planned to turn Eliana's friends into mindless robots.

No one else saw it this way, though. Mental shields had deteriorated almost entirely, rendering everyone's collective thoughts palpable and coherent. They all drank Olalla's lies, and they would drown in them.

All except Nero's mind reader, Jerry Watkins, who now glowered at Eliana, his pink eyes harboring more emotion than she'd ever seen from the dull boy.

Focusing on Watkins seemed silly, because he wasn't the *only* person immune to Olalla's deception. Every citizen of Periculand was spellbound, but the Wackos, although dazed, hadn't retained Olalla's explanations as reality. Many of them side-glanced William's body and remembered how the woman had convinced him to take his own life.

Had Danny trained them in this art? The Wacko leader seemed unfazed himself, but…how?

"It pleases me to finally witness a Principal of Periculand who has the same ideals as our organization," Danny said, his words spoken fluidly but judiciously. "Perhaps there will be more development to this alliance in the future. For now, we'll leave peacefully…once we have my sister in our grasp."

"Oh, Daniel, I might have let you have her if you weren't so oblivious."

Olalla's eyes flew beyond his shoulder, to where Ashna crouched within the crowd. Eliana had forgotten all about her plans and motives. With Olalla's real nature exposed, Danny seemed more of a gnat than a beast.

"Your sister has been here this entire time and you've failed to notice her. How imprudent of you. I think for your lack of focus, I'll keep Ashna for myself. Her abilities intrigue me, to say the least."

Anyone remotely close to Danny staggered back when his body literally began to glow. The black leather encasing his skin swelled, and any visible tattoos turned from black to the color of incandescent flames.

In the same moment, however, every one of Periculand's Affinities assumed an offensive stance, threatening the spark of another battle.

Eliana knew it would be fatal, and she sensed the Wacko leader knew it, too, even if he couldn't read minds. After the tentative peace that had been proposed, igniting another brawl seemed foolish. He could have incinerated them all, Olalla included, but his horde would be among the charred, and Ashna, the very prize he sought, wouldn't survive.

For a solid minute, the decision warred in Danny's brain, his thoughts open to Eliana now when they had been guarded before. Surrendering had never been an option for him, but if he didn't give in now, he would lose. To walk away would give him the chance to return with an even greater force—to kill Olalla without sacrificing his followers—to demolish her in a way that even her cadaver would remember, if there was even a body left afterward.

Besides, though Eliana didn't know the specifics, Danny had a bargaining chip back at the compound that he was *sure* Olalla would trade Ashna for.

"We'll be in touch," he stated vaguely, as he dipped his chin and then spun on his heel, signaling his minions to follow. Every one of them did—even Naretha, who looked as if she'd rather stick around and tear through Olalla's flesh with shards of salt.

"Thanks for killing the Regg guards for me!" the mind controller called after them with a self-satisfied laugh. The Wackos ignored her completely, marching through the hole in the fence with impressive restraint. If Eliana had an army behind her, she would *not* have walked away, not until Olalla's head was on a spike.

The flames throughout town finally started to die down, but it seemed as though they'd descended even deeper into hell. Periculand was eerily silent now without the Wackos, and the space before the Residence Tower was strangely empty without their presence. Perhaps Eliana felt alone because any form of diversity—singularity—*freedom*—had disappeared with the terrorists. Now it was only her, Jerry, and Olalla—numerous Olallas.

"Nero."

The brute stumbled forward. Her influence hadn't warded off

the effects of the bee-stinger's venom, but he still stared down at her attentively.

"I believe you want to apprehend Ashna, don't you?"

"*No*," the girl growled, backing away as she held up her hands in defense. It was then that Eliana realized a fourth personality dwelled here: Ashna's. Somehow, with her infinite Affinities, she possessed the ability to deflect Olalla's manipulation, and the new principal knew it. "Don't touch me!"

Ashna threw up a force field that momentarily inhibited Nero from reaching her, but the shield didn't encompass her entire body, and so the acid-spitter and Demira snuck behind and grabbed her, Dave burning her arm with his acid and Demira encasing her torso with a metal chain.

"Here." Olalla chucked a pair of handcuffs at Nero, and he turned just in time to catch them. From this angle, Eliana couldn't study them very well, but they were definitely more advanced than normal shackles, and Ashna groaned in pain the moment they were slapped onto her wrists.

"Glorious." Tipping her head back toward the sky, Olalla closed her eyes. The clouds and smoke had dissipated, paving the way for the stars, but even they didn't shed any light on this situation. Periculand would have been better off if Danny had leveled it completely, or if everyone had combatted Olalla and died in the process. Hastings's fate seemed humane compared to this.

Now, bow.

The reaction was instantaneous. All of Periculand instantly wanted to bow before Olalla—their *queen*. Tray, Lavisa, Ackerly, *Kiki*—even Hartman, though on the ground, lowered his head in servitude. Only Ashna and the two holding her remained upright—and Eliana.

Bow, a voice hissed at her, but it wasn't Olalla's this time; it was Jerry Watkins.

Though he hadn't succumbed mentally, he knelt along with the rest, and Eliana scrambled to join them. The last thing she wanted to do was show Olalla respect, but even more than that, she didn't want the woman to realize this small grain of power the mind readers held over her. The two were immune to Olalla, and while it seemed useless now, they needed every bit of leverage they could obtain.

Eliana wasn't a prophet like Kiki, but she knew this immunity could potentially lead to a cure, and for her friends, she would find one.

For Kiki, whose pinkish hair was mangled, whose pretty face was to the pavement, whose feelings Eliana had shattered and now desperately needed to mend, she would find one.

39

The Fire External

As the Wackos trekked through the scorched entrance of Periculand, the only positive thought to cross Jamad's mind was that Danny had been too distracted by the unexpected turn of events to notice his dog was injured. The mood Olalla Cosmos had left him in was highly unstable; even the slightest trigger would set him off. So Jamad clutched Shards tightly to his chest and prayed his leader wouldn't glance back at them.

Lavisa's kick hadn't killed the dog, but it had cracked a few ribs, and Shards whined softly at the pain. Although the slices and bruises he'd earned had him limping, Jamad tried his hardest to blend in among the Wackos—to not look as distraught, confused, and *scared* as he felt. Despite Danny's notorious invincibility, they departed Periculand without his sister, and Jamad knew someone would pay for it. He hoped Danny's wrath was reserved for the woman who'd urged their departure with her powers of manipulation.

As far as Jamad could tell, though, the manipulation that swayed them into leaving hadn't been supernatural. He'd heard the woman's voice warbling through his brain, but it hadn't affected him, and as they approached the herd of black vans, he recited every truth in his head.

Olalla had convinced that Regg to kill himself. Olalla had forced all of Periculand into her submission. Olalla, with the same Affinity that had taken Hastings's life, had now seized the town—Jamad's town.

Even as they abandoned it, half in ruins, half aflame, Jamad still saw it as his town—his home. He hated leaving it almost as much as he'd hated arriving here with the task of destroying it. At Headquarters, the concept of invading Periculand had seemed the perfect test: if he could demolish this home, he could demolish any home, including his parents'. As soon as the thin white line that was the Residence Tower had appeared on the horizon, however, he'd gone cold with how wrong this was.

He inhaled the frigid night air and then sighed. They would return to Headquarters now, and Jamad would have to live with what he'd done. It was a choice he'd made, to stay with the Wackos, and there was no turning back now. Avner and Maddy were too far away, physically and emotionally, for him to ever join them again.

What bothered him about their escape from the compound had not been that they'd wanted to ditch the Wackos. Hell, at this point, Jamad wanted to ditch the Wackos. The problem had been the way in which they'd chosen to escape—without him.

Maddy hadn't conferred with Jamad about the possibility of rescuing Avner. She'd waited until he was safely out of the picture. His two friends would have been perfectly content to leave him with the Wackos. Only because he'd obstructed their path had they invited him along. Otherwise, they would have abandoned him.

That was what had enraged him.

Avner was wrong about a lot of things, but he was also right about a lot of things. The Reggs—specifically the Regg researchers—deserved punishment, and the Wackos would give them that. But the Wackos *were* terrorists—or, at least, destroyers. Jamad couldn't stand behind Avner's self-righteous quest for peace, nor could he support the Wackos in their unnecessary aggression, meaning he was stuck in this unpleasant limbo, wedged between two contrasting sides, unable to fully commit to either.

What would Zeela have done? Would she have taken Danny's deal, or would she have rotted away with her boyfriend, only to escape and leave Jamad behind? He wanted to believe she would have sided with him, especially after how the Reggs had treated her, but he didn't know, and it gnawed at him as much as the mystery of her whereabouts. Her destination should have been Periculand, but she hadn't been there, which meant she could be anywhere—which meant she could be...*dead.*

"Are you *crying*?" Naretha demanded. Stumbling, Jamad halted his strides beside their van, the one they'd taken here alone after the incident in the weapons room—the one he'd hidden in until stupid little Shards insisted on joining the battle.

"What—no, no, I just—the wind—it's burning my eyes—"

Naretha's flat, impatient look quelled his stammering. "I wasn't aware cold wind had any effect on you. Good to know your Affinity is as useless as you are."

"I'm not *useless*..."

"Your one job was to keep the rat safe, and you couldn't even manage that." It wasn't until her narrowed eyes landed on Shards that Jamad realized "the rat" was actually the dog. "If Danny asks, we blame it on Jez. From what I observed, he didn't make it out of Periculand, which means he probably never will. There have been enough casualties tonight. I don't want to add your name to the list."

Jamad's eyebrows rose slowly as he cocked his head. "You... *don't*? That's a surprise."

Naretha yanked the driver's door open, impeding his opportunity to gloat. "Get in."

Hurrying to the other side of the vehicle, Jamad heeded her command, partially because he knew her attitude was mild for the amount of indignation that must have festered inside, and partially because he couldn't stand to look at the flickering orange landscape any longer.

Putting on his seatbelt with Shards in his lap proved a difficult feat, but he accomplished it—right before the back doors flew open.

The van bounced and jostled as the Wacko leader hopped in and crept forward to kneel on the floor behind them, settling between their seats. Jamad tried not to look too guilty when Danny's eyes settled on his broken dog.

"Is he dead?" The apathy in his tone was unsettling to Jamad, and Naretha attempted to expel her nerves by turning on the vehicle.

"N-no—"

"Good," was all Danny said as he averted his gaze toward the town he'd razed. "All is well, then. This worked out better than I ever could have imagined."

Naretha was about to shift the van into reverse, but his statement stopped her. "How so?"

Danny made no effort to hide his aura of superiority. "Well, with *Cosmos* in charge, my sister will be even more eager to escape Periculand than she was to escape the compound."

"And you think she'll come running back to us?"

"Where else would she go? You must know she's going to return and try to usurp my position. There are Wackos in our ranks who are loyal to her. You must be shrewd enough to sense it, darling."

Naretha ground her teeth together to keep her mouth shut. At first, Jamad assumed she'd grown tired of his pet names, but then it dawned on him that she might have been one of those Wackos loyal to Ashna.

Either way, Danny disregarded her muteness and plunged on with the details of his plan. "If Ashna *doesn't* escape—well, I have the perfect object with which to trade for her waiting back at Headquarters."

Blanching, Naretha opened her mouth but didn't muster a reply.

"Olalla seems powerful enough," Jamad said carefully. "Is it really a good idea to *give* her anything she could use as a weapon?"

"Oh, this can hardly be considered a weapon," Danny retorted, his voice dancing with manic mirth. "He lacks the hunger for violence."

Shards nearly toppled from Jamad's lap when the realization hit him. Still, he wouldn't believe it without verbal confirmation, so he choked out a strangled, "*He*?"

"Your old friend Avner, of course," Danny affirmed, draining the air from Jamad's lungs.

"Wh-why would Olalla want Avner?"

"You didn't notice the resemblance? For someone who was so close with Olalla's son, I would have thought it blatant."

There was no hope in replenishing his empty lungs now. Of course he hadn't noticed the resemblance between Olalla and Avner—he'd never looked for it. Apparently, neither had Avner, for he'd never expressed any thoughts on the woman beyond her being a positive vice-presidential candidate for the Affinities. Now the notion that Olalla was anything positive had been quashed, while the notion that she was Avner's *mother* was unearthed.

The familial connection alone would have been jarring, but coupling it with the fact that Danny wanted to use Avner—who had escaped—for a trade had rendered Jamad speechless.

"Oh, those pesky Stromers." The man's tone was light, but his scowl was set darkly on Periculand. "I'll be glad to exchange Avner for my sister. Once the Stromer family's together, I can incinerate them all at once. How delightful."

Jamad echoed a throaty, "Delightful." Naretha remained silent. When she finally did shift the van into reverse, her movements were gradual, as if she wanted to prolong their journey back to Headquarters to avoid the calamity of their return. Jamad didn't know if there were any cameras in the weapons room, but he knew they'd be dead meat if there were.

Though it had been unspoken, he and Naretha had, in the end, agreed to let Avner, Maddy, and Zach escape. Either one of them could have killed all three, but they'd chosen not to. Danny would know this, and he would know they'd kept the entire breakout a secret to him. Naretha didn't seem inclined to tell him now, and Jamad didn't want to be the one to spill the information.

As they maneuvered away from town, the flames snaking out from beneath Danny's leather collar reflected the fires scattered throughout Periculand, and the fires scattered throughout Periculand reflected the inferno festering in his eyes.

"We'll see you again soon, Periculand," he said to the town, and any lingering flames bowed toward him, as if hearing his words. "The next time we part, you won't be burning—you won't be suffering. You'll be a graveyard."

Adara awoke within a casket of burning rubble.

For a few brief seconds, she actually savored it. She was immune to the heat of the fire and, apparently, the pain of the rocks piled atop her body. After a month of staring at the same plain walls, it was refreshing to see they'd crumbled around her.

Then she remembered she wasn't the only person the walls had collapsed on. Even though the fire licking her skin didn't affect her, it would definitely affect the King and the Prince.

"Thank the devil I'm not dead," she muttered, staring up at a slab of concrete inches from crushing her skull. A few other boulders propped it up around her head, saving her from fatal injuries. The rest of her body had not been as fortunate, but the rocks sprinkling her arms, legs, and torso were light and easy to swat and kick off. Groaning, she finally shifted out from beneath her rubble casket and embraced the aches and pains that accompanied freedom.

"Isn't the phrase, 'Thank *God*?'"

The familiar voice split a grin onto Adara's face. Rubbing her eyes open, she found the jail cell was half ruined, the gaping hole above still showering debris from where the ceiling had once been. There was too much smoke for the night sky to be visible, and Adara was impervious to the chilly wind, so nothing had altered, really.

Except the fire that had claimed nearly every surface.

At least the three walls of their cell were still completely intact, along with the bars, leaving no method of exit. Adara was really, *really* eager to scale the burning walls and climb out through the ruptured ceiling that had almost crushed her to death.

"You really think God saved me?" she questioned as she staggered to her feet. Her threadbare shirt had various holes from her outburst and her flimsy pants had burned up to mid-thigh from the explosion, but not even one hair on her body fried. Other than a few bruises from the rocks, she was completely unscathed. "I'm a *demoness*, your Majesty. God's probably crying up in his palace because I'm still alive."

From where he stood in his designated corner of the crumbling cell, Angor stopped dusting off his ash-ridden prison garb to frown at her. "You're lucky I'm not a religious person. Otherwise, I believe I'd be deeply offended by your sacrilege."

Even atop a mound of concrete, his head didn't reach the lip of the wall. Both of their metal slabs had been flattened, which meant they would need to pull themselves up via the small window to reach their only route of escape. Climbing the wall had never been a serious option in Adara's mind—too much effort—but she felt doubly screwed knowing it would be physically impossible.

"Remind me to kill Danny next time we see him. The freakin' guy couldn't even knock down these walls for us? Rude, if you ask me."

Angor snorted as he resumed brushing off his garments. To Adara, it seemed like a silly thing to do during a time such as this, but maybe it was an attempt to distract himself from his own injuries. Like hers, his pants had been singed at the bottoms, but unlike hers, his skin was susceptible to burns, and the sight of the swollen red marks on his calves was disconcerting.

"I will remind you, actually. I'm curious as to how you'd go about killing a man with Daniel's talents."

"The method that seems most appealing to me is probably suffocation by donuts, but that might be too sweet of a way to die for Danny. He deserves suffocation by Brussels sprouts, or something equally as disgusting."

"Well, now I am offended." Angor managed to glare at her even as the smoke provoked a cough. "Brussels sprouts are my favorite vegetable."

"Eugh—and I was starting to *like* you. Clearly, I was mistaken in my judgment."

Angor tried to chuckle, but it came out as coughs when the smoky air infiltrated his lungs. After a moment, he finally decided to cover the lower half of his face with his shirt. "The smoke doesn't affect you? I should have assumed it wouldn't. I suppose the heat doesn't, either."

Adara stroked her chin as she considered the redness of his skin and the perspiration dripping from his face. "I guess there are a few perks to this Affinity of mine—I'm not sweating buckets like you, and I could probably become a chain smoker. Now I'm considering it just because I think it'll piss off Tray—"

A chunk of rock plummeted from above, and Adara had to lurch toward Angor to avoid it. At this closer proximity, she saw a few pieces of his hair had been scorched, and welts were present on his arms, as well. Perhaps there were more than a few perks to her Affinity.

"God—you *are* trying to kill me, aren't you!" Adara called up toward the indiscernible sky. "I told you He's angry," she added to Angor. His eyes were the only visible part of his face, and he didn't hesitate to roll them. "I wouldn't be surprised if we're already dead. This seems like hell to me."

"I believe we're alive…" Angor began, scanning the area, "but…"

The moment his gaze settled behind her, Adara knew what caught his attention. She'd tried to avoid glancing beyond the bars, but it was unavoidable now. Spinning around, she squinted through the veil of smoke to where the Pixie Prince lay in the hallway, face pressed against the unforgiving floor.

Naively, she'd hoped he'd fled during the avalanche—such an unrealistically optimistic thought that she hadn't wanted to check its validity. Now that the reality was spread out before her, she could barely formulate a thought.

"I don't think he's dead," Angor stated, gingerly stepping over a few flaming pieces of wreckage to stand beside her. "I can feel the nerve impulses connected to his heart, and it's still beating."

"You…can?" She turned her head toward him—mostly to stop herself from looking at Calder's motionless body—but Angor focused acutely on the Pixie Prince.

"Yes—the heart is a muscle, as you know."

"I didn't, but thanks for making it sound like common knowledge."

He graced her with a withering look, which she enjoyed immensely. Annoying Angor pried her thoughts away from Calder, unconscious and drowning in a sea of flames. None had reached him quite yet, but…he was surrounded.

"The heart is a muscle that works involuntarily," Angor explained. "I have not tested my abilities in regard to it, nor do I wish to under this circumstance, but I can sense the impulses traveling from his sinoatrial node—"

"So you're saying he's definitely alive, right?" she clarified impatiently. Judging by the shimmer of mischief in his pink eyes, the King now made an effort to repay her obnoxiousness with some agitating remarks of his own. "Can you wake him up?"

"Unfortunately, no. Sleep and consciousness go far beyond my powers—as far as I've investigated, at least. Now doesn't seem like the proper time to test that, either."

"Now seems like the perfect time to test it—he's going to die out there!" Restraining her emotions, she added, "If we're going to be stuck in this cell indefinitely, I'd rather not have a burning corpse in our company."

"Well, I'm glad we agree on something," Angor mused, tilting his head toward Calder. "Why don't you absorb the flames that threaten his life, then? It would benefit everyone if you did."

Adara's fists clenched at her sides, and the fires flared even brighter. "You know I can't."

"You *think* you can't. I doubt you acquired your Affinity by needing to *create* fire. It seems more likely that your ability originated from the need to *stop* a fire—to save yourself from burning. Now you've been presented with the need to save Calder from burning, and you claim you can't? Adara...this is your purpose—this is your natural inclination. You can spark fire, and you can quench fire. The only inhibitor is your own mind."

Adara had about five snarky comments to combat the King's oh-so-majestic advice. Before she could pick which one she wished to utter first, a massive chunk of the ceiling broke loose, tumbling down into the corridor outside their cell.

At the impact, both Adara and Angor buckled to the floor and coughed at the wave of dust. Blinded by the cloud, she fought to clear the air by waving her hand in front of her face, only to find the concrete boulder wedged between the bars of their cell and Calder, who had yet to awaken. She was about to verbally thank the devil that the lethal slab hadn't flattened him when she noticed the blaze had crept closer to him with the boulder's collapse. Wisps of fire flicked at his jeans until the fabric began to combust.

Suddenly more alert than she'd been in weeks, Adara scrambled toward the metal bars and used them to hoist herself upright. Beside her, Angor panted, but at her quick movement, his vision whipped into focus. Noticing the flaming jeans, he immediately screwed his eyebrows together and stared intently at Calder. Although the Pixie Prince's eyes remained closed and his mouth continued to droop, his body started to push off the floor and roll back and forth in the hall, smothering the fire that had ignited his clothes.

The problem was that the fire was everywhere, growing at a pace too rapid for Angor to thwart. Every time the rolling quelled one fire, another flame latched onto Calder's clothes.

"Can't you make him walk out of here?" Adara demanded, clutching the bars so tightly she could barely feel her hands.

"I can," Angor conceded, relaxing his eyebrows as he pushed to his feet. Calder stopped flopping throughout the hall, and Adara knew it was only a matter of minutes before his stagnant body became a pyre.

"Then *do it*," she snarled, the heat of her irritation increasing the intensity of the conflagration, putting the Pixie Prince in even more danger. "He needs to get *out*!"

"If Calder stands and walks out of here, he will continue to burn along the way, and I don't know how far the range of my abilities extends. I might be able to guide him out of the building, but I might not be able to extinguish the fire once he gets there. He will burn inside or outside of this police station. You're the only one who can stop that from happening."

The words were stated with a calm Adara could not fathom. She'd been uneasy earlier when she'd thought Nero would pummel Calder, but this would not be a beating he could recover from. This would be the end of the Pixie Prince, and she would be the cause of it. No, she hadn't detonated the building, but she possessed the power to save him now and didn't use it.

The flames spread to his sweatshirt, eating away at the black material and threatening to sear his skin. Though the fabric was thicker than that of her prison attire, the fire would still consume it—and then it would consume his flesh and his bones and his soul and she could stop it but she couldn't—

"Wake *up*!" she cried, shaking the bars as if the attempt hadn't proven futile already. "Wake up and drench yourself, you lazy sack of water!"

The taunt should have provoked him, but he was still dormant, still doomed to die.

Abandoning the bars, she sprinted across the cell and launched toward the sole window embedded in the unharmed wall. Her fingers grasped the ledge, but when she attempted to heave herself upward, her elbows barely bent. She was too weak to pull her own weight, and if she couldn't get over this wall, she couldn't drag Calder out of the police station and save him. Mere feet away from her, he would burn, and she would have to watch.

"I should have trained with you," Adara complained, sounding so pathetic that she even pitied herself. In a lame attempt, she shoved the concrete wall, but her own momentum shoved her back, and she stumbled until she was against the bars again, so incredibly close to the Pixie Prince but so incredibly far.

"I'm afraid it would take more than a few weeks for you to accomplish a pull-up," Angor informed her without any consolation.

"I'm not talking about your exercising shit. I'm talking about—about *this*." With a grand, imprecise gesture, she motioned toward this entire blazing building. Angor didn't have to ask to understand.

"Adara," he said, brushing some of his ash-laden hair from his face, "any one of your friends could have found a way to free you from this prison over the past month. Calder had multiple opportunities—in fact, I'm surprised he never used his mysterious lock-picking skills to simply open the door for you. I've seen him sneak into many places throughout campus—the boy's got a real knack for—"

"Does this rant have a point other than to *enrage me*?"

"The point," he amended hastily, "is that anyone could have freed you, but they all wanted you to free yourself. Calder's been encouraging you for weeks to gain control of yourself. He wants you to be strong and capable—he doesn't think you need rescuing."

Biting her lip, Adara closed her eyes and involuntarily *felt* the flames riddling this room, permeating this town. Unlike ever before, their presence was soothing to her, as if she had hundreds of friends dancing brightly in the night. Her flame-friends were demons like her, though, plagues that would gnaw away at places and people and…the Pixie Prince.

His Affinity's instinctive water secretion repelled the fire temporarily. Normally, he could have soaked this inferno with the snap of his fingers, but now…his fate was in her hands.

"Do you agree with him?" Adara asked quietly—*timidly*. Emerging during this crisis was her true self: a fearful little girl who wanted nothing more than to curl up under a blanket and watch movies while eating donuts with her friends. Maybe that's all she'd ever been—a coward hiding behind a monstrous façade.

"When you believed I'd killed Hastings," Angor said, "you didn't hesitate to step forward and avenge him. You didn't think about erupting in flames; you simply *did*, because you knew it was what you needed to do. Don't wonder if you can, Adara. Just know what you need to do and *do* it."

Her eyes inched open, and she found the former principal standing before her, eyes filled with faith. "You know," she began dryly, "you're really good at sounding inspirational, but not so good at actually *training* me to use my Affinity. No wonder you decided to be principal and hired a bunch of teachers do all the hard work for you."

Affronted, his lips parted for a reply, but she didn't give him the opportunity to speak, because he'd already said all he needed to say. She *hadn't* hesitated to avenge Hastings, and she *couldn't* hesitate now, not with the heat starting to melt Calder's skin.

This was not an outburst, as it had been after Hastings's death. This was not what Adara was good at. She had never practiced control because she'd never thought she had it. Her parents had abandoned her, her brother had left her, and her bully had tormented her, all shaping her life without her consent. The struggles of her childhood had led her to relinquish power over the one thing she could control: her reactions. Emotions ruled her, and now they ruled her Affinity as well.

There was one skill she was practiced at, though. It wasn't necessarily the *suppression* of her fury, but the *capturing* of it—the willful act of saving that useful emotion for a more appropriate occasion. Since arriving at Periculand, she hadn't bothered to utilize the talent, but her formative years had been characterized by the bottling of her wrath against Kiki, which she then chose to release by playing sports in the backyard with Seth, verbally harassing Tray, or sneaking into the Belvens' mansion.

Before it had been a habit—a defense mechanism—but now she had the chance to apply that aptitude to a situation of actual significance, an act of selflessness.

Shutting her eyes, Adara drew in all of the anger and alarm overwhelming her. They were the same sensations that had always arisen due to Kiki's victimization, and so she imagined she was back at that wretched high school, snuffing her sarcastic remarks and pretending nothing miffed her.

She pictured each flare as an insult, because as with Kiki's jabs, fire didn't bother her any longer. For the majority of her life, the two had been her greatest fears, both remnants of her childhood that haunted her daily. In her eyes, the anxiety had been a weakness, but over the years it strengthened her, forging her into a creature that basked in that which plagued her youth.

Now she beckoned for it, siphoned from it, thrived in it. The heat seeped into every pore, flowing from every corner of the room to fuel her. Flames were not her friends, she realized, as they rippled into her skin; they were her servants, and she was their master. The power she had always craved was finally in her grasp, absorbing into her flesh, merging with the fabric of her soul.

Angor had been right. Even Calder had been right. For when she squinted her eyes open the police station was desolate, utterly devoid of light and fire—except that which radiated directly from her.

It didn't terrify her, not anymore. In fact, she relished this view of the world through the glow of her flames, because they belonged to her now, and she would wield them to her advantage.

Stepping forward, she reached for the bars with her rock-encrusted hands, but this time she didn't have to wrap her fingers around them. Just her proximity melted the metal, disintegrating it into pool of silvery liquid that Angor scampered to avoid. Any rational person would have been apprehensive, especially when the slabs of *concrete* softened, but Adara simply smirked, sauntering through the puddles of substances that should have been solid like she was walking through a shallow pond.

The hard part, she acknowledged, had not been summoning the flames but would be extinguishing them. They weren't consuming her clothes—for the moment, she possessed that much control, at least—but she couldn't remain a fire demoness forever.

Only once had she been this monstrously ablaze, and then she'd been thwarted by unconsciousness. She would have to accomplish it by her own volition this time, and she had no idea how.

Positioning herself atop a slowly thawing mound of rubble, Adara stared down at Calder and tried not to fall prey to the helplessness this predicament bred. The rage had dissipated, but the fire remained. How was she to douse a conflagration that's source was already depleted?

Ease your mind, Adara, a voice cooed from within her, too sweet to be her own. Advice usually didn't sit well with her—even good advice, like Angor's—but this voice compelled her to believe without question—without even *wanting* to question. *Release your emotions, positive and negative. Even happiness can drive you out of control.*

Happiness had never been a familiar concept to Adara, but there had been a spark of *something* in her chest after summoning the fire, disintegrating the bars, and saving the Pixie Prince. Perhaps that moment of elation had perpetuated the flames.

But how could she remove herself from the situation entirely? There was no way for her to deny that she was proud of what she'd done—and that she was relieved to have finally accomplished it. What was the point of doing something that had no impact on her?

Sometimes we must do things not for the sake of ourselves but for the sake of others…

Her jaw clenched at that. *That sounds a hell of a lot like doing something for the 'greater good,' and you know I'm not into that bullshit, Brain.*

There was definitely an amused lilt to her brain's voice when it responded, *Maybe not, but you still have to turn off your emotions. Now.*

The need for feelings immediately evaporated. All worry, fear, pride, and relief drifted away, banishing the fire's presence and morphing her into a hollow volcano. The dark layer that had enveloped her skin soon withered as well, leaving the same filmy ash she'd become so closely acquainted with over the past few weeks. She felt nothing. She was nothing.

Then her numb eyes settled on Calder.

At some point, her mind had instructed her to walk forward, because she stood above him, safely away from the swiftly solidifying metal. Angor's forced rolling had left Calder lying on his back, head tilted to the side, eyelids peacefully closed. She had been ordered to dispel her emotions, but without them, this new wave hit hard, dragging her to her knees.

"Are you all right, Adara?" Angor called from afar. He was in the cell, probably, but between the darkness and the dizziness, Adara couldn't see him. Everything was a blur except Calder. Her eyes barely had to adjust to the lack of light for her to distinguish his ash-coated cheeks. His hair had come undone from its typical bun, and it cascaded around his face like motionless waves. The sweatshirt was in ruins, exposing most of his torso, the skin now red and crusted with dried blood—and burns.

Adara had not seen serious burns in quite some time, but the sight of them now dredged up memories of her past, of scars that had completely faded. She'd always been convinced she had a tough stomach, but staring at the welts induced a sense of nausea that she couldn't fight.

Doubling over, she heaved out the contents of her last jail meal—into Calder's splayed locks of hair.

"Shitnuggets," was the next thing that spewed from her mouth.

Calder's lips contorted in disgust. For a brief, disoriented moment, she thought nothing of it, but then she realized it was a voluntary movement—that he was awake.

"That's really all you have to say right now?" he groaned, squeezing his eyelids together before revealing those deep blue irises. Though they were glossed with pain, there was still a crafty smirk surfacing on his face.

"You—you're—*That* was what it took to wake you up?" Adara spluttered, lamely attempting to mask her mortification with incredulity. "I just had to puke in your hair?"

"Oh, no—I've been awake," he grunted as he tried to lift his head. The effort provoked an intensely pained wince, and Adara almost helped him lower back to the ground—almost. She had never willingly touched him—not in a kind way, at least—and to do so now when he was in such a fragile state…she was afraid she would break him. Also, she didn't particularly want to touch her own vomit.

Mostly, she was too paralyzed to consider doing anything, because Calder had said that *he'd been awake.*

"For *how long*?" she demanded in a voice shrill enough to pass as Fraco's.

"Since you started worshiping the devil for your undeserved longevity."

"You—" Her wide eyes cut toward his burns, the ones he'd somehow suffered consciously, without screaming or crying or moving an inch. Calder had been awake the *entire time* and she'd had no clue. "How? *Why*? What the hell is *wrong* with you?"

Even through his grimace, he managed a roguish grin. "A lot of things, obviously." His eyes dipped down toward his injuries, which he somehow looked at without barfing. "As for the *why*—well, I think that should be obvious by now, Stromer. Like Angor said, I wanted you to do it on your own. What would you have gained if I'd done all the work for you? As for the *how*, I staved off the fire with my Affinity."

"Not very *well*," she growled, glaring at his face since she didn't want to view the damage he'd endured—for *her*. Because for some twisted reason, he thought the development of her Affinity was more important than his own life. And for some equally unfathomable reason, she hated that.

"Well enough," he dismissed. "I'll heal."

Adara couldn't compile an adequate answer to that. Her mind was still bogged down with the weight of what he'd done—the absolute trust and the unnecessary sacrifice.

"Did *you* know?" She whirled around to glare at Angor. He was positioned in his corner of the cell again, a healthy distance from the hot metal that obstructed his path to the hallway.

"I had a hunch," he admitted with a shrug.

"You sick bastard—he could've *died*!"

"I was in complete control of the situation." Calder inclined his head toward her in protest. Apparently that was enough to trigger pain, because he cringed before adding, "Mostly."

"Clearly *not*." Expelling a breath, she ran a hand through her greasy hair and shook her head at him. "You are *insane*. I don't even feel bad for you. You deserved to be puked on."

"That sounds incriminating," a voice huffed, and Adara swore aloud before her eyes even confirmed it was Nero. His silhouette was unmistakable in the half-crumpled doorway to the front lobby. As he glanced between Adara and Calder, his lips curled around his teeth, not in a snarl but in a grotesque smile, like he'd stumbled upon a priceless prize. "You burned him to a crisp and now you wanna puke on him, too? Should've joined me, Mardurus. I've always told you Stromer's a lost cause."

"Oh, don't be so harsh, Nero," a female voice chided as three other figures appeared behind him: Mr. Grease, Devil-red, and the Affinity ambassador. Though Olalla blended with the shadows, her amethyst eyes gleamed through the dark, almost entrancingly. "Adara's the one who saved this town from disaster. Buildings were burning until she conquered all the flames a few minutes ago. She's a Periculand hero."

"A Periculand hero?" Adara repeated, oblivious to the woman's deceptive tone. "Let's erect my shrine right next to Hastings's then, shall we? Oh wait—the Reggs never bothered to commemorate him because they *murdered him*. Where are those assholes, anyway? I'll gladly reignite the fire to end them."

"The Rosses have received their punishment…for now," Olalla said in a way that should have disturbed Adara but didn't. She was too peeved that she hadn't been the one to dole out the punishments for the Rosses—her own freaking *parents*. She *supposed* Angor deserved his own revenge against them, too, and she gladly would have shared the privilege with him, but he seemed unfazed about the Rosses had finally being overthrown—suspicious, almost.

"Hold on"—Calder lifted his head just enough to narrow his eyes at Olalla—"did you say Stromer saved the *whole town*? I didn't think she was capable of *that*. Sounds like a joke to me."

Adara rallied her most dramatically mocking voice to say, "I thought you *believed in me*?"

His lips parted but didn't utter a word; his gaze was trained warily on Nero now, and he swallowed uncomfortably at the way the brute continued to simper. It was the first time Adara had ever seen him appear genuinely frightened of Nero, his beloved ally. Perhaps it was his vulnerable position, lying injured on the ground, or perhaps it was because he knew anything that brought Nero pleasure would bring others pain.

"Considering all the fires abruptly disappeared, Adara must have been the savior." Olalla's gaze slipping cleverly in Angor's direction. "I assume you've been training her?"

"Adara's competent enough to have taught herself," Angor said carefully—distrustfully. Wedged in the corner, he looked like a trapped animal waiting to become a meal. His expression surrendered to placidity when he noticed Olalla's companions were Fraco and Aethelred, the two standing at her side like personal butlers. The placidity wasn't relief, though; it was more akin to resignation—like Angor knew what would come next and had accepted this doom.

"That's reassuring, since you won't be her mentor any longer," Olalla said, and Adara felt the chill—not in the air but in her mind. The coldness slithered into the crevices of her brain, numbing any sense of skepticism.

"Have the Wackos left the town?" Angor asked, but his inflection indicated he already knew the answer. People as powerful as Olalla and Nero wouldn't have been here in the police station if the battle wasn't over.

"With no help from you," the Affinity ambassador confirmed tartly. Stepping into the corridor, she studied the melted and now cooling metal with a satisfied air. "You were too busy behind bars to defend Periculand, so I did. Classic, isn't it, Aethelred, that Periculy screws up and I have to swoop in and save his ass?"

"I can't say this was the first time," Devil-Red agreed with a nod. Adara was curious about the elusive nature of this exchange, but for once, she didn't feel compelled to intervene.

"Don't worry, you'll continue to pay for your crimes," Olalla soothed, as if doing him a favor. "This jail might be ruined, but I have an even better place for you to decompose. You'll be in the good company of our mutual friend *Artemis*. I suppose I'll have to detain Ashna there as well. To her misfortune, she can resist me, and we can't have her forming a coup against me. No, she needs to be caged until her brother comes crawling for her."

"Ah, now that's something we can all make a toast to—a non-alcoholic toast," Adara reassured with a smug smirk in Nero's direction. His delight finally faded with that. "I've heard underage drinking is taken *very* seriously here in Periculand. Wouldn't want to end up beside Unicorn Fairy in chains. At least she earned imprisonment. That bitch broke my Greenie's heart."

"Which obviously merits incarceration," Calder chimed in sardonically. "Angor should be freed, though."

"No, he shouldn't." Nero made the threat plain through his gritted teeth.

Adara made her insubordination plain through her careless eyebrow raise. "Yes, he should. He didn't kill Hastings. The Purple Almost-Vice-President knows that. Why else would she have locked up my nasty mother?"

Olalla emitted a laugh, but it was too spiteful to warm Adara's chilled thoughts. "You're going to make me hate myself, aren't you?" The girl's brow creased, but the woman plunged on without explanation. "Angor murdered Hastings—didn't you?"

Features twisting with shame, the man solemnly closed his eyes. "Y-yes…I did."

"See, there you have it." Olalla gestured toward him like his confession clarified everything, and…somehow it did. Somehow, the pieces snapped into place for Adara; all the clues they'd gathered led to the conclusion she'd first deduced—that Angor was guilty. Of course he was. He was *evil.* She was so sure of it that she was tempted to erupt and finish the deed she hadn't been able to accomplish last month.

"Now that everything has been made clear to you all, we can move forward," Olalla announced, and Adara didn't defy her. She didn't *want* to defy her; she wanted to *follow* her. "You can call me the Purple Principal, if you'd like."

Olalla's permission should have made the nickname less enjoyable for Adara, but she felt delightfully devious as she said, "I would like that."

"Good," the Purple Principal purred. "Now, I'd like you two to return to campus and clean up. New rules will be implemented now that I'm in charge, and I want everyone to be present for the assembly. I do hope you don't skip out this time," she added to Calder, who feigned innocence.

"I don't know what you're talking about."

"We all know what she's talking about," Adara said with an eye roll. "You have proven to be excessively stupid tonight, though, so I wouldn't be surprised if you've actually forgotten. What are you gonna do with the son-murderer?"

"You'll see soon enough." As Olalla spun to depart, an object on her head sparkled in the faint light of the moon, and Adara realized it was a crown. Her only opinion was that its gaudiness would have suited Kiki's taste...and that she secretly would have liked one herself.

"Grab him," Olalla commanded to Nero, who heeded her words without question. Marching over the mess Adara had made, he stalked into the cell and grasped Angor by the throat, hauling him away without a hint of mercy.

Adara had the urge to feel, but she felt nothing. There was no vindication, nor was there remorse. Not when Olalla commanded Fraco and Aethelred like robots. Not when Nero dragged Angor away. Not when Angor glanced back at her in sorrow.

There was no outburst this time because there was no need for an outburst. And so the fire was dead.

Acknowledgements

So far, Nerve has been my favorite book to write and my least favorite book to edit. I could not have finished this monstrosity if not for outside help. I *would* thank the devil, but that would probably be socially unacceptable, so I'll thank these mortals instead:

- My parents, for letting me live with you since the costs of publishing make me poor
- My grandma, for reading Blood even though you thinks it's "too long" (can't wait to see your reaction to Nerve, Granny)
- My grandpa, for understanding my weird sense of humor
- My husband, Phil, for keeping me sane throughout the process of finishing this book (and for always listening to me rant about my own characters)
- Daniëlle, for being a wonderful a friend (and for being a weird writer like me, finding inspiration while on the subway and such)
- Jasmine, for taking the time to read my books even when you're insanely busy (and for leaving the best comments)
- Ilona…I don't even know how to begin to thank you for all you did for this book. Your amazing art, your insightful suggestions, and your willingness to tolerate me and

my barrage of questions—I would be lost without you (dramatic sobs ensue)

- My Patrons on Patreon (Amelia, Isabella, NewRa, and Tawnie), for your support and encouragement (and for being patient throughout my long hiatus)
- And to all my other readers. Whether you found me on Quotev years ago or just discovered this series recently, I'm eternally grateful for your encouragement and support.

About the Author

In books, Kirsten loves drama, unhealthy relationships, and violence. In real life, Kirsten loves solitude, laughing with her husband, and not killing people. Her only friends live hallway across the Earth, but at least she has hundreds of characters in her head to keep her company. You can probably find her cuddling with her pups instead of writing. Nerve is her second full-length novel, but there are more to come. Find her online for more info:

www.kirstenkruegerauthor.com
kirstenkruegerauthor@gmail.com